Twixt Two Equal Armies

A Novel inspired by Jane Austen's *Pride & Prejudice*

GAIL & TINA

Meryton Press

Oysterville, WA

TWIXT TWO EQUAL ARMIES

© 2009

Gail McEwen and Tina Moncton

Copyright held by the authors.

ISBN: 978-1-936009-08-4

Editing and layout by Mary Sharples
Graphic design by Ellen Pickels

As, 'twixt two equal armies, Fate
Suspends uncertain victory,
Our souls — which to advance their state,
Were gone out — hung 'twixt her and me.
— John Donne

Prologue

Before it all began, for many, many years,
there were two girls, two cousins, two friends...

WHENEVER she looked back on that summer, it seemed she had laughed most of the time. Laughed, giggled, tittered or chuckled. And the best thing about it was that she had not done so alone.

It certainly had not started out that way. That spring her mother had taken a commission requiring her to stay in Edinburgh and then to accompany one of the economist fellows of the University on a tour of the mills around the north of England. Mrs Tournier made it perfectly clear she did not regard this dedicated and vagrant life as fit for her daughter, and that her work would be much sooner accomplished and much better executed if Holly did not join them. Since her father had passed away only a little more than a year earlier, her mother decided she should travel to Hertfordshire and befriend her Bennet-cousins and family.

Holly cried every night before they left Scotland. She cried for most of the journey too, except when shooting her mother daggered looks in response to her attempts at conversation, and she cried and sulked and avoided speaking to anyone when they arrived at Longbourn.

Then one day when she sat with her cousins, Jane and Mary, and her Aunt Bennet, quietly sewing and moping in her indescribable longing to be back at Rosefarm Cottage with just her mother, she caught a glimpse through the window of Elizabeth walking

3

across the lawn to the house. She was accompanying Holly's Uncle Bennet — though one should perhaps say she was jumping and skipping around him, laughing and talking and catching his hand. Something hard and cold gripped Holly's heart as she watched father and daughter from behind the window and she thought she would burst out crying at the sight of them. She bit her lip even harder and though her eyes swam with tears and she could not make out any stitches, she bent her head to her needlework and felt her heart slowly break all over again.

A few moments later, however, her world changed. Having left her father in his study, Elizabeth came into the parlour and straight away crossed the room to where her cousin sat so quietly. She perched beside her for a while, neither of them saying a word, listening to Mrs Bennet's chatter, Holly still struggling to pick up her work again and Elizabeth casting glances at her futile efforts. Then, quite unexpectedly, Elizabeth took her hand.

"Do you want to see my tree house?" she quietly asked. "It's just mine and it's a secret, but you can go there if you want to be alone sometime. Come, I'll show you right now."

Holly never remembered if she had agreed or not — probably not — but Elizabeth pulled her out of the house anyway, with no bonnet or shawl, and led her beyond the village lane, behind the green and through Farmer Wilson's pastures until they came to the woods behind it. There, Elizabeth explained, she and her father had found the perfect tree and he had quietly commissioned the construction of a tree house. Its existence and location was their secret, but since he never came there except to find her to go walking with him, she wondered, would Holly...*could* Holly share this secret with her?

"I come here to be alone; if you want, you can too. I have some books and a pillow and even a candle. Just tell me and I'll leave you alone — I have plenty of other secret places around here. I'll show them to you as well if you like, but none of them is as good as this one."

Whatever Holly answered and whatever her intentions regarding her cousin's offer had been, the rest of the summer turned out quite differently from what she had expected. Perhaps because her life had been so devoid of laughter and happiness lately, it did still strike her as if she had laughed her way through those months at Longbourn. In her cousin Elizabeth, she found someone with whom, despite the fact that her position in life and disposition were so different from her own, she could share a whole world in common in that tree house, and elsewhere too. Elizabeth, who delighted in the absurd, found Holly's every attempt to question her mind and opinions to be a personal challenge. She never feared to use that sharp tongue of hers or to gently tease where others would respect or accept, to make her laugh when she needed the silliness and to leave her alone when she needed the solitude. As the summer progressed, Holly found she needed that solitude less and less. She and Elizabeth would sit in the tree house talking, reading to each other and revealing secrets they would never utter to another breathing soul. Holly found that she could hold Elizabeth spellbound with the stories her father had loved to tell her and

4

she eagerly shared all her parents had taught her to love and esteem: knowledge, the use of one's own judgement, being proud of one's abilities and intellect, as well as the responsibility to use them.

"But, Elizabeth, you're so clever. Don't you think you *ought* to use your abilities to help others?"

"Of course, Holly, but only if I can do it through the command of my very own pirate ship!"

Holly giggled. "And what good would you do with your pirate ship?"

"Sail the seven seas, of course, and rob and hunt treasures and make Billy Watson walk the plank for breaking my butterfly net. But I would refuse to wear the eye-patch!"

"Or the wooden leg!"

"Maybe we could have lots of parrots instead!"

"Quiet, timid, little parrots!"

"Who would never get a word in edgewise!"

They laughed and Holly poked her cousin in the leg. "But what would you do with all the spoil? Think about how much good we could do."

"Mm." Elizabeth picked out a stolen cherry from the basket between them. She spit the stone out of the tree house and they heard the rustle as it fell through the leaves. "Well, I *would* keep the pearl and diamond tiara..."

"And I would keep the soft and luxurious Cashmere shawl..."

"But other than that, I suppose we'd have to help the poor starving children of Peru."

"We would be *very* rich, Elizabeth. The poor starving children of Bengal too."

"*And* the poor starving children of Nubia!"

Their laughter rang out again.

"That would be heaven," Holly said when they quieted down.

"Very appealing, I agree," her cousin said and leapt to her feet, "but until then, why don't we feed the poor starving lambs down by Mr Wilson's? I'm sure they are quite as adorable as any Bengal or Nubian children. And they eat grass!"

"Fair enough," Holly conceded. She nudged Elizabeth, who sat closer to the makeshift tree ladder. "Go!"

Elizabeth laughed. "I will!" she said and scrambled down.

So it turned out, when Holly left Longbourn to rejoin her mother and to return to the life she had so fervently wished for earlier, once again her heart was wounded. She had left part of it in that tree house and in the care of her cousin Elizabeth — her friend in laughter and companion in secret confessions.

Chapter 1

In which a young Hertfordshire woman and a young Earl find refuge in Scotland fullfilling their friends' expectations most admirably

M ISS Elizabeth Bennet set out for the north at the time of year when migratory birds and people with sensitive health elected to head south. Elizabeth had never suffered from ill health and neither was she the sort to choose her abode according to personal comfort. As a consequence, she felt nothing but hope and relief as she sat in the post and chaise for the third day in a row on muddy roads and in the company of morose co-travellers. For such a long time now she had kept her own council on so many things. Her beloved sister Jane would normally have been privy to her thoughts and speculations, but Elizabeth was fully aware that Jane, with her sweet ways and compassion, could not be burdened with her most uncharitable and desperate feelings. At any rate, Jane was now occupied in her own immediate happiness, just as she deserved to be. Whatever preyed on Elizabeth's mind, making her lie awake at night weighing tragedies and embarrassments in their most wicked form, was not for Jane now. She would not have it so.

She gave a fleeting thought to the fact that this must have been the same road on which her youngest sister and her husband had travelled to Newcastle scarcely a month before. That thought brought with it a renewed sense of shame and regret. She had never told anyone exactly how her sister's marriage to Mr Wickham had made her feel. No one knew everything she knew. No one had been there and seen the look of anxiety in Mr Darcy's eyes when faced with the knowledge that his sister's secret was out and in her hands; or witnessed the fragile, shy demeanour of the one who had to be rescued from lies and falsehood too early in her young life. Even worse than that, only she knew how she had made Mr Wickham's cause her own for all to see on such flimsy and unworthy grounds. Only she knew how her injured dignity at a country ball had overcome her precious judgement and sense and led her astray.

She looked down at the gloved hands on her knees. They danced an unconscious little dance and she realised they were practicing — the first movement of Mozart's piano sonata in A — as she had found herself doing so often since she first played that piece back in August on that magnificent pianoforte in that magnificent music room of that magnificent family... No, not magnificent. Kind. Diffident. Generous. Suddenly another recollection intruded: *You will never play really well, unless you practice more.* Against her will she smiled a little, remembering Lady Catherine's thoughtless remark. Then her smile faltered as she remembered the thoughtless remarks that came later in the Hunsford parlour amidst declarations of love and admiration. Well, at her aunt's home in Scotland she could oblige both Lady Catherine and herself, for she would certainly be in nobody's way there.

Sighing, she stopped her hands as her mind turned to that unexpected visit by Lady Catherine de Bourgh just a few days earlier. She had played that encounter over and over in her mind a hundred times already and she still did not understand it. What had possessed her? Why had she fought like a tigress to keep from giving one inch to a woman she had no interest in? Why had she defied all laws of common courtesy due an older and more distinguished woman from a young, unmarried, provincial slip of a girl?

Pride. That was part of it, of course. She possessed pride in abundance, but not even that could completely explain why she should feel the need to stand so stubbornly against Lady Catherine's demands. She sighed. It was because of him. With such conflicting memories now, how could she be certain of anything? And without certainty, how could she make promises? He was kind — he was mortified, he sought her out — she repelled him. He had done so much for her family — all was true and yet nothing could fully explain how she had answered his aunt's accusations. What was it about him? Was her determination a credit to herself, or more of what she had so readily accused him of — vanity and pride?

Soon, however, the thoughts that had been forced to flow back and forth in her mind in screaming silence for so long would finally be able to be articulated freely. She could tell her aunt and she could tell Holly. Everything and anything. And they in turn would be more understanding than Jane could be; they shared her pride as well as her doubts and disappointments with human nature. Asking just the right questions, following her own faltering thoughts, they would be more sympathetic than her father would be; they were women with lives lived behind them. Oh, how she had practiced at that exchange with them! It was all she could do to keep from saying it aloud here and now.

Soon the Borders, then the Southern Uplands, then Clanough village and then Rosefarm Cottage. And then her aunt and cousin and the society of women who would challenge her, but at the same time let her rest in who she really was as a person.

Mr Darcy sat at his writing desk in the library looking out at the London street beneath his second floor window. The noise outside barely penetrated his consciousness as he sat straight in his chair with his eyes fixed beyond the immediate view. He was perfectly still and to the chambermaid, who in her error thought the room empty and came to remove the ashes from the grate, he seemed asleep. She quietly tip-toed out again and her Master never blinked an eye. He simply had not noticed her. His body might be motionless, but his head was swirling with thoughts and plans.

On the desk in front of him lay a letter from his aunt. He gave it a glance and set his lips in an even firmer line. The letter had reached him at Netherfield but he had not dealt with it there. He had simply done what he had set out to do and then left Bingley to it.

His jaw relaxed slightly and a crooked smile crept over his features. Yes, he was certain Bingley would have some very happy news to share upon his return to Hertfordshire. His friend had been quite touching in his reaction to his confession and opinion. At first incredulous at Darcy's motives and actions on his behalf, he was quick to understand, forgive and dismiss.

Darcy moved his gaze closer to rest on his right hand, still lying on the letter. Bingley was a good man and perhaps he was right. If there is a chance at happiness, one should perhaps just grab it and not question. Impulses do not always have to be rationalised. Feelings are not always by default inferior to reason. In fact, reason often encourages the very feelings it seems to be at odds with. So here he sat, contemplating whether he should allow his feelings and impulses to guide him to where his reason was telling him there were possibilities for success.

His aunt, Lady Catherine de Bourgh, had come to see him, not only to emphasise the indignity of the rumours she had reported in the letter before him, but aghast at the response from the young lady who, along with himself, was the subject of those rumours. But she brought stronger ammunition as well, or so she had thought. When she stopped over at Longbourn to give Miss Elizabeth Bennet a piece of her mind, a piece which was promptly returned to her ladyship by the said Miss Bennet, she discovered that on that very morning, Miss Bennet was preparing to leave for an extended visit to relations who, once they were known to Lady Catherine, shocked her greatly. As she later spelled out to her nephew just exactly *which* relations Miss Bennet was visiting, Mr Darcy was certain he did not look quite as repulsed as she expected. Her response lit a hope and a suspicion in him quite contrary to the one Lady Catherine had intended or his own reason for so long told him he had no right to entertain.

Miss Bennet was leaving to visit her relations, scandalous relations according to Lady Catherine, but what interested him more was that these relations lived in Selkirk, Scotland. Providence had thrown him a circumstance and he impulsively decided, right then and there, to take advantage of it. He now smiled to himself. After having regretted his decision to interfere on Bingley's behalf because of reason, he was now planning how to do the exact thing again to another friend because of instinct. For perhaps the first time in his life, he would take a chance that was not calculated, but that would push his interests towards what his heart told him was right and might just work out to his undefined advantage.

As for that friend, despite his earlier mistakes with Bingley Darcy believed his interference could not help but be beneficial. When Lord Baugham was bored, he was apt to play such games as Darcy had no stomach for himself, therefore he always strove to distance himself from the intrigues and amusements his lordship tended to surround himself with in while in Town. That he happened to witness the rapidly escalating situation between his friend and the two present ladies of his particular attention a week ago at Wellstone Manor had surely been providential. A quick word in a willing ear and his lordship would surely see the wisdom of withdrawing rather than playing the game to its natural, stormy conclusion. This time he was right to interfere. For both their sakes.

The opportunity for such an intervention came sooner than he anticipated, but it was not entirely unexpected. That very evening he found his friend in perfect time for dinner, in his hall, ridding himself of his outer clothing and throwing them at his butler.

"I happened to pass by and thought I'd see if I should find you at home!" Lord Baugham grinned up at him. It was an infectious smile and quite successful in hiding the impertinence of his action. But then, it was the result of a lifelong study and had served his friend very well in the past, and not only when scrounging dinners he could very well afford to give.

Darcy assumed a leisurely pose at the top of the stairs and looked down at him, but not without a smile himself.

"Dressed for dinner?"

"Well, I thought I'd make certain you wouldn't refuse me entry because of etiquette. Are we dining alone?"

Darcy raised an eyebrow. "You don't surprise me, you know. Not as much as you think. I was told there would be veal tonight and so I have been expecting you."

There was a genuine laugh from his friend. "All is right in the world then, eh? One wouldn't want to disappoint by suddenly turning unpredictable. Or is that predictable?"

Lord Baugham made his way up toward his friend after a quick wink to the butler and the assisting footman. With his long legs and quick pace it was soon done.

"And when am I to find out who, of my staff is the guilty informant on my menus?"

Baugham shrugged and walked before his host into the drawing room.

"Perhaps the delectable fumes of Monsieur Chrétin simply drift across to Berkeley Square and I pick them up. Or perhaps the downstairs maid's sister's son apprentices with the butcher and his cousin runs as a link boy for me occasionally."

Mr Darcy gave him a lopsided smile and reached for the claret.

IN THE TYPICAL MANNER OF men, Lord Baugham and Mr Darcy would have described themselves as "the best of friends." Had they not gone through university together, studying the same subjects, defending the reputation of the same College, competing for the same prizes and earning honours enough between them both on and off the sporting field to cause considerable notice among the tutors and masters?

Now, as adults, they attended many the same social gatherings, held many acquaintances in common, shared interest in the same pursuits and voluntarily spent a respectable amount of time in each other's company. They were both tall and good-looking, both were men of status and fortune, and both commanded attention when entering a room. On the surface they were very much alike — how could they *not* be the best of friends?

Such an easy relationship between two such different tempers, however, might still be an enigma to those not privy to their history. Certainly there had been a fair amount of jostling and vying between them, but for two competitive minds the rivalry had so far been confined purely to sports and academia and never tried in other, more immeasurable areas of life, and so far both had felt the friendship of the other to be a great privilege, adding understanding and equality in the society between them. Not an easy thing to achieve considering the requirements of both.

Darcy now studied his friend in his post-dinner repose. They both sat comfortably in front of a generous fire with generous drinks beside them. Baugham relaxed with his long legs stretched out before him and his normally so brilliant blue eyes half-hidden behind lazy eyelids. He wore a contented smile, however, which was no more than right for dinner had been excellent. It always was, of course, but this time Darcy felt the groundwork had been laid well enough; it was time to set to work.

"I've had an offer from a canal building company in Stockport. They want to build a canal through the northern part of my Glossop land."

There was a nod from his friend. "Makes sense. How much are they offering?"

"5000 pounds."

His guest gave a low whistle. "A pretty sum of money."

"Mm. It'll cut the land in half. It's grazing land, too."

"Well, if they offered me 5000, I wouldn't care if it cut Cumbermere right in half and buried the main drawing room under water!"

Darcy looked down into his glass. "Perhaps. But what if it were Clyne?"

Lord Baugham's lazy eyes opened and a hint of mischief washed over them. "I'd tell them to take their offer to the devil!"

"And you'd be right, too. Not that I don't think we will be forced to share the burden for what the industrialists are doing to the country in the name of progress and prosperity soon enough somehow."

"Well, they've already made farmhands and maids a scarce enough natural resource up north. All gone to Chester to work at the mills. Not to mention all this talk about ending the Corn Laws… Damn it, Darcy, I thought you promised me a nice quiet evening without vexations and politics! You know how I hate being reminded of the fact that I am an indebted landowner after a good dinner. It really ruins a fine meal like nothing else."

"I promised you no such thing," Darcy noted dryly. "You should just be glad I restrict myself to agricultural politics, since you've had plenty of other sources of vexation lately — of a considerably more personal nature."

Lord Baugham waved his hand dismissively.

"In fact," Darcy went on, "you've really outdone yourself in blatant disregard of the facts and circumstances in search of some silly way to relieve boredom this time."

"Nonsense!"

"Wellstone did not look like nonsense to me. Sisters, Baugham? What in the world can you have been thinking? No, never mind — I don't want to know. But, may I remind you; you deemed the situation serious enough to warrant an early leave-taking and that not without some embarrassment to your hosts as well as yourself."

Baugham's eyes were now directed at his host and had lost all of their peace. "Are you preparing one of your lectures? If so, spare me!"

"No. You're beyond lecturing in this, my friend."

There was a deep grunt from his lordship.

"I think you know it, too."

There was no protest, so Darcy bided his time, finished his drink and refilled both of their glasses before he continued.

"And I suspect you would not be sorry to come across a good way to extract yourself and end the whole fiasco sooner rather than later."

"Nonsense!" was the answer again, but Darcy knew his friend was speaking more of his own performance in the society drama he was embroiled in, than his friend's suggestion.

"Weren't you going to Clyne anyway?" he said smoothly. "Couldn't you just leave a little earlier than originally planned?"

As always, the mere mention of his lordship's Scotland estate made Baugham smile. "Not that much to shoot yet."

"Well, with the sorry skills of marksmanship you've displayed here in Town lately, I think that might just be as well."

He received a sharp look and acknowledged his misplaced quip. "But you cannot deny it would solve a thing or two."

"Two things, certainly," Baugham said with a raised eyebrow.

Darcy shook his head. "I think you should go," he said quietly. His friend gave him a long look and then sighingly sunk down even deeper into his chair.

"Perhaps I should," he said and closed his eyes.

THE JOURNEY PROVED TO BE one of the more comfortable ones Lord Baugham had experienced on these roads. It was true he had the hospitality of his old friend, Lord Grifford, and his most comfortable arrangements at Millby Hall to thank for one night, and although the beautiful lady of the house begged him to stay a few days more, he was eager enough to be on his way to spend the next night on the road, much less comfortable but much closer to his final destination.

Yes, he had left Town early, but upon reflection he had no regrets about that. If he had been a more self-searching individual, he might perhaps have regretted more the circumstances which necessitated the decision to leave sooner than planned, instead he felt only relief and anticipation — and boredom. Lord Baugham sighed as he stared out at the landscape that was so numbingly dull and unchangeable. Mile after mile of the same muddy road, batches of trees and sleepy hamlets. He could not even make out any landmarks to tell him how far he had come; he only knew there were at least two more nights on the road before he arrived.

On the other hand, as the distance from London grew, any possible lingering thoughts or regrets on the two lovely sisters, Mrs Ashton and Lady Merriwether grew more distant as well. Yes, two sisters, equally lovely and spirited and safely married to older doting husbands and both equally as interested in the young Lord Baugham, who seemed unhindered, willing, and able to brighten up a dull season with some flirtation, fun and, well…more. How could he have been expected to choose between them? And who would have supposed that sisters talked of such things amongst themselves? Surely it would have been more dangerous for him to profess a preference for one over the other? As it was, neither of them had been happy with sharing his attentions, once discovered, and it had very nearly come to a scene at Wellstone Manor, where the delightful clandestine flirtations and relationships risked exposure in a most embarrassing manner. The whole business had suddenly and definitely lost its charm for him and the truth was Darcy's urgings that perhaps it was high time for him to follow through on his frequent threats to leave the whole business behind him and run up to Scotland were received with a willing ear. Since his friend usually took great pains to distance himself from his affairs, Baugham had been surprised at his friend's sudden interest in saving him from scandal, but he had to admit that Darcy was right; the situation *was* close to spiralling out of control and the advice was not unwelcome.

He sighed. Trust Darcy to keep on the sidelines and just enjoy the spectacle with a mix of incredulity and amusement only to suddenly take matters into his hands with a definite opinion and a well-thought out solution. Of course he was right, there had been nothing else to do but go, and having taken definite steps to do so, Baugham was not especially surprised at the relief and happiness he felt by quitting Town and leaving society behind.

CHEERED IMMENSELY BY THE SIGHT of a few fine and massive specimens of the otherwise long-gone Ettrick Forest oaks and sunny weather after two days of incessant rain, Lord Baugham strode into the Caledonian Thistle post house in the village of Clanough on an early October afternoon and cheerfully greeted Mr Robertson, the proprietor. He was splattered with mud from head to toe, his coat was filthy and his manservant would most probably experience palpitations upon observing the state of his boots and breeches, but he was in a splendid mood. He had escaped the confines of his carriage and ridden the last stretch of his journey, he was home, or would be within the hour, ahead of schedule and just picking up his mail before disappearing from the surrounding world into the haven of peace and anonymity called Clyne Cottage.

As the small stout figure of Mr Robertson disappeared to fetch possible missives for his lordship, Baugham leaned leisurely at the bar and sipped at the tankard that had been drawn and placed before him without question. He wiped the sweat off his brow, sighed deeply and listened absentmindedly to the busy noises of a coaching inn preparing for the departing Edinburgh stage. There was some sort of commotion at the door and suddenly it was flung wide open and a cloaked, stooping figure pushed a large bandbox through the door. He watched as this figure, a young lady as it happened, placed the bandbox to the side and began dragging in a trunk. Absently, he wondered where the boy was that should be helping her with such heavy work.

The young lady, Miss Holly Tournier, was wondering the same thing when the strap she had been tugging on suddenly snapped and nearly sent her onto the floor on her backside. Holly looked around in embarrassment, but thankfully saw that the room was nearly empty, except for Mr Robertson, who had his back to her at the moment and apparently did not notice her distress, and one other gentleman leaning against the bar — watching her with a smirk on his face.

"Quite heavy those things, aren't they?" he said in a refined drawl, partly in her direction, partly at Mr Robertson who had returned with his mail. He slipped the proprietor a third coin in addition to the ones for the ale and the service and, nodding towards the lady, gave him an encouraging look. Consequently, Mr Robertson disappeared again in search for Tommy.

Holly stared in disbelief, not only at his smile and callous remark, but at the fact that he could simply stand there and watch her struggling and not even *think* to offer any kind of assistance. Of course, at the sound of his voice she thought she knew exactly who the gentleman was; he was that lord who had bought the Clyne lands up by Nethery Farm a few years earlier. On further reflection it did not surprise her that he should be so ill-mannered. What else was to be expected from a rich member of the peerage, brought up to a life of idleness and privilege hiding away at his little plaything of a cottage and probably engaged in unspeakable sloth and indulgence? She rolled her eyes at his comment and gave him her best smirk in return.

"*Please*, do not trouble yourself, sir," she replied in a voice that she hoped reflected the full level of sarcasm she intended. "I am sure I can manage it quite well on my own."

"Oh, I have no doubt about that!" The reply came in the same cheerfully lazy drawl. "I'm always amazed at the amount of stubbornly capable women in this part of the world. Can't make it easy for aspiring chivalrous men."

"Well, it is certainly obvious you have learnt that lesson to heart, sir," Holly muttered, shuffling her luggage out of the way across the floor.

Her comment was lost in the sound of the bandbox scraping the floor and Lord Baugham threw a glimpse over his shoulder towards where Mr Robertson had disappeared.

Holly stood up and tried to straighten her clothes. She was tired, her limbs ached, her nose was full of the dust of the road and the odours of her fellow passengers and on top of everything she now had to stay dignified in the face of a rude and boorish man who had left all his gentlemanly habits south of the border, thinking people up here were not entitled to his good manners. It was almost too much. She just wanted to be home already.

She felt her throat constrict and concentrated on looking haughty and fixing Lord Baugham with her best dark look, perfected over all her years as a schoolteacher.

"They're in such a hurry these days," the man she was busy disliking suddenly said. "The stage I mean. You know, I was told once by this fellow I met out with a shooting party that the passengers on the stage he came on were given three minutes over a hundred miles to get something to eat over two stops! Reading and Millsby, I think. Or Millston. In Linconshire at any rate. Can you imagine, he came to join us for shooting by taking the stage!"

"Really? How shocking." Holly did her best to ignore him but found great relief in answering him in her iciest tone. However, Lord Baugham did not seem to notice her frosty reply but carried on.

"Well, of course, he never heard the end of it! Imagine! Guns and such on the stage! I'm amazed the stage master didn't throw him off. Although, perhaps he had no time to do so since, as I said, there was very little time to stop anywhere. But it just goes to show you."

Holly briefly closed her eyes and then gave him a disgusted look.

"That the stage is really rather impossible. I suppose they just threw down your luggage outside and left you to fend for yourself, didn't they?"

Somehow it galled Holly to no end that he was absolutely right. She had barely climbed out of her cramped seat on the coach before it set off again and she found the luggage unceremoniously left in the middle of the courtyard with no ostlers or post boys or anyone in sight to help her. It seemed so humiliating to her that he should have guessed at her humiliation, too. *It must be written on my face,* she thought.

She swallowed. "*Some* people," she said sharply, "have no choice whether to take the stage or no. *Some* people are happy not to have to sit on the roof or walk. And some people don't mind very few and short stops because they could not afford any fare or drink at the exorbitant prices avaricious landlords charge at their postal inns anyway."

It was an outburst she had not planned and she had to admit she felt rather better for having succumbed to it, but the way the man opposite her hitched up his eyebrow and gave her a long look with what she noticed were exceptionally bright blue eyes in such a dimly lit quarter as this, was slightly uncomfortable.

"Well," Lord Baugham said slowly, "I suppose you have a point."

"I know I do," Holly answered, not quite prepared to admit that she was done with him. "And that is perhaps one additional reason for this imposed self-sufficiency to which you seem to take such offence, my lord."

Baugham tried to give her a friendly smile, but she merely narrowed her eyes and turned away. Just then Tommy breezed in, stammering apologies and taking charge of her belongings, looking confused as the lady slipped him a coin for his services. Baugham just cleared his throat and shook his head, smiling. There was a moment where the young lady glared at Tommy for what she must have considered extremely peculiar behaviour and inattention and then caught his lordship whistling a little tune to himself. She gave him a stare, but as he seemed oblivious to her displeasure she silently articulated a few more very uncharitable thoughts about "gentlemen" and "nobility" and turned on her heel.

Baugham stole an amused glance at her while he watched her walk out the door, then flipped through the mail, discovered nothing but business from his steward and secretary and, giving a small sigh of satisfaction, pulled on his gloves to leave again.

JUST DOWN THE WAY, IN a snug little parlour crowded with newspapers and unfinished books piling up on the empty chairs and tables, Mrs Arabella Tournier sat upright, reading, her handsome face set in its habitual frown. She was by no means an unpleasant or disagreeable woman, but there was little enough cause for smiles and happiness in her life and so they were seldom seen unless she was in the presence of her daughter. Suddenly, however, a small chuckle escaped her, because the only other thing guaranteed to relieve the perpetually down-turned mouth and knitted brows was her correspondence with her family in the south. She was contemplating a missive just arrived from her sister-in-law all the way from Hertfordshire. The correspondent's polite amazement at the speed of His Majesty's Mail Services and, in the next line, her sincere assurances that Elizabeth was very welcome to stay up north as long as possible and even a bit longer than that, if you please, were met with a wry smile and distinct amusement in her lively and intelligent eyes. Mr Bennet's protests, she was very candidly told, were not to be heeded. Elizabeth was much better off with her aunt where she would be far less trouble and might possibly come to realise and regret her shameful treatment of her mother in the midst of the harsh and grim weather they must surely be suffering from at this time of the year. Life in Hertfordshire at the moment was perfect, and Mrs Bennet intended to enjoy it as a just reward for all her struggles. Mrs Tournier had no qualms in allowing her the right to do so. Especially since it meant Elizabeth's removal to their home was one part of it. It could be said a letter had seldom been sent and received with equal, yet quite opposite pleasure in both sender and recipient. The receiving of Mrs Bennet's letters was an expense Mrs Tournier would be loath to forego but perhaps not entirely for the reasons her sister-in-law imagined.

Notwithstanding the excellent news contained in this particular letter, what Mrs Tournier was so fond of in her sister's infrequent letters was that there was no art about them. They perfectly mirrored their authoress' tone and personality, not to mention were most informative about the wealth and prospects of her future son-in-law and his impressive connections and Mrs Tournier, however much she was glad the writer was not there in person to deliver her news and opinions, appreciated that. They were so very different from her brother's letters. Mr Bennet was a most unreliable and frequently exasperating correspondent, because though Mrs Tournier felt no regrets in leaving the place of her birth and girlhood, she did retain an affection for it and, more importantly, for her nieces. Her brother could never be relied upon to be as candid about the goings on in Meryton and at Longbourn as his wife was certain to be.

The most welcome letters from Hertfordshire were, of course, those from her niece, Elizabeth. Mrs Tournier gratefully acknowledged that her sister-in-law's candidness and her brother's wit were perfectly married in Elizabeth's letters and she took great joy in keeping up a regular correspondence with her. As few others of her family would, Elizabeth Bennet confessed to great curiosity about her aunt's life and exploits, but even more readily she confessed to being very fond of her. Whereas Mrs Tournier's previous life as the wife of a French Revolutionary, exiled when the movement turned violent and bloody, and now a purveyor and collaborator with various periodicals and publications of the intellectual circles in Edinburgh, was not generally talked about within the Bennet family, Elizabeth almost defiantly kept up a warm and close relationship with her aunt. And, perhaps even more importantly, with her cousin Holly.

When Mrs Tournier was widowed eight years previously, she had chosen to stay on at the small cottage called Rosefarm where the family had made their home after their flight from Paris at the Jacobins' rise to power. First it had been insisted upon by the Pembrokes, who originally provided the little family with a refuge from a rootless existence in exile. The terms and rent were very generous, and if at first grief held Mrs Tournier and Holly close to where Jean-Baptiste Tournier had lived and worked, it soon became apparent that economy would continue to do so. Additionally, she was obliged to work for an income, and as much as she hated the necessity, it was evident that her daughter must contribute as well. This her daughter did through teaching at a respected seminary for young girls in Edinburgh. Hockdown School was respected but uninspiring. Elizabeth's visit would be a treat Holly well deserved, and probably desperately needed.

Mrs Tournier let her hands smooth the sheet of paper in front of her while looking out at the darkening October evening. Soon it would be dark enough to require another candle and *that* she could ill afford, especially for familial correspondence. She shifted her eyes to the empty paper and the quills that lay untouched in their etui. She could write her brother — she *should* write her brother — and offer her congratulations and thanks for allowing Elizabeth's visit. She knew it was a sacrifice for him to let her go and she felt she ought to acknowledge as much directly to him.

Her good intentions were forestalled by the sound of a closing door on the other side of the house, and the muffled squeals of Mrs Higgins in the kitchen. A smile spread across her face as she dropped her letter on the desk. Brisk steps, one hallway, a few doors, and she was there. Her daughter had just pulled her bonnet off and was working on her gloves when she spotted her.

"Well this is a surprise, Lie-lie — " was all she was able to get out before she was smothered in hugs, kisses and tears.

16

As HE SET OUT FROM the inn, Lord Baugham reflected that although four days and three nights in fairly adequate lodgings on the way was extremely tiresome to a man of such an impatient disposition as himself, it was worth it once he could finally look upon the sweeping hills, the luscious green glens and big skies. He felt his heart swell and his mind clear of all the clutter in anticipation of finally reaching the place he loved best in the world — Clyne Cottage.

His ancestral home in Cheshire, Cumbermere Castle, had never held his affection. Both an unfortunate relationship with his father and his dislike for the ostentatious trappings of the estate and its obligations contributed to his spending only the absolute minimum amount of time required to attend to unavoidable business affairs. He had been left very little else by way of fortune from his late father; just that mismanaged estate and a glorious, yet chequered, past. The Castle was completely without modern improvements, decayed, in decline and uncared for. His lordship viewed his prime obligation, owed not to his squandering father, but more to the generations of honourable Cumbermeres before him, to save what he could of the seat and estate and restore some of its importance for the local tenants and other dependants.

This goal did not entail the frequent presence of his own person at the estate, as his friend Mr Darcy advised, but rather the discovery and employment of industrious and reliable persons to perform those obligations for him. "I will not rest until I have at least attempted to do my duty," he had informed his friend, "but my talent does not lie in managing, you must see that. My talent surely lies in harnessing the abilities of others, allowing them to work without interference, and securing what profit I can from it."

Any affection for land and property he reserved for Clyne Cottage, and when finally the carriage drew up in front of the view he had waited so long to behold, he felt something indescribable swell in his chest — a poet might have called it love. The day was rapidly waning, but the whiskey-coloured sandstone building, nestling against the rolling hills and faintly reflecting the scant sunshine, was clearly visible to him through the shielding monkey-puzzle trees and Scots pine. Behind it, he knew, the river languidly meandered, only to struggle through rough and rocky passages just half a mile further down. As visible as the cottage was to him, was his carriage to its caretakers, so when he stepped out and stretched his long limbs, his smiling face met those of Mr and Mrs McLaughlin, both happy to see him and eager to wish him welcome once again.

After a warm exchange of greetings, they informed him that Riemann had arrived only a few hours before and was busy arranging his quarters to his satisfaction. Mrs McLaughlin soon extracted a promise to be allowed to send into town for meat to sustain them for the coming few days before his lordship would be able bag some game for his own table, and Mr McLaughlin was granted an audience to address the situation of the wine cellar.

As was his habit, his lordship immediately bullied his man into interrupting his arrangements to help him change out of his travelling clothes and into his country clothes, and then dismissed him from interfering with his dress for the rest of their stay. Childishly happy and humming tunes with distinct romantic notions of nature, Lord Baugham retired to his library with a book and a drink to wait for dinner. But before that, he availed himself of the last remaining light of the day to compose a letter:

Clyne Cottage
Tuesday

Dear Darcy,

Just a short note to tell you I have indeed arrived and am comfortably sitting at my writing desk with the Kye River flowing smoothly beyond my window in front of my eyes as always. You may be amazed at the condition of our roads, for I have never known a journey to be so smooth and swift. Alas, I will never be completely satisfied with the Almighty's plan of putting the place I love best so far away from the places I am bound to inhabit, but I suppose that is all in his great plan of teaching me humility and patience. So far his success has been nominal — as our last conversation no doubt has convinced you. Nevertheless, you are not to worry. I have put all troubles and regrets behind me and I find I have not the least bit of concern for what is now being said or done in my absence. I daresay by Christmas all will be forgotten. I am now at home and at peace and take this opportunity to wish you all the best.

Your friend,
Baugham

Chapter 2

*Pasts are left behind and Hearts and Minds find Rest
in and around the Village of Clanough*

As always with her homecomings, Holly felt emotionally drained just reaching that small parlour and being in her mother's presence. Consequently, there was little talk and much touching of stray hairs and smudges of ink or mud on faces and hands as they loosened their initial embrace. For anyone familiar with the habitual expressions and faces of the two women, it would have been remarkable how tenderly Mrs Tournier's eyes rested on her daughter, and how shiny and soft Holly's expression turned when her mother touched her face and took her hands once more.

They sat down, wordlessly, on the sofa and, with sighs of relief and happiness, settled down to a few moments of silence when all in the world seemed right and well and just as it should be.

"You know, my dear," Mrs Tournier finally broke the silence, "as much as I am enjoying your unexpected early arrival, your stomach will soon have its revenge by interrupting our perfect harmony and happiness with vulgar sounds if I do not soon offer you tea."

Holly sat up with a smile and could not hide her delight.

"And," her mother said with a smile of her own, "to celebrate and to restore, we will both have sugar with it. I haven't had any for a week and I have been very hard at work with Mr Harrowdash's latest thoughts on the ballast of France's republican past in its new imperial age, so I definitely deserve some tonight."

Holly froze. Her mother had used a light tone, but she knew her fondness for richly sugared tea when she was working, and if she confessed to having had none this past week, that meant that she was economising. Tears welled up in her eyes as she realised she must divulge her predicament as soon as possible and perhaps spoil this perfect moment. She grabbed hold of her hand, preventing her from moving away to call Mrs Higgins.

"Maman…" she said in a desperate tone.

Her mother frowned at her as she looked down.

"What is with all this emotion, daughter? I know you are always happy to be home, but it has not been that long since you last were here."

"Oh Maman," Holly choked out between sobs that were full of bitterness as well as relief and worry. "I haven't just come home for a visit this time…I have been *sent* home. For good."

Not waiting for her mother's bewilderment to express itself in words, she plunged on.

"But I have been thinking on the way and the first thing tomorrow I plan to send out letters in search of another position. But…I also thought that maybe I might try find something closer to home, instead. I mean…I'm a miserable seamstress, but I can cook — or serve. Do you think maybe Mr Robertson at the inn might have a place…?"

She stopped when she met her mother's eyes watching her. Slowly Mrs Tournier sat down again and folded her hands in her lap.

"What happened?" she said.

Pressing her lips together to keep them from trembling, Holly looked down at her own hands.

"You were right in everything you tried to warn me about, that's what happened. I should have kept to lessons in music and French and not attempted anything more. The headmaster called me into his office and…it was just as you said, no one was interested in having the girls learn anything of educational value — he said I was wasting my time, and theirs. And, Maman, they learned about my going into the city and the boys' lessons and that's…"

She looked up and attempted a smile, even as the tears fell freely. "It appears that I am a subversive influence and a poor example of virtuous womanhood. After five years of service, I am no longer acceptable."

Mrs Tournier stroked her daughter's cheek and for a few minutes she listened to her tearful exclamations. When she finished, she addressed her calmly and softly, but not without some sternness.

"Oh my dear child, all these tears! Now Lie-lie, you must stop this nonsense straight away! As far as I can see, you have nothing to reproach yourself or your conduct with, other than idealism that I suppose you cannot help. Therefore, there will be no tears spilled on account of Mr Hockdown and his establishment. Why should you see this as such a great calamity when you were uneasy and unhappy at that place, your conscience is clean and you are loved and appreciated right here? It makes no sense."

Mrs Tournier could see the protests springing to her daughter's lips, but she headed them off with a look.

"Truly, I can see no other reasonable source for your tears other than exhaustion and relief. We will manage; we always do. Something will come up. And since you have no reason to lament, there is no reason why your homecoming should not be a source of great joy and celebration instead. If your stay should be of some longer duration than originally planned, all the better!"

"But Maman — "

"Lie-lie," the mother continued sternly, "I will allow you to cry and mope all you wish tonight, but your cousin is coming soon and I plan to enjoy her visit, as should you.

"Sit with me a while. We do not have to say a word. Indeed, I hope we do not since once your eyes grow used to these familiar surroundings you will find that your life is not so hopeless after all, and there is no reason for such desperate tears. Rather the opposite, since I will now try once again to ring for tea."

Holly felt herself relaxing — it felt good to be home and in her mother's care, just like when she was a child — but when the tea arrived she was not quite ready to tend to it.

"It is not the fact of my leaving that has upset me, but that I was sent off in disgrace and shame like a common..." here she broke off, not trusting herself to continue without more tears. After a moment she looked up at her mother with an odd smile. "Maman, tell me — how did you know I was uneasy and unhappy at Mr Hockdown's school? I tried so hard to hide it from you in my letters."

Mrs Tournier gave a most undignified snort for a lady with pretensions of sense and wit. "*Tried,* being the operative word, my dear. There is no such thing as successful concealment of your feelings from your mother, although I have tried very hard not to put you at a disadvantage because of it. And if your desperate attempts at inducing sense and compassion into your charges, or those after hours forays into the city for charitable education were not telling enough, I know your disposition well. Remember, I have known you all your life! You have never made any secrets of your likes and dislikes. Even if you very rarely express them out loud, they are written on your face plainly for anyone to see who takes the trouble. And you never did take to letter writing as an art. Your own sweet self shines through in every line."

The slight smile on her daughter's face induced Mrs Tournier to take her hand and clutch it.

"So then, what is this shame and disgrace you talk of? You are by no means the first capable and intelligent young woman to be dismissed for unfathomable reasons. Surely no one who knows you can doubt your character and your diligence?"

"I had thought not, Maman, but it seems that old prejudices are more highly regarded, and less easily replaced, than poor young teachers. Maman, Mr Hockdown implied that my dealings in town involved... less than respectable actions as well. I don't know how he could say such things; how could anyone say such things about me?"

Mrs Tournier was not a timid woman by any measure. She had also seen enough of the world and man's folly, greed and cruelty not to be easily impressed by renewed evidence of it. Furthermore, having been quite a beauty in her day and blessed with a sweet countenance, she did not portray dismay or rage very convincingly — which perhaps had always been the saviour of her sometimes more than trying manners and bluntness. Now, however, she definitely could have inspired the most sanguine of her fellow men to recoil. She looked at her daughter, her calm vanished, eyes flashing and her brows laid in deep wrinkles.

"Infamous! So that is how the land is laid, is it? That horrid man! That sad, desperate excuse for a human being!"

She clasped the locket around her neck with her late husband's portrait as she always did when agitated and, rubbing it for a few seconds, managed to compose herself.

"Nothing surprising, nothing extraordinary, but I am incensed all the same. 'Less than respectable', indeed! Oh, I do believe I am too put out to make any sense! But rest assured, I shall spend a sleepless night articulating my chagrin and tomorrow after breakfast I shall be glad to spell out my injured sense of justice and propriety in carefully worded phrases to Mr Hockdown! We may be without recourse, but we are most certainly not without voice! You may be certain of that."

Strangely enough, this show of agitation had a calming effect upon Holly. This was what she was accustomed to; her mother had always been her most vocal champion, and now that she had shared her burden she was sure that somehow, between the two of them, things would be put right.

She pulled her mother to sit down beside her, laid her head upon her shoulder and rested a moment in the comfort she found there. Then after pouring two cups of tea and mixing them properly, she handed one of them over.

"When does Elizabeth arrive?"

Mrs Tournier pursed her lips and patted her daughter's hand.

"As if you have not been counting the days for the past month. But I will allow your unnecessary question as a very welcome change of subject. Elizabeth will be here in two days' time, and, as I have been able to procure a copy of Mrs Burney's latest play, you and she must fight over the part of the romantic heroine I think. I'm convinced that it will rally your spirits. I think we must arrange a little soirée around it, don't you? I know Elizabeth with be highly disappointed if we do not and will insist on reading it out loud herself and commenting on the wit of it all, whether we have an audience or not. If only we can contrive some way of keeping any undeserving young men we find ourselves obliged to invite from insisting on the part of the hero, we shall be well entertained."

Holly smiled and concentrated on her tea. She watched her mother unload three lumps of sugar into her cup, stir it reverently in silence and sip it with her eyes closed. As she opened them again, she looked at her daughter.

"And Lie-lie my dear," she said firmly, "Mr Robertson will not have a place for you at his inn. Ever."

"Maman, this is no time to be proud. I will do what is needed."

"Of course you will," her mother said and leaned back with a blissful look on her face. "You just will not work for Mr Robertson that is all."

"Maman? What is going on?" Holly asked beneath lowered eyebrows. "Why do you have that smug expression on your face?"

Mrs Tournier opened her eyes and they sparkled. "It's the sugar," she said and laughed. "Oh how I do like my sugar!" She patted her daughter's hand and put away her tea cup. "And tomorrow my dear, we will pray for a fine day so that you can potter about in your garden and I can sit at my desk watching you as I write my letters. I have quite a few I must attend to."

Seeing that further questioning would be futile, Holly put her cup away as well and simply sat quietly next to her mother. She was home, Maman was not worried, and even if they must live without sugar, somehow all would be well.

LORD BAUGHAM COULD NEVER ABIDE being anything but happy at Clyne. His plans, therefore, simply consisted of staying there for as long as he remained so, and leaving just as soon as it was no longer the case. The very first morning of his stay, he made plans to venture out with poles and tackle and the avowed intention of catching his own dinner, to Mrs McLaughlin's surprise, but was interrupted in his mission by a majestically proportioned thunderstorm. Needless to say, that most gothic of weathers frightened away the fish more effectively than his oaths or the wet spectacle of himself did, though he did manage to bring down two unsuspecting birds on his way back. His man, Riemann's, fussing and Mrs McLaughlin's potions failed to bring him any benefits or enjoyment, but when he was comfortably tucked in front of a warm fire, reflections upon man's insignificance against natural forces and his folly at thinking himself able to disregard the signs sent to warn him, led him to poetry.

The storm without might rair and rustle,
Tam did na mind the storm a whistle.

The lines from his favourite poem made him smile. But circumstances were not favourable to philosophical thought and poetic ramblings. Instead, he found himself planning the small excursion northwards Mr McLaughlin had seen fit to recommend for tomorrow, probably covering a few days, to inspect the salmon passages before winter set in. This was all he needed and he sank further into his chair. Weeks of the same activities, the same landscape, the same pursuits stretched before him and he smiled. He was home.

HOLLY HAD GONE TO BED with a vague sense of guilt for the relief she felt when contemplating that she really, truly would never have to return to Hockdown School ever again. It was true that she also possessed a fully developed sense of outrage at the injustice of her dismissal, but she could not look around her small, comfortable, room, warmed and illuminated solely by the frugal fire, without a smile.

In the morning, she sat up with a start upon first seeing the sun streaming through the window, fearing she had overslept, but it only took remembering where she was, and why, to decide to snuggle back down under the warm blankets and let herself slide back into a decadent, second slumber. By the time she woke again, the sun was much higher and her stomach was grumbling about a missed breakfast.

A doting Mrs Higgins had saved a plate for her and, while she ate, Mrs Tournier kept her company with a cup of coffee. Afterwards her mother, with that same smug expression she had sported the night before, pleaded letter writing duties and excused herself, leaving Holly to choose how she would spend her first morning home. It was no surprise to any of them that she went directly to her garden.

She had meant to simply walk around and check out the state of things, pulling off the odd dead blossom or dried leaf as she noticed them, but once alone in the chill October air, she could not stop the train of thought and worry. As she played the humiliating inquisition in front of the Directors over in her mind, as she recalled the vile insinuations, as she worried about how they would manage to make ends meet now that she was no longer earning a wage, she found that she was growing more and more agitated.

She had not cried. Throughout all the humiliating ordeal of being summoned from her classroom in the middle of the day, being subjected to impertinent questioning, being accused of "masculine" behaviours simply because she believed the girls had intellects that ought to be nurtured, she had not cried. Worse was the lecturing; each pompous gentleman on the Board of Directors in turn, chastising her at length for trying to expand her pupils minds and give them something to think on besides fashions, dances and men. Worst of all was Mr Hockdown, the Chairman, who came last.

"Miss Tournier," his stentorian voice rang out, "is it true that you have been stealing out to the sordid quarters of the city in the night, alone, in a seditious attempt to educate the filthy rabble, to stir them up to pretensions of equality and worth?"

Lifting her chin defiantly, she had answered grimly, her mouth tight and her eyes flashing, "They are not filthy rabble, sir…"

In need of activity, Holly took a knife and snips from the greenhouse and what started out as a tour of inspection soon turned into a full blown cleansing ritual. Anything brown or overgrown, in need of trimming or cutting back before the frost, received her attention. She cut, pruned, trimmed, raked and piled as she thought about what had been, what was, and what might come. The physical labour provided an outlet for the restless wanderings of her mind. Yes, she was prepared to do anything that might be necessary in order to assure their continued support — but at the same time, the thought of becoming a cook or a serving girl depressed her spirits. She had always dreamed of being so much more. The legacy of her parents, and her idealisation of their struggles and sorrows, was a very powerful influence on her aspirations. She wanted to *do* something, to *be* someone — to make a difference.

"And more seriously," Mr Hockdown had continued, "I cannot but question your assertions that charitable motivations and misguided views on education are your sole incentive for these secret forays into the city to meet with men clandestinely. Miss Tournier, these activities cast a shadow over your moral character and respectability…"

Holly had thought she had found a way to make her situation bearable and to live up to her parent's republican ideals, but it had been taken from her and turned into something ugly and sordid. While she had detested being a teacher of deportment, drawing, music and French, at least it was a respectable profession and could be seen as having *some* sort of impact on the lives around her, but to think she might be reduced to wiping tables and filling mugs simply to put food on the table... As much as she hated to admit it, her pride rebelled at the thought of facing Elizabeth and telling her she was to become a serving maid at the local public house.

Holly then grew disgusted with herself for succumbing to such snobbery, pulling a few innocent plants out by the roots in the process. Since she was old enough to obtain a position she had always worked, her mother worked, and she had been raised to believe that the labourer possessed as much, nay, more, nobility than the so-called upper crust of society — she would *not* be ashamed!

By this time her thoughts had grown as dark and ominous as the storm clouds gathering overhead, her pile of refuse in the corner had grown almost as tall as she was. She put a flame to it, watching as all the dross and litter caught fire, sending shimmering waves of heat and feathery bits of floating ash up to the skies. She listened to the crackling of the flames and wondered if there was any symbolism to this act of hers. Would she be a phoenix rising from the ashes? Or was she merely watching her hopes and dreams go up in smoke?

Mrs Tournier was preoccupied with her letters, but she suddenly smelled something burning. Looking up, she saw smoke oozing from a pile of leaves and garden debris and her daughter standing with her arms crossed beside it watching intently. The rain was beginning to fall, extinguishing the flames, but Holly was still focusing on it as if expecting something to happen.

"A bonfire, eh?" Mrs Tournier thought ruefully and put down her quill for a moment. "All that smoke can surely not be welcome to someone bent on symbolic significance."

Suddenly, however, a gust of wind shook the hedges and a swirl of a dozen or so yellow and withered leaves rushed past the bonfire, got caught in the warm air rising with the smoke and lifted the round, golden leaves first high up and then scattered them like gold coins over the nearest patch of earth.

Mrs Tournier smiled. "Making money," she thought. "Well, let us see, Lie-lie, if my method isn't more reliable after all."

She carefully put a few more finishing phrases to her letter and in a strong, sure hand signed it, sprinkled blotting sand all over her spindly writing, folded it up and addressed it to the Board of Directors at Hockdown School for Fine Young Ladies, Edinburgh. She had deliberately striven for brevity at the expense of a full articulation of her sentiments to restrict herself to one, uncrossed and plain sheet of paper and, even if she had muttered additional comments to herself vigorously during the process, she was pleased with her effort.

Putting it aside, she drew out a new page, hastily ran over what she intended to write in her mind and set to work.

Rosefarm Cottage
Clanough
Selkirk

My Dear Sir John Ledwich,

As always at this time of year, I am once again asking for your congratulations on the return of my prodigal daughter. This time, however, you may even be so bold as to envy me since it has transpired she will be home for a longer duration than originally planned. Nevertheless, not to abandon our old customs altogether, this letter is that traditional invitation for you to come and see us at your convenience to take pleasure in the fact that I have my Holly home with me. As usual you can expect Mr Jones from the Chronicle and Mr Kershaw, too, since Parliament is adjourned. Do not be surprised if Mr Grant sees fit to join us, too. I can hardly refuse him since his Aunt Grace is coming and she is bringing the Pembrokes and you know I could not refuse them even if I should want to.

This time if you should take a fancy to conducting some of your more picturesque thermological experiments in the kitchen, I am afraid we shall have to dismiss Mrs Higgins beforehand, since she cannot abide any pyrotechnics or explosions causing havoc on the hearth. She has no natural curiosity about the world around her, poor thing.

So now that you have a fixed engagement and a promise of lively, but civil, conversation, mandatory intelligent discourse, a few pretty girls and stimulating company to brighten up your rainy Edinburgh academic toil, I shall put another matter of great importance to you quite bluntly.

I know you are hard at work on your newest treatise on Heat and Voluminous Expansion and although I am rather inclined to think illustrating test tubes and pipettes must be the height of tedium, I am certain Holly would find both pleasure and challenge in perfecting your visions and conclusions. As you are already fully aware of her artistic talents, I have no qualms over pressing her services upon you and I will not do it cheaply, so there is your means of excuse, if you will have one, for not considering her. You are, after all, an important man these days and can afford to pay her handsomely. She, on the other hand, can aspire to the title of an established artist, so I will not sell her short.

Please let me know post haste of your decision and then we can spend several agreeable hours haggling over fees when I welcome you here in our modest home on the 20th.

Yours cordially.
Mrs Arabella Tournier

26

HOLLY POKED HER HEAD IN the door once more to check the time. That the post chaise was running late was not unusual, but that she was so anxious for it to arrive made the minutes drag by intolerably slowly. Mr Robertson gave her a smile and a wave and told her not to fret, the coach might be delayed, but it *would* arrive sometime this day. Didn't she know the punctuality and reliability of the English post was the envy of the civilised world?

She returned his smile and resumed her pacing on the lawn in front of the Caledonian Thistle. So many times, a wait on this lawn had only meant that she was leaving home again on the Edinburgh stage, but this time her spirits were high. Elizabeth was coming and she could hardly wait. Elizabeth's visits were always a special time, set aside for laughter and enjoyment, for deep talks and confessions, and for freedom, at least for a short time, to be her long forgotten, girlish self. She was determined that no worries about past or present would mar the visit — there would be time enough for that later.

At the sound of the carriage wheels, she shouted for Tommy and ran up the road to meet it. Of course, it did not stop until it came to the inn yard, so Holly had to turn and run back down the road again alongside it. All the while she smiled and waved into the window, hoping that the shadowy figure waving back was her cousin.

Finally a head popped into view, a frantic unclasping of the window ensued and all the while Holly could hear her cousin's muffled laughter behind the glass.

"Oh Holly! What are you doing? You dear silly girl!" were Elizabeth's first words as she finally was able to open the window. She leaned out, laughing happily the rest of the way until the carriage came to a stop, jerking her back into her seat and momentarily hiding her from view again.

Holly, breathless and grinning from ear to ear herself, stopped and composed herself while Tommy unlocked the door and unfolded the steps. The first one to emerge was her cousin Elizabeth with her bonnet strings untied and her arms stretched out to be caught.

"Oh, Holly!" she said. "What a welcome!"

Through happy tears and laughter Holly cried, "Oh, you *are* welcome. So very welcome! I am so happy to see you."

She did not even wait for the luggage to be unloaded before she was tugging her cousin down the road toward Rosefarm Cottage.

"I have arranged it all with Mr Robertson already. They will bring your trunk down directly, but I am in no humour to wait for it. You must come and say hello to Maman. Then we can have something to eat and you can rest in your room if you need to." She tugged again. "Come, Elizabeth. Hurry."

"Hurry? I have been hurrying the whole day! The horses were lazy, indolent creatures only interested in vying for opportunities to cast off their shackles and admire the scenery, and if I weren't so mortally afraid of getting a good scolding from all those slovenly inn keepers and coachmen, I should have refused to pay them anything for their slothful services! How *can* Clanough be so far away?"

She held her cousin at arms length and took her in. "No, Holly, I just want to look at you." She winked her eye at her and pinched her cheek playfully. "I do believe you've grown."

"Grown?" Holly laughed. "I do believe the rough coach ride has addled your brain. I have grown…Elizabeth, I *am* grown and have been grown for several years at least! Now you on the other hand…are exactly the same size as the last time I saw you—and I will say that you look very well. But aren't you the least bit hungry? I have been waiting here all afternoon; shan't we have some tea at home?"

Elizabeth looked at her cousin. Holly's eyes sparkled and there was an energy about her she had missed. An energy that matched her own restless mind as well as her elation perfectly. Carefully she linked her arm through her cousin's and kissed her cheek.

"Of course we shall. I will want for nothing once I have tea with you and Aunt Arabella. But," she turned them around and slowly guided Holly down into the road, "I insist on a majestic approach to our final destination. I shall hurry no more. I shall heed the words of the philosopher who claims the journey is more important than the destination. You shall lead me down the road to the very place I've thought of and missed and longed for so desperately, but I insist on dignity. Even if I burst first!"

Elizabeth smiled at her cousin, who smiled back and for a moment they were silent as they began to walk back towards Rosefarm Cottage in almost exaggerated poise and composure.

"There!" she then said conspiratorially. "Now your neighbours know we are capable. Shall we run the rest of the way?"

And run the rest of the way they did. Laughing, shrieking, nearly losing their balance a time or two, bumping into each other and finally, bursting through the gate at full speed and hitting the kitchen door with a thud. Once inside, they skipped past a stunned Mrs Higgins and charged arm in arm into the parlour to find Mrs Arabella Tournier at her desk.

Gasping for breath and stifling their giggles, they watched Mrs Tournier turn around and remove her spectacles.

"So the whole neighbourhood now knows what I see. I must tell you, I could hear you coming all the way from the tinker's yard. So, welcome Elizabeth!"

Elizabeth dropped a curtsey and her aunt gave her a little crooked smile.

"Very nice, niece," she said, "but not quite how we do it around here." She rose and embraced her niece warmly and received many equally affectionate kisses on both of her cheeks amidst laughter and smiling.

"I'm sure you had a perfectly beastly journey," Mrs Tournier said when Elizabeth finally let go of her, "and knowing you, you think the only way to remedy that is to take a long walk this instant. However, since you are now in my care I will insist on tea first."

"To which I could have no objection, my dear aunt! I would sincerely love a walk to admire Scotland's beauty as soon as possible, but since I know very well you don't share my fancy and would not accompany me, I will gladly have tea instead."

"I'm very glad to hear it," Mrs Tournier smiled. "Besides, there are a great many happenings at Longbourn that I must hear about instantly, so the walking will have to wait."

Elizabeth flushed a little, but quickly found her seat and thus hoped her aunt had not paid too much notice to her hesitation. *Let Lydia take the blame for my wavering,* she thought. *That certainly is a subject I do not care to have a frank discussion about so soon after my arrival.*

"Of course!" she said aloud. "I should tell you first of all that Jane sends her love and fondest regards; that which she can spare from Mr Bingley, naturally. She is very happy."

"Well then we shall be thankful for Jane's endless affection and regard for all and sundry despite circumstances and distance. However, if my daughter can leave you alone for a quarter of an hour, you are to run upstairs, fling off your dirty garments, have a wash and catch your breath only to skip downstairs to us again and then be at our disposal for the rest of the evening."

Elizabeth smiled and embraced her aunt once again.

"I will. Thank you, dear aunt, so much for having me! I will be right back!"

Holly followed her out to tend to tea and Mrs Tournier looked after the two girls with a thoughtful smile.

THE FOLLOWING MORNING, LORD BAUGHAM awoke at dawn after a heavy dreamless sleep. At first, the faint sound of rain slowly penetrated his perception with its heavy patter on the thin windowpanes, gradually lifting him to the surface of consciousness, until he finally drifted awake murmuring "Well, I'll be! I wonder if the dam will hold." That thought stayed with him as he slowly opened his eyes and stretched his limbs, aching after an exceptionally still slumber. He slowly accustomed himself to the morning and found himself thinking about his planned expedition, which not even the rain could spoil. He felt his eyelids shut again and as he listened to the rain slowly fading away, he realised it was far too early to leave this blessed drowsy state and so he let himself be dragged down into sleep once more.

But a few hours later, when he woke again, he was itching to rise and wasted no time in throwing off the covers and ripping the drapes open to ascertain whether his ears served him right and the rain had stopped. Indeed, he was right and he hastily washed himself and dressed in his trousers, boots, shirt and simple waistcoat. The necktie could wait; he had business this morning out on the brook by the end of the wood. The bridge was near collapsing, Mr McLaughlin and he had noticed on their way back yesterday, and he needed to walk over to ascertain the damage before he set out on any pleasurable communing with trout or other wildlife.

He found Mrs McLaughlin in the kitchen by the fire, plucking a grouse.

"We need more groose," she said as a way of greeting. "Ye've not bagged enooch this sennicht."

Baugham scanned the kitchen. Somewhere there must be an apple tart. His nose very distinctly said so.

"Yes, well, I have been busy, Mrs McLaughlin."

There was a growling noise from the housekeeper.

"What with? It's autumn. We need meat on the table and in the aumrie."

"Aumrie?" Baugham said still looking around. "Oh, pantry!"

He went over to the door at the centre of Mrs McLaughlin's culinary kingdom and opened the clasp. There it was! Untouched as well. He took it out and reached for a knife on the kitchen table. A quick look from Mrs McLaughlin and he arrested his movements.

"I am going to repair the bridge with Mr McLaughlin later today. I need my strength," he said sternly.

"Aye, well, I'll mind that when I pack yer nacket later on before ye leave," she calmly said.

Baugham reluctantly put down the tart.

"And more than tairt ye need meat," she finished and calmly went back to her plucking.

His lordship threw one more longing look at the apple tart and then went on his way to find Mr McLaughlin to tell him to pack up.

While that was being attended to, he took a turn around the stables to look over his horses before he returned to the house. One more surreptitious check on the kitchen revealed that the housekeeper was still standing guard over the pantry, so with a sigh he strode out again to meet the waiting Mr McLaughlin. Together they set out to their destination.

They worked for a fair while, replacing the half-rotted planks with newer, safer ones and sharing some of Mr McLaughlin's cheese and bread for lunch. Pleased with their day's work, Mr McLaughlin coaxed his lordship into taking a detour to the west of the estate on their way home to inspect another collapsed bit of road. It was agreed that something had to be done about it before the heavy autumn rains set in and this problem was further pondered over in his lordship's study, accompanied by a welcome pot of strong, hot coffee and the rest of the now surrendered apple tart.

THE END OF THIS DAY could not come too soon for Darcy. He had already endured two long days in a comfortable carriage, two sleepless nights in very fine inns, but by assuring himself — through the prodigal distribution of coin at the last stop — of the freshest horses available and pushing his driver to his and the beasts' limits, he hoped to reach Clyne Cottage before the night grew too late.

He was stiff and tired and his jaw ached. At first he had wondered about this last inconvenience, until he realised that every time his thoughts threatened to go off the disciplined track he had set for them — to wonder at the folly of what he was now doing, to worry at what Miss Bennet's reaction would be upon their meeting, to wonder how he would go about finding her, and the thousand other random anxieties that threatened to overwhelm his mind — he would set his teeth, perhaps twenty times an hour, and turn his mind back to the present. A present that consisted only of a journey, and a sore jaw.

He would think no farther than reaching his destination: a fire, a meal, a bath. Baugham would be there, and that would mean company and conversation, then a marginally comfortable bed. He would not think of Miss Bennet until tomorrow…he wondered if Baugham was acquainted with her relations. If that was so, things would proceed more smoothly and naturally, but his lordship always boasted of the isolation of his Scotland existence. Knowing his personality as he did, Darcy could not wholly credit his assertions, but even if it was so, he would at least have *some* knowledge of such unusual neighbours, even as far as knowing where they lived. Miss Bennet would go for walks, he was sure, maybe he could…

A quick jerk of his head brought him back to the present, the journey, and he felt a sharp pain in the muscles of his jaw as he set himself to think no more of Miss Bennet. Once again.

Chapter 3

*In which Two old Gentlemen Friends settle down for a Peaceful
Time at Clyne and an Interest in Local Families is Revealed.*

WELL, I must say I do not envy my sister Bennet one jot," Mrs Tournier told her niece. "Despite the happy news about Jane, it is with some astonishment and disbelief I find that she managed to reach the age of twenty-three without marriage! The good Lord knows that fact does not bode well for her younger sisters."

Elizabeth tried to give her aunt an affronted look, but only managed to break out into a laugh.

"It is perfectly true, though," her aunt went on, "if you subscribe to the notion that marriage is the only respectable profession for you. In keeping with that sentiment, I must say that my brother's indifference and my sister's obsession between them do little to further your interests."

"Ah, but could not one say that since the eldest sister — belatedly I admit — has managed such a splendid match in both love and importance, and the youngest managed the complete opposite at a far too early age, all the remaining sisters will have every chance at achieving something in between the two?"

Holly smiled as Elizabeth put down her teacup after that statement with an innocent look on her face. It was a great pleasure just to sit, watching and listening, while her mother and cousin talked as if no more than a week had passed since they had last sat with each other. *Bennet women.* Although age, situation, life and distance separated them, there was something so inherently familial in the way they conversed. The way they turned a phrase, hitched one eyebrow at a crucial point of argument, the sideways smile that revealed deliberate exaggeration or mischief and that same low, almost husky laugh.

Holly smiled as her mother poked her cousin in her arm to make a point and Elizabeth laughingly took it and shook it about, refuting her argument.

Holly had no memories of her Bennet grandparents; therefore she supposed she was really more of a Tournier woman. This was, of course, a fancy she had constructed herself, for she had even less knowledge of her French family than her Hertfordshire one. Nevertheless, it was an assumption she happily made based solely on her memories of her father and what he had meant to her. Yes, even if she would be no one else, she would be her father's daughter.

"And you have been fortunate yourself, Elizabeth, in being able to decline our cousin, Mr Collins' offer I understand." Mrs Tournier's blunt question brought Holly back to the conversation before her and she raised her head to hear the answer.

"I suppose Mama told you — I'm quite out of her good graces still, even though I think Jane, the dear unselfish creature, has made some progress toward remedying my disgraceful behaviour."

"I heard from your father, yes. As you know I have never corresponded with Mr Collins, just as I did not with his late father. I prefer to think of it as his prejudice, but the truth is I would not have the stomach for it even if he were to approach me."

"Are you quite sure that was wise, Aunt?" Elizabeth smiled mischievously. "You do have an attractive, unmarried daughter that you might have tried to interest him in. I believe you have missed your chance to secure your own return to Longbourn."

"Well, I shall be sorry to see Longbourn pass out of my brother's direct line, but I have no desire to again call it home. Once is quite enough, as you might well understand."

"I do. And as I am convinced that Mr Collins' suit could not have been successful with Holly either, I am glad she was saved the mortification of hearing his violent professions of affection."

"At least Mr Collins had the grace to accept your refusal in time," Holly joined in, laughing. "You must count yourself as lucky to only once have to endure such an inappropriate declaration!"

A strange blush crossed Elizabeth's face and Holly feared that her jest may have been perceived as unkind. She hastened to explain herself.

"And lest you despair, let me just tell you that we are at odd ends of the same dilemma, for every time I return home for a visit there is a gentleman, Mr Grant, who persists in proposing, no matter how many times I refuse him. He takes heart in the general opinion in the neighbourhood that we are a likely match and he simply will not hear me. It is unfortunate that there are no Miss Lucas's in the vicinity, for he is quite a catch — sadly, I obviously am not sensible enough to take advantage of it."

Holly's tragic tone made Elizabeth laugh. "And what is wrong with Mr Grant that he is not worth considering despite his eligibility?"

"Poetry," Holly groaned. "He quotes poetry — extensively — and not just any poetry. He is excessively fond of Byron and Blake. That, as you can imagine, makes any alliance impossible to contemplate."

"Yes, I can see that. Quite," Elizabeth said. "Perhaps I will do the gentleman a favour when we meet and share with him your love of Burns."

"Do and I shall never forgive you," Holly playfully smacked her cousin's hand. "I will not have my love for Robert Burns sullied, thank you very much. It is a pure affection, and thankfully, one with no danger of unwanted offers."

"It appears, Holly, as if there is no hope for us. As I can boast of *no* offer that actually qualifies as serious or proper, and you state that repeated offers and poetry are no less vexing, I wonder if we ought to consider foreswearing all of our marital ambitions at once and be done with the business altogether!"

"Excellent idea!" Holly stood and solemnly pulled her cousin to stand in front of her. "Let me go first. Take my hands and bear witness: I, Hortènse Amelie Marianne Tournier de Caisson, hereby renounce all pretensions to fine matches and swear to reject all prudent considerations. I vow to be a poor spinster, content in the company of intelligent and interesting females — to the exclusion of any member of the male sex."

Elizabeth gasped. "Oh you are bold! But that is easily sworn standing in this room and in this company. In fact, that is hardly a sacrifice at all! Now add that no man shall ever be worthy of your regrets and that nothing less than insanity shall ever persuade you it is right to throw yourself at a man's fickle mercy."

"Agreed," Holly continued the joke. "But I think we can make some exceptions — we will allow ourselves to enjoy the company of pleasant old men, and scholars such as Sir John Ledwich, and good-natured married men such as Mr Pembroke — the elder Mr Pembroke I mean — our landlord. But any man younger than the age of forty will be strictly forbidden to come into our vicinity."

"Agreed!" Elizabeth laughed. "There! Is that not a relief? The root of all our problems solved at once! I must say I look forward to how free and easy our lives will be from now on. There is only one thing we have to fear now."

"And what is that, my free and easy cousin?"

"Why, love!" said Elizabeth and her merry eyes twinkled.

"I expect we are quite safe from that, way out here. Unless you have designs on Mr Grant, as he is the best and only prospect in our little village." Holly's smile turned sly. "And if you do, I will say right now that I happily relinquish any prior claims on his affections."

"You are so eager to entice me into breaking a most solemn vow already! You temptress, you! No, unless love comes and claims my sanity and my will, I am right here beside you at the carefully drawn battle lines, cousin. Depend upon it! And if it does come," Elizabeth shrugged. "I'm sure the spectacle of it will quite make up for the disappointment of such weak restraint."

"Well, even if you are determined to give yourself a way out, Elizabeth, do not think that I will release you from your vow so easily. We are sworn sisters in this endeavour and any man who has the temerity to make you fall in love with him will have to prove his worth to more than just your father."

THE SUN WAS SETTING BEHIND a thin veil of clouds, coloured in shades of purple and rose, when his lordship directed his horse through the back gate after several days' absence. Mr McLaughlin followed his Master and they reached the stables in mutually agreeable silence. As was his habit, Lord Baugham stripped down to his shirtsleeves, unsaddled and groomed his horse before considering his day's work to be complete, then left his companion to unload the guns and re-deposit the effects.

The night was already upon him, and to his great delight his lordship could see the stars above his head as he crossed the yard. He opened his front door with a contented sigh, ready to call for a bath and a fire.

Riemann met him in his chamber and — as expected — was quietly busy preparing for his lordship's pleasure upon his return. The fire crackled wildly, battling the last remnants of chilly air in the room and everything Baugham had looked forward to was being laid out, prepared and arranged. His lordship sighed contentedly and stretched his limbs. He was sore and tired, his arms ached, his feet hurt and the mix of dried sweat and cold limbs made him feel exhausted and slightly detached from reality.

He undressed slowly, stretching his aching muscles as he pulled his shirt over his head and threw it with the rest of his clothes on the floor. He arched his back and smiled as he heard Riemann come back into the room.

He was just about to undo his breeches when his valet's voice behind him made him freeze.

"My lord," Riemann quietly said, "were you aware that Mr Darcy is sitting in your library?"

Baugham turned around and saw his man standing behind him, not with his dressing gown and slippers, but with a fresh change of clothes.

"No," Lord Baugham said and, snatching the clean shirt from his valet, stalked out the door.

Riemann watched as he walked out, heard the door slam and sighed before going down to the kitchen to postpone the bath and dinner.

Darcy was sitting by the hearth, deeply immersed in a book. Baugham felt no doubt he was genuinely unperturbed by the commotion caused by his unexpected arrival and he took in his leisurely pursuit before he entered, walking to the mantelpiece and assuming a nonchalant pose.

"Darcy," he said in a flat voice. "What are you doing here?"

With the studied arrogance of complete self-assurance, Darcy carefully closed his book on his lap, ready to resume his reading in just a few minutes.

"I came to see you."

Darcy let his eyes linger on his friend, taking in every detail of him, but Baugham stared at the fire, shifted his pose and picked up a poker. He did not look at his unexpected guest beyond that quick initial glance.

"Well, you're very lucky then," he dryly said. "I've been gone for three days."

"I know," Darcy said calmly.

The air between the two men was heavy. Baugham felt an inexplicable resentment upon being served with the exact behaviour he so frequently exercised towards his friend. To arrive unannounced and unexpectedly at any of Darcy's establishments was his prerogative. It was an unspoken means of equalising the power balance between himself and his fastidious, but rich and self-sufficient friend. Darcy had always accepted this as Baugham's privilege and never complained or questioned; there were other ways to keep his unpredictable and mercurial friend from besting him. Now the tables were turned and Baugham was annoyed by Darcy's presumption and perceived arrogance. The careful balance between them was slightly off-centre because of it.

They circled around each other without moving, trying to find a balance. Baugham offered Darcy a whiskey; Darcy complemented him on the taste. Baugham asked about his family; Darcy thanked him and asked about the hunting. Thus they continued for a while, letting the immediate dust settle between them.

"So," Baugham finally said. "Now you have seen me, what next?"

Darcy looked at him for a while.

"Dinner, I should think," he said at length. "If you're so inclined."

"Oh, I think so, however sore and tired I am. I will go wash; Mrs McLaughlin will be displeased enough as it is, thanks to you. I see you've made yourself quite at home already, so if you'll excuse me..." Baugham's words tapered off as he left the library.

Darcy gave a crooked smile and waved an impatient hand at his back. When he heard the door close, he found himself abandoning any thoughts on his awkward arrival and his host's wounded sensibilities, instead pondering whether it would be too soon to inquire about neighbours and inhabitants of near-by villages as part of the upcoming dinner conversation.

THE GIRLS WALKED PAST THE trees dotted with the chaotic lumps of black crows' nests. The inhabitants screeched as they passed and some spread their dark wings against the blue sky and flew away.

"They remind me of what it was like to walk into Meryton after the news of Lydia's elopement," Elizabeth said dryly. "So many hurrying off to spread their screeching opinions on the state of our nest, even though theirs were hardly models of propriety themselves."

"You must have been very angry," Holly said. "I mean, knowing what he was."

"Yes. Angry. Ashamed. Desperate. Sad."

They had set out that drizzly morning with baskets to scour the countryside for wild herbs and mushrooms before the frost set in — and to talk. They had walked a fair way before either said anything, but when she finally spoke, Elizabeth told her all about that terrible time of worry and confusion, when they did not know where Lydia was, or with whom, what her plans were or if she was safe or even alive.

Holly stole a look at Elizabeth walking slowly beside her. "Were you perhaps also sad for yourself?"

"Of course I was sad for myself," Elizabeth answered with a short laugh. "If you had been at Longbourn during that time, you would not need to ask such a question.

36

Who would not be sad to cut short a pleasant holiday in Derbyshire and return to such a scene?" She attempted a smile, but could not hide the edge of bitterness it held. Her cousin simply looked at her, so Elizabeth continued more sombrely.

"Yes, Holly, I was sad for myself — sad and disillusioned. At that time I was already feeling that too many of my strongly held beliefs had been proven wrong through the actions of others. I had proudly held such clear ideas on Charlotte's sensibility, on Mr Bingley's love for Jane, on his friend's abominable self-conceit, and Mr Wickham's goodness — even my own family's behaviour, which I had always viewed as harmless folly — but Holly, how could I ever have imagined that Lydia's morality would be as scant as her sense?" She sighed. "And through her actions came such censure and judgement upon the rest of us. Right at the time when I thought..."

Leaving the path upon spotting a patch of currant bushes, Holly waited for Elizabeth to continue. When she did not, Holly tried to reassure her as she carefully plucked the berries and leaves.

"Don't be too disheartened; at least one of your judgements has ended up being true. Mr Bingley's love for Jane was steadfast after all, and incidentally, I doubt whether his friend has changed much in character, so you are likely safe in that area as well.

"And, as far as censure and judgement... it is obvious Jane is not suffering from it, and you have said yourself that the opinion of the neighbourhood is that the Bennets are now the luckiest of families — Lydia's scandal is all but forgotten in the excitement of Jane's marriage."

"It is not just the opinions of the fickle locals that matter..." Elizabeth began as they returned to the lane.

"Nonsense!" Holly cried with a light-hearted smile. "What else *does* matter? Who else would even know or care of it beyond your own small circle in Hertfordshire? And even if they did, what effect could such a thing have on anyone else?"

"Mr Bingley's friend learnt of it and I fear it affected his opinion greatly. Holly, is not that mint over there by the stream?"

"Yes, Eliza, very good, I'll make a scavenger of you yet! And look, there is Valerian close by as well." In no time they were scrabbling down the bank and filling their baskets with more bounty from the countryside.

"But why should you care about Mr Bingley's friend? We have already settled it that he is a proud and disagreeable man, but even so, he did allow Mr Bingley to return to Netherfield and propose to Jane, so the knowledge cannot have affected his opinion so greatly.

"Truly, Elizabeth, I doubt that anyone in 'high society' would bat an eye at Lydia's behaviours — they likely seem tame in comparison to the goings on in Town during the season — but then, there do seem to be different standards for acceptable behaviour that vary considerably according to one's circumstance, or one's sex."

"Well, you are perfectly right in that, Holly. It is only the sex of the offender that determines whether the offence receives winks and nods, or censure and shame." Elizabeth's brows wrinkled. "Holly, I cannot tell the Valerian from the weeds. Why don't I gather the mint and you can carry out the difficult work."

Holly agreed and began pulling and stuffing the roots into her basket. "That mint will be a nice change in the teapot, will it not? Oh, I had better leave some room in my basket for the rose hips. Further on down, toward the grounds of Clyne Cottage, are some hedges that have grown wild. Since we're so close, we might as well see if there are any left from last year.

"But, about what you were saying, while there is a marked inequality in matters of morality, at least those who suffer from it are suffering due to their own actions and decisions. What *I* find to be even more grievously unfair are the antiquated attitudes toward education — as if only men, and only those men who are rich and high-born at that, are capable of improving their minds or even deserving of the chance to attempt it."

"I should have known our conversation would somehow end up on your favourite subject!" Elizabeth said. "But you may have a point. I wonder... if Lydia had been taught something other than the importance of catching a husband, would things have been different for her. Of course, we were all brought up similarly, and it was impressed upon all five of us that we should seek to marry above all things, but what would the result have been if even a small attempt had been made to expand Lydia's mind, and Kitty's too?"

"Exactly," Holly declared. "As it says in *Vindications,* most of us are taught only what we need to know to attract husbands and little of what is necessary to become desirable partners after the marriage takes place. What is so wrong with broadening the mind of the female so that she can carry on an intelligent conversation? Or have an opinion, well-thought out and of her own reasoning? Not everyone has *your* natural inclinations, Elizabeth, or Jane's innate goodness, but most can be taught to think at least a little bit and control their impulses."

Elizabeth was about to say something but stopped short. Holly sent her a quizzical look while she carefully bowed down over a cluster of hedgehog fungus and folded the withered leaves away.

"Elizabeth?"

"Impulses," Elizabeth said. "Controlling one's impulses. Is it a good or bad thing at the end of the day?"

"What do you mean?"

"I mean an impulse can be offensive and rude and completely unwelcome and misguided and yet... there is always some truth in all impulses, don't you think?"

"I suppose that depends on what you mean by truth," Holly answered carefully as she cleared away the detritus hiding the mushrooms from view. "I would say that our impulses are more a reflection of our nature — they urge us toward what we *want,* but not what we *ought...*" She laughed softly. "I am not explaining myself well at all, but I mean to say impulses are true, but it does not necessarily follow that they are good or right."

"No," Elizabeth said slowly, "certainly not always good or right. But a reflection of our nature — yes, that is well put. And isn't nature always true?"

Holly looked thoroughly confused as Elizabeth met her gaze squarely. She stood up with a sigh.

"Holly, there was another proposal. And if Mr Collins' offer based on pretentious aspirations and misguided feelings of propriety was too ridiculous to accept, this second one was scrupulously honest and forthright and equally impossible to accept as it was offered against all reason and sound judgement."

All attempts at work were abandoned and Holly stared at her in confused amazement.

"I don't think I understand you correctly, Elizabeth. *Who* proposed to you — and why would any such proposal defy reason and sound judgement? What possible argument could anyone have against you? It is preposterous!"

Elizabeth tried smiling wryly, but she did not quite succeed and looked pained instead.

"Mr Darcy. And rest assured his reasoning was good — excellent in its logic, in fact." Her smile faded away. "His professed emotions were…well, at least very sincere and passionate. In fact, I suppose I cannot fault him for any of his words. Only the coupling of them together while forming an unexpected proposal of marriage."

To Holly's amazement Elizabeth seemed to wipe away something in the corner of her eye.

"Stupid," she muttered.

"Mr Darcy? That unpleasant friend of Mr Bingley's?"

Elizabeth nodded, apparently not trusting herself to speak quite yet. At the sight of her cousin's distress, it took all of Holly's self control not to give into impulse herself and begin a long rant against anyone who could cause her pain. A rant, however, is difficult to manage when one is as curious about the details as she was, so she deferred it momentarily.

Taking a deep breath, she asked as calmly as she could manage, "Will you tell me about it? What did this man say to you — what possible objections could he have had? And if they were so great, why did he propose at all? Has he no honour?"

Elizabeth hesitated. Of course, she remembered every word he had said to her that evening at Hunsford, but could she explain why she felt so very differently about them now than she had then? Nevertheless, this was the exchange she had so often rehearsed in her mind, anxious for the relief of putting words to her thoughts, so she began at the beginning.

"When Mr Bingley arrived in Hertfordshire last fall, he brought a small party of friends to the assembly rooms…"

When she finished by repeating all Mr Darcy's confessions and all his objections, both of them were blushing with emotion and the baskets with mushrooms and herbs had been abandoned on the ground.

"But you must understand, Holly, at the time I dismissed it as an embarrassment and despised him as before. But then there was the letter and then — "

Holly's head shot up and she fixed her eyes upon her cousin's.

"Elizabeth! Do not tell me that you think *anything* he wrote in that letter in any way excuses the way he spoke to you just the day before! I see nothing in it that redeems his behaviour at all."

"But Holly, he *did* warn me about Mr Wickham. He had very good reasons to doubt his character, but I was too pre-occupied with upholding my prejudices to take him seriously enough. And now Lydia is paying the price for my negligence."

"Nonsense," Holly scoffed. "Even his explanations about Mr Wickham were given too late and only to excuse himself — where was his concern when that scoundrel was freely roaming about Hertfordshire, charming your neighbours and defrauding the merchants of Meryton? His conscience was only raised when it reflected badly upon himself. So, not only has he participated in the downfall of one Bennet sister and actively sought to ruin the prospects and happiness of a second, he then proceeds to insult and degrade a third — along with the rest of your family. What excuse can there be? What does this man have against you, Eliza?"

"Besides my championing Mr Wickham's cause at the expense of his own reputation, cheering my sister's capture of his friend in opposition to his wishes and the publicly disgraceful behaviour of my entire family? Why, I have no idea, Holly."

There were a thousand protests on Holly's lips and she would gladly have given vent to each and every one in turn, but Elizabeth talked on, staring at her hands and not even noticing her cousin's outraged expression.

"And despite all of this he admitted he 'admired' and even 'loved' me enough to want to make me his wife. Perhaps that is my greatest sin — making him want to go against everything he believes in. Making him give in to impulses he is ashamed of. Maybe that is why he dislikes me so much. And when I was at Pemberley with Aunt and Uncle Gardiner and there was a safe distance from our differences, he was civil and even — courteous. Until he found out about Lydia. His regrets must have turned to relief in an instant."

Holly's face grew dark and angry. "*Your* sin! *Making* him go against *his* beliefs — give in to *his* impulses! What sort of rubbish are you speaking, Eliza? If you had deliberately set out to attract him I might understand your regrets, but…"

With this, Holly snatched up her basket and, too outraged to sit still any longer, stood up and began furiously plucking what few leaves remained on a nearby bush.

"I…I am speechless…" she sputtered. "What right…oh! how dare he…if it is possible to truly despise a person one has never met, then I must say that I do — so intensely — dislike this Mr Darcy that I could easily…agh! 'I would eat his heart in the market place'!"

In spite of herself, Elizabeth had to smile.

"Thank you, Holly. Your outrage on my behalf is really very comforting and if I had to choose a champion on whom I could rely to gladly overlook all my faults and stupidities and fight for me to the bitter end, I would, without hesitation, chose you. Thank you for letting me wallow in my self-pity and misery for a while. I rarely do get the chance and it was very refreshing. But all this is nonsense. Things are as they are and Mr Darcy is as he is — whatever that is. I must stop. I want to stop. And I hope I never have to turn over Mr Darcy's most inconsiderate and annoying unpredictability again."

She came up to her cousin and lifted up the basket that was lying askew on the ground at her feet.

"Come Holly. We are even further away from Mr Darcy's and my troubles now than I thought I was in Derbyshire. And I would like it to stay that way for this little while, at least, now that I am here with you."

To both men it was inconceivable to tarry over breakfast, or spend more time indoors than absolutely necessary. Their motives for this restlessness were not the same, but the result was that one offered a tour around the immediate grounds which the other accepted with alacrity despite the slight drizzle.

As they walked around the house to admire the view of the river to the east, Baugham's housekeeper, Mrs McLaughlin, and another woman came towards them up the slope. Darcy paid them scant attention at first, but after Baugham sent both of them a smile and a good morning, he took a closer look. They were carrying baskets of eggs and other crudely wrapped victuals and a pail of milk — presumably bought for their enjoyment the next morning.

"I must say you live more frugally than I would ever have expected of a man as fond of his comforts as you," Darcy said as the two women made their way up past them again. "Only two maids and a stable hand?"

"One maid. Or actually, one housekeeper and no maid; Mrs McLaughlin takes care of all I can ask. Mrs Higgins is Mrs McLaughlin's cousin. She works down in the village for some old French widow and her daughter. Comes up here to gossip with her cousin as often as she can, I believe. Although it is hard to know which cousin has the most to impart about the scandalous manners and habits of her employer."

Darcy felt his heart contract.

"A French widow? That is unusual."

"I dare say it is. I think her husband was some sort of revolutionary; he was exiled from France and died here in Clanough. Although strictly speaking I think the woman herself is English. She's notorious enough, but you hardly ever see the daughter. Mrs McLaughlin tells me she is a teacher at a seminary for young women up in Edinburgh."

There was silence and Baugham's thoughts drifted to the cutting of wood, then to trees on his estate in danger of collapsing with the first autumn storm, and whether walking would be preferable to riding if he took Darcy with him on a more extended tour to check on them.

Darcy on the other hand had one fixed thought in his head: *That must be them!*

By the time they passed the stables, Darcy's train of thought had moved on from hesitation and doubt of his good fortune to a definite resolution and plan of action.

"Clanough," Darcy said. "Any society worth mentioning? Or visiting?"

"No," Baugham said shortly. "Well," he amended, "Mr Robertson down at the Caledonian Thistle Inn has decent ale and takes in papers from Edinburgh. But to be fair, I don't know anyone else. Nor do I wish to. I don't think I have missed much."

"That French widow sounds intriguing though. Why here? And you said she was English."

Baugham shrugged his shoulders as they walked back toward the warmth of the house.

"And the widow of an exiled Frenchman," Darcy was unwilling to let the subject drop so easily. "Hardly well off then. Do you know her history?"

"I do not. I know Mrs Higgins works for them and they live at something called Rosefarm Cottage at the end of some village lane by the backfields. That's all. Surprisingly enough for me, I am not curious in the slightest to know anything else about them."

"You have no interest in romantic pasts or gallant revolutionary tales," Darcy said tartly.

"No. And if I did there are plenty of horridly tawdry novels I could indulge in to produce the desired thrills that would not involve actually meeting these people. It is much easier to close a book than it is to break an acquaintance. I'm sure I would never get away from them if I made the mistake of showing an interest. People like that live only in the past and have no interest in a present that does not suit their old notions and preconceptions of the world. Tiresome and vulgar."

Darcy's face was grim, but he said nothing.

"And considering the fact that you sent me away from Town because I had too much to do with women, you can hardly expect me to seek out any female company here," Baugham said.

"I didn't send you away. I gave you good advice and you took it."

"True," Baugham said quietly. "And I am glad I did. You were right. But it does not affect my antisocial inclinations."

Chapter 4

In which Company is Enjoyed, Endured, Sought and Found

"So will there really be no young men inclined to dance and no music at all?"

Elizabeth took a few elaborate dance steps together with her rake. Holly stopped in the middle of cleaning the steps and stone slabs in front of the cottage and leaned on her broom.

"We-ell…" she said slowly, "usually it is useless to even try, for no one can really hear any music over all the chatter and talk and, I believe, given the wretched condition of our old spinnet, most of our guests would agree that it is a blessing."

"That old thing truly is a disgrace," Elizabeth laughed. "I cannot understand why you keep it still."

"Well, first of all it doesn't take much room. Second, it was left for us by the Pembrokes — so we are not really at liberty to dispose of it — and lastly and most importantly, it serves as a convenient piling station for books and papers and when closed it is just the right size to hold the tea tray."

"The Pembrokes sound like very kind friends. They have a son, do they not? Is he handsome? Does he dance? Oh, tell me he does not quote poetry!"

"Yes they have a son and yes, he is handsome." Holly said in a level voice and, not looking up, attacked the same spot she had just finished sweeping. "No…no poetry — he fancies himself a scholar. But he will not be coming. I expect he is busy."

Elizabeth skipped around the growing heap of leaves she had gathered and then gave a formal curtsey to her tall and thin dancing partner.

"A pity. Oh well," she said generously. "I am looking forward to the party all the same, even if I am to be deprived of the pleasure of a quadrille partnered with a handsome young man."

"Are you forgetting our vow so soon, Elizabeth?" Holly smiled shakily, "Our pleasures will come from stimulating conversation and Sir John's spectacular displays. No men, remember?"

THE ONLY THING THAT PREVENTED Darcy from requesting that his friend tie his hands to the armrests of his chair was the fact that he was still depending on Baugham to somehow bring him closer to Rosefarm Cottage and its inhabitants. The rain had kept them inside for most of the afternoon and that definitely had a depressing effect on his lordship's mood. Darcy could not deny he felt the same. In his case, however, his nerves were further tried by what a day cooped up with only his friend for company did to his plans to find Miss Bennet.

He had just formed a firm resolution to start taking his daily exercise by riding up and down the Clanough village lanes, when a commotion and the sound of female shrieks were heard out in the hall. Lord Baugham's nervous finger tapping stopped and Darcy immediately found himself eternally grateful to whoever was responsible for the interruption.

A minute later, Mrs McLaughlin walked through the door with a tea tray and what looked like a wet rag stuffed in her apron pocket. Darcy frowned slightly at this singular sloppiness but Baugham did not seem to notice.

"What was all the hubbub, Mrs McLaughlin?" he asked. "Not another guest, I hope."

He gave Darcy an impish grin which was returned by his friend's pursed lips and derisive look.

"Noo, it was Mrs Higgins dropping the hot kettle. Ye must excuse her, m'laird, she's fair nervish tonight."

Baugham nodded and transferred his attention to the tray's cold cuts and preserved plums, but Darcy's attention was firmly caught.

"Nervous? Why?"

"Because she's been driven out of her kitchie while the women have their party."

Now Baugham looked up too, but it was more due to the housekeeper's scornful tone of voice than pity or concern for the fate of Mrs Higgins.

"Really? How odd."

"The Tourniers?" Darcy interjected, ignoring the abundant display of food and beverage in front of him which seemed to have broken Baugham's concentration on the issue at hand once again. "A party?" Immediately his mind turned to the probability of the guest list including young female relatives from Hertfordshire.

"Aye," was Mrs McLaughlin's short reply since Lord Baugham was by this time perched behind her, anxious to get his hands on the cheese.

"And do these parties take place at Rosefarm Cottage often? You must have an intimate knowledge of the family and their guests, Mrs McLaughlin."

Baugham stopped the shovelling of meat onto his plate and stared at his friend in stunned silence. Mrs McLaughlin gave a snorting throaty sound as she finished pouring the tea.

44

"What else goes on besides explotions in the kitchie? I don't know that I want to know ought else."

"I take it they are an eccentric bunch then," Darcy went on calmly.

Mrs McLaughlin shrugged and surveyed her finished work.

"Aye, well. They have that niece from the Sooth staying with them. She's respectable enough, it seems."

Baugham was still staring at Darcy when Mrs McLaughlin decided question time was past and sailed out again. Darcy shrugged, but felt a growing sense of triumph moving about in his chest even as he tried to return to his book in a detached manner.

"Just curious," he muttered when he felt his friend still watching him.

"So I see," Baugham said and resumed his finger-tapping.

Darcy sighed.

HOLLY HEARD VOICES IN THE hall downstairs and she rushed to stick the last pin into her hair, threw one more look at herself in the small looking-glass on the wall and pinched her cheeks. Not too bad, she reflected. She would never be a great beauty, but her time at home had eased the worried frown on her forehead and her eyes were not the hard ones that usually looked back at her. She'd do. After all, no one would be in attendance this night that she needed to impress with her looks; if she could get through the evening with some attempt at spirited conversation and well-argued opinions, she could count it a success.

As she flew down the stairs she heard Elizabeth's voice and she could tell it was choked by barely contained mirth.

"You *must* be Mr Grant," she was saying.

Holly rolled her eyes and bit her lip, but then remembered Elizabeth would be by her side and her frown turned into a smile.

A young man was bowed over her cousin's hand as she entered the parlour. Instantly he looked up at her and Holly recognised Mr Grant's usual stunned expression.

"Mr Grant," she said. "I see you have met my cousin, Miss Bennet. How do you do?"

"Miss Tournier," the young man said and flushed wildly. "I...I am charmed. By you both, naturally." He swallowed hard, giving Holly a moment to exchange a look with her cousin. "*She walks in beauty like the night,*" Mr Grant said in a constrained voice. "You...you look lovely, Miss Tournier. As always. As always..." he muttered and kissed her hand again.

"Is that poetry, Mr Grant?" Elizabeth asked in a cheerful voice. "Or is the lighting too dim for your tastes?"

Mr Grant looked bewildered. Holly, not meeting Elizabeth's eyes lest they both burst into laughter, smiled politely then turned to welcome the other guests in an attempt to extricate herself from his attentions. It was not an easy task; Mr Grant was nothing if not persistent and he followed her possessively as she made her rounds.

BAUGHAM TWIRLED THE EMPTY WINE glass in his hand. He eyed the decanter that stood on the table, but could not quite decide whether he wanted any more. He sighed.

What now then? They had discussed plans for roe buck hunting, whether the trout might be worth the small trek up stream, the upcoming social calendar of the locals including the traditional Martinmas fair, church attendance and the quality of the preaching, as well as if Clanough had anything to offer in the form of attractions. Historical attractions, Darcy had felt it necessary to add.

Baugham told him about the effigy in the local Presbyterian chapel. "Sir Robert Ramsey. I haven't seen it myself, but Mrs McLaughlin tells me it is a fine piece, bronze I believe, and quite the destination for sight-seers from Edinburgh in the summertime. She does not approve of their audacity in picnicking on the church lawn."

After that, more silence. The evening passed with nothing specific decided upon, but Darcy nevertheless expressed — several times — that he had not travelled so far simply to stare at dusty stag heads above fireplaces or sit in cramped quarters unless the weather absolutely made it necessary.

"And I cannot believe you find any enjoyment in staying cooped up here either," he said sternly. "Just because your boredom enticed you into playing inappropriate parlour games in London, there will be no cure for that in sitting inside all day."

Baugham protested he certainly did not sit inside all day — quite the opposite as his very absence when his friend had seen fit to arrive had proven.

"But neither can I see how mingling with tiresome provincials at every opportunity can afford me any more enjoyment than I already find very well on my own. I did not acquire this place to enjoy effigies in local churches or admire fat cows at country fairs!"

OLD MR PEMBROKE WAS WEARING a Turkish fez perched on his head. His bushy hair spilled out on all sides and he proudly displayed, to a very entertained Elizabeth, his wife's ingenious use of hatpins to keep it safe from falling off.

"This is my party hat," he cheerfully explained, "and it is reserved for occasions when familiarity and ease mingle with excruciating intellectual sharpness, conspiring together against my poor fuzzled head."

"Or when there is real danger Sir John will singe your eyebrows off," his wife interjected. "As you may gather, the fez is an essential accessory when we travel to Rosefarm."

After Elizabeth enthusiastically agreed, Mr Pembroke smiled at her paternally. "It is too bad, my dear Miss Bennet, that you could not have timed your visit to Rosefarm for earlier this summer. My son, Mr Jonathan Pembroke, always comes to spend part of the summer season here with our good friends, and I am sure he would have been delighted to make your acquaintance. Although," he conceded as he looked around, "I doubt poor Rosefarm Cottage could accommodate *two* extended visits at once. Mrs Pembroke and I have always regretted that we could not offer the Tourniers a more spacious residence, but it seems to have served them well through the years and they have made it a very comfortable home."

"And hospitable too," chimed in Mrs Pembroke. Then she turned to her husband, "But you forget, my dear, that Jonathan has plans to break his journey here in a few

46

weeks' time.

"He always enjoys his stays here, whether they are brief or long," she added to Elizabeth. "So you will have the chance to meet him after all. I declare, I am sure he won't know which way to turn, with two such pretty young ladies in the parlour to attend to."

Elizabeth smiled. "He needn't be uneasy on that account; neither my cousin nor myself require much attending."

Across the room, Holly picked up an empty platter that had been full of food just a few minutes before, sighing over the appetite of her mother's friends. She had thought they could get by very well on some of the leftovers until Sunday, but apparently wit and conversation did not prosper on an empty stomach. Now it seemed highly unlikely there would be any leftovers at all except for the stewed cabbage. Well, maybe one could make soup of it. Or hide it in some form of pie crust…

The sight of Sir John beside her cheered her, and he smiled as she caught his eye. "So my dear, *has* Mrs Higgins been sent away?"

"Well, you had better come and help me set things up in the kitchen then," Sir John continued when she nodded and gently took her arm to steer her away from her chores. "Ah," he smiled as he spotted a young man in the crowded parlour. "Here is a colleague of mine I would like you to meet as well. Dr McKenna!" he called across the room. "This is the young lady I have been telling you about."

Dr McKenna was a large, well-built man with broad shoulders, a long frame and an open, friendly countenance, a physician by profession and an aspiring geologist by choice. Holly gave him a smile and greeting when he came over and they all three went into the empty kitchen together. When they returned a few moments later, Holly's cheeks were a bright red and her eyes sparkled with excitement. She shot out of the door with Sir John and the doctor following slowly and likewise smiling behind her, and almost ran up to her mother.

"Oh Maman!" she said and clutched her mother's hand, quite interrupting her argument with Mr Kershaw. "Sir John has made me such a wonderful offer!"

"Really?" her mother asked. "And does his wife know about this?"

Holly blushed, but Sir John came to her rescue.

"Of course she does," he said cheerfully. "I would never make such an offer without consulting her first."

"Well, I am glad to hear it," Mrs Tournier said with a mischievous glint in her eye. "One can look forward to a perfect marriage of words and image then?"

Holly met her mother's eye and they both smiled.

"Well, I shall certainly do my utmost to fulfil my obligations," Holly said and felt as if she was floating slightly above the ground with happiness. A commission! Colour plates to Sir John's Treatise on Heat! And compensation equalling her entire income for one term at Hockdown School! "Thank you so much, Sir John, you will never regret giving me this opportunity, I promise you."

Both Sir John and Dr McKenna laughed, and the doctor piped up. "And I can promise you, Miss Tournier, that once I am fortunate enough to obtain funding for my own treatise, you will be the only artist I consider to illustrate it." Holly looked at him in surprise. "Well, if Sir John trusts you with his work, I can only conclude that your abilities are excellent," he explained. "And... if it allows me to make you as happy as you appear to be tonight, it must be worth any compensation."

She thanked him kindly and even sent a friendly smile to Mr Grant, who was perched behind the sofa regarding Dr McKenna with slight suspicion and her with a possessive eye.

Elizabeth stood at the other side of the room and the cousins' eyes met. Her cousin gave her a proud and happy look and Holly answered her with a contented smile. Then they laughed a little before returning to their own circles of conversation.

Mr Grant, who had been suffering cruelly while Holly had been privately sequestered with the gentlemen in the kitchen and conversing so happily afterwards, came up and, taking advantage of the next lull in conversation, positioned himself in between her and her friends.

"Is this true what I have overheard," Mr Grant heedlessly blurted out. "You are home for an extended stay?" At her hesitant nod, he plunged on. "Why, that is very good news indeed! And may I hope that, perhaps, this circumstance is in some way a favourable reflection on my offer — "

"Mr Grant," Holly interrupted hastily. "Please. Such personal matters should not be... this is not really the time or the place to discuss... I fear I have been neglecting our other guests for too long already and Sir John's proposition is really all I can contemplate right now." She knew with all her stammering she was not making herself clear and that her excuses were not helping her cause at all, but all she could do was continue. "I have only just arrived home, you understand, and I am sure that Maman will not wish me... nor am I in any rush to... please, it must wait. Surely you are in no particular hurry?"

"Hurry," muttered Mr Grant, "oh, no! No, I am, of course, fully content with — well, it is a very nice evening. And you are right. Of course."

Holly watched as Mr Grant took a step back. The look on his face told her that her attempt at forestalling his questions had somehow given him the wrong impression and now he was proceeding on a false hope she would hear yet another proposal from him at a more convenient time. She despaired that she would ever learn to handle a difficult situation without somehow turning it into an even bigger problem.

"...which, you must agree, is exactly why Lord Sidmouth's position defies all common sense," Mrs Tournier, having turned back to her discussion, said in an uncharacteristically patient voice to her companion. Undoubtedly he would have answered her in the same vein, because even though the tone was light, there was passion in their eyes and heightened colour to their cheeks that betrayed an earnest debate. That was not to be, however, for Mr Grant sat down beside her with a heavy sigh and dramatically put one hand up to his brow.

"*In what distant deeps or skies. Burnt the fire of thine eyes? On what wings dare he*

48

aspire? What the hand, dare seize the fire?" he declared to Mrs Tournier with another sigh.

His hostess regarded him in silence.

"I trust, Mr Grant," she finally said with pursed lips, "you do not mean to imply that my dinner has given you indigestion."

Mr Grant gave a start and apologised for his ill-timed use of Mr Blake's sentiments.

"I was merely...Mrs Tournier...it is that your daughter, she is exceptionally lovely tonight and she did favour me...but perhaps I am too hasty in my hopes...Mrs Tournier..."

Mrs Tournier could bear it no longer. She stood up and addressed her daughter in a strong voice that carried over the room and left no room for interpretation.

"Holly! Mr Grant suffers from indigestion; time to set up Sir John's tubes and valves and what not!"

THE EVENING DRAGGED ON INTERMINABLY, and the competition between the days-old newspaper and the increasing drowsiness that threatened to overcome Lord Baugham was interrupted by an explosive sigh from across the room and the sound of books sliding and hitting the floor.

He dropped his newspaper slowly and fixed a narrow gaze upon his friend. "Having troubles, Darcy?"

By that time Darcy had gathered the books again and drained the last drops from his glass of port. He shot an irritable look at his lordship and asked, seemingly out of nowhere. "How can you live like this?"

Baugham knit his brows together, "Now what sort of a damn-fool question is that, Darcy?"

"A desperate one; this library of yours is a disgrace! I cannot find a single thing I should care to spend any of my far from valuable time on, and what I do find is covered with dust and so mistreated the pages disintegrate if I so much as breathe on them."

Darcy demonstratively wiped his hands on his handkerchief and then dropped it on a side table.

"I should have brought my own," he muttered, not quite out of ear shot.

"Yes, well, perhaps you should have brought your own," his friend simultaneously muttered from his chair.

"However that may be, my friend," Darcy paused and opened one of the books he was holding. "you cannot deny that these are a disgrace. Look! The first twenty pages have been cut out." He then opened another one and pulled a face as a few pages came loose from the binding. "This one says, 'Happy thirteenth birthday to my dear nephew, David,' signed by an 'Uncle Horace' Not a very precious gift, it seems."

Now it was Baugham's turn to sigh heavily, and feel uncharacteristically peevish at Darcy's digging around through his old books. True, his library was a shameful mess, and true, the books were sitting, lying, balancing and perching perilously here and there openly on the shelf, but he had never intended *this* library to be anything but a private sanctuary and not a showcase for avid collectors. Why should he have to explain to Darcy that the copy of *Treasure Island* he regarded with such a disdainful expression was indeed an exceedingly precious gift? A book that had been read to pieces, and had been a friend and means of escape during his boyhood years. That this and many other such gifts from his uncle had been lovingly transported to the library of the one place he felt most at home? He dropped his newspaper with a snap.

"I have a perfectly fine collection in London that serves my needs most adequately. You cannot go around expecting Pemberley standards just because you are bored."

"Surely there is something between 'Pemberley standards' and…this? Surely it would be kinder to let these…volumes die a dignified death on the grate rather than keep them here, abused and wretched for all to see?"

By this time the paper had gone back up and Baugham muttered behind it. "If I should ever want advice, or *anything*, from somebody who was never invited in the first place."

Darcy pretended not to hear. "If this is all your father left you with, why leave it out like this for you to be reminded? Clear it out! Take up the responsibility to your name! Clean up your library!"

"If you consider what my father left me," Baugham said, "this little bit of library is very far down on the list of family disgraces. I, however, don't care to dwell upon the legacy of the sixth Earl while I am here at Clyne."

"With this mess about you, it is a wonder you can avoid it. Yet what about the responsibilities of the seventh?" Darcy persisted. "Have you not taken into account the legacy you will leave for the eighth Earl of Cumbermere?" His voice was steady, but there was a sly smile on his face.

Baugham did not see the smile, nor would it have improved his mood if he had. He abandoned his paper, silently cursed slow moving clocks and long autumn evenings, and walked to the decanter to fill his glass.

"As far as ancestral obligations go," he said in an attempt to discomfit him enough to drop the subject. "Perhaps you had better worry a little more about the continuation of the Darcy line and a little less about my own business. You are the master of forethought and scheduling—I cannot believe you have gone so long without planning for the furtherance of your own legacy."

This time the smile on his friend's face was unmistakeable. "Oh, I think I am beginning to form a plan. A very promising plan."

Sir John's experiments in the kitchen were a resounding success and although explosions and vapours and changing matter elicited close interest and suitably impressed remarks, nothing was broken or burnt, nothing was spoiled and Mrs Higgins was put to shame for having no faith in science.

There was a reading of Mrs Burney's play, which was a great success as well, for Mr Grant was cleverly persuaded by Miss Bennet that she absolutely depended on him to support her in her role as the old hypochondriac wife by playing her long-suffering, and thus heroic, husband. Holly was left to enjoy reading the spirited heroine with all the witty retorts and moral superiority against a perpetually chuckling Mr Pembroke. His fez fell off early in the first act due to this mirth and apparently he considered the reading harmless enough, for he left it off for the rest of the evening.

And there was dancing after all. Holly and Elizabeth performed a Scottish jig — with more enthusiasm than skill or concentration, it must be admitted — to the cheers and laughter of the crowd and Mrs Pembroke's improvised accompaniment. All the guests except one seemed to enjoy this little variance to the usual curriculum heartily. Mr Grant, however, kept clutching at his heart and turning pale whenever Holly lifted her skirts ever so slightly off the floor to manage some of the more intricate steps required. In the end, he was compelled to sit down for quite a while and certainly looked more exhausted than the two dancers.

Tick.

Tock.

Tick.

Tock.

Baugham looked up at the clock for the fourteenth time in as many minutes. He then returned to his study of the board in front of him and, once again, had to reorient himself as to the arrangement of the pieces.

Any further attempts at reading long since abandoned, the gentlemen were attempting to pass the time until the hour became acceptable to retire with a game of chess. The minutes, the seconds, passed in excruciating slowness.

Darcy shoved a pawn recklessly in the way of Baugham's bishop and suddenly declared, "We should have tried to acquire an invitation to that gathering! Mrs Tournier sounds like an intriguing woman, and in any event, an evening at her home could be no worse than having only each other for company."

"Absolutely not," Baugham muttered as his hand lingered over his bishop. "That's a terrible idea."

Darcy frowned at him. "Don't hover," he said tersely.

"I don't hover. I am approaching."

"Well, approach a little less slowly then. Or I'll call it fidgeting instead."

Baugham moved his bishop and fell back into his chair.

"What we should do is stop pretending we have any social obligations towards each other and retire so we can get an early start for the trout tomorrow. This is simply mind-numbing."

"I am certain," Darcy retorted, "that the happenings at Rosefarm Cottage are anything but mind-numbing. How could they be otherwise with Sir John Ledwich as one of the guests?"

"Sir John Ledwich? Sir John is there?"

Baugham's attention was suddenly caught and his hand stopped right over his queen.

"You're hovering again," Darcy said calmly.

"Never mind that. What on earth can he be doing there?"

"Mm." Darcy carefully positioned his queen. "Check. 'Explotions in the kitchie', if your housekeeper is to be believed. Worth finding out at any rate, wouldn't you say?"

Baugham hastily moved his king out of the way and into safety.

"I cannot believe you would want me to suffer the agonies of polite chit-chat with old hags and their spinster daughters and other dull females just to talk to Sir John. I had much rather commandeer his carriage back to Edinburgh and have my conversation there."

Baugham swung his rook so that one of Darcy's pawns fell off the board.

"Darcy, I neither know those people, nor do I wish to. That is the whole point of my stay here."

"And I cannot believe that you take your pretensions of a hermitic existence to such extremes," Darcy said as he calmly surveyed the board. "What can be the harm in making yourself agreeable to the locals here? It is, in actuality, a form of duty and a form of showing respect to them. An occasional appearance here and there is all that is needed. You *do* at least plan to attend church services while you are here, do you not?"

Baugham sat back, still waiting for Darcy to make his move.

"Do not think that it is necessary to continually preach duty to me, Darcy. Do not forget that I have my own seat in Cheshire, where I make all the proper appearances when I am there. But Clyne is not Cheshire, and here I do not jump through hoops for the entertainment of the locals."

"They are not 'hoops'," Darcy said darkly. "It is respect and due expectation. You are a landowner. How many of the people rely on you for their livelihood? And not just their livelihood but their future? You are an unknown greatness in such a small place as this and you owe it to the people who rely on you in various ways, to declare yourself and instil a sense of security for them. "

"Check!" Baugham said and slammed down his knight. "What is it that you want?"

"What gives you the impression that I want anything?"

Counting on his fingers, Baugham proceeded to explain.

"One: Instead of your habitual discouragement of my preference for coming here rather than joining in more exalted pursuits, you encouraged me quite ruthlessly that I should not only leave London immediately, but that I should specifically remove to Clyne. Two: You are here as well, in Scotland, of your own accord. Three: You are not only here, you are anxious to socialise with the local populace — in Scotland. That, my dear friend, is suspicious enough! And four: I know you and I think you are up to something."

"What you think I might be up to, so far away from civilised society, I cannot guess."

"I cannot guess either," said Baugham, "but I will wager that it is some way connected to the events at Rosefarm Cottage this evening, or to the family you find so fascinating residing within."

For a brief moment, Darcy's guard was down and Baugham saw something flit across his face, something akin to irritation. "I would simply like to meet them. That is the extent of it," he answered weakly.

"Well, if you let me checkmate you right now — in less than three moves — we'll be sitting in the parlour of Rosefarm Cottage, having tea, within three days. I'll contrive a meeting somehow. No questions asked."

There was a silent moment as Darcy met his lordship's eyes. Baugham smiled. He knew it! Darcy was hesitating. This was something he wanted, but still he hesitated and would not yield. It was harder for him — damn his pride and sense of honour! — to lose a game of chess on purpose than to have what he so desperately wanted and plotted for to be served on a silver platter no questions asked.

After a long time, with only the ticking of the clock making any sound in the room, Darcy reached out and wordlessly made his move. Baugham could not suppress a smile when he saw that with that one move his friend had not only spared his last remaining knight, but he had put his own queen in danger as well. It would be less than three then. This turn of events would almost certainly prove to be very interesting.

"What a wonderful party!" Holly kicked off her slippers and massaged her ankles and toes.

"You didn't sprain your ankle from the jig, did you?" her cousin smiled and tugged at her bodice while she fanned herself with a piece of paper.

Holly laughed. "Oh no! Split seams more like it, but I loved every second of it!"

Their eyes met and both burst out laughing.

"Mr Grant!" Elizabeth said and hid her face in her hands. Holly shook her head, but could not stop laughing.

"*Never seek to tell thy love, Love that never told can be; For the gentle wind doth move, Silently, invisibly,*" Elizabeth declared with her hand resting on her brow and head leaned back in a dramatic pose.

This launched another fit of laughter from the girls.

"Oh you are infinitely to be preferred, Eliza!" Holly said and wriggled her stockinged toes. "The way *you* do it, it is very enjoyable."

Elizabeth caught her aunt's stern eyes upon her. "Well, perhaps I do him wrong. The way we have been abusing young men among us lately I suppose I should show mercy and call him 'very agreeable.' After all, if you decide to accept him one day I shall have to endure that and more, and might even come to treasure him as someone who at least openly appreciates your virtues and good character as he should."

"Oh, he is not so bad, I suppose," Holly sighed. "I might have been a little hasty in portraying him to you in such a ridiculous light. Although you must admit it would be hard to be happy with a man who possesses such an extensive knowledge of the poetry of Blake."

"And who is so eager to let Mr Blake or Lord Byron speak for him on every occasion!" Elizabeth laughed. "*She walks in beauty like the night...*"

But she got no further before Holly held up her slipper in a threatening manner

53

and Mrs Tournier sat down on the sofa beside her with a thump.

"Girls, the hour is late! Spare me, simply show me mercy and spare me. I want no more of this speculation on Mr Grant's hidden virtues. And you, Elizabeth, must stop encouraging him in living out his ridiculousness."

"That is what you must expect, Aunt, if your guest list includes so few attractive young men. Aside from Mr Grant and Sir John's handsome doctor friend, why, one would think you mean to encourage Holly in her quest to avoid men. It's a pity you could not invite Mr Jon —" She was stopped mid-utterance by the strong grip of Holly's hand on her arm.

Mrs Tournier stood up and straightened her back. "I am exhausted," she said, tight-lipped and looking far from tired. "Goodnight."

"Oh dear," Elizabeth said as soon as the door closed behind her. "I hope I did not say something amiss."

"Maman does not care for Mr Jonathan Pembroke," Holly said quietly. "That is all." She stood up then and began gathering the leftover food from the scattered trays around the room. Elizabeth moved to help her despite Holly's protests.

"I am not a guest, dear Holly, I am family and I must earn my keep," she teased. "I would not have my visit send you to the poorhouse."

"It will do no such thing, Eliza!" Holly said, cheering up immediately. She dropped the platter she carried onto the sofa before dancing over to the fireplace to stoke the last of the dying embers. "I have a commission to make colour plates for Sir John Ledwich's latest treatise! And the distant promise of another. The handsome Dr McKenna is bringing round the manuscript and sketches Monday morning. I can start straight away!"

She twirled around a few times more, to her cousin's delight.

Elizabeth stopped as well, picking up the piece of paper she had been using as a fan.

"Well, I shall freely admit I understand nothing of what he proposes for you to do. 'Connected valves in triangular positions...' It is very impressive, though. How shall you find the time with your obligations at Hockdown?"

Holly stopped abruptly. "I'm not going back to Hockdown," she said calmly.

Elizabeth looked stunned. "You are not? But...why?"

Elizabeth pulled Holly down to sit beside her on the sofa and searched her face with a worried frown.

"Holly," she said. "What happened?"

Holly smiled a little wistfully and regretted the wonderful evening would have to include revisiting the events before she left Edinburgh, but at the same time she was glad Elizabeth had asked. She needed to tell her.

When she was finished, Elizabeth looked pale. "That is not possible," she finally said. "That is appalling. I...oh, I wish I had a horse that could take me there right now and I would tell them a thing or two about your character!"

"You don't ride, Elizabeth," Holly said dryly, "especially all those miles on a dark and wet night."

"If ever I could, I would this instant! I am so sorry, so very, very sorry."

Holly smiled a little sadly and stroked her cousin's hand that held on to hers very tightly.

"I must apologise to you, Holly," Elizabeth said quietly. "I have yet again been too lost in my own selfish concerns to even notice there was something wrong or to ask you how you are. And you have listened so patiently and faithfully to my stupidities and self-indulgencies."

"No, Elizabeth," Holly said steadfastly and fastened her own grip on her cousin's hands. "Don't say that. Can't you see how happy I am right now? I am! I am happy because I am home, I have that commission, I have the party and most of all I have you here with me. Can't you see? And I am happy because for once I do not have to wallow in my own self-pity and miseries, but I can share yours." She smiled. "We always do that, you know: we are honest and we tell each other what we want the other to know. I would have told you in time, I swear I would have. But right now I just want to revel in my good fortune and the fact that you are here."

"I *am* here," Elizabeth said. "And I am so very happy to be so."

Mr Darcy glanced at his watch once again. He was sitting in a chair in his friend's room watching him try on yet another coat.

"Perhaps we should have gone fishing after all," he muttered. "Assuming trout don't merit the same esthetical consideration as your fellow human beings."

"They are Presbyterians, Darcy," Baugham answered as he straightened his sleeves. "Not the fish," he hastened to clarify, "the human beings. They believe in predestination. And I am predestined to be late — there is nothing I care to do about that — so I might as well look my best. Everyone's going to stare, you know."

"How much more 'your best' can you possibly look after trying on four different coats?"

"The devil is in the details. So are you still bent on going? Or shall it be the trout after all?"

"I always attend when I am in the country. It is a moral duty."

"From what I hear, you always attend more to comparing the tenant roll to the congregation at Pemberley and then pester your sister to remember everyone's name rather than the sermon."

"Who told you that?"

"Your sister; she claims you make her visit the absentees under the guise of charity."

"It *is* charity. No one owes me any explanation. She could have told you that, too."

"She did."

Baugham sighed and seemed finally to have settled on a choice. Darcy threw one last glance at himself in the mirror beside his friend before he picked up his hat and gloves. Yes, people would stare. They always did. But in this case, attention and gossip might just be a good thing.

"Are we to visit all the local congregations in the name of moral duty? Shall we go up north to the Catholic church next week?" Baugham asked his friend as he considered his old hymnbook.

"'One God and Father of all, who is above all, and through all, and in you all',"
Darcy said and strode out ahead of him. "It is a fine day. Let us walk."

"True enough, I suppose," his lordship muttered and followed him out, "but if the
trout don't bite tomorrow, I am holding you responsible."

The walk was accomplished in silence, interrupted periodically by his lordship's
sighs, which gradually grew into laments about the waste of fine fishing weather.

"You know, Darcy," he said. "It is entirely possible to bask in the presence of our
Creator while also taking pleasure in His handiwork. It isn't too late — oh, apparently it is. I see that we are here."

BAUGHAM DID HIS BEST NOT to fidget under the stern glare of his friend, but it was
difficult to sit still when he could feel the eyes of the entire congregation directed at
them. Church attendance was not conducive to his plans to remain separate and aloof
from the local populace and he could hardly understand how he had let himself be
talked into coming. While he tried his best to find a comfortable position, the voice
of the reverend droned on, seemingly endlessly.

Sneaking a sidelong look, Baugham was gratified to see that Darcy himself was
not paying the strictest attention to the discourse, but appeared to be surreptitiously
surveying the gathered worshippers. Smiling slyly, he leaned in and whispered to his
friend, "Eyes forward, son. It wouldn't do to offend the locals."

Darcy glared but turned his attention to the sermon. His lordship had just settled
into a deep spiritual and not so spiritual contemplation on how church pews contributed to the Christian experience when he was startled by Darcy sitting up abruptly
beside him.

"Amen," he said in a terse voice. Thus ended the service. Hardly had the reverend
closed his book of discourses before Baugham felt Darcy nudge him hastily with
his elbow.

"It is over," he said. "Let's go."

He groaned and awkwardly slipped his tall frame out of the ancient seats wondering at Darcy's apparent eagerness to exit the building before anyone else. He stretched
his legs carefully as he replaced his hat and slipped on his gloves. The small church
was warm by now, although the service had been short and to the point. As a result,
Baugham felt kindly towards the northern form of reformed faith and even had a
smile for the curious who now could take a closer look at them.

His friend was already pressing resolutely towards the exit. Indeed, Baugham
thought his haste and near rudeness as he pushed himself past the crowds a little
funny, since he was the one who had insisted they would come and so eloquently
had persuaded him to desert his trout.

Finally he caught up with him, but only because he was standing still and letting his gaze sweep over the departing congregation on the immediate outside of
the building.

"Look no further," Baugham said as he reached him. "Here I am. I must say I was — "

But he got no further before Darcy interrupted him without ever having given him a glance.

"Miss Bennet!" he said in a loud, clear voice.

Several people turned and looked, but one young woman stopped dead in her tracks and stared at him.

"Mr Darcy!" she said in an astonished voice.

And that was it. That was the extent of the conversation. Baugham looked at his friend, then at the object of his unwavering attention; a slight young woman with fine eyes staring straight back at him, and ultimately at her darker friend, who was possessively holding onto her arm and narrowing her eyes at the silent, but resonant, scene. The way she held her head high, giving Darcy openly hostile looks and squaring her jaw told Baugham her determination hid a considerable temper. It did lend spirit to her otherwise stern countenance, though, he admitted, and had she not been an obvious prickly one, she might even have been considered handsome in a fiery, Gallic way.

A slow grin spread across his face as realisation took hold of him and various curious details in his friend's behaviour over the past week were explained.

"Aha!" said Lord Baugham and his face broke out into a brilliant smile.

Chapter 5

*In which Mr Darcy's First Ambition is finally Realised
and Reactions thereto are Varied*

Allow me to introduce myself!" his lordship said as the silent scene before him in the churchyard threatened to slip into embarrassment. "My name is Lord Baugham. And you must be Miss Tournier?"

The darker young woman turned her eyes on him and Baugham almost took a step back at the strong, unbridled resentment in them.

Holly recognised the name of the effectively absentee Clyne estate owner and she grew defensive immediately. From the moment she had heard, several years earlier, that an impoverished Sir Donald Clyne had sold his lands at a bargain price to an English peer who had apparently made the purchase on a whim of fancy, she had formed an early and strong dislike toward that peer, whoever he might be. What right did a stranger have to swoop in and gobble up the local land, especially such a beautiful and treasured place as Clyne? Combine this with the fact that he was now here with the man who had caused Elizabeth so much pain, both looking far too grand to grace a sermon at an obscure country church, and Holly found it nearly impossible to be civil.

Ignoring his look of puzzlement, she then turned to her cousin and tried to catch her attention away from this Mr Darcy who had so unexpectedly appeared. Darcy's friend, however, apparently had different ideas, for he immediately engaged her in inane conversation.

"We are practically neighbours," he went on in spite of the young woman's obvious reluctance to take their acquaintance any further. "I own Clyne Cottage — well, I say *practically* neighbours, because we are separated by some backfields, of course, and that little patch of woodland."

Reluctantly Holly confirmed his assumption of her identity while she kept a careful eye on her cousin, quickly calculating how soon she could rescue Elizabeth from what was obviously a terrible discomfiture. But that peculiar friend of Mr Darcy's talked on and on and she could not break his onslaught of social pleasantries, however hard she tried to give him her best stern schoolmistress eye. *Good Lord*, she thought while she waited for an opening to present itself, *is this chatterbox really a friend of that arrogant Mr Darcy?* They looked like Tom and Jerry strutting about in such a ridiculous fashion outside their own natural surroundings! Well, she would not let Elizabeth or herself play Kate or Sue to them. She would get her away from there — soon!

Her cousin remained subdued and awkward until Mr Darcy, apparently as the result of some super human effort, was able to silence his friend and addressed Elizabeth on some polite nonsense about her family. Elizabeth relaxed slightly and answered him, accepting his congratulations on the upcoming marriage of her sister. Mr Darcy could not take his eyes off her, though he wore a distinctly confounded expression and was shifting his weight from one leg to the other, seemingly anxious to take his leave. There was a small lull in the conversation when the questions on families and health were exhausted and Holly wasted no time taking advantage of it.

"I am afraid my mother will be expecting us back," she said. "She would not want us to be late for her tea."

She tugged at Elizabeth's arm; she was still staring at Mr Darcy, hypnotised by what Holly recognised as a very dangerous look in his eyes.

"Perhaps we will have the pleasure again soon, Miss Bennet?" Mr Darcy said. "Miss Tournier?" He turned to her, adding her name as an afterthought.

"Perhaps," Elizabeth said quietly and Holly did not answer at all. She simply raised her eyebrow at Elizabeth and steered her away.

The men stayed rooted to the spot, looking after them as they hurried down the knoll and onto the village lane. After they slipped out of sight, Baugham concentrated on his friend, who stayed gazing after them for a long time.

"Well," Lord Baugham said breaking the silence after a good while, "tea would have been nice."

ELIZABETH STORMED DOWN THE LANE and Holly found she was forced to take small running steps to keep up with her.

As Rosefarm appeared at the end of the narrow road, Elizabeth suddenly stopped and faced her cousin.

"Holly," she said, "I cannot go home yet; I must have a few minutes. Please humour me. I will meet you shortly at the big elm by the crossing."

"Of course," Holly said, "but what…"

She had time for nothing more before Elizabeth stuffed her hymnbook and shawl into her arms and broke out in a run, leaving her cousin behind. Holly had to confess the respite might be good for her as well — the appearance of Mr Darcy and his friend had also shocked her and she felt very uncertain of herself. Angry and jealous and disappointed, this was not what she had expected from Elizabeth's visit. Curse those men with their easy smiles and self-righteous lordly manners! They cared nothing for anything but their own will and fancy! Holly wandered the lanes for the requested few minutes and then slowly made her way towards the agreed meeting.

She spotted her cousin standing by the old, nearly bare tree, looking out for her. Holly quickened her pace and soon caught up with her.

"Better?" she asked quietly and slowly gave back the shawl and book.

Elizabeth smiled and fiddled with her effects before she answered. "Marginally; at least I know now what is bothering me enough to make me bolt like that and cause a spectacle in the middle of a Sunday afternoon.

Holly said nothing and Elizabeth took a deep breath.

"Holly, I am so confused. I do not know one fact from another anymore. What is he doing here? The nerve of him! To happen upon me like that when I had no idea and could not prepare myself! Or can you give me a reason I even *should* prepare myself? Why do I feel like I should?"

She clenched her fists and hugged her hymnbook tight in an effort to calm down.

"Did you see how he looked at me and how nice he was? I cannot help but think maybe he has changed…and then, Holly, I must say this out loud even though the thought rightly frightens me. Do you suppose he is here for me? Or just to visit his friend? Is this a terrible co-incidence, and if not, then what exactly is it? What is he on about?"

"But Elizabeth, that makes no sense at all; why would he come here to seek you out?" Holly cried in puzzlement, as much to convince herself as Elizabeth. "After such an arrogant and insulting proposal this spring, then such strange behaviour when you saw him in the summer. All politeness and condescension until he heard the news about Lydia…"

Elizabeth was pacing, only half-listening and muttering to herself. "Oh, why is he — how do I speak to him? What should I say? How should I act? How do I feel? How *should* I feel?"

Holly's brows almost met in the middle as she tried to sort out all that Elizabeth had told her earlier, combined with what she could see of her reactions upon seeing the man again, and then fit it in with her own sentiments and fears about the astonishing events of the morning.

"He purposefully sets out to destroy Jane's hopes and happiness, but then has an apparent change of heart concerning her and Mr Bingley, only to abruptly leave Hertfordshire after having scarcely spoken ten words to you the entire time he was there. And then, Lady Catherine comes to call for the sole purpose of insulting and threatening you. Then he unexpectedly appears *here*, apparently only to continue his taciturn ways and stare at you shamelessly? Yet you cannot reconcile your feelings toward him?"

Elizabeth was so agitated and confused that she could not answer, so Holly continued: "You must forgive me for asking, but have you lost your wits? What in the

60

world can your dilemma be about this man? I can tell you precisely what you should feel about him!"

"Holly, no! I know it seems strange, especially when you lay things out in black and white that way, but I suspect there is so much more to him than all this. I truly believe he is a good man. He certainly is a good, caring brother. And there are times, when he looks at me with such an expression of tenderness, like — "

"Tenderness!" Holly interrupted snorting in disgust. "Spend enough time fending off the advances of fathers and brothers of schoolgirls and you'll recognise that look for what it really is! I am sorry to be so blunt, Elizabeth, but he has made clear, in no uncertain terms, his opinion of you. He has no respect or esteem for you — he desires you; that is the extent of it. A man with a strong desire will couch it in any terms necessary to gain his ends, including looks of tenderness and even proposals of marriage or holidays in Scotland if he grows desperate."

Elizabeth looked at her cousin shrewdly for a moment while drumming her palm with a dead twig.

"Don't think me a simpleton, Holly, simply because 'brothers and fathers' are relatively unknown to me. I know what *that* look is. But as well as I recognise it, I also recognise that it is not everything." She sighed and threw away the twig in one hasty gesture. "It's not so much the way he looks at me or what he says — it is what he will *not* say and what he does *not* want me to see in him. If he were consistent in his actions and words, I would have no hesitation." She sighed. "Oh, it was much easier when I had made up my mind and was so certain about what I knew he was!"

Holly smiled tightly, uncomfortable with her cousin's struggle to explain away the man's behaviour. "Yes, consistency would be a blessing indeed, but I'm afraid *that* quality is sorely lacking in humanity in general. Ourselves included I fear; for I would hazard a guess that if Mr Darcy were not half as handsome as he is, your feelings about him would not be quite so confused. Men are not the only ones to let a pretty face go to their heads or affect their judgement, are they?"

Holly's expression grew serious as she continued walking beside her cousin. "Do not believe that I think you are a simpleton, Eliza, or anything of the sort. You *have*, however, led a protected and sheltered life in Hertfordshire, and it's happy for you that you have. But, cousin, men can be scheming, and devious — and it can be very hard to discern their motives, especially when we ourselves are conflicted in what we feel about them."

Elizabeth gave a hard little laugh and for a moment Holly thought she saw a shadow of fury flicker across her face.

"Don't think that men like that are strangers in protected and sheltered places. On the contrary, it seems to me they actively seek those places out."

Holly looked at the ground for a moment and then quietly said, "I suppose you mean Lydia."

"And by Lydia I mean her husband," Elizabeth said sharply. "Yes, there is a fine example to enlighten our conversation! An apt to illustration of how a sheltered life can be the most dangerous gift someone can give you in the guise of love and care."

"Forgive me, Elizabeth," Holly replied, keeping her eyes lowered. "I don't mean to come across as all-knowing and worldly wise. Heaven knows there are enough such men in the world to meet us wherever we happen to be — even tucked away in a tiny village in Scotland." She kicked at a pile of gathering leaves on the edge of the path. "And there are plenty of us who are more than willing to listen to them."

Elizabeth looked at Holly curiously, saying nothing in case this reflection had some foundation in experience she might want to relate. Holly did not elaborate, though, and soon Elizabeth's thoughts wandered back to the events of the morning and all the unpleasant memories and regrets the sight of Mr Darcy had conjured up.

"I was fatally mistaken in Mr Wickham. I could be just as mistaken in Mr Darcy and then my fault would be great indeed."

Holly smiled. "You, dear cousin, feel you are too quick to judge a man — not that I can see much evidence that you have judged this Mr Darcy wrongly — but then, *I* am too apt to mistrust, so I may be ascribing sinister motives to his strange behaviours when upon further examination they may be perfectly innocent.

"But as much as I try, as I think on it, I cannot reconcile myself that he just *happens* to be visiting a nearby friend at the same time you just happen to be visiting us. And such a friend as that... how close can they really be, Eliza? They appear to be so very different in temperament — not that I care so much for Mr Darcy's manners, but as questionable as they are, they are to be preferred to those of that Lord Baugham."

"Oh, Holly. Surely we have Lord Baugham to thank for not ending up as the topic for conversation and speculation at every dinner table in the parish! He really did us all a service even if it was quite a silly one. I was so very awkward and silent... as for Mr Darcy..." Elizabeth sighed and seemed to be watching something far away beyond the clearing and the rolling hills. "I wish I understood what he was about. I wish... I wish for once I knew the motive for his actions or words. If I knew that, then perhaps..."

Holly watched her. For some reason Elizabeth's words unsettled her. She wanted to ask her if she loved Mr Darcy, but she could not. Strangely enough, she was frightened of the answer. If Elizabeth was regretting her choices and actions over the past year despite all protestations of reason and facts, if she was still, when seeing him face to face, undecided as to what her feelings for him were, it seemed their old, familiar, safe relationship was changing, and right now she needed to know everything was just as it always had been with them.

The strong winds of the night before had shaken the trees and blown away the brilliant leaves. Now the trunks stood black and naked against the green of the grass and pines. They stood silently side-by-side until Elizabeth reached out her hand and took Holly's.

"Whatever is the truth about Mr Darcy, I have come to realise that the follies and inconsistencies I so enjoy observing and laughing at in my fellow human beings can be found very much closer to home. I should start with myself the next time I want

62

to marvel at how ridiculous people's actions and words can be."

"Oh, Elizabeth, don't be too severe with yourself! Don't make the same mistakes in the opposite direction. You do not know why he has come; you could still be right."

Elizabeth sighed, but she was smiling now. "You are right, I could. I am certainly selfish enough to hope I am, even in the face of overwhelming evidence to the contrary. I suppose that is a peculiar brand of optimism, but I find it has served me both well and ill in the past so I am loath to relinquish it."

Holly looked at her pleadingly. "Elizabeth, don't let your guilty conscience over hasty words and uncharitable thoughts make you blind to the fact that this man has yet to do anything other than prove his power to you. Not respect or esteem or even love. And until he does convince your heart as well as your mind..."

Elizabeth nodded. "Yes. That is what I think as well. And, more importantly perhaps, feel. Mr Darcy probably has as many regrets about this affair as I do. I have yet to see anything that proves the opposite."

She could have added "unfortunately" and the word hung in the air between the two girls, both equally aware of it. But still, Holly thought, even if interpreting Mr Darcy's actions in the best possible light and knowing her cousin's honest feelings on the subject, there was still a long way to what she knew Elizabeth wanted and deserved in a man.

She kept hold of her cousin's hand, feeling the need to break away from this subject, this feeling of upheaval that was in the air. It was stupid, she knew, this wish that they could always go on as they had before. Of course Elizabeth would marry someday, hopefully to a man who deserved her, and changes were coming to her own life as well — whether for good or ill she could not see. But for this little span of time, Holly only wanted to enjoy her cousin's company, and remember what they had always been to each other; she wanted to be a carefree girl again. She squeezed Elizabeth's hand tightly and began their old game.

"Here I bake..."

Elizabeth glanced at her for a moment, then smiled and continued the childish rhyme.

"Here I brew..."

Holly's grin widened.

"Here I make my wedding-cake..."

"And here I mean to break through!" Both girls then, hands clasped, began to run down the path, remembering the days when their dream wedding cakes had been carefully crafted out of mud and sticks, breaking through the recriminations, regrets and worries that surrounded them and determined, for the time being at least, that nothing and no one would break them apart.

THE SURPRISE ENCOUNTER AT THE church that morning seemed to have turned the tables regarding the tempers of the gentlemen. Lord Baugham was in a splendid mood and Mr Darcy hardly said a word as they walked home again. Baugham had exchanged a few words — all condescension and ease — with the reverend, complementing him on the service and confessing that if all Presbyterian sermons were as enjoyable as this morning's, all they had to do was to change the pews into slightly larger and more comfortable ones and he would convert on the spot. Darcy, frowning at this frivolity, suddenly objected to his attempts at fulfilling a landowner's social responsibilities and merely wanted to be on his way again.

This, however, could not be accomplished before the local representative of the landed gentry, a Sir Torquil Tristam complete with wife and three daughters in tow, made himself and his family known to his lordship in a long and detailed speech. Once they extricated themselves from his exuberant conversation, Lord Baugham stopped to wave cheerfully at Mr and Mrs Robertson, of the Caledonian Thistle Inn, and their brood of children making their way down the slope. Only then was Darcy successful in dragging him away.

"And now you suddenly don't approve of my landlordly duties?" Baugham quipped. "Just when they may come in handy to you too."

"What do you mean by that?" Darcy asked sourly, his only wish being that he could find peace and quiet enough to contemplate that morning's results. He still could not quite decide whether it had been a success or a failure.

"You still want to break down the door to Rosefarm Cottage, don't you? Or have you established an abduction scheme now that you know the lady ventures outside."

"Well, it is quite obvious my company is not enough for you for tea anymore," Darcy answered coldly.

Baugham gave him a long sideways look. "Darcy. Who is Miss Bennet?"

"She is an acquaintance of mine. And of my sister. Mr Bingley is betrothed to her sister."

"And you have come to see her. Or has she come to see you?"

Darcy looked straight ahead, controlled his features and, with an air of calm, answered his friend's questions.

"I came to see you. I told you as much."

"Why? Is that your only purpose in coming here, Darcy?"

Darcy looked up at the sky. "It looks like rain," he said. "We had better hurry home."

"Holly," Elizabeth gasped. "Stop. Please. I can't run any further."

"No, not until you have chased all your vexation and doubt away!" Holly cried, tugging at Elizabeth's arm.

"I have! I swear I have," her cousin panted and laughed, planting her feet and refusing to run another step. "Tea…I need tea."

"Very well, I relent! But only because tea sounds like an excellent idea right now; I am starved!"

This time the walk to Rosefarm was accomplished in better spirits, though with no less confusion for both girls. Once there, Elizabeth was able to speak calmly of Mr Darcy's surprise appearance to her aunt, and to temper somewhat Holly's less than flattering description of Lord Baugham.

"Lord Baugham, eh?" Mrs Tournier said and looked thoughtfully at her daughter. "I know that name from somewhere — "

"Of course you do!" her daughter scoffed. "He is 'practically our neighbour'." She looked down her nose and drawled. "And I say practically because I would never condescend to consider someone little better than a crofter a true neighbour, however close we live to the same fields and woodlands."

Holly pulled a face, but her mother was unimpressed.

"I wonder…" she said and tapped her foot. "What is it I almost remember about that name? He must have had the place for nigh to three years already…"

Holly ignored her mother just as she had been ignored and lifted her eyebrows to Elizabeth. Elizabeth shook her head and remarked that whatever the gentlemen were about, she was thankful to be home.

"And you did not think to invite them for tea?" Mrs Tournier suddenly returned to the conversation.

"I am sure," Holly answered, her eyes narrowing, "that there were better prospects awaiting them than what we could offer."

"Pity," her mother answered and picked up her book. "That might have made me remember. Well, certainly it will come to me soon."

Just then Mrs Higgins came in with a tray that could not belie Holly's assertion. A pot of steaming hot tea that had been stretched with dried herbs from the larder — from the aroma, it was raspberry leaves this time — a plate of toasted bread, a bowl of fruit preserves, a small sugar dish and a cream pitcher. Sufficient for family and close friends, but not what one would customarily serve to proud, young society men from London.

Elizabeth offered to pour and could not help but smile when she realised that, as usual, the small pitcher held not cream, but honey. On earlier visits she had learned the strange secrets of the Rosefarm tea tray: no cake or biscuits unless guests were expected, cream was never wasted in a tea cup, the white sugar was for Mrs Tournier — her one indulgence when it could be afforded — or company. Elizabeth had been assured many times over that she could avail herself of the sugar bowl as well, but since Holly invariably sweetened her tea with honey or treacle, insisting that she preferred it that way, she felt it was only fair to do so as well, leaving the expensive treat for her aunt to enjoy as long as possible.

In fact, the tangy, herb-laced cup of tea sweetened with honey was a distinctive taste and memory that she associated with Rosefarm Cottage, good conversation, and happy times. She would have been disappointed to be presented with a traditional cup loaded with cream and sugar when there. It would have seemed too bland and ordinary for the surroundings.

BAUGHAM STIRRED HIS RICH, SWEET tea carefully in silence while Darcy fastidiously declined the cake as he assembled his meal. Mrs McLaughlin had laid out a delectable spread of scones, cakes, biscuits, meat, various preserves and pie for the gentlemen's enjoyment, but neither of them paid it much attention.

"I think you had better tell me the whole story," Baugham said and sat down opposite his friend in front of the roaring fire.

Darcy stared ahead into the flames with his fist to his mouth.

"Evidently I must. Otherwise I will never find peace from your relentless curiosity I suppose. However, it is not a simple tale."

"Simple tales bore me," his host said. "And whatever you try to convince yourself and others, things are never that simple with you."

"Leave the reviews on my life until I'm finished," his friend said dryly. "You would not want to pre-empt your scorn and pity."

Baugham made a conciliatory gesture and settled down.

"I am in love with Miss Bennet," Darcy said. "Fatally, humiliatingly, totally and inescapably."

He stopped, as if that was the extent of it.

"Right?" Baugham prompted him. "And?"

"That is why I am here: to see her."

His friend sighed, got up from his comfortable chair, took a turn around the tea tray to add some more sugar to his tea and then slowly walked round to his desk, rummaged through his drawers and pulled out a clear, long necked bottle filled with a golden liquid. He brought the bottle round to his seat and poured a generous dollop into his cup, silently offering Darcy some, too. With the slightest of nods, his friend accepted.

The sat in silence again, feeling the whiskey slowly flow into their stomachs, seep into their veins and spread a warm glow through their bodies.

"I asked her to marry me once. In Kent. She emphatically turned me down. In fact, she told me I was the last man on earth she would marry. I remember the words quite clearly. But when I ran into her again — "

"Ran into her? You have seen her since?"

"Yes. On several occasions. And I cannot quite see — but I think, perhaps, she does not think so ill of me as then. In fact, that is what I need to know from her. Her opinion of me. I have tried very hard and I would hope she would recognise that. I thought she had."

There was a pause when Mr Darcy sank into his own thoughts and his friend tried to make sense of this confusing statement. Darcy? In love? So Darcy's cousin Anne was out of the equation then? How interesting! How fortunate! But how very, very strange.

"Why have I never seen her in Town? How curious. She must be much sought after to think herself in a position to refuse your offer... one of these provincial heiresses, is she?"

Darcy straightened his back and drank the last of his tea. Without feeling the need for polite pretence, he poured a new drink of the whiskey straight into his teacup.

"Her fortune is nothing to speak of, perhaps a thousand pounds, perhaps less…"

"What?" Baugham sat up, dumbfounded. "A country girl with fifty pounds a year at the most? I don't understand. And notwithstanding your foolery in offering for such a woman, what in the world gives her the audacity to turn *you* down?"

"I suppose I should feel flattered by your blind faith in my endless qualities, but she did not love me," Darcy answered quietly.

"What in God's name does that have to do with it? Love!" Baugham scoffed. "I don't love you and I'd marry you! — well, you know what I mean," he amended, seeing his friend look at him with something between exasperation and boredom. "You are a prime catch for any woman, my friend. You don't smell; you possess manners, money and pedigree; have no vices to speak of; and any woman's life as your wife would be very comfortable, very secure and very fine. And still, whoever said that love and marriage ought to be mixed? — if love exists at all, and on that matter I have my serious doubts. You are much better off to marry a suitable woman you can tolerate reasonably well, and then discreetly take your enjoyments as you may. It is much simpler that way. Saves everyone from grief, trouble and silliness."

"Yes," Darcy answered, emptying his cup once again. "I can see how your philosophies have simplified your life immensely and kept you out of troublesome situations."

"But Darcy," Baugham smiled, "I make no pretensions of wanting a simple, untroubled life when in Town. Unlike you, I enjoy a little intrigue and spark now and then. And anyway, refusing your offer of marriage makes no sense for any woman."

"Excepting when one does not have a very high opinion of my character."

Baugham stared at his friend. "How is that possible?"

Darcy shifted in his chair and had just made up his mind to tell his friend about his efforts on behalf of his friend Bingley with regards to Miss Jane Bennet when Baugham turned around and eyed him excitedly.

"Unless she is afraid of you!"

"What?" Darcy was completely taken aback.

"Well, a timid young woman might be somewhat…wary of you. And she did simper a bit when we met her outside the church and her friend obviously thought she was fragile as glass the way she held on to her. There's all that wealth and responsibility of yours, and then you do tend to scare the living daylights out of people with that stare of yours when really in the mood."

"Miss Bennet is not frightened of me. In fact, the more one tries to intimidate her, the more she recklessly and provokingly questions you. And very cleverly she does it, too," he added more quietly.

"Well, then," his friend was undaunted, "perhaps her affections are engaged elsewhere and that is why she refused you, which makes her a very foolish young woman in my opinion."

"Once again I'm touched by your blind faith in me."

"It's a simple matter of reason," his friend said calmly.

Darcy looked at him carefully.

"You have no idea of what I am speaking, have you? You have no idea what it is to have a woman turn you inside and out and put all your truths to shame and transform your certainties into follies?"

"Of course I do!" Baugham bolted out of his chair and went to stand by the hearth instead. "But that, my friend, is not love. That is something else entirely and something better not let into a marriage. Especially when so much is at stake as in your case: family, estate, duty, obligations, reputation — why get hung up with this... Miss Bennet?"

"Do not think I have not asked myself that very question a thousand times, but the answer is always the same. I need her. I want her. I love only her. And I cannot abandon that hope or my principles of honesty and sincerity unless I know, unequivocally, that there is *no* hope."

"Darcy, the woman you marry — and of course you must marry, I quite see that — must be worthy of you and all that you are. A Miss Bennet, from somewhere in Hertfordshire, poor as a church mouse, for heaven's sake, who turns you down on the pretext of having a poor opinion of your character when all she needs to do is look around her to see how you inspire devotion in friends and underlings alike, can hardly be thought to be worthy of you and your principles. At the very least she is foolish beyond reason!"

He grabbed the poker and executed a rough swirl into the burning logs although it was completely unnecessary and only served to send them crashing down to smother some of the underlying embers.

"At worst," he continued grimly, "she is a scheming, capricious, husband-hunting tease."

Darcy was standing now too, glaring at his friend. "Baugham! You forget yourself — I have told you how I feel about Miss Bennet and what's more, your ignorance of what is really at stake here does not qualify you to insult her. Or me, for that matter. I will have her as my wife, and my wife on terms of respect and mutual affection. This is about my happiness and, for once, recognising what is true and what is merely pompous parading of principles. If, that is, *she* will have *me*."

Chest heaving and eyes blazing, Darcy turned and stalked out of the room without another word.

"Fool," his lordship muttered when he heard the door slam, but his irritation was gone and there was a hint of sadness to his sneer.

LEAVING THE YOUNG WOMEN BEHIND her in the sitting room, Mrs Tournier went by the kitchen to have a word with Mrs Higgins, their housekeeper. She found her sitting at the kitchen table scraping turnips, sat down and wordlessly came to her aid.

"Higgins," she said, "what do you know of the owner of Clyne Cottage?"

Mrs Higgins, being accustomed to her Mistress' inquisitive mind on a variety of subjects, was not surprised.

"Not much, ma'am," she confessed. "It's a verra private gentleman. He calls himself Laird Baugham but I hear he's really called the Earl of Cumbermere. My cousin, Mrs

McLaughlin and her husband wirk and take care of the estate. For an estate it surely is. The cottage itself isn't as grand as ye'd think, ma'am, but the grounds are large. Verra secret gentleman, she tells me."

"So I have heard. He and a friend of his caused quite a stir at church this morning, I believe. And my daughter apparently finds his presence much decreases the value of the neighbourhood."

"Aye, well, from what I've heard from my cousin he's as good a Master as they come. But then, Heather always had a soft spot for saucy young men … ever since her Jack was killed in the Peninsula. And young Miss Holly surely is the most particular young leddy when it comes to young men, ma'am. The truth belike lies somewhere in the mids, I should think."

"I am very certain it does," Mrs Tournier answered. "Well, perhaps we'll one day clear up this mystery of the Master of Clyne, who leads a solitary existence only to pop up in church as cordially as you please one day out of the blue, with a friend in tow. The Earl of Cumbermere, eh? Well, well, I know that name well enough. This must be the son then …"

FATALLY. HUMILIATINGLY. TOTALLY. *INESCAPABLY.* IT was not the words that kept echoing in his mind, it was his friend's voice. Darcy confessed himself to be in love and it had not seemed to have brought him much of the joy Romantics promised. Baugham had never declared himself the owner of any romantic sentiments and thus he was not surprised.

As long as he had known Darcy, his friend had been the sternest advocate of reason, temperance and detachment when dealing with affairs of the heart. Beware of fortune hunters, beware of the matrons, and beware of tricks and debts and ulterior motives. And Baugham had been an avid pupil of aloofness in personal encounters with the opposite sex. Some degree of experience and adventure was desirable, but not attachment or commitment and certainly there had never been any cause to abandon reason. That philosophy had served him well so far and he had, together with Darcy, always been committed to maintaining that love had nothing to do with it.

And now Darcy was in love. Baugham had mixed feelings about this. Shock, to be sure, that his friend would succumb to the weakness. Irritation that he should do it so readily and openly. Fear that it would serve him ill and he would suffer the ills he had always warned his friend about.

This Miss Bennet, who was she? What was her motive? How would she use his friend and to what end? Love was, after all, the one area of life where women ruled, exercising their endless power in humiliating and selfish ways. What would be his friend's fate?

Baugham hesitated for a while, but decided to wander down to the kitchen. Perhaps Mrs McLaughlin could be of some help to unravel the mystery of the woman down at Rosefarm Cottage who had his friend in such an uncharacteristic clutch.

Mrs McLaughlin sat at the large kitchen table, drying and polishing the crystal. Every glass Darcy and he had used for before dinner drinks in the library, through the wine and the water and the sherry with the soup, to the port and the whiskey afterwards, stood like a company of soldiers in front of her, lined up according to size.

Baugham lifted up a sherry glass, but hastily put it back after Mrs McLaughlin gave him a look.

"What do you know about the Rosefarm ladies?" Baugham launched into his questions without ceremony. It was fruitless anyway. If he came round to the kitchen at this hour, Mrs McLaughlin knew he either wanted to ask questions or plunder her larder. Asking questions usually produced more results more quickly and with less effort.

"Dinnae know that much. Good employers, although not too plump in the pootch."

"Oh, come now, Mrs McLaughlin," his lordship drawled and picked up a wine glass. "Really."

"Well, I cannae launch into all I know straight away, now can I? Not without any clues to what yer looking to know. I'm sure ye'd expect Mrs Higgins to do the same at Rosefarm."

"She'd tell them I'm a good employer although not too wealthy either?"

Mrs McLaughlin snorted, but hid a smile as she turned around to put away the seltzer glasses.

"She'd tell them they'll have to wirk a wee bit harder than that if they want to learn anything."

"Right. Well, more specifically Miss Bennet then. What is she like?"

"A bonny lass. Gleg and trig and smairt." Lord Baugham looked pained and Mrs McLaughlin tried very hard. "Sharp. Quick-witted. Clever," she said slowly. "Does a world of good for Miss Holly. They be like sisters really. And Mrs Tournier is right fond of her niece. Thy're two women cut from the same tree, alright."

Baugham felt slightly disappointed. "Anything else? Anything… important?"

"Well…" Mrs McLaughlin carried more of the glasses away and stacked them carefully on the upper shelves. "It do seem as if Miss Elizabeth is come to git away from her kin down south. Some gunk or other. Disappointment," she explained slowly. "A mutual disappointment. What it be, I dinnae know. Nor is it my place to really."

"Oh? Well, should you find out more about that…gunk of Miss Bennet's…"

Mrs McLaughlin looked at him haughtily.

"Well, maybe not then," Baugham muttered and rose from his seat.

Chapter 6

*Social Life in and around Clanough picks up and
Intelligence is Gathered about the Other Side*

"ELIZABETH, I am sorry that I cannot come with you this morning, but Sir John's friend will be here any time now and I don't want to keep him waiting. He returns to Edinburgh on the two o'clock post." Holly apologised as she smoothed nonexistent wrinkles from her skirt and brushed her handkerchief over the table to remove invisible dust from its surface, "I don't know why I am so nervous, I already have the job. I just hope that I will be able to do it properly."

Elizabeth reached out and stopped the nervous movements with a soft touch on her shoulder. "Holly, stop worrying, you will be fine, you know you will — and so will I. I am perfectly capable of walking out by myself, and to be honest, I rather welcome the chance to think and sort out my feelings in solitude."

"Of course you must. I shouldn't be so selfish to require you to always be in my company, so I give you leave to go without me," Holly smiled. "I trust when you return you will be all sorted and thought out."

"You may count on it," Elizabeth laughed as she tied her bonnet and walked out the door.

Sir John's friend, Dr McKenna, was kind, friendly and an easy conversationalist. He was knowledgeable about Sir John's work and requirements and full of encouragement and admiration for Holly's preliminary sketches. The morning passed quickly as they paged through the manuscript, the doctor pointing out the places Sir John had marked for the colour plates, helping her decipher his notes, and explaining any concepts which were unclear to her.

Elizabeth returned shortly before noon and, along with Mrs Tournier they shared a light meal in the parlour.

"So," Mrs Tournier began with her customary directness to their guest, "you are an aspiring geologist? Whatever for? I believe I can claim the privilege of hostess to have you explain to me, Dr McKenna, exactly what it is that makes rocks so fascinating and worth your passion. I assure you, although it at present is a mystery to me, I am by no means unwilling to see your reason and even learn a thing or two."

Dr McKenna smiled and met Holly's eyes. Holly recognised an intelligent man in his look and realised Sir John most probably had warned him about her mother's unguarded behaviour and eagerness for debate, even with virtual strangers. The rest of the conversation consisted of pointed questions and intelligent answers, good natured teasing, laughter and not a little bit of knowledge shared around the room until it was time for their guest to leave to catch the coach to Edinburgh.

THE MORNING SUN WOKE LORD Baugham the moment it peeked over the fell. This was by no means unwelcome to his lordship, and he was restless to get up and take advantage of the clear weather.

He was somewhat surprised, however, to discover that his otherwise fastidious friend did not appear at breakfast. He still had not shown himself after Lord Baugham had had a good rummage through the kitchen for provisions from Mrs McLaughlin and the gun room for equipment from Mr McLaughlin. In the hall, impatient to be on his way, he questioned Riemann while he prepared himself for his outing. Since the valet would not answer his inquiry of Mr Darcy's whereabouts, he concluded nothing was to be done.

"Well, when you see him lurking about somewhere again, tell him I've gone down to the trout rock by Nethery Farm and that I shall try to catch dinner for us before lunch. He might join me if he wishes; I shall be there for as long as I can manage. Glorious weather! Can't wait to see if it has bewitched the fish as well as myself!"

With that he was off, whistling, down to the place where the fish always bite and the stream always sings. It was a fair way to walk but the sun had done an admirable job of drying out the worst of the rain from the last few days and so he could keep up a good pace. The place he was heading to was a very secluded spot by a narrow part of a brook that took an elegant turn just around a large flat boulder only to almost tie a bow on itself as it tried to catch its own tail again on the other side. Consequently, a large pool of water lay quietly just under its rocky path, letting the river catch its breath before it cheerfully rolled on.

His lordship set himself down on the flat boulder, admiring the scenery and the glittering, bubbly stream rippling by his feet. He could see no fish yet, but they would come. They always did. He laughed softly to himself and shook his head. "Darcy must be the most perfect fishing partner imaginable with his cursed taciturnity and then he ends up not coming!"

The sun, the fresh air and the inactivity of the trout made Lord Baugham hungry for his lunch at an early hour. He sat down beneath a large elm, resting his back against the trunk, cutting pieces of bread and cheese while watching his rod peacefully bobbing up and down on the twirling water. It was very pleasant in the shade and quiet — the only sounds were the rippling of the water and the birds singing in the tree above him. Before he could make a conscious decision, he had slid down the trunk, crossed his arms behind his head and placed his hat over his face. Approximately two minutes later, Lord Baugham was fast asleep.

"Baugham!" a voice bellowed.

His lordship jerked in his sleep and shifted his long frame splayed against the tree. His hat tipped and slid down on the ground. Without opening his eyes, he sighed and only considered getting up when he heard twigs being crushed by determined footsteps close by. When he looked up, there was Darcy poised above him, frowning.

"Are you awake?"

Baugham sighed again. "Evidently."

"You look terrible."

"And you look much too agitated. What is it?"

"You promised me tea at Rosefarm within three days. Get dressed. We're going."

Mr Darcy stalked off. Baugham jumped up and called after him.

"Now? Why?"

"Because we have received an invitation and we do not wish to disappoint. It was hard won."

With that Baugham had to be content, for Mr Darcy had a coat to consider back at Clyne.

"Perhaps you should tell me who invited you," Baugham said later on as they directed their horses over the fields at a trot.

"Miss Bennet," Darcy said calmly and kept his eyes on the emerging village beyond the trees.

"And does the rest of the family know of this invitation?"

"In a manner of speaking. Miss Bennet mentioned her aunt was always fond of lively company."

"Which is why I am being dragged along?"

"Something of that nature, yes."

Baugham contemplated his friend's short answers and remembered the look of unbridled dismay on the face of Miss Bennet's cousin when they met after church. He sighed. That, and an old widow, would certainly require all his effort if the afternoon was to turn out to be lively. He decided Darcy owed him at least a hunting trip up towards Blechan Fells if he managed to serve his appointed purpose.

Mrs Tournier was enjoying herself immensely. Spontaneous jigs, guests in fezzes and spirited arguments about Poor Laws were all very well, but a live drama of four young, determined characters, meeting and playing out their various agendas right in front of her was infinitely to be preferred as far as unexpected entertainment was concerned. On occasions like this, she had to admit she missed London society and the menagerie of the perpetually intriguing *ton*!

She glanced at her daughter. Holly's jaw was set and her dark eyes looked warily from under her long lashes as she filled teacups. Her niece sat straight-backed on the edge of the sofa with her hands in her lap. Her speech was effortless and she led the conversation easily, but her uncommon stiffness spoke louder than her easy exchange.

And best of all — the gentlemen! Mr Darcy smiled easily, but had difficulty in meeting the eyes of any who addressed him. They strayed all too often to admire the back of the sofa, the arm rests of the sofa, the fabric of the sofa, the carved legs of the sofa and, in doing so, often hastily skimmed over the woman who sat in the middle of it all, apparently obscuring his view and study.

Mrs Tournier was, however, most entertained by the young man sitting beside her. He could hardly know why, but she was both listening to his constant flow of light conversation and trying to see the father in the son. It was not easy. Mrs Tournier had met the notorious sixth Earl on a few occasions in London in her youth, fully aware of his grim reputation. He was a gambler, a libertine and a drunk. His infrequent appearances in polite society were most likely motivated by a need to apply for loans from his more reputable associates and he had always quickly disappeared again to more depraved pursuits, which no one in her acquaintance had ever witnessed firsthand, though everyone claimed to have detailed knowledge of their degree of wickedness.

She could see but little of the father in the son, excepting for those blue eyes that were detached, though by no means hard or unfeeling. He returned her silent thoughts on his family by asking about hers. She answered honestly, to which he showed a remarkable degree of intelligence and interest for a man with such easy manners.

Once the tea was poured, Mrs Tournier derived another source of pleasure in guessing what thoughts were running through her daughter's mind as the guests helped themselves generously to the offerings from the tray, and most specifically, from the sugar bowl. In receiving her own cup from Holly's hands, the unmistakable fragrance of mint gave evidence that, however lofty the status of their guests, she had not felt they deserved the privilege of being served pure, black tea. The gentlemen's faces were portraits of polite surprise, Elizabeth's of subdued curiosity, and Holly's of scarcely contained suspicion and defiance.

"So!" Lord Baugham said and broke the silence surrounding the first sip. "Here we are, travelled all over, restless in our pursuit of novelties or peace, yet never before having been to tea in Clanough. I must thank you, Mrs Tournier, for opening your door to show us what we have been missing."

"If you are referring to the tea itself, my lord, I think it is probably about time you were treated to new sensations. As for our company, I would suppose a man like you is not inclined to come to obscure Scottish villages with an eye toward enlarging his social circle. Perhaps you feel we ought to be spectacular in our singularity in order to warrant another visit?"

"Oh, no!" Lord Baugham laughed. "You are singular enough in the fact that you have failed to live up to my prejudiced expectations! And I assure you, madam, you have failed in a most charming manner!"

"You are surprised at the quality of society outside your own circles, my lord?" Holly sat down beside her cousin, stirring her cup slowly.

"Perhaps, but such surprise is nearly always the fault of the expectant party — as it surely is in this case — and the triumph of those being visited."

Holly arched her eyebrow and looked at Lord Baugham. What a smug face he had! It was all sport to him, this whole thing.

"I suppose," her cousin broke in, "Scottish society is by no means foreign to your lordship. I would venture a guess that you are intimately acquainted with its wilder forms."

"That is very true, Miss Bennet," Baugham said cheerfully. "I am not overly familiar with the society here, other than the wildlife. I tend to visit Scotland when I am in my more subdued frame of mind, to enjoy the solitude and quiet — and I must say beauty — of the place."

"And I see that when you *do* require company," Holly added, quietly, but with a noticeable edge to her voice as she glanced at Mr Darcy, "you prefer to import your own rather than seek out what may be close by?"

Lord Baugham gave her an amused look, Darcy shifted in his chair and Mrs Tournier smiled smugly into her teacup.

"Now Holly!" Elizabeth laughed uncertainly and stood, ostensibly to fetch some more cheese. "Take care! As your own imported companion, I must ask you to have pity! Or else quickly praise my bravery in venturing so far north!"

Lord Baugham watched Miss Tournier for a few more moments, and then shifted his attention to Miss Bennet.

"Well, Miss Bennet, I will certainly praise you then and ask you to entertain us with your travel exploits all the way from Hertfordshire. Travel guides being all the rage, perhaps you might inspire us!"

"I do not know how well I can inspire one who has undoubtedly made the journey countless more times than I have, and since my aunt and cousin make the reverse journey but rarely, I have exhausted my gift for description of the picturesque beauties of the roadsides long ago. They grow quite out of patience with me sometimes. It is hard to believe, my lord, but living here as they do, they do not appreciate my raptures over the green of the landscapes, the grandeur of the wild storms or even the fickleness of the weather as they ought — but do not you agree that, though the journey is long, the pleasures awaiting us at the end of it make all the inconveniences worth while?"

"My sentiments exactly, Miss Bennet! Although I must be honest and admit to generally being of a romantic disposition and longing for whatever exact landscape I just left behind."

"My cousin and I walked to the edge of your grounds the other day — you have a lovely estate, my lord, and certainly no reason to want for any other surroundings." Elizabeth appeared happy to be able to converse with Mr Darcy's easy friend, while at the same time her eyes frequently darted across the room.

"I am glad you approve," he said, bowing his head in recognition of the compliment, though his smile momentarily tightened. "But," he brightened again, "never having been to Hertfordshire, Miss Bennet, you must awaken my interest in it. It is, as I said, in my nature to be curious."

Holly listened as Lord Baugham skilfully steered the conversation to rest on Elizabeth, questioning her in a friendly, but particular, way on her family, her home, her interests and opinions. Holly had no wish to sit quietly and listen to her cousin being grilled in this manner — however good-natured it seemed on the surface — but she could not think of a single thing to say to break the conversation that did not seem impolite. And Mr Darcy certainly was no help! He sat there, as he would, seemingly quiet and poised and content, but with a restless look in his eye and no conversation. *No* conversation! Holly saw that whatever his professed feelings for Elizabeth might have been, he would be of no help in rescuing her from the interrogation of his friend.

With a sigh she waited for his lordship to take a breath and jumped in the middle of their talk, resigning herself to the appearance of rudeness in order to defend her cousin.

"Lord Baugham," she blurted out the first thing that came to her mind, "I hope you have no plans to correct that bit of lower ground that tends to go boggy in the spring. It does give a lovely place to watch the birds as they come through."

It worked. Lord Baugham paused in his extended questions on how the social life in Meryton compared with that of Clanough and looked at her. Holly suddenly felt self-conscious under such a direct and very clear blue-eyed stare, and flushed.

"I . . . I trust you know that which I mean."

"Oh, of course," his lordship said regaining some of his ease. "I did not realise that you . . . well, that is to say, it is rather far off the path through to the north fields. I was not aware of it being such a favourite spot. Of anyone's."

"Well," Holly stammered, now wondering whether she should have just left Elizabeth, who had really seemed to be doing quite well, to fend for herself. "I do . . . that is, when I am home, I tend to wander a bit far afield. I sometimes forget to mind the property lines."

"Hmm," his lordship said and could not prevent a shadow of disdain from passing across his face. He had always thought of Clyne as a personal sanctuary, and it did not please him overly to know that she knew about the places he had come to consider his private and intimate sources of pleasure and comfort in the short time he had been in possession of it. *He* had only come across that patch of land last year, and had been pleased to think of it as his own secret discovery.

The look in his eyes was easy enough for Holly to read. Yes, it *was* his property, but she felt a twinge of resentment in being made to feel like an intruder in the places she had loved to wander since she was a child.

"I will be certain to pay closer attention in the future. Forgive my trespassing, please," she said, sitting back in her chair and turning her attention to her teacup.

"It is perfectly in order to have my grounds enjoyed by those walking through them," his lordship said airily. "Think nothing of it, Miss Tournier." But it was quite clear *he* did.

THEY LEFT SOON AFTERWARDS AND rode homewards in silence. Darcy seemed calm and almost happy. Certainly the corners of his mouth were relaxed and he sat easily on his horse looking at the surroundings with interest.

Baugham's predicament was greater. On the one hand, he was surprised and pleased at his encounter with Mrs Tournier. Far from the dull widow he had expected, he found her to be intelligent, informed, witty and frank in a manner that gave him great delight and she was also a surprisingly handsome woman. He had liked her very much and had not been sorry to spend an afternoon in her company.

On the other hand, was the dilemma of Miss Bennet. There was no doubt she was an intelligent woman herself and his suspicion that she might find his friend intimidating and for that reason be averse to his advances he soon discarded. Not that his friend had done anything to counteract his inclination of repulsing unwanted addresses. He had sat on his chair, silent and relaxed and quite content to observe the proceedings around him. Baugham had the sneaking suspicion that the visit had been arranged as much to give him an opportunity to assess Miss Bennet as for his friend's own benefit.

If that was the case, Miss Bennet had given a fine performance. And, as it *was* a performance, it was better not commented upon. Perhaps there would be other opportunities to speak with her and to observe. Baugham reflected that he should not be sorry to do that either, and the puzzlement he felt at that realisation soon made him abandon any further deliberation on the subject of Miss Bennet's personality and sincerity.

"Oh, I need to thank you, Darcy!" Baugham said instead and moved his horse closer to his friend's. "I enjoyed myself very much back there!"

Darcy gave him an arch look. "I'm glad to hear it."

"What a remarkable woman! And all the way in this little place! Astounding."

"I assume you mean Mrs Tournier."

"I do indeed. I am most impressed. And, I don't mind telling you I liked her very much. Do you know, she turns out to be the widow of Jean-Baptist Tournier, the revolutionary and Girondist! I read his pamphlet 'On the Necessity for the Abolishment of Noble Privileges' when I was fifteen and it was rousing stuff, let me tell you. He was a lawyer but frightfully clever with words. Even my French teacher, old Monsieur Vallée thought so. Tournier had to flee Paris in '92 with his wife and daughter and they eventually settled here. Sadly, he died quite soon afterwards. He was a very clever if, of course, frightfully radical man. Isn't that quite amazing!"

Darcy, never a man to endorse revolutionary sentiments, however prettily written, grunted and shook his head.

"And easy on the eyes still, too, wouldn't you say?" Baugham winked, knowing he had successfully managed to irritate Darcy on all the points he felt strongly about in one go.

"And I remember the daughter now, too," he went on more thoughtfully. "I have seen her about on occasion, I suppose. She's a teacher. I wonder how that rhymes with her father's views and her mother's frankness!"

His lordship chuckled and Darcy gave him an almost imperceptible headshake. "Well," he said, "I suppose I owe you that fishing trip."

"Ah!" his lordship said and his thoughts drifted even further away from Rosefarm Cottage. "Angling! Yes, the great leveller of men, a sport for gentlemen of all social standing, a pursuit where the master meets his servant on common ground!"

"A sport of quiet and reflection?" Darcy smiled.

"And therefore more of a challenge than one would think," Baugham laughed and to his great happiness, Darcy grinned broadly.

They made plans, then and there, to go up to Brachen Falls and trick the trout as soon as possible. Darcy appeared to look forward to the trip and asked his friend a number of detailed questions pertaining to geography and terrain. Baugham answered him happily, feeling his mind and heart already racing off ahead to the best and most beautiful spots.

"Darcy," he said after a while with a sheepish smile, "you know, I really did enjoy myself very much today."

His friend looked at him carefully. "You did?"

"Yes," Baugham answered. "I did. But I don't know that I quite understand it all. Yet."

"Don't fret," Darcy said calmly. "One day you surely will."

HOLLY WAS LYING ON HER bed, unable to close her eyes. It was a small room, right under the roof. A maid's room, if there had been a maid. When it rained the patter of the drops was so close it was guaranteed to lull her to sleep in an instant. It was not raining now, however, and she could not sleep.

This had always been her room, it was completely familiar to her, and yet she loved going over the things and checking that they were still where they had always been. Her chest of drawers, her small cabinet, her table and chair by the window that held few books and a looking glass perched on the side. It was mostly empty now, but when she was younger the table had always been covered with papers and paints and easels and gathered treasures of every kind. Her bed was narrow, but the blankets and pillows were familiar and smelled old and sweet.

There were no sewing samplers on the walls, but they were far from empty. On every available spot there was a drawing or a study or a sketch and on the slanted ceiling, just above her head, where it was impossible to hang anything, she had instead drawn butterflies and other insects making their way across the whitewashed space.

Holly sighed and watched the wasp that was just above her. Just on the opposite side of the hall was an identical room where Elizabeth was lying in a bed just like hers. She did not have insects to look at above her bed, but Holly was certain she was not sleeping either.

When the gentlemen left them that afternoon, she had wanted to speak to her to come to some sort of common result and judgement of the visit, but Elizabeth had been evasive. She instead asked her to write a letter to Jane with her — she was due, she explained, and Jane would never forgive her if Holly did not speak to her directly. Holly was eager to oblige and somehow they ended up being very silly in their serious pursuit, once again finishing each other's sentences and Holly drawing silly little portraits of the two of them in the margins.

She threw her covers aside, jumped off the bed and wrapped herself in her dressing gown, pulling on some thick socks. She picked up her still lighted candle and traipsed hurriedly across the hall and gently knocked at her cousin's door. She was right; Elizabeth was nowhere near sleep either.

"I was hoping you'd come," she smiled. "Get in here, you must be freezing."

Holly skipped over to Elizabeth's bed and dug her legs and feet in under the warm blankets.

"I need to apologise," she said.

"Not again, Holly!" her cousin smiled and prodded her with her elbow. "It seems all we do these days is apologise and I think we should stop before we are afraid to do anything to provoke reaction from the other anymore."

Holly smiled back. "Well, perhaps. But just this once though. Then I will stop."

"Only if you let me do it once more too after you've finished."

Holly could not help but laugh. "Very well. Me first though. I apologise for tea. I was very rude to you and I let my emotions get the better of me when I should have kept my peace and stood by you calmly. I don't know what got into me! At the very least, I could have made better use of my rudeness to shield you from Mr Darcy rather than to irritate his friend."

Elizabeth reached over and took Holly's cold hand in hers, dragging it under the sheets.

"Yes, that was highly curious, I must admit. But please don't worry about Mr Darcy on my behalf. I think I did very well not speaking to him *at all*."

"He never said anything!" Holly said. Oh, how she had waited to be able to say that! "He just looked at you and never said a thing! To anyone!"

Elizabeth looked at her cousin. "Holly," she said quietly, "my turn. Let me say that when Mr Darcy does speak — which is, I grant you, a rare occurrence — he speaks very well."

Holly was puzzled and showed it.

"I talked to him earlier today; we met while I was out this morning. I don't doubt he had been looking out for me, hoping to catch me walking. He said as much and he has done so before: once, in Kent. The morning after…well, that was when he gave me that letter explaining his actions and I am glad to say he did nothing of the sort this time. But he asked if he might accompany me and I had no objections so we walked. We said perhaps ten words all together. Most of them concerned whether it was convenient for him and his friend to call. I said yes."

"You said yes…" Holly repeated slowly, "and by 'yes', did you mean *'yes, if you must*' or *'yes, please do'?*"

Elizabeth was quiet. "Neither," she finally answered. "I meant, *'come if you will and I will see what you are about'*."

She sat up and tenderly adjusted Holly's dressing gown to cover her properly. "Holly," she said, "I apologise for not telling you earlier."

"You are forgiven, of course. But Eliza, did you feel that you wanted, or needed, to keep it from me?"

"Neither, again. That is why I owe you an apology. It is no secret — I could never keep it a secret from you. I have none but childish and cowardly reasons for not waiting to tell you. Had you asked me what I thought of that walk, what happened, and if I had been sure of myself right away, I could not have told you anything that could have satisfied even myself. So I kept quiet and hoped if the gentlemen should call, you could see a little more for yourself and then perhaps not need me to tell you things that only make me more uncertain and unsure of myself."

Holly sighed and thought back over the strange visit of the afternoon.

"I wish I could say that I had seen something, but his behaviour today was just as mysterious as all your descriptions of him in Hertfordshire. Did *you* see anything; are you any closer to satisfaction as to his feelings? Why does he seek you out only to remain aloof?"

"Why do you think I am still awake? I went to bed two hours ago, Holly!"

Holly smiled and pulled her cousin's head onto her shoulder and stroked her hair.

"Don't worry Elizabeth, we are intelligent and resourceful women and we won't let this man disturb our time together. And that friend of his!"

Elizabeth sighed. "Lord Baugham. What a curious man! And what a curious man for Mr Darcy to have as a friend! Could there be two more diverse men claiming friendship? Except..." and here she laughed. "I wish you knew Mr Bingley! Now what does that say about Mr Darcy, I wonder, having friends like that?"

"Something like 'tell me who your friends are and I shall tell you who you are'?" smiled Holly. "If Mr Bingley is as agreeable as you say, I think it only one more puzzling contradiction about Mr Darcy. This friend was not so agreeable at all!"

Elizabeth raised her head and looked at her cousin thoughtfully. "Do you really think so, Holly? Once again, I think we owe him a great debt for keeping our little party somewhere near ordinary, polite discourse."

Holly snorted. "He was so...smug!" she said violently. The idea of being indebted for anything to a man like Lord Baugham disgusted her. "Very well," she conceded, "but he was so annoying. And quite full of himself and his own sparkling wit. And so eager to impress Maman and flash that smile and play the gentleman, when all he really wanted was to expose you and find something to ridicule us about!"

But Elizabeth was frowning and was obviously worlds away from Holly's long-awaited outburst about her 'practical' neighbour.

"Really?" she said absentmindedly. "Well, perhaps."

THE HOUSE WAS QUIET AGAIN and Lord Baugham felt a great sense of peace come over him. It was true he had been more confused by his introduction and conversation with Miss Bennet than he at first expected. The biggest fault with that lay with his inability to fit her into the picture he had formed of her. Of course, he rationalised, that was partly Darcy's fault. How was one to successfully envision the woman Darcy confessed such violent feelings for? There was no precedent, only sketchy figures of youthful admiration, never discussed and quickly exchanged by Darcy for new pursuits or peace.

Baugham did not believe in love. It was not that he did not believe in its existence, he rather did not believe in it as a goal worth striving for or as a means to achieving happiness. He had not needed love for the twenty-eight years of his life and when it had been given to him it had been complicated, tinged with tragedy and sorrow. Love was a thin veneer over selfishness, desperation and helplessness; it took more than it gave and what it did give was more aptly called by other, less noble, names.

The truth was that if Darcy confessed to love for a woman, Baugham was caught in territory he knew nothing about and viewed with suspicion. That in itself was cause enough for him to be curious. Who was Elizabeth Bennet? And more to the point, what was she? Why did Darcy love her enough to propose marriage despite her obvious reluctance and then keep returning to her when she so clearly had denied him? And why had she denied him? It still made no sense at all. What kind of woman was she?

He looked around the hall after leaving the bright, warm drawing room. There was still the whiskey bottle and perhaps Darcy could be persuaded to come back to the library. Baugham had a vague feeling he perhaps owed his friend something akin to an apology — or sympathy.

According to Mrs McLaughlin, Miss Bennet was fleeing from a disappointment. But what sort of disappointment? Had she set her sights on someone even higher than Darcy and that was why... but no, that was so far-fetched an idea that Baugham dismissed it immediately. Whatever it was, his lordship thought, it must be *gunk,* indeed. Shaking his head, he abandoned the idea of further conversation about this confusing matter and took to his chamber instead. The fire was burning, but there was no sign of Riemann except in the form of his laid out nightclothes on the bed and the perfect arrangement of a glass of wine and the volume of Donne's poems he had left open in the library yesterday. Baugham's amusement was evident when he discovered that his valet had marked the exact spot of his interrupted reading and inscribed the piece of paper with the date. He was certain this was Riemann's subtle comment on his habit of reading several works at once and leaving them open upside down all over the house. Then his lordship disturbed the perfect picture of order and took them both to bed with him.

Since so, my mind
Shall not desire what no man else can find;
I'll no more dote and run

To pursue things which had endamaged me;
And when I come where moving beauties be,
As men do when the summer's sun
Grows great,
Though I admire their greatness, shun their heat.

A wise sentiment, and very aptly put. He could certainly live with that and be very comfortable. Very comfortable, indeed.

Chapter 7

*Friends and Family Keep Abreast of the Developing
Friendship of Miss Bennet and Mr Darcy*

HOLLY sat at her worktable amid a jumble of manuscript pages, half completed sketches, tubes and pots of paint and pastels as she tried to decide just exactly how she wanted to organise and portray Sir John's air pump experiments. There was not much evidence of progress to show for her long day's work excepting for a growing list of discarded or unworkable ideas, but however much her brow was wrinkled in thought, it was work she enjoyed and found much more fulfilling than her attempts to educate the spoiled daughters of Scotland's elite.

The sound of Elizabeth's book snapping shut, therefore, startled her from her concentration.

"Holly," said Elizabeth, "I have something both to tell you and to ask you."

Welcoming the opportunity to drop her pencils and stretch her tight shoulders, Holly slid her chair back and lifted her arms above her head.

"Perfect timing," she yawned. "I am just ready for a break."

"I have been doing a great deal of thinking, as you might imagine, last night and today," Elizabeth began, "and I think I must go for another walk."

"Well, of course, I can be ready — "

"No, Holly, *that* is what I had to tell you. What I ask of you is this: I would like to go alone. There is a chance I may run across Mr Darcy again; indeed, I think there is a very good chance of it, and I have thought of a few things that we might talk of somewhat easily. I can ask him about his sister, or Mr Bingley, or his plans for staying or leaving, simple things — Holly, please do not give me that dark look. I have thought this over carefully, and I would like to have the opportunity, just me, to talk with him again now that these first uncomfortable meetings are over with, to see how he acts toward me. If I can but watch him in a relaxed or unguarded moment, I might discover some inkling as to his feelings and then might be able to be clearer as to my own."

It was not hard to understand Elizabeth's need, but that did not make Holly any more apt to like it. For the hundredth time since her cousin's arrival, she silently cursed the name 'Mr Darcy'; fervently wishing she had never heard it. Elizabeth looked at her, silently asking for understanding, so she put on a mild face, declared that her plan made perfect sense, and wished her a nice outing.

"Go!" she smiled.

"I will," Elizabeth answered and jumped off her seat.

It was not until after the door closed behind her that she let out an explosive sigh and flopped gracelessly down on the sofa.

"Ahhhhh!" she yelled out to the ceiling, childishly kicking at the arm of the sofa. "*Why* did he have to come here? Stupid man! Stupid, stupid man!"

When her outburst was over, she jumped up and looked around hurriedly, hoping her mother had not heard. She tried to settle down to her work again, but soon discovered that it was impossible. Her mind kept wandering outside to where Elizabeth walked, wondering if or where she might meet up with that man. What if her initial fears were right and Mr Darcy's motives were not honourable? What if he had followed her to Scotland in anger and frustration? He had already admitted on more than one occasion to purposefully seeking her out, looking to find her when she was alone.

The more Holly pondered these questions, the more concerned she became. Even as she told herself she was being ridiculous, that despite his faults Mr Darcy appeared to be an honest and respectable man, the doubts persisted. Elizabeth herself trusted him and believed him to be good; there was no cause for her to worry. But then again, Elizabeth had believed that same thing of Mr Wickham, and had admitted how mistaken she continually felt regarding Mr Darcy.

Holly was pacing now. Elizabeth was out there somewhere — looking to speak to this man alone. Night fell fast this time of year…what if…what if…

"Enough!" Holly declared before grabbing her cloak and heading out the door herself. It was nothing, she was sure, but she would not be easy in her mind until she found her cousin and made sure she was safe again at Rosefarm.

Mrs McLaughlin glanced at the door. All was quiet.

"Well now," she said. "How's things at Rosefarm these days?"

Her cousin, Mrs Higgins, concentrated on her turnips a moment longer before looking up with a shrewd smile.

"Same as here I should think."

Mrs McLaughlin returned the smile and said casually, "She asked aboot him, then?"

"Aye. Just as he did aboot her?"

The two women shared a quiet laugh.

"Nosy folk these southerners," Mrs Higgins said. "And always in need of a bit of help with the snooping, aye? I tell ye, I could have burst out laughing when the gentlemen walked through that door. And to think, just the day before, Mrs Tournier was asking me about his lairdship"

"His lairdship asked most especially about Miss Bennet though."

"Well, I know why she is of such interest. It's that friend o' his. The way he gaups at her..."

"Mr Darcy?"

Mrs Higgins proudly wiped her knife on her apron and nodded.

"Like he wants to eat her and give her a set-down at the same time."

The women burst out laughing.

"Aye, well, then there's nothing else for it, is there?"

"No, indeed. Only cure for that particular trouble is marriage, aye?"

FIRST HOLLY LOOKED CAREFULLY UP and down the lanes leading from Rosefarm Cottage out of the village and into the countryside. Nothing.

Then she returned to Clanough and canvassed the central, and then the peripheral streets for any sign of them. Nothing.

Then, with a hurried pace, as evening was drawing near and the sun was close to setting, Holly turned up the road that led from Clanough toward Clyne Cottage. The further along she walked the dimmer the light grew — as the sun began to sink her feelings of fear increased. Soon she felt as if she was on the verge of a panic and her pace quickened so that she was nearly running. In no time she was on the grounds of Clyne itself, but once there she stood frozen, not knowing where to go next. To her great relief she saw someone crossing the fields, a lone gentleman making his way straight through the fields in long, unhurried strides. It was Lord Baugham, obviously just returned from a day of hunting. Recognising someone whom she could involve in her desperate search and mounting worries, she ran up to him.

"My lord," she gasped. "Please... I must beg for your assistance."

Baugham's eyes registered first shock and then strangely narrowed into something resembling suspicion. He looked her up and down in the dusky light and although he wore a friendly smile, it did not quite reach his eyes.

"Why, Miss Tournier, don't tell me you're out trespassing again. That would be slightly disconcerting, wouldn't you say, considering your promises of just yesterday." Fighting to keep his voice on a courteous level he looked at her a little closer. "Or have you come across any more interesting sights on my land that you believe I should familiarise myself with?"

"What?" was Holly's confused reply. "Trespassing... no, please do not think — oh, for heaven's sake, there is no time for this... we must find them! He is *your* friend!"

"I am sorry, Miss Tournier, but find who? What is it you would like me to do for you?"

Exasperated, Holly stomped her foot. "You must come and help me! Mr Darcy has made off with my cousin and we must find them. Now. Hurry!"

His lordship resumed his slow and steady walk toward the house. "Made off? I am sure there is no need to worry, Miss Tournier. But if it will make you feel better, I'll send Mr McLaughlin out. He can see you safely home and then — "

"No!" her determined insistence surprised him. "It is getting dark, we must find her now!"

They stood watching each other, though Holly kept looking around her hoping she could catch a glimpse of Elizabeth and even hoping Lord Baugham might tell her he had seen them or knew where they were heading or... anything! Without realising it, she drew her breath and it came out again as a quiet, distressed whimper.

"Now please don't concern yourself," his lordship finally said. "Of course I will help you but... well, this is a bit extraordinary and I am sure Mr Darcy and Miss Bennet — "

"Sir!" Holly said, exasperated. "It will very soon be dark and my cousin is unfamiliar with the grounds around here. I have looked everywhere else I know she likes to walk except here. Do you wish to have that on your conscience?"

Baugham was not quite sure what Miss Bennet's ill-advised outings with or without his friend at this time of the day had to do with him, but he found himself mumbling something about being glad to be of assistance.

"Oh, I hope she hasn't gone to the bit of everwood down east," Holly suddenly said impulsively. "She would, though, she was fascinated by that last time she was here."

"What? *My* bit of everwood? That patch north of Kye?"

Holly rolled her eyes at him and set off eastwards towards the even darker sky. "Before it was yours this and yours that, my lord, it was mine too. All of ours. I have lived here since I was eight years old and I have as much affection and right to wander here as you have. Maybe more."

"Well, if that is so, it is only because the previous owner was too lax to enforce his property lines! Or take care of the place, I should add. It certainly did not do any of the local inhabitants proud, the way it was mismanaged."

"It was enjoyed all the same."

As they reached the thickening growth of the wooded patches, they stopped, both of them realising how dark it was fast becoming. The trees were already heavily shadowing the path, obscuring the colours and textures of the thick undergrowth.

"Oh, I hope she didn't consent to venture off the path..." Holly muttered. "She so loves that patch by the stream..."

"Truly, Miss Tournier," he protested, "all this concern is quite unnecessary. Miss Bennet is a grown, capable woman and Mr Darcy will be sure to see her home safely. If she is with him she is in no danger I can assure you."

"*If* she is with Mr Darcy! If she is with him she is very much in danger — I don't trust him and I don't trust his motives concerning my cousin. I don't know what your scheme was in bringing him here to harass Elizabeth, but you can be sure that I will not let it go unchallenged."

"Harass? My dear Miss Tournier, you are speaking nonsense! My friend is utterly reliable and if they have been foolish enough to wander off the path at this hour, I am sure they have only Miss Bennet's 'love of nature' to blame."

She turned on him and gave him a vicious look.

"Yes, you would say that, wouldn't you? You men all plead female folly to excuse your own licentious motives and then pretend you were led into situations that presented no alternative. I need to find my cousin. Now."

"And I am not surprised to hear *you* say that," Lord Baugham shot back. "After all, it is *never* a woman's intention to deliberately lead a man into a compromising situation and so to force his hand in order to satisfy her own *avaricious* motives. Is it, Miss Tournier?"

Holly gasped, "What are you implying, sir? She is not thinking clearly when it comes to him, that is true, but by no means is she intending such — she only sought him out to ascertain his…" she stopped abruptly, angry at his lordship for goading her in to admitting that Elizabeth had set out to deliberately meet Mr Darcy, however innocent she knew her intentions to be. "How can you possibly think — "

Baugham knew he was being unreasonable, but the way she kept directing fierce comments at him, obviously expecting him to cower before her either out of gentlemanly sentiments or fear, caused him to want to lash out, to make her as angry as she was making him.

"Quite easily, my dear Miss Tournier. I begin to wonder just what exactly is Miss Bennet's reason for seeking out my friend, in the waning light and in such an out of the way location. I think you must try to persuade her that daylight and respect for one's neighbour's territory are good and prudent means to prevent such a predicament in the future."

"*Her* reasons? I think you would do better to ask *his* reasons for his year-long campaign to destroy her peace and comfort. Why does he follow her here, only to stare at her like a mute and disapproving schoolmaster? I cannot blame her for wanting to find out what he is about, though I must say that *I* don't think him worth the trouble."

Steadying herself so as not to trip over the tangled brush, Holly pulled at her hem as it caught in a bramble.

"But you really ought to think a little less about your own feelings of ill-use and concern yourself with others a little more. I see now that I was in error asking for your assistance. Please, don't trouble yourself further. *I* will find her out."

The smallest smirk appeared on his face. "Are you able to find your way home from here? If not, I would be happy to point you toward the shortest route."

"I know the way, sir! I know things about this place that you could never imagine, even if you made it your home for the next twenty years! And if I need your help, it is only to keep that friend of yours a respectable distance from — "

Suddenly his lordship shushed her, stopping her short. Before she could take proper offence, Holly followed his gaze and saw the object of her frantic search walking arm in arm with Mr Darcy, turning through the wood to reach the field just beyond it. She stood as if rooted to the ground when she saw Elizabeth's head lift up and the sound of her laughter ring through the damp evening air. To her great surprise, Mr

Darcy's rich, deep laugh joined with her cousin's and in that moment it was quite obvious to her that Elizabeth was exactly where she wanted to be at the moment, in no danger and extremely content with her companion.

All she could do was turn to her own companion with a look of deep relief mixed with utter confusion on her face and say, "Oh…"

Baugham watched as Miss Tournier seemed to lose all her energy and go limp beside him. Suddenly, she looked vulnerable and any impulse he had had to answer her with an "I told you so" vanished.

"Well," he said gently. "All's well that ends well, then."

"Yes." She was still looking at him with a frown, but then turned her head to catch the last glimpse of her cousin and Mr Darcy turning down the slope towards the village in the dying light. They looked magical, somehow, against the gathering evening fog at their feet, Mr Darcy slightly bent towards Elizabeth in explanation of something.

Before the silence between them threatened to turn embarrassing, Lord Baugham cleared his throat.

"So may I escort you home now, Miss Tournier?"

"No," Holly said absently, still looking after the oblivious couple down the slope, "that won't be necessary."

Baugham's smile was a little warmer this time. "But my dear Miss Tournier, a moment ago you were concerned for your cousin's safety and worried about the coming dark, and you don't even have a suspicious gentleman to add to your protection. Please let me perform that function. You can hardly want for less comfort than your cousin. What is good for the goose, and so on."

Now she looked at him with a puzzled expression.

"No," she said calmly. "It will be all right. You forget, I know these lanes like the back of my hand. And I am not like my cousin."

With that she left him standing and made her way towards the village too. Baugham looked after her a while as she slowly followed the previous walkers. Then he shrugged, picked up his things and made his way home again.

HOLLY ARRIVED ONLY A FEW minutes after Elizabeth, causing her to suspect Mr Darcy had taken his time getting her home. She had taken her own time, sauntering the longest way she could contrive without leaving the safer lanes and paths.

Elizabeth sat in the parlour with her mother and Holly could instantly see she was happy. One glance at her mother also told her Elizabeth had seen fit to share with her the reasons for her long walk and sparkling eyes.

"So, Holly!" she cheerfully greeted her and rubbed her hands against the small fire in the grate. "Were you as lucky as your cousin here, to meet a protective gentleman who allowed you to stay out far too long and talk far too much as well?"

"No," Holly said carefully, "but Elizabeth did?"

"Yes, I did," her cousin answered cheerfully. "And Mr Darcy was kind enough to indulge my incessant love of the scenery and he took me up to the Pillidon Cave. Remember, we went there once determined to live the glamorous life of a highway man, but were chased home again by the bats? We must have been no more than thirteen, I think. And oh! the scolding we got, even though we thought my dear aunt would appreciate the female courage in our career choice!"

Despite herself, Holly had to laugh. "Yes, I do remember that. The stones in the cave were cold too. And you had forgotten to bring the butteries left over from breakfast so we would really have been forced to rob and pillage if we had stayed any longer."

"Well, this time I saw no bats, but the stones are still cold."

Holly smiled and gave her mother a glance. She was smiling, too. Elizabeth saw the exchange and took Holly's hand, making her sit down beside her.

"Ask what you need to ask, Holly. I have no secrets from either you or Aunt Arabella," she said gently.

Holly looked at her cousin's happy expression and open face.

"And Mr Darcy?" she asked. "Does he still have secrets from you?"

"Secrets? Probably. But we are very good friends now and have forgiven each other numerous times for all manner of trespasses and misunderstandings — wilful and accidental alike."

"And...what will he do now?"

"Well, considering I gave him quite a dressing-down when he last laid his feelings open to me, I fear he will not soon want to risk that again. But who knows? Perhaps I shall be allowed back into the drawing room at Pemberley one way or the other — if I behave myself."

Holly smiled, happy for her cousin's happiness even in the midst of her own confused feelings on the matter. She suppressed a sigh as she realised how much this visit had changed from what she had earlier anticipated. It would no longer be one last escape into a carefree past. Instead, she was witnessing the beginnings of Elizabeth's emerging future — a future richly deserved and filled with promise. *And what of me, I wonder*...for as pleased as she was for Elizabeth, she could not escape the feeling that she was losing her; she was being left behind.

"And that is as much as I will hear on the subject of male motives and other guess work," Mrs Tournier said forcefully. "Things are as they will be, my dears, and I have no doubt even the most taciturn of gentlemen will forget himself and give some inclination of what his intentions are if he keeps meeting you so accidentally around country lanes and fields."

"And caves," Elizabeth said mischievously and winked her merry eyes at Holly.

"So," Mrs Tournier said, giving Elizabeth a stern look, "show some female sense and set about planning what you intend to wear next week to Lady Tristam's little *soirée-musicale,* or whatever she prefers to call it. That is as much planning for the future as is prudent right now."

"Darcy. How are you and country balls these days?"

Darcy eyed his friend sunk deep into his chair, his long legs stretched out on the fender of the blazing fire. It looked like he was preening his nails with the end of a long penknife. A penknife, Darcy reflected, that probably seldom saw other work and especially rarely was called upon to perform its original assignment.

"They seldom serve to interest me solely on their own merits. Why?"

"Well, it seems the gregarious Sir Torquil Tristam is holding what his wife referred to as a *soirée-musicale* next week and thanks to your pushing me all the way to church last Sunday, we are invited."

"And did you perchance accept?"

"Well, I said we would be delighted, if our hunting plans gave us an opportunity, to which Sir Torquil replied he would be pleased if we could consider his home as a worthy hunting ground — for pleasure — for one evening."

Darcy sighed. "Oh these country squires and their wit."

"He has three unmarried daughters," Baugham added, his mouth twitching.

"That is not what I would count as adequate additional incentive to attend a country ball, I'm afraid."

"No…" Baugham said slowly, "but I do hear most of local society puts in an appearance."

Darcy gave him a long look and his mouth curled at the edges before he went back to his book. "Then I would say it would be impolite not to do so also," he said, eyes concentrating on the page before him again.

Chapter 8

Lord Baugham meets Ladies in and around Rosefarm Cottage

Lord Baugham awoke to the sounds of Riemann shuffling in the background, discreetly moving in and out of his bedroom and dressing room to fetch shirts, water, combs, shaving equipment and whatnot. Baugham surprisingly felt none of his usual inclination to jump out of bed and start the day

The events of last night preyed upon his mind and he was not quite certain which caused him the most unease. He settled on Miss Tournier's ice-cold voice repeating:

I know things about this place that you could never even have imagined, even if you made it your home for the next twenty years.

Was it true? Was he a stranger, after all, in the place he most readily called home?

But he loved this place. He was not so certain about the village down the road and even less inclined to profess any interest or concern for the inhabitants of that village, but he loved the countryside around Clyne, and surely, if you love a place it is not necessary to count years of residence as proof of devotion. Did he really have to earn that degree of feeling or relationship? Couldn't he claim that an irrational and spontaneous affection, leading to a slightly chancy purchase of an estate so far away from his usual business was folly enough to prove a worthy affection beyond a doubt? Surely there were enough people who lived their whole lives in one and the same place, calling it home and hating it?

Like Cumbermere Castle. He stopped his thoughts and forced them in another direction. He had no wish to think of his ancestral home and the obligations that were forever being forced upon him from that quarter, by stewards and lawyers and land contractors and purveyors, not to mention interested local parties missing what they saw as the rightful head of the local community.

Then there was Darcy and his quest, adding to his feeling of disquiet. Last night his friend had been quietly content, writing long letters of pleasure to his friend Bingley and his sister, and even longer letters of business. There had been no mention of his outing earlier in the day. He had, however, almost cheerfully admitted to having neglected his affairs shamefully, but it being worth every minute of it so far.

Darcy cheerfully admitting to neglecting his duties was a disturbing thought to dwell on. Then an even more intriguing idea floated into his mind. If he, himself, was prepared to ignore the agonies of travel and the utter boredom of the road to reach Clyne, and Darcy was happily abandoning the principles and sense of duty that had been his guiding light since his early adulthood to take a few walks with Miss Bennet, perhaps love was possible without misery after all.

That thought put an effective end to his loitering abed, and he made up his mind on the spot to engage himself in some distinctly unsentimental and challenging discourse, and, perhaps, to stand up for his friend's happiness all in one go.

He left a very pale valet scuffling to put away discarded clothes as he walked down to breakfast. Riemann had not taken his cheerful announcement that he intended to go visiting a lady very well, protesting he certainly had no fitting attire prepared for such an occasion and he would beg him to postpone until he could arrange something more appropriate. Baugham simply shushed him and left him to seriously worry over how his future reputation as a gentleman's gentleman must deteriorate, the way he allowed his Master to walk out of his chamber into polite society.

THAT SAME MORNING, DECIDING TO take advantage of what promised to be an unseasonably warm day, Holly hauled a bushel basket of peas up from the cellar and sat shelling them in the sunshine. Elizabeth was inside writing to Jane again, no doubt apprising her on her recent walk with Mr Darcy, so she was left alone with her thoughts.

Mrs Tournier ventured out soon afterward, just as a deep sigh escaped from her daughter.

"Lie-lie, please tell me that you are neither pining nor pouting over this latest development of your cousin's."

Holly frowned. "No, of course not, Maman!" but then she met her mother's eyes. "Well, perhaps just a little. I cannot help but think that, no matter what she says to temper her hopes, things will be changing very soon and very fast, for Elizabeth. I think I am happy for her, but at the same time, I cannot say that I am equally happy for myself."

"Ah, so the world does not unequivocally love a lover after all."

"I do," she protested. "At least one of them."

Her mother smiled and turned her face against the sun. It was fairly successful at warming her up as she sat against the stone wall, which was the only reason she had consented to take herself outside to keep her daughter company. Even so, she felt she needed a little reparation for the wind that was still blowing courageously around the yard.

"So you want to fall in love yourself? Is that it?"

Holly's head shot up in surprise. "Whatever makes you say that? I was referring to Elizabeth and Mr Darcy, of course, not myself. I love her very much and I want to see her happy, but…" she tossed the peas vigorously into the bowl on her lap, "I just don't like the idea of that Mr Darcy showing up and taking her from us, that is all. And he isn't even charming about it! He leaves that to his noble friend, though he is not always so successful at it either. Why last night he — "

Her hand rose to her mouth as she remembered. "Oh, Maman. I made such a fool of myself last night."

"Sounds as if you are indeed well on your way then to falling in love then," her mother said in a teasing voice. "Did you find yourself a companion to walk the woods after all? Or did you refuse an eligible one?"

She dismissed her mother's teasing without remark. "Neither really, but I did drag poor Lord Baugham all over his grounds searching for Elizabeth. Oh, I was so sure that she was in some sort of danger and he was so infuriatingly sanguine about it — I'm afraid I was rather rude with him — but it turns out, of course, that he was right all along and Elizabeth was perfectly safe — with Mr Darcy."

Mrs Tournier gave her daughter a searching look. "And what was it, exactly, in that which made you feel foolish?"

"Because he was right and I was wrong," Holly laughed. "And I was so insufferable in my convictions… I would have preferred it if he had been just as insufferable right back once he had been proven correct, but instead he offered to see me home, as if it was the most natural thing in the world for me to have done what I did."

"Some men don't revel in the victory, Lie-lie, they prefer the fight," her mother smiled.

"Well then," she laughed as she stood and kissed her mother, "I will wish him a proper shrew for a wife, and may he be happy all of his days." She laughed again as she carried the basket round the corner to the kitchen.

WHEN HIS LORDSHIP WAS ALMOST at the gate, he saw a dark figure with a light-coloured apron flapping about her in the wind rise up from her seat, and an older woman's hand simultaneously come up to pat the cheek of the younger one. The older woman sat in the nook of the stone wall by the house, warmed by the sun and sheltered from the wind. He could not make out the lady's words as she addressed her daughter.

He was mentally rehearsing his planned assurances to Mrs Tournier of Darcy's impeccable character when he was startled by the sound of laughter ringing out. It was a rich, musical laugh with a pearly, sparkling twang to it that sprang deep from the young woman's being. The ease and spontaneity of it surprised him; everything he had seen and assumed about Miss Tournier's disposition was inconsistent with the scene before him. The sight of her bright smile and open countenance was puzzling to say the least. He looked up and saw the young woman, still smiling, bend to kiss the top of her mother's head while she briefly answered her. Then she picked up the basket that had been sitting on the bench and slowly walked off around the corner of the house.

Baugham stood looking after her until he felt he had been spotted. He doffed his hat to Mrs Tournier, but quickly and inexplicably changed his mind about his errand and turned his horse in the direction of The Caledonian Thistle and Mr Robertson's excellent ale.

Chapter 9

How a Small Change of Unfortunate Weather can Spoil and Save your Day

THE extraordinary spell of warm, sunny weather could not last and so it was no surprise to anyone that it rained for the rest of the week. This caused hunting trips to be abandoned, walks to be postponed, outdoor work not to be attempted — while young women looked out windows sighing away at the dull greyness while, similarly, young men cursed the rain streaming down and leaving a grey dullness over everything. The only thing the weather did accomplish were a few colour plates being finished sooner than expected, and Miss Bennet acquiring some rudimentary knowledge of the physical reactions of matter to heat.

At the end of the week there was a small lull in the miserable circumstances when a letter was received from the soon to be Mrs Bingley and the rain had lessened to a misty drizzle. Watching Elizabeth immerse herself in her letter, Holly seized the opportunity.

"I must go for a walk," she said. "I cannot stand it any longer!"

Elizabeth looked up, obviously torn. "Well, a letter can wait," she then said firmly, "the rain — as we so clearly have been witness to — cannot."

"Oh no!" Holly was already flying about the hall gathering her things and rummaging the cupboard for her basket. "You must stay! Letters can wait, but I think visits cannot. With this break in the weather, someone will most probably take the opportunity to call and if you were out trampling the muddy fields and woods searching for mushrooms that I cannot even assure you are there anymore, I will never forgive myself. Neither will Mr Darcy," she said cheerfully and hurriedly shrugged into her light cloak and simple straw bonnet. Elizabeth watched her with a frown.

"Perhaps, but if he professes to know me any better than a perfect stranger, he will be very well aware of the fact that when it comes to walking in impossible weather, I am quite my own irrational mistress. Holly, are you sure you are dressed warmly enough? It is certain to rain again."

"Quite sure! I thought I'd go see whether there is anything left of the winter chanterelles over by Georgie's Patch. There might not be, but it's usually a place of abundance and with the rain and all…but it's a fair way to walk, I will be fine."

Elizabeth obviously did not believe her, but she fingered her letter and held out Holly's basket to her and bid her to be careful and take care or else she would come looking for her.

The weather was still grey, but the drizzle had stopped and the woods smelled fresh and pungent. The birds were equally grateful for the break in the rain and there was rustling in every bush, and twittering, and the curious flapping of wings everywhere. Holly kept up a brisk pace. Partly to keep warm, for it was chilly — her breath whirled around her in a misty smoke as she bustled up the hills and through the undergrowth, taking advantage of a few shortcuts — but partly because it really was a fair way to walk up to her little secret cornucopia of winter chanterelles. The shortest way would have been to cut across the Clyne estate, but she was determined to avoid that. She walked around with pleasure, after all, she had not been out of the house in four days and her nerves needed the exercise as well as her body.

She smirked a little when she thought about her hidden cache. Yet another thing to prove that you could pay as much money as you wished and put up fences and display fancy deeds with seals and lofty language, but you had to work, walk, explore and spend your time to understand and bond with the place you called home. You had to let the secrets come and reveal themselves to you through time and patience and curiosity. Then, slowly, you would find the best spot for watching Kingfishers dive into the river for their prey; know where the foxes bred under which fallen tree and where the juiciest brambles, the richest mushrooms and the shortest paths were.

The rain started to pick up again, although hidden under the trees as she was, she hardly noticed it. She was excited too, for she had been right, the mossy knoll under the spruce was cluttered with light brown caps peeking up from beneath the rich green cover, promising even more if one gently pushed aside the wet and soft ground. Holly spent what felt like hours carefully excavating the tender brown and yellow stalks, gently laying them in her basket and very cautiously treading from one spot to another not to trample the precious bounty under her feet.

She did not stop until her basket was nearly full. It was only then she became aware of the cold drops of rain rolling down the brim of her bonnet and that her back was soaked through. Straightening, she finally realised the rain had come back with increased force and intensity. She felt happy nonetheless and vowed she would drag her cousin here next time all the same. After all, even if the frost came, the winter chanterelles would still be here.

On her way back, however, her mood soured despite her proud bounty. The rain turned icy, the wind picked up and the walk across the open spaces back was tapping her strength. To cap it all off, she stepped into a boggy patch, soaking her boots and stockings and her toes were rapidly feeling the freeze of the cold water and going numb.

Holly stood panting, her light cloak, now heavy and wet, snuggled around her, dragging at her legs and feet, and looked down the slope. She was tired to the bone but she must not stop and rest. If she did, she would only grow colder and wetter and that might be dangerous. To reach home as soon as she ought, she would have to cut across the Clyne estate. She winced at her proud resolution to stay away from the easiest path to prove her point, but she realised it would be foolish now to persist. Gnashing her teeth, she turned and set off across the fields as close to the house as she dared.

She was so tired. Her feet felt like lead. She was cold and her arms and shoulders ached. Her head throbbed and she slipped and slid through the mud on the small path. The rain came down in streams and the brim of her bonnet sagged before her eyes. She felt close to crying and she certainly whimpered when her skirt was caught once more in twigs and branches on the ground and sticking out in front of her as she stumbled on. And so when she glimpsed the house through the trees she had no strength left to fight. *A quarter of an hour in the kitchen*, she thought feebly, giving in to her misery. *He will never know.*

She snuck successfully around the house to what she presumed was the kitchen entrance. All was quiet except for the rain that came almost horizontally and Holly shielded her face as she knocked on the door. The light and warmth and figure of a large woman that emerged almost made her sob.

"Mrs McLaughlin?" she managed. "I'm so sorry but I was out gathering the last of the winter chanterelles and I was caught in the rain. I'm ... I'm ... I was hoping — "

A strong, warm hand reached out and grabbed her arm, pulling her into the kitchen and firmly closing the door behind her.

"Well, for heaven's sake child, dinnae stand out there in that fool weather! Come in and sit down. Ye're in a frightsome state. You need to dry off this minute or you'll catch yer death o' cold."

Holly almost collapsed with relief. "Thank you," she said and made it to the nearest chair by the wall. "Perhaps only for a few minutes," but her hostess had turned her back to her and was busy setting water to boil and bringing out butter and bread and cold cuts from the larder. Holly watched her, feeling drained and almost detached. She slowly removed her cloak and bonnet and draped them over the chair.

"Take off yer hose and boots." Mrs McLaughlin did not even turn around, but her tone of voice was such that Holly realised this was an order and not a request.

It felt strange, and not a little daring, to peel off her garments in a stranger's kitchen, but as soon as the drenched and heavy leather and the soaking, cold wool was off her feet she felt better.

"Oh," she said involuntarily and slumped back.

"Come, come!" Mrs McLaughlin urged. "Dinnae sit there in the draft. Up here by the ingle! Come on then!"

Holly was numb and mute in the face of such efficiency and she allowed herself to be pushed to a chair in front of the burning stove and could only watch, with her protests dying on her lips, as Mrs McLaughlin hung her stockings over the fire and put her muddy boots on a rag nearby.

"Well then?" the woman said and eyed her with a stern look. "Kelter out of that petticoat young leddy or ye'll never be dry enough to go home again. I'll not have ye leave this place with cold, slitterie linens on ye. Git it off now!"

She blushed deeply. Mrs McLaughlin was right, of course; she needed warm, dry clothes next to her skin on her last leg home. Fortunately, the petticoat was not as bad as the stockings, although the hem was nearly destroyed. Holly, who was no friend to needlework, sighed as she realised she would have to cut it up and stitch it back together once she got home.

"Och." Her hostess, picking up her cloak and bonnet and catching sight of her basket brimming with winter chanterelles interrupted Holly's thoughts. "I thought it was past time fer these. Where did ye find them? Or is it a secret?"

"It is no secret. By Georgie's Cave. I suppose with the rain and the mild weather we've been having lately…"

"Och aye. I didnae know about that place. I for ordinar go down beyond Cold Fell, plenty of penny buns in the wood there still I hear. Imagine that, born and bred on Ross' paddock down in the glen and never heard of the chanterelles of Georgie's Cave! Just goes to show, ye learn something every day."

Holly remembered her uncharitable thoughts about buying one's way into a home and kept quiet.

"And to think, it was the Frenchie's lass taught me that, too!" Mrs McLaughlin laughed. "Begging your pardon," she added, though she did not look at all remorseful.

"Not at all," mumbled Holly and got up to hang up her petticoat by her stockings.

"Now sit ye down and I'll poor the tea. Ye have some bread and cheese and just sit there." Mrs McLaughlin cast another eye at Holly's basket. "Half of that for a muir fowl?" she said thoughtfully. "A big one an all, since ye have visitors."

Holly stared at her. "It is no secret place and you're welcome to whatever you can find. I left plenty."

"Ye want to bargain, do ye? Aye then, a muir fowl and one un-skinned rabbit just in."

Holly snapped her mouth shut. "Done," she said, surprised. Mrs McLaughlin looked pleased. "I think I'll have some of this tea myself," she said, carrying the tea tray over.

HOLLY WATCHED HER PLACE THE sugar bowl on the table — fine, white sugar — and she very carefully, almost afraid lest some of the grains did not make it all the way to her cup, heaped two spoons of the shimmering crystals into her cup and watched them sink to the bottom. After a generous helping of cream — but not so much as to drown out the taste — she stirred carefully, feeling the strong, rich, acid smell of black tea find its way to her nose and she sighed. She must still wait a little, she would not want to scald her tongue and spoil the experience. She could wait...just a little more. They drank slowly and Mrs McLaughlin did not seem to have much to keep her busy.

"Aye well, I would have if the gentlemen got some shooting done instead of just sitting around here, or going on walks and visits. As it is, there's nae much to put away for the winter and we'll have to buy the beef. And speaking of lounging round about the house..." Mrs McLaughlin cocked her head to the kitchen door. Too late, Holly noticed the heavy footsteps of a man drawing near, and all she could do was look down, clutching her teacup more closely to her chest for reassurance and hoping he would walk right past.

A blond head popped through the door. "Mrs McLaughlin," it said in terse notes, "if this infernal rain does not stop and Mr Darcy does not cease his constant shifting between smug contentment and nervous frowns, I will go myself to Brachan Falls tomorrow even if it pours and — "

He stopped short and Holly lifted her head to find his startlingly clear blue eyes staring at her in amazement. "Miss Tournier!" he said and stepped inside the door.

Holly firmly pressed her feet together in what she hoped was the middle of her sagging skirts, far enough from the hem not to be seen even a glimpse of.

"Lord Baugham," she said in as dignified a voice as she could manage. Her hair had become slightly unpinned when she had pulled off her soaked bonnet and she was aware she must present a picture resembling someone cast ashore from a shipwreck in her wet and sorry state.

He eyed her curiously, but at least not with hostility.

"Have you taken refuge from the weather in my kitchen?"

"As you see, sir," she said. "I was out by Georgie's Cave to pick the last of the mushrooms there — keeping away from your property I assure you — and I was...surprised."

Instead of nodding and excusing himself, Lord Baugham walked in and surveyed the offerings on the table before him. Holly winced as Mrs McLaughlin calmly got up and put one more teacup on the table.

"You show an admirable optimism if you venture so far out after the weather we've been having," his lordship said and sat down, wasting no time in attacking the loaf of bread before him. "Or was it either that or complete insanity at being cooped up indoors too long?'"

"Possibly a little bit of both, my lord," she attempted a confident smile. "I think I *was* a little mad to get out of the house — and from what I heard just now, I think you can understand my feelings perfectly."

Lord Baugham leaned back in his seat, pushing his chair away from the table and stretching his legs.

"Ah, well, I am better now. But I think you have a kindred spirit in Mr Darcy. He left just a few moments ago. It seems you have traded places!"

The slightest sigh escaped her. "I expected as much. It appears that neither of us have enough sense to stay in out of the rain. Though his incentive holds quite a bit more charm than my own."

"Miss Tournier! Are you slighting the comfort of my kitchen or Mrs McLaughlin's hospitality?"

Holly could not tell by his tone if he was teasing, questioning, or taking offence, and she suddenly became acutely aware that her damp skirts were clinging to her legs underneath the table and that her undergarments were hanging on the hearth in plain view. It made her feel vulnerable, which in turn made her straighten her shoulders and answer him with spirit.

"Not at all. But you forget that your kitchen was not my first object, and I do hope you will agree with me that my cousin holds far greater charms than that basket of mushrooms over there."

"I most certainly will agree with you on that point. Although..." Baugham cast a saucy look at Mrs McLaughlin, whose eyes were a mixture of scorn and softness. "If Mrs McLaughlin can get hold of some of those mushrooms and I could manage to bring her something akin to a roe buck to dress and roast and garnish, I fear Miss Bennet, for all her charm and grace, will not be half as tempting. For myself, I mean. I cannot — and would not! — speak for Mr Darcy on this point."

"I cannot say that I wouldn't be tempted to trade her myself for a haunch of roast venison," Holly smiled, unconsciously pressing her fingertip into a few spilled grains of sugar on the tabletop and bringing it to her mouth.

"Ye bag the roe buck and ye'll have yer wish, my laird," Mrs McLaughlin said with no attempt at disguising her wounded pride. "That's nae where the problem lies at all."

There was a brief moment when Holly caught Lord Baugham's eyes and stifled a smile and Lord Baugham looked back feigning complete innocence. The housekeeper got up to fill the cups and Lord Baugham let her pass. As she swished by, his eye caught the arrangement above the hearth of one pair of stockings, a petticoat and a bonnet hanging to dry.

Of its own accord his eye then swivelled back to the owner of said garments and immediately and unconsciously ascertained that the petticoat was indeed missing. As soon as he noticed her deep blush he realised what he had done and looked away, gazing fixedly into his plate instead. Teacups were returned but, as his lordship was about to excuse himself, the clatter of dropping silver sounded.

"Please, let me get that for you, Miss Tournier," his lordship cried, feeling a sudden need to be chivalrous. Holly, at the same time, felt very much like crawling under the table and was making ready to duck down herself to retrieve her dropped spoon. Her movements shifted the careful arrangement of her skirts and Baugham found himself kneeling at the base of her chair, spoon in hand and in full view of two well-turned but quite bare ankles, and ten, it must be admitted, attractively plump toes.

This time it was his turn to blush scarlet, and he rose with alacrity, returned the offending spoon and quickly excused himself, pleading — well, he hoped it was a somewhat coherent excuse.

SCARCELY MORE COHERENT WAS HOLLY as she rushed to gather her garments from before the fire, despite the housekeeper's protests. "No please, they are quite dry enough, really. It's just a short way now, and I really must…"

She struggled to pull her damp stockings up as Mrs McLaughlin, shaking her head and muttering under her breath, placed the game in her basket and fixed a cover of oilcloth for the journey home.

"Should I nae have Mr McLaughlin bring ye home in his lairdship's carriage? The rain's not yet stopped."

"No!" Holly exclaimed as she tied her petticoat and shrugged into her cloak, still cold and heavy from the soaking rain. "Fine. I'll be just fine. Thank you for everything, Mrs McLaughlin," she called behind her as she grabbed her basket and practically flew out the door.

Mrs McLaughlin stayed looking after her, shaking her head, and then returned to the heap of winter chanterelles now awaiting her attention on the kitchen table. Muttering to herself she cleaned and cut and spread them out on a piece of gauze on the warm hearth to dry. Just as she was finishing, Lord Baugham returned, again poking his head around the door, but with much less alacrity than the last time.

"Ah…I think I forgot. I *am* going to Brachan by myself tomorrow — even if Mr Darcy will not. Would you be so kind and prepare something in the way of fare. I shall leave first thing in the morning."

And with that he was just about to withdraw again when Mrs McLaughlin made a threatening, distinctly Scottish noise in her throat.

"What?" said Lord Baugham, sighing at what he knew was a sign of serious annoyance by his housekeeper.

"Next time I'll thank ye to be a wee bit less chivalrous round women taking refuge frae the rain, my lord."

"Oh. So you would have me forget my manners while I am here?" his lordship teased, giving her his best charming smile. One look told him that his attempt at disarming her was unsuccessful, so he tried another tack.

"Really, Mrs McLaughlin, it was just an innocent mistake. Unfortunate, I grant you, but no harm done I am sure."

"Well, ye did nae maybe notice her running out of here, red in the face as a lobster. I tell ye plainly enough, my lord. I'll have none of that sport in my kitchie. She's a douce young lass although of, maybe, misfortunate kin and circumstances and she is as good as promised to a young man, too, so she's nae game for any of that wicked London stuff."

"Mrs McLaughlin, honestly, I hope you don't think… Promised? Promised to whom? Someone in Edinburgh?"

"To a Mr Grant — a friend of the family." Mrs McLaughlin, realising she had perhaps been engaging in what could be construed as gossip that bordered on speculation based on neighbourhood tittle-tattle, busied herself in her larder once more. "Will the cottage pie from yesterday be sufficient for ye for the morrow, my lord? I'll pack some cider as well."

"Yes, that would be fine," he answered. "To Mr Grant! The gentleman from Crossling? Are you quite sure? He doesn't seem quite the type to... Are you *quite* sure?"

Since she was far from sure, Mrs McLaughlin simply made a Scottish noise again and hoped his lordship would not press the point. From what she had seen of the young woman today, and from what Mrs Higgins had told her, Mr Grant was eligible, suitable and respectable but would be a clear catastrophe for Holly Tournier to marry.

LORD BAUGHAM FINALLY HAD HIS way with his friend the next day as Mr Darcy confessed he was most eager to join his lordship on a fishing expedition. It adhered to all the rules of masculine camaraderie in that the fish, and the success and skill with which one caught them, was the primary object for conversation and debate. The weather cooperated for the most part, the food was Spartan, but enjoyed in silence with a good bottle of whiskey by an open fire. Topics larger than life were kept to one's own thoughts and communication as to direction and timetables were kept to a minimum.

At dusk, when they made their way back across the fell heading towards the darkening eastern sky, the return to civilisation seemed to prompt little more philosophy and chat.

"How long will you be staying?" Baugham asked as Clyne Cottage could already be seen casting its shadows over the slope behind the River Kye.

"Well, there's a wedding in Hertfordshire I must attend soon. Bingley has asked for my assistance. I shall be going down to Netherfield shortly."

"A wedding, eh?" Baugham said thoughtfully. "Just one?"

Darcy gave one of his indeterminable low laughs. "Christmas is a popular time of year for weddings."

"So I hear."

Darcy gave him a quick look and he could read hope and determination in it, but it was not confirmed with words.

"Chess later?" Baugham said.

"It would be a pleasure," Darcy said. "Although I do not plan on letting you best me this time."

"You didn't plan it last time either."

"Ah, but I have luck on my side these days," Darcy grinned.

"AND I TELL YE, ROSIE, I put him right straight on that kind of foolery! I said I will nae have this sort of conduct in my kitchie and I would thank him to keep out of it in the future if he cannae behave himself!"

Mrs McLaughlin was still reliving her indignation at Lord Baugham's misdirected chivalry towards Miss Tournier a day later when her cousin came over.

"The cheek!" Mrs Higgins had the good sense to say and look extremely appalled. "But... surely quite innocent when it comes down to it? I mean, bare toes..."

Mrs McLaughlin slammed down her rolling pin so that the open jars on the table rattled.

"She was a visitor and he made her ill at ease and it is sore unfair for such a fittin and well-favored man to take advantage of his situation and with the young woman practically promised an all — "

Mrs Higgins looked up from her potato peeling. "Miss Holly is promised?"

A faint blush spread over Mrs McLaughlin's features, but she pressed on with the dough.

"Heather, ye don't mean Mr Grant?! I should surely hope not!"

"You did say…"

But it was useless. Mrs Higgins stopped her industry and gave her cousin a stern eye.

"Cousin, that was nae right. I said *he* made out as if it were a done deal. I said *nothing* about her."

The two women faced each other in silence for a moment until Mrs McLaughlin slammed a bowl in front of her cousin.

"There's two fine birds there if ye'll have them. Fat and all."

In silence Mrs Higgins inspected the birds. "Och aye," she finally conceded, "they'll do."

"And I merely wanted to put him in his place. He had no business acting like he did."

"I dare say," Mrs Higgins muttered, "but still — "

"Och, he'll forget about Mr Grant soon enough an he'll show Miss Tournier some respect in the future. Which is as it should be. Right?"

IF NOTHING ELSE, THIS PARTICULAR sojourn to Scotland was unique, Lord Baugham decided as he once again sat in the parlour at Rosefarm Cottage waiting for tea. So far from his cherished solitary existence here, he seemed to be seeking, rather than avoiding, company.

What possessed him to accompany Darcy to Rosefarm when his friend obviously no longer needed his assistance to be welcomed there, he could only attribute to a vague curiosity of wanting to see how his friend acted while around his declared love. It was perfectly clear to anyone with normal sight, hearing and understanding that Darcy and Miss Bennet got along very well indeed, and that the looks exchanged between them spoke of more than friendship. If there was a deeper understanding than that, it was hard to tell. Mr Darcy was not one to wear even the most violent feelings on his sleeve for anyone to gawk at and Miss Bennet addressed him with remarks that could just as easily be interpreted as impertinence as intimacy.

Also, Lord Baugham was acutely aware of a nagging feeling that he needed to atone for the uncomfortable, unfortunate scene that took place in his kitchen a few days earlier. Not that he could mention the matter, of course, but at least he could show Miss Tournier that he felt the affair to be of no great import — to put her mind at ease in the event she was feeling uncomfortable.

And really, he *did* enjoy Mrs Tournier's company quite a lot, and what better reason could there be to accompany his friend to Rosefarm than to show respect and kindness to such a woman?

Polite chatter filled the room and soon Mrs Higgins brought the tea tray in without ceremony. Baugham's attention was diverted momentarily when he noticed Miss Tournier stand and quickly meet the woman as she set it down. A few moments of hushed conversation, gestures, and nods captured his notice. He watched as Miss Tournier took a dish from the tray, handed it to Mrs Higgins with some obvious words of instruction. Mrs Higgins shook her head but left, apparently acquiescing, returning a short time later with that same dish filled to the brim with lump sugar, and with a rather sour look upon her face.

His attention was taken up again by his hostess and he thought nothing more about it until he was served a short time later. The tea was poured and prepared to everyone's liking, but though he was not one to usually notice such things, Baugham did see both Miss Tournier and Miss Bennet bypass the cream pitcher entirely and choose the honey pot over the sugar bowl. A picture then flashed through his mind of Miss Tournier in his kitchen, her finger in her mouth after collecting a few stray grains of sugar off the tabletop. His eyes then darted around the room — a work desk where Mrs Tournier performed editing and clerical duties for pay — a rickety drawing table with a half-burnt tallow candle, covered with colour plates in various stages of completion that Miss Tournier, no longer employed as a schoolteacher, was commissioned to make for an old friend, the smell of tea stretched with herbs gathered wild from the countryside or perhaps even from the garden outside, and he could only picture the basket of winter mushrooms found by Georgie's Cave that must be now drying in the kitchen. His eye and mind took this all in and, when he next sipped his drink, he was suddenly aware of how very sweet a cup of tea with three lumps of sugar in it really was.

He put down his cup after hastily draining it to escape the realisation of his failure to be more aware of his surroundings. The sweet liquid stuck in his throat and he grimaced. Miss Bennet, who was sitting beside him, noticed his predicament and smiled.

"It takes some getting used to," she said in hushed, tones her eyes winking at him in sympathetic conspiracy, "but after a while I find that I prefer it this way."

Baugham felt uncomfortable, but then he realised Miss Bennet was no stranger to his dilemma and he smiled back.

"Tea is mostly about the company it's taken with, I believe," he answered, "and therefore I know you are absolutely right."

"My aunt is a very hospitable woman and so I have ample proof of my assertion. And I think, my lord, you are beginning to enjoy your tea more and more each time we see you."

"I think so, too," Baugham smiled. "And you, Miss Bennet, seem to positively blossom in the fragrance."

Elizabeth laughed but declined to answer.

"Tell me," his lordship continued still with a smile on his lips, "how would you rate the tea when Sir John Ledwich comes to call compared to today? Or Mr Grant?"

At that Elizabeth burst out laughing. "Mr Grant? Oh goodness me! I think those two persons are exact opposites of how tea benefits from their discourse. My aunt tries to serve Sir John as little as possible so that he may speak as much as possible. With Mr Grant, a strong cup of tea that is never allowed to ebb out does much for the quality of her enjoyment."

Baugham wrinkled his brow. "Really? And is this a universal strategy among the inhabitants at Rosefarm?"

Elizabeth nodded. "You mustn't think we don't value Mr Grant's presence and company. Rather, we enjoy it better when he is not tempted to stretch his conversation with words borrowed from others." She took a sip and tried to look serious. "Mr Grant greatly admires Mr Blake."

Baugham pulled a face of surprise. "Does he indeed?"

"My cousin is never so diligent with her duties concerning the teapot as when Mr Grant comes to visit. She takes that task very seriously."

Baugham returned Miss Bennet's smile and then looked over to the tea tray that was conspicuously free of the presence of Miss Tournier. *Well, just wait till you find that out, Mrs McLaughlin!* was his next spontaneous thought as he sorted the information in his head.

MRS MCLAUGHLIN WAS CARRYING THE heavy bundles of laundry from the kitchen to the linen cupboard upstairs. It was tedious work since the washing, once delivered, had to be checked and some of it put aside for more meticulous ironing to reach Mrs McLaughlin's standards of what constituted a respectable linen supply. She was carrying the sheets and pillow cases with two hands when a door opened in the hall below and her employer stuck his head out from the library.

"Mrs McLaughlin!" he said in a voice of both sternness and triumph. "I would be much obliged if you would cease repeating your unfounded speculations concerning Miss Tournier and Mr Grant. It is completely groundless and I would not have you accused of idle gossip or ill-will."

The housekeeper was by no means rattled by this unexpected rebuke by her master, but simply looked down at him over the banister.

"If ye say so, my laird," she said airily. "Not that there're many other prospects for her and she is nae fool. She'd do best to marry and that's a good prospect."

"That is as it may be," his lordship said haughtily, "but she is not marrying *him*."

He withdrew his head again and closed the door.

"Och aye, it's like that, is it?" Mrs McLaughlin muttered and continued her ascent.

Chapter 10

In which a Young Man comes to Call Causing Anguish and
Chivalrous Impulses both at Home and Abroad

"I CANNOT believe what this visit of yours has got me into, Darcy," Baugham grumbled later that night, well into his third glass of whiskey. "Church going, morning calls, God knows how many tea parties, not to mention rain-soaked females in my kitchen, and now, a soiree-musicale?"

Darcy's unrepentant smile only served to irritate him further, so he refilled his own glass and glared across at his friend.

"I came to Clyne to escape all this nonsense — at your behest I might add — and here I am back in the middle of it all and all because of your penchant for involving yourself with troublesome women!"

"*My* penchant?" Darcy nearly sputtered in his drink. "Need I remind you, Baugham, of the reason I suggested you ought to leave in the first place? Troublesome women appear to be your specialty, my friend, not mine. And I sincerely hope you do *not* find yourself in the middle of any such nonsense as what you left behind."

Baugham, highly affronted, drew himself up with great dignity.

"Darcy! *That* is not what Clyne is about! Nor what I am about *at* Clyne." He leaned forward to emphasise his point, trying hard to maintain his upright posture. "Clyne is my *sanctuary*, Darcy, and I'll thank you to keep that in mind. And since you are here, having chased a woman all the way from Hertfordshire, I will take the liberty of calling her troublesome indeed."

He leaned back, smugly.

"I *never* had to chase a woman as far as that."

"No, Baugham," Darcy's smile was unruffled, "but you did have to run up here to escape two troublesome…sisters, were they? Nor did I, on the other hand, ever find myself, at the tender age of twenty years, in the rather dubious position of fighting to defend the honour of my — "

"Continue along that same line, Darcy, and I will find myself in that same position once more," Baugham's eyes were narrowed and dangerous. "Talking about such things will not do. Tit for tat, my friend, and you know it. I seem to recall a certain young woman at about that same time, with a lovely voice and an amazing ability to make you spend half your allowances on trinkets and her follies, remember?"

Darcy glared at his friend, though it did little to stop him.

"But if you like, I can show my magnanimous nature and declare that women in general turn out to be troublesome regardless of their virtue or motive. It seems it is an inevitable consequence of their sex. Perhaps they cannot help it…" His lordship was growing distinctly philosophical, swirling his glass around to emphasise his reflective mood.

His glare fading fast, Darcy could not help but smile at his friend's observations.

"Is it so much that all women are troublesome, Baugham? Or that we simply aren't able to withstand the effect that *some* of them have on us?"

He sat for a few minutes smiling at the fire, while Baugham tried to focus on his face.

"I am all too familiar with the effects marginal actresses and singers have on University students, my friend, or the attraction of energetic and lively sisters as a pleasant diversion when one is bored with Town life. What I don't understand though," he leaned forward, once again imperilling his upright state, "what I'd really like to hear from you, Darcy, is what makes one particular woman worth all the trouble."

Darcy reached out for the bottle and filled his glass with a healthy amount.

"What makes her worth the trouble…" he repeated thoughtfully, after several equally thoughtful sips. "I don't know that I can exactly say what it is. It's just that, before I even knew what was happening, she was always in my thoughts, and I kept looking out for excuses to run into her, or speak to her…"

Baugham brought his drink unsteadily to his mouth, hardly spilling any in the process.

"Nothing new there, Darcy."

"No, Baugham, this time is different. This time it is…I mean there's a…" He thought another long minute before suddenly slamming his glass down on the table in inspiration. "*This time*, Baugham, I'm not simply thinking about what I want…what's best or most desirable for me…*this time* it's not just the outward appeal that…"

He paused, trying desperately to capture his feelings with words. "Baugham, without Elizabeth Bennet in it, my life would be…less. And, I think — *I hope* — it is the same for her. That's the only way I can explain it."

Baugham looked at his friend with a sceptical eye.

"Next you will tell me she is perfect."

Darcy shook his head and smiled.

"Oh, she is not perfect. Perfection in a woman does not have the kind of power that she has over me. A perfect woman's words do not cause the havoc that hers inevitably do to me. In fact, she is distinctly imperfect. She professes opinions simply for the effect they will have. She forms strong judgements and keeps to them in spite of evidence and fairness. She laughs at people instead of pitying them. Actually, she laughs rather too much all in all. She is entirely too fond of obeying her own mind when a little care and reticence would be prudent, but she never does so out of malice. And she is the sort of woman whose loyalty, affection and love is a hard-won thing, but, once achieved, is absolute and invincible."

There was a pause while Darcy drained his glass and Baugham still stared at him.

"Darcy," he finally said, "I must surrender to your eloquence. You have me convinced. That was the longest speech I have heard you give in years."

If Mr Darcy had had the unfortunate tendency to blush, he would have turned a rosy hue at this moment. As it was he simply averted his eyes.

"Well," he muttered into his already empty glass, "perhaps you will see for yourself one day."

"I think not," Baugham said lightly. "Such agonising and illogical sufferings as you go through, my friend, are really not for me. I enjoy tangles that are more easily solved and that less sleep is lost over."

"It is not really a choice, you know," Darcy said quietly while reaching for the bottle.

"Of course it is! Either you lay yourself open to such irrationality or you don't."

Darcy shook his head but said nothing.

"You are just pretending it is inevitable and unavoidable to rationalise your own confusion and surrender."

"Harsh and hasty words spoken in pure ignorance, Baugham," Darcy said and took a sip.

"Nonsense. Never shall a woman, regardless of character or station, be she ever so impertinent and opinionated, cause me to abandon my own rule over my heart and — more importantly — my mind. Hold me to it!"

Darcy smiled. "I wouldn't dream of it. Despite your foolishness, I still have hope for you."

"Ach!" Baugham gave a disgusted snort and a vicious look. "You had best give up *that* hope right now. As pleasant as I find female company in general, I have no intentions of letting one into my life permanently." He leaned back and closed his eyes against Darcy's infuriatingly self-satisfied smile, enjoying the pleasing sensation of floating on air instead. "Nothing but trouble..." he grumbled, "and more of that, I don't need."

Lord Baugham took advantage of a break in the weather to slip out for a ride to the Caledonian Thistle to look after his mail. His conversation with Darcy the night before had ended in silently finishing the bottle, which seemed to suit his friend perfectly, but which left him restless. After a brief but troubled slumber, he woke in the middle of the night and then been unable to go back to sleep. Instead, he tossed and turned and cursed and grumbled until he had finally found rest in the early hours before dawn.

So he definitely needed a ride and a change of scenery to break out of his mood. To his great delight, aside from the London newspapers, the only correspondence directed to him was a brief note from Mr Townsend, informing him that all was running smoothly in his Town home and not much else. The inclement weather insured that the public room of the inn was nearly empty, so he decided to enjoy a pint while he was there. He took his time, and an occasional sip, as he sat at a table near the window, leaning back in his chair and watching the clouds break apart revealing slivers of blue sky and sunlight, then joining together again, darker and more ominous than before.

His contemplation was broken by the sound of the door as Tommy entered and crossed the room to the bar.

"Mr Robertson, Miss Tournier is outby asking after the post."

Baugham's ears perked up at the sound of the name, but he told himself that whatever his friendship was with Mrs Tournier, there was no reason to make an occasion simply because a neighbour of his was picking up her mail. He could very well sit here and finish his drink — if Miss Tournier happened to still be about when he was ready to leave, well, he would wish her a good day before he went on his way back home. He watched as Mr Robertson returned from the back room with an envelope, he watched as Tommy carried it outside, and he watched as the boy returned tossing a coin up and catching it as he walked.

Hmm... the bottom of the mug so soon? Just as well. In no time he was tossing a few coins of his own on the table, grabbing his hat and gloves and heading out the door. No sense in tarrying — he should be going before the rain started again. Taking a deep breath of the crisp autumn air, he looked around as the door closed behind him. Miss Tournier *was* still there, standing in the grassy area and reading her letter while leaning against the trunk of a tree. He must, of course, now speak to her; it would be rude to ignore an acquaintance, however much she was apparently engrossed in the page before her.

"Miss Tournier," he doffed his hat in greeting as she looked up in surprise, "I hope I am not disturbing you."

Her face was hard to read as she quickly closed the letter.

"Not at all, my lord. I was just trying to decide how to break the news..."

Her odd expression troubled him. "News? I hope everything is well? Is there anything I can do to be of assistance?"

She smiled. "No. Everything is well, thank you. It is just that... it looks as though we will have another houseguest as of tomorrow and Maman is not quite as fond of this one..."

She trailed off and again that unreadable look came over her. He waited for her to continue, but when she did not, he sensed the weight of the silence and felt the need to break it.

"Another cousin?" he asked.

"No, it is Mr Pembroke. He is an old friend of the family. Or the son of friends at any rate. The Pembrokes own Rosefarm Cottage and have been very good to us. Their son, however — "

She stopped suddenly but the disjointed manner in which she spoke disconcerted him somewhat and he felt compelled to continue the conversation.

"I can imagine, with the limited space at Rosefarm, that too many guests at once can be quite inconvenient. It must get a bit crowded."

As soon as the words left his mouth, he prepared himself for the probability that Miss Tournier would take offence at any perceived slight of her home, but to his surprise she did not.

"Yes, there is that. Rosefarm will most probably be short of both space and patience for the next little while. Maman and Mr Pembroke do not get on well, you see."

"I think my sympathies must be with your mother."

Holly looked out at the road ahead of her.

"Well, spare some sympathy for my cousin as well, if you would, my lord, for she will have to move into my room for the time being," she said absentmindedly.

"Really?" Baugham drawled. "I thought girls liked that sort of thing."

Holly snapped back to give him a contemptuous glance.

"I suppose girls do, yes; however, when a valued friend has travelled a great distance to visit, it is nice to feel that you can provide her with a comfortable place to sleep and a small space to call her own."

"Well then, this friend, Mr Pembroke. He ought to postpone his visit to a more convenient time."

Holly shook her head. It was obvious that Lord Baugham had no concept of living under obligation to anyone. As if a simple letter of explanation would have any impact at all on Mr Pembroke's feelings of entitlement regarding Rosefarm Cottage.

"Mr Pembroke does as he pleases," Holly retorted.

"I wonder at your use of the term 'friend', then, Miss Tournier. It would seem to me you are far too liberal with that epithet. No one in my acquaintance could earn such a name based on so little."

"Yes, I am sure that you would never be required to consider such a thing, or be forced to place a more pleasant face on an unhappy and uncomfortable circumstance. One is not always lucky enough to be able to choose their 'friends', my lord. Nor plan the timing of their visits."

"I would not call that luck, Miss Tournier, precaution or prudence would be more appropriate. Which, well applied, would render your other hesitations redundant."

"If you harbour any doubts as to the proper running of our home, whether prudence or precaution is exercised in a manner that you feel is inappropriate, or if you have objections as to the suitableness of our friends, I suggest that you take it up with my mother, sir!"

Baugham narrowed his eyes. "Miss Tournier, you mistake my meaning. I was merely trying to express my concern for your dilemma and perhaps offer some perspective, but I see you are determined to misinterpret my words and my intentions."

What an infuriating woman! There she was, shooting daggers at him and twisting his words to make him seem petty and spoilt when all he wanted to do was to have a polite conversation on dispassionate matters. And in the end, being forced into saying insulting things after all due to her stubborn insistence on misunderstanding his every word!

As he stood there, lips pressed tightly together against the flow of words threatening to spill out at her, at the same time flabbergasted as to why he should be so angry as to nearly lose control — something he never did — she pulled her cloak around her and said decidedly, "I should be getting home now; there is much to do to prepare. Good day, my lord."

Baugham watched her stalk off and suppressed an oath. Somehow she had left him with the feeling that he was by no means finished with her but at the same time he realised that to continue could only be more disastrous. He shook his head both in loathing and self-disgust and turned on his heel to get himself home.

"Maman... we have a letter... it's... it's from Mr Jonathan Pembroke..." Holly hesitatingly handed the page to her mother. "He is coming tomorrow."

Mrs Tournier watched the letter with her mouth curled in disgust before she took it carefully between her thumb and forefinger.

"Tomorrow?" she said in a cold voice. "Well then!"

Letting the sheet of paper float down on her desk and then to the floor, she got up and walked out of the door. Picking up the letter, Holly almost gave a little shriek of surprise as the door slammed shut with a bang. She listened as her mother made her way through the house to the kitchen, slamming every door in her wake. After a few minutes she came back and told her daughter she had spoken to Mrs Higgins.

"I'll be in my room, Lie-lie," she said her jaw clenched so hard the words hardly came out. Holly nodded and once again stayed listening as her mother took herself up the stairs until at last her own bedroom door was shut with a resounding bang that made the walls shake.

Holly sighed. She had better warn Elizabeth.

All of Elizabeth's belongings had been moved across the hall to Holly's room and the two girls were now crowded into her narrow bed. The arrangement held great promise for keeping them both warm throughout the night, but did not bode quite so well in assuring an early or especially restful slumber.

"Holly," Elizabeth whispered, "why does my aunt dislike Mr Pembroke so? She has been positively ill-tempered ever since she heard he was coming."

Holly lay still, wondering how much she could or should tell about Mr Pembroke, but of course she soon realised that she could do nothing but be upfront and honest.

"Elizabeth," she spoke into the darkness above their heads, "I... we don't talk about this, Maman and I, it is the only thing we cannot talk about... since that night she has never..."

Elizabeth strained her eyes to see Holly as she stammered through a most astonishing admission that her cousin and aunt had a subject they avoided between them.

"I was very foolish when it came to Mr Pembroke once," Holly said. "Very, *very* foolish…"

The unspoken, but obvious, meaning hung in the darkness between them. Elizabeth swallowed.

"Oh," she said. "And…he still comes here? Why?"

"Well, not for that original silly thing, to be sure," Holly scoffed. "I think…. No, I shouldn't. I cannot be fair or even reasonable when it comes to him or his motives. You had better see for yourself. And I have no doubt you will see exactly what he is about very quickly. But it is just for a few days thankfully."

Elizabeth stayed quiet, but the oddest sense of protectiveness towards both her cousin and her aunt filled her. Holly did not seem overly distressed, but it was quite obvious she was anxious and fearful on her mother's behalf. To be at the mercy of someone like that! Elizabeth clenched her fist. Oh this world really was full of undeserving young men and it seemed not even an intelligent, sweet and reasonable girl like Holly was completely safe. It is a hard thing indeed to learn from such mistakes, but thankfully it seemed they had been spared the worst ramifications of such an error.

IF ELIZABETH HAD BEEN PRESENT during any of Mr Pembroke's previous visits, she would have recognised that dinner on the night of his arrival was typical of all dinners in which he was in residence at Rosefarm. Mrs Higgins would serve in a tight-lipped and perfunctory manner, Mrs Tournier would be uncharacteristically quiet and excuse herself after only a few bites, while Holly, not entirely at ease herself, would feel the burden of responding to their guest's pronouncements and opinions and keeping some sort of polite discourse going.

She could not forget Holly's confession of the night before and her own astonishment at the presumption of the man to continue visiting as often and for as long as he did under those circumstances, so when he turned to her and began to lay before her his future plans and his past struggles, she found that she was hard pressed to show any interest or sympathy. For the latter, especially, he was relentless in his quest, explaining to this newest captive listener his struggles to find acceptance among the scholarly community for his innovative ideas on economics and the redistribution of wealth among the populace.

"Miss Bennet," he said, leaning forward and fixing his intensely passionate eyes upon her, "you must understand that even during my University days, I was subjected to the bitterness and jealousy of my peers and my instructors. I knew I could find neither recognition nor encouragement in such a stodgy and stifling atmosphere, so I came to Scotland where free thinkers are generally welcomed and encouraged, and to a house with a legacy of fighting for justice and equality, but even then I met with resistance…" his gaze shifted to Holly, who was quietly eating her dinner and offering no comment or even appearing to hear his conversation. "It was a rare thing to find someone whom I *thought* understood me completely."

Holly's eyes shot up then quickly returned to her plate, but Elizabeth noted a new tightness around her mouth.

Pembroke continued as if oblivious, but he now directed his gaze at Mrs Tournier, who was scarcely able to keep her countenance civil, and then back to Holly. "*Very* few ever understood the importance of my work and how much it took out of me, and even among those who did, none had the courage to stand by me in support. So you see, Miss Bennet, I now must struggle on in a solitary — "

He was unable to finish his tragic history due to the interruption of clattering silver and a scraping chair as Mrs Tournier abruptly threw her napkin onto her plate and left the table without a word.

Rising next, Holly managed a quiet, "If you will excuse me, I must speak with Mrs Higgins," before leaving as well.

Elizabeth was incensed at his shameless manipulation of what was necessarily a painful memory between mother and daughter, and at his apparent willingness to use it for his own amusement, for he sat there with a self-satisfied smile, his eyes bright with undisguised mirth.

In a tone exhibiting heroic self-control, she asked him mildly, "And even after all these years, the professors and the great minds of the universities do not accept your way of thinking? How tragic for you."

He sighed and shook his head, drawing his breath to speak but Elizabeth would not give him the chance.

"Well, as tragic as that is for you, I suppose that it *is* for the best that learned, old men — the authorities of our age — should take everything under sober consideration and cannot be as easily beguiled as innocent and idealistic young girls. I suppose *they* cannot be swayed by passionate appeals and shameless playing upon their romantic notions surrounding a beloved late father."

Elizabeth brought her napkin up to her lips and then rose from the table as well. "I do pity you though," she added in an apparent afterthought, "for it seems that even idealistic young girls can find the capacity to resist such tactics."

THE LADIES OF ROSEFARM COTTAGE spent the afternoon of Lady Tristam's grand event in the kitchen. Partly due to its consistent warmth and partly due to the fact that, since Mr Pembroke had taken over the writing desk in the parlour, it was the only place where the three could gather to discuss and plan the occasion. Additionally, Mr Pembroke's absence from the kitchen assured that Mrs Tournier would be present, and the girls very much desired her company.

"Now you see, Holly," Elizabeth said, plying her needle as busily as she was employing her tongue to convince her cousin that the evening had definite possibilities of actually being enjoyable, "this dress will be perfect once we replace the lace around the bodice and ruffle up the hem a bit. It has such classic lines, no one will know that it isn't this year's latest."

"No one," Holly muttered as she vigorously applied the brush to three pairs of dress slippers, "except those who have seen it twenty-five times at least. I never thought I would ever miss Hockdown, but at least if I were there I would not have to go to this thing."

"Why should you be so against a *musicale*, Holly? You are very fond of music."

"I am fond of music," she answered, "but you know how these things always degenerate into long displays of marginal female talent and since I can't sing a note, I will have to play and that usually ends up...Elizabeth. Maman. You must both promise me that I won't be trapped at the instrument all night, playing the dances."

"They have engaged musicians, Lie-lie," Mrs Tournier assured her. "You may both be as untalented and uselessly beautiful as you wish this evening."

"Oh, we will be, Aunt. I have such a good idea for fixing Holly's hair, too." Elizabeth held up the completed gown to Holly, "Here, see? With my embroidered stomacher and your new shawl it is a completely different dress."

MRS HIGGINS PULLED OUT A chair and offered her cousin a seat at the kitchen table as she took the parcel held out for her and began unwrapping the contents.

"Thank ye for coming by, Heather. With everyone gone to this party, here's the first moment's peace I've had in days. Och! This little bit of coffee will be a rare treat for the Mistress."

Mrs McLaughlin leaned forward and pointed to the rabbit carcass at the bottom of the basket. "Now, Mr McLaughlin snared that one his own self, but ye just tell Miss Holly if she asks, that I took too many of the mushrooms and couldnae rest until I made it right."

She pulled a small packet of recovered leaves out next and rose to sprinkle it into the kettle to make her cousin a proper pot of tea.

"So, it's been a noisy time around here with all the company? It's little enough room ye have for it, that's certain."

"Ach, that's the problem, Heather. It's nae noisy at all — it's been quiet, very quiet, but a louder quiet I've never heard, if ye know what I mean."

"This Mr Pembroke..."

Mrs McLaughlin pronounced the name hesitantly.

"Aye," was her cousin's only reply as she reached for the cups.

"I thought they were friends of the family...?"

"The parents are. Good people they are, but the son..."

Mrs McLaughlin could not quite understand and her expression showed it freely. Mrs Higgins sighed and sat down to wait for the water to boil.

"He takes advantage of their dependence on his parents," she said, "and you can guess what that does to the Mistress of this house."

Mrs McLaughlin nodded.

"But it's more than discourtesy and disrespect. What it is though, I cannae rightly say. But I do know this. Mrs Tournier hates the man. Miss Tournier despises him.

114

And it's as plain as parritch Miss Bennet loathes him, too."

"And you?"

Mrs Higgins squared her shoulders and gave her cousin a rare, unbridled look. "Well, let me just say that were he to fall down the stair and howl for help or break his neck, I'd be much too busy watching the bread dough rise to be of any assistance."

Chapter 11

The Soirée-Musical at Tristam Lodge

"ARE you quite sure about this, Eliza?"

Holly sat on her bed and, holding up her small mirror, tried to catch her cousin's work on her tresses at the back. Elizabeth was twisting and puffing up and Holly could not quite make out what she was about, wielding the hot iron tongs that she was brandishing about Holly's hair.

"Yes, I am quite sure," Elizabeth said and let a few curls loose from the red hot instrument. She skipped off the bed and shoved it into the fireplace to heat up again. Deftly she pinned some of the curls up towards the crown of Holly's head while letting a few others fall freely around her ears. "Your hair is just as thick and strong as Jane's and she always wears it like this. Well, except that she is fair. But other than that you know she is quite twice as beautiful as me so she is worth emulating."

"I usually put it up in small braids all over," Holly muttered, still having a hard time catching the over-all arrangement of her hair in the small mirror.

"And how usually is usually?" Elizabeth said in a mock stern voice. "When was the last time you dressed up to go to a fine *musicale*?"

Holly smiled. "Three years ago. Oh actually, Sir John took me to the theatre once in Edinburgh last year. I dressed up then."

"And sat hidden behind people in the back shadows of the box for the whole night watching a performance no doubt," Elizabeth said. "This is a party! There! Done. Now it is your turn. I want the braids you usually have!"

Her cousin climbed off the bed, still in her shift, nearly hitting her head on the low ceiling in the process and settled down in front of Holly, who started to braid Elizabeth's smooth, dark hair into an impressive bun high on the crown of her head, leaving one on either side to frame her beautiful eyes. When she was done, they helped each other struggle into their dresses. Afterwards, Elizabeth held up the small mirror and tried to show as much of the two of them as possible. Elizabeth was a fair vision in fine, sheer muslin with some exquisite work on her bodice and a skirt that came down in three layers to show her satin slippers. Holly was all smooth lines in a simple but richly coloured green velvet dress with a small train.

"The neck is too low," she muttered and pulled it upwards by the fine lace trimming.

"No it isn't," her cousin said and tugged at her waist to bring it down again. "And anyway, that's why I left these tendrils here at the side and back. If you exposed all that milky white skin of yours without any protection, you would have the men swooning in your wake."

Holly had to laugh. "I doubt it," she said, "unless Mr Grant is there. Not that he needs this much skin to do that."

Elizabeth pulled out one of the small satin flowers she had worked into her hair and pinned it into Holly's. "There," she said, "in case there is anyone who does not know we go together. Aren't we perfect!"

They stayed admiring each other for a little while until Holly looked at her small golden watch hanging from her waist — the most precious piece of jewellery she owned.

"Oh dear!" she said. "Maman!"

Mrs Tournier was not normally a woman of great patience when obliged to leave her house to go to something as tiresome as a *soirée-musicale* given by Lady Tristam. The girls rushed down the steps in the hope that she had not lost her temper waiting for them already, but they were met by a calm lady standing in front of a mirror in the hall adjusting her shawl to exactly the right and fashionable angle.

"I beg your pardon, Maman," Holly gasped. "Will we be late?"

It was a very different Mrs Tournier who turned around and awarded them with a gentle smile. The girls gave her a surprised look as they took in a very elegant lady, perfectly poised and dressed in the perfect shade of blue to set off her auburn curls under a soft sweeping feathered turban and bringing out the colour of eyes more usually seen peering narrowly over a pair of spectacles.

"I think not. The carriage is not here yet."

"You look very beautiful, Maman," Holly said and kissed her mother's cheek. "Do you think anyone will believe I am your daughter?"

"Well," Mrs Tournier said, gratified, "vanity keeps dotage at bay. The day I don't feel tempted to run late by just a tweak here and a tuck there to make me look my best before I show myself to the local elite, is the day you can put me in the poor house. You both look very nice as well. So that is what your cousin thinks your hair needs. It is very nice. I do believe you will not be able to avoid dancing later tonight."

Holly looked at Elizabeth. "Dancing! Oh, it has been so long!"

"And if your courage fails you I will solicit the first one and force you out into a quadrille!"

Sir Torquil Tristam, despite his place at the top of local society, was an amiable gentleman, devoid of all pretension save one: Lady Tristam — and perhaps his oldest daughter, Primrose. Together they planned and put on a yearly *soirée-musicale*, insisting on calling it thus, as if by giving it a name void of established meaning, they would be celebrated for bringing forth something unique and dazzlingly spectacular. In reality, it was just as Lord Baugham had presented it to his houseguest: a country ball. But they were readily forgiven by the local society for this aspiration to singularity and exclusivity, for Lady Tristam always insisted on bringing the very best musicians and players from Edinburgh to perform, the atmosphere was formal and as genteel as could be managed in the Southern Uplands of Scotland and the invitation list was long and varied. Miss Tristam possessed a marginal vocal ability, but, through prodigious distribution of food and drink, the guests were generally in an amiable mood by the time the evening's highlight took place and she treated them to an aria, accompanied by Miss Prudence and Miss Patience on the harp and pianoforte.

Holly ran her gloved hand over the seat beside her. They were waiting in Mr Darcy's carriage, especially sent to convey them all to Tristam Lodge. Mr Darcy had chosen to go with Lord Baugham in a separate conveyance and Holly wondered how Elizabeth interpreted that. She looked up and watched her mother and her cousin sitting opposite her. Her mother looked almost regal, she thought. She looked like she belonged in such a fine carriage with the finest inlaid wood and smoothest velvet seats. Her cousin, too. It felt like a fairytale and they could be fine ladies on their way to a grand ball. She only hoped the carriage would not turn out to be a pumpkin and her carefully arranged shawl and cloak would not reveal tattered rags at some point in the evening. In all honesty, she felt like she was already wearing those tattered rags and hoped that the lighting at the party would be dim enough to hide the threadbare spots on the velvet of her gown that Elizabeth had been too polite to mention while working on it. But for now she tried to put it out of her mind and turned back to her companions; there was no reason for anyone to pay any particular attention to her or her clothing that evening. Elizabeth was gazing out of the window with a faraway look in her eye while still arranging her skirts; Miss Bennet sitting in Mr Darcy's carriage. Would she soon be Mrs Darcy, sitting in the same carriage and calling it her own?

Elizabeth turned her eyes and popped them wide open in reaction to Holly's silent scrutiny.

"Really, Holly!" she said.

Holly was caught off guard and was startled.

"Stop it!" her cousin went on, but with a smile on her face. "I know what you are thinking and I will not have it."

"Have what? You cannot know possibly what I am thinking."

"Of course I can! It is written all over your face! And besides, it is exactly what I am trying very hard not to think myself."

"Well, you cannot stop me from doing so in any case," Holly laughed, "and I think you had better get used to the idea. It is a lovely coach."

"Yes, it was very friendly of him," Elizabeth said quietly and Holly thought she could see a slight blush sweep over her cheeks as she looked outside again.

The exuberance of the ladies was cut short when Mr Pembroke belatedly climbed in and plumped down beside Holly. Elizabeth's open countenance clouded over and Mrs Tournier steadfastly stared out of the window.

Mr Pembroke, unable to catch another friendly eye, had to be content with winking at Holly and apologising for being late without a flicker of remorse to his voice or demeanour. Mrs Tournier cut him off by knocking on the roof with a force that took them all aback and the carriage set off on its journey towards the evening's entertainment.

TRISTAM LODGE WAS SPLENDID IN the early darkness of a November night, Baugham reluctantly admitted as he and Darcy approached. It was brilliantly lit, the owners sparing no expense, and the first glimpse of it when coming up the drive was an impressive sight not easily forgotten.

Lady Tristam displayed a barely contained enthusiasm as the gentlemen entered the already crowded rooms. Music could be heard coming from one of the salons and people had gathered to listen, but she came swooping in at full speed when informed of their arrival.

"My lord!" the lady said, completely out of breath and evidently suffering from the ambition of tightening her stays to the measure enjoyed in her girlhood. "Mr Darcy! I cannot. Tell you. How pleased. I am. My husband! My daughters! Here. Somewhere. I cannot believe…"

Scanning the crowd with a look of breathless vexation, Lady Tristam sailed off as suddenly as she had arrived, possibly in search of the missing members of her family to present to the gentlemen. They did not tarry to see whether she found them or not, instead plunging into a crowd of curious whispers and stares. Darcy adopted a grim set to his mouth.

"Well, I don't profess to love this any more than you do," Lord Baugham said to him with an exasperated sigh, "but you must promise me not to relieve your frustrations by going around spouting sarcastic comments that will only confuse the provincials."

"That will not be possible to refrain from, I'm afraid," Darcy said dryly, "but I will promise to try to find someone who will enjoy them."

Baugham noticed Darcy's attention shift and his demeanour change. It did not become any less stiff or imposing, but a subtle difference came over him — a measure of apprehension and a new kind of irritation. The source of this transformation, of course, was not hard to discern and Baugham looked at the two women standing where the music still gently flowed out of the well-lit room.

"Music will play second fiddle tonight, I see," Baugham murmured. "I think you owe me a two-day hunting trip and at least a stag for this."

Baugham stole a glance at the obviously reluctant companion he was left with after

Darcy so skilfully directed Miss Bennet's attentions elsewhere. His first impression of her as he had crossed the room in Darcy's wake had been a favourable one. She looked very well. She looked soft and vulnerable. Perhaps it was the candlelight and the attempt at making the best of what obviously was an old dress. The hair was different, too, but very becoming. Baugham gave an inward smile; an old dress, but a very fetching one. Women were strange sometimes. Who cared about the age of a dress when it was otherwise perfect? So even stern schoolmistresses knew the benefit of a low neckline and a flattering colour!

But what on earth was he supposed to say to her?

HOLLY WAS LOATH TO LET Elizabeth accept Mr Darcy's invitation to find a seat for the music on display, but purely for selfish reasons. She was happy on her cousin's behalf because she was so obviously happy herself, but for her own part she could have done without the company she was left with. It was awkward to stand so conspicuously together with Lord Baugham in a place where they were spotted by every single passer-by and with nothing to say. He was, of course, dressed as only a man who made his habitual residence in London could be and, with his height and looks and appearance, he stuck out like a sore thumb. She was so obviously a poor match for him in her old gown and her strange hair. She looked down at her feet. Oh no, not her feet! She swayed her gown awkwardly so that the tips of her slippers were no longer visible and looked out over the crowd desperately searching for something to say.

The feeling of discomfort was obviously reciprocated by Baugham.

"This seems a popular event," was what finally popped out after a long deliberation.

"Yes, it is," she managed. "Very."

"Quite crowded."

"Certainly; Lady Tristam is most generous with her invitations." *Like inviting the likes of us*, she thought. She stole a quick glance at him to see if that was what he was thinking, but his lordship was looking out at the crowd he had so admired and did not react.

"It is my first time here," he said and frowned.

"Yes. I know."

There was a growing desperation in their stilted conversation. Holly kept her eyes on other parties and prayed for a distraction that would break them up. *Any excuse*, she begged silently, *any little thing. Please…*

Unfortunately her ardent prayers were answered by Mr Pembroke, who had gathered a party of young persons around him and was apparently entertaining them with his wit and observations and eliciting a rapt response. He glanced over at her and his lordship, causing the rest of the party to follow suit. Five pairs of eyes watched her for a moment before Mr Pembroke turned back and made a comment that caused his audience to break out into adoring laughter while shooting sidelong looks in their direction.

Holly turned crimson and felt her ears burn. She prayed it had gone unnoticed by her companion, but Lord Baugham had been watching the scene as well.

"Who is that?" he asked casually.

"That is Mr Pembroke, our...guest," Holly managed, unable to hide a desperate note in her voice.

Lord Baugham watched the adoring court around Mr Pembroke and the man himself, posing and prancing with wide gestures and a cocky step and his romantically curly hair being swept aside in a studied gesture every so often.

"Miss Tournier," he said with surprising alacrity, "is your mother here tonight?"

Holly was hardly surprised at the question. Naturally he wanted rather to talk to her mother. Well, it was a way out and quite a welcome one. She led him to the music room and, with a huge sigh of relief, he left her side and made his way to the company she realised he had much rather be saddled with than her.

UNFORTUNATELY FOR HIS LORDSHIP, THE music room was filled to capacity and though he could see Mrs Tournier seated directly in front, he could not get to her without disturbing the majority of those enjoying the performance. He stood on the outskirts of the crowd, listening, until he became aware that more sidelong glances were being directed his way from the audience than were trained on the string quartet before them. He made a great show of looking around and, pretending to spot an acquaintance out in the hall, did his best to quietly slip out.

"I can see them!"

There was a female flurry hurrying past him, forcing her way among the people and a gentleman struggling to keep up. Baugham took a step back and went unnoticed as one of the Tristam daughters stopped, put up her fan and proceeded to survey the room while vigorously cooling herself.

"Oh," the lady said as the gentleman reached her and tried to put his arm about her in protective familiarity, but the lady unceremoniously moved aside and he had to be content with standing shoulder to shoulder with her in an intimate whisper. "It's just the dark one — Mr Darcy. And he is with that...niece of theirs."

Baugham narrowed his eyes and took half a step forward. Shielded by an older lady still believing in the virtue and style of a towering powdered wig he was protected enough to overhear but not to be seen by who he now recognised as the eldest Miss Tristam and Mr Jonathan Pembroke.

"Jonathan," Miss Primrose whispered quite audibly, "cannot you introduce me? I want to meet them. Both of them."

"Oh, Primmie!"

The disgusted tone of Mr Pembroke was simply answered with a quick snap of the fan and a vicious look.

"Do you know how rare an occasion it is for a man like that to find his way into this deserted back garden of the world?" she hissed. "Never mind two! Mr Darcy is fabulously rich and his friend is an earl! You must introduce me!"

Mr Pembroke did not answer, but obviously looked over to where Mr Darcy and

Miss Bennet were sitting and sharing some detail of the musical rendition.

"Well, right now is highly inconvenient," he muttered back.

A pout came over Miss Tristam's face and she lifted her chin before snapping open her fan and once more putting it between them.

"In other words you cannot. Or will not," she said scathingly. "Really, Jonathan, for all your boasts and talk you really are so...inept, aren't you?"

She sighed and looked out over the crowd again. "I suppose I'll just have to ask my father then..."

Baugham watched as Mr Pembroke grabbed Miss Tristam's elbow and turned her back towards him.

"Don't be silly," he said smoothly, but not without obviously struggling at keeping his voice level. "Of course I can do it. You wish to meet Mr Darcy and Lord Baugham? It is no trouble and quite easy. My tenant at Rosefarm, old Mrs Tournier, will make the introductions as soon as I ask her. She knows the gentlemen quite well. They're in and out of the house all the time!"

Miss Tristam turned and a concerned look flashed across her face. "Then I think you had better see to it at once, Jonathan, hadn't you?"

Baugham could not help but smile to himself as Miss Tristam turned on her heel and walked away from her vantage point, once again making Mr Pembroke struggle to keep up with her through the crowd. By taking just one step to the right, Baugham was able to put himself in Mr Pembroke's way and it would not be unfair, although not exactly flattering to his lordship's manners, to say he took immense pleasure in the look of chagrin and even desperation on Mr Pembroke's face as he half bumped into him and then hastily had to apologise before running after Miss Tristam, who was well on her way to the other side of the room where Mrs Tournier had sat herself down. Pembroke hesitated, looked after Miss Tristam, looked Baugham in the eye while obviously struggling with his next step, but his lordship just gave him a smug smile and withdrew into the crowd once more. Perhaps it was not right, but sometimes the tediousness of country balls must be relieved by taking one's opportunities for entertainment as one found them. Now all that was left to do was to look forward to the second act and he had to confess he had great trust in Mrs Tournier's pivotal performance.

WHEN HOLLY TURNED AROUND FROM the music room, it was only to find Mr Grant bearing down upon her with a determined look on his face. He watched Lord Baugham's back all the way into the music room and then rather possessively held out his arm to her. Unable to see a way to gracefully decline it, she took it lightly and allowed him to escort her to the refreshment table that had been set up in the great hall in the hopes that whatever he had to say to her would be accomplished as they walked and would not therefore be witnessed by too many.

"Miss Tournier, might I just tell you that you look stunning this evening? I must say, I think that gown is my particular favourite — each and every time I see you in it, I think you must be the most beautiful lady in the county. *The pale which held that lovely deer…"*

Mr Grant could not have made a more unwelcome comment to Holly at that time, and combined with his ill-timed verses, she found herself feeling a terrible mix of embarrassment and humiliation and she fervently wished a large hole would open up in Sir Torquil's magnificent marble floor and swallow her up. But, no obliging crack appeared in the stone and Mr Grant would continue along his theme.

"…can surely see it is truly in *your* best interests as well as my own. And as much as my devotion to you is steadfast and true, not even I, Miss Tournier, can wait interminably for you to grant a favourable answer to my heartfelt pleas."

He stopped in the middle of the room and took both of her hands into his own as her face flushed with mortification.

"Miss Tournier; I simply cannot wait. I must have an answer, once and for all. Will you do me the great honour — "

"Please, Mr Grant," Holly hastily interrupted. "I am very sorry, but I cannot see my way to an answer different than the one I have given you many times in the past."

"Well, I suppose there is no rush, Miss Tournier." Mr Grant *would* keep talking, and as expected, he was not daunted in the least. Despite his claims of mere seconds ago, he declared, "I will not give up hope just yet. *Then let us teach our trial patience, Because it is a customary cross.*"

She was aware that they were drawing curious stares from the other guests, and what was worse, Lord Baugham had just entered the hall and was looking at them too. Too desperate to be choosy, she quickly drew her hands away from Mr Grant's and meeting his lordship's gaze, seized the opportunity that was presented to her.

"Mr Grant," she hurriedly began, "have you met Lord Baugham?"

"I have not yet had the pleasure," Mr Grant said stiffly, not looking like he particularly regretted the deprivation.

Lord Baugham's greeting, on the other hand, was all that was polished and polite, making Mr Grant display features remarkably resembling those of a petulant child and so Mr Grant hastily solicited dear Miss Tournier's permission to fetch her a glass of wine since it was obvious from her flushed, but charming, face she was in need of one urgently. Holly was certain that her supposed flushed features were a result of Mr Grant's frustrating behaviour, his lordship's contrasting manners, and a feeling that this evening had all the hallmarks of a disaster, but off he went and she let out a sigh. Lord Baugham turned to her with an amused expression, though he said nothing. All too soon, they were right back to where they had started: both struggling to find a suitable topic of conversation, standing awkwardly side by side looking out over the room.

"I believe I see Sir Torquil," his lordship said, taking a step away. "I should go and — "

He was interrupted by a voice behind them.

"Ah, here you are, my dear! Goodness me, how quickly you are able to take advantage of such a rare and privileged opportunity! I must say, I am impressed at your skill."

Holly's blood ran cold at the sound of Mr Pembroke's acid drawl behind her. He was quiet enough at Rosefarm, when surrounded by universal dislike, but here, in his element…It churned her stomach and she was suddenly afraid the underlying contempt that must be inevitable in their relationship would very soon be expressed both vocally and publicly. In fact, despite his smiles and attempts to appear good-humoured, she felt certain by the sarcastic tone of his voice that Mr Pembroke neither wanted, nor was able, to avoid it.

Trying to recover her equilibrium, she took a breath, squared her shoulders and turned around to face the unwelcome intruder. Intending to be frostily polite and to carry herself with dignity, when she saw Miss Primrose Tristam leaning on his arm with a smug smile, she shrank back. Her voice, that she had intended to be strong and forceful, came out in nearly a whisper.

"I don't know what you mean, sir"

Mr Pembroke laughed a strange, airy laugh and smirked at Miss Tristam before returning his attention to Miss Tournier. "Oh, my dear, it surely cannot be a surprise to you that you owe your presence at this fine event to my being at Rosefarm," Mr Pembroke said smoothly. "It would appear that Lady Tristam's willingness to oblige me as a very dear and old friend outweighs her customary discretion and standards," he chuckled, belying the cold look in his close-set eyes as he looked her up and down thoroughly, "but never mind that now, hm? As you've so deftly attached yourself to her loftiest guest, perhaps you would condescend to make an introduction to a couple of old, dear friends?"

It was perfectly obvious to Lord Baugham that Mr Pembroke's attempts to solicit an introduction from Mrs Tournier had been unsuccessful. It was equally obvious that the man was now going to attempt the acquaintance through Miss Tournier instead. He sighed inwardly, prevented by their arrival from completing his leave-taking, but he supposed it was best to get the business over with. However, he could not help looking on in surprise when he heard the unusual temerity in Miss Tournier's voice. The man was obviously a boor — that he had concluded upon first setting eyes on him — but from all he knew of Miss Tournier, he could not fathom why she would be so disturbed by his presence as to give such a weak and ineffectual answer. Where was the thunderous brow, where was the famous frown of disapproval? His shock at this was great; however, it paled in comparison to what he felt when Pembroke next opened his mouth.

"Well, what do you say…Holly?"

If Lord Baugham had still been planning on making a quick escape, it became impossible now for at Mr Pembroke's impertinence, Miss Tournier suddenly and instinctively clutched at his arm.

Speechless, he felt an incredulity bordering on disgust. It was worse than his earlier glimpse of him had ever led him to believe! His prejudices about the manners of young men relying on their father's blind charity and their own self-importance was once again confirmed as he watched and listened to Mr Pembroke, standing rather too close to Miss Tournier and giving her distinctly patronising looks — and having the nerve to speak to her in such an intimate manner, aiming to give the impression that…. He glanced at her and an odd feeling crept into him to see her so obviously upset. Their eyes briefly met and she quickly withdrew her hand from his arm. He cleared his throat as he pulled his eyes away with difficulty and addressed the man who had not even given him more than a glimpse until now.

"Sir," he said in a tight voice fixing his cold blue eyes on the offending man, "I do not believe I have had the pleasure. I believe I should introduce *myself*, since the circumstances in your address are so… irregular. My name is Lord Baugham." He hesitated for a second but then boldly added: "Mrs Tournier and Miss Tournier are good friends of mine. And you are?"

"Lord Baugham?" Mr Pembroke broke his scrutiny of Miss Tournier for a moment and pulled himself up to his full height, which, unfortunately for him, did not match Lord Baugham's careless posture. "I am Jonathan Pembroke. Of course I know who you are, sir. Heard of but rarely seen, aren't you? Well, that explains it, I'm sure. And in view of that, my lord, surely I am not mistaken in presuming that you cannot be *too* familiar with our Miss Tournier here." He laughed slightly and rolled back on his heels. "You are neither of you then familiar with the finest local society, which I'm sure, makes taking refuge in each other's company quite understandable. She, also, is not in the habit of frequenting the best society Clanough has to offer, I'm afraid, but not from lack of trying, I suspect. Some people have no sense of place, or shortage of ambition, it seems."

Baugham could not help breaking out into a terse smile.

"Mr Pembroke. Indeed. You must forgive my presumptuous nature, sir, but you do rather *heighten* my esteem for Miss Tournier, and any resolution of hers to stay away from such social gatherings. From what I see at present, there is nothing but good sense in such a course."

"How droll you are!" Mr Pembroke said while Primrose Tristam's brow was temporarily clouded over with a frown. "I hesitate to assume, my lord, that you suffer from a lack of discernment, so I must assume that you are either operating in ignorance, or blinded by more… personal motives. However, it is of course quite clear that as a mere schoolteacher, Miss Tournier has her connection with my family to thank for the Tristams' attentions and I am sure her absence from most gatherings is due less to her own resolution than it is to that of the hosts. It is common knowledge here, but, of course, I would not imagine you to have been aware of it. If I were not around, it is very unlikely she would have received any such attention, much less the opportunity to attach herself to such a noble personage as yourself, even if just for the evening. Isn't that the case, my dear?"

Baugham frowned and took a step forward, attempting to shield Miss Tournier from the man's impertinent stare.

"You are perfectly right," he interjected, his voice tight and clipped. "I know nothing of Miss Tournier's local reputation or social ambitions, but in the very short time of our acquaintance I have known her to show much judgement when dealing with folly, impertinence and rudeness, not to mention admirable affection and loyalty to those fortunate enough to earn her friendship. As I can discern that you are in fact, no friend to her, I think I can only esteem her excellent judgement even more highly than before.

"I suppose you are to be congratulated as well, Mr Pembroke, on how very successfully you are able to demonstrate how one can rise to societal acceptance and claim connections as desirable as those of our hosts this evening without appearing to possess any sort of manners or sense of propriety. Society has always been extraordinary in that regard, bestowing attentions even when they are utterly groundless in terms of merit. I find it, and in turn you, excessively diverting in a perverse sort of way, but I am certain Miss Tournier would advise me against the folly of allowing you to incriminate yourself any longer."

Mr Pembroke did not take these observations in good stride and his eyes narrowed further and he seemed to puff himself up in order to answer his lordship while all the time casting glimpses at Miss Tristam by his side. The lady in question looked bored and irritated, which no doubt did not have a beneficiary effect on his next choice of words.

"It's a wonder that Miss Tournier doesn't advise you against incriminating *yourself* by openly associating with a woman who was dismissed from her place of employment for disgraceful and immoral behaviours."

"That really is quite — " Baugham began, but he was interrupted by Miss Tournier's gasp of horror.

"*What*? How did you...who has said such things to you?"

The fact that Miss Tournier was mortally upset was evident from her rapid breath, her flittering gaze and her fingers pressed to her mouth. Baugham very firmly took hold of her arm, almost yanking her back to his side and executed a slight bow in withdrawing from Mr Pembroke.

"You forget, my dear Holly," Pembroke persisted, "that I have many friends and associates in Edinburgh. The news is by no means a secret, no matter how you might try to hide it from your illustrious new acquaintances." He turned from his lordship's pale and speechless companion to the man himself. "You must judge for yourself the value of allying yourself with Miss Tournier and her family against the cost to your reputation, but I would surely warn you against it. If you attach yourself to this — well, I'm sure you would find, in doing so, you have most foolishly discarded the possibility for any *good* and *valuable* society; however, I am told your stays here are brief, and perhaps you prefer your pleasures to be fleeting and...common. If that is the case, my lord, I beg your pardon and wish you a good evening," he huffed and then stiffly returned the bow before stalking off.

STUNNED, HOLLY FELT LIKE SHE had just been struck. Her head was spinning, the room was excessively warm, and she was not feeling very steady on her feet. She was grateful for Lord Baugham's interference and support, but right then she wanted nothing more than to leave. She looked frantically around the room for her mother, but though she had seen her clearly only a few moments before, everything was a blur to her now and she could not find her.

"I find Mr Pembroke to be quite a ridiculous man," Lord Baugham slowly said, apparently in no hurry to release her. "I also find myself deeply regretting any doubts I may have expressed when speaking to you about his letter. Perhaps it is a good thing I find him so laughable, for if I were to dwell seriously on his behaviour, I might be forced to resort to illegal measures and demand my satisfaction of him. I make no promises, however, that I will not change my mind at some point and follow up on any murderous impulses."

Desperately trying to hide her distress, Holly smiled feebly at his attempt to lighten the mood. He was looking at her intently with his piercing blue eyes and she wished he would leave her alone to calm her breathing and rapidly beating heart that for some reason were not easing, even though Mr Pembroke had gone. Instead he very calmly reclaimed her hand, placed it on his arm and let his own reassuringly rest upon it a few seconds before he slowly led her away from the scene that had caused not a few eyes to turn and watch.

"Perhaps we should go join your mother," he said as together they walked in the opposite direction.

Holly relaxed a bit and found that she was oddly content to lean upon Lord Baugham's strength for the time being. She was grateful to him. She was grateful that he fought this battle for her; in the one battle that she felt incapable of fighting on her own, he had stepped in and defended her. At that moment she felt that she could call him a true gentleman and she vowed she would show him more charity from now on.

"*Ye ugly, creepin, blastit wonner,*" his voice sounded quietly beside her. "*Detested, shunn'd by saunt an' sinner*"

"Robert Burns?" She stifled a gasp of surprise when she heard the lines from her favourite poet. "You like Burns?"

"Of course I do, Miss Tournier," his lordship smiled. "And I find the lines that follow are particular favourites of mine: *How daur ye set your fit upon her, Sae fine a lady!*"

Momentarily flustered, she then found herself growing calmer with the realisation that she not only had a gentleman at her side, but maybe even a friend. She felt her heart stop its frantic beating and no longer noticed the curious stares, but as they approached the drawing room and she once again was aware of her surroundings, she stopped him.

"Please," she said as she extracted her arm gently. "I think, my lord, I would rather take myself outside for a few moments — for some fresh air — before joining my mother. I thank you for your kindness. You must go on and enjoy the rest of your evening."

"A splendid idea," Lord Baugham declared, "but I will not hear of you going out unaccompanied. I see the windows to the garden are opened. That would be perfect, I think."

He once again offered his arm — this time simply holding it out to her and silently waiting for her to accept it, which she finally did. They walked in silence through the crowd of people who were clearing the floor in the anticipation of a dance. She turned a thankful smile upon him as he escorted her into the crisp, cool air of the Tristams' garden.

"Perhaps I might claim the privilege of fetching you a glass of wine, Miss Tournier?" he asked quietly.

Nodding, Holly realised she must relinquish her hold on his arm in order for him to carry out his task, but she was strangely reluctant to do so.

She did, however, and with a smile Lord Baugham left her standing. She felt strangely bereft even though she had presumed solitude was what she craved most of all at this point. As she stood, watching the breeze swaying the trees, she realised she was waiting impatiently for his return.

Chapter 12

Lord Baugham claims privileges and Miss Tournier discovers she is thankful for them

BAUGHAM left her on the terrace and wandered in search of the promised glass of wine at a leisurely pace. The offer to accompany Miss Tournier to the garden had been automatic and natural, but once he was away from her he wondered at the impulse. What had possessed him to attach himself to a woman in distress and, in particular, this woman with whom he could scarcely hold a civil conversation? Perhaps if he took long enough about his task, she would have time to collect herself and, hopefully, to engage another acquaintance to keep her company. Surely, despite Pembroke's assertions, she had plenty of friends in attendance. He stood for a moment and weighed his own options: everyone with whom he could claim more than a passing acquaintance was occupied. Darcy and Miss Bennet had joined the dancing; the brilliance in Miss Bennet's eyes and the smile on Darcy's face convinced him they were better off enjoying each other than entertaining him. He saw Mrs Tournier speaking with a lady on the sofa, but her hands were flying about and she was so obviously in the middle of a heated conversation that he could not interrupt.

His lordship could never be accused of being a socially awkward man and, if he had cared to, he could have adopted his carefree London persona, sought out his host and intimated himself into the best company, joining in the frivolity surrounding him, indeed becoming the life of the party. Or, if he was so inclined, he could ask to become acquainted with any of the ladies present, beginning a friendship that could very well lead to... but no, Clyne and Scotland were his escape from all that nonsense. So there he was, back where he started, with everyone of his particular acquaintance otherwise occupied — everyone except for the woman waiting in distress alone in the garden. There was nothing for it but to fetch the wine and return to her.

So, he found himself walking back again with a glass in hand. She was standing just where he had left her: by the open doors with her back turned to the room, which he took as an encouraging sign that she was not desperate to escape him or his assistance. She looked oddly relieved when he returned, but she appeared so agitated and restless standing beside him that he then began to suspect she must share his misgivings. He once again cast a glance into the salon through the opened windows to find some other means of relief for her obvious distress.

"Lord Baugham, please stay for a moment," she suddenly blurted out. "I have not had the opportunity to thank you for coming to my aid." With a little smile she added, "As you can imagine I do not often find myself at a loss for words, and I am more grateful than I can say that you were not."

She cleared her throat.

"And…" Her voice was unsteady but she pressed on regardless, "among those words were some that were very kind to me yet, at least in your case, quite undeserved. You praised my judgement to Mr Pembroke, and we both know that in my dealings with you, that quality, on occasion, has been sorely lacking. I am sorry that this has been so, please forgive my impertinent behaviour."

Looking up to him earnestly, she then asked a question obviously most important to her. "Please… please do not believe the vile things that he said about me."

With that plea, her thin veneer of composure cracked. She turned away as tears she could not control began to stream down her face.

IT WAS A SURPRISING MOVE on her part in his lordship's eyes, one that left him dumfounded. Added to the shock of such unexpected behaviour was his own intense discomfort, because there were few things that made him more ill at ease than a woman crying. Somehow he had the presence of mind to hand her a handkerchief and quietly guide her further out to the garden without finding a single comforting word to offer her. They sat just beyond the windows, protected by the darkness of the night. There they would be safe from prying eyes since the dancing continued and the room was filled with music and laughter and steps on the floor. Her shoulders shook quietly and she seemed so alone and vulnerable and utterly desperate. Still he had nothing to say, but his position was very quickly becoming unbearable.

"Oh please, Miss Tournier" he shot to his feet when his discomfort became too acute. "Please do not cry! Oh, this is terrible. I am so sorry. Please, is there nothing I can do?" She shook her head and buried her face and quietly sobbed more deeply into the white fabric of his handkerchief. Baugham got up in a violent movement and started pacing.

"Please, Miss Tournier, I know we have not always seen eye to eye, but I would never wish to see you in such pain. I beg of you, disregard Mr Pembroke. I certainly do. He is his own worst enemy and no one could be of any doubt of his character once they spend more than ten minutes in his presence. I know all the blame and fault must lie with him and whatever the accusation is he makes must be groundless.

And so must anyone who knows you and your family. Of course I pay no importance whatsoever to his words. To do so would never cross my mind. Please do not distress yourself or ever doubt that."

She seemed to have calmed down a little and was silently drying her eyes, stealing what looked like incredulous glances at his restless movements. In the dark it was impossible to see her face clearly or hear if she was still softly sobbing. Baugham drew a breath and ran his hand through his hair.

"That villain, that fiend! You do realise that I shall now have to run my sword through him after all? It will be a pleasure, I promise you, but I need to assure myself that you will be well before that. Please?"

He stopped in front of her. When she turned her face toward him again, Lord Baugham was surprised to find her smiling.

"Thank you for your kind offer," she said, with a slight sniffling giggle. "I so wish I could take you up on it, but such a man is not worth the trouble you would bring down on yourself for the deed."

Looking down at her lap as she folded his handkerchief over and over, in a quieter voice she continued. "And thank you for your kind words just now…and for not believing him."

She straightened her shoulders and he could see her struggle to keep a cheerful expression on her face.

"I am really quite well now if you wish to go back to the party."

Baugham was so relieved that the tears were over he let a grin spread on his face and settled himself opposite her on the balustrade, crossing his arms.

"I am glad to see you have recovered so well, Miss Tournier. You know, Mr Pembroke is likely to encounter stiff opposition from me if he ever hopes to repeat his performance. I will henceforth jealously protect my interests, for I am quite certain it is *my* unique privilege to be uncivil and rude to you. I am so very good at it, after all, and will not readily share it with pompous amateurs."

This time her smile was less strained, although her big, dark eyes were still soft with recently shed tears.

"I am quite content to bestow to you the sole right to behave rudely and uncivil towards me," she replied, "but only if I am given that same right in return. I believe we have both shown our skill and determination to excel in that area, we should both be rewarded, don't you think?"

"It would be an honour to be insulted by you at regular intervals, Miss Tournier. I absolutely accept your proposal!"

She smiled and sipped her wine. Despite the chill in the air and his earlier reservations, he found he was rather comfortable out there in the quiet, away from the increasingly boisterous crowd inside the house. But, he realised, they really should be getting back. It was not wise for her to stay away so long after a scene that had surely been witnessed by others. He stood up and reached out his hand to her, giving his most brilliant smile, hoping his charm would work on her reluctance this once at least.

131

"Now, my dear Miss Tournier! No more Mr Pembroke and no more skulking around in the shadows, hiding the brightest jewel of the evening. It has been my experience in life that good name and position will very often hide maggots and rot, whereas a diamond will shine in any gutter if you only let yourself see it."

Her face might be indiscernible in the dark, but her voice betrayed good-natured surprise.

"Are you saying I am in the gutter, my lord?"

"No, not at all," he laughed. "Surely not even I would dare slur our host's dwelling like that, but as Chinese generals have known for over two thousand years: all warfare is based on deception. So even if you do not feel it to be tempting, you must trust me on this — you need to dance!"

To his surprise, she accepted his offered hand, stood and accompanied him back into the house. As they walked, she turned a genuine smile upon him.

"I *will* trust you on this. Though I must say I am a trifle disappointed in you. You missed a prime opportunity to insult me just now."

He did not even give her a glance, but his blue eyes sparkled as he surveyed the room to find a conspicuous enough place in the dancing line to fulfil his goal for her.

"Oh, there will be others, Miss Tournier. Plenty of others…"

She removed her shawl and draped it on the back of a chair, the old dress all but forgotten. Taking his arm again she allowed herself to be led to the dance.

"I quite depend upon it, my lord."

ONCE THE DANCE ENDED, THERE was not much left of the despondent, sobbing and shaking woman he had helped out on the terrace a little while before and Lord Baugham was very much grateful to her for that. She had done very well, holding her head high in almost childish defiance which, he found to his amusement, he had liked very much. Also, she had not once let her eyes stray outside the dance and had shown quite a graceful turn. He could now very well see that his stubbornness and even liberal actions on that lady's behalf had paid off. Her cheeks were glowing and she looked radiant and happy from her turn on the dance floor as he led her away again.

His train of thought was interrupted when his partner's attention turned from him to her soft and laughing cousin, cheerfully approaching her and exclaiming the obvious.

"There you are, Holly!" Miss Bennet said. "Did I not tell you that you would enjoy yourself this evening? Such lively music! Such fine dancing!"

Baugham let Miss Tournier's arm slip out of his before he heard Darcy's voice behind him.

"Miss Tournier," he was addressing her with a twinkle in his eye, "I think I must thank you for being a lovely enough incentive to cause my friend to break his annoying isolation from local society sooner than my nagging ever could have done. He had all but sworn to me he would not dance this evening, and now he has! Twice! With you! It leaves me quite hopeful, because I, for one, have never met anyone who knew less of what, or who, surrounds his home."

Baugham gave him a look and a theatrical sigh of resignation.

"Quality before quantity, Darcy," he said. "Do you really want to argue with me on that?"

"Not at all, my friend, but I should still like to see you become more involved in..." Darcy glanced toward Miss Bennet, who was leaning in close to her cousin, laughing and speaking animatedly. "Perhaps Miss Tournier could provide you with a few, useful introductions?"

Darcy was so obviously seeking to turn Miss Bennet's attention away from her cousin and onto himself again, that Baugham turned back to Miss Tournier and smiled. He had no particular wish to become acquainted with anyone else, but Darcy's challenge was less than subtle so he played the friend and offered her his arm. Miss Tournier smiled, too, and allowed him to lead her away.

"I THINK," HIS LORDSHIP SAID as they slowly made their way across the room, "you really must forgive me, but as much as I am loath to disappoint the expectations of my friend, I find that currently I have no interest in soliciting any company in addition to what I already have found."

For no discernable reason Holly felt a slight flush rise in her cheeks, but his lordship chatted on, apparently not expecting any reply.

"But there is a confession that goes along with this stubbornness, which I hope will excuse me in your eyes, lest you think me devoid of all polish or politeness, or hopelessly taciturn and hermitic, in choosing to go through an evening with as few introductions as possible! You see, Scotland never sees my social side. I have a very complicated life in London. And elsewhere. The reason I come here is because I love Clyne and I love my freedom and my solitude and for various reasons, I do not care to share or expose my sentiments to a wider circle. I am afraid I cannot explain it better. I meant it when I said that I do not encourage social connections when I am here. It disserves my affection for this place and its importance to me. I have a house in London and an estate in Cheshire. Both of them are useful, but I have a home at Clyne. And that is necessary. I trust I can rely on your understanding?"

Holly felt slightly ashamed of the way she had so blithely held Lord Baugham's attachments and feelings for Clyne in contempt, as well as a bit confused at Lord Baugham's confession, and she could not help feeling curious about what sort of "complications" his life in London held. It was not her place, however, to pry and she thought she should at least acknowledge his right to love the area as much as she did. After this night's events, she hardly owed him any less.

"I think I understand your feelings for this place, my lord. I must confess that for all the years I spent in Edinburgh, I never lost my yearning to be here...home. And, despite everything, I am very happy to be home now, I *hope* for good."

"So then, there is nothing that could persuade you to leave? That is, if I am not being presumptuous in my questioning, you would want to stay at Rosefarm? Always?"

133

"Oh, I do not mean that I would never wish to travel. I have an extensive list of places I wish to see, however unlikely the possibility is, but, my home and my heart are right here in this village and at Rosefarm."

"I see. Quite understandable. I thought perhaps the memory of your father might induce you to confess to a partiality for other places as well."

Holly smiled a little sadly.

"Well Paris, of course, is at the top of my list. When I was a little girl, my Papa would tell me stories of how beautiful and how magical it was. The museums, the gardens, the salons…someday…" She turned to him. "Have you ever seen Paris, Lord Baugham?"

He intently fixed her eyes with his and was quiet for too long a time.

"No," he finally said. "It has not been possible to do so in very many years, as you know."

He realised they had walked the whole length of the room and ended up on the opposite side without speaking to a single person beside each other. They paused by the windows and Baugham faced her, smiling.

"I see I have had the good fortune to stumble upon the one inhabitant of my neighbourhood whose company cannot be bettered. I was right: apparently there is no one in the entire room who can satisfy me better than what I already have found of my own accord. I must regard myself as a very skilful and very lucky man at the same time then."

"Lord Baugham, you are entirely *too* skilled at flattery," she lightly jested. "No wonder your life elsewhere is so full of complications. I shouldn't wonder if they were all of the female variety."

IT HAD BEEN A PERFECTLY pleasant moment, Baugham reflected, standing there with such unexpected company, chatting away as one does in ball rooms all the time, but some unhappy recollections now intruded on this pleasant scene. While in residence, he was perfectly happy with his way of life in Town — complications and all — but once he was away he did not always look back at his doings there with complete satisfaction. He did not wish to reflect upon such things here, nor was he comfortable that his conversation with Miss Tournier was touching so near to that aspect of his life. This was not where he wanted to go nor the game he wanted to play here.

He surveyed the room and caught sight of Mrs Tournier, somewhat more subdued, sitting on the same sofa.

"I think, Miss Tournier, I have been ignoring your mother for far too long. She will not forgive me easily or attempt to restrain her reproofs if I do not remedy it, I think. Will you join me?"

He caught her looking at him with a curious glance. He answered it openly and the faintest blush crept across her cheeks.

"Oh, I am just trying to decide how much to tell Maman about Mr Pembroke. She has a very strong opinion of him and I am not sure what her reaction will be if she discovers he...what happened earlier, I mean."

Baugham smiled when he saw her anxiety and was reminded of Mrs Tournier's direct ways.

"Why, you must tell her the truth, of course," he slyly whispered. "That you have engaged me and my sword to discipline him at the slightest trespass against you, and that that makes him a marked man and in mortal danger. Really, all things considered, that should make your mother pity him."

MRS TOURNIER MET THEIR EYES as they made their way towards her and, although she smiled, she did not look at all pleased.

"So, you have come to rescue me at last?" she asked as her daughter sat down beside her. "And you, my lord, do not even contemplate leaving again straight away for I am quite put out! I know one should never expect decent conversation or interesting discourse when at Lady Tristam's *musicale*, but I had no idea my only salvation from an extremely dull evening would be dependent on a young priest from Fife! He was well-read enough, but I am now so bored I could cry!"

"Oh Maman!" her daughter sighed and gave Lord Baugham a desperate glance.

Mrs Tournier looked at her daughter, and then she quickly glanced over to the gentleman to see what his reaction was. His lordship was standing still by the chair and wearing an amused, but completely non-committal, smile.

"The only thing that has given me any kind of pleasure or entertainment so far this evening was seeing the two of you out on the dance floor and conversing without a single temper tantrum or sulking face between you. Quite remarkable! By the looks of it, it was not as easy as it appeared from the outside. My daughter, I think, is quite exhausted from the experience. Exhausted, but very bright-eyed, I might add."

"Oh, I have every confidence her fatigue is wholly due to the dancing," his lordship mused. "I suspect Miss Tournier does not get to dance as much as she should. It is very beneficial exercise, I find, for a wide variety of ills. And it suits her well. I would venture to say looking happy suits her very well."

Mrs Tournier looked at her silent daughter.

"Indeed," she curtly said. "All this dancing of yours makes me quite long for a glass of wine; how about you, my dear?"

"Say no more!" his lordship laughed. "I am on my way!"

As he left the ladies, Mrs Tournier looked after him with narrowed eyes for a long time and then turned to her daughter.

"The reason I am most displeased with my evening so far is that I have not been able to take part in any of the truly interesting events. I see there were words exchanged between Mr Pembroke and his lordship in your presence; I saw you disappear with Lord Baugham in tow; I saw you dance and laugh with him; I saw my niece and her admirer fending off interruptions to their apparently fascinating study of the view from the eastern windows, and now I have you here beside me looking weary, but with blossoming cheeks and kind eyes on his lordship and I have no inkling of what

135

is happening. How am I supposed to support any of it?!"

Holly closed her eyes and leaned against the back of the sofa to rest her head for a moment then began to speak in a quiet voice:

"His lordship was very kind when Mr Pembroke came up to me and…he wanted an introduction and…well, Maman, you know how he can be sometimes. I was caught by surprise and couldn't respond myself. Lord Baugham was very kind…. He said I should dance and so I did. It did take my mind off things but I am very tired now…"

Holly took her mother's hand in hers and squeezed it, falling silent. For the time being, that was all the information her mother could get from her.

Mrs Tournier looked at her daughter with regret, for she could see all was not well with her in spite of her smile and flushed cheeks. If she had anticipated that Mr Pembroke would have accosted her daughter for the requested introduction to his lordship and Mr Darcy, she never would have refused — in her typically caustic manner when forced to speak to the man — to perform the service herself.

WHEN BAUGHAM RETURNED HE SETTLED beside the two ladies and watched them: Miss Tournier a little pale and quiet, Mrs Tournier developing a mischievous glint in her eye.

"Lord Baugham," she began, "I am told you performed one kind service to my daughter already this evening; are you quite finished playing the hero, or may I make one more appeal to you?"

"As always, I am at your service, madam," was his answer. "How may I be of assistance?"

"As you know, Mr Darcy very kindly sent his carriage for us this evening — if I could prevail upon your kind assistance by way of an escort when it is convenient for you. Mr Pembroke, I am sure, would not care to have his merriment so soon interrupted, nor am I opposed to his spending time in other company.

"At the same time, I have not yet had anything of interest happen to me this evening and even though I presume my daughter has found much more to her delight than she anticipated, she is very tired. This is all provided, of course, that you can do without the imminent vocal performance by Miss Tristam, accompanied on harp and pianoforte by her sisters. "

His lordship stood with remarkable speed.

"You may rest assured nothing would give me more pleasure than to personally see you home. I will find Darcy this instant to inform him of the change of plans."

He hesitated and leaned over the back of the sofa to catch the ear of Mrs Tournier.

"I have a request to make of you, madam," Baugham whispered urgently. "Ostensibly Mr Darcy is here to hunt. Game, I mean. Well, *that* is not going very well and my housekeeper is sorely disappointed in our efforts so far. I wonder would you be so kind as to forward an invitation to your…guest, Mr Pembroke? Perhaps he would be interested in aiding our hunting ambitions on an expedition or two?"

"Are you going to take him down the glen and shoot him?" Mrs Tournier asked.

136

"That would be a favour on *your* part, indeed."

Lord Baugham laughed softly even though Mrs Tournier's statement sounded perfectly serious. He gave Miss Tournier a hasty look, but she was watching the crowd although still holding onto her mother's hand.

"So I understand," Baugham said, "however, on Mrs McLaughlin's displeasure that would have scant effect and I am soliciting on my own selfish behalf here, madam."

The lady gave him a shrewd look. "There's a great career as a house whip awaiting you should you be inclined to enter politics," she said. "Persuasive powers that promise something for everyone, is it?"

"Perish the thought!" Baugham said with feeling. "All I want is meat on my table and for my housekeeper to stop nagging me."

"Certainly I will forward the invitation if you insist upon it, but I am not convinced myself of Mr Pembroke's sporting prowess."

"Well, my friend's aim improves significantly with his level of frustration, so I think we shall be well provided for." Baugham winked at Mrs Tournier and with a mischievous smile on his lips, he departed.

When Mr Darcy was found — once more by a dark window, enjoying a dark view with his luminous and sparkling partner — he was more than happy to declare his readiness to see Miss Bennet home safely once the festivities were over, if Miss and Mrs Tournier preferred to leave early.

"Oh, I am not going anywhere!" Mrs Tournier said, lifting her eyebrows. "What a notion! Did I not say nothing of interest has happened to me yet? I will most certainly not leave before something does! But, Mr Darcy, I will most willingly accept you as a more suitable substitute on the journey home."

His lordship's carriage was quietly ordered and, due to the bustle that accompanied the Miss Tristams' impending performance, in which it was difficult to determine whether the number of guests moving in to the music room was quite equal to the number making their way out — they managed to leave without attracting notice. The ride to Rosefarm was quiet, a circumstance for which they both were grateful, and Lord Baugham was everything that was polite and proper as he handed Miss Tournier out of the carriage and escorted her to her door. Then with a smile and a bow he was gone, leaving her to wonder at the strange turn of events.

HOLLY PUSHED THE DOOR OPEN and stood still in the small hall after closing it behind her. It was cold and eerily quiet, not a sound to be heard in a household that otherwise was more cramped and restless than usual. She could hear the clock ticking in the parlour as she quietly moved along the hall, removing her gloves and untying her cloak. Peeking inside, she watched how the moonlight cast a long silvery shadow across the dark room. It looked magical and she tiptoed inside to enjoy it.

The light lay over the sofa and Holly sank down into it quietly. She slipped off her shoes and, drawing her feet up underneath her, all she could hear was the slight creaking of the springs of the sofa and her own stays. Then there was a deep sigh, which filled the room like a shout. She was slightly startled herself and, as if fearing to disturb the sleeping house itself, took pains to sit perfectly still and quiet for a few minutes until peace returned.

She was alone, but not lonely in her home. A wonderful feeling, even though the evening itself had been quite stressful. Without really noticing it, she slipped into thoughts about her companion in the carriage ride home. Was he sitting in a dark and silent room like herself, thinking about what had passed at the Tristams'? And how was he thinking about it? He seemed pleasant enough on the way home and had been more than generous and gentleman-like when she had needed it, but on reflection, how did he view the evening and her part in it?

She jumped up off her seat. She did not want to think about Lord Baugham and, even less, concern herself with what he thought of her or her misfortunes. She walked steadfastly out of the room again and climbed the stairs to her room, for once not avoiding the creaking floorboards on her way but rather aiming for them with determined steps.

THE MASTER OF CLYNE WAS not particularly fond of empty or silent houses and so he did not share Miss Tournier's quiet reflections in the moonlight at any point. He chatted amiably to Mr McLaughlin as he brushed down the horses, he wandered down the hall and noted the light in the kitchen as Mrs McLaughlin sat up with some silent chore awaiting her husband, and he met Riemann in his chambers and thanked him for his excellent choice in evening wear

It was not until he lay in his bed and debated putting out his candle versus picking up his book that his thoughts turned to the evening's proceedings.

The event itself was everything he had come to expect from a country squire with pretensions of condescension and importance, but Sir Torquil was an outgoing and friendly man and Baugham could not fault his hospitality. Nor, when observed dispassionately, could he blame him or his wife for putting their daughters forward to any likely prospects that might appear. From what he had observed, Mrs McLaughlin was correct in her assessment: a young lady's opportunities were severely limited in this little corner of Scotland. That went a long way to explaining the general expectations of the neighbourhood concerning Mr Grant and Miss Tournier. Not that the poor man had any chance, he smiled and recalled the desperate look in her eyes as she called him over to make the introductions. No, poor Grant was doomed to be disappointed.

His mind idly wandered through the crowd, wondering if there were any other likely candidates, but though she and her cousin had surely attracted much notice among the male guests that evening, none of the gentlemen had warranted much notice from Miss Tournier in return — until that Pembroke fellow. He reflected with satisfaction that he had been able to do her some little service in that instance. Yes, the look on the man's face as he left them, and the opportunity to make up for his own too frequently unforgivable behaviour in the lady's presence, pleased him.

"Baugham, my lad," he smiled to himself, "take care. One would think you are

138

getting rather too fond of rescuing rural schoolmistresses in distress and wasting your breath on putting down boorish country squires. That will never do. Even if you do decide you're tired of squabbling Town sisters."

Suddenly he was confronted with a feeling of distaste when reminded of his idle dabbling with Mrs Ashton and Lady Merriwether. He could not even classify them as pursuits, for neither one had required much pursuing. The contrast between these women who would so lightly enter into indiscretions and one who was completely mortified by the mere suggestion of it, rather turned his stomach and shone an un-flattering light on his own behaviours.

He tossed his book aside; he snuffed out the light and turned over to sleep. *No matter*, he thought as he closed his eyes, *no sense in dredging these things up now. I am at Clyne. That part of me is left behind for now.*

Chapter 13

A Willingness to Challenge the Weather Brings Surprises

BAUGHAM glanced at Mr McLaughlin sitting beside him on the bench in the stables cleaning and greasing a saddle. He himself had absentmindedly been taking his gun apart for cleaning for the past half hour, lost in his thoughts.

He had wandered down to the stables with the expressed purpose of finding Mr McLaughlin to arrange for the spur of the moment hunting trip, but his genuine quest was for the opportunity to vent his thoughts in a new setting.

So he sat on that bench with the always quiet Mr McLaughlin at his side, exchanging not more than a few words about weather, state of saddles and horses. Still his lordship made no progress in clearing his muddled thoughts.

Now what? His gun was clean. Mr McLaughlin had been given his assignments. It was still early in the morning and Darcy would most probably be off for hours yet and then come back and continue in his infuriating self-satisfaction. Baugham nervously tapped his fingers against each other and looked out into the swirling mist through the stable door.

A ride. That's what was needed, despite the damp and fog, it was movement and exercise he craved. He had been idle and trapped indoors for too long now — no wonder his mind was unsettled and apt to wander in odd directions.

THE NOVEMBER FOG LAY THICK over the village also. Holly could hardly see her hand in front of her, but the cottage was so cramped and her thoughts likewise kept jostling for space and order in her head, so she had taken herself outside anyway. She stood with the rake in her hands and made feeble attempts at scratching soaked leaves from the ground into an ordered pile that might someday be dry enough to be burnt.

A very apt metaphor for her own state of confusion, she thought. Should she burn the conclusions that her scattered thoughts piled into or leave them be? No matter, they would perish and be hidden when the first snow came anyway.

From somewhere in the mist came ghostlike sounds of squeaking carriage wheels and horses whinnying as they passed by on the road without ever being seen. She sighed and breathed in the damp air. The window in her mother's bedroom gave out only a faint light even though she was right underneath it. Mrs Tournier had hardly shown herself downstairs these past days and if Mr Pembroke made good on his boastful promise to go and shoot with the gentlemen tomorrow, Holly would forcefully drag her down from her room and make a point of sitting her in her favourite chair and indulging her as much as she could. *Poor Maman*, she thought, *she acts like a wounded beast.*

Normally she would have used her need for space and solitude to walk to the inn and pick up the post. These days, however, Elizabeth always was the one to do it and she would not relinquish the task. Jestingly, she said she was fascinated by the various ways one could accidentally meet acquaintances on such a short walk, but Holly knew that besides Mr Darcy taking his walks around the same paths she did these days, Elizabeth wanted to be the one who paid for the postage. She should feel embarrassed for that obvious concession to their lack of resources, but Holly was only grateful. So instead she stood in the gloom while her mind played the scenes from last night's party over and over.

After she had tortured herself long enough with Mr Pembroke's words and Primrose Tristam's looks, she turned to Lord Baugham's behaviour. It was puzzling to say the least. She had thought him to be shallow, but a shallow man would have either turned from her immediately, or even joined in the scorn and censure. He had done neither, showing himself to be a true friend and gentleman. But now...now she stood wondering whether the unforgiving light of day and distance from the immediacy of the situation had changed his opinion of her. And she wondered why she cared.

The sound of slow hoof beats brought Holly out of her reverie. She looked up, and to her surprise the very gentleman who had occupied her thoughts so persistently materialised through the mist. He reined his horse to a stop at the gate and she was suddenly unsure of what to do or how to act, but when he removed his hat and inquired as to her health and the health of her mother, Holly reverted back to the comfort of etiquette. She made her curtsey and greeted him.

"I am well, my lord, thank you. Maman is well too. Please, will you come in and have some tea?"

"I thank you, but I cannot stay," said his lordship, looking slightly awkward. "I was merely out for a ride and thought I might enquire as to...well, I can see that you are quite well this morning."

"I am, thank you, my lord," Holly managed to say.

"Good, good..." his lordship murmured. "I am glad to hear it..." His voice tapered off and he cast several glances around.

A sudden dread of reliving the discomfiture of the night before, of desperately casting about in her head for something to say, made Holly thankful he did not dismount, but he also did not appear to be preparing to ride off just yet either. He just sat there on his horse and looked down at her with a smile.

"I see you don't consider a late night to be an adequate excuse for staying inside, Miss Tournier. Very admirable! Tell me, do you enjoy working out of doors? I myself seem to be always looking for some bridge to repair or fence to mend. Any excuse for being outside and active."

With a sheepish smile, she gestured to her meagre pile of leaves.

"I'm afraid my mind has been a bit distracted and I haven't made much progress this morning."

She took a step forward, recalling that she owed him a debt of gratitude.

"But I should... I would like to thank you, yet again, for offering your aid and assistance to me last evening. I'm afraid I monopolised too much of your time and ruined any chance you may have had to enjoy the evening."

Somehow it seemed her words had an unexpected effect on his lordship and it was quite obvious he was struggling to answer her.

"Not at all, I assure you. You are not to think anything of the kind. I have made a vow never to tolerate tiresome people here in Scotland out of mere politeness, so you may rest assured that if I had preferred to be in any other company last night, I would have sought it. Since I did not, you may take that as an indication that your acquaintance is nothing but delightful to me."

If they had not been saved by the distraction of a small breeze scattering the pile of leaves and catching hold of the hem of her cloak, there might have been an awkward moment. His words came out a trifle more serious than he had planned and he saw a blush creep across her cheeks and her hand rise up to her tug at her earlobe. As she made no immediate reply, he smiled and shifted uncertainly in his saddle. With nothing more to say, he really should be getting on.

"Well I suppose I should be — "

"My lord!" she interrupted. "I would like to ask one more favour of you if I may. I would like to give you the correct circumstances surrounding my dismissal from Hockdown — I would not have you think any of the slanders spoken last night had any real basis."

"There really is no need, Miss Tournier, if it makes you uncomfortable." Baugham said gently. "As I have already told you, I give no credence to Mr Pembroke's uttering whatsoever and I do not wish to imply that it is any of my concern. You really do not owe me any explanations. I told you I have the highest regard for your character, and I do."

She looked him full in the face and smiled.

"It seems that I am continually thanking you lately. And so I will say it again: Thank you." He waved it off and looked down again to see a sly smile on her face.

"Miss Tournier?" he questioned, his own smile returning.

"I was just thinking, my lord. If you continue to behave in such a gallant manner, I will think you have forgotten the very exclusive privilege you were granted to insult me at every turn."

"I find that you are now being quite unfair to me, Miss Tournier, in challenging me to do what, at this moment, is impossible," Baugham answered with a glint in his eye.

The smile on her face grew broader and suddenly she burst into laughter; it was good to see her laugh after all the distressing emotions he had seen her go through. It took her a few moments to regain control and he enjoyed watching her efforts to do so.

"Oh, my lord, I believe you are a true master! Rest assured, if *at this moment*, I have given you no cause to abuse me — I am certain the future will provide you with ample opportunities. You are very skilled at combining flattery with insult."

He smiled at her, impressed that she read his subtle jest so easily, and since she had done so, relieved that his gamble had paid off.

Soon, however, the laughter slowed and turned into smiles, and presently he found that, even after the merriment subsided, he had kept his eyes on her. Her eyes sparkled, her breath was still coming heavily with the residual mirth and her cheeks were flushed with the release. With an effort he turned his gaze away, wondering at his rudeness.

"Ah, well…" he said.

"Yes," she said and looked away, too.

"You will give Mrs Tournier my regards? And Miss Bennet?"

"Of course. Thank you."

He felt giddy. Something was not right and he should go. He was suddenly very impatient to do so and turned his horse while taking his leave. He fancied he could feel Miss Tournier's eyes on him as he went on his way again.

A SHORT WHILE LATER, ANOTHER faint figure appeared at the garden gate; Holly gave a start, but then she recognised her cousin's figure. Strangely enough, Elizabeth moved more slowly than usual when back from her walks to the post office. When she came closer, Holly could see there was quite a bundle of mail so she should have been showing much more eagerness to relay them forward.

"Eliza!" Holly called to the clearly distracted figure. "You must say something. You look like a ghost walking out of the fog if you don't."

Elizabeth came closer and Holly could see she looked contemplative, but not sad.

"How about if I let you read a letter I received? You will find me an all too real, but fickle friend if you do."

Holly was disturbed by the tone of Elizabeth's voice. "What are you talking about?" She let her rake fall to the ground and hurriedly went up to her. "You could never be that!"

Elizabeth laid an opened letter in her cousin's hand and looked at her. "My father," she said. "You had better read it yourself." She looked around them. "Let's not stay here though. It's an eerie day and I'm sure the spirits are out to cause mischief. Let's find a little sheltered, warm corner of our own, shall we; where no one can find us for a while?"

UP IN HER ROOM, ON the bed supported by blankets and cushions and each other, Holly could not help but smile as she folded her Uncle Bennet's letter again. The tone was so familiar and his way of speaking through writing to his favourite daughter reminded her of her mother. Not that her mother would ever have written such a letter begging her to come home. The sentiment might be the same, but the unabashed need would have been cloaked in much more subtle language.

"He loves you very much," she said.

"I know," Elizabeth sighed, "and you, if anyone, can understand what a father's love does to a woman's determination."

They looked at each other in silence and Holly held out her hand.

"Go," she said.

"I will," Elizabeth answered as she took it in hers.

Then they smiled and leaned into each other, temples touching but eyes looking elsewhere. They sat silently for a long while in the little room.

"Do you remember who said it first?" Holly finally asked and sat up a little straighter. "'Go'. I think it was always you who instigated it. And I always stubbornly answered 'I will'. Again and again."

Elizabeth smiled. "No, I think it was you; when we were going to climb that enormous elm by the parson's farm. Then we fell down and hurt our behinds and it was so humiliating. People thought we had done something quite naughty and been punished, the way we could not sit down without wincing for a week! I'm sure that was your idea."

Holly gave a little laugh. "Well, I know it was you when we were going to cross the river in our bare feet, and you dared me and just would not shut up! Until you slipped and ended up too wet to pester me anymore."

"We were younger, though, when we climbed the tree," Elizabeth said, "twelve perhaps. The summer after…after your father died."

"Perhaps you're right," she sighed. "Our lives have certainly changed since then." She gave her cousin a shy look. "And I think yours will change even more soon."

Elizabeth did not answer but twisted her fingers through Holly's.

"And you?" she said. "What do you want out of life now?"

"Not so much anymore," Holly replied softly. "Regular letters from you, sugar for Maman's tea…and that Sir John's friend will find funding for his publication."

"Holly! So little?"

Holly stared at the swirling fog outside the window.

"Oh, Elizabeth, it feels like those wishes are ambitious enough in themselves lately. Once they are achieved I might set my sights a bit higher, but…"

She could feel her cousin's eyes upon her and though she continued to gaze out the window, she could just picture the creases of concern on Elizabeth's brow.

"I know," she went on. "I used to have such lofty dreams, didn't I? But Elizabeth, they were just dreams, too ambitious for a girl to achieve. I had always hoped that, with such parents as mine, I could make a difference in the world. Even after my own dreams had wilted, I, at least, hoped that I could teach and inspire others, but that only leads to slander and disgrace."

"My dear Holly," Elizabeth cried out in distress, "please do not sound so bereft! It tears at my heart."

"And don't *you* sound so despairing!" Holly turned to her cousin and gave her a half-smile. "It is nothing more than coming to terms with realities and my own limitations. I have always wanted my life to be meaningful, but I wonder if I have been looking for that meaning in the wrong place. Maybe for me, the daughter of Jean-Baptiste and Arabella Tournier, my duty is not to inspire those coming after, but to care for the one who has done her duty and suffered for it. In short, Elizabeth, I will do my best to take care of Maman and see that she lives in comfort and without worry. What loftier goal can there be for a daughter?"

Elizabeth narrowed her eyes and tried to speak sternly, "It is a lofty and admirable ambition indeed, but I don't believe that one must exclude the other. I know that you have already touched many lives, despite the fact that those horrible men stopped you, and I am sure you will touch many more. You might be discouraged right now, but you have always lived with such passion! I will never believe you can abandon it completely."

"Very well then, cousin, I promise that if any opportunity for the betterment of mankind comes across my path, I will pounce upon it. And now, in a demonstration of my philanthropic intent, I am going to charge into Maman's room, throw myself on her bed and disturb her piles of books and papers, and allow her to yell at me until her heart's content — and I think you should join me."

"I will."

DARCY WAS DIRECTING HIS BEST glare at him. The one that made footmen shiver and maids break out in uncontrollable sobs. Baugham had great respect for that stare, but at the same time he viewed it with more interest than fear. And besides, he was right in this and he knew it.

"I spent half an hour in the same carriage as that...man last night and I'll be damned if I will spend anymore under any other circumstances."

"You owe me a stag, remember?" Baugham said calmly and put down his glass.

"I did not promise it in Mr Pembroke's company. How is he going to contribute towards it exactly?"

"As I told Mrs Tournier, your aim is flawless when you are fuming."

The glare, however ineffective, had not diminished. "And why exactly was my aim a topic of conversation between you and Mrs Tournier?"

Baugham calmly pulled the stopper from the bottle and topped off his drink. His silent gesture of offer was waved off by Darcy in irritation.

"I offered to take him off of her hands for a day." He held up his hand to forestall the coming protest of indignation. "Darcy, you had your fill of him after thirty minutes in a carriage; the ladies have been trapped in that small cottage with him for *days*. Where is your sense of chivalry? Do you not wish to be of service to at least *one* of the residents of Rosefarm?"

Darcy leaned back in admission of defeat, though his demeanour had by no means changed.

"Your tactics, Baugham, are underhanded and detestable. Very well, I will agree to it, but at the end of it I will never owe you anything more — ever! Mark my words, by the end of the day you will see just how right I am."

Taking a sip, his eyes grown a little colder, Baugham replied, "Oh, I don't doubt that. Not at all."

WOMEN'S LAUGHTER AND VOICES INTERRUPTING one another filtered into the Rosefarm kitchen from the parlour. Mrs Higgins put her used iron back on the hearth and picked up a hot new one.

"That Mr Darcy is such a fine and considerate gentleman! I wonder if he realised just how much service he was to this house when he asked Mr Pembroke to come and shoot with him and his lairdship?"

Mrs McLaughlin was helping her cousin by dipping her fingers into the water bowl and sprinkling the fabric at regular intervals, but she suddenly stopped.

"Mr Darcy? It was nae Mr Darcy who came up with that thought. His lairdship it was. For some queerie reason," she added muttering.

Mrs Higgins also stopped with her iron for a moment. "Really? Aye, well he wasnae aware of the gentleman's true nature, I would suppose."

"And ye are, Rosie?"

"I've seen enough of his behaviour the times he comes to stay to know what sort of man he is. Which makes me just as thankful as the rest of the household to his lairdship — whate'er his motives."

There was a slight silence when Mrs Higgins let the heavy hot iron gently smooth over the wrinkles of a petticoat and Mrs McLaughlin played with her fingers in the water between sprinklings.

"What is it with ye?" Mrs Higgins gave her cousin a suspicious look.

"His lairdship is a good man," Mrs McLaughlin slowly said, "but he is nae charitably inclined, as ye might say. Especially here at Clyne. He doesna go out of his way to oblige folk if he can help it."

"So?"

"So there must be something in this that gives service to him, too. Or someone."

MR DARCY HAD FULFILLED ALL expectations and was not only instrumental in bringing down a magnificent stag with two well directed and very cold-blooded — if not foolhardy — shots, but also had been very busy adding to the gentlemen's bounty by shooting practically every piece of fowl that crossed the sky on the way up and down to the hunting grounds. Despite this obvious triumph, his glare was worse than ever and his jaw was set so tightly he had long ago ceased trying to wrench it open to take part in the general conversation as they returned home to Clyne.

Baugham on the other hand, whose irritation rather expressed itself in restlessness and sarcasm, had a very light bag and a very dry mouth. The bottle of whiskey had very soon been emptied and not only by his lordship. Pembroke was a decent shot, but he was evidently more anxious to prove it through nonchalance and boasting than by actual deeds.

They left their helpers to deal with the carcass and following in Mr Darcy's urgent strides, headed towards Clyne with their bags filled from Darcy's work.

Baugham marched on, listening to the crunch of the dried brush and leaves under his feet, regretting the empty bottle in Mr McLaughlin's pack and steeling himself for his next unpleasant task. Soon enough, a marginally gracious invitation to dine was offered and accepted, with only one indiscernible grunt emanating from Darcy as a consequence. The gentlemen headed to their quarters, Mr Pembroke was given the use of a guest room and in half an hour's time they were seated in the library, washed up and somewhat refreshed — and conversing awkwardly while awaiting dinner.

Darcy's temper had recovered sufficiently to try to take some of the pressure off of Baugham, so he started a conversation while their host generously filled three glasses.

"Do your plans keep you in Clanough for much longer, Pembroke?" was all he asked, but he felt quite pleased with himself for managing that much.

Pembroke accepted the glass from his lordship, sniffed it inquisitively and took a small taste. He then, to Baugham's great irritation, lifted it up in acknowledgment of its quality and gave him an approving nod. Exhibiting a great deal of self-control, Baugham smiled back tightly and availed himself of a large swallow of the commended substance.

"Oh," Pembroke finally replied to Darcy's question, "I think I will be here for several more days. I have some writing to complete before I return to Edinburgh and Rosefarm Cottage is a quiet, convenient place to work. I find it to be a very satisfactory arrangement."

"I wonder," Baugham drawled, "how convenient or satisfactory your hostess finds this…arrangement? The cottage is very small and they do already have one houseguest."

"I suppose," Pembroke smiled, "that is the advantage of being the landlord. My convenience takes precedence. And Miss Bennet appears happy enough to share with her cousin. Girls like that sort of thing, you know."

Lord Baugham was not at all pleased to hear his own words repeated by this pompous, inconsiderate man, and he felt a renewed sympathy for Miss Tournier's irritation at hearing them from him. They had a paternalistic and patronising sound, and he was sorely tempted to repeat the lady's response to the man across from him. Thankfully Darcy jumped in at that moment.

"I suppose that space will not always be so much of a problem on future visits. Miss Bennet will be returning home and Miss Tournier will surely marry at some point. After that, you will only have Mrs Tournier for company."

Baugham could see a comment rising to Pembroke's lips, a comment, if spoken, he was certain he would find offensive and then be compelled to ask the man to leave. Trying to keep to his purpose of providing a very much needed respite for the ladies, he deflected it with the first thing he could think of to say.

"It's a bit curious," Baugham began quickly, "in my experience, country girls tend to marry and settle down earlier than Town girls, but yet neither Miss Bennet nor Miss Tournier are married — nor are either of them spoken for I believe."

He watched to see if Darcy would take exception to his hasty remark, but to his surprise, Pembroke spoke up instead.

"Well, I know nothing about Miss Bennet's prospects," he snorted, "but Miss Tournier has had more offers than one would expect."

Baugham's eyebrows rose slightly at this intelligence, "Indeed? And she has accepted none of them?"

"Nor will she, as long as she is in the clutches of that mother of hers."

"So," Darcy smiled tightly in an attempt to inject some humour into the exchange, "one must court the mother in order to win the daughter? This has the makings of a Shakespearean farce."

"Don't fool yourself, Darcy," Pembroke said, "this drama will not tie itself up as neatly *or* as quickly as that. I have spent the past five years trying to get back into that woman's good graces. It can't be done, I tell you. She doesn't believe anyone is good enough for her precious daughter, and Miss Tournier is fully ruled by her mother in that regard."

"*Back* into her good graces, Pembroke?" Baugham idly questioned, but to his irritation, Pembroke seemingly lost interest in the subject and returned his attention to the glass in his hand and Baugham's best whiskey.

"The Tourniers are very lucky, you know," he drawled, "and not the poor pitiful country bumpkins you make them out to be. They have been treated very generously by my parents who, even though their original friend, Monsieur Tournier, is long since deceased, and Mrs Tournier is in no way without relatives of her own she might appeal to, have let them stay on at their property on *very* generous terms. A bit too generous one could even say, since they seem to object to the actual owner of their cottage using it for his immediate needs on quite reasonable terms."

At the mention of Mrs Tournier's relations Darcy lost his resolution to contribute to a civil conversation and drained his glass in one go. He thrust it out towards his friend, who promptly filled it to the rim. Looks were exchanged and Darcy sunk into a morbid silence.

Baugham sighed. This was going to be a long evening indeed.

WHEN THEY FINALLY SAW THE back of Mr Pembroke, Darcy had practically turned into an effigy of stone and Baugham contrasted his friend's pale and set countenance with his distinctly flushed and agitated one. As the door closed behind him, Baugham grabbed the poker and viciously attacked the dying embers in the grate, sending a flood of sparks upwards in a final display of fury. Darcy looked at him and, while still maintaining his exact position in his chair, the corners of his mouth twitched ever so slightly.

"Never," he said darkly, "never have you inflicted such pain upon me before, my friend. Not through broken ribs from fist fights or sparring matches ending in bloodshed or mental agony over hurt pride and lost challenges. The only comforting aspect is that you suffered as much as me."

"I did," Baugham said through clenched teeth. "God, if I have ever done anything so painful before in the name of charity..."

"Next time," Darcy said, "make a subscription to some worthy society instead."

"Like 'The Society for the Forceful Eviction of Pompous Persons from the Homes of Deserving Women'."

"Or we could just kill him," Darcy added darkly. "He is the sort of man who plans his own funeral meticulously. It would be a shame to miss it."

Wry smiles spread over the men's faces as they finally relaxed into a peaceful silence and the comfort denied them for so long. They sat, they drank a little more, they watched the glowing logs turn to black charred remains as the rain slowly picked up and began to drum on windows and roof.

"Rain," Darcy remarked. He got up from his chair and faced his friend. "One stag and I lost count of how many birds. The debt is yours, my friend. You will repay it handsomely when I invite any interested party from Rosefarm Cottage for tea tomorrow."

Baugham groaned. "Just not Mr Pembroke!" he shouted, as Darcy was about to walk out the door.

"I'll certainly do my best," was the answer before the door closed behind him.

Chapter 14

*Tea is once more Enjoyed and Important Thoughts are Shared at
the Eve of Departure Ending in Both Tears and Hope*

"WE will walk," Elizabeth said firmly. "Whether we are offered a carriage home or not probably depends upon how well 'we' can behave ourselves, but I will risk it. In fact, walking both ways is not an entirely unappealing prospect at this point."

Holly just smiled. As soon as Elizabeth had told her there was an invitation to Clyne Cottage for tea, she had gone around to the kitchen to see if her boots had dried up from her last venture outside that morning. Now her cousin and her mother stood facing each other in the hall 'discussing' the mode of transportation available and Mrs Tournier was frowning at Elizabeth's refusal of Mr Darcy's carriage. Mr Pembroke sat in the parlour swinging his crossed leg, listening to them with an amused smile. This was about him, he was certain. Since the carriage was refused and the young women were going to walk, he had declined the invitation, as had Mrs Tournier. If the carriage had been accepted they would have all gone.

"Holly needs this," Elizabeth said tightly and both women knew they were referring to an absence from Mr Pembroke. Mrs Tournier narrowed her eyes.

"And I do not?"

Elizabeth said nothing but returned her gaze steadily.

"You are entirely too stubborn for your own good, Elizabeth," her aunt finally said.

"Sticks and stones, Aunt," Elizabeth said and smiled.

It was a grey day, but the rain from the previous evening had stopped and the air was filled with scents and fresh reminders of the dormant green and earthy world. The two young women who made their way through the village, over the fields, and across the woods felt as if they had been released from a dungeon.

To her great surprise, Holly had felt a surge of happy expectation when Elizabeth shared Mr Darcy's invitation. Despite her difficulties with the present owner and the more than confusing way in which he had been acting lately, she had always viewed Clyne with curiosity and a wish that she might one day be so bold as to actually see what it was like inside. The old owner of the property had never earned the respect of anyone in the neighbouring village; it was common knowledge he preferred his other estate in Perthshire when he was not in Town pursuing a political career, and the estate had been all but ignored. But the house, with its warm coloured sandstone and unsuspecting prospect down to the river had always held promise — and, of course, the dilapidated estate of an absentee landlord was an ideal playground for disrespectful local children, which explained her familiarity with the grounds.

The inside of the house, however, was still a mystery; except for the kitchen. Holly told the story of her humiliation to Elizabeth, warning her against getting her feet wet. Elizabeth laughed and threatened to do just that, saying the prospect of digging her bare toes into a thick rug at a lord's lair was fast becoming too irresistible to ignore.

"I TRUST YOU ENJOYED YOUR walk, ladies?" Mr Darcy's mouth twitched slightly without ever losing its pleasant curve when he greeted them in the hall outside the drawing room where Mrs McLaughlin had escorted them.

"Of course, sir," Elizabeth said, smiling pleasantly. "I think I told you I would enjoy it. But I am rather surprised to see you did not feel a corresponding need to walk as a consequence."

Darcy sent her a smile and then turned to Holly and took her hand instead, welcoming her as well. It was a good thing he did so, for Holly felt slightly overwhelmed when finally confronted with the interior of the house. She looked around her: not grand, not fashionable, not overly impressive as far as furnishings at all, but it was a surprisingly warm and welcoming house, comfortable and certainly far more homelike than she had ever imagined. True, that stag head over the fireplace in the drawing room was very imposing, but other than that the room had a certain feel of domestic blindness to any desire to impress and an obvious inclination to bow more to the comfort and indulgencies of the inhabitants.

Just then the inhabitant himself stepped out of his drawing room to greet them.

"You took us quite by surprise!" the owner of Clyne Cottage said and smiled at them when Mr Darcy ushered them in. "Or me, rather. Darcy here was quick on his feet as usual."

"I think Mr Darcy could have told you we would most likely take the opportunity to walk, had he wanted to. He is well acquainted with my stubbornness on that subject," Elizabeth smiled. "Then you could have positioned yourself in the window, too, and been prepared."

Darcy gave what was a ghost of a smile, but Lord Baugham laughed.

"How well you know my friend's habits! But I will give you the best seat in the room if you guess my excuse."

"Sleeping, perhaps?" Holly said quietly.

Lord Baugham cast her a quick glance. "I see I shall have to do with the second best, Miss Tournier," he smiled. "What betrayed me?"

Holly gestured to her cheek and Lord Baugham wiped his with his coat sleeve.

"Printing ink?" he laughed. "Well, I am glad the offending newspaper has been banished from the room already. But you are here for tea, not parlour games, I hope."

His voice was pleasant enough, but a surprising question ran through his brain when Miss Tournier pointed to her cheek: *Is there no privacy from that woman?*

However it had begun, it turned out to be a very harmonious company that sat down for tea. As Mrs McLaughlin brought in offering after offering, even the gentlemen raised eyebrows at the abundance on display.

"I think Mrs McLaughlin was never convinced you would come by any other means than walking," Baugham finally observed. "My dear woman, there's enough here to feed an army!"

"We shall certainly be able to march on our stomachs back home again," Elizabeth remarked.

That exchange was typical of the afternoon. Elizabeth mostly kept up the conversation with able help from his lordship, while Mr Darcy was obviously content with watching Miss Bennet push back Lord Baugham's attempts at snaring her with her own words. Holly felt immensely cheered by the walk and the friendly atmosphere and was perfectly content just sitting within close range of the cream and sugar and her teacup near enough to her face to take in the heavenly smell when she was not actually drinking it.

During a lull in the conversation there was a sudden gust of wind through the trees outside, enough to make the windowpanes rattle. All four turned their eyes to the window to catch the branches of the closest trees swaying and rustling ominously.

"Rain," sighed Elizabeth. "You know, I used to blame Mr Darcy's solitary disposition in company as the reason he always showed such preference for gazing at prospects out of windows, but I have come to realise my error. Weather is an integral part of conversation in polite society and ignorance of it is an unpardonable sin. I know I have often been guilty of it when my optimism has got the better of my intelligence as to the conditions outside. Does it always rain here?"

"Yes," said Holly vigorously at the same time as his lordship emphatically said "No."

"Well, I blame my southernmost ancestry for my poor capacity to come to terms with Scottish weather sometimes," Holly smiled. "I don't suffer the worst of it very well, I'm afraid."

"Which would be most of the time in November," Elizabeth sighed.

"I think you must take care, Miss Bennet," Baugham said, "criticism always offends the newest convert the most and when it comes to the comforts of staying in Scotland that would be Mr Darcy. His resentment is a terrible thing, you know."

Mr Darcy gave a broad and calm smile towards Miss Bennet after directing a less openly interpretable look toward his host.

"I know Miss Bennet well enough to know she never means to offend. Only to challenge and laugh," he went on.

Elizabeth laughed. "There you are then! Or to chase away my fears by ridicule. This kind of weather makes me think of ghost stories. My cousin tells excellent ghost stories! The one of the Piper's Cave never fails!"

Holly shook her head gently. "You always want to hear it and then you always end up lighting far too many candles and singing merry tunes all night to chase your fright away."

"Well, with such a prospect I think we must insist upon hearing about the Piper's Cave, Miss Tournier!" Baugham leaned forward.

"You will be sorry if you do," Elizabeth answered before Holly could protest herself, "for then I will be forced to claim your carriage for the journey home instead of taking my cousin's narrow and dark shortcuts through the woods."

Darcy sent her an indulgent smile but reserved his words for Holly. "Miss Tournier," he said, "we really must insist. A story that has such an effect on Miss Bennet must be entertainment for us all — intentional and unintentional, I am sure."

Holly settled back. She would tell them a ghost story then. She smiled to her audience, a subtle change in her demeanour commanding their interest. If there was one thing she knew how to do, it was tell a story. Her mother's friends knew it and the girls at Hockdown knew it. She also enjoyed it herself, both because and despite the audience.

She dropped her voice to a melodic hum — warm but still full with the promise of unexpected twists — and held the rapt attention of her audience perfectly between glances at Elizabeth's face, which predictably paled as she proceeded through the story.

"Marquis Alexandré had an only daughter, the beautiful Isabeau," Holly began, "whom he would never let out of his sight. Men from all across the land would be pleased to seek her hand but the marquis, ever jealous of anyone who would take his daughter's love from him, had vowed that he would never allow her to marry. He proclaimed a terrible death awaited any man who dared to woo his daughter.

"One night, Isabeau was awakened by the most beautiful, haunting music she had ever heard. Unable to help herself, she was drawn to it — it was hypnotic. She followed the sounds outside and there she saw a handsome young piper, a young man from the village. He stopped playing and smiled at her — the loveliest smile she had ever seen — and then he spoke to her: tender words of love and longing. All night long they were together; Isabeau dancing while the piper played, they traded words of love and promise and when the sun came up he left, vowing that someday soon he would return for her and take her as his wife."

She could not help glancing at Mr Darcy then, but he sat motionless in his chair, listening and watching her tell her tale.

"But, the marquis had spies everywhere on his estate and they told him about this young piper. He flew into a rage and had the boy arrested and brought to him. Even under the cruellest torture, he would not renounce his love for Isabeau or his intention

153

to marry her, as poor as he was. The marquis was pitiless in his anger and fear and he threw the boy into a cave by the sea, chaining him to the rock face and threatening to bring Isabeau down to him to witness his degradation. The piper pleaded that he would do no such thing—'Please!' he cried, 'Do not let her see me this way.' But the marquis would not relent."

"Oh!" her cousin said in an involuntary little gasp. Holly smiled but went on.

"That night was a fierce storm, the worst that had been seen for untold years. Isabeau's poor lover was battered and beaten against the rocks as the angry sea surged into the cave. When Isabeau was brought to him the next morning, his body, still chained to the wall, was broken and he was nearly-drowned. She reached him just as he drew his last breath. 'Isabeau, my love,' he whispered, 'Dance for me, and I will forever play for you.' He died in her arms.

"Isabeau screamed and cried and shook him as if she could awaken him from that eternal sleep, but it was not to be. She reached into his pocket and took his pipe, holding it up to the marquis. 'He will play, and I will dance, Father, I will dance!' she cried."

At this point Mr Darcy was looking at Elizabeth with an expression partly of complete puzzlement and partly of worry. The lady herself had paled visibly, but did not notice that she had become a rival to Holly for Mr Darcy's attention. Holly moved a few inches and caught Elizabeth's hand, squeezing it playfully.

"She ran up to the highest cliff and, clutching the pipe to her breast, flung herself down to the rocks below. Her father, mad in his grief, took up her body, as beautiful in death as it had been in life, and carried it tenderly into the very cave where her lover had perished. There he sat for days upon days, moaning in lament, crying in his guilt and when the storms arose again he simply sat there, allowing the remorseless waves to beat and batter him against the rocks until he, too, was dead.

"Since that day, all the people around are afraid to venture near the Piper's Cave. They say that even now, when the wind is cold and the icy storms sweep across the frenzied sea, you can see them and hear them there, Isabeau and her lover, two ghostly white figures dancing and playing in the dead of night, together at last and forever. And the marquis, his terrible moans and cries echo endlessly through the cliffs while the waves crash against them, his grief and sorrow as eternal and relentless as Isabeau's joy—and it is said that you must beware, for if a man hears that terrible wailing while the seas rage, it is a sign that his dearest love is bound to die."

"Oh!" said Miss Bennet again, very much relieved that the story was ended and her colour began to return. Mr Darcy flashed a small amused smile, but Lord Baugham still stared at Miss Tournier in concentration even though the story was clearly over and she broke the spell of the terrible tale by laughing a little and patting her cousin's cheek. Not until Miss Tournier realised she was still being watched even though she was silent, and sent a questioning look to his lordship, did he avert his eyes and mumble something about it having been a well-told tale.

ELIZABETH WAS HAPPY. IT WAS obvious. Holly had been watching her again as
154

she shook away the effects of the story. It was sight for sore eyes to see her cousin so lively and gay, with an inner peace to her that shone through. But why were *her* eyes sore? She was happy if Elizabeth was happy. She was certain of that. What was this melancholy that penetrated even her sincerest wishes of joy?

Was it perhaps the fact that Elizabeth would be gone in a few days? Or the realisation that once her colour plates were finished there were no more immediate commissions or sources of income waiting for her except a vague promise of a young un-established geologist who had probably forgotten both her and his promise long ago. Holly sighed — she should start soliciting for work. Perhaps talk to Sir John or her mother's friends in Edinburgh. Perhaps start considering a position as a governess or teacher. Only as a last resort though. Pray to God it would not come to that! She looked down at the still abundant display of tea before her on the table and thought of her mother's fondness for her sugar. It just might yet come to that...

She hardly registered that Mr Darcy had moved over from the sparkling warmth of her cousin and came to stand beside her to fill his teacup. She performed the task and gave him a hasty smile, expecting him to move away from what must be the depressing sight of her brooding mood, but he did not.

"That was a gruesome story for such an educated and fine young woman to tell," he smiled. "You had me quite spellbound, which, of course, was your object."

Holly stared at him.

"Mr Darcy! I...well, perhaps you're right, but a father with an only daughter has no choice if he wants to pass on the legends of his childhood, I suppose."

"I suppose not. But it certainly was a tale worth risking a young girl's sensibility to pass on. You told it very well."

"So did he," Holly said in a smaller voice than she intended. That was all that she needed — to slip into melancholy over her father as well!

She cleared her throat and straightened her back to shake off the sadness that had almost gripped her, but Mr Darcy hastily began talking before she could open her mouth to move to another subject herself.

"My own father was a master at ghouly tales," he began in a more light-hearted tone. "It seems strange now, that one's favourite memories should be connected to such infinite frights."

"I think any time spent with a busy and adored man must be precious; even if it came at the price of sleepless nights and skittishness."

"Yes," Mr Darcy said quietly, "exactly."

He gave her a look and in that instant Holly saw something in the combined smile on his lips and the frown on his brow that she recognised. Mr Darcy's father had been well-loved by his son.

"Still, I think I was a little more fortunate than you were," Holly smiled as she poured herself a cup of tea, carefully slipping as much cream into the cup as she dared while continuing.

"In the matter of fathers or of ghost stories, Miss Tournier?" Darcy asked.

"In the matter of my sex, Mr Darcy; as a little girl, I had the privilege and ability to crawl upon my Papa's lap and hide my face in his coat if his stories frightened me. Somehow," she continued, "I doubt that young Master Darcy would have done likewise."

Darcy's laugh was soft and barely audible, but heartfelt, "No, you are right about that. No matter how frightened I would become I would have never admitted it — but I cannot recount how many nights I laid awake, hearing the sounds of organ music in the wind and listening for footsteps on the path outside." He smiled again. "It's funny, but the ghost always seemed to take the very path that led beneath my window."

"Yes, and every hollow in every rock became the Piper's Cave for me, no matter that we lived nowhere near the sea. But... I could not wait to sit at his feet again and watch his face and hear his voice as he would..." she stopped momentarily to swallow the silly lump that had risen in her throat. "What I wouldn't give..."

There was no need to finish the thought. She turned her eyes toward Mr Darcy, his face was soft and distant, feeling and knowing exactly what she meant. The sounds of laughter carrying across the room brought them back to the present, and after exchanging understanding smiles, they parted. Mr Darcy moved directly back to Elizabeth's side, Holly walked to the fireplace and sipped her tea thoughtfully.

THIS QUIET EXCHANGE HAD BEEN noticed by Lord Baugham. While Miss Tournier was busy telling the story, he had seen her come out of her quiet contentment, obviously enjoying herself without any self-consciousness or self-conceit at being the centre of attention. Then she had withdrawn and looked puzzled again until Darcy had spoken to her. Strangely enough, his taciturn friend, who could do a fair imitation of a stone effigy himself, had managed to draw Miss Tournier back into the light again.

Curiosity was his chief fault, he knew that, and this was irresistible. The evening at Sir Torquil's gave him even more fuel for thought, so he tentatively came around to stand next to her by the fire.

She smiled briefly at him as she noticed him approaching.

"Warming up your chilled bones, I see," Baugham said. "I think I need some reassurance that I am still among the living, myself."

Something in what he said seemed to make her frown for a moment, but she found her footing quickly. "I am glad to see my cousin recovering more quickly than usual," she nodded towards Elizabeth, who was obviously talking about quite other matters than ghost stories with Mr Darcy.

Baugham shuffled his feet.

"Miss Tournier, you must allow me — that is, I fear I neglected to properly welcome you. I find myself quite out of practice at playing host here in Scotland, you see. As I have already explained, I keep a very secluded household and company here. We have very few visitors and I must admit I prefer it that way."

"Well then, I am indeed privileged," Holly replied somewhat shortly, remembering his efforts that night at the Tristams' to explain his desire for isolation, and realising

156

he was now making it a point to bring it up again. "We do appreciate your sacrifice in receiving us despite your preferences."

Baugham wondered at the guardedness that overcame her countenance and tried to speak lightly. "Not at all. In fact, I am very happy to be able to welcome you properly into the rest of my home. Mrs McLaughlin's kitchen is very clean and comfortable, but I would hate to think that your knowledge of Clyne Cottage would end there."

Did he really have to bring up that afternoon in the kitchen? She groaned inwardly, concluding from his smile that he must have been excessively amused at her predicament then. Irritated and trying desperately not to allow the blush that threatened to rise, she changed the subject.

"Well, I *am* happy to at last be able to see the inside of the house. As you know I trespassed shamelessly on these grounds when I was a girl — the pool by the stream was one of my favourite spots — and more than once I walked through the woods to look at the house. I often wondered what it was like inside."

She looked around curiously. "The child in me always imagined grand rooms and fine furnishings; I see now I was quite off the mark…though I cannot say it is not better the way you have furnished it in reality. It seems…a proper house for its purpose and your affiliation with it."

Baugham felt very uncomfortable talking about his home as if it were an open house to be judged by its furnishing and style, as if it were a showpiece of the aristocracy, made to mirror the inhabitant's position, wealth and stature. And then yet another reference to his private sanctuaries! All he needed now was for her to tell him how to best catch the trout in that stream. He felt irrationally jealous. Anyway, this self-effacing manner of hers was most irritating. She was of an ancient and noble family on her father's side, the name she bore was a proud and splendid one, why did she insist on making out she was poor, humble and worthless? As if her income and how she came by it had anything to do with it?

"I am so happy you approve." He knew his voice had lost some of its warmth and the reply was mechanical, but he was powerless to stop it. And why should he? She looked at him with her large dark eyes as if completely innocent and childishly delighted with her discoveries and opinions, excitedly sharing them with him as if she was doing him a service to acquaint him with his own property! He cleared his throat. "I must confess I did not know that what I thought of as my private and most treasured spots around the grounds were common knowledge. I cannot say I have seen many trespassers. Not that they would have been wondered at, of course. It is, after all, the beauty of this place that convinced me to call this my home."

"Well, my lord, it would be hard indeed if a part-time resident would deny the beauties and joys of his land to the village children simply in order to keep them to himself when and if he happens to arrive. I cannot imagine anyone thinking himself harmed to know that his stream was giving happiness and refreshment to a few boys or girls."

Her eyes gave a flash directly at him, but then looked elsewhere. Baugham shrugged and looked elsewhere, too. His face was indiscernible but his eyes seemed to cloud over.

"Not harmed, Miss Tournier, simply jealous. Always jealous..."

But she turned back and gave him an incredulous stare.

"Jealous! Jealous of what? That these little children, who must join their parents in daily toil in order that they may be able to eat; that these little ones, who are destined to grow up to toil daily with their own children; that these little ones who have no hope of *ever* attaining such property but whose brightest hope is to be employed by one who does...

"You are *jealous* because they rob your stream of some pleasure and maybe a few fish?"

For a moment he felt his features harden and his heart quicken in indignation. He knew he must have looked cold as stone, but he also knew that his unreasonable anger was perfectly mirrored in her dark, flashing eyes and a mouth set tight into a line. She nervously touched her earlobe in an attempt to distract herself from her resentment and Baugham unconsciously stretched a few inches to be able to shift his eyes elsewhere.

"...unless you want to risk another fine rendition of the headless man walking the woods at night," Miss Bennet's voice rang out and interrupted the peculiar stand-off.

Holly turned away first and directed a strained smile towards Elizabeth. "Since I am the one who will have to endure any nightmares that will plague you, my foolhardy cousin, I am done with tales tonight."

Holly cast one last glance at Lord Baugham, but he was already looking elsewhere and did not catch the scorn in her eyes. On the other hand, his lordship was careful to direct his eyes to the window to make certain Miss Tournier did not catch the unbridled irritation in his.

AFTER THE LADIES LEFT, DARCY softly closed the door behind him and settled himself back in his chair.

"Now that was not so bad, was it?"

Lord Baugham still kept his back turned to his friend and stared out at the brown wet leaves swirling around in the gusts of wind over his lawn.

"Hmm."

"What?"

"Nothing."

Darcy looked at his friend for a moment.

"You are standing in front of the window assessing the view and the weather. That is my usual prerogative."

"Hmpf."

Baugham broke away from his idleness with a jerk and walked around the drawing room.

"I'll be in the library. Where is that newspaper?"

THE FOLLOWING DAY, THE GIRLS WALKED to the posting inn slowly, as if to delay the inevitable separation looming before them and enjoying one last private, heart-to-heart conversation.

"What do you think, Holly?"

Holly was quiet a while. "I think he loves you very much," she finally quietly said. Elizabeth smiled.

"But…" Holly went on, hesitating, "I'm sorry, but I have to say this too. I don't know *how* he loves you. I mean, are you *sure* of what he wants from you? I'm sorry to be blunt, but there it is. I keep looking for a sign of selflessness and understanding in him. Sometimes I think I see it — well, lately that is, but I still feel like I must say it."

Elizabeth's face turned grave and she took her cousin's hand in hers.

"There was something I never told you, Holly, about Mr Darcy. I did not because I was certain I should never see him again and the information was regarding a third party I thought… I thought I should protect her."

As they walked, Elizabeth, in quiet tones, told Holly about what Mr Darcy had disclosed to her about his sister and her misfortunes with Mr Wickham.

"And Holly, despite this he was the one who took care and found poor Lydia. And he paid for everything. My uncle was allowed to do nothing! My father thinks he must have paid Mr Wickham at least ten thousand pounds to extract him from his debts and convince him to marry Lydia."

Holly was speechless.

"Why?" she finally said. "Why would he do that?"

"I think he felt it was his mistake to correct."

"But Lydia — " Holly began and then stopped. There was no way of continuing without casting light over her aunt and uncle's negligence and Lydia's thoughtlessness.

Then suddenly she understood. She saw it clearly and she smiled as she thought back to what Mr Darcy had said about his father. Something she recognised so well herself.

"Elizabeth," she said, "I think Mr Darcy has been the victim of living in the shadow of an ideal. A larger than life figure that showed him what greatness should be, but he missed an important lesson: the fact that greatness comes not from living up to an example, but from living up to your own convictions."

"What do you mean? Do you mean his father?" Then a softer look swept across Elizabeth's face. "And yours?"

"Yes, I do. I think Mr Darcy desperately wants to do right and serve his father's memory to be a worthy successor, but he forgot to make allowances for his own fallibility and humanity as well. We are not perfect just because we display a perfect front. Mr Wickham threatened that image of perfection by hurting him where he was proudest — his affection and care for his family, even by proving him wrong to have trusted a childhood friend and a favourite of his father's. Such a thing does not go away until you admit you were mistaken and stop trying to hide your faults at all costs. At the cost of others. At the cost of Lydia and from what you tell me, countless tradesmen's daughters."

Holly stopped and grabbed Elizabeth's other hand too and looked at her earnestly.

"What he did was wrong, but he told you the truth and then when that was not enough, he faced his failure by rectifying another one. That was very brave of him — and generous. Not the money, but the laying himself bare to accusations and blame and the shameful truth of his association with that scoundrel."

"So…?"

"So I think he is a good man. You told me so once, remember? And I think you were right."

"Yes," Elizabeth smiled and looked down at their crossed hands, "I think I was."

There was a pause; Holly knew Elizabeth needed to go on with something important still left unsaid.

"Holly," Elizabeth said quietly, still looking down, "about that foreswearing we did so happily just a few weeks ago. I might have to break my pledge."

Holly smiled. "Please don't worry. I'll keep it for both of us."

She attempted to resume the slow walk not to be late, but Elizabeth held her in place.

"No, Holly. Please don't hold on to it too tightly. Promise me that if there is the least evidence — or the slightest doubt — that you will open your heart to the possibility of breaking it, too. Promise me you will learn from my mistake and not let prejudice, or pride of the mind, overrule your heart completely."

Holly frowned, but now Elizabeth met her gaze squarely. "If reason and emotion should meet in the same person, promise me you will have the courage to be persuaded and not hide or be afraid?"

"That is a tall order for any person to achieve," Holly said still frowning.

"True," Elizabeth said, "but it has been known to happen and I just want you to believe that you deserve it, too."

All too soon the coach arrived. Elizabeth's trunks were loaded and she was hurried aboard to keep to the tight schedule of the post. Holly leaned in and the two cousins exchanged tearful goodbyes and before either of them were ready, the door was shut and Elizabeth Bennet was on her way to Hertfordshire and Holly was left, alone and desolate, at the roadside.

She stood watching until the coach diminished into a mere speck and then disappeared altogether. She fought back the sobs, but her tears ran freely down her cheeks; she would miss Elizabeth profoundly. Her interval of respite and enjoyment was at an end, and now it was time to make some very hard decisions. She drew in a shuddering breath as the growing chill in the air convinced her that her prolonged study of the horizon would do nothing to bring her cousin any closer. Shivering, she turned and began the slow walk back home.

She had not taken three steps when she noticed, from the corner of her eye, another figure on the edge of the green in front of the inn, facing the same direction from which she had just turned. Mr Darcy. A grateful feeling arose in her heart to him; he must have been fully as sorry as she was to see Elizabeth leave, but he had allowed them their time together, a quiet goodbye unimpeded by his presence. She took a step toward him and, as if suddenly noting her presence, he made his way across the green as well. They met in the middle and he offered her his arm without a word. She took it silently and they walked slowly down the road to Rosefarm Cottage. Not a word was exchanged between them, nothing needed to be said — Elizabeth had gone.

He escorted her up to the gate and it was there that she finally broke the companionable silence.

"I envy you, Mr Darcy."

He looked at her, his expression confused.

"You do? May I ask why?"

"Because," she smiled sadly, "you have the means and the opportunity to go after her. That *is* what you mean to do, isn't it?"

A sudden smile spread across his features and Holly noted how it changed his whole appearance.

"Why…" he hesitated. "Yes," he then firmly said. "You are absolutely right in that." His beaming face betrayed his every thought and wish, "It is, in fact, exactly what I mean to do."

"I should hope so," Holly said. "Go!"

"I will, Miss Tournier, I will!"

JUST AFTER SUNSET DARCY WALKED into the library. "Baugham, I thank you for your hospitality but I leave in the morning."

Baugham turned in his chair and watched as his friend sank back into his. "This wouldn't have anything to do with Miss Bennet having left this afternoon?"

"It would. And I want to be able to put myself at Bingley's disposal if he should ask me."

"He hasn't asked you?"

"No."

Baugham could not help but smile. "Good Lord, Darcy, you have become very meek and subservient in your old age! Six months ago you would have taken it for granted that Bingley was incapable of getting married without you!"

Darcy returned the wry smile. "That was six months ago."

A moment of complete understanding passed between them and Baugham got out of his chair to find the appropriate companion for this silent, combined celebration and farewell. The glasses were filled, homage was paid to colour, smell and taste and they settled to enjoy the rare and ancient brew.

"Well, I should add good luck to that, I suppose," Baugham said thoughtfully after a few moments alone with his whiskey.

"I hope I shan't need luck," Darcy answered him. "But thank you."

That was all that was said for a long time thereafter. Both men seemed lost in their thoughts, feeling silence was the proper respect to be shown to this moment. After a while, however, Darcy looked at his friend and the sheer force of his concentrated gaze made Baugham look up from his own reverie.

"What?"

"Thank you." It was said in a different tone this time. A tone that made Baugham smile sheepishly and wave away his friend's gratitude with an impatient and embarrassed wave of his hand.

"Not at all," he muttered. "It has been an interesting experience. From the sidelines, so to speak."

Thus they sat each content with his own efforts in the matter of Mr Darcy's short Scottish holiday. Finally Darcy got out of his chair.

"I shall see you in Town then perhaps?"

"Perhaps." Darcy hesitated as he was about to walk away. "Will you continue your acquaintance with the Rosefarm ladies although I am gone?"

"Possibly. Well, probably. I like Mrs Tournier."

"And Miss Tournier?"

Baugham snorted. "I was predisposed to, but I have never met a woman who made it more difficult for me to like her. Or indeed just sharing a superficial acquaintance. She is the most exasperating, annoying thing, isn't she? Scrutinising, judging, bothersome and quarrelsome. Besides, she clearly doesn't like me. Other than that?" he shrugged, "I can hardly avoid her now."

Darcy hesitated.

"Baugham...behave yourself, will you?"

Baugham sent his friend a look of affronted exasperation.

"Well, I needed to say it," Darcy answered, "regardless."

Baugham shook his head and went back to his book. "I sincerely hope you realise that my calm incredulity at your really quite insulting suspicions does everything needed to refute any notions you might have of me being unable to act like a gentleman."

"Quite." Mr Darcy looked at him for a moment before walking through the door. Baugham watched him leave and then returned to his silent contemplation of the fire.

Chapter 15

Normal Life is Tried but Found Wanting in Clanough and
Old Habits Make a Disturbing Re-appearence

THE week after Elizabeth's departure was spent quietly at Rosefarm. Letters to
Longbourn were written and posted and letters from Longbourn were anticipated long before they could possibly have been sent. Mrs Tournier spent a great
deal of time reading and working upstairs in her chamber, consigning the parlour to
her daughter's artistic endeavours and whatever pompous nonsense Mr Pembroke
was hard at work perfecting at the cost of more candles than she cared to consider.

The rain was intermittent, but the cold was growing deep and constant, and any
outings Holly made necessitated her heaviest outerwear against the sharpness of the
wind and weather. Despite this, she availed herself of a long walk at least once a day
to escape the tensions in the house and her feelings of isolation.

The day that she completed the final touches on the last colour plate was one of
mixed emotions for her. As she looked them over she was proud of her accomplishment, they had turned out as well or better than she had hoped and she knew Sir
John would be pleased. Yet, at the same time it signalled the end of her commission.
She was now, again, without gainful employment. Sir John's offer of compensation
was generous and she was grateful, but it was a finite amount and she knew that she
must at once begin looking for something else.

She sat deep in thought, idly letting her gaze wander across the room until it rested
upon their visitor. There had been hardly any interaction between them since that
fateful night at the Tristam soirée. Of course, such were the conditions at Rosefarm
there was hardly any opportunity for private encounters, but it also seemed to Holly
that Mr Pembroke was keeping his distance deliberately. What had passed between

the two of them and witnessed by Lord Baugham was never touched upon. Holly never told her mother or her cousin and likewise it seemed he was perfectly content with pretending that incident had never happened and that he had never directed any words to her that night. For the moment, he was still here and still acting as he always did. From experience, it was certain his sojourn would not last very much longer. There was already an impatience in him, a boredom setting in and an obvious disinterest in raising any topics with his hosts, even ones that would put him in a favourable light.

A chance idea sprang into her head and she was suddenly struck with the possibilities it held. Her mother would not like it...but once she had entertained the prospect she could not let it go. It may be impulsive, but action needed to be taken. She would ask.

"Mr Pembroke?" Holly managed to say after several false starts and hesitations.

He looked up from his page and turned toward her, obviously surprised she would even address him. "Yes?"

"When do you leave for Edinburgh?"

"STILL QUATE, AYE?"

"Like the chuchyard."

It was a rare moment. Mrs McLaughlin had walked over from a household in perfect state of organisation and pristine cleanliness to spend the rest of her afternoon helping her cousin. But as she arrived and swung her heavy basket to rest on the kitchen table, she realised her cousin needed no help. The Rosefarm kitchen was silent and Mrs Higgins was sitting in her chair by the hearth, knitting, though perhaps spending more time pulling at the yarn and twisting it idly between her fingers than around her knitting needles. She looked up, ready to be interrupted and glanced at Mrs McLaughlin's load.

"Is that what I think it is?"

"Well, I didnae know what to do with it and since I now make dinners for only one — and rarely proper ones at that — and you still have three to see to, you're welcome to it."

Mrs Higgins slowly lifted herself out of her chair and came to inspect the basket.

"Mm," she said. "Nice. His lairdship had good luck then?"

"He shoots at everything that moves it seems," Mrs McLaughlin said sourly. "I cannae tell what it is about him. If he were bored, he'd leave, so that's nae it. But it is something. Probably that Mr Darcy's fault somewey."

"Things aren't the same here either since Miss Bennet left," Mrs Higgins said, but with much more regret for the departed than Mrs McLaughlin was able to muster. "Although that's nae all her fault."

The silent accusation against the last remaining houseguest hung heavy in the air and needed no words to be shared.

"Well, at least we'll have meat for dinner. And proper meat. Thank you, Heather."

164

"No, you're doing me a good turn. Donnae mention it. Just eat it."

BAUGHAM WAS INDEED AT LOOSE ends. He could not articulate why, but once Darcy had gone and he was left to himself again, he was beset with a sense of restlessness and incapacity. Somehow, whenever he sat in his library trying to let a book transport him away from his own thoughts and surroundings, their last conversation ran through his mind as fresh as if the words had just been spoken.

"Behave myself!" his lordship swore. "Who is there to take offence when I do my behaving in perfect solitude and internment indoors!"

That same pained sentiment was repeated on the days when, weather permitting, he set out on his own to hunt away his frustration outdoors,

"Well?" he asked the pheasant as he picked it out of his dog's mouth. "*You're* quite offended, I dare say, but I hear no other complaints as to my behaviour."

Slowly he managed to shake off Darcy's uncomfortable implications that his Town self could not be separate from his Clyne self after all, and that there was danger the two should somehow mix. Not that he could understand how Darcy had even thought there might be females around here worth setting up in such a game as one could enjoy with ease in London. But still. Even if he could, he never would. Such a notion was ridiculous and really quite insulting. As if that was not the essence of the whole idea of Clyne! That it was separate, different and a shelter. Damn Darcy when he got onto his high horse and played at that ridiculous notion of *noblesse oblige* and moral high ground!

When he could finally leave his indignation and that nagging little voice questioning the force of his reaction behind, there was still the matter of what his friend had led him to understand he was about. Why was there no news? Aside from Darcy occasionally putting his sense of chivalry before his belief in their friendship in the most annoying way, he was usually a most loyal friend and no news of his professed mission in Hertfordshire was puzzling. Why was there no letter?

Baugham sat on his horse after having driven him hard over the fields up to the highest fell in the neighbourhood and looked down at the rolling landscape below. Far away he could see the hazy contours of a church spire and a few dark spots gathered around it. Clanough.

"No," he muttered. "I will not. If there is news, he will tell me himself. I know he will."

IT WAS AN EXCELLENT AND rational resolution to stay away from any potential source of news on the matter, and it took him a further day to find an even more rational and excellent reason to break it. He had a packet from London; no letter from Darcy, alas, but there was a bundle of newspapers. Also, Mrs McLaughlin had given him a foul look when he came home that morning with two partridges tied together over his shoulder.

"I will take them to someone who will appreciate them then," Lord Baugham announced a little too merrily for Mrs McLaughlin to take as an insult and she quietly packed the birds up for him without comment.

But his expectations were cruelly disappointed and his cunning strategy wasted. It had started out well enough, with Mrs Tournier joining him after a little waiting in her parlour. He had a chance to look around him during that time and, to his surprise, noted that she seemed to have taken her work and her usual personal belongings elsewhere. The writing table held neither the familiar chaotic correspondence, newspapers and periodicals of the Mistress of the house, nor anything that looked like her daughter's drawings and paraphernalia. Instead there was one sheet of paper, a few well-sharpened quills, an unopened inkhorn, and a thesaurus lying at aesthetically pleasing angles and looking like they had hardly been touched at all.

He was intrigued, but had no time to express his curiosity before Mrs Tournier followed his gaze and promptly stated that he was admiring the physical expression of a mind so convinced of its own perfect reasoning, it could not produce one piece of evidence or argument of its genius to convince the world's doubters.

Baugham understood and quickly steered the conversation elsewhere and into more pleasant areas. When he inquired after Miss Tournier, however, he was informed that she had gone out on an extensive walk and should be back later. He took the news with what he supposed was indifference, feeling neither disappointed nor relieved.

They spent a very rewarding quarter of an hour as Mrs Tournier gratefully perused the periodicals brought by her guest, pointing out her acquaintances in the latest edition of the Chronicle, enlightening him as to whose output was worth his time and then moving on to the latest speculations on the war and its impact on domestic affairs, including Lord Sidmouth's latest statements in Parliament.

Baugham enjoyed himself very much during those few minutes, but it was not to last. Once Mrs Higgins brought in the tea, Mr Pembroke joined them. He was astonished that the man would have the nerve to show himself at all after behaving so rudely at the Tristams, but he appeared to think nothing of it, rubbing his hands in anticipation and confessing he was starving for some cake and cold cuts, apparently in that order, for he made himself very much at home by helping himself to a large slice before sitting down very close to his lordship and leaning in confidentially.

"I say, I think I will somehow contrive to have you invited for tea every day for the remainder of my stay. The offerings today are much more suitable than what is customarily laid out." He lifted his chin and sniffed the air disdainfully. "Unfortunately I cannot say as much for the tea…but do not despair, I have discovered a way to make it *nearly* tolerable."

He raised his voice and addressed Mrs Tournier, who was then pouring. "Just half a cup, my dear, as usual."

Lord Baugham was affronted for the lady at his tone and term of address and he could see her lips were so tightly pressed together they were beginning to go white. He stood and quickly crossed the room to take his cup from the lady. The question of cake caused a brief internal debate, but in the end he accepted the offered piece graciously, in the same spirit with which it was given.

He was in the delicate process of deciding just how to prepare his tea when Pembroke sauntered over to claim his half cup. With a wink directed at Baugham, he lifted the sugar dish and raked a prodigious amount directly into the cup. Next he added cream until it nearly reached the rim. Leaning in once more to his lordship, he muttered, "There now. Almost tolerable," before returning to his seat with a generous helping of cold cuts as well.

The intruder's presence — for despite the fact that he himself was the visitor, Baugham could not think of Pembroke in any other terms — put a damper on the conversation and soon he, in what would be a humorous turn were he not so annoyed, resorted to the very question Darcy put to him a few days earlier, through rather the same clenched teeth.

"And just how long will it be before you travel to Edinburgh, Mr Pembroke?"

Pembroke leaned back with an inexplicable, self-satisfied smile. "Actually, I will be leaving the day after tomorrow. Poor Mrs Tournier will be deprived of all her company almost at the same time."

"I am sure," Baugham addressed the lady, "that you do not look upon having only your daughter for company as any sort of hardship."

"Not at all," was the terse reply.

With a rather irritating smirk on his face, Pembroke raised his cup and emptied it. Baugham watched in disbelief as he returned to the tray, served himself another helping of cake and reached again for the teapot. He was aware of Mrs Tournier's seething resentment as she sat in her chair, strategically placed as far away from the tea tray as it was from the writing table, but she neither spoke nor reacted to Mr Pembroke's elaborate display of another splash of tea followed by a good dollop of cream and several spoonfulls of sugar.

"Such a dreary day," Pembroke said, moving his spoon lightly back and forth in the liquid. "So fatiguing to have nothing to do. What does one do with oneself in such beastly weather in this tiny corner of the world anyway?"

Baugham could not remove his eyes from Mr Pembroke's light grasp on the spoon and his ineffectual blending that seemed to go on and on without any attempt at reaching the bottom of the cup, but just swirling around in the liquid on the surface.

"Just stir it!" he impulsively thought, not realising he had uttered it out loud until Mrs Tournier looked up and the ghost of a smirk moved across her face.

"I beg your pardon?" Pembroke stopped his movements and stared at his lordship.

"Nothing," Baugham muttered. "I... I was thinking of... what to do. When the weather is like this. Stirring things... up. So to speak." And he went on vigorously stirring his own very sugarless and creamless cup.

"Stir things up?" For some reason Pembroke's smirk returned. "Hm, sounds... intriguing. Perhaps I might just take your advice, my lord."

Baugham refused to acknowledge him with anything but a thin smile and for a while the clinking of china and the ring of silver was all that could be heard. He tried to resume his conversation with his hostess, but apparently she had no stomach for discourse in the presence of her guest. Therefore the topics remained the difficulty of the weather, the difficulties of the conveyance of the mail all the way from Edinburgh and the difficulty of living with the burden of talent generally.

It did not take long until Baugham had had enough. At the earliest possible moment he rose in order to excuse himself, but there he was pre-empted by Mr Pembroke.

"You must excuse me," he said languidly, "I think I shall take myself upstairs and rest for a while before dinner. No, my dear Mrs Tournier, please do not exert yourself, I shall take my last cup of tea with me, that will be quite sufficient.

Mrs Tournier's cold eyes followed him as he piled the rest of his dishes on the cushion beside him with a clatter and rose, heading for the tray once more.

Baugham turned to Mrs Tournier. "Thank you, madam," he said curtly. "Most sincerely. Until next time."

He cut off Mr Pembroke's advance, sweeping past what was left of the display of tea, snatching the sugar bowl from the middle of the left-overs and, without so much as a glance at Mr Pembroke, stalked out of the room, headed for the kitchen and thrust the sugar bowl into the hands of the astonished Mrs Higgins.

"Hide it," he said. "And if anyone other than Mrs Tournier asks for it, tell them I took it with me."

Then, without waiting for a reply, he swept out the door in long and urgent strides and within minutes he was galloping the long way back to Clyne.

IF ONLY HER ARMS WERE an inch or two longer, much embarrassment and discomfort might have been very easily avoided. As it was, Holly was presently perched precariously on a stone, leaning out over the bank of the Kye River and reaching across for all she was worth for a bit of tangled line.

Lately to Holly, any day, or afternoon, or hour without rain was an occasion to escape outside to walk and think and plan. This afternoon she took the opportunity of what promised to be an extended period of clear skies to make the long trek to gather the last Agrimony plants of the season. And just in time too, she reasoned, because the icy wind that blew through her cloak told her a hard frost was on its way, if not tonight then very soon. She drew it tightly about her and pulled the hood down as far as she could as she made her way rapidly to the quiet pool near the river that bordered the Clyne grounds. Yes, she knew that she was, strictly speaking, trespassing, but she reasoned that it was not her fault that the Agrimony grew on Lord Baugham's side of the river. Also, she rationalised, she had collected it every year since she had found it growing wild there. Was she supposed to just let it go to waste because his lordship felt peevish about it? A brief irritation flashed through her as she found herself having to justify an action that she had never before thought twice about.

However, Holly had more important matters to think over and, despite her wicked intentions, the long walk was welcome for the opportunity to do so in peace. As unpleasant as she anticipated it would be, her trip to Edinburgh with Mr Pembroke was settled. There she would deliver her finished work to Sir John and bring home a very welcome remuneration. He would be more than pleased with them, she knew, and she was sure she could enlist his help in obtaining introductions to other scholars and scientists who might be in search of an illustrator. She also had plans to look up Dr McKenna, remembering his promise to engage her as soon as his funding materialised. She was certain that something fruitful would come of her efforts. Edinburgh was bustling with discovery, knowledge and the brightest minds of the time — where else was opportunity to be found if not in such a place?

She was, however, not nearly as sanguine about informing her mother of her planned journey, or her means of travel. She would tell her tomorrow, Holly decided, giving her as little time as possible to fret and stew.

At last she found herself at the pool and to her dismay she realised that she had left her basket behind in her hurry to get out of the house. She gathered as many plants as she could carry back herself and sat on the bank to braid it into a bundle, but the stems were wet and muddy; her hands were numb from the cold and her fingers were clumsy. Just then she spied a discarded length of fishing line she thought she might use to tie it off instead, tangled in the rushes along the bank and she climbed down to grab it.

If only her arms had been an inch or two longer, she would have been able to reach it without stretching so precariously far out over the water. She had just brushed it with her fingertips when the inevitable happened. She lost her balance and, before she felt herself sliding down the muddy and wet slope towards the river on her rear with her skirts folding up in the mud and dirt underneath her, she had the most undignified collision with the ground.

The oaths Miss Tournier yelped while sliding downwards, just barely managing to halt her progress by clutching onto a few wilted tufts of grass and digging her heels into the wet riverbank before more of her was bound for the ice cold water, were definitely not of the approved variety for a young genteel women, but they were in French so she at least sounded quite sophisticated to her rural surroundings. She did not feel so, however, when she crawled up on the bank again on her hands and knees muttering the same obscenities between her teeth.

"Home," she muttered. "I have no choice, I must go home directly. Oh... *Maudit*!"

Having been vulgar enough to forget her anger and feel rather audacious instead, she calmed down and scrambled to her feet, sighing and shaking her wet skirts. The shortest way, she decided. Her toes were already losing their feeling in the soaked boots.

BAUGHAM DROVE HIS HORSE HARD over the fields and kept his eyes fixed as far ahead as possible. It had been an unmitigated disaster! What misguided, foolish, insane notion had convinced him he needed to risk his perfectly organised life at Clyne for tea and conversation at Rosefarm Cottage? He intensely regretted having set foot in that house today. Well, ever, really! Fair enough, the game they were welcome to and Mrs Tournier's face as he forgot himself from Mr Pembroke's fiddling with his tea had been rewarding, but other than that...

Baugham felt like pounding his head against something hard. How dim-witted was it permissible to behave in the face of, admittedly, hazardous provocation? What had that imbecile said? He was leaving the day after tomorrow. Well, he would return after that to apologise to Mrs Tournier.

That damn, stupid, infuriating, selfish pup…

And where was Miss Tournier — the usual terrorising guardian of the sugar bowl — in all of this? Not that her presence could have made any difference to the dreadful overall experience, but she might have saved him from losing his temper and being forced to take matters into his own hands. Out walking? For the better part of the day?! How selfish! In fact, wasn't she obliged to rather stay home and help her mother withstand that cretin in the parlour than skip around the countryside like a schoolgirl? There might be visitors — like him! What about their acute pain in being subjected to such company without a moderating force present? And at the expense of newspapers and partridges! Really, it was most inconsiderate!

HOLLY WAS COLD TO THE bone and no amount of rapid walking would warm her up, it seemed. Her gloves had fallen and were lost forever, but despite that fact, she stubbornly held the scraggly, but hard won, bundle of vegetation tightly to her chest, which in turn made her cloak all the more muddy and cold. Her hood came untied and fell back from the wind, her hair escaping and blowing into her eyes and face; her ears burned, her head ached, but she was too clenched against the cold to be able to contemplate stopping to tie it back again — if she could even get her numb fingers to move well enough to work the strings. All her attention and energy was focused inwardly as she concentrated on moving her stiff and frozen feet forward one step after the next, so she did not hear the sound of the galloping horse as it rapidly came toward her. All she could see was the few feet of lane in front of her and all she could think of was the fire in Mrs Higgins' kitchen.

IN THE MIDDLE OF MOST unkind thoughts about daughters taking selfish long walks at the expense of suffering mothers and innocent gentleman visitors, Baugham spotted a familiar figure coming out of the woods. *His* woods!

"But of course!" he said through clenched teeth and approached her. "Miss Tournier!" he called, not in greeting but in demanding tones. "I wonder," he said cynically, noticing the distinctly miscoloured back of her clinging skirts, "did you find the water in my river very wet?"

She looked up in disbelief, not only that he should come upon her once again in the same embarrassing predicament, and worse, but that he should speak of it in such a callous manner. Of all the insensitive, self-centred… the French oaths threatened to bubble out again, but she swallowed them down. She could not quite swallow the sentiment that accompanied them.

"I beg your pardon, sir. Do you worry that I carry too much of it away with me?"

"Not at all, I assure you. Only that you perhaps carry it away a bit too often."

"In that case, you are right. I can see where it would be doing you a great deal more good were it still in the river rather than soaking my boots and skirts. You must forgive my selfishness."

She tried to stomp away, but the brief pause had already stiffened her muscles and the short steps she could manage caused a searing pain in her frozen feet.

"Oh really!" Baugham said impatiently, but not without appearing to feel some pity for her situation. "That won't do! You'll be frozen through before you get over the field."

He jumped down and reached out his hand to her in an impatient gesture to help her into the abandoned saddle. "Didn't anyone ever tell you you'd be better off at home, where you could be of real use and out of danger in such weather and at this hour?"

The look this observation earned him made him step back instinctively. He had seen that expression before and on several occasions it had been followed by a hard slap to a cheek. Fortunately for him, Miss Tournier did not seem willing to let go of the muddy bundle clutched so tightly to her chest. Instead, she turned her shoulder away from his offered hand with a jerk.

"As a matter of fact, no!" she sputtered. "No one has had the effrontery to so openly contradict the teachings of my parents that I may know and follow my own mind!"

"I beg your pardon," Baugham continued with his eyes hard as steel and devoid of any emotion. His voice grew icy and his demeanour impossibly stiff and remote as he fixed his eyes on his horse that fidgeted nervously in the presence of such unbridled hostility between the two. "I seem to be labouring under a misapprehension regarding your sensibilities. I was under the impression that directness and even rudeness was a sign of affection and respect in your family."

Her eyes narrowed into angry slits, fueled as much by embarrassment as anger, she snapped, "My lord, your misapprehension is grave indeed if it leads you to presume that you have either the ability or the right to make judgements on the basis of a few week's acquaintance! How dare you presume to possess such knowledge concerning my family?"

"Why, I believe about as much as you have to presume anything about me, Miss Tournier! But then I suppose people aspiring to pretensions of intelligence and reason claim the privilege of demanding civil and polite discourse from others while they feel free to practice prejudiced assumptions based on fancy and their own conceit. But you are right. I could not make that general claim about all your family. Your mother can at least give as good as she gets!

"Now will you be so good as to reclaim some of that professed reason, accept my assistance and get on the horse! No doubt you can see the sense in proceeding lest you should freeze to death for the sake of pride and a tantrum."

"I do not ride, sir," she replied coolly, a perfect picture of affronted dignity. "Nor do I throw tantrums. Now, if *you* will be so good as to let me be on my way, I should like to get home where I can be of some *use*."

BAUGHAM SWALLOWED HARD. HE NEEDED a moment to master this. Why did he spiral into a mindless rage every time she looked at him with those defiant eyes, shooting daggers and lightning at him? *Now then,* he told himself silently, *keep to the issue at hand. Get this impossible, soaked, stubborn, blazing, bothersome, infuriating woman home! And then go and finish it by cutting logs or something in the privacy of your own home.*

"Do not refuse me my right to be of use in my turn," he said after a deep breath, "I will see you home and if you do not mind, I shall be infinitely grateful if these are the last words we exchange today. But get on the horse!"

Her anger was temporarily replaced with a look of disbelief. "Are you *ordering* me around, my lord? You might be an earl and used to having your own way, but I am *not* your underling to be commanded!"

"Don't be ridiculous," he sputtered, "I am doing no such…oh, for the love of…" He stopped and took a deep breath to compose himself and his temper. "*Please*, Miss Tournier, allow me to help you onto my horse and let me see you home safely."

"I suppose," she said, "that, however unnecessary it is, I do not have the power stop you if you feel you must. No more than you have the power to get me up on that horse. I will walk. Follow if you must."

She whirled around as well and set out down the road. He fought a brief but overwhelming urge to sweep her up and deposit her bodily in the saddle. But he mastered himself and simply stayed beside her, grim and silent, leading his horse and breathing disapproval with every step.

Holly, on the other hand, once the conversation had ceased, quickly returned to her inward focus of cold hands, cold feet, chill wind and one step after the next. The walk to Rosefarm felt interminably long, and only once was it interrupted by Lord Baugham repeating his assertion that she had much better ride than walk. That was enough to spur her on the rest of the way, and once the cottage was in view she quickened her pace and scarcely took the trouble to give him a perfunctory nod before she rushed to the kitchen door. Home. Warmth. Fire.

Baugham watched the door close behind her, cutting off Mrs Higgins' surprised exclamations mid-stream. He mounted his poor, confused horse, tightened his collar against the cold wind and once again galloped for home. *Troublesome,* he dismissed them all, *nothing but a troublesome family.* He had been right and Darcy had been wrong. Utterly and completely. One last visit of apology and he need never be bothered with them again.

Chapter 16

A Very Unpopular and Frustrating Trip is Taken

ROSEFARM Cottage was quiet, the inhabitants having retired to their respective rooms early again, but the mother and the daughter of the house were definitely not asleep. Mrs Tournier lay in her bed, her pillows fluffed and towering up behind her head and shoulders just the way she liked it, her hands folded on top of the blankets. Her candle was snuffed out and she was ready to leave another day behind her. But she could not. In the silence of the house, she could hear her daughter's soft steps in her room, no doubt preparing for tomorrow's departure. Mrs Tournier clenched her fists at the thought and tugged at her sheets in frustration.

She closed her eyes and tried to breathe slowly. "Oh Jean," she finally sighed. "I am so angry; all I can see and think about is her."

She realised that in order for her to successfully conjure up her departed husband's face, she needed to calm down. She twirled her wedding ring like a talisman and then rubbed the locket with his picture in a secret ritual. "She's pacing around there right now, preparing to go to Edinburgh with that... man," she said dryly. At that thought, her resentment threatened to destroy the faint image she had been able to summon and almost reverted to her daughter again.

"*Oh non,*" Mrs Tournier whispered. "*Depart-pas! Reste avec moi qu'un petit instant, Jean.* I need to talk to you."

Fiercely holding on, she managed to turn her husband's face towards her once more and even made him smile at her. "She is so like you, isn't she? But I don't trust that man and I don't want her to go with him. That's all. It is unnecessary and... you know I will never forgive him."

Sighing a little at her own passion, she nevertheless could not resist a wry smile.

"*Oui, je sais, je sais.* Now you tell me I don't trust *her.* Well, perhaps. It is just that she has a kind heart and he knows it. And therefore the thought of them alone together makes me ill."

She fingered the old, soft sheet and ran her hand over the quilt to smooth it out after her restless outburst earlier.

"Well, that's all. I suppose nothing can be done about it. I just felt I had to let you know. Just because you so very inconveniently had to die, does not mean I do not intend to burden you with parental worries. They're inescapable, even in paradise."

She sighed.

"Sometimes, *mon chéri*, I miss you for more than one reason. Like right now."

THE PAST FEW WEEKS HAD been quite hard on his lordship's man, Mr Riemann. His master was an erratic man at best, shunning form and abhorring predictability almost compulsively at times. At Clyne, that usually meant refusing to allow Riemann to perform the very duties he so relied upon when in Town. He was allowed no discussion or assistance with clothing or attention to detail about his personal appearance. Also, his lordship could be absent for days on end and his sojourns in this place he so professed to love always ended abruptly, Lord Baugham losing interest or pleasure in it sooner than anyone else could suspect it might be time to remove again.

However, these days his lordship was a puzzling contradiction of obvious discomfort that did not lead to any decisions about leaving, and a keen social interest that led to opinions being asked and options being tried out regarding available clothing.

So here they were again. Riemann regarding his Master in the full-length mirror; the Master frowning and sighing but apparently dead set on finding the perfect match between country comfort and town elegance to once again go visiting in the village.

Once his lordship finally settled on his choice, his valet could tell he was still uncomfortable, annoyed and determined, all at the same time, from the way he hurried away from him., From his vantage point, he could see Mrs McLaughlin poke her head out of the kitchen window, stopping his Master as he walked over to the stables. The housekeeper stretched out her arm through the window and his lordship trotted through the flower bed underneath it to receive a bundle of fowl of some sort. A few words were exchanged, the result of which was that Lord Baugham looked thoughtful and Mrs McLaughlin triumphant. Shortly thereafter, the Master of Clyne took his birds and rode off.

BY THE TIME LORD BAUGHAM reached the outskirts of the village, he had settled on a course of action. Apologising to Mrs Tournier was no hardship. He certainly owed it to her and he had no qualms admitting he had acted rudely in her parlour and toward her guest; the fact that she had secretly approved of his action naturally contributed to his eagerness to settle things between them. At the same time, he was painfully aware that he owed a greater apology to the daughter — one which would be far more difficult to deliver and articulate. It was not the substance of the apology that he doubted, but he could not understand why he had acted in such a heedless and stupid manner — why, in fact, he usually did when it came to her! — and so his remorse was muddled with other sentiments. Least of all did he spend time contemplating what he owed Mr Pembroke. He confessed he would be very pleased if the man had already left and did not particularly worry about either Mr Pembroke's opinion of him or how to state his apology for his abrupt behaviour the last time they met. He would have to do with short and simple — that was all that was forthcoming in this case.

Rosefarm Cottage seemed quiet enough when he tied his horse to the post and made his way through the gate. Lightly swinging his birds as he walked, he rounded the house and peeked into one of the kitchen windows at the back. Someone was moving about with her back towards him, but the uneven window panes made it hard to see anything besides the combination of colour and movement.

He knocked, he took his hat off, he peeked around the door to greet Mrs Higgins. But of course, with the luck he had been having lately, it was not Mrs Higgins at all.

THE KITCHEN TABLE WAS COVERED with various piles as Holly busily sifted through all her sketches and sorted them into categories: definites, possibles, unlikelys and scribbles. Not wanting to appear too eager or needy, she had decided to only take a few of her best. After much deliberation she chose six that she felt best demonstrated her abilities in the various scientific disciplines, regretting that she had never thought to sketch any rocks. She then walked to the pantry and pulled out the crockery jar that held their household ready cash.

A quick count after she emptied it on the table confirmed her in her conviction that she was doing the right thing. Pulling out just enough to cover the trip home and a meal or two during her stay, she was just putting it in her pocketbook when she was interrupted by a tap on the kitchen door. As Mrs Higgins had earlier thrown up her hands at Holly's mess and declared that since she could get no work done as it was, she was heading out to the market, Holly answered the door herself. Her surprise at beholding Lord Baugham standing there with his birds, rather than the expected tradesman or peddler, was interrupted by the accompanying burst of wind that threatened to scatter all her papers.

"Oh dear!" she cried, torn between the visitor at the door and all her hard work on the table. "Please excuse — do come — can you… Oh! Just a minute!" and she left the open door and flew across the room to rescue her sketches.

His lordship quickly closed the door behind him and rushed to assist her. Once everything had been restored, Holly turned to give him a proper greeting. The memory of their last meeting was obviously at the forefront of both of their minds and an awkward silence followed until Baugham recalled his several missions. He held out the bundle he had brought with him.

"Miss Tournier," he began, "I am here on a selfish quest. It seems that no matter what I do, I cannot escape my housekeeper's wrath, since I have gone from not bringing in enough meat to now bringing her too much. I wondered if you would be so kind as to protect my domestic tranquillity by giving these birds to Mrs Higgins?"

HER BROW WRINKLED, WHETHER IN suspicion or confusion Baugham could not tell, but she took them from his hand. He decided to plunge in with his next duty: best to get it all over with at once and be done with troublesome acquaintances once and for all.

"I am also here to beg your pardon for my words and behaviour the other day. It appears that I have taken my exclusive privilege to the extreme and somehow manage to anger and insult you at every turn. That was never my intention. I can assure you it will not happen again and I beg your forgiveness that it has happened at all." Suitably formal yet humble, and best of all, final.

She granted it readily, and may even have been asking his pardon as well, but his attention was diverted by the scene in front of him and his infernal curiosity got the better of his judgement. Taking a step closer to the table, he bent down to examine the drawings scattered upon it.

"And I must add my apologies for interrupting and disrupting your work. Are you organising a showing, Miss Tournier?" he asked with a ghost of a smile.

"No, sir," she shook her head and set to straightening the piles, but not without the smallest smile of her own. "I am preparing to go hunting myself."

"Ah," he said, slightly puzzled, "then I shall not keep you from your task. If you will excuse me… that is, is your mother in the parlour? I believe I owe her an apology as well, along with that… your guest."

"Yes, Maman is in the parlour having her tea, as it happens, which…" when she did not continue, Baugham hesitated. To his surprise, she was holding her hand over her mouth and trying to stifle a giggle.

A grin slowly spread across his face. "Ah yes. Thought as much. I take it you heard, then? I hope Mrs Higgins interpreted my hasty remarks correctly and included you in the secret of the whereabouts of the sugar bowl?"

"Yes, well, Mrs Higgins actually thought it best to tell me before Maman asked for it," she said, quickly returning to organising the drawings and straightening already immaculate piles of paper. "And it was not hidden in so very a secret place for those who live here. There was never any danger of Mr Pembroke coming to look for it himself in here."

Baugham looked at her and then returned to the sketches he was still holding in his hand. "No," he muttered, "I suppose not."

"I do appreciate the gesture, however," she said, "and I confess, I am very sorry I was not here to see it. There have been many times I have had to fight the impulse to do the same thing."

Noticing how closely he was scrutinizing the page he held, Holly stepped in to see what had commanded such close attention. "Do you have a special fondness for bees, my lord?" she asked when she saw that it was a page of idle scribbles she had made one lazy afternoon.

176

"Ah…so they *are* bees…" he murmured absently.

"Yes, of course. It appears that you have had so much practice in insult lately that I think you have forgotten how to flatter. Therefore I think you need to now praise the excellence of my drawings, Lord Baugham. Do not you think this particular bumble bee is exceptionally well portrayed?"

He lifted his head and returned her gaze before he again looked at the picture. Then his mouth twisted into a curious shape and his blue eyes glittered.

"Ah well, there you have me. That is impossible, I think. I'm afraid I must invoke my original privilege. You see — as you must, I hope — the proportion of the fore-wing as to the rear wing is off. The tibia is far too long and with the way the tegula is situated on the thorax…I'm afraid this little fellow would never have made it to the next daisy. The pencilled line of his flight is very charming…however, if you really think I should practice praising your work, I will try. But we must choose an easier subject than these bumble bees."

Holly shook her head and smiled. "I cannot really fault you, for these were done in idleness and escape from my true commission for Sir John."

Baugham looked at her with renewed interest.

"So you're finished then? And this is it? I thought…I was given to understand it was just a few colour plates. And on the Propensities of Heat. These are of bees and…" He turned the few leaves over in his hand, "heather?"

Holly laughed and moved around the table to his side and looked at the drawing.

"*Calluna vulgaris* — yes, heather. But a very rare form of white heather. I only saw the one little specimen a friend of my mother's brought over. He wanted me to recreate what must have been a magnificent scene he encountered on his exploration in the Highlands for a piece he was doing." She gently took the drawing from Lord Baugham and looked at it closely. "But this was not what he had in mind."

"You never saw it yourself?"

"No" said Holly and put away the picture.

BAUGHAM STOOD UNCERTAINLY. HE WAS finished here; he should move on and look up the others he owed a visit, but he was suddenly fascinated by Miss Tournier's work occupying the entire kitchen table.

"Hunting…" he said slowly. "What exactly are you hunting for with these, Miss Tournier? If I may ask?"

She straightened her shoulders and spoke matter-of-factly.

"For work, of course. I am leaving for Edinburgh this afternoon to deliver Sir John's plates and I hope to find something else while I am there."

"This afternoon?" Baugham checked his pocket watch. "Miss Tournier, I'm afraid you have already missed today's post. I hope my arrival has not delayed your journey."

"Thank you for your concern, but no. Mr Pembroke has hired a private carriage and he has said I may ride with him. We will be leaving within the hour."

It was then that he noticed the collection of coins and banknotes on the table, spilled out from a crockery jar. She turned and raked the coins back in discreetly, folding the notes into her palm.

"So as you see, I should be getting ready to leave. You will find Maman in the parlour."

Baugham did not hear her last statement. He stared at the money being shuffled and was still trying to understand her.

"Him?" he said incredulously, almost aggressively. "You're going with *him*?"

"It is the sensible thing to do," she said, looking slightly annoyed. "As I said, you will find my mother in the parlour."

Baugham's eyes were drawn to the banknotes in her hand and he felt extremely uncomfortable. He also felt a sudden anger building up. Where exactly it came from was not quite clear to him, but he strongly suspected it had something to do with the power of money over people and how they must put their own dreams and pleasures aside for more practical concerns. The thought of Miss Tournier being forced to solicit for work under such circumstances, regardless of her own obvious feelings and certainly those of her mother, was infuriating and did not sit well with their proud independence and self-reliance.

Of course she must go, he understood that, and at this moment he felt incredibly frustrated at his own helplessness in the face of his strong feeling that Miss Tournier should not have to be in the position to have no choice in the matter on *how* she was to get there. It seemed to him her decision could only be humiliating and downright dangerous and should be avoided at any cost, knowing what he did about Mr Pembroke's uninhibited treatment of her. That sentiment, however, he was not at liberty to express and so he swallowed his chagrin and attempted a smile.

"Forgive me. But allow me to…that is, there is no need to follow Mr Pembroke's schedule and convenience. I will gladly offer my carriage at your disposal for the same. I have no need of it. And my man can follow you and, uh…perform some errands for me at the same time. All things considered, I find this is a much better scheme."

"There really is no need to trouble yourself. My trip is already arranged, no such schemes are necessary."

Placing several drawings in her case, she stacked the remainder together and replaced them in her folder and gathered everything from the table to carry away.

"Now, if you will excuse me. I really must prepare."

He swallowed hard, once again feeling an irrational rush of anger toward her. He averted his eyes from her face. He clenched his jaw. He counted to ten. Slowly. Only then was he certain he would not utter a useless protest that could only serve to re-ignite the anger on both sides that always seemed to be hiding just under the surface. This woman, with her infernal pride, was impossible! Even in her ridiculous stubbornness, she made him regret his principles and go back on his resolutions! She coaxed him into being grateful for receiving simple, polite conversation and she made him bend over backwards in search of the certainly sweet nature that was hidden under all that anger and temper and haughtiness!

"Very well. Of course you must do as you see fit." His voice was tight and angry and it was apparent in her obstinate expression that she could sense his disapproval, but she turned without another word. That was it. He would be forced to leave her in this mood of dissension because the visit most certainly was over. *One more try,* he thought. He would approach her where her heart surely must be at its softest.

"I would not want to keep you from what must be necessary preparations. But I would be very happy if you would tell me if you think it would be appropriate for me to visit your mother and... well, perhaps see that she is comfortable while you are gone?"

Miss Tournier turned one last time before she walked out of the kitchen. Her face was softer and he could see the lines between her brows ease a little.

"That would be very kind of you," she said. "Thank you."

He shook his head as she softly closed the door behind her, staring down at his boots. Then he paused. His eye was caught by a piece of paper lying half obscured by the wood basket on the hearth. It was a small scrap of Miss Tournier's sketching paper that had strayed in the gust of wind earlier and had been overlooked in its hiding place He picked it up, uncertain as to exactly why — more bumble-bees — and he watched the flawed creatures making their way across the page, between illegible scribbles and delicately drawn daisies, roses and sweet peas. Involuntarily he smiled, folded up the paper and pocketed it.

MRS TOURNIER WAS INDEED SEATED just where her daughter had insisted; on the sofa in the parlour. She looked up as if disturbed out of deep thoughts when his lordship entered and he noticed she had a tight grasp on something on a chain around her neck that she did not let go.

"Mrs Tournier," he began, "how fortunate it is to find you here. I came to — "

Mrs Tournier stood up before he had even finished his greeting. "And it is very good to see you, my friend," she said. "Come, sit by me, will you?" To Baugham's infinite surprise, his hostess took hold of both his hands and pulled him to sit by her on the sofa.

"Are you quite well?" he asked, more suspiciously than he had intended.

She gave a wry smile. "Probably not. But never mind about that."

Confused, Baugham decided to push on with his original mission.

"Well, I wanted to come by and apologise for my rude behaviour in your presence and as your guest the other day — " Again he was interrupted.

"Yes, yes," the lady said and waved away his words, "that's all good and well but of little consequence. In fact, *I* should be thanking *you* for it if I weren't so... " She looked at him earnestly. "Lord Baugham, you may as well know. My daughter is going to Edinburgh with Mr Pembroke."

Baugham could not help raising an eyebrow at her bitter tone of voice.

"Yes, quite," Mrs Tournier said dryly. "So you see I'm far too upset to handle any silly self-abasing apologies right now and instead am busy trying to calculate a way to use your arrival to prevent her from going."

Baugham gave a slight smile. "I'm afraid you are wasting your time, Mrs Tournier. I spoke to your daughter in the kitchen just now and clumsily enough tried to influence her decision to go myself. I think you grossly over-estimate my powers in that regard."

"Silly fool!" Mrs Tournier said, and it was unclear whether she meant his lordship, her daughter, or even herself.

It remained unclear, for at that moment Miss Tournier came into the parlour in search of her notebook. Looking at the figures of her mother and Lord Baugham, she could recognise an alliance of disapproval, but she simply steeled herself and refused to take it as a sign of concern or affection. Instead, she told herself they were both of them interfering where they should stay out and trust her, and her face showed it clearly.

"Maman," she said. "My lord."

Lord Baugham sensed a silent conversation being played out between the two women and felt acutely ill at ease again. Why he should be compelled to insert himself into the situation, he could not fathom. True, he knew Pembroke to be an arrogant ass, and Mrs Tournier obviously held an even harsher opinion of him, but Miss Tournier was a grown woman, capable of making her own choices. As it was, however, he could not escape a feeling of kinship with the woman beside him in believing that such a journey must be prevented.

"Miss Tournier," he therefore said, "I was just about to explain to your mother that I have placed my own carriage at your disposal... and how disappointed I am that you will not take me up on it."

Holly looked at her mother before she met his lordship's eyes. *So,* she silently asked, *not only an alliance, but a conspiracy, too, Mother?*

Call it what you want, her mother eyed back, *as if I would not try anything at my disposal...*

"Well, my lord," Holly said calmly to Lord Baugham, "all is explained then. I came to get my sketchbook."

Baugham coughed discreetly and, from the ice cold looks exchanged between mother and daughter, hastily decided he would keep his peace henceforth.

"Mr Pembroke has informed me that he is ready to leave. This is goodbye then, Maman."

Holly ignored Lord Baugham and went up to her mother. She took the hands that would not release their tight grip on one another and so were covered by her daughter's hands. Holly kissed her cheek.

"Wish me luck?" she said quietly.

"You don't need luck," her mother told her sternly, but her eyes held a different message of sadness, joined with care and affection.

Holly smiled and gave his lordship a glance.

"Good luck," Baugham muttered, looking glum.

Holly opened her mouth to reply, but in that instant the door opened and Mr Pembroke swept in.

"Ah, my dear," he said lavishly, "come, come. The hour is upon us. I must away. *Must* away," he said and gave Baugham a meaningful look.

180

Baugham ground his teeth and stood, glowering darkly at the man as he bowed farewell to the lady. Mrs Tournier never turned her eyes away from her daughter. Mr Pembroke likewise ignored his hostess and gave a perfunctory bow in her direction while offering his arm to Holly in an exaggerated gesture. Holly gave her mother a last look before she was swept out the door, leaving Baugham standing by her mother, both with conflicting emotions and barely contained frustration seething through them both.

The door closed and the coach lurched into motion, but Holly could still feel the two pairs of disapproving eyes that watched her from the window. Though she did feel wretched that her mother was upset, this really was not as bad a decision as everyone made it out to be. How else could she travel to Edinburgh so quickly and comfortably, and most importantly, at no cost? Upon coming down that morning, she had steeled herself to withstand her mother's mutterings and huffs and sidelong glances, but Lord Baugham's arrival, along with his unwarranted and unwelcome interference, had taken her by surprise.

Of course, he probably assumed that her mother would welcome an ally, as well as someone to vent her anger to once she was gone. But that he should insinuate himself into such a private family matter as this... *No, that isn't fair,* she corrected herself, *he has no knowledge of the circumstances.* Nor was she afraid that her mother would speak of it to him. Mrs Tournier spoke of it to no one.

She was a grown woman now and she was certainly in no danger from Mr Pembroke at present. Without an audience, he was merely background noise, his conversation quite easily ignored behind the covers of her book. So well rehearsed and familiar were his stories of ill-usage and thwarted dreams, that she was able to give the proper reply to all of his complaints without taking the trouble of listening. But, as Edinburgh grew closer several new words caught her ear and demanded her attention. *Business, increase,* and *effective immediately* caused her to lower her book and focus on his words at last.

"I thought that would finally get your attention," Pembroke's lip curled. "Have you got it all, or shall I repeat everything I have just told you one more time?"

Holly narrowed her eyes but her tone was meek enough. "Repeat it please."

He leaned back in the comfortable seat and looked across to her. "I suppose I should not be surprised that you will avail yourself of the hospitality of my private coach yet still barely make an effort to be civil to me. Such seems to be the pattern between your family and mine — or it has been until now."

He crossed his legs, taking up much of the shared room.

"But, as I was saying, not for long. My father is at last taking his physician's advice and retiring from all business affairs, leaving the disposition of them to me. As you know, it is beyond question that you and your mother have been taking unfair advantage of him and the generous terms he gave to you in the wake of your father's death. Surely by now, if you had been industrious in the practice of economy, he should have seen *some* increase in the amount of income he derives from Rosefarm rent. He has always been soft, too soft to demand it from you, but you of all people should know, Miss Tournier, that I am not."

A sinking feeling of horror slowly filled Holly's stomach as her eyes grew wide and she tried to reason with him.

"But surely, your father must have made some stipulation — "

"None, Miss Tournier!" he snapped in triumph. "None, but that I am to do what I think is best and not to trouble him about anything. Doctor's orders! Nothing as sordid as emotional appeals and sentimental scenes must disturb him. And what I think best is half again as much rent as you are currently paying, and coming due this current quarter."

He stretched out a little more as Holly fought a rising feeling of panic and nausea. Her pride told her not to plead with him, but the harsh realities of life won out.

"Please, sir, so much? Can we not speak to your father? Or may we at least have more time — "

A sharp laugh cut her questions short, "Certainly not! No more time, no speaking to my father. All his business affairs have been passed on to me, legally and binding. If you are not willing or able to meet the new terms of your tenancy, there are others who will be. Miss Tournier, I hope for your sake that your arrangement with Sir John was lucrative, and that there is more coming." His mouth curled and his eyes looked at her with pitying scorn. "It is simply a matter of business, *Holly*, and I am sure you would not want to trespass or take advantage of my father's good will and continue in rendering him ridiculous?"

His eyes were cold, his face was set; his decision had been made and Holly would not further demean herself by asking anything more of him when he so obviously enjoyed her distress and equally obviously had no intention of relenting. Mercifully the coach drew to a halt a short time later and Holly, numb with disbelief, mechanically collected her bag and began the walk from the coaching inn to the University Buildings. Once there she would deliver the colour plates to Sir John Leslie, and pray that there was some work out there for her, somewhere.

Chapter 17

*How Miss Tournier's Remaining Friends and Family Passed
their Time in her Absence and what her Return Entailed*

Edinburgh,
Ledwich House

Dearest Maman,

*You may rest easy upon receiving this letter, hearing that I am arrived in Edinburgh
and am now safely in Sir John and Lady Ledwich's care. I will also give you the
satisfaction of admitting that you were perfectly right and my journey was every bit as
unpleasant as you predicted. However, it is done with and I have emerged relatively
unscathed.*

*I trust that you will not be cross with me when you read that I will remain here in Ed-
inburgh for a few days longer than I had intended, to inquire into some employment
opportunities that Sir John and his friend have so kindly suggested. It appears that no
commissions will be forthcoming any time soon, and — it also appears that my need to
find work is more pressing than we had anticipated.*

*I will explain when I arrive home, hopefully with gainful employment. Look for me
either on Friday or Saturday, I'll be coming by the stage as usual.*

Your loving,
Holly

THROUGHOUT THE WEEK THAT FOLLOWED, Lord Baugham made good on his expressed intentions to Miss Tournier and was a regular visitor to Rosefarm Cottage in her absence. He found Mrs Tournier's company as stimulating as ever, even if she was understandably even more prone to debate than usual.

The day after her departure, his lordship came upon her as she was reading the letter from her daughter. She did not look displeased to see him, even if her eyes lingered on the note while he entered.

"Well, my lord," she said and waved the letter in front of him before crisply folding it away. "I am pleased to report that she has survived her journey and is now with Sir John."

"Does Miss Tournier write of her plans to return then? Do you expect her soon?"

Tossing the letter sharply onto her now reclaimed desk, Mrs Tournier's face grew grim.

"She stays a few more days at the least."

Baugham was surprised to see a sudden change in her demeanour at those words. Even more surprising was what followed.

"She is always leaving!" The statement sounded matter-of-fact, yet almost wistful. "She comes home, I grow accustomed to her presence... then she leaves and I miss her." Mrs Tournier then took a breath, straightened her shoulders and shook off her regret.

The familiar gesture tugged at Baugham's heart. He had seen it from Miss Tournier several times and he wondered how often this small, proud family had to shake off disappointments and sadness and, from somewhere within, find the strength to carry on.

"So," she interrupted his reverie, "what have you brought today? Partridges, or opinions?"

"Both, madam," he smiled.

"WELL, MY DEAR, OF COURSE I will ask on your behalf, but I think you must be prepared to consider other options, too."

Holly held on to Sir John's arm as he steered her out of the dark winding closes by his rooms and the laboratories. The University being scattered in all manner of buildings all around the center of Edinburgh, Sir John had his workplace and lecture rooms in a cramped building near Grass Market, but its location was nonetheless convenient, for it offered him access to the Faculty's laboratories to the west of the Castle. Holly looked up at the magnificent building on the hill, ancient and imposing even though dusk was already falling and obscuring its features. Looming, she thought. Why was every feature of the city suddenly an omen of impending doom?

"Thank you, Sir John. I cannot tell you how much it means to me. I... well, there is no disgrace in admitting we do need the extra income."

"Of course you do. I wish Dr McKenna could have been more specific with his prospects, but as usual, science must await the currents of economy before it can aspire to its universal goals."

Holly recognised Sir John was not in a particularly optimistic mood. He always

184

muttered obscure philosophical sentiments when he was dissatisfied with his work or troubled by real life concerns. But then his features lightened and he squeezed her arm.

"Now, I will renounce these gloomy thoughts and so must you! I have you for myself for just a little while before you go back and I will take you to see the latest developments around New Town. I am much impressed! Such a difference from these dirty, confusing and ancient streets around here. My wife says we could perhaps take rooms in Princes' Street and I must say I favour the idea. The ordered plan and the well-laid out structures are so much easier on the working mind of a natural scientist like me. You must come with me and give your opinion on what she has in mind!"

Holly smiled and agreed to accompany him. A little beauty and faith in the future of city planning would do her good. And New Town was what she always imagined London to be like — at least her mother had said it rivalled anything she had seen in the way of harmonious and handsome architecture when she had been living there.

They had a very pleasant afternoon of it, with Sir John conducting her on a short walking tour of the parts of town she was less familiar with. They returned to the University to take tea, where they were joined by Dr McKenna and Holly was introduced to more of their colleagues, but the answers to their discreet inquiries on her behalf were all very much the same. Coupled with the genuine praise and admiration of the quality of her work, were equally genuine regrets that wartime economics, internal wranglings for power and influence within the University, and sporadic labour unrest in the printing shops, not to mention the alarming rise in the cost of paper, were all combining to make publication especially difficult for the time being.

Dr McKenna returned with them to Sir John's for supper and they spent the evening reviewing possibilities and making lists. Holly was grateful, not only for the kind solicitude of the gentlemen, but for their treatment of her as a rational, capable being and not as a mere fragile thing to be protected. It grew late as they talked and planned, and suddenly Dr McKenna looked at her as if he was taken with an idea. She waited to hear him, but he merely apologised for keeping them up till such an hour by his visit and quickly took his leave.

"Geologists," Sir John smiled. "One can never know what to expect of a man who spends his life looking down at the ground. Now, my dear," he bent down to kiss the top of her head, "it is time to retire. I daresay we will have better success tomorrow."

Sir John climbed the stairs, quietly vowing to rattle as many academic cages on Miss Tournier's behalf as he could on the morrow. A few moments later Holly went up, vowing to start out first thing in the morning to make full use of the lists of schools and families of whom she might enquire about a position. Dr McKenna, once he entered his room in South Bridge Street, wasted no time in pulling out pen and paper and making good on his own private vow of writing a letter to his father.

"NOW DONNAE YE START WITH me Heather McLaughlin! I have quite enough of that from the Mistress these days as it is. I will make my cottage pies just as I always do — except with a bit more paitrick meat than usual — and that will have to be good enough for both of ye!"

"Well, donnae gnap my head off! I can see ye're in a mood all right. Pass me the rolling pin, I had better handle the dough."

"This household, Heather, is in a right state, I can tell ye that, and I am getting grey hairs — even more grey hairs, I should say — because of it."

"Is this about Miss Holly's trip again? Have ye heard nothing from her? I expected she would be back by now."

"There was a letter a few days ago saying she was raking around for work up there. No other explanation, but it has the Mistress in a regular tift."

"Well, why doesnae she simply come home and find work here?"

"Why, indeed? I reckon she's going back to what she knows, and there's nae much need for fine teachers such as her hereabouts."

"That's so, but why the sudden need? I thought she was all fixed for wages with her picture work, you said she was making enough to get along a good while, being cannie as always."

"Aye, but it goes out faster than it comes in, don't it? I just wish she'd come back soon. It done the Mistress no good for *him* to leave, since Miss Holly left with him. In fact, she might be even worse off now than when he was here."

"Oh, Rosie, speak about Masters and moods and I'll give ye an earful myself. There's something queer about him this time around. Goes out visitin' more than I ever seen him do, but coming back full glum and dark. I thought once that guest o' his left...but..."

"But what?"

"But the mood is unlike. For ordinar he's happy and keeps to hisself, but now he's nae happy and still keeps to hisself, restless like, and murmlin under his breath and all. Grumpy, that's what he is. Usually when he's like this he leaves and goes to London or wherever it is he goes when he's nae here. This time he's just stayin'."

"Ye know, he was right here the morning Miss Holly left. I wonder..."

"Oh, I know what ye think and however highly I think of Miss Holly, I will not have her home-comin be the answer to every problem and cross mood in the shire!"

"P'rhaps nae *every* cross mood..."

"Well, Mrs Tournier is far certain used to being on her own."

"Ay, but she has more company than you might expect, what with visiting lairds and all. But the way she hardly stirs from that writing desk, composing letters and writing on her reviews all through the night, hardly pausing for food and tea, is nae right. So I'm that grateful his lairdship comes by to take her mind from it some. She will make herself ill and then where will we be?"

"She'll be home soon, though, Rosie?"

"Should be."

ON THE FIFTH DAY FROM Miss Tournier's departure, Lord Baugham was cursing his sofa. He had stretched out on it in an attempt to take an undisturbed nap in his quiet house while the grey day outside slowly gave way to evening dusk, but the damned thing was not cooperating. It was too short for him and his feet stuck out over the armrest that chafed on his calves. Pulling up his legs was no better and the pillows he had so carefully thrown behind his head kept sliding around in the wrong place. What a nuisance of a thing! What on earth had possessed him to acquire it?

He sighed when he remembered he had not actually chosen it himself. It had come with the house and either the previous owner had been a shorter man than he or was not fond of naps in his library. Either way, Baugham had no understanding for his taste in furniture.

Abandoning his nap, he looked around him instead. The gaping shelves were entirely his own responsibility. Lately he had received rather too much comment about the state of his library to be completely complaisant about that either. Previously, its sorry state had never bothered him particularly; he travelled with the books he cared to read and whatever collection he could claim was reserved for his London house. Of course, that was nothing compared to Darcy's collections divided between Pemberley and his London addresses — each exemplary and impressive in its own right. But then, Darcy employed a librarian who kept up the purchase and inventory and sent around to all of Europe for catalogues by the finest publishing houses, diligently searching for any missing pieces. Baugham was rather more eclectic, acting only on his own preferences and fancies since, whatever the Cumbermere collection once had been, it was now both neglected and scattered, thanks to his father's negligence and sorry financial affairs.

So the library at Clyne, with its shelves filled with everything but books, never really gave him a bad conscience. Until now. He looked at the rolled up prints, the old fishing hat and skewed deer head that were lying where proud rows of leather bound backs of books should have stood and narrowed his eyes. Piles of paper, old quills and small boxes with no content supported old volumes. *Stupid,* Lord Baugham thought, *I never needed a library here, why should I hanker after one now?*

Squirming on his back to reach a better view that would not annoy him quite as much, his hand brushed over the pocket of his waistcoat and drew out the little booklet he had developed the habit of glancing through on occasion: *Sur la nécessité d'une Republique et la Suppression des Privilèges de la Noblesse" par Monsieur Jean-Baptiste Tournier.*

He fingered it before he randomly picked a page and read a few lines on the now-so-unfashionable republican cause of gone-by days. Monsieur Tournier's arguments were well formulated and elegant, but of course they were impossible to read without reflecting on what had passed in the world since he announced his convictions and principles.

Baugham yawned. Reaching into his other pocket, he fished out another piece of paper, carefully folded up. Looking at it made him stop yawning, his face showing a mixture of a frown and a smile. Those amazing bumble bees, flawed as their artistic execution was, were bravely making their way across the page in what looked like confidence and joy. He carefully folded the paper again and slipped it into the middle of Monsieur Tournier's most passionate argument for the transformation of *des Etats Généraux* into a true reflection of the French will and interest of the French people.

"No game today, madam. You will have to satisfy your hunger by reading the Inquirer instead. And it is only two days old, so supper might just be forced to wait after all."

"However fond I am of grouse, my lord, the Inquirer is surely far more succulent in its arguments, so I thank you."

"Well, I hope it will entertain you. I confess I rushed through it because I was too anxious to hear your opinion on the Lord Rector's scheme of financing the new University Study Hall by subscription."

Lord Baugham made himself comfortable in what had become his accustomed chair and stretched his long legs.

"Blasted rain!" he said. "Couldn't even see the fat pheasants flying two feet above your head, if, indeed, they were as stupid as the hunter and ever came out of the snug holes they keep themselves to. I hope you have grown tired of game."

"If not exactly tired, I can certainly appreciate Mrs Higgins' baked turnips and leek soup more these days. It seems his lordship giveth and his lordship taketh away in equal shares lately. My lord."

Baugham gave her an arched eyebrow, to which she pursed her lips to hide a smile.

"Well, one day we may be blessed to have stray mutton on our tables, for I was down to Nethery Farm with Mr McLaughlin yesterday. Apparently some of their sheep had wandered over to the river on the Clyne side of the property line and they needed to be returned to their rightful owner, except apparently good Farmer Nethery was a trifle vague on how many of his sheep had actually gone missing. He thought we might have driven them down to the market to make a profit out of them ourselves. Or put them on our table. What a peculiar fellow!"

"The only thing peculiar about that Nethery is how he still is in possession of his farm with the mismanagement and drink that seems to occupy him instead of providing for his family."

Baugham looked at her thoughtfully. "I understand from Mrs McLaughlin that we take in laundry from Mrs Nethery."

"A sorely needed source of income for them, I should imagine. The oldest boy is seventeen now, so one can only hope he can take over from his father soon."

Baugham nodded quietly. He had entertained the same hope himself after speaking to the father and ending up settling the details of Farmer Nethery's drunken accusations with his son Duncan standing by. The simple labour of sawing down a murky tree by the entrance lane together with Mr McLaughlin had been a glum affair after that.

HOLLY SAT AS FAR BACK in the seat as she could, attempting to minimise the contact between herself and the fat, smelly man beside her. She had been away a full week, the stage was behind time and its progress seemed unutterably slow. Her spirits were depressed, though not so much from the tiresome journey as from her own thoughts. She had visited every reputable school in the city, followed every lead and suggestion of families in search of a governess, and although everyone she spoke to seemed impressed by her knowledge and accomplishments, they also all asked for references from her last employer. In several schools, just the mention of Hockdown appeared to trigger recognition of her name. Her former employers had done a thorough job of insuring that her reputation was well and truly wracked within her immediate circle of opportunity.

She turned toward the window to escape the attentions of the fat man and cheered herself up with the thought: *Only a few more hours. I should be home by sunset at any rate. Home by sunset*... Home. She had spent so much of her young life longing for home, she could scarcely accept that she would soon have to contemplate leaving it again.

Just as the sky was beginning to darken, the stage pulled in front of the Caledonian Thistle on the outskirts of the village. She stepped out of the coach, tipped the driver and grabbed her carpetbag. The air was dry and cold, winter had definitely arrived, and she pulled her coat tightly about her as she walked down the lane in the evening light.

The shadows lengthened and disappeared by the time she turned the corner into the lane that led to Rosefarm Cottage. There it stood, warmly lit and welcoming. She slowed her pace, taking in the sight and recognising the horse tied on the gatepost.

Just as well, she thought wearily, *he's one more person I might ask.*

"THAT, SURELY, IS A MATTER of principle!"

"It is only a matter of principle because you have a fixed opinion on it!"

Mrs Higgins quickly deposited the tea and made her way out of the parlour again, because to her mind it distinctly looked as if the Mistress and her guest were having an argument. She was very used to arguments being held in all their vigour, leading to loud exclamations on any number of topics, but she was not so certain this was one of Mrs Tournier's usual disputes. And Lord Baugham did look a little too agitated for the circumstances, and him a young man at that.

Noticing the servant's hasty withdrawal, Mrs Tournier halted her rhetoric and gave a snort.

"I think you are frightening the servants, my lord."

"I am certain I could not be intimidating enough for that on my own."

Mrs Tournier unexpectedly sighed and gave a sad smile.

"You are perfectly right. I have been in a frightful humour all week and the only thing that seems to lift my spirits is getting into fruitless arguments over principles with you."

"And when will Miss Tournier be home?" Baugham asked quietly.

"Therein lies the answer to my current distemper. I have been half-expecting her all afternoon. Now, it appears that I will spend tomorrow in watchfulness as well."

"She had not anticipated being away for so long, I believe. Pardon me if I'm too inquisitive, but has her trip been successful?"

The woman's face turned grim and she shook her head slightly. "She is now seeking another position."

"A position…" his lordship repeated carefully, "As in…at another school?"

"Or with a family, or wherever!" Mrs Tournier snapped. "But away nevertheless…away from here. Away from home. Again."

"Ah…" Baugham said slowly. "Not entirely unexpected, I would assume. But, perhaps, disappointing?"

"Quite," Mrs Tournier crisply said. "But I have no qualms admitting to you that a disappointment of this sort is no easier to bear simply because of its necessity or inevitability."

She stood up and walked over to the window, glancing out at the road.

"It is just her and me. This is her home; she belongs here. For a moment all was as it should have been again and now the pieces of my life are once more broken up and jumbled, waiting for us to lay them out in order again. I find that I do not take to it as well as I used to. Not that it alters anything."

Baugham listened quietly to Mrs Tournier's matter of fact statement, delivered as it was without a shred of drama or self-pity. In the silence that followed they were both startled by the sound of a door creaking. Mrs Tournier turned around and fixed her eyes on the door. Baugham scrambled out of his seat, at a loss as to why his heart suddenly seemed to be pounding with anticipation.

She burst into the room and looked around her with some amazement. Then she dropped her carpetbag, giving a quick curtsey toward his lordship, while her eyes searched for another. Once found, she ran into her mother's embrace right where she stood and, barely holding back tears of fatigue and worry, expressed her relief at being home.

If Lord Baugham had paid as much attention to such things as he usually did, he would have noticed straight away that there was mud all over Miss Tournier's boots and on the hem of her simple brown skirt and travelling coat. Loose strands of hair had escaped all around her face and collar and her smile was tired. But he noticed none of this because he was so taken aback by her sudden appearance and a surge of indescribable emotion gripping his stomach — which he presumed was the effect of the perfect surprise — that he noticed nothing else. Next came relief and he felt a grin spreading over his face. Mrs Higgins rushed in, anxious to relieve the traveller of her effects, adding her exclamations of surprise and welcome to the mix but he found he was still silent. He only looked at her with a pleased smile. He told himself it was relief for her safe return, but in honesty he knew it was something else. He had missed her.

"Well!" had been Mrs Tournier's only utterance when her daughter burst into the room and no one — least of all herself — could have discerned whether it was a mark of pleasure or irritation. When Holly sat down beside her, she could still not utter anything except "Well!" but this time it was clear that she was well pleased with the return.

"You must have some tea," she then sternly said, although the light in her eyes and the warmth with which she regarded her daughter could not be mistaken. "You look quite freakish, my dear, you must have walked all the way from the inn. I shall take that as a compliment, but I will insist you go up and change as soon as possible. Mrs Higgins! Bring some fresh tea, if you will!" With a wink to her guest she added, "And the sugar bowl. As you see, I have been quite well entertained while you were away and hardly have had time to miss you at all."

Miss Tournier only smiled at her mother's gruff manner and leaned in to kiss her on the cheek. "Well, I have missed you dreadfully," she said softly.

Baugham watched it all with unexpected pleasure, enjoying the sight of Mrs Tournier showering her daughter with unaffected love, while at the same time staying true to her accustomed directness. Miss Tournier was obviously relieved to be home and in her mother's care again, simply smiling at her and holding on to her hand. It was a pleasing sight, indeed.

He soon realised that he must be intruding and although he was loath to withdraw from witnessing such a warm, familial scene, he realised he must. Miss Tournier had had a long and arduous journey and he was satisfied with the knowledge that she was now restored safely and properly to her kin. That was what mattered, and what had been his concern all along, after all.

"Miss Tournier," he said, still smiling as he stood to leave. "Since you are now returned, I feel happy in relinquishing the pleasant company of your mother to you without hesitation. I wouldn't wish to further intrude on your homecoming. I am sure I will see you again soon; I've grown so dependant on your mother's company and conversation, I fear I won't be able to forsake it even now that you are home."

SHE RETURNED HIS SMILE. IT seemed he did not hold a grudge against her over the unpleasant manner of their parting and for that she was grateful. Hard feelings on his part would have made her avowed task all the more difficult, though she was determined to see it through all the same. After taking a breath she stood up and stepped toward him. In a quiet voice she spoke: "Tomorrow I thought I might walk out to visit... with Mrs McLaughlin... I wondered if I might take a moment of your time while I am there?"

He was quite taken aback. She was asking him for a private word. That was most unexpected. Suddenly a feeling of her hunting not having been successful struck him. But what on earth did she think *he* could do? She didn't think he *could* do something, did she? Was he supposed to *do* something?

"I am at your service, Miss Tournier, as always," he said in what he hoped was a carefree tone. Then he smiled once more reassuringly, took her hand gently in his, kissed it and bowed to take his leave. "Let me say that it is very good to see you again and I hope to see you tomorrow then. Have a good and restful night."

Chapter 18

Offers are Anticipated, Dreaded, Pre-empted, Made and Accepted

MR McLaughlin listened to the approaching footsteps in the yard outside the stables. He paused in his labour and sighed. Not even mucking dung was safe today. It was, naturally, his lordship coming to look him up. He had hidden here originally from his wife, but that was Lord Baugham's doing, too. Whenever his Master was in a queer mood like today – restless, angry, upset, bored — he took it out on Mrs McLaughlin by following her around the house and making sport of her chores and monosyllabic communication. He would tease her until her gruff answers gradually receded into glaring looks or sighs and when there was no more response to be had out of her, he would then move on to her husband, looking for physical chores that might offer him more resistance.

By now it was already too late for him to maintain any hope of a peaceful day. After having taken one look at his wife when he came in for his lunch, he quickly gulped down his cock-a-leekie soup and went out to the stables and the horses' manure. Mr McLaughlin sighed. He was a simple man, and one of the best things about his position with his lordship was the relative peace and quiet in which he could do his work. That rarely changed, even when Lord Baugham was in residence, and normally he quite liked his company — though he did talk a lot, even for a southern man — and even admired his familiarity and ready acceptance of the dirtier chores of the estate, but when he got into these moods of his ... McLaughlin could not understand them and therefore stayed wary of them.

He listened closely again. Yes, he was definitely heading this way. McLaughlin stuck his shovel into the dung heap and decided there were rabbit traps a few miles west that needed inspection. Alone. This instant.

How curious, Baugham thought as he shook the handle of the shovel back and forth a little in the dung heap, he could have sworn he heard someone digging about just when he was about to turn the corner. But no matter. Obviously it was work in progress and he might as well dig in himself. Taking off his coat and turning up his sleeves, he set to work emptying the remaining dirt in the wheel barrel.

It did not take long for him to finish and return to his own rooms, feeling somewhat more serene than when he had left them that morning. He could still not understand what Miss Tournier could think merited a private conversation between them so soon after her return from Edinburgh. Or, to be more accurate, he could still not understand how he would be able to avoid involving himself in something he was not prepared to undertake. That was more to the point. He knew her well enough to expect anything from her and that was a frightening thought. In his calmer moments he thought that perhaps her urgency had something to do with her cousin and Mr Darcy. Perhaps something along his own impatience for news and intelligence on how things were faring in Hertfordshire these days. In his more anxious moments he conjured up desperate schemes and arrangements that made him cringe and a light panicky sweat form under his collar. What if she was still on the hunt? Underneath all this, however, was unbridled curiosity and impatience. Did she actually mean not to make her call until teatime? What awful complications could ensue from such a late meeting? Disagreements over tea in his parlour? Disappointments to be nursed by walking home in the dark and refusing carriages and any aid? Tears? Good Lord, anything but tears!

Baugham sighed. He needed to clean himself up, change and then assume some perfect pose of indifference and feign an engrossing occupation in some appropriate location while he waited to receive her and find out what this was all about.

Despite her weariness, Holly had not slept well. The intervening days had done nothing to alleviate the memory of Mr Pembroke's pronouncement or of her worries about finding work. When the morning dawned, she crept out of bed, dressed quietly, and went downstairs to think and worry some more.

She shared a cup of tea with Mrs Higgins, catching up on the little bits of home life she had missed while she was away: Mrs Tournier — as Holly expected when she was not there to look out for her — had spent far too much time working at her desk, but she was gratified to hear that Lord Baugham had been a regular visitor during that time. *It was very kind of him,* she thought, *and Maman likes his company…*

Holly left the thought unfinished. She busied herself around the house and in the garden. She visited with her mother and helped Mrs Higgins in the kitchen and anything else she could think of to occupy herself, until she could put off her errand no longer. Grabbing a basket and filling it with some dried bundles from the root cellar, she finally headed out to Clyne Cottage.

The long walk gave her time to think about what she would say to Lord Baugham. It really was a simple request — he spent much of his time in London and must be acquainted with many families. She was not as convinced that he would be aware if any of them had need of a governess, but even just a few names would give her a place to start. If they could manage to make the trip to Hertfordshire for Jane's wedding, it was only another half-day's journey to London. Just a name or two … and perhaps he would know of some schools as well. But, by the time she had reached the kitchen door, she was still not quite sure of how to approach him with such an unusual question.

A few minutes in the Clyne kitchen, exchanging her own surplus herbs for a few that Mrs McLaughlin's cupboard held in abundance, and she found herself being quickly escorted by the unusually tight-lipped housekeeper to the library.

Lord Baugham was standing by his desk in front of stacks of paper and there was a steady thumping noise as he was throwing old newspapers in a pile on the floor beside him, presumably to be got rid of. Mrs McLaughlin's mouth narrowed further and she gave a huffing noise before disappearing straight away.

Holly looked after her in surprise, having expected some sort of introduction before being left alone, but before she could reflect on how to introduce herself, his lordship had turned around and spotted her.

"Oh," he said. "Miss Tournier. Is it teatime already?"

"I, uh …" Holly stammered, "I don't think it's quite … Mrs McLaughlin …" Then she dropped a quick curtsey and asked, "How are you today, my lord?"

He bowed to her over the growing pile of newspapers on the floor, which looked slightly strange, and Holly could not suppress a smile.

"Very well, thank you. And you?"

"I am well, thank you."

"Quite restored from your travel?"

"Yes, thank you."

"Glad to hear it." There was a small pause during which Baugham wondered if he should resort to the whole ritual of polite greetings and then decided he would certainly try. "And your mother? Is she well?"

"Very well, thank you my lord. She sends her regards and thanks for your visit yesterday. And for your … assistance, I think was what she said."

"Not at all. It was my pleasure. Did you walk? The weather was not too cold?"

Holly looked at him suspiciously. Had they ever engaged in such a thorough exchange of civilities during their entire acquaintance? This was very odd. However, since she could not quite decide how to approach the reason for her visit, she played along, wondering how far he would take it.

"Actually, the day is quite nice. Perfect for a brisk walk. And you? Are you liking the change in season?"

He looked at her and then could not help himself, but broke into a smile.

"A change in season, is it? As in change from cold rain to ice cold rain and now we are all eagerly anticipating the soon to come change into sleet?"

His smile was disarming and Holly, suddenly aware of how brightly his blue eyes twinkled when he did so, could not help but return it.

"That's very true," she said, trying not to stare. She dropped her eyes, feeling confused.

"I brought Mrs McLaughlin some Agrimony. It's good to take if you are caught out in the weather... icy rain... sleet... that is what I was gathering when I slipped in the mud... So I thought I should bring her some."

"Ah well," Baugham answered awkwardly as they both remembered the unpleasant end to that adventure. "I do my best to avoid Mrs McLaughlin's potions if I can possibly escape them. A hot drink and a good fire are all that are necessary to ward off a chill. Better than those barbaric tonics she tries to foist off on me."

Holly opened her mouth to protest his prejudice against time honoured traditions and remedies, but thought better of provoking another scene. She was here to ask a favour of him and it would be best to come to the point. She began abruptly, "I want to thank you for taking the time to speak with me today. I know that my asking this of you is highly unusual."

Baugham realised she was about to launch into her reasons and he almost winced.

"Ah, yes... well, um... that is, I am happy to be of service."

Never had more uncertain words been spoken, he reflected and moved a few papers around to hopefully seem casual about what was to come. Whatever it was.

Taking a deep breath and plunging ahead, Holly began, "You know my purpose in going to Edinburgh was to — "

"Miss Tournier!" Baugham blurted out. "I wonder, could you do something about my library for me?"

The moment the words left his mouth, he was shocked into silence. Had he just said that? He had not even thought it before he was suddenly making an offer! It seemed she was shocked as well. She stared at him while wrinkles formed on her forehead and her eyebrows drew together in incomprehension.

"I beg your pardon?" she said slowly.

"I... I need someone to restore my library for me. Perhaps you could? It is a shambles. Mr Darcy says so all the time. So I thought. Perhaps. You could?"

"You mean... work for you? Here?" Her hand sought her right earlobe and tugged at it gently in confusion.

Was that what he had meant? He supposed so. In a way. And why not? Miss Tournier was in need of employment, he was in need — apparently — of a librarian. A librarian was not a dependent. It was a skilled craftswoman, an expert, someone with respectable knowledge and independence.

"Well... yes. As you can see there is a great deal of work, and it might take some time..."

But Holly was scarcely listening. All she could think of was that Lord Baugham had just offered her an opportunity to earn some badly needed funds close to home. Looking around she quickly decided that in its current state, his lordship's library might just keep her in work until Dr McKenna could engage her. She would not have to leave, at least not yet.

The more she considered it, the more excited she became and she nearly had to stop herself from jumping up and down for joy. She could not stop the brilliant smile that lit her face or the enthusiasm in her voice as she accepted.

"Yes! Yes! I will! Thank you, thank you!" She was babbling, she knew, but she could not help it. "When should I start? Do you have anything particular in mind? Tomorrow? Shall I come tomorrow?"

Baugham felt like someone had left the doors to the stables open and he was in the process of witnessing his horses escaping to freedom. It was a beautiful sight certainly, but at what cost?

"Um…" he said hoping to form some opinion on just what exactly he had in mind by changing the subject. "Tea? Would you like some tea?"

Holly returned his hesitation with a smile that nearly spilled out into laughter. "Oh no! I promised Maman I'd be home for tea." Suddenly she stopped, afraid she had seemed rude. "That is, I thank you, but I cannot. Maman is expecting me. Oh…"

She frowned a little, lost as it seemed in her own thoughts.

"My lord, it is very kind of you to offer and I gladly accept your commission, but I think I need to discuss this with my mother before I can settle any details. I hope you understand."

Understand? He was gratefully relieved!

"Of course. That is entirely appropriate."

"Then perhaps…" She looked at him, her eyes sparkling, not even attempting to hide her happiness and excitement, fighting hard against bouncing with joy. "Perhaps you would care to take tea with us…some day…tomorrow? Today?"

Baugham looked at her. She was a puzzle, this woman. Usually when they met she was irritating and bothersome. When she had walked in to his library, she had looked sad and strained. As she was now, she was almost beautiful.

"Well, if you are intent on not staying for tea and must hurry home, why don't we kill two birds with one stone and I will walk with you and speak to Mrs Tournier. It will be getting dark soon," he added.

Again, she looked at him with an open, almost teasing expression. "Oh! Well, I suppose it is only fair that you should be the one to tell her of your generous offer. Not that she is not excessively fond of you already, I think, but this might just make her openly declare her rare admiration and esteem."

Baugham was slightly confused by this, but she smiled so openly and without a hint of mischief that it was contagious.

"Right then. I'll just get my coat." He walked towards the door and was almost opening it before he stopped, reminded of her original reason for seeing him. "Oh, I must beg your pardon, Miss Tournier. I think you wanted to speak to me about something…"

She had moved to one of the shelves and was fingering the books and carefully touching the backs of the ones standing up when she looked back at him, her big dark eyes laughing and a contented smile that made her face glow.

196

"Oh no! No, it was nothing, my lord! Nothing important at all!"

"Did I not say that it was a lovely day for a brisk walk?" Holly continued the chatter on the way to Rosefarm. "Have you read Montaigne's *Of Experience*? There's a line in it that always pops into my mind when I walk: '*when I walk alone in a beautiful orchard, if my thoughts have been dwelling elsewhere, I bring them back to the walk, to the orchard, to the sweetness of this solitude, and to me*'. Of course, this is not an orchard, but I always think of it when I go through the woods as well."

She reached out and plucked a bronzed leaf off of a branch of a nearby tree. "I don't usually like to walk through the orchards this time of year. They always feel so empty and desolate. My favourite time is in the spring, when the trees are bursting with flowers and bees, and everything is so busy and full of life."

Baugham could only watch her in amazement. Who was this chattering, skipping person talking about orchards and spring? It seemed every time she opened her mouth he was even more amazed at what came out of it. Holding his peace, he listened to her rattle on, hardly pausing to gasp for breath.

"But, of course that makes this time of year excellent for the kind of work you have offered me. Did I already tell you how thankful I am?" She smiled and a slight blush spread across her face. "Oh, I am certain I did, didn't I?"

Baugham gave a dismissive gesture and swung his cane through the wilted grass, still saying nothing.

"And I will work very hard and it will be a pleasure at the same time. And even if that commission of Dr McKenna or any other is offered to me, I promise you will still have my absolute diligence and commitment. There is, I know, a lot of work to be done and your library is sorely lacking in attention and dedication. I am sorry to say it, but I think you must agree. Still, I am certain I can make something out of it that you can be proud of and enjoy all at the same time. That is what libraries should give, don't you think? Both pleasure and knowledge — a whole world in a little space — so many friends and even authorities for your personal joy! It is like a little university in your own home, don't you think?"

Baugham shook his head slightly while he smiled at the ground.

"What? Oh, I do go on, don't I?" Holly laughed and ripped the leaf apart sprinkling the ground with the dry remnants as they walked on. "But this means so much to me," she said more quietly. "To us. My mother and me."

"So it seems," he said. "And your promise of industry is impressive. Though it does leave me slightly breathless."

"Oh!" She averted her eyes and bit her lip. "Well, when I get excited I do… well, I do lose some of my composure I suppose, and buzz about."

He looked at her and smilingly said:

"The bee goes out, and honey home doth bring,
And some who seek that honey find a sting.

Now would'st thou have the honey, and be free
From stinging, in the first place kill the bee."

Baugham had been thinking of the lines for a long time. They would perhaps be seen as impertinent, but they seemed to fit this exhuberant moment and surely she could not know about the scrap of paper serving as a bookmark now.

HOLLY LOOKED AT LORD BAUGHAM for a moment, reminded her of her poor unscientific bumble bees that could not assure themselves of even insincere flattery.

"Really, my lord, that is terribly unfair to the poor bee — to destroy it because you will not take the time to learn how best to get the honey. I presume that is a dilemma many of us face — there is no other insect that can provide the honey, yet we shy away from the bee because we are afraid of its sting. We need it, but it frightens us."

She walked along a few more steps, and then, feeling silly, turned to him, "Well, you need not fear me in any case. I promise that *I* will not sting unless it is absolutely necessary. Instead, I will be a model employee, docile and unthreatening in every way."

"You know, Miss Tournier," he said, "you do me great wrong. I have absolutely nothing against industrious bees. I am excessively fond of them for their own sake — not just the honey. And after all, if the bee did not sting, it would not be a bee, but some simple fly. And I find simple, docile, unthreatening flies to be quite boring. Especially when compared to those amazing bees whose thorax and wings are so deliciously challenging its whole capacity to fly."

Holly gave a small, embarrassed laugh. "Well, I cannot continue that metaphor in any way, my lord, that will not make me seem impertinent and possibly ungrateful. You are safe this time."

"I'm sorry your trip was unsuccessful," Baugham said quietly after a while. "I would have wished the initial inconveniences would have ensured its success."

Holly nodded and took a few steps to the side of the path to ostensibly inspect some sort of wilted plant, but in reality she did not want to discuss that particular topic or even think about it in his company. Mr Pembroke was gone and she would think of him no more. It was enough to know that the threat he had hung before her and the imminent notice on the rental conditions could be met with something more than ineffectual despair and outrage.

Baugham noticed his kindly meant comment was not to Miss Tournier's liking and he pursed his lips and stayed silent again. Their pace picked up, there was no talk now and the light was fading. But his remark still hung in the air. He realised he had broken an unspoken rule by alluding to Miss Tournier's difficulties. It was, in such a relationship of employer and employee as theirs had become, presumptuous and possibly threatening to a woman as proud and as desperate for work as she was.

He took a deep breath. Well, here was just one more time he would bend his carefully laid out rules for this family.

"Miss Tournier, my father, the late Earl of Cumbermere, left me with precious little of worth. He squandered most of his fortune and sold off countless valuables to pay his debts and obligations. So, among other things, I inherited quite a ramshackle library that once had been lovingly assembled by my grandfather and my uncle. My father sold off most of the valuable pieces, apart from the ones that his secretary and my mother could save."

She looked at him, surprised, but said nothing and continued to walk on the grass beside the actual path.

"This rather embarrassing remnant of the Cumbermere pride and joy I have brought with me to Clyne," he continued. "It certainly is no library for a discerning gentleman, a fact Mr Darcy loses no opportunity to remind me of, and so far I have found solace in the knowledge that Joseph, my father's secretary, is taking very good care of my own collection in London. But I cannot bring him here to do the same and, the more I stay at Clyne, the more I feel the old Cumbermere library and whatever I have purchased since, does me no credit and brings me no joy. That is why I need your help in bringing it to order. I have no idea what is in it, what treasures, if any, are still in my possession, or what needs to be compensated."

To his relief she had once again joined him on the path, but kept her head bowed down and her hands behind her back, eyes averted.

"On my own, I would hardly know where to begin," he then said softly.

They passed out of the woods and made their way along the little stretch of Kye River that ran up to Clanough. The bridge creaked as they both walked over it and they exchanged a brief smile. Holly took a step to the rail and threw in the rest of her crumbled leaf and stem. They stood for a while in silence, looking out over the water and tracing the twirling water bubbling just a few feet underneath them. Holly considered Lord Baugham's revelation about his family affairs and pondered all the information he had shared with her. Though she was sure he felt himself to be matter-of-fact in his statements, she could tell that there was much emotion beneath the surface as he spoke of his father. She was not curious about the father — it was the same story told many times over across the kingdom — but she wondered about his mother, and about him . . . Here he was, a young man, trying to hold together and rebuild the remnants of his legacy. Did he have a guide? or was he trying to find his way on his own? It was no wonder to Holly that he had become so attached to her mother — if ever there was an unchanging anchor in the world, it was Arabella Tournier.

"I see," she finally said. "Thank you. I will, as I said, do my best."

"I have no doubt you will," he smiled, leaning against the railing. "I will, of course, allow for a helper and you must continue to see to your other obligations. I dare say the chaos will keep for a while yet without complete ruin. I must say, though, that I am afraid you may think twice about agreeing to this commitment when you see what a mess I find myself in. It won't do to pretend it is anything else than on the brink of hopelessness."

"Lord Baugham, I hope I am not the kind of person who will go back on my word simply because there is labour involved in keeping it!"

He smiled at the faint, familiar note of irritation and could not hide his amusement.

"Oh, I am positive you are not! But I am equally certain that neither are you a person wholly convinced it is impossible to force twenty-five hours of work into a twenty-four hour day if you feel it is required to meet your standards, and then where would I be with your mother?" He laughed. "Oh yes, I believe a bee is a most appropriate description of you, there are no two ways about that!"

He stopped and looked at her with a curious expression, but not without considerable warmth and spark in his brilliant blue eyes. I wonder, he found himself unexpectedly and silently musing, I wonder what is it about her... Only when her expression became confused and curious did he realize he had been staring and he pulled his eyes and thoughts away.

Again they turned and watched the swirling water until the silence became uncomfortable.

"My mother will be very grateful," she replied quietly, showing the turn that her own thoughts had taken, "as I think you must know."

"It is no secret that she is happier when you are home," he said, "and if I can be of some service to her in that way..." he tapered off before blurting out: "You must forgive me, Miss Tournier, I know you call Clanough your home and say you would be content to never again leave it, but after what I have come to know of local society, and of your landlord, I wonder that the two of you choose to stay. That is, your time in Edinburgh must have shown you that there is something beyond provincial attitudes and prejudices. There surely must be other places you can go. Places without the memories and circumstances that must burden you here."

"My lord," she said quickly, stiffening, "if you are regretting your offer, please retract it at once, before —"

"Not at all," he assured her. "You have my word."

"Thank you," she smiled with obvious relief, then still leaning on the rail, she turned to him, her brow wrinkled in thought. "But I must tell you that the memories here are no burden to either of us, my lord, they are a blessing." Her hand came up absently to tug on her earlobe as her face changed and her expression grew distant. "I think they are exactly what keeps us happy here, and the people and their mind-set; most of them are very nice, the rest... they just don't matter. It is the place. When we first arrived, Papa would make me walk with him all over the village — to learn all about our new home, he said. He was well-liked here, you know, despite his... well, Frenchness. Perhaps there is still something left of that Auld Alliance that made the people here very generous when a Frenchman sought refuge in his obvious distress, even in this day and age. Maybe that's why I love it so much; every inch of it reminds me of him. The paths, the lanes, even this bridge. Especially this bridge."

Curious, for reasons of his own, to hear how memories of one's childhood and one's father could be seen in such a different light from his own, Baugham could not help but ask, "Why this bridge?"

"It was our spot," she said with a look of tenderness. "Wherever we would walk, we always tried to end up here; we'd stand here like this for what seemed like hours and watch the water, or have some sort of silly contest…"

He looked at her in astonishment. "Perhaps I am reverting back to my own shameful boyhood memories of what sorts of contests are held while looking out over bridges, but, don't tell me Monsieur Tournier and his very refined daughter engaged in a… spitting contest?"

She looked up at him, and despite the slight blush that coloured her cheeks, raised her chin and smiled.

"Perhaps."

The laugh that came from that admission and the mental picture it conjured up was instant and spontaneous. Miss Tournier joined in.

"But I was sworn to secrecy and so must you be, my lord. Do not breathe a word of this to my mother."

"Upon my honour," he gasped. "Your secret is safe with this co-offender." Then, catching his breath, he realized that though it was probably time to continue on their way, he did not quite want to yet. He looked down at his feet, then leaned over to pluck two pebbles lodged between the planks of the bridge that were no doubt left by some village boys from a throwing contest. He laughed when he weighed them in his hands.

"Tell me," he said, handing one over to her, "did your father teach you to throw as well?"

"Of course he did." She smiled mischievously, challenging him to make the first throw. "But, you should know," she cautioned, "he taught me well. I am a very good shot, my lord. You had best beware."

He fixed his gaze on her once more, his blue eyes twinkling and a wry smile hovering on his lips.

"Oh, Miss Tournier, I think it is a little too late for that!"

She stepped back from the railing and quickly averted her eyes, nervously smoothing her skirts and tugging at her ear while her eyes darted everywhere but to meet his. Lord Baugham suddenly realised they had skated from apologies and awkward confessions, through teasing bantering and thoughtful conversation and on into full-fledged flirting without him even having noticed it. That thought gave him a jolt and he stood straight.

"I'm afraid, Miss Tournier," he said a little more stiffly than he intended, "that however pleasant this moment is, we really should be getting on. Please…?"

Very slowly they turned and, as if careful not to tread and shatter a delicate thing that lingered around them, they made their way in silence towards Rosefarm Cottage and the comfortable ritual of its tea tray.

Chapter 19

*His Lordship's Library Finally gets the Attention it
Deserves and a New Avid Reader is Introduced*

B AUGHAM was suffering from acute embarrassment. He sat in his chair in the small parlour where two women on the opposite sofa were beaming at him and sending him grateful and happy looks, all because of a strange impulse he was now having doubts about, if not outright regrets. He really did not like to be reminded he had that kind of power over persons he hardly knew, and the fact that a mere whim and indiscernible fancy of his could make such a difference to someone was disquieting to say the least. These women were now obviously depending on him and, more to the point, they were to be a feature of his daily life here that he could not control and that he had never intended or particularly wanted. It smelled of exactly the kind of thing Darcy was always going on about — duty and obligation — and he thought he had guarded himself well from that sort of involvement while at Clyne.

"Well, I really cannot stay," he said as he got out of his seat. "I'm happy my suggestion meets with your approval, Mrs Tournier. If it is at all convenient I would suggest Miss Tournier could perhaps pay Clyne a visit tomorrow and make an initial assessment of the work and then we could proceed."

Holly stood up, still smiling but a looking a little surprised at the abruptness of his speech.

"Oh! But can't we offer you — "

"No, no!" his lordship said and took a step closer to the door. "It is late; I would not wish to inconvenience you any longer. We will meet tomorrow and then we will see where we are."

He took his leave and left the women looking after him. Just as he closed the door behind him he heard a female shriek from the parlour window and he hesitated. Rolling laughter followed it, however, so he briskly went on his way again, not looking back.

ONCE HIS LORDSHIP LEFT, HOLLY at last could give in to her long suppressed urge to jump up and down in excitement. She then ran to her mother and nearly smothered her in an excited embrace.

"Maman, is this not the finest thing in the world? I have found work, right here in Clanough! And I'll have time enough to look for more before —" she broke off suddenly.

"Before what, Lie-lie?" Mrs Tournier asked.

"Oh, I really wish I didn't have to talk about it right now," Holly began, "but as unpleasant as it was, I think it was a good thing I took that ride with Mr Pembroke after all."

Her mother looked at her tartly, but held onto her hand. "Well, that is the one thing you will never manage to convince me of."

For a moment Holly's exuberance and joy gave way to a more serious expression. "Maman, during that trip I was able to learn something, something that it is better to know as early as possible. Mr Pembroke is taking over his father's business affairs, together with the management of his properties, Rosefarm included."

Her mother's face progressively grew more severe as she waited for her daughter to finish her sentence. "Is he letting us go?" she asked tightly.

Holly sighed, sorry that this discussion was taking the joy out of the moment, but it was best to get the truth out quickly.

"He is raising the rent — significantly — and it will come due this Christmas. But Maman, we are well provided for now, because I have the money from Sir John we can use for that, and now with my work for Lord Baugham, we will have something to live on as well. That gives us the next three months to solicit work enough to prepare for when it comes around again."

Her mother looked at her with narrowed eyes. "And this is why his lordship offered you employment?"

"Heavens no!" Holly was shocked. "I wouldn't share our private matters with anyone, Maman. Certainly not with him. What a thing to suggest!"

"Hm," Mrs Tournier said.

"It really needs work," Holly said seriously. "That library is a disgrace."

"Oh, I'm certain it is," her mother said, "and time consuming as well. Have you agreed upon a suitable salary for such an extensive renovation?"

"Well, no," Holly admitted. "Not as of yet. It was a spur of the moment decision, you see. But I'm sure everything will work out easily."

Mrs Tournier looked at her and simply said, "Yes. As easily as everything works out between the two of you. But in any case I would suggest you agree to terms soon, and also that you should arrange for some additional help."

She got up and her daughter stayed where she was looking thoughtful.

"Yes, his lordship did mention something about more help."

"As he should," Mrs Tournier nodded. "You'll need a suitable young man to help you with the heavy or dirty tasks who could also benefit from escaping from his daily grind and perhaps get more out of assisting you than wages for his work. I think his lordship's sense of charity can well stand it."

"You already have someone in mind, don't you?" Holly said suspiciously.

"Certainly I do," Mrs Tournier answered calmly. "Hamish Nethery."

IN SPITE OF TAKING THE shortest way home, Baugham found himself surprised at just how soon he could see the lights of his windows showing through the trees. He had spun round in the same thoughts all the way without being able to reconcile them or make sense of their relation to one another. When he left the laughing women he had been overwhelmed by a sense of wryness. Well, he had done a good thing, even if it was from complete ignorance and lack of moral deliberation. It had just popped out of him! It had, however, been for the best and he felt pleased he could help a friend like Mrs Tournier keep her daughter beside her for a few more months.

Apart from that, however, he tried hard not to think of what he had done to his well-established routine and purpose at Clyne. He had invited a woman into his house — a quarrelsome, bothersome, opinionated woman — one with whom it took all his efforts to remain on civil terms and who really had the most unfortunate habit of making him feel ill at ease and doubtful of his own resolutions. A woman who gave him inviting glimpses of a laughing temperament and a spirited and mischievous nature, but who could show a general resentment toward him and who he was, just as easily as she could fall into friendly banter. A woman who had looked so troubled when she came to see him at Clyne with her still unknown appeal, that he had impulsively given in to charity to save her from the shame of making a request of him or to see her suffer.

He did not like that last thought at all. And so he returned to the first thoughts on his surrender to keep his privacy absolute and every local dignitary, personality, denizen or neighbour out of his house and life. Mrs Tournier was happy, and he had been glad to do his friend a service. But *she* would be there, perhaps *every day*... He sighed as his thoughts continued around the same track once more.

MRS McLAUGHLIN WAS JUST THROWING the last soiled cloth in her laundry basket for tomorrow and giving one last proud glance at the shining copper pans and silver laid out all over the table, when there came a discreet knock at the kitchen door. Proud with her work that morning, she opened the door and let Miss Tournier in.

"Ye'll be here to look at the library then, Miss Tournier? His lairdship told me ye'd be comin'. He's in there now, if ye can show yerself the way." Mrs McLaughlin said, beginning the task of returning the metalware to its proper place. She gave the young woman a glance as she gathered her cloak and bonnet to stow away and shook her head grimly to herself as Miss Tournier gingerly made her way down the hall.

204

Feeling a bit out of place, walking through the rooms and down the halls of Clyne Cottage unaccompanied, Holly found the door that she thought must be the library and softly tapped on it. To her relief she heard a muffled voice on the other side and brisk footsteps. Before she was quite ready, the door opened and she was face to face with Lord Baugham.

"Good morning," she said hesitatingly. "I hope … that is, we never settled on a time yesterday so I wasn't sure … Is this inconvenient? Me coming now, I mean?"

"Now is as good as ever!" Baugham said in what he hoped was a cheerful tone that did not give away his own hesitation. "Come in! Come in! I'll send for tea, shall I?"

Although she had taken a good strong cup before she left home to sustain herself and not be forced to take anything in the form of food or drink while working, she quickly nodded. It was something to keep busy with, a prop to help them through what must be the initial awkwardness of a new relationship. And anyway, the tea served at Clyne was nothing like the tea she drank alone at the kitchen table at Rosefarm, so this was an entirely different meal, she rationalised to herself.

She slowly moved around while Lord Baugham busied himself with finding Mrs McLaughlin. It was a beautiful room, richly furnished with dark woods and leather, well lit by large windows and warmed with a lively blaze in a great brick fireplace. She walked about, admiring the floor to ceiling bookcases along two full walls — deeply breathing in the beloved smell of paper, ink, wood smoke, and what might have been the smell of old tobacco — she examined the jumble of titles within her reach.

She looked up and down the shelves. It was a fair sized room and obviously one in which a large amount of time was spent. Leisure time, she concluded, for it was strewn with newspapers, books opened and left to wait for their reader's pleasure, little knick knacks obviously picked up from other parts of the house or outdoors and left as keepsakes or for convenience. The furniture was worn, but of good and comfortable quality, emphasising that the owner of the room rather spent his time reading and lounging than studying or working. There was a working desk but it was cluttered with things — the chair included — and it was quite obvious it was not used for its original industrious purposes.

But the bookshelves did betray neglect. Many of them gapingly empty, some of them filled with anything but books; some of the books that *were* there were in terrible condition and little more than loose stacks of pages, some of them were new and bunched together in one area as a little isle of order and pride in a vast sea of chaos and abandon.

She pulled out a few volumes carefully: Catullus, the Iliad, Burns, Shakespeare's 'As You Like It' with commentary, and three volumes on the Caucasian peoples and the old Silk Road.

"Oh, so you found my fancies?" Baugham came back through the door, almost startling her. "That particular selection you must blame me for. I'm sure you can find another Burns — the second edition, I think — around here, too. In tatters though, I shouldn't wonder.

"You see," he continued, picking up a volume only to put it back again straight away, "you are now in what I like to call 'my' corner. That is, the things you see here are books I've mostly purchased here, or on my way here, or had sent up from Hatchard's. Nothing remarkable, I believe, although I did lay my hands on that most curious treatise by John Craig through Mr Blackwood's assistance. And perhaps the *Hortus Kewensis* might interest you — it's somewhere on the lower shelf. But I have bought them myself without any intension of fitting them into anything besides a bookshelf or a travel satchel.

"And so here, on the other side," he said and walked over to the darker corner of the room, "is the Cumbermere side." He shrugged and pulled a face. "I have no idea why they are still here or what is their use or value. I just hauled them with me at one point in some fit of optimism they could actually be used to make a library out of this room. No treasures though, I suppose, since those would have long been sold off. Although I know my Uncle was regarded as quite a quirky old Astronomy enthusiast. I dare say I remember there being some curious, old Italian works no one quite knew what to make of. Very interesting engravings though, I seem to recall. Also, there are old botanical works — Jungius and Tournefourt certainly. The old man was fond of that sort of thing, but any Linnaeus I think must be gone."

Holly was certain that her expression must be showing more than she intended about the condition of the library, a thought confirmed by his lordship's next statement.

"Well," he said in a soft voice, quizzing her with his blue eyes very much on the alert, "I think you will agree there is a great deal more work in this assignment than you might have thought, but tell me, is it as hopeless as your countenance leads me to think?"

She looked around her. "No," she said. "Not hopeless…"

"Yes, but maybe a bit more than you thought you were taking on?"

BAUGHAM FELT A MEASURE OF unspoken criticism in her attitude and looks and felt strangely obligated to apologise for proposing she do the job at all, "Now that you have looked it over in the cold light of day, you are perhaps feeling sorry that you agreed to do this yesterday? If so, I will completely understand. Only you can measure the value of your time…"

To his great irritation, she appeared to take offence at his suggestion.

"Lord Baugham," she replied, "please believe that I have no wish to go back on our agreement. I am perfectly willing to keep to my word, as I assume you are also?"

Baugham raised his eyebrow and felt his lips tighten. He felt an irresistible urge to snort at her and admonish her not to be childish. He suppressed the impulse, however, and retreated to feigning a bland expression and studied indifference.

"Then we understand each other perfectly, Miss Tournier. I wonder if you could be prevailed upon to close the last details of our understanding now? I am here at your service."

She put down the volumes she was still holding and gave him a determined look,

"Oh, by all means, let us settle this business at once. Then there can be no more questions about my intent to keep my word. If you will be so kind as to tell me what you require, I will do my best to accomplish it."

"Certainly." Baugham did not quite realise it, but his answer amounted to that overdone cordiality he usually employed when his attorney called upon unpleasant business.

"As we agreed, in exchange for just compensation, you undertake to arrange this assortment of written material into a passable collection worthy of the name of a library. You will commit to a certain timeframe and regular attendance, and you may engage an assistant as well if you deem necessary. I would suggest coming at least twice weekly to begin with. However, you are surely the best judge of what your other commitments can allow you to spare.

"Should I remove from Clyne, you may, naturally, arrange your hours as you please. I suggest your work should include a purchase recommendations list, a written card record of content and a shelving system. I trust you can comply. I would be happy to accommodate any thoughts you have on this subject and I trust this agreement can be concluded as an oral agreement only?"

"I have no quarrel with that, my lord. However — "

Lord Baugham sent her an exasperated frown and a barely concealed sigh.

"Oh good heavens!" she snapped back. "Do please stop that! I was going to tell you I *will* need help and that I have found the perfect assistant. Subject to your approval, naturally."

Baugham's face broke into a smile at her impatience with him.

"I'm sorry," she muttered.

"Not at all. The misapprehension was all mine. I'll behave now."

She smiled back, but tried to send him a chastising look all the same. "My mother suggested that young Hamish Nethery would do very well. He can more easily be spared from his duties around the farm at this time of year, and she thought that such an opportunity would do him good. If you agree, I should like to run down to speak with his father this afternoon."

"Nethery, eh? The one with the renegade sheep?"

She looked at him, puzzled. "I suppose they keep sheep, my lord, but … Hamish is just a lad. They wouldn't be *his* sheep, though it's possible he might have responsibility for them. But," she asked, her brows knitted together, "why are we talking about sheep?"

Baugham laughed and proceeded to tell her — as humorously as one could when it came to hunting for the stray sheep of a cantankerous neighbour on a wet day — his previous connection with the Nethery farmers. When Mrs McLaughlin brought the tea around, he was still in the process of describing Duncan Nethery's comments to his father and they quickly agreed that Mrs Tournier was correct in feeling the younger son could only benefit from some scholarly occupation away from home. Mrs McLaughlin was asked as well and she confirmed Mrs Tournier's somewhat downbeat assessment on the head of the family, but she was well-acquainted with

Hamish, declared him to be a clever, well-behaved boy and said that she had no objections to him coming to work at Clyne. If he could be taught to wash his hands before he touched the furnishings, that is.

"Then it is all settled," stated his lordship as he finished his cup. "But Miss Tournier, I would be obliged if you would permit me to make the arrangements for young Hamish's employment. From what I have heard and seen of Mr Nethery, I would not wish to subject you to any close negotiations with the man."

This suited her very well; her relief at being spared the necessity of dealing with the drunken, possibly greedy, and probably belligerent father of a boy she had not even met, showed on her face as she accepted.

"Now," she stood, "if you will excuse me, I should be getting home now. Shall I come tomorrow morning to begin work?"

"Excellent," his lordship replied. "If all goes as planned, your assistant will be here as well."

She took one last look around the library, smiling slightly as she did so.

"Till tomorrow then," she said as she walked out the door.

Baugham leaned back in his chair and thoughtfully watched her leave until a distinct grunt from Mrs McLaughlin reminded him of his duties. He jumped up and dashed down the hall, in a few strides catching up to Miss Tournier walking in the direction of the kitchen.

"Please, let me see you to the door," he said, turning her around towards the front entrance and ignoring the bemused looks and raised eyebrows it earned him.

LATER THAT NIGHT HIS LORDSHIP returned to the library and stood, glass in hand, in front of a roaring fire. As he struggled to make sense of his scattered thoughts, he felt two eyes boring into him. Looking up at the dilapidated stag's head over the mantle, he smiled and addressed him.

"Well Rupert!" He lifted his glass of brandy and smiled. "It appears that I have engaged a librarian to come and sort out this mess you keep complaining about that is my library. And an assistant. Although, strictly speaking the assistant doesn't know about it yet, but I am convinced he will be agreeable. And the best part in all of this is — and why I feel so particularly smug — is that I have managed to follow an opinionated old lady's advice, rescue a young woman from indigence and misfortune without her pride suffering one bit, *and* do good to a local family whose sheep habitually stray onto my lands, all in one very self-serving way. Clever, eh?"

Rupert said nothing, but continued to stare.

"Well, now, if you think that is odd, this will surely make you laugh! It is Miss Tournier! She and I are now business partners! Yes, I know what you will say, 'What on earth were you thinking?' Sadly, I must admit to you that I was not thinking at all, so yes, I must agree that it has every chance of turning against me." He laughed but then sank into a thoughtful mood. "But…it is a very lovely and charming librarian I have hired, Rupert. No doubt I have banished peace and quiet from Clyne for a good while, but I dare say both the collection and my fencing skills will benefit."

The stag's expression took on a decidedly sceptical turn.

"Certainly I am going to fence! I don't think I could hardly expect otherwise. Only verbally, of course, but that can be quite as exhilarating and deadly as fencing with swords, you know. Especially with such an opponent."

A few moments of silence accompanied a battle of wills, as Baugham tried to stare down those irritatingly knowing brown eyes.

"You can just as well keep such speculations to yourself, Rupert," his lordship snapped. "I cannot deny that Miss Tournier can be pleasant company when she cares to be, but this proposal came upon me as a result of her need rather than any scheme of mine."

His glare had no effect on the creature.

"You are worse than Darcy!" he muttered. "A business proposition, nothing more.

"Fear not, I have every intention of 'behaving myself'. In fact, I will protest that there is, was, and will never be, any such stuff in my thoughts and I will thank you to remember that I am a gentleman and Miss Tournier is a lady.

"Suffice to say, her pride is intact, her situation is temporarily settled and I will be rid of your constant nagging about your substandard surroundings. All in all a very satisfying end to many problems, I would say."

The room was very dark when his thoughts once more returned to the present; several candles had burned down, but as he let his gaze wander over the obscured walls and rows of volumes standing on parade in the shadows, his mind involuntarily wandered off again. He felt himself smiling at the thought of a busy librarian — a very pretty librarian, her figure clothed in light coloured muslin and no doubt a severe frown on her pretty, concentrated face — bringing order into chaos in his collection, and possibly chaos into his ordered existence at Clyne. He had to confess to himself he might even be looking forward to it. Then, with one last glare at Rupert over the mantle, he snuffed the remaining candles and went up to bed.

Lord Baugham was in his library, seated in his favourite chair — a recoup he was enjoying though he did miss Darcy in other ways — reading the newspaper, when there was a slight knock on the door. He glanced at his watch and, noting it was close to ten o'clock, got up, straightened his waistcoat and bid the visitor to enter. The door opened very slowly and revealed Mrs McLaughlin, clutching a tall, scrawny boy by the shoulder.

"M'laird," she said more quietly than was her habit. "This here is young Hamish."

Baugham looked the boy over. He certainly did not fit the picture of a strong and quick helping hand where physical labour might be expedient, but underneath that fringe of overgrown, tangled, curly hair a pair of watchful, bright eyes peeped and regarded him with unabashed curiosity. He had outgrown his clothes and apparently his providers did not think the season was advanced enough to yet procure him new ones. Baugham noted his tattered boots with disbelief, but then he recollected himself, winked at him and bid them to come into the room.

Mrs McLaughlin gave him a look, but pushed the boy in front of her until he was standing close enough for his lordship to reach out his hand and greet him.

"Well, how do you do, Hamish?" he asked lightly smiling. "You must be wondering what on earth you are doing here."

The boy instinctively warmed to this larger than life figure who addressed him so casually and seemed glad to have him trampling all over his fine gentlemanly rooms.

"Well…aye, sir, I do…a wee bit."

"I shall be glad to tell you," Baugham continued. "The thing is, you see, that it has reached my ears — by way of Mrs Tournier down in the village, don't you know — that you are a clever and good young man who could perhaps help me out. And in doing so, also help my hired librarian, who, I should tell you, is on her way here as we speak and is the daughter of Mrs Tournier. So you see, we're all old acquaintances and eager to help each other."

He grinned and was happy to note the boy smiled shyly and gave a slight peek at Mrs McLaughlin, too.

"You shall of course, be paid for your services. What those services will be, I think it's best we wait for Miss Tournier to specify, but I have engaged her to bring order into the confusion I call my collection." He watched the boy, amused, as he looked around him, eyes round with astonishment, no doubt unable to imagine how such a place could be described as chaos by any measure.

"Yes, I know," Baugham continued, leading the boy to one of the shelves and dragging his long finger over a row of leather-bound volumes. "It's quite a mystery. But I think you might enjoy it all the same. And, if you should happen upon something that takes your fancy, you are welcome to read it — within the limits set by my librarian, of course." He leaned closer to the boy and said in a conspiratorial whisper. "She will be here soon, so I shall take the opportunity to give you a hint beforehand. Miss Tournier used to be a stern schoolmistress, so you must take care. But I have found," he said his lips twitching and smiling warmly at Hamish, "that a bit of flattery never does me any harm with her when she's in one of her moods. And if that should fail, you should not hesitate to call on me. I am quite experienced at being scolded by her sharp tongue and to tell you the truth, I rather enjoy it."

The boy returned his smile, obviously having lost his heart to this fairytale figure in this fairytale surrounding. Mrs McLaughlin, however, pursed her lips and felt it was time to intervene.

"Aye, that's all good an' well, but before he meets anybody, schoolmistresses or nae, I am taking Hamish to the kitchie and giving him a right meal and a good wash. Ye cannae work in here with grubby hands, muddy feet and a churning belly."

"Quite right, Mrs McLaughlin!" Baugham said and returned to his seat. "And I think, perhaps, your first wage should be in the form of a pair of boots. After that, we'll see."

AFTER ARRIVING ON THE CLYNE grounds, Holly entered through the kitchen again and was soon introduced to Hamish, who was sitting at the table with Mrs McLaughlin, devouring a large bowl of soup. She accepted the housekeeper's invitation to sit for a minute, but she was startled to see the boy's expression turn from ravenous to fearful as she took her seat.

"Good heavens, lad. Ye'll need to learn quick enough not to put so much stock in what his lairdship says," Mrs McLaughlin snorted. "Miss Tournier is nae anything to be afraid of."

Young Hamish found himself flanked by two formidable women and though he was able to manage a shy, thankful smile to the housekeeper as his bowl was once again replenished, Miss Tournier was quite another matter, especially when she asked him what his lordship had said of her to make her seem so frightening.

At this he had to turn to face the scary schoolmistress, and poor young Hamish suddenly and unexpectedly found himself lost in her deep, brown eyes and he found it impossible to speak anything but the truth — even to protect his new-found friend and benefactor sitting in his comfortable library.

"He said, miss — he said ye'er quite stern, and that ye hae 'moods' and I should flatter ye."

Mrs McLaughlin gave another snort that almost resembled a laugh as she left the table. "Aye, ye'd be better keeping your mooth closed and yer eyes open, lad. Now get off with the both o' yese, I hae work to do."

Holly found nothing funny about Hamish's statement at all, and showed it freely on her face, but, after realising that it was, in fact, not his fault, she spoke to him as gently as she could manage.

"Hamish, you need to know that his lordship is mistaken. I am neither frightening, nor stern. It's just that I cannot abide foolishness. Nor can I abide false flattery, so please do not be persuaded to try it through bad advice."

Hamish nodded sheepishly, wondering to whom he had done the worse service with his honesty — his lordship or himself — but since Miss Tournier then smiled and asked him to come with her, if he pleased, he decided perhaps he would be allowed to prove himself neither foolish nor insincere.

Together they walked down the hall and into the library, where they found Lord Baugham idly wandering around and apparently taking stock of the contents. Holly could not help shooting him a dark look before returning to the boy still at her side.

"Hamish. Before I decide how you can help me, I must know how far you have got in your education. Can you read?"

"Aye," he agreed with enthusiasm. "We'el, a wee bit."

"Well, you need to practice then. You will, after all, be working with letters and words and texts and our goal will be to make sense of it all."

She smiled at him and patted his shoulder before calling across the room, "Lord Baugham, do you have such a thing as a reading primer in this muddle?"

His lordship turned around at her voice and showed a deceptively innocent and surprised look. "Why, Miss Tournier," he said sweetly, "I had rather hoped you would be the one to tell me that. And indeed, if I am guilty of such a shocking oversight, you must purchase one on my behalf."

Holly was quite unimpressed with his charm. "Well, I rather doubt that you are in need of one at this stage in your life, so I shan't go to the trouble. I thought perhaps you might have one left, in with your childhood books."

"That is a distinct possibility, though you will earn my honest admiration if you are able to find anything of the kind. I have just been looking the situation over again, Miss Tournier, and I think, perhaps, considering the circumstances, you will be within your rights to demand a king's ransom for your services."

"I don't know why some people persist in bringing up matters that have already been adequately laid to rest," Holly mumbled to no one in particular as she examined the jumble of titles within her reach.

Realising his lordship was quite possibly right about her chances of being able to discover any one particular book, she suppressed a sigh and turned to Hamish.

"Well young sir, I think we do have a very large job ahead of us. Right now I need you to take a careful look around and see if you can spy a blue book about this size," she indicated with her fingers the thickness of the needed volume. "If you are lucky, it will be very high up and you will have to use this extraordinary ladder to get at it!"

Lord Baugham stood, leaning on the back of one of the high-winged chairs, and watched his librarian, together with her assistant, start rummaging around the bookcases. The boy was lifting his gaze upwards and Miss Tournier apparently could not resist touching every single volume with her fingertips as she went through them. It was a pretty picture, and since he had detected a distinct surly disposition in his librarian today, he chose to observe the scene for a while before interfering. After a while, when their search had produced no results, he approached them.

"Perhaps you will have better luck among the Cumbermere books," he volunteered.

Still perturbed at what he had told Hamish, Holly simply nodded and crossed the room. The Cumbermere side of the library had somewhat more order to it than the other, that is, the books looked like they had been packed into trunks by the shelf but unpacked and re-shelved by the armload, with no mind given to their proper place in the arrangement. However, about halfway up the far wall toward the corner she spied several clumps of familiar bindings — yes, they were definitely schoolbooks.

She pointed out the needed book to Hamish and gave him permission, after looking to Lord Baugham for confirmation, for him to use the ladder to fetch it. There was a great rumbling screech as the boy jubilantly pushed it into place, but even louder was his gasp of surprise shortly after scrabbling up the rungs.

"Is this an adventure book?" he called down holding a slim volume in his hand. "M'laird, may I have a look? You said I could…"

"An adventure book? What a find!" Baugham exclaimed "Bring it on down here, boy, and let Miss Tournier quiz you on something more interesting than the primer."

Holly meant to send him an annoyed look, but when she turned to his lordship she could not help but share in his smile at the boy's enthusiasm.

Once he was down, Holly gently pulled the book, *The Life and Adventure of the Famous Captain Singleton,* from his hands. Directing him to sit next to her on the sofa, she turned to the climactic battle scene and pointed to a word here and there, asking if he could read them. She was pleasantly surprised at his abilities. She indicated a paragraph, "Why don't you read this passage to me?"

Baugham had the distinct feeling that his presence was no longer needed, but he stayed anyway, quietly admiring the tableau on his library sofa. Miss Tournier had that soft look that he had seen but rarely, and Hamish was beaming and reading out with vigour:

But the next question we had among ourselves, was, how we should do to trust them, for we found the people not like those of Madagascar, but fierce, revengeful, and treacherous; for which reason we were sure that we should have no service from them but that of mere slaves; no subjection that would continue any longer than the fear of us was upon them, nor any labour but by violence.

Holly smiled at the boy. His enthusiasm was greater than his punctuation, but he read well and intelligently nonetheless.

"Hamish, I am very pleased. You have used your time in school well and have accomplished much more than I had hoped for. I am sure we will work very well together and turn this into a proper library Lord Baugham can be proud of."

Listening with pleasure, Baugham recognised that particular passage very well! The book had been his father's and most probably his Grandfather's, too, and had been read to shreds by now. He listened to Miss Tournier's calm voice praising her assistant and smiled.

"You know," he interrupted softly, "that's when he became 'Captain Bob' to his men, and I will have you know I forced my mother to call me by that same name for weeks, in the vain hope that the Navy might recognise my qualities at the tender age of thirteen and take me with them to more exciting places than my draughty old schoolroom. I hope you can be persuaded to stay here, though Hamish."

Hamish merely smiled shyly and turned back to the book, but Holly laughed at the image in her head of a young, swashbuckling Lord Baugham insisting on being re-baptised as "Captain Bob." She looked at him closely, trying to imagine him as a thirteen-year-old boy and he grew slightly uncomfortable under her scrutiny.

"Ah well, I know you have much to review so I shan't disturb you any longer. I will be in my study if you need me. Please do not hesitate to ask me anything, although I must admit my knowledge on any inventory subjects is sketchy to say the least. Perhaps you might like tea in a few hours? I shall ask Mrs McLaughlin to be so kind."

With that he bowed to both of them and left them to their work.

Leaving Hamish to finish his exciting battle, Holly took a tablet of paper from the desk and began, as she wandered around the room, to make notes on possible ways to categorise the veritable stew of volumes.

She soon came to the conclusion that, at least to begin with, everything must be classified by subject — which meant that all the shelves must be emptied, and the books sorted and returned before she could go any further.

Ready with her plan, she interrupted Hamish from his adventures and they began pulling books down and stacking them on the floor all over the room.

An hour of furious activity convinced Holly that she had been too ambitious in her plan and that there were many more books in the library than it appeared at first glance. They had not even emptied one wall and there were stacks everywhere. The air was clouded with dust and both herself and Hamish were covered from head to foot. She stood with her hands on her hips, a puzzled expression on her face as she considered her next move.

"Hamish, if you can make your way across the room, I think we need that window opened," she said. Dodging furniture and climbing over piles, the boy managed to reach the window and unlatch it.

The fresh, bracing breeze helped to clear her thinking, and she made her decision. She sat on the floor and began sifting through the piles,

"Let's start in small steps, shall we? We'll sort these we already have down, list them by subject and then move on. So, poetry here and history...over there." She sighed. "It certainly seems we shall need that tea in a few hours, after all..."

Chapter 20

The Dreary Work of a Librarian's Assistant gets its Reward, a Library gets Demolished and Employer and Employees find Much to Talk about

HAMISH looked down at the books he was holding. He shifted them around and leafed through them for the umpteenth time. Miss Tournier was sitting on the floor with her paper and pen, writing on her list with a concentrated air. Every now and then the wind from the opened window caught her loose strands of hair and twirled them about her head. She seemed not pay the slightest notice to it, but got up every now and then to fetch or return a book from another pile. The notices with *Natural Science, History, Travels* and all the others written out in precise long-hand, fluttered in the breeze as they were stuck between the books. He sighed.

"Miss Tournier," he tentatively said casting a shy glance at her.

"Mm?" was the disappointing answer as she once again scribbled a note and stuck it between two books on the floor.

"Miss. I dinnae know... I hae one here that is about botanic history in Greece and one that is in a language I never saw before. What do I do with them, miss? And this one — what do we do with the ones wantin' half the pages? I think I saw some loose pages behind the French novels, but this other one here must hae the wrong covers, the pages are all the wrong size and there are something that looks like notes spilling out of the binding..."

His supervisor gave him a long look and sighed.

"Is it... might it soon be time for tea, miss?" he asked in a hopeful voice, glancing over at Captain Bob on the table.

IT HAD BEEN A SHORT but satisfying nap in his chair and Lord Baugham languidly stretched his long legs as he opened his eyes again. He glanced at his watch. If he wanted to, he certainly could finish those accounts sent over by Mr Tilman for approval before tea, but he realised he did not. He got up from his chair and walked over to his desk. There was a slight chill in the air and as he shuffled the papers and ledgers together, he made a mental note to attend to the fire both in the study and the library.

With a few long strides he was out of the door, on his way to the kitchen to request Mrs McLaughlin to bring the tea tray into the library before going into the room itself. What met his eyes caused him to feel a curious mix of astonishment and delight. Among what looked like an ocean of books, papers, leaflets and booklets, two figures were huddled in the middle of the floor. The window had been forced open and a fresh breeze swept across the room.

Hamish looked up immediately as he entered and scrambled to his feet to greet him. Miss Tournier glanced at him, but at the same time raised a hand as if to silence him while she finished writing something on a sheet of paper resting on a chair. After a brief pause she lifted her head and it almost startled him to note she was smiling. It instantly stuck him that she looked happy, and that realisation made him return her smile generously.

"Well!" he said looking about him. "I dare say to an uninitiated eye like mine, you are hovering on the brink of disaster, but I can tell you must have some successes to inform me of! Will you tell me how you are coming along if I stay for tea? Mrs McLaughlin will be with us presently."

Her assistant's eager expression and her own stomach made Holly welcome the suggestion. Rising from the floor as gracefully as she could between piles, papers and the fact that she had been sitting in one position so long that her feet were growing numb, she happily accepted his offer.

"Hamish, I believe the air has cleared enough, shall we close the window? Oh my goodness, you would not believe the dust we loosed upon this room."

He curled his mouth into a wry smile and watched her smooth out her skirts.

"Actually, Miss Tournier, I would."

He motioned to his own shoulder with a wiping gesture and watched, amused, as she first looked at him in surprise but then realised his hint. Her eyes then shifted to the dust on her dress and with a small "oh!" she furiously rubbed it with her hand, a most becoming blush spreading over her features.

"Allow me," he said and handed her his handkerchief.

Holly did her best to brush off her dress, suddenly struck by another thought, which produced several sideways glances about the room in order to check for any nearby mirror. No, there were none that would not take acrobatic skill to reach. So she did the only thing she could. Summoning up her sense of humour she addressed his lordship gravely, "Might I ask you to assure me of the fact that my face, most particularly my nose, is free from smudges?"

He raised his left eyebrow just a smidgen and obviously had great difficulty matching her seriousness. Something tugged at the corners of his mouth and he pressed his lips together to control it, instantly giving him an air of gravity.

"Certainly!"

He sent a quick glace towards Hamish, who had quietly ploughed his way through to where Captain Bob was waiting for him, then navigated a bit closer. With one pile of books between them, he leaned in and, narrowing his eyes, studied her face for quite a while, lingering particularly and most tenaciously over her chin, nose and forehead.

Holly gave him a stern look, not quite appreciating the theatrics as much as he was enjoying them, but determined to keep her countenance.

"Hm," he said and held out his hand for his handkerchief. He crumpled it together and carefully reached out to wipe her left temple, contriving to keep his expression perfectly serious, but when he detected a slight flinch as he touched her face, he broke out in a wide grin and his blue eyes sparkled mischievously.

"There. I believe you are perfectly presentable to have tea with Hamish and me now!"

Handing her the handkerchief once again, he made his way back through the maze of books and opened the door for Mrs McLaughlin.

Holly wiped her hands and, not knowing what else to do, folded the square neatly and placed it on top of the *Natural History* pile. Then, lifting her skirts in order to navigate successfully across the room, she set out to clear the papers, pencils and notes from the table so Mrs McLaughlin might set the tray down.

She picked up a stack of books from one of the chairs and looked around for a place to set them that she could reach, that she would remember, and that would not disrupt her system of organisation. After a moment she spied an empty spot of floor, but with her hands full she could not get to it.

"Lord Baugham, take these books over there please. Right by the *Astronomy* pile. And then this pile here," pointing to the other chair, "will have to go next to *Foreign Travels*. Mrs McLaughlin, you can put the tray right here."

"The Laird preserve us!" cried the housekeeper as she navigated through the room with her burden. She set the tray down on the designated spot and stood with her hands on her hips and a dark frown on her face. It was perfectly obvious she was horrified at the scene before her eyes.

"The Laird preserve us!" she could only utter for a second time, adding a shaking head. Baugham smiled broadly. "Don't worry, Mrs McLaughlin. I have a strong suspicion Miss Tournier is in full control of events. And it looks like they're doing the dusting, too, so don't you fret!"

Holly was already sitting down and ready to pour out before she realised she had just ordered Lord Baugham around like he was one of her students. And what's more, he had done exactly as he was told, with a meek look and without uttering a word. Had she been able to see his eyes, she would have perhaps noted that they had lost none of their sparkle, that he was biting his lip most determinedly and that his shoulders shook slightly as he complied.

Looking around for a place to sit, Baugham opted for the armrest of the sofa, since there was no other space left on it — apparently it had been designated as a harbour for *Poetry and Verse* according to the note sticking up behind the cushions. He crossed his arms over his chest and waited for the tea to be poured. Then he caught a glimpse of Hamish, shyly waiting with his hands grasping the book behind his back.

"Have you got as far as the Cape yet, Hamish? What an adventure, eh? I think it would be a good idea to try to find Crusoe and the Military Memoirs, too, in this mess before they're safely stowed away in a Brave New Order of Things."

"Hamish," Holly retorted, "would you kindly inform Lord Baugham of the distinct possibility that until Mr Crusoe is safely stowed in our Brave New Order of Things or anything else than this awful mess, he is likely to remain marooned and alone for eternity? As for Military Memoirs, I ask, what military man worth his training would be satisfied to remain in such disarray?"

Since Hamish obviously did not care to relay the information to Lord Baugham or hazard an answer to her question, Holly smiled, handed him his cup and plate and nodded her permission for him to go off and read.

Pouring for his lordship next, she asked, "So, how *do* you like the jumble we've made of your lovely room?"

He took the cup from her hands and smiled.

"I like it prodigiously! Very refreshing. And exciting. Although I still worry that you have taken too much upon yourself. It looks...well, right now it looks daunting. But I must admit you are doing me a great service."

"Oh, it *is* daunting, and overwhelming, and exciting!" Holly's eyes sparkled as she spoke, then her face grew softer.

"But I am finding it curiously peaceful too. To take one small piece of the world, even as small as these few shelves that are sitting empty right now, and bring it from disorder into harmony...To make sense out of the confusion..." she smiled, feeling a bit foolish at her Romantic notions. "As you can tell, I perhaps have been looking too much at poetry books today."

"Mm," he looked at her thoughtfully. "Perhaps that is the key. To make sense of the confusion little by little. The temptation is to think one must take it all on at once, isn't it? One could say my fault has been a misunderstanding of that notion; trying to attack too large a piece at once it leads rather to inaction instead. I have not always been the most diligent servant to my family's memory and legacy, but this certainly goes some way to what I owe them."

His words reminded her of what he had earlier told her of his father, and she felt she must say something to him.

"My lord, forgive me if I am overstepping my place, but you must know that a proud name and heritage cannot be erased by the actions of just one person. To do such a thing takes the cooperation of several generations. I cannot imagine that *you* would wish to be cooperative in such an undertaking."

He smiled wryly. "I thank you for your concern, but there really is no need for it. I am very happy in my more than privileged life and not such a dour figure at all. You are very right in your assessment, of course. Still, perhaps if you had lived in that world…" He hesitated but then put down his teacup and turned around to browse through the volumes on the sofa.

"*What's gone and what's past help, should be past grief,*" he said a little wistfully. "That is very true and I believe it.

"I don't know," Holly sighed. "It seems there are some things — or people — that when they are gone, are never past grief. However, as I am discovering, we must *can* the little piece of life we are given and try to make sense of it as best we can." She looked up at him. "What else is there for us to do?"

He still did not fully meet her eyes and seemed preoccupied with the poetry volumes. It was impossible to read from his face what he was thinking and as he put down the books and once more raised his teacup to his lips, his eyes had clouded over and were fixed on his boots.

"I think you must be right. Some things are worth our grief, and some are not. I should think your father…he would have been worth much — if you will forgive me for being presumptuous. I think he would have been very proud of you. But all the same, he would not wish you grief, but happiness."

Holly smiled wistfully. "Oh he was always very proud of me, in all of my childish accomplishments. And no, he would not wish me to grieve, and truly I do not all of the time…but it is something I will always carry very near, and it meets me in the most surprising places. I don't know why, suddenly, he is so much on my mind."

He looked down, momentarily at a loss for words, but he realised that she was not really expecting a response, so he glanced around him and smiled.

"Quite a metaphor in action, don't you find? Demolish to rebuild?"

Trying to shake off the melancholy mood that had descended upon the library, she looked around and gestured to her handiwork, "I don't know that I like that term — 'demolish' — I prefer to think that I am jarring them out of their complacency and satisfaction with their merely tolerable existence and introducing them to their best destiny as…" she raised her teacup in salute, "a proper library!"

The smile was back in his eyes. He met her toast and watched her quietly for a moment.

"I have every confidence that you will do just that, and I am truly most grateful that you accepted this assignment. I wish…Miss Tournier, I am hoping you will treat this library, and Clyne, to freely come and go as it suits you. As strange and even unsettling as this room now appears, I am happy you are here. What Mr Darcy would say if he ever returned, I know not!" he laughed. "You might be called upon to defend me against his censure and disapproval at having his favourite chair thus occupied by…" he lifted a volume, "…Mr David Hume no less!"

He looked at Hamish still absorbed in his book before he turned back to her.

"Now, if you will excuse me, I will leave you to your work."

"Of course. I will finish sorting through this last pile and then I must be going. I should be able to return soon however, perhaps tomorrow."

With that Holly recalled Hamish from his adventures around the Cape and they resumed their positions on the floor. Lord Baugham took a last look at the tranquil pair working quietly in the midst of the turmoil that was his library, he bid them a good afternoon and returned to his study.

The shadows were lengthening by the time Holly tapped lightly on the study door. When his lordship looked up, she quietly said, "I have left Hamish with his book for now. Would you please fetch him in half an hour and send him off? It would not do for him to be late in arriving home." They both smiled at the image of a boy so engrossed in his reading he would miss supper and risk disapproval to just get through one more chapter. They quietly bid each other a good night and, wrapped in her shawl and bonnet against the cold, Holly walked home toward Rosefarm Cottage and her waiting supper.

HAMISH WAS JUST RELUCTANTLY DEPOSITING the dashing Captain Bob on the shelf again. He sighed and let his hand rest on the cover a moment before he turned around to find his lordship smilingly watching him from the doorway.

"Well, Hamish," he said in a gentle voice, "I think that's quite enough work and excitement for one day. I am sure you will continue the adventures when you go to bed. Perhaps even challenge a few savages while you make your way home to Nethery. And you know there is more where Captain Bob came from next time."

Hamish smiled shyly and nodded.

"I suspect you enjoyed yourself," Baugham said. "I am glad. And your supervisor was not so bad, am I right?"

Hamish looked at his lordship, this time boldly in the face. It was hard to tell in the growing shadows of the library, but he did feel his lordship might have been teasing him. He still decided he should speak his mind.

"Well, I did, sir. Very much. But I think... If ye pardon me, sir, I feel ye are wrong about Miss Tournier. She is very kind and I could nae say that she was in any particular mood at all, sir, however clumsy and stupid I surely was about many things."

His benefactor was quiet and Hamish began to feel he had perhaps been too bold. But he surely felt this honest and brave stand was what Captain Bob would have done, so he decided to suffer any consequences.

"Yes," Lord Baugham finally said in a kind voice, "you are quite right. She is a remarkable woman, is she not? I certainly think so. But I tell you this Hamish, remarkable women are often hard to make out. That is what makes one remark them, after all. Now, you must hop along if you mean to be back here tomorrow, as I suspect you do."

After Hamish left, Baugham closed the door behind him and walked back to his library. It was growing dark, but the darkness suited his thoughts. In reality he wanted to take in the chaos that reigned in the room without being obligated to present either a stoic and confident appearance, or being forced to respect the on-going work by keeping his hands off his own books.

The smell of dust and old paper unleashed upon opening the door was startling in the quiet dark. Baugham lighted a work candle on his desk and shuffled the heaps of volumes around to see what exactly his collection of *Classics – Greek* entailed. Depressingly little, it turned out, and all of it in disturbing condition. He sighed and let them go.

His eye was caught by a white piece of fabric lying on top of another pile of books. As he lifted it and made out the smudges on the material, he smiled. She had left his handkerchief on a pile of books after using it. He hesitated. Did that mean she intended to use it again?

That thought made him break out into a wide grin. How many times had he given his handkerchief to a woman, whether in real need or play? And how many times had it simply been abandoned after having been used? Very seldom, Baugham conceded. A woman of the *ton* would never simply abandon a gentleman's extended handkerchief, regardless of the original purpose. She would use it for more than that. She would take it and somehow draw attention to its change of ownership later — publicly or privately. She would give it back, invariably with some elaborate gesture. She would plot and ponder just who should know she held onto it, or she would hide it as a token. But she would never just abandon it where she had used it; strip it of any coquettish or playful meaning and treat it as a mere … handkerchief.

Baugham looked down at the bit of fabric, lightly sliding it between his fingers. He found that he was very content regarding that white piece of cloth as a simple tool of necessity and not as a prop in a game. He suddenly felt ashamed of what he could, and on occasion had, used such an innocent piece of material for. Intricate games, flirtations and clandestine messages.

This handkerchief — used and abandoned — was neatly folded so that the smudges were left on the inside. It looked innocent and precise, its use nobody's affair or concern. Was it possible to go back to the time when a handkerchief was just that — a handkerchief? Here at Clyne it was. Suddenly he longed for it to be possible elsewhere, too.

Baugham put the handkerchief back where he had found it. It was just a handkerchief. If Miss Tournier had further need of it, he had better leave it. If not, Mrs McLaughlin would collect it and see to it. It was as simple as that. He sat a while, surprisingly enough feeling quite content in his present situation. Then he got up, took a last look around in his topsy-turvy library, smilingly fingering the note with *Juvenile Literature* written on it before he picked up Mr Defoe's greatest adventure and headed up to his bedroom.

"The rippet, Rosie! The mess, those old, filthy, tattered books all athort the place! All athort the chairs, tables, sofa! The floor, Rosie! The floor is covered with the things! And not all of them are books either. If I'd hae known it would be coming to this, I would hae thrown those disgusting, smelly things away a long time ago. Laird knows, I nearly fell off the ledder with the chore of dusting them on many occasions!"

Mrs Higgins, usually more quiet and subservient to her elder cousin's obvious expertise and housewifely experience, felt Mrs McLaughlin was really being very ignorant.

"Well, she's cleaning them up now, is she not?" she tried while neatly stitching through the worn heel of a thick stocking.

"I'll believe it when I see it," Mrs McLaughlin said with disgust. "I don't know what they're thinking could be done to it. I'll wager she'll suggest they'll throw out most of it after she's had a look through. That is if she has any sense."

For some reason her cousin's quick glance at her made her add, "And I know she has sense, Rosie."

"Aye, well, some of these people have an odd attachment to any book. Dear things, ye know, and some of them they treat like treasure."

"No treasure there, I can assure ye," Mrs McLaughlin said and bit off her thread. "It's all what the old Earl left and that's a paltry lot. Everything he could get any money out of he sold off. Nothing left but *novels*, I shouldnae wonder."

The way she spoke the word made her cousin look up.

"Novels?"

"Aye. Although I'm nae saying his lairdship hasnae done his best to get something a bit less vulgar. He reads much poetry. And he likes the travel books. Well, some of the things those savages get up to are no better than reading novels, I know."

"Och well…" Mrs Higgins began, not quite certain how she could tell her cousin what Mrs Tournier had explained to her: that novels could be both useful and educational if chosen with care. But Mrs McLaughlin interrupted her.

"All I'm saying is I hope they dinnae think they can turn the whole household tapsalteerie, just on account of some dirty books. And I know his lairdship feels the same way. I'm sure he doesnae like his peace or ways disturbed and ruined like this."

"Well, if he doesnae, why did he ask her to do it?"

Apparently that was a question Mrs McLaughlin did not want to answer.

"I need the thread, Rosie. And the thicker needle. If ye please."

THE NEXT DAY, HAMISH WAS standing on the soft carpet of the library in a pair of hand-me-down boots Mrs McLaughlin had thrust into his hands the moment he entered the kitchen. It was very quiet and very empty. His lordship was apparently out and Miss Tournier had not yet arrived. Of course, he had left all his chores at Nethery in a hotchpotch as soon as he could, not to be late. His mother had scolded him, but fortunately his father and Duncan were out in the field and had not borne witness to his eagerness to rub shoulders with the Quality up at Clyne.

His father had had a few choice comments about the summons from his lordship out of the blue three days ago, but his mother had acidly remarked that it was not as if his efforts on the farm provided them with as much opportunity of buying new boots before the winter, and he should just let the boy be.

So Hamish had run practically all the way today as well and arrived breathless in Mrs McLaughlin's kitchen. She had looked him over and inspected his hands and nails and given a grunt, which, he supposed meant she approved, given him an apple to munch on while he waited and then sent him out to go and announce himself at the library.

"Ye work here now," she said, "and I have no time fer announcing anyone in the middle of me own work."

Slowly Hamish slipped the new boots on his feet and wriggled his toes. It felt strange after the summer of bare feet and the memory of his old boots that had grown too small already by May. He took a few steps to try them and smiled to himself. Slowly he made his way to where he had last left his explorations and picked up *The Life and Adventure of the Famous Captain Singleton.* Perhaps if he just had a little time before anyone joined him, he could have a look at the illustrations of Captain Wilmot's famous pirates...

UNLIKE HAMISH, HOLLY DID NOT run all the way to Clyne Cottage, but she did walk at a brisk pace. Wrapped up in her heavy shawl and bonnet, she was quite warm and enjoying the clear, crisp late autumn morning. The trees and shrubbery along the road had long ago dropped their foliage and, when no one was around to see, Holly scuffed and kicked through the fallen brown leaves along her way.

After arriving on Lord Baugham's grounds, she entered through the kitchen and greeted Mrs McLaughlin before making her way to the library where she saw Hamish enthralled in his book. Unwilling to interrupt the boy's raptures, Holly merely watched him, smiling as she remembered how she, as a little girl and truthfully even now, loved to lose herself in a good story.

Hamish had just immersed himself in the great battlefield scene off the coast of Angola and was unconsciously biting his lip as the savages were resorting to throwing lances at the gallant crew of the ship when he was aware of not being alone. He looked up quite startled and saw Miss Tournier watching him with an amused smile. He jumped up from his seat and slammed the book shut.

"I beg yer pardon, Miss, I didnae hear ye come in. It's...it's most exciting, miss. That's why I didnae...I mean, I was jist waiting for ye..."

"Oh, but I know! It is exciting isn't it? What part are you on now? The battle? When I read the battle for the first time, I'm sure I missed both my dinner and my tea!"

She moved into the room to begin another work day and the boy relaxed as he realised he would not be reprimanded and he even ventured a smile.

Aside from his lordship popping his head through the door a time or two to inquire after their progress and whether they required anything, Holly and her assistant passed the day busily and quietly in work. They stopped only when they noticed the shadows begin to creep into the corners of the room.

"Well, Hamish," Holly said with finality, "I think we have done yeoman's service today and so, tomorrow — "

"Oh, miss! Tomorrow is Martinmas!" Hamish interrupted in a rush, but then dropped his eyes. "That is...I could acourse come if ye in particular wish me to..."

Holly laughed.

"Oh, I had not forgotten about that! How could I? Of course neither one of us will work tomorrow. I'm quite certain his lordship would not even have suggested it. You be sure to enjoy your day off. Now run along Hamish and come again on Monday."

Bowing hurriedly to her, Hamish ran out, very much prepared to fight off any savages daring to cross his path through the woods home, but at the same time equally eager for tomorrow to come as soon as possible.

As Holly walked home in the growing darkness, the first snow of the season fell over Clanough and its environs and as usual, the event divided the world into two camps. There were those, who by occupation or situation stood or sat inside by a window and admired the slow descent of white soft flakes all the way from the grey skies to the brown earth. Then there were those out of doors, who felt the weather on their face and back and could neither see the beauty nor the necessity of it. Both knew, however, that this time the phenomenon would be short lived. There was no lasting winter frost in the air yet and the ground around the lanes and houses swallowed up the white flakes almost as soon as they touched. It was a moment, nonetheless, that made everyone realise the passage of time. The year would soon be out and a hard season would begin. They would either grow tired of the snow, or used to it, before spring would come and present them with new annual wonders. But for now, a white world caused them all to stop for a while and think about things a little bigger than household chores, the demands of editors, letters to stewards or the classification of works on economic history.

In the grand city of Edinburgh, however, Dr Philip McKenna stepped out of his classroom, down the corridors of the quad and out into the chill evening air thinking of distinctly more mundane things. Pulling his gown about him against the cold wind, he walked to his rooms, wondering if a letter would be waiting for him when he arrived.

Normally his father's forgetfulness and habit of allowing too much time to lapse between the receipt of a letter and the writing of its response did not distress him. Rather, it was one of Mr McKenna's eccentricities that everyone around him accepted and readily excused as the by-product of a kind and generous, if somewhat scatterbrained, nature. After nearly a week of anxious waiting, however, his son was feeling distinctly *out* of patience with his father's usual habits and he was seriously considering sending a second letter by express, and instructing the courier to wait for an immediate reply.

It was an unusual request he knew, and that was probably why he had received no answer as of yet. His quarterly allowance was generous and he had never before felt the need to ask for an advance. And to be truthful, this had not been an appeal for an advance on his own funds as much as it was a request for a loan from his father's, and he could imagine the old man's confusion and applications to his wife to please clarify this unusual turn of events. Why should their son unexpectedly be possessed of such an urgency to complete his often put off treatise; a treatise that had been in the planning stages for a number of years, subject to numerous revisions and delays

224

and that he had been used to consider as a far-off possibility at best? Why, my dear, should Philip have the sudden need to hire an illustrator?

McKenna smiled, but the smile faded when he opened his door and saw, once again, that there was no letter in the tray. He tossed his gown over the back of the sofa, rekindled the fire and moved the kettle over it, in between repeated glances at the empty mail tray. He briefly considered inquiring of the landlord if perhaps something had been overlooked, but he knew it would be futile, as well as insulting to the conscientious man. Instead he unwrapped the bread and cheese on the table in the corner and cut himself a few slices of each for supper. Taking his plate to the cluttered desk, he cleared a spot and wrote a quick note:

Dear Mother,

I fear my latest letter has thrown poor Father into confusion, and I do apologise for it. Please let me assure you (and through you, him) that all is well with me. I simply have been presented with an opportunity that I wish to take advantage of.

I do not write to ask you to petition in my behalf, I simply ask that you take pity on your poor son who sits on tenterhooks and urge Father to send his decision — whatever it should be — soon.

Love, as always, to you, Father, Peter and Emilia.

P.

With a sigh he then pulled out an overstuffed file and began paging through its contents. If he was going to hire an illustrator for his book, he supposed he ought to bring his notes and ideas together into some semblance of order.

Chapter 21

Local Customs Prove Impossible to Resist for Practically Every One of Clanough's Inhabitants and Lord Baugham takes Delight in Simple Country Traditions

BY the time Lord Baugham finally found another living soul in his house the next morning, he was convinced there had been some sort of emergency, perhaps even a French invasion.

"Where the devil is everyone?" he confronted his valet without ceremony. "Have I been deserted? Have my vile habits finally broken the backs of Mr and Mrs McLaughlin?"

Riemann turned around just in time to catch his lordship's coat from falling off the chair he had thrown it on.

"My lord," he said, "Mrs McLaughlin is at church regarding the effigy and Mr McLaughlin is engaged with the ale."

Baugham stared at his valet.

"What?"

"I believe the occasion is the Martinmas Ramsey Run, sir."

"The Martinmas Ramsey Run," Baugham mouthed. "What in God's name is that?"

Mr Riemann gave his employer a faint smile. On the anniversary of one Sir Ramsey's death, he explained — which happened to fall on Martinmas — the village of Clanough celebrated the good knight's courage and gruesome fate by arranging a horse race along the exact route that the knight had taken in his attempt to flee from his barbarous English persecutors. It was a good two miles, starting from the church where the old manse had once stood, the pursuit ending with him being captured when attempting to cross the Kye. He had been thrown off his horse and brutally killed — some say by breaking his neck in the fall — but the villagers rather supported the theory that he had challenged at least four of his oppressors and shown a gallant hand at fighting with his broad sword before being cut down by a particularly vicious and cruel enemy.

So every year, the race from the church to the supposed site of the slaying by the river was organised in the village. Young men were encouraged to take part and each was supplied with a small pouch of pig's blood that the winner of the race was privileged to empty into the river Kye in commemoration of Sir Ramsey's bloody end.

One would have thought that this spectacle of legend, horseracing, young men and pig's blood would have been quite enough for the villagers' entertainment, but over the centuries other important additions were made. One was the polishing of Sir Ramsey's effigy in the church. Only married mothers who had lost a child, preferably in battle, could participate in this annual mourning ritual honouring Clanough's greatest patron. Another was a free tankard of the season's ale that the elders provided. Happily everyone, regardless of family circumstances, was entitled to participate there. Also, since the wait for the winner at the banks of the Kye was tedious and often cold and wet, a market for entertainment and refreshment had slowly sprung up. And since people did come from nearby villages to view this spectacle, a small but welcoming and entertaining fair was set up around the starting point of the race, complete with more refreshments, impromptu judging of farm animals and items for sale that could remind them of this extraordinary event.

"Well, if that isn't the stupidest thing," Baugham snorted. "And Mrs McLaughlin is now... polishing his effigy in church? Well, well."

Another person who was rather less impressed with the local traditions surrounding Sir Ramsey and his race was Mrs Tournier. Her daughter had walked out early to where Sir Torquil had marked out the traditional route for the race. In fact, Holly had tried to coax her mother to indulge her childish curiosity and come with her, but Mrs Tournier had no wish to accidentally run into the master planner himself walking along the route, calculating distances and curves, placing out warnings in the form of poles and commissioning simple wooden bars to be erected at the most dangerous spots. There had, in the past, been plenty of accidents when young hotheads, having not been able to procure the necessary horse, had run along with the riders anyway. Sir Torquil believed the possibility of injuries in such situations demanded planning and preparation and took his task very seriously.

"I will wait for you to tell me all about it when you return," she said to Holly. "If I go out now, I might be obliged to have a polite opinion and, surprisingly enough for me, I suppose, I really have no wish to form an opinion on an obstacle course."

THE SNOW FROM THE PREVIOUS afternoon was, of course, long gone by the morning of the Martinmas Ramsey Run and the sun peeked through woods and hung low in the sky instead. This was an unusual occurrence at this time of year and enough for Lord Baugham's curiosity and sense of fate to make him determined to take his customary ride by the village today.

The grounds on the field behind the church were already packed with people despite the early hour. To a more metropolitan eye, it was hardly more impressive than an ordinary street scene, but for the local populace it was the most exciting event of the season and the mill of fellow villagers, as well as kin and friends from farther away, was heady.

The number of displays, amusements, refreshments and sights — not to mention the inevitable fights and the drunks and the fools — gave the participants the knowledge and assurance the day would provide them with ample cause for discussion and gossip for a long time to come, regardless of how the actual Ramsey Run itself turned out.

Lord Baugham steered his horse away from the main throng of people and leaned forward in his saddle taking in the sight. He was interrupted in his study by a man, followed by three young women and several more young men, hurrying towards him, shouting breathless greetings. Baugham sat up again as he recognised the gregarious Tristam family. The two men behind them were carrying poles and a bag of tools so he supposed he had the privilege of catching Sir Torquil making last minute corrections to the course before the race began.

"My lord!"

Sir Torquil apparently was not too busy to stop and engage an onlooker in conversation. Baugham doffed his hat and jumped off his horse.

"Sir Torquil. Glorious day! You must be very busy."

"Oh yes, yes!" the man stuttered. "Of course. But everything is as it should be now. Or will be very soon. Adam, John — you go on and fix that pole right where I told you. I shall be with you shortly."

Baugham gave an inward sigh. The assembled Miss Tristams had by then joined their father and were standing just behind, blushing and flushed from the exertion of keeping up with him.

"Miss Tristam, Miss Prudence, Miss Patience," Baugham said and executed a bow. "Here to admire your father's handiwork, as I am?"

The two youngest girls tittered, but Miss Primrose Tristam was more aware of herself than that.

"Oh no, not at all, my lord! I'm the prize, you see. And my sisters were simply too curious about the competitors to wait at home until it all begins."

"Prize?" Baugham said and glanced at Sir Torquil.

The father blushed. "Well, my lord, perhaps it is slightly provincial and unsophisticated but ... well, it is such an ancient tradition. The winner is granted a kiss from the village's most prominent, unmarried young lady. All in good fun and properly done, I assure you."

"Well, how very *urbane*," Lord Baugham said gracefully and smiled at Miss Tristam. "I know quite a few fine ladies in Town who have bestowed the same sort of graceful gratitude for a race well won." *And not always stopped with a kiss,* he thought.

Miss Primrose looked extremely pleased and her father somewhat relieved. The younger girls tittered.

"Oh!" Miss Tristam suddenly exclaimed. "But I hope you are entering the race, my lord!"

The two sisters joined her in a little gasp and a squeak. Sir Torquil lighted up.

"Oh yes, my lord! It would be such an honour."

"Oh say you will, my lord! It would be so exciting!"

Baugham looked at the eager faces in front of him and cringed. "Ah…well. Thank you but I could not. I am simply here to watch the fun. And admire the course. I am quite certain you have done a marvellous job of it, Sir Torquil, and I am most eager to see it in action. "

Just then a voice sounded behind him.

"But surely the course can best be admired and the action best judged by one taking part in the race itself?"

Baugham recognised the voice and instantly met her eyes as he turned around.

"Miss Tournier," he said with both delight and wryness.

"My lord," she answered.

Gone was the matter-of-fact, modestly dressed librarian and scientific sketcher of bees and physiological experiments, and before him stood a gentlewoman of simple but decided elegance. That hat she was wearing framed her face and dark eyes in a very flattering manner and she had tilted it charmingly, just so. Her shawl was draped gracefully over one shoulder and allowed to linger over her other arm displaying her figure very well and, if not exactly of exclusive quality, its colour and style had obviously been chosen with assured knowledge of what became the wearer. *Very unequivocally French,* his lordship reflected amusedly and greeted her with an appreciative smile and bow. He offered her his exclusive notice without so much as thinking about the rest of the party, for he felt an irresistible urge for selfishness and curiosity today.

"Miss Tournier," he said again, a boyish smile playing on his lips. "You look absolutely charming! I cannot tell you how annoyed I am that you have decided a librarian must not betray her exquisite sense of style in her employer's dusty library. I feel quite cheated!"

Holly flushed at his forthright praise and obvious appreciation and she was not quite sure how to respond. Was he having fun at her expense? Primmie — Miss Tristam that was — seemed to think so. She sent Holly a smug and not overly kind look while her father busied himself with taking a few steps closer to them to hear what was being said and to be able to step back into the conversation as soon as the opportunity presented itself. Of course, some sort of reply was required so after stammering her thanks she countered, "You do not think it would be somewhat ridiculous if I came to work in your dusty library in my finest clothes? How could I ever get anything accomplished?"

He smiled mischievously as he took in her obvious indignation and narrowed eyes.

"Why, I cannot believe you are telling me efficiency and intelligence can only be achieved at the expense of loveliness and charm, Miss Tournier? On the contrary, you might find yourself with an extra pair of hands to order around and do your bidding if you did. And no dust would surely dare cover an inch of such a lovely lady."

He inspected her left temple in mock earnest, perfectly repeating his previous performance.

"No," he murmured, "thought as much."

She tried as hard as she could to maintain her serious expression, but Holly saw the good-humoured twinkle in his eyes and could not refrain from smiling herself.

"Ah, so now I see the way it works. The real secret to efficiency is not to do my own work, but to find a way to compel others to do it for me. Quite enlightening... but sir, are you so easily swayed by fashion that you will allow yourself to be ordered about like a schoolboy merely due to a change of gown?"

Baugham leaned towards her in a conspiratory fashion. "I have been known to, yes." He smiled and continued, "But a gown is never just a gown, as I am certain you know from the way you wear yours today. It is so much more and I must say if you claim anything else, I will swear you spent an exasperating amount of time before the mirror to get that sleeve ruffled just right. And I must say it was worth every second of it."

"Well, this is distressing, Miss Tristam, is it not?" Holly, suddenly uncomfortable with such exclusive and close attention, asked Primrose before turning back to his lordship. "Tell me, my lord, are all gentlemen so well aware of the efforts we girls go to make ourselves look effortlessly beautiful? Please tell me you are a singular case because, I confess, you are perfectly correct, though I shall deny that I ever admitted to such a thing."

He smiled at her, "You must never admit anything of the sort. You are quite perfect."

This last exchange did not please Miss Tristam. After all, *she* was the prize, the most prominent young lady in the town. How that Holly Tournier dared to think she could compete with her for the attentions of an Earl in that old, turned out dress, she did not know. She swished her new blue silk daintily as she stood and turned to Holly.

"*I* have nothing to fear if his lordship possesses such knowledge, Miss Tournier. But I suppose that when one resorts to employing such tactics, it must be very disappointing to be found out."

Holly had known Primrose Tristam long enough to be able to generally remain unaffected by her spiteful nature, but she wished that Lord Baugham's presence had tempered her tendency to nasty remarks. She sighed and stepped back, "I suppose you are right. Now, if you will excuse me, I think I will see what treasures are on display in the churchyard.

"My lord," she nodded. "Good luck in the race."

"But..." Baugham could only stammer out one word of protest at her assumption and hasty retreat before Sir Torquil stepped into the void with additional, sincere appeals to honour him, his daughters, and the local populace by participating in the Ramsey Run.

For some reason, he felt compelled to follow Miss Tournier, to make sure that she had not taken Miss Tristam's remarks too seriously, or if indeed she had, that she did not somehow hold him culpable for the implied insult. Unfortunately, it appeared that the only way he would be able to escape from the now combined entreaties of the entire Tristam family, was to agree to join the race and afterwards – regardless of his fortunes – to come to a celebratory supper at Tristam Lodge.

The thanks and exclamations of gratitude and joy were hardly less effusive than their pleas, but at last he was able to extricate himself and walk off in the direction of the churchyard. Progress was slow as he was waylaid often by greetings, introductions, and the general confusion of the ever-growing crowd. At last he saw her, speaking to a stallholder and lovingly fingering some colourful trinkets. He saw her smile and shake her head at the vendor before wandering away again.

"That was quite presumptuous of you, don't you think?" he demanded when he finally caught up to her standing by another stall, surrounded by the sweet smell of roasted nuts in cinnamon, syrup and cloves.

"I beg your pardon," she said with a frown.

"To consider the matter of my participation in the race settled. I presumed you knew me better than that."

"However well I may or may not know you…" Holly stopped and tried to read his expression. "Does this mean you have *not* been persuaded to enter? If that is the case, I must say that I am impressed. It's a rare gentleman who can withstand the persistence of Sir Torquil and his lovely daughters."

Baugham gave a slight, self-deprecating laugh.

"Oh, I think I must enter. But certainly not because of Sir Torquil or his formidable trio."

"Out of the goodness of your heart then? Or, perhaps it was the incentive of the winning prize that tempted you away from your resolutions to remain aloof from the local populace?"

"Oh no! Though I must say such a prize must raise some interest… my dear, Miss Tournier! You look positively intimidating. Please don't tell me you don't know this is all your fault."

Holly gasped. "*My* fault!"

"Why yes. You see, if I thought you wished me to enter, which I do not precisely think at this moment, my instinctive reaction would be to absolutely refuse. But if I thought that you did *not* wish me to, but had rather I remained in my bad hermitic habits, I think I would have put my name down sooner than Sir Torquil could have gathered his lovely daughters around him. At the moment, I am not quite certain what you wish me to do, but I *think* I have entered regardless. In fact, from the way you keep giving me such frowns, I get the distinct impression you actually wish me to be gone as far away from this field as possible, and therefore I think I must stay close and in the Ramsay Run after all."

Holly shook her head slightly and pursed her lips.

"Sometimes, my lord, you are entirely too clever for your own good."

Baugham gave a sheepish smile, which she assumed was entirely calculated but, nonetheless, quite disarming.

"I know I am and I apologise. I hope I can rely on your forgiveness since my foolish words are not uttered out of spite. Just as you seem to admirably put up with those that are."

Holly gave him a quick look but then turned her head away.

"The contestants are beginning to gather, my lord," she said. "It's time you were at the starting line. And if I may repeat myself: good luck."

"Well then. And thank you," Baugham smiled and gave a bow before he left her.

HAMISH WAS LEANING AGAINST THE railing of the course. This local horse race was, of course, nothing to Captain Bob and his gallant fights against savages and natives, but as far as adventure and excitement went, it would be quite unsurpassed this particular afternoon. He spied his employer hanging about on the other side by the hot chestnut vendor and he pulled his mother's sleeve.

"Mam!" he said urgently. "There he be! His lairdship is taking part. I told ye soo!"

The whole of the Nethery family was standing just behind him. His father and Duncan were wearing sullen looks and could not quite bring themselves to the same level of enthusiasm about follies of the local gentry, but his mother looked eagerly over to where her second son was pointing and then turned to her neighbour, another stout farmer's wife surrounded by her copious offspring.

"Aye, there he is indeed. I tell ye, Sarah, Laird Baugham has never been up to these things for as long as he's owned Clyne and now, with Hamish telling him what a grand affair it surely is, nothing would please him more, don't you know, than to come."

Her friend muttered something and slapped one or two of her children's heads as they were trying to push each other over the fence.

"Ooo," Mrs Nethery went on without heeding her husband's cold looks and her friend's obvious scorn, "he's such a clever boy, our Hamish, that nothing would do but for his lairdship to particularly ask for him when he needed that library cleaned out."

"We're nae 'cleaning it out', Mam," Hamish protested, but not very loudly.

The neighbour thought it time to put this self-important woman in her place a little.

"Well, I for one would nae let my bairn go to an English laird's house all alone, with no one to guarantee respectability except that queer Tournier woman's daughter. Half French and all! Really, Maggie, I wouldnae!"

"She's nae queer!" Hamish said hotly, feeling Captain Bob's spirit overtake him once again in the face of injustice and threat. "Miss Tournier is very nice and she has nae moods at all. And his lairdship says she's remarkable and I quite agree!"

"'Quite agree', do ye?" the neighbour mocked. "Aye, what fancy talk is that, then? Now who has aspirations of gentility all of a sudden after running errands to a laird and a half-French schoolteacher?"

Mrs Nethery was just about to grab her son Duncan by the ear and pull him and Hamish apart since this uttering had the additional effect of compelling Duncan to pinch the back of Hamish's neck and call him a poofed-up toad and Hamish slapping Duncan's hands away in a gesture Captain Bob surely would not have contemplated

232

if not in the utmost distress, when it was announced that the race was about to begin. This had a calming effect not only on the children, but also the adults, who refrained from further comment and all settled down to watch, two of the party heartily wishing his lordship would show their jeering fellows just what he was made of and the rest no doubt hoping Ned McMahon, who had served in the army and had been engaged in two campaigns, would whip that fancy Quality right into the mud.

BAUGHAM FELT LIKE AN IDIOT. He felt like leaning his forehead against that big, thick oak on the west side of the church, thumping it against it until he could see stars dance in front of his eyes and he no longer felt like swearing in every language in which he had a working knowledge — including Latin. What on earth had he got himself into? True, he had taken part in his fair share of races and wagers ever since he was old enough to be out of his short coats. He had participated in foolish bets and raced against the finest horsemen in the country. He had lost gallantly and competed earnestly for any number of silly and strange victories, but this was ludicrous.

Looking around him, he spied Miss Tournier in the distance giving him a glance. "Good luck," she had said and had actually sounded as if she meant it, but whether it was a wish for victory or for something else, he had no idea. She smiled at him, then addressed a group of village wives who had walked up to her. Baugham groaned; more attention from the locals was just what he did not need. He waved back as cheerfully as he could, though, and at the same time Miss Tristam managed to catch his eye and send him a coquettish smile. He returned it and when he turned his eyes towards the group of women again, Miss Tournier had turned her back to him and was speaking to someone else.

A tall man leaned against the fence just a few yards from his lordship. While Baugham patted his horse and whispered his apologies to the beast, the man — obviously a former soldier — had gathered quite a crowd around him. The eager looks and greetings and tugging of his coat sleeves were met with a patient air and an indulgent smile.

"Ye're going to win, Ned!"

"Ye dinnae need any luck!"

"My money's on ye, jist so ye'll knoo!"

The other contestants were already gathering, tying up their horses by the same fence and looking defensively both his and Ned's way. Most of them were boys, barely dry behind the ears, and most of the horses had not seen any other race than possibly the one for the best oats in their trough at home in the stables after a hard day's work. But there was a fair number of them and they all seemed to take this thing rather seriously and so Baugham supposed he was obliged to do the same.

A man came around with a tray of ale tankards on it and a number of small pouches tied to a stick. Baugham thankfully accepted the tankard but looked at the pouches with puzzlement.

"The blood…m'laird," the man muttered. "Ye must take a bag of blood, too."

"Right," muttered Baugham and carefully untied one of the small pouches, weighing it in his hand.

The tall military man leaned towards him and smiled. "Be careful ye tie it to yer saddle where it cannae get in the way. It breaks easily and pig's blood is nae something ye want to have all over yer britches when ye come home."

"You're certainly right there," Baugham answered as he thought of the combined deterrent of Mrs McLaughlin and Mr Riemann.

THE KNOLL BY THE CHURCH had not quieted down, but the crowds lessened considerably as the start of the run loomed. Left were the drunks and the vendors taking a rest, the animals and the competitors getting ready. A young boy went around and collected hats and coats and other effects and he took a little extra time with Mr McMahon and wished him good luck in his run with his eyes sparkling from an acute case of hero worship. A few boys who wanted to see the runners off, counting on various short cuts through the woods to catch the victor arriving by the river at the other end, were waiting around as well. The rest of the spectators had moved to the finishing spot by the river to get a good vantage point.

Lord Baugham calmed his horse, stroking him gently between his ears and speaking quietly. He was still young and nervous and the presence of the other beasts in such close proximity made him fidgety. On the other hand, Baugham was quite certain that when it came to speed and agility there was no match for Weimar in this run. If he could just quickly put the rest of the men behind him and distance himself from them, he would have no difficulties winning the Run and the privilege of emptying his bladder of pig's blood in the stream at the end of it. On the other hand, he remembered Miss Tournier's words; did he *really* want to win this run?

Nevertheless, when Sir Torquil finally determined that the moment was right to release the riders, Baugham quickly let Weimar outpace the slower, more massive beasts and manoeuvre himself to take the lead. To his surprise, however, he soon noticed that the military man's horse was a good and steady mount and could keep up with him through sheer effort, if not grace or swiftness. The two of them, and a third young man, quickly outpaced the rest of the pack and sped along Sir Torquil's masterpiece without really admiring it at all, but rather calculating and avoiding the hazards of it.

The track was not very broad. After a nice easy stretch along the village lane with people standing beside it or peeking out through windows, it deviated in through the woods, and there turned into nothing more than a cow path at times. Sir Torquil had been forced to disobey his natural inclination for straight and clear roads and had marked out the way by hanging pieces of red cloth on the branches of the trees overhead or sticking poles into the ground to lead the riders. Baugham found, to his amazement, that he was forced to maintain a good pace and struggle hard, compelling Weimar to follow his leading against his own instincts while racing through the trees and over the uneven ground to keep his lead.

234

The steady thumping of hooves followed him and for a moment he gave in to the realisation that he was enjoying this. Not as a race to win, but the speed, the agility of his horse and the thrill of competition with a worthy opponent, who was answering the rhythm of Weimar's graceful strength with steady determination just a few paces behind him.

As he listened to Ned McMahon baiting his horse nearer and nearer to him, he became aware that there was just the two of them now. Anyone who had the means and skill to keep up with them into the woods had now faded back, and he realised he was going to have to not only rely on Weimar's superior pedigree to stay ahead, but also some sort of strategy.

Baugham could see the end of the wooded stretch and the fields that lay beyond it. With a crash, both of the riders broke out into the free ground and Baugham could feel as well as see Ned McMahon out of the corner of his eye. There was a fair bit to go yet and the closer they got to the river, the more people they could make out standing some way back or up on the slopes to catch the fine view of the leading horses of the race running neck to neck now.

Baugham threw a glance at his rival. McMahon noticed it and gave him a sideways grin.

"Beware of the grassy bit down there, m'laird!" he shouted good-naturedly. "A fine horse like yours could easily step awry on the tufts!"

Baugham made a fleeting gesture to his head in thanks. The slope down to the river was indeed uneven ground, with tufts of grass hiding soft spots, holes, and rocks. Baugham decided he could not risk it, reining his horse in just enough to let McMahon pass him before he picked up the pace again.

In the distance, on the riverbank, he could see a large red flag flying above the heads of spectators. Behind that, the river Kye flowed, quiet and clear, over a bed of pebbles, a few trees leaning over it. As soon as the end was in sight, the crowds began to move and a low hum reached them as the people geared into action and speech.

They were neck to neck. Some of the spectators retreated up to the banks behind the goal to make way for them, and soon they found themselves close enough to think about the necessity of stopping. Baugham was ahead now again. Slowing down to fling himself off, Weimar struggled briefly and threatened to run right through the crowds to the river. Baugham cursed and restrained him as best he could. Meanwhile Ned McMahon had reached them and was calming his own mount. Baugham could have flung himself off there and then, leaving Weimar to pace himself alone, but he stayed mounted. There were too many people around. Children were excitedly creeping closer to get a better look. The pebbles on the ground were slippery and the animal was edgy and nervous, giving a frustrated snort and shaking his head wildly, eyes bulging in excitement and fear. Then Weimar slipped and whinnied in alarm. Ned McMahon gave him a look as Baugham's horse danced around wildly, finding his balance and recovering some of his dignity. *Will he keep?* the look asked. *I'll keep him,* Baugham's own quick glance answered back. Ned McMahon grabbed his pouch, slipped out of his saddle and landed in the cold water. He threw the pouch on a sharp pebble and stepped on it. Bright red blood flowed out, instantly colouring the river from a deep red to a light pink and a huge cheer went up into the air.

This did nothing to sooth Weimar's sensibilities and Baugham was forced to guide him a little to the side, on the grassier patch, before he slid down himself and went up to the horse's head to talk to him in a soothing voice. Weimar stepped around, a little calmed by the removal and the fact that his master was beside him on the ground.

His fumbling defeat was embarrassing, to be sure, but of course a very good and diplomatic outcome considering the sentiments of the local populace, who could not be bothered with the refinements. All they cared about was the victory of their dependable hero and the joy was great.

Baugham was simply relieved the whole thing was over and offered his congratulations to Ned McMahon, offering to buy the victor a pint at some more convenient moment. The placid man smiled and assured his lordship he had every respect for his abilities and that he had been lucky in his great fortune to be able to meet him in such a close race. They parted on the best of terms and Baugham lost no time leaving Ned McMahon to his admiring neighbours.

Holding on to the reins, Baugham dragged the stubborn horse — now apparently very comfortable with staying in the river and quenching his thirst — onto the bank. A few people gave him a look and some offered him mumbled words of congratulations on the best run in years and Baugham nodded quietly without offering answers. Suddenly he was aware someone was watching him. Miss Tournier stood a few feet away and he met her eyes, startled by two conflicting thoughts at the same moment. At the one hand, he willed her to come over and offer him company and protection in this awkward situation, but on the other hand his impulse was to turn around, throw himself on his ungrateful mount and take the shortest way back to Clyne again.

He had not time to decide which impulse he preferred because just as Miss Tournier was coming toward him a loud shot rang out and the crowd turned in the direction from which it came and grew silent. Sir Torquil was standing on a platform, holding the starting pistol in one hand and Ned McMahon's arm triumphantly in the air with the other.

"Ladies and Gentleman, your Champion!"

Cheers and applause filled the air, as well as numerous caps, and McMahon grinned bashfully from the adoration of the good men and women of Clanough.

"And," Sir Torquil continued when the din died down a little, "his prize!"

Primrose Tristam made her way up the steps in a slow and stately pace amid polite applause, a few catcalls and at least one, "Make it worth yer while, Ned." coming anonymously from somewhere in the crowd. Baugham's attention was called from the ceremony by a quiet voice beside him.

"My lord," Miss Tournier nearly whispered. "That was a very fine race – in all respects. You needed no luck for doing what you did."

Just as he was about to protest, he heard his name booming across the crowd.

236

"And we salute Lord Baugham, for his kind condescension in joining in with our traditions and finally giving Ned here some stiff competition and providing a good show for all the spectators." He gestured toward Baugham, "My lord!" and the crowd erupted in cheers again. Baugham tried to diffuse the adulation by a bow and wave.

The ceremony of the crowning of the victor went on as it had every year since Ned McMahon had returned home from the war and Miss Tristam gave a good performance as always, if slightly more hurried than the previous years.

Baugham sighed a genuine sigh of relief that made Miss Tournier look at him curiously.

"Sometimes defeat has unexpected benefits", he said smiling.

She bowed her head and gave a small smile, arranging her shawl around her shoulders against the growing cold and he reflected once more how her unexpected gracefulness and elegance pleased and surprised him. There was most decidedly something about these French women, he reflected, that did not blossom well under stern, frugal Scottish circumstances and with a family like hers, the home she had grown up in surely was more akin to the circles in Town than this part of the world, however much Edinburgh cast its metropolitan light not far away.

"Tell me, Miss Tournier," he therefore asked, "I have been curious for long. What was it that made your family settle here after leaving Paris?"

She gave him a surprised look.

"Oh, we didn't. First we were in England for many years. Or it seemed like many years — I was very small, only three, when we left Paris."

"Do you remember much of that time?"

"No," she shook her head, "Maman will not talk about it, but do I remember living in many different places. Sometimes it was only the three of us, but mostly we stayed with friends. I remember when we stayed at the Pembroke's townhouse, it seemed so grand to me; I thought it was a palace. I used to sneak into the parlour and climb up on their enormous damask chairs and pretend to be a French princess. *La Princesse Royale Holly*!" She laughed. "Quite a secret little game of mine in those circumstances, I think you can understand."

Baugham smiled and could somehow well picture a stubborn little girl's refusal to give up her fascination for princesses, despite her family's outspoken sentiment on the monarchy itself.

"They are the friends who provided us with Rosefarm Cottage, of course," Holly continued but not as lightly as before. "They are very kind, and he never used to trouble us if we were late with…but now Mr Pembroke has given over his business interests to his son who is not quite so…"

Silently cursing her stumbling tongue, Holly abruptly stopped herself and glanced over to his lordship to see if she had done so in time. He seemed to be preoccupied with stroking his horse's muzzle and not to have heard what she almost said, so she turned back to the subject of her family.

"Papa still believed in the movement and continued to lecture, to write and to do what he could, though he had to be very careful and quiet about it, of course, but over time — as everything became so horrible over there — he lost all faith and hope and became ill. Our friends thought that living here, so far away from the turmoil and memories, would be beneficial…but he died anyway…"

Lord Baugham did not look up, still keeping his attention on the horse, and Holly, too, found herself tentatively reaching out and touching the animal's side. It was warm and soft, with the feel of surprising strength beneath. Something made her continue speaking where she normally would not.

"Maman, when she will speak of him, tells me he died of a broken heart," she said, focusing on the silky feel beneath her fingers. "Is that not a surprisingly romantic notion for her to hold? But, I have often wondered…if he had only…"

Here Holly did break off, turning to stare out at the lingering crowds before them for a moment in order to collect herself. When she looked at his lordship again, it was with a smile on her face.

"And that is the long and uninteresting story of how the Tournier women ended up in Scotland. Do you have a similar tale to tell of how the Earl of Cumbermere came to be here?"

For a moment there was no reaction from her companion. Then he looked over at her.

"Oh, are you referring to me? I am sorry, I do not heed well to that calling." He gave a grin. "There is no story. I came hunting a few years back and fell in love. With Clyne. In actual fact I was staying north of Melrose in Roxburgh, but then I drifted south and west and here I am. And that is the full, uninspiring history." He smiled. "I am, however, not in the least bit surprised to hear your mother harbours romantic sentiments. I could not doubt it for a moment, for I cannot help but think her heart is as big as her mind."

Holly had fully collected herself by this time. "Well, I must say that is a singularly dull tale. You came hunting, saw it, liked it and bought it! I am disappointed. So you must humour my romantic disposition, passed down so successfully from my mother, and tell me a better story than that!"

"Miss Tournier, I can assure you that you would not enjoy any story I would attempt to share," he laughingly said. "I have no patience for well-built up suspense, surely you are the master of tale telling in this particular company. I will confine myself to quick and shallow insults as I have pledged in your case."

"Well, I must say you have been very idle on that front lately, too", she said and sent him a sly look. "You've not grown tired of it, I hope. It would be a great disappointment to me, you know."

She watched and waited uncertainly, unsure of why she would have said such a thing.

"Quite right," he said dryly, not meeting her eyes but smiling. "You are quite right of course — nothing in the world would top my experiences today better than attacking you out in front of all these good villagers, thereby adding poor sportsmanship and boorish behaviour to my list of questionable achievements of the day. I do believe I am much better off to bow out gracefully, if such a thing is still possible, and return home. Still, I would appreciate it if you would allow me to salvage *some* pride and self-respect. You must allow me to thank you."

"I certainly will allow it, sir. But might I ask your reasons for feeling it necessary to offer thanks to me?"

"For the happy conclusion to this day and for ensuring that it did not end up in the reds after all. It did look like this strange Run would have gone down in history as the most unfortunate excuse for the upholding of country traditions to my mind — and let me confess country traditions certainly were never favourites of mine to begin with. But, thankfully, as a result of these few moments, I find myself regarding this day with both fondness and pleasant surprise now. "

He smiled. She gave him a delighted smile in return.

"You are very welcome, sir. And may I return the same thanks to you?"

"Of course," Lord Baugham tipped his hat. "If you return the courtesy and tell me why."

Holly lowered her voice.

"I saw you," she said with a more serious tone. "I saw what you did when your horse... And I think you — "

She was interrupted by a familiar voice. "My lord! Oh, my lord, you must think I have not a decently grateful bone in my body... The prize ceremony... Mr McMahon... I was delayed..."

Sir Torquil was wading through the crowd, his eldest daughter very ably keeping up with him as he struggled up the little slope.

Lord Baugham took a step away from Holly and, in light of what she had just been about to tell him, she felt oddly bereft.

"The aldermen," Sir Torquil breathed, "our distinguished Dr. Smellie... I must beg to introduce..."

His lordship threw a hasty look at Miss Tournier, but she was busy looking at her feet and then Primrose Tristam sided up between them so he could never receive the amused look he had hoped to share with her before Sir Torquil hastened him away to a party of small men in somber dress a few feet away.

Holly watched him walk away. It really was his own fault, she reflected, since he would never deign to venture out into their little provincial circles. Perhaps he found them tedious, perhaps vulgar, but they would catch up with anyone who took to living here for any period of time. These little formalities were important to them and should not be mocked — but, as she watched him being introduced to the local dignitaries, she had to own he did not look mocking at all. Quite the opposite. Which made her wonder why...

"So," a pointed voice said beside her, "what on earth shall *we* talk about so exclusively now? You can hardly expect *me* to talk to you about books as well."

Holly smiled and slowly turned to Primrose Tristam. "No," she said slowly, "I cannot claim to expect that."

"Well, then," Miss Tristam said.

"But we didn't talk about books," Holly went on. "We talked about — "

"Oh?" She was interrupted by a snorting sound from Miss Tristam. "What else could you possibly have to talk about? Really, Holly!"

Holly frowned. "I'm afraid I do not — "

"You're the hired help," Primrose Tristam said and leaned into Holly ever so slightly, at the same time as she pretended to share a confidence. "What else could you properly talk about to your employer? Certainly nothing of a personal nature. Holly, dear, such things are…unseemly."

"I…" But it was a useless beginning to a protest that had no foundation. Primmie was right.

"Let me give you some advice, my dear," Primrose said and looked at her with sickly sweet concern. "Because we are *such* old friends and all that. I know you haven't had the experience of many servants in your household, and you have no gentlemen about, so you may not be aware of their unfortunate tendencies to trifle with the help. I cannot tell you the stories I have heard, from Mama and my aunts, of how so many sweet young girls are brought to ruin because they mistook the intentions of their masters. Some so foolish as to even think he might marry them." She paused for a tittering laugh before resuming her mission of mercy.

"His lordship is all that is charming and affable, but you must be sure not to mistake any…interest he may show in you for anything more than what it is. After all, it is obvious that when he marries, he must choose a bride from among his own set. But, no man is past seeking out a little diversion with the hired help in the meanwhile. Books and the weather do not an attachment make!"

Miss Tristam drew even closer and assumed an air of confidence, despite the fact that Holly remained resolutely silent. "To be truthful, Holly, I don't understand why you don't just accept Mr Grant and get it over with. He's really your best prospect and if I were you I would move quickly before news of your current…*work* is spread too far abroad. He may begin to question the wisdom of wanting to marry a servant girl."

Dr Smellie really was a marvellous man, his lordship thought, perhaps because of his unfortunate name, for he was a man of dry and precise humour. The kind of humour that did not lend itself to friendship very well, but served as the perfect antidote to Sir Torquil's anxious reassurances and interventions. There was an amusing comment about the fate of being smallbuilt when trying to catch the final dash into the Kye and the spilling of the pig's blood and Lord Baugham laughed with his new acquaintances. His laughter, however, was stopped mid-stream when he happened to catch the eye of Miss Tournier. She was still standing in the spot where he had left her, but there was something about her expression that struck him. Suddenly this play was not so amusing; the attention not as gratifying as it had been just a moment earlier. Having allowed it to go this far, he was now obligated to see it through, but his thoughts were now on quickly extricating himself from this public display.

After begging various pardons and promising possible future meetings, he was able to take his leave and retreat back to where Miss Tournier was standing motionless with the eldest Tristam daughter chatting to her in perfect cheerfulness.

"Oh, very good work, my lord," Primrose twittered as he came up to them. "Those dreary old men, I'm so glad you're not one of those who find their company invaluable. I know Mama complains about Father being so embarrassingly fond of them that he stops and drags them around where ever he seems to meet them. You're much better off back here with us."

Lord Baugham smiled and said he could hardly argue with that.

"I must go."

He stared at Miss Tournier, but she would not meet his eyes.

"Of course you must, my dear", Primrose said and leaned over to catch Holly's hands and give her a kiss on her cheek. "You dear creature."

She had hardly let go of her hands before Holly stepped away.

"Miss Tournier!"

She stopped, but seemed reluctant to turn around.

"I . . ." What could he say? He struggled with the appropriate words for a moment. "Thank you. Again. For helping me and guiding me through my first Run. I enjoyed it."

"You're welcome, of course," she muttered before turning away once more.

"And now you must let me help you a little, my lord," Primrose interjected, turning his attention back to herself. "A little supper . . . I know Mama and Father are most anxious . . . can't let your employees carry all the weight . . . not paid . . . my pleasure . . . "

Holly could hear Primrose chatter away as she took herself down the slope and away from the last scene of the Ramsey Run. What she heard next should not have come as a surprise, but when Lord Baugham's cheerful voice carried back to her, proclaiming that although Ned McMahon had won the race, it certainly turned out that he was carrying off the prize himself, accompanied by Miss Tristam's delighted laughter, it made a great hole in her enjoyment of the day all the same.

But it's only to be expected, she rationalised, *after all, I am merely an employee, not one of the "prominent" young ladies of the village.* Despite herself, she turned and watched him being led away, Primmie clutching his arm comfortably and possessively, smiling and bowing to the accolades of the crowd. Once she thought he briefly caught her eye, but his expression as he swept past her seemed to confirm her own relative unimportance and standing among such company. She turned from the sickening scene before her and began to walk towards Rosefarm Cottage, filled with an unexpected and, she scolded herself, irrational disappointment; she had thought that perhaps she and his lordship were becoming friends . . . now she was corrected. If he was more at home with the false flatteries and simpering attentions of Miss Tristam, then he was welcome to them. She would remember her place and trouble him no longer with any attempt to be anything other than a hired librarian.

Chapter 22

On Gentlemanly Behaviour and Justifiable Defeats

Hamish was gutted. He was no stranger to feelings of shame or disappointment, but the result of the Ramsey Run seemed to him to have offended some higher principle and he had felt compelled to quickly slip away from his family as soon as he saw his lordship rein in his horse and hesitate, giving over the victory. The only satisfaction he could claim was that Duncan's instant jab in his ribs had prompted his mother to sharply smack her eldest's head. Now he wandered alone back to the church knoll among the drunks and the giggling girls, past the fortune-tellers and the ale stalls behind the animal enclosures to be alone. He kicked at the heaps of straw in his path and wallowed freely in his misery. His lordship had lost in a humiliating way to Ned McMahon, upsetting Hamish's newfound world order. Now, Ned was a good man, of course, and a local hero, and it was not really his person that had offended Hamish's sensibilities. Certainly, his family's victorious shouts and his neighbours' gleeful looks had stung him, but the more he thought about it, he really did blame Lord Baugham for his present misery.

"Ye could hae beaten him!" he muttered angrily. "I know you could've. Why didn't ye make a real effort?"

To Hamish, his employer's dignity and success seemed the most important things in the world, but in his eyes, his lordship had simply not taken the competition seriously enough. He had done his part, bravely standing up for him among the locals, despite the opposition, but Lord Baugham had failed him. In conceding defeat so readily, he had not lived up to his promise of a heroic model. That was the wincing and incomprehensible defeat.

He could not help but think of Captain Bob and how that gallant hero was also destitute on his return to England and how he was determined to overcome his desperate fate. In just a few days he would be there with a true hero again, facing insurmountable obstacles and valiant fights and that thought cheered him. Having no wish to go back and hear the rest of the jeers and remarks his family had thought up for him since he left, he wandered down the slope and dodged the carts and bands of youths making their way to the grounds for more riotous fun as the evening approached.

Suddenly he saw a familiar figure walking slowly down the church lane by the wall and he recognised Miss Tournier. Now, it was hard to know whether a gallant and protective spirit was awakened within him upon seeing this lonely figure walking, or whether he thought he had finally spotted someone who could give him the sympathy and reassurance he still felt lacking. Whatever the case, he set out in a trot and breathlessly called her attention to him long before he reached her side.

"Miss Tournier! Miss! Oh, am I glad to see ye, miss!"

Miss Tournier turned at the sound of her name and gave a genuine smile of delight. When he reached her, a little short of breath, he greeted her.

"Good evening, miss. Ye should nae be out here on yer own like this. Where's his lairdship?"

Holly was touched by his concern and her expression showed it. "Well Hamish, I am very happy to see you. His lordship has found more appealing company than I am able to provide. But if I might take *your* arm as I am walking, I would feel much safer indeed."

Hamish did not believe that company more appealing than Miss Tournier's could be found by anyone, but he very proudly held his arm out and beamed as she softly laid her hand upon it and allowed him to lead the way. "Where to, miss?" he questioned shyly.

"Home, my friend. I should be getting home and so, by the way, should you. It is late."

"It's nae that late, miss," Hamish protested. "I'm quite used to staying out late. But I'll go after I've seen ye home if you wish."

He was obviously happy to be of service and Holly smiled her thanks as he cheerfully guided her onwards.

"So tell me Hamish, what did you think of this year's Run? Did you find it exciting?"

Hamish's spirits sunk. The elation and pride he felt at being able to be of assistance to Miss Tournier faded when once more his lordship's shortcomings were recalled. He did not quite know how to answer her, so he looked down at his feet once more while they walked on.

"Hamish?" she soon gently prompted. "Did you not enjoy it?"

She had once told him she could not abide foolishness, and although he had an inkling his sentiments might be considered foolish at best and even childish, he did think — and from all that he had heard in the way of morally educational tales from his teachers and the Reverend, it was true — that honesty never could be considered to be wholly foolish. Imprudent, perhaps, but he did so much want to tell her.

"Yes, ma'am, assure I did. It was...exciting. But..." He took a deep breath and stole a glance at her to ascertain she did not frown or even laugh at him. "I cannae deny I was...surprised at...at the outcome of the Run."

He could tell she regarded his laborious confession with a straight face and admirable patience.

"It's just that he was so much better than Ned!" he burst out with a pleading look. "I know he was! He is! And that furlie horse of his is...magnificent! And he lost and I dinnae think he should have."

The boy's words made Holly recall her own, very opposite, impression that Lord Baugham had conceded a certain victory for the noblest of reasons. She smiled. Silly thoughts to be thinking considering how they had parted just now...and now she wondered if perhaps he had not lost out to Ned McMahon so voluntarily after all, since he had so readily snatched up the 'prize' in the end. However, she did not want to say as much to a boy in the throes of acute hero worship.

She turned her smile upon Hamish and tried to ease the boy's disappointment. "Hamish, we must allow even those people we admire to be human and imperfect. Yes, Lord Baugham lost to Mr McMahon, but I hope you noticed how gentlemanly his behaviour was in doing so — he would not endanger others for the sake of his own glory."

Hamish pondered this — to his mind — very generous interpretation of the obligations of a heroic horseman. As far as he could deduce from all the adventure stories, the prime reason for engaging in displays of gallantry was to beat the enemy soundly and, if possible, through the utmost exertion of one's capabilities and skills. It still seemed to him Lord Baugham had failed in that, seeing as Hamish was convinced his lordship surely could have beaten anyone in the most dashing way he chose to.

But still, if Miss Tournier was of the opinion that gentlemanly behaviour included losing with grace and affability, he supposed he could grant that Lord Baugham did possess gentlemanly manners.

"Aye, miss," Hamish said hesitantly, "I daursay ye're right. Although I do think in all fairness," he said a little more determinedly, "that it would also be gentlemanly to treat a sporting engagement seriously."

Or, Holly thought darkly, to treat a friend, or even employee with respect enough to allow her to finish her sentence and not ignore her just because someone else comes along to flatter you and invite you to supper. But this was not about her and her bruised feelings, or even his lordship's manners truly, this was about Hamish, and she did want him to learn the principles of gentlemanly conduct. She swallowed her feelings of bitterness and put the best face on Lord Baugham's actions that she could.

"That is just it, Hamish. This was a sporting competition, not a struggle for freedom or a battle to preserve life and limb. It was a friendly race between neighbours. Sometimes a gentleman must choose which battles are worth fighting, and sometimes it demonstrates more strength to be humble than to swagger and lord it over others."

Hamish, having just benefited from a prime display of swaggering and lording by his own family, began to see the sense of what Miss Tournier was saying. He also reflected that his lordship's kind indulgence of his absorption with the adventures of Captain Bob and how he so understandingly took part in his fascination might be comparable to what Miss Tournier was saying about his chivalrous behaviour on the racecourse. In that light, of course, his lordship did seem quite heroic indeed.

"Yea, that's so, an all," he said eagerly, suddenly remembering something else praiseworthy. "And did ye see how he had to stay on his horse when all the wee ones was crowding in? He couldnae hae very well jumped off and let him loose, could he?"

Hamish, almost restored in faith and spirit, looked at Miss Tournier with wide-eyed wonder.

"But I do wished he would hae won. Don't ye, miss?"

Holly, who would by no means weaken the admiration of this boy who until now, had few, if any, heroes in his life, returned his wide-eyed stare. "That was a very fine thing he did indeed. I am sure he could have won if not for that."

And it was the truth, she thought. That, after all, is what she had tried to tell him herself.

This answer seemed to satisfy the boy, for he nodded his head gravely and walked on beside her in silence.

"Miss," he said at length. "Are ye and his lairdship just being chivalrous to me, too? I try my best but I cannae help but think... me not in school an all. Haen't been for two years, though when I was, Mr Crossly used to say I did well. I should like to know even if ye are, you know."

The earnestness behind those bright eyes made Holly pause and carefully consider before making her answer.

"Hamish, the code of chivalry proscribes good manners and proper behaviour. So, if I were merely being chivalrous toward you, I would give my curtsey and greet you politely when we meet on the street or in church. Lord Baugham, to be polite, would give you a nod as you passed him by. This is all that is required for good manners.

"You, Master Nethery, have been noticed because of your worth. You showed yourself to Mrs Tounier to be quick-witted, able, eager and willing to work. That in turn is what led her to recommend you to Lord Baugham. You have proven to be all these things, in addition to being a very pleasant walking companion."

Blushing, the boy walked quietly by her side obviously pleased with her answer. Holly was thoughtful, pondering his previous words. Just as they reached the gate of Rosefarm Cottage, Holly broached the subject.

"Hamish, I know you were taken out of school and I can see you are sorry for it. I would be happy to work with you in continuing your education if you like. I believe there are great things ahead for you, Hamish, and I would be honoured to help you achieve all that you are able."

"Oh Miss Tournier!... yes," he stammered, "... thank ye, miss! That would be... I would like that very much, please!"

The smile he gave her warmed her heart. In truth, she had not seen that kind of smile and gratitude mingled with enthusiasm for a very long time. Not since she left Hockdown School, when she had been dismissed and sent home. But it was not the smiles of the girls at the seminary she suddenly remembered with regret. It was those young boys at the penny school that she had been told was such a disgrace. How could doing anything that awarded a smile like that ever be a disgrace?

The thought stayed with her as Hamish hastily removed his cap in a salute before setting off in a run back to the village. Suddenly she felt a desperate need to talk to her mother. Common sense would drive away this curious mix of regret, sentimentality and ire the Martinmas fair had left her with.

Mrs Tournier was energetically stirring her tea when she heard the sound of voices coming down the lane. Looking up in the expectation of company when the door opened, she was slightly disappointed when her daughter walked in alone. She hardly let the girl kiss her cheek and bid her a good evening before she demanded an account of the fair.

"Did I not hear two voices outside?" she asked, "Who has been so gallant as to drag himself away from such entertainments as to walk you home? And why is he not worth a cup of tea for his troubles?"

"That was Hamish Nethery, Maman," Holly said sternly. "Practically the only gentleman in attendance today — in practice, if not in station, at any rate — and he needed to get back to his family. I am very sorry to disappoint you and your frightful need for gossip, but I could not have asked for a better or more amusing protector on my way home from that... affair."

"You think I want gossip?" she asked. "Oh, very well, perhaps I do, but spare me the cows, pantomimes and Sir Torquil's conversation, Lie-lie, and tell me something that is not enacted every year, in exactly the same way every year, under the tiresome demand of heeding to tradition. I take it, then, that his lordship stayed well away from the spectacle?"

Holly helped herself to tea and toast before taking her seat. "No, he was there. But really Maman," she smiled, "I think the livestock was the most interesting and I wish you would let me tell you about it."

Mrs Tournier huffed. "Livestock!" she said in contempt. "But I'm glad you ran into Hamish. Tell me, how is that boy doing?"

"Oh, he is doing very well. I like him very much — although he has quite the case of hero worship and had a hard time reconciling himself to the fact that Lord Baugham lost his bid for victory in the Ramsey race."

Holly took a bite of toast before continuing, with a wicked glint in her eye, "Are you sure you do not want to hear of the cows? Then I could tell you that Primmie Tristam took quite an interest in his lordship — but that is no surprise, is it? And, I might add, found it necessary to warn me about getting too high for my station!"

Her mother cocked her head and looked curious.

"Oh yes!" Holly went on, now realising that a good acid response may have been impossible when Miss Tristam was so busy pouring all that poison into her ear, but that she had every right to attempt one now. "She very helpfully instructed me to remember my place' she even advised me that books and weather were the only subjects I should ever attempt to discuss with his lordship, since everything else would be tantamount to flirting. I, you understand Maman, am merely the hired help and in danger of being trifled with at every turn like any common scullery maid! Can you believe it? Primmie warned *me* about being trifled with!'"

"Cows indeed…" Mrs Tournier groaned. "That girl is such a trial on one's thin veneer of civility. I hope that some gentleman will offer for her soon and relieve poor Ned McMahon — it *was* he who won the race again, was it not? — of the obligation of that yearly kiss. I can imagine that her mother did her best to foist her off on one of the gentlemen in attendance? That would have been a kindness she would have enjoyed."

"Oh there was no need for that, she very quickly foisted *herself* off on Lord Baugham, and he was by no means unhappy with the fact. I am sure they enjoyed a great deal of inane conversation together. I left soon afterwards — I can never abide silly flirtations — I just do not have the stomach for it."

Holly then launched into an account of the race, and descriptions of the people and marketplace, adding a few derogatory comments on her nemesis when she could slip them in without seeming to be too affected, as well as a few choice words on his lordship's spine in choosing his company, but Mrs Tournier only looked thoughtfully at her daughter after her spontaneous outburst, scarcely listening at all.

"Oh, and she pressed the poor man into joining them for 'a little supper' just as I was leaving. He must be regretting his choice now… and I tell you, I cannot wait until I get back to that calamity at Clyne he calls a library and prove myself to be a saviour rather than 'nothing better than a maid'!" she finished.

"Really?" her mother said slowly. "And there are no redeeming features of that lordly collection at all?"

"Maman, there are so many books to sort and classify that I must admit I have hardly been paying attention to the titles, except to decide which category to place them in. Even as bare as the shelves appear, once they're stacked on the floor, there seem to be four times as many of them. But, if you must know, most of it is rubbish. I'm sorry to say", she added with false charity.

Holly proceeded to describe the progress of her work, far beyond the capacity of her mother to endure such details of explanation. She pushed aside her work, took off her spectacles and put them in her pocket.

"It is time we had some supper ourselves, I think. "

As they walked to the small dining room, Holly's thoughts reverted to another point of permanent worry and annoyance over the fickle behaviour of gentlemen as she once again shared her confusion and frustration at the lack of news from Elizabeth.

"I just don't understand what the delay can be. Mr Darcy appeared so eager, his intentions toward her were so clear… you saw him with her… I thought for sure he would have made an offer by now."

Mrs. Tournier sat down across from her daughter and they waited while Mrs. Higgins filled their soup bowls.

"Yes, I surely did see him with her. And her with him. There was no shortage of encouragement from your cousin, nor is there any shame in it when one takes into account the man's obvious affection for her. But are you so eager after all, Lie-lie, for Elizabeth to be married? You were not so keen on the idea just a short time ago."

Holly paused, spoon halfway to her mouth. "It would make her happy, Maman!"

"And you can live with that?"

"Of course I can," she protested, but then looked thoughtful, "Well, I suppose I didn't like the idea at first — but after he went to such lengths to pursue her I was convinced.

"Although I wonder," she said, occupying herself with scraping the last drops of broth and cabbage from her bowl, "do you think maybe I should ask Lord Baugham if he has heard from him? Perhaps Mr Darcy might have gone to his estate in Derbyshire first and been held up with business? His lordship might have some news that I can include in a letter. That is, if such a subject is proper for the hired help to broach with her employer."

Mrs. Tournier merely raised her eyebrows as she sipped her soup, watching Holly spoon a large helping of cottage pie onto her plate.

"Upon my word, how things have changed. There was a time when you could hardly keep a civil tongue in your head about, or towards, his lordship and now here you come home, very much put out over the idea that your conversational subjects ought to be limited. I would be very interested to know what it is you *have* been talking about. Surely books and the weather were never a real option despite Miss Tristam's concern?"

For some inexplicable reason, Holly felt a blush rising to her cheeks. Feeling stupid, she took her time before answering casually, "Oh, we just talk of general things. Books — yes, but also art, education — those sorts of things. He asked how we came to settle in Scotland. Actually, I think he is very curious about you and Papa; he asks a lot about our family though he does not speak much about himself.

"Lately I am finding him, *had* found him to be, curiously easy to talk to … that is, when he isn't being inattentive or irritable."

She watched as her mother poured out the tea for her.

"Notwithstanding the spiteful motive behind her words, perhaps it would be for the best if you follow Miss Tristam's advice and keep to civilities and business with his lordship. I like the man. And although I do not think he is the sort to be frightened away from visiting by the offensive manners of a girl, I should find it very tiresome to have to always enjoy his company away from you or suffer the consequences. After all, he will most likely be leaving soon and I should like to have the pleasure of his visits for as long as he is still here."

Oddly, Holly was not making an attempt at taking the steaming cup from her hands but was looking at her strangely,

"Leaving soon? Why do you say that?"

Her mother raised her eyebrows. "He does not live here permanently, Lie-lie. In fact, he hardly stays here at all, which leads me to ask you what you are going to do once he is away again."

Holly sat still. "I don't know what you mean, Maman."

Mrs Tournier folded her hands and leaned forward.

"I mean, have you made any arrangements concerning continuing your work in his lordship's library when he removes himself."

"I... He has mentioned no such plans to me," Holly said defensively.

"It is my understanding he rarely does," her mother answered dryly. "He has shown remarkable constancy this year as it is, I am given to understand. He will leave — probably sooner than later — but your work will go on. I presume."

Holly was overcome with a strange feeling of confusion. "Yes... yes, I presume it will."

"Well, then," her mother said pushing the cup into her hands, "I should say it would be prudent for you to prepare for that eventuality. What you are to do when — not if — he leaves. Wouldn't it?"

Holly looked down at her hands and forced herself to stir her cup even if there was nothing yet added.

"You are right, Maman," she said quietly. "That would be prudent. I will."

She stared in silence for a few minutes while her mother watched and waited.

"He... his lordship did mention to me the other day that I was to come and go as I pleased in his absence, but I did not think he meant..." Holly finally said in what was meant to be a conversational tone. "It will be a strange house without him though."

"Then it is a strange house for the greater part of the year," her mother said gently.

"I know. It's just it will be strange working alone. It is work that requires a certain amount of consultation."

"I suppose it does. But you will have Hamish to help you. And I understand Mrs McLaughlin reigns supreme in the household in her Master's absence. No doubt she will be of great assistance."

"No doubt," Holly said and carefully put down her spoon again. "I like Mrs McLaughlin."

"Well, then," Mrs Tournier said.

Holly gave her mother a feeble smile. "Yes. That is that, I suppose."

"And then there is this, of course." Mrs Tournier reached into her apron pocket and brought out a folded up letter.

Holly gave it a curious glance but made no effort to take it, even though her mother demonstratively put it on the table between them.

"Don't you want to find out what it is?" her mother said, slightly irritably.

"Of course", Holly said, taking a little and curious pleasure in annoying her. "Why don't you tell me while I finish my supper?"

She attacked her food again and avoided her mother's look.

"It is from Dr McKenna."

That earned her a glance and a surprised expression. Secure in her triumph again, Mrs Tournier continued more gently.

"You have been offered a commission, Lie-lie, to illustrate his book. Scenery, as far as I can make out. Involving rocks, no doubt."

"Oh! But…"

"And that is a good thing", Mrs Tournier went on more sternly again. "Don't you agree?"

The fleeting doubt in Holly's mind that she would be able to set aside and abandon Lord Baugham's library for something else so soon fluttered away again.

"I do", she said more determined than she felt. "It is."

"Well, then", said the mother and pocketed the letter again. "I will write him and say you accept." By express, she added to herself.

Chapter 23

When Frustrations are Up and Defences are Down and Tea is Served…

ANOTHER day of dry weather enabled Baugham to make his customary annual tour around the northern boundaries of his estate. The terrain was good, the air was crisp and cool, and his horse was in a splendid mood — no doubt pleased he was not required to display his obvious talents to any undeserving country nag. Once the circuit was complete, he made his way homeward through the village, picking up his mail and scheduling an appointment with the gunsmith. With nothing left to delay or distract him, he slowly, almost reluctantly, headed toward Rosefarm Cottage. It was a visit he was obliged to make and had not been able to find a way out of, even after a long and arduous ride. The manner of Miss Tournier's departure yesterday was puzzling and even unsettling. It was not impossible, of course, but he had searched his mind for whatever he might have said or done that had not been taken in the spirit of his pledge of exclusive insult, but he could not remember anything. She had been upset, but why?

As he rode up to the gate he was surprised to see her on the steps, bracing the wind to trim the climbing roses entwined around the entrance. She turned around the moment he rode up and immediately straightened up despite her flushed countenance and steady grip around the thorny wilderness. There was a quick smile of recognition that gave him heart and he decided to try his luck on a lighter note.

"Miss Tournier! How fierce you look with that knife in your hand!" Baugham tried to sound cheerful. "Remind me never to invoke any privileges of mine when you are thus armed."

Holly, however, simply hoped her smile would disguise the dismay and confusion she felt at his arrival. That immediate feeling of being caught unawares soon yielded

251

to a wry voice reminding her of her mother's words from yesterday. *He'll soon be gone again,* it echoed, *and these bothersome visits will stop. I shan't let him trouble me.*

Knowing she looked messy and ridiculous with locks of hair falling in her face and the breeze blowing strands across her eyes, she ignored the embarrassment, dropped the knife and with one hand welcomed him.

"Maman will be pleased to see you have come," she said in as cheerful and unaffected voice as she could manage under the circumstances. "If you can wait a moment while I tie this back up, I will bring you in."

"Oh no, no! I beg you would not trouble yourself. My visit today can only irritate her for I cannot stay." He looked at her closely, a mischievous smile playing on his lips. "But in the light of what I just said, you will think me extremely foolhardy, but the temptation is irresistible. I must know: do you mean to tie up the roses or your hair?"

She winced. Of course he would call attention to her unkempt appearance. Miss Tristam, she was certain, would never be found in such a state of disarray. *Never mind, Holly, he will soon be gone...*

"Well, I see you had enough sense to wait until I had dropped the knife before provoking me." She tried to smile playfully. "But considering that I am, with some difficulty, attempting to keep this branch from dropping onto my head, it is safe to assume that I am referring to the roses."

Lord Baugham leaned forward in his saddle.

"I must confess I hoped as much. It seems quite as lovely as it ever could be just as it is. At least compared to the roses," he hastily added.

She gave him an arch look, but he only laughed. Then, after a slight pause, he impulsively descended from his horse and tied the reins loosely around the garden gate.

"I think you have forgotten my resolution to also flatter you. If so, you are instantly forgiven since I find myself wondering if I have not caused it myself by some unfortunate remark yesterday."

She looked up with surprise in her eyes.

"Oh, well," he said while glancing back at his horse. "You left rather suddenly."

She averted her eyes, too. "Yes, I suppose I did." There was a flicker of uncertainty on his face and she went on. "Please don't think it had anything to do with you. I enjoyed myself very much yesterday. It was simply... I simply had to leave, that is all."

It was obvious that her words in no way went far enough to satisfy his curiosity, but he did look slightly more at ease for having been exonerated.

"I understand," he said. "I left very soon after as well. The Tristam's very gracefully invited me to take supper with them, though I expect you heard... It was a good day and yet..."

"Yes," she said dryly and turned to her roses again. "And yet."

"I'm sorry," he said without really knowing why.

She was struggling with the vines again and he watched her for a moment before he reached out and grabbed a particularly stubborn branch, swinging in the wind above her head and avoiding capture, As he held up the thorny stems and tried to

252

keep them out of her face and hands, she quickly and tightly wound up the heavy vines. There were no words; she was putting great concentration into her efforts and he found he had to do the same. But as she turned and stepped back to assess their work and remove her gloves, her apron strings got caught in the thorns. Baugham looked at the strips of fabric tangled in the barren twigs and gently loosened them from their hold.

"*Pluck a red rose from off this thorn with me,*" he muttered and let them fall again behind her.

She turned around quickly and looked at him. To her surprise he met her gaze and did not look away for a very long time. He seemed on the brink of saying something, but then hesitated.

"Mrs Tournier," he said instead and directed his gaze beyond her to the door of the house.

Holly swallowed and looked behind her. Indeed, her mother had appeared at the door and stood watching them quietly. Holly could not quite read her mother's mood from the look on her face, but she very quickly directed a smile at her and gave her hand for Lord Baugham to kiss.

"Miss Tournier is correct," Baugham said and gave a bow. "I must decline. Not only because of my impertinence, but also I am obligated to take tea with the Tri — with friends."

"I am sorry to hear that," Mrs Tournier said dryly.

"However," Lord Baugham added almost immediately, "perhaps I might take the time for a quick cup to ward off any desperate need for refreshment I might otherwise experience far too soon, though it is more than I deserve under the circumstances."

"It is exactly what you deserve," Mrs Tournier smiled narrowly. "Tea, Lie-lie?" she said.

"In a moment, Maman. I'll just finish up here first. You go ahead."

Mrs Tournier lingered a moment as did their guest, but since Holly began to look around for her sweep, neither of them had any choice but to walk inside.

SITTING IN THE UNIVERSITY LIBRARY that same afternoon, Dr McKenna was having a difficult time keeping his mind on the lecture notes he was preparing. The letter from Mrs Tournier had arrived at last yesterday and it contained the welcome news that Miss Tournier would be delighted to accept his offer. He stared ahead, feeling a curious sense of relief and not a little confusion over why it should be the case. He knew the prospect of finally publishing *The Geological Formations and Features of the Scottish Countryside* was only a small part of it, because up till now he had been content to bury himself in the halls of academia or lose himself in his treks of exploration and not concern himself overly with seeking recognition or, in fact, even completing what had become a years-long work in progress and somewhat of a joke among his colleagues.

But suddenly, once he had seen Sir John Leslie's finished work — the bound leather cover, the fine paper, the quality typesetting and the lovely, yet still clear and concise illustrations that added just the right level of professionalism, taste and beauty to the text — he was now very anxious to see his words and findings in print as well.

Then his mind wandered back to that night in Sir John's dining room, when he, Sir John and Miss Tournier talked and plotted and planned a way for her to find work, and further back to that evening at Rosefarm Cottage, in the kitchen, and how her face lit up when Sir John offered her his commission.

McKenna smiled to himself. Miss Tournier needed the work, and he was anxious for his treatise to be at last completed. Once he was able to bring a few more aspects into line, he would make the journey to Clanough to settle the matter. She had appeared so sad and defeated upon leaving Edinburgh when he had last seen her...he decided that he would very much enjoy the opportunity to bring that light to her face once again.

"I WAS TAUGHT BY PEOPLE who still believed in the ideals of the enlightened era, my lord. I was taught that natural sciences were the foundation on which the advancement of mankind — economic and social — as well as the welfare of the people was based. Only through knowledge of the world and resources around us can we build our wealth as a nation and as a people."

"And now it is all belligerent nationalist politics?"

"Quite. Fine principles have deteriorated into a contest of arms and violent strength. I find that hard to bear sometimes. We no longer benefit from the finest minds of different nations competing and sharing their discoveries in an attempt at reaching the same goal. The furthering of knowledge for the betterment of mankind has given way to patriotism and the quest for power and riches, built on the ashes of foreign nations and the bodies of strange soldiers."

"Well, as a Cambridge man, steeped in the conviction that only study of the classics will carry mankind anywhere close to higher learning, I must accede that you are absolutely right. The limits set by conservative notions of education and faculties have most certainly damaged my respect for proper learning and application of knowledge. I have not honoured my Alma Mater with what I was given. I spent three dissipated years at University, took great delight in displaying my talents and none in applying them to anything that was not to my own advantage or amusement. I sometimes wonder if I should have done better at another discipline than mathematics, which was so disastrously designed to allow me to show off. But you see, nothing but Cambridge was to be considered. And philosophy makes me quite ill."

"If you ever have a son, my lord, I hope you will remember that."

Baugham laughed.

"You should not be uneasy on that score, madam! My family has a grand tradition of filial disobedience. I have every confidence that any son of mine will stay well away from Oxbridge and take his learning as an attached apprentice of some sort. I should be very happy were he to consider anything as orthodox as natural sciences at Edinburgh."

254

"As much as I do not believe you mean one word of that, I would very much love to witness it. A noble Anglican son surrounded by all those nonconformists…"

Mrs Tournier looked at her friend when there was no response to her challenge. He was staring out the window and had quite obviously abandoned their discussion for the view of the garden.

"Well?" she said impatiently.

"She is there," he said and then turned his head towards her and gave a sheepish smile. "I can see Miss Tournier in the garden these past fifteen minutes, ma'am."

"Really?" Mrs Tournier said and could not hide the acidity in her voice.

"She seems not prepared to leave it, though," his lordship continued. "The thought of tea must be very unattractive to her for some reason, for I cannot see that she is employed in anything useful. In fact, I suspect she is piddling."

Mrs Tournier stood up and joined him watching out the window.

"My daughter likes her garden," she said. "She apparently feels it is a more comfortable place at the moment than my parlour. However, she rarely piddles."

"Just today or as a rule?" his lordship asked softly.

"Do your plans keep you in Scotland for much longer, my lord?" she abruptly asked the preoccupied young man staring out the window, but it made no impact.

"No fixed plans," he said distractedly before standing. "The wind is picking up. If you will excuse me, I think I should let Miss Tournier know that the tea is getting cold and you wish her to come in."

"You are ascribing protective maternal feelings to me that I make no claim to at present, my lord, and which would most certainly confuse my daughter," she stated, but he was already on his way to the door, leaving Mrs Tournier to huff in irritation, and then to sit and wait in impatient agitation for their return.

HE FOUND HER SITTING ON a rickety garden bench beneath what, under more favourable seasons, was a large apple tree but now was more like a tangle of ancient and lichen covered branches at impossible angles. She was twining wilted weeds between her fingers, deep in thought and if she heard him approach, she made no sign of it, looking steadfastly ahead out into the farther end of the garden where there was nothing but the same barrenness to be seen.

"So," Baugham said softly as he reached her, "here we are. You hiding out in the garden, braving the elements and me wondering how to execute your mother's wishes and bring you in."

Holly turned at the sound of his voice, her expression curiously and uncharacteristically empty.

"Please do not trouble yourself, my lord. I am not hiding; I am simply enjoying the solitude. I am perfectly capable of deciding for myself when I ought to come in from the cold, as my mother is well aware."

She pulled her eyes away and went back to staring at the emptiness in front of her.

"Well, then," he said, "let me confess a selfish motive. You really cannot deprive me of your presence while taking tea in your parlour, thinking I shall be content with the charming and excellent company of just one woman when I could have the pleasure of two. More especially since I was so helpful with some very thorny vines just now. I thought I was forgiven for whatever crime you will not concede I might have perpetrated yesterday?"

She gave him a cold look. "And I thought you would have discharged your obligation to my mother and been happily on your way to the Tristam's by now. Indeed, if charming company is what you look for above all else, my lord, I am very surprised that you stay. That is the one thing they can more than adequately provide you with and I cannot imagine why you would delay joining such 'accommodating' company only to come here to pine for it."

She was about to turn back to watch her bleak garden and wish him long gone, but the way he returned her cold gaze arrested her. He was looking at her so strangely she found herself unable to stop meeting his eyes. She should look away, make him realise she had no interest in continuing this game, but the way his blue eyes bore down on her made her stay still. Both stubbornness and fascination kept her just as she was.

"The Tristams?" Baugham said incredulously and could not keep his voice from rising to a near shout. "The 'charming' Tristams! You imagine I *pine* for their company?"

"Well you certainly seem to enjoy it well enough," she said, believing herself to be calm, but in fact sounding quite sharp. "Supper yesterday and tea today. And since the flattering attentions you receive are obviously returned with equal measure, I can only wonder that you would forsake such fascinating company just to mingle with the hired help. Truly, *my lord*, such condescension is not necessary. I will complete your library without any need for flattery or further incentive."

"Miss Tournier! This habit of yours…" he sputtered. "Why you insist on portraying yourself as a poor country lass of no consequence rather than the daughter of proud and noble heritage that you are — you know you are not merely 'hired help', and referring to yourself as such reeks of false modesty and misplaced humility."

"Modesty and humility," Holly scoffed. "Two qualities that I am not surprised are unfamiliar enough to you that you cannot tell the genuine from the sham! In case you have forgotten, I *am* the hired help; I *am* a poor country lass of no consequence, whatever my father may once have been. You have no place in such company; truly, it only wastes your time as well as mine. Go conduct your business elsewhere, somewhere more profitable and pleasing to you. There is nothing here that is worth your time!"

He met her blazing eyes with narrowed, cool ones.

"Business? What business do you think I am in then, Miss Tournier? Do you suppose me to take pleasure in the company of one who simpers and blushes and flatters, scarcely having the ability to hide a predatory nature, or do you suppose I enjoy indulging in insincere flirtations with females to pass a boring afternoon?"

She swiftly stood up and took a few steps away from him, instinctively wanting to distance herself from those ice-cold eyes. He spun around and closed in, just as instinctively denying her the safety. That menacing gesture strengthened her resolve and she dug her heels in. She concentrated hard on returning his direct and foreboding expression while he went on in a very tight and harsh voice.

"It is by no means compulsory to have a sense of humour when aspiring to pretensions established by polite society. I can even comprehend why a woman of your character and situation would not place much value on fripperies and inane chatter. But I fail to see why you are intent on misconstruction every time I open my mouth. Pray, what is it about me that makes you feel so defensive and so anxious to show me my trespasses at every single turn?"

She stood to face him, drawing as much dignity as she could gather.

"You, sir, rely far too much on your novelty value in this confined country circle! No doubt with your easy manners you think you only engage in good-natured teasing. Well, it is a relative term at best. Some men are harmless flirts that can be easily seen through and so cause no mischief. Others… well, others cause more damage than they realise through their carelessness. You trifle and charm and flirt and *play* your way through the lives of people you hardly know and think you can go back to your London circles and everything will be as it has always been here. Well, it will not! Do you imagine that we disappear into our little holes as soon as we are not needed for your entertainment anymore? Well, we do not! We are left with exactly what you leave us with in terms of irresponsible behaviour and hopes and interpretations…" She forced herself to stop, turning the subject in a more general direction:

"And though on such a short acquaintance I would not presume to know what sort of company you take pleasure in, or how you prefer to pass a boring afternoon, I can say that you do seem to make it your business to charm and endear yourself to every female you happen upon. That, sir, is your choice if you wish to go about the countryside gathering a court of admirers and raising expectations. And I am sorry if it disappoints you that I do not wish to be among that number… one of many…"

Baugham gave a snort and threw out his hand in a desperate gesture.

"Indeed! And this is your honest opinion of me? Fantastic and extraordinary, I must say! How unfortunate of me to fancy seeing a disposition that enjoys spirited and ready conversation in you. Perhaps I should have interpreted your capricious temper in a less positive way! Perhaps I should not have assumed that an informed mind such as yours is capable of an honest exchange of opinions under any other guise than romantic aspirations! And perhaps I should not have overestimated your ability to keep name, prejudice and character separate in your mind!"

"Romantic aspirations?! You flatter yourself, my lord! I fear you have become so used to fawning and flirtation that you forget the value of honest communication. If words spoken in truth and feeling are so offensive to you, I give you leave to go elsewhere. I am sure there is a Miss Tristam breathlessly awaiting your arrival who will be happy to tell you exactly what you wish to hear! Go to them!" She gave an irritated wave of her hand. "Line them up and pour out your considerable charms before them. That way you can quickly determine which is the most cloying and therefore, the most agreeable to you."

She stomped her foot in frustration.

"Hateful, spiteful man..."

Something warm and stifling travelled up his throat and settled in his mouth. He felt his mind shot through with a thousand flashes of what he wanted to say and what he felt. His head swam with strong impulses and he struggled to make any sense of them at all. But as he was hard at work sifting through the words he really wanted to fling at this impossible wench who dared throw him into such a rage and render him so completely at the mercy of his temper, he caught sight of her lips trembling with rage and how she suddenly bit the lower one when she had finished spitting out her malice.

He was mesmerised. He must have stared at those lips for an inordinate amount of time — perhaps all of five seconds — unable to articulate any of the sentiments he was so intent on expressing with full force.

"Lord, help me," was all that he could manage before his hand reached out and lightly touched her cheek. She gasped, but his impulse was too overwhelming and her features flickered in front of his face as he bowed down and resolutely pressed his lips on hers.

The sensation was stunning. They were soft and warm and she tasted of honey and dew. As his brain and body registered all the feelings that kiss caused within him, he felt her grow even softer and warmer. The stifling feeling in his throat melted away and was replaced with something far more exciting and urgent. As it caught up with him, he sharply drew his breath and released her.

In absolute silence and amazement he stood watching her, looking deep into her dark, smouldering, bottomless brown eyes, unable to withdraw and even less able to comprehend the world around him and how he found himself in this most surprising and precarious situation.

Holly felt as if a bolt of fire had just shot through her body. She could not tear her eyes away from his, even though her mind was racing. She knew what had just happened, but she was confused — he had kissed her... *he had kissed her*...

She considered it; the experience was nothing like she had expected, but it was not at all unpleasant — no, not at all. In fact, she was certain she had kissed him back and she realised that she was, even now, clutching the sides of his coat with her hands. She quickly dropped them.

She felt warm and flushed and she thought that she must be angry, but he was looking at her still and in such a way that she felt the bolt of fire return and she drew in a shallow breath. A small sound escaped from her still parted lips and she knew that what she had been denying to herself for so long could be denied no longer.

But his eyes were changing. His expression was growing more guarded and she could see he was trying to pull his eyes away — and then he succeeded...

Damn him!

Coward!

No!

Determined to respond to this bewildering situation with strength and equally determined that he must acknowledge what had just happened, she found her voice.

"Please explain yourself, sir. What is the meaning — why did you...do that?"

Baugham felt his feeling of panic rise. He knew his eyes were restlessly glancing about and could no longer meet hers. His heart raced and his blood rushed in his ears. How could this have happened? How could he have been such a fool? How could he have lost control so utterly?

He retreated ever more firmly behind his reserve and was determined to escape and put an end to this folly as soon as possible.

"Miss Tournier," he said slowly, hearing his own voice distantly. It seemed to him to be so very cold and stiff, just like his own pose. "I...I am mortified. I have...I have just proved your reproaches beyond a doubt. I must beg your forgiveness."

He noticed the light had gone out of her eyes, too, and she regarded him with a most appalling mix of negative and desperate feeling.

"I cannot explain myself," he said helplessly. "I...I have no excuse to give. I can only promise you that...It will not happen again, I assure you."

Holly turned and took several steps away. She closed her eyes and breathed in deeply in an attempt to regain her composure. It took longer than she wished. When she felt equal to facing him again, she turned around, but avoided his eyes.

"Please see it does not. Your apology is accepted."

She took her bonnet up from the garden bench and tried to tie it upon her head but her fingers were not working well. In frustration she pulled it back off again and turned toward the outer gate.

"I would beg you to leave now, sir. I will make your excuses to my mother."

"Thank you. I will. I — Give her my warmest regards..." The words stuck in his throat. "Say what you must."

He simply bowed to stop his babbling and then, as if in a daze, began walking toward the gate. He stopped there, lingering for a while; following her with his eyes as she, just as slowly but with a great dignity, turned her back to him and headed toward the house. As he watched he felt all of his acute embarrassment and shame envelop him once more. Then he uttered an oath under his breath he had not used since he was a very much younger and more impulsive man and turned on his heel to find his horse.

Miss Tournier would return without him, and Baugham realised her mother would almost certainly deduce from her daughter's countenance that something was amiss. He rode off in confusion, finding himself hoping that Miss Tournier would not disclose his reprehensible actions to Mrs. Tournier, but everything he knew about her told him that she would likely confess all. Added to his already acute feelings of remorse and mortification was a deep regret that by committing an unpardonable sin against a lady of character and good reputation, he had wronged her mother as well. That afternoon, in one moment of thoughtlessness, he had lost two friends.

Mrs Tournier was a naturally curious woman. Her interest and curiosity caused her to question many accepted facts and she was very fond of any process that could lead her to the discovery of new truths and revelations about the world around her. This, naturally, made her quite a reader and constantly thirsty for scraps of knowledge, and although she was always quick with her opinions, she did consider a good argument on the opposite side of a debate to be as essential and interesting as her own researched point of view.

That same noble and unusual trait in a woman also made her insufferably nosy at times. For someone who judged fact as truth, the limits of the personal sphere and inner doubts were sometimes hard for her to comprehend or even to respect. She knew she was once again pushing against those boundaries of respect when she stayed by the window even though her daughter and their guest could not be seen from it, but when the door slammed and just one set of footsteps could be heard, so obviously Holly's, she abandoned all pretence of discretion and opened the window to peek out.

Her rudeness was not awarded. She could see no one, so she returned to her seat and waited on pins and needles, fighting the urge to run out of the room and find her daughter and insist that she reveal everything. She was certain there could be nothing too surprising in their failure to appear together in her parlour. Very likely there had been "words" exchanged between them again. But still. Why were they not busy keeping up appearances and fighting their sour countenances there in front of her?!

At that moment her daughter came in with a cup of tea and a piece of bread in her hand.

"There you are!" Mrs Tournier said, quite excitedly and losing all pretence of detachment. "What on earth has been going on?"

Her daughter gave her a look, but calmly put down her cup of tea and dipped some bread in it. It was evident from her pale face that *something* had happened, but as obviously as her feelings could be read from her countenance, just as stubbornly was she able to withhold any details or confessions about it if she chose.

"Nothing worth mentioning," Holly said calmly and hoped her ears did not explode into a crimson colour at the blatant lie. "His lordship had to attend to his horse — he's quite a nervous specimen I understand — and he had to take his leave. He was quite shamefully late, he said. He begs your forgiveness, of course. I understand tea was cold so I made some for myself just now. Or would you care for me to warm up the pot again?"

"Never mind the pot! As if tea is the answer to every single predicament in life! What about before that?"

Holly looked up. "What do you mean, Maman?"

"Did you manage to behave civilly to one another or were you able to find something to argue about in the quarter of an hour he was out there?"

Holly said nothing for a full minute or longer. Why had she thought she could return to the parlour and simply resume normal life, to act as if nothing was wrong? A sudden apprehension that nothing about her life would ever be normal again swept over her and she struggled to keep her face calm and unaffected. Her mother was watching her expectantly; she must answer her question. But what could she say? If she confessed the kiss, what would her reaction be? Would she rail against Lord Baugham in anger, or would she somehow blame Holly for her unguarded behaviour? Or worse yet, would she dismiss it or laugh it off as a thing of no consequence?

The tea was bitter in her mouth, the bread sat like a stone in her stomach; unconsciously, her hand moved up to her ear. She must answer.

"We…we were simply discussing…he was asking me for purchase recommendations for the library. That is all." Satisfied with herself for coming up with a fairly plausible story, she elaborated further, "He was asking my opinion on the works of de Forges when Mr Campbell's dog ran too close to his horse," her speech grew more rapid as she went on, "and he grew skittish and his lordship tried but could not calm him so he thought it was best to try to ride it out of him so he asked me to beg your pardon and he left."

Without looking at her mother, Holly carried her cup to the tray and walked to the doorway.

"I think…I'm rather tired, Maman. I think I will go lie down for a while."

Without waiting for an answer, she left.

Her mother watched her leave closing the door very carefully behind her. She was by no means impressed by the fact that the author of the poem *"Goddam! Goddam! par un French-dog"* and Mr Campbell's harmless and docile pet together made up an explanation for his lordship's absence, but there was not much she could do. Her daughter would not talk to her. For now, anyway.

HOLLY RAN UPSTAIRS AS QUICKLY as she could, her breath coming roughly. What had just happened ran over and over in her mind and it took quite some time before she could form any kind of coherent thought.

The thinking only made it worse. He had kissed her; he had looked at her in that way and then he had drawn away, cold and detached. And he had left without a word of explanation, only apology. The worst part to Holly of course, was that, because of that kiss and that look, she was fully aware of feelings which had been hidden from her before. *No,* she thought, *be honest, not hidden, you have just refused to admit them.* But now, here it was, she must acknowledge what she felt — though there was no good in it.

Her thoughts were in such turmoil — he had kissed her. Her first kiss, and instead of coming as a prelude to, or the result of, a declaration of love as she had always imagined, it came as a surprise, the result of temper and a prelude to regret — for him. As for her…his reaction gave her no room for any feelings save despair. She paced around her room wildly, the scene continuing to play in her head. She was wretched. She was miserable. She was mortified that she had responded to him and returned his kiss. She was embarrassed and ashamed and angry.

His words, her words, the warnings of Miss Tristam, tormented her and though it was still mid-afternoon, she stripped to her chemise, crawled into bed and covered her head with her pillow — willing sleep to come and rescue her — at least temporarily — from her distress. But she could not escape the facts. He had kissed her. He had kissed her and then he had walked away.

Netherfield
Hertfordshire

Baugham,

In keeping with all the traditions of our longstanding friendship, it is my pleasure to inform you of the fact that I have once again, as is my habit, bested you. For not only have I proven the existence of true, disinterested love as I watch the happiness of my good friend Bingley — I have at the same time secured that same love for myself, in the person of Miss Elizabeth Bennet. As for you, since Bingley and I have at this point secured the affections of the two brightest, liveliest and most beautiful women alive (although the exact numbering and order remains a matter of much debate between the two of us), I'm afraid you will be left with third best — if you should ever decide you are no longer satisfied with being a bystander to love and muster up the courage to enter the fray.

As I assume you mean to quit Scotland after Christmas and return to Town for the winter season, I have no hesitation in telling you that I would be much obliged if you could see your way to leaving a bit sooner than planned, staying here at Netherfield with Bingley and me until the ceremony. Your presence and company will be greatly appreciated . . . if for nothing else than to keep the rest of the Bennet family charmed and occupied.

I must confess to one more favour I must ask of you, if you still maintain your friendship with the ladies of Rosefarm Cottage. It appears that the presence of her cousin and her aunt are necessary for Elizabeth to be completely happy on the day of her wedding so I would ask you to deliver the enclosed missives to them. And . . . if Mrs Tournier appears to balk at the arrangements I have made for their travel, that you will do your best to smooth things along and assure their arrival.

Yours in triumph,
Darcy

So Baugham sat in his darkened library, looking at the letter in his hand even though there was no longer enough light to make out any of the words. The news it contained was not unexpected, but its contents had sent him into turmoil nevertheless. *When it rains, it pours . . .* he thought. Now why should he make that deduction?

It was a happy letter; a letter he knew had been on its way and a letter, the contents of which he had been impatiently waiting for.

He separated the two additional folded up sheets from within the letter and looked at the directions. They stared back at him, the one made him wince, the other made him feel acute shame. He sighed. After an excruciating hour at Tristam Lodge, surrounded by smiling and giggling girls, unfortunately all lined up on the parlour sofa just as Miss Tournier had said, he had at last been able to take his leave and go home, expecting shelter and peace to sort out his necessary feelings of doubt and shame and regret. But he was faced, not with a place of refuge, but a letter which further accentuated his crime, rubbed his nose in his shortcomings — all of them — and most effectively not only conjured up his broken promise to his friend, but also imposed further obligations to live up to his friend's expectations and atone for his sins

Among the sundry thoughts swirling through his mind was the question: how the devil was he supposed to deliver the enclosed letter to Miss Tournier with how things now stood between them, and knowing what news the letter contained? Under his breath he cursed Darcy for putting him in such an awkward position, then he cursed himself as well.

"…if you still maintain your friendship with the ladies of Rosefarm Cottage." The phrase mocked him.

Pompous, presumptuous ass, was his next thought. Giving instructions to smooth things over for him — as if that was even possible any more, as if he still had a right to set foot through their door. And now, if he was to try to execute the office given to him, he would be faced with the necessity of first finding out from Miss Tournier whether her mother had been informed of his… behaviour.

He resisted the urge to crumple Darcy's letter and toss it into the dying embers of the fire, emptying his glass in one swift motion instead as more phrases swirled around in his thoughts: "if you should ever decide… left with third best…" A disgusted snort escaped from him in the gloom: *as if she could be relegated to…* Before that thought was allowed to proceed any further, he shot to his feet and sent the empty glass into the fireplace instead. The sound of shattering glass was satisfying, and he strode out as quickly as he could make his way among the piles and chaos still reigning in the room, never questioning why he had chosen the library as the place to try to sort out his troubled thoughts.

Those troubled thoughts were not placated by that sudden display of violence, however. When Riemann finally closed the door to his bedchamber, Baugham sank into his chair once again and signalled his relief by letting a huge sigh escape him. He reflected today would have been a better one had he never ventured out into company at all.

Perhaps then he could have avoided jeopardising so much that he could only just admit to himself that he valued. The loss of Mrs Tournier's friendship and yes, that of her daughter, too. And not only friendship, a business relationship as well. The terrible thought seized him and he had to physically leave his chair not to be paralysed by it. What if she would not come again? What if he had not only driven her away as an acquaintance and friend, but also as an employee? What had he done? Was it not enough to risk her reputation and treat her with disrespect, did he have to force her to leave her source of income as well?

He once again relived the anger, the frustration and tried to understand how he had ended up giving in to inexplicable impulses. He never did that, why this time? Had he really wanted to kiss Miss Tournier or was it something else? If so, what? And what now? What did he want from her now and what was he prepared for? What were his feelings when examined? What were hers when one closer reviewed the case? It was confusing, but how much should one trust one's impulses in cases like these where reason was wholly absent?

And then, to his great surprise, he remembered the sensation of her being, and the rush to his senses when he realised what he was doing. He shook his head. When such things preyed upon one, it was hard — no, impossible! — to make a fair judgement and decide what was right and true.

He got up and paced the room back and forth to the dark windows, but the air was too cold and he felt exhausted. So he lay back on his bed and tied his arms behind his head.

"But it is of no consequence," he muttered, "for I promised her it would not happen again..."

Chapter 24

The Letters that Finally Came and the Talk they Necessitated

ORNING came finally, after a night in which Holly did not feel that she got any rest at all. For once, she was up before her mother and she quickly and quietly dressed herself and stole down the stairs.

Her night had been spent in confusion. She was engaged to go to Clyne in the morning, and she fought with herself for hours while she tossed and turned in her bed. At times, her Romantic side screamed against the idea of having to face him again — then her Pragmatic side would remind her that Hamish would be waiting and he would not understand if she neglected her promise. Romance cried out that it would be tragic to spend many hours in Lord Baugham's presence and she would be justified to leave his library in the same turmoil that he had left her mind and emotions.

But, as was usual for Holly, she forced Romance to be still when Pragmatism reminded her that she had entered into an agreement that she must fulfil: there was work to be done and wages to be earned and that was all there was to it.

However, that was not all there was to it, because her ever helpful practical side also reminded her that she must find a way to hide her feelings from him — a skill she had never mastered very well with anyone.

She waited downstairs for as long as she could, but still left for Clyne far too early. She lingered in the immediate grounds outside until she saw Hamish walking in from Nethery Farm. Happy to see his friendly face, she jumped up to meet him.

"Miss Tournier, how're ye doin' this mornin'," he said with his typical grin.

She returned his smile as well as she was able and hooked her arm through his.

"I will be fine, Hamish. It will be fine."

Hamish's smile turned into a frown at her answer.

"Oh," he said, "I'm late, aren't I? I thought I was early, but I must be late since yer waitin for me?"

"No! Heavens no, Hamish you are not late at all! I am just very early, but I did not wish… I thought I would wait for some company before going inside. Shall we see if Mrs McLaughlin has anything left in her kitchen from breakfast before we begin? I hope you are ready to start your studies."

Hamish happily admitted that he was quite ready to begin and cheerfully led the way into the hall. Taking a deep breath and summoning all her strength, Holly accompanied him through the door, wondering what might await her on the other side. To their great surprise, they almost bumped into Mrs McLaughlin, who seemed to be expecting them.

"Och, there ye are!" she said and placed her duster inside her apron pocket. "Ye'll be hungry, Hamish, I'll venture. Come here, first food, then work!"

She gave Miss Tournier a questioning look as she opened the kitchen door and let the smell of apple crumble and apple loaves drift out into the hall.

"Miss?" she asked. "What about ye? Do ye want to join us? There's plenty of it before his lairdship gets his paws on it, but then ye'll be hard pressed. I've not seen him this morning yet, although I venture he'll be smoked out of his hiding place soon enough when he gets a snowk of this."

Holly declined, certain that she would not be able to eat a bite, but she gratefully accepted a cup of tea. Sitting at the table in the warm, comfortable kitchen, she wished she could stay there all day and not have to venture down the hall and into the library.

Then a realisation struck her! Lord Baugham had as much reason to wish to avoid her as she had to wish to avoid him. He must know she would be there, so he would undoubtedly stay away from where he knew she would be working. She felt herself relax as some of the tension of the situation left her.

"On second thought, Mrs McLaughlin, maybe I will have a small piece."

BAUGHAM HAD BEEN STUDIOUSLY SITTING in his study all morning pouring over the books sent over from Cumbermere. "Quarter Day. The most hideous two words in the English language," he sighed to no one in particular.

Usually he made it his business to go down to Cumbermere to be present and submit to his steward's diligence in person. This year, however, Clyne had kept him busy, although in retrospect he realised that it would perhaps have been beneficial to have adhered to tradition. He also did not wish to reflect too closely on just *what* at Clyne had commanded so much of his undue attention. It was no use anyway. He had spoilt whatever reason he might have had for lingering during those few foolish moments and he really should spend more time thinking about what could be salvaged than…

Suddenly he lifted his head from the neglected numbers before him and drew a breath. He sniffed the air and wrinkled his brow. Was it? Yes it was. And it was coming from the kitchen. That decided the issue. He had long been looking for an excuse to take a break from the work he did not want to do and the intrusive thoughts he did not want to dwell upon, and Mrs McLaughlin's apple loaves were not only an excuse, they were an imperative. She would, of course, be grossly offended if he slighted them in the least, so it was only right that he should interrupt his efforts and pay his respects to her efforts.

No sooner were these thoughts formed than he was down the hall where the enticing smell grew stronger. Baugham smiled and blessed his housekeeper for having the knack to know exactly what he needed at every moment.

But when he opened the kitchen door he was met with more company than Mrs McLaughlin and the steaming treats. For a moment he stood, open mouthed in disbelief. She had come after all! The sudden shock immediately gave way to acute shame. What circumstances, what need must Rosefarm Cottage be facing for her to still continue in his employ after…after yesterday? He had put her in a position where she did not even have the choice to snub or distance herself from him. Well then, all that could be done was to make the best of things and not make it any harder than it had to be for her. All these thoughts swirled in the briefest of moments behind a face as blank as a mask.

"Ah!" he said and tried to not make his voice sound flat. "I see have rivals for the loaves." He smiled tightly at the small party gathered around the kitchen table in an attempt to lighten the atmosphere. "Please tell me I am not too late."

Mrs McLaughlin got up and directed him to sit in her chair.

"Of course not! Ye work too hard for me to oversee that," she said and placed a plate in front of him.

"I am so glad to hear you say that," Baugham sighed. "You are truly a treasure, Mrs McLaughlin. I have no idea what I would do without you or your apple loaf."

As soon as she saw him, Holly's first instinct had been to leave the kitchen as quickly as possible. She had already put down her cup and was beginning to push away from the table when she suddenly stopped and sat back in her chair. She had done nothing wrong. She would not run away.

Composing her features as placidly as possible, she stole a glance in his direction while he was speaking to Mrs McLaughlin. He was his usual calm, polite and charming self — as if nothing out of the ordinary had occurred. Instead of feeling the relief that she logically knew she should feel, she grew angry. How dare he do such a thing and then pretend that he had done nothing! Could he possibly think that she was the kind of girl who would allow such liberties? Was Primmie right, and he was merely looking for a little diversion with the help? Why hadn't she slapped him?

As she sat, in a turmoil of anger, humiliation and acute discomfort, she suddenly realised that though she should not run away in fear or shame, she would be perfectly justified in leaving for other reasons. She simply did not wish to be in the same room with him.

Every eye turned toward her as she suddenly stood up.

"I believe I will be getting to work. Hamish, I will be waiting to hear your lessons when you are finished here." She saw the boy's expression turn to regret as he eyed the second piece of apple loaf Mrs McLaughlin was just putting on his plate, so she added, "No need to hurry."

She turned to the housekeeper, "Mrs McLaughlin, thank you," and neither speaking to nor looking at Lord Baugham, she left the kitchen, walked to the library and began furiously pulling books off the shelves. The sooner she could be finished with this project, the better she would like it.

BAUGHAM SAW PERFECTLY WELL THE look of sadness and even disappointment on her face when he had come in. Even more obvious was her stern look as she left. He toyed with his cutlery and teased Hamish for a little while longer before he too got up and made his excuses. As much as he thought they both wanted to leave the appalling incident of his trespasses behind them by not touching upon the subject, it was clear some things still needed to be said.

He knocked on the door and quietly entered, leaving it slightly ajar. She was on the other side of the room, with that sea of books between them, stacking volumes and moving them from shelf to shelf.

"Miss Tournier," he said in a quiet voice. "Forgive the intrusion. I do not wish to inconvenience you but ... "

He cleared his throat and took a few hasty steps closer to her.

"I fear I am completely to blame for disturbing your peace of mind and I should like to assure you that if I thought it would aid you, I would start each of our conversations henceforth with an apology. You certainly deserve nothing less. But I would beg you to believe I will honour your wishes and keep my promise. I could not bear to have you in doubt of my respect for you and appreciation of your work here."

Holly had much she wanted to say to Lord Baugham or to ask him, but pride and decorum kept her silent on the one question foremost in her thoughts.

"My lord," she said quietly instead, "please do not feel the need burden yourself — or me — with continued apologies. Yours given yesterday was accepted and I believe for everyone's sake, the ... incident ... should be forgotten so that I might concentrate on my work here in order to be done as soon as possible."

She turned back to her shelves, but a moment later turned round again and impulsively asked the question that had been turning over in her mind since the day before.

"However, I cannot help ... I must say ... At the Fair, my lord, Miss Tristam insinuated that I am perhaps naïve about certain aspects of working in a gentleman's home. I had thought she was just being unkind ... but now I begin to wonder if perhaps there is ... if you have ... expectations ... concerning our arrangement."

A thousand protests sprung to his lips, but he could see in her face that she was debating something within herself and so he waited. Soon she appeared to come to a decision. She lifted her chin and spoke again.

"My lord, have I in ignorance seemed to agree to anything more than organising your library?"

His frown deepened and his folly seemed fresh and doubly treacherous again. Closing his eyes, he let out a breath filled with remorse. As unfortunate as the question was, he had to admit that her concern was legitimate considering the position he had put her in, and he also acknowledged that she was brave to ask it. So he must do his best to reassure her — if such a thing was possible.

"You fear, I suppose," he slowly said, "that my action against you can only have been a result of a disrespect of your person; that I have such a low estimation of you as to be able to insult you and impose upon you simply because I am in a position to do so, as a means to humiliate you and punish you for your... frankness. In light of my crime I understand your concern, but I assure you most emphatically nothing could be further from the truth. I have the highest regard for your character and integrity, Miss Tournier. The blame is mine alone.

"I appreciate your candour and I shall return it. At no point have you been guilty of misreading the very simple and clear understanding we came to concerning your work here. There can be no doubt about the terms and conditions — they are and have been purely business in nature. It was never my intention to take advantage."

Not quite able to meet his eyes, Holly began to idly sort through a pile of books.

"My lord, I had not thought you held me in such low estimation and I am glad to hear I was not mistaken. But for such a thing to be done... We live in a very closed society here, my lord, not well traversed in intricacies and games of more sophisticated minds and places. I could not help but wonder."

He sighed quietly. She was once again asking for an explanation, and he was once again unable to oblige her, however much he would like to. But how could he explain away such a thoughtless, impulsive action? There was no justification, no reason, no excuse, no defence — only blind stupidity and unending regret on his part. He could not explain, so he did not attempt it. Instead, he knew he owed her the power of his next question.

"Of course, if you in any way feel your position here in this house to be untenable, you have only to say so. I could not, of course, in light of the circumstances, penalise you for leaving the job unfinished and I would fulfil my agreed obligations in full, just as promised."

He hesitated.

"I hope, however, that will not be the case. It would grieve me greatly to have caused so much irreparable harm. I will not trouble you any further, should you wish it."

During her long, sleepless night, Holly had determined that he would never see how she had been affected, so she forced herself to look at him directly.

"I have a job to do — and I expect you will not be surprised to find that I intend to complete it. My mother thinks highly of you and values your friendship, as I know you value hers, and I would not wish to... if I were to suddenly quit here she would ask questions that I could not help but answer... I see no reason to allow something so obviously meaningless to change the way we go about our lives. I believe it will be best to continue on as we have."

That last declaration used up what was left of her strength so she quickly turned and busied herself with shuffling random stacks around.

"If that is indeed your wish, nothing could make me happier," he said in a subdued voice. "I . . . You must let me say, Miss Tournier, I am very grateful for your decision. I will endeavour to be worthy of your trust and forgiveness."

Her answer was inaudible and he sensed she had rather he left. He would. But there was still one more thing. He touched the sheets of papers he held in his pocket and slowly drew them out.

"Miss Tournier."

She did turn around and he could almost see the despair in her face. He hastily pulled forth the letters and showed them to her.

"I received these yesterday. From Mr Darcy. In Hertfordshire."

Holly looked at the letters in his hand but did not move. Baugham sighed and slowly put them on the table beside him.

"I believe they contain the happiest of news. And perhaps long expected news as well. My congratulations to you are in order."

Holly looked at him with a puzzled expression. "To me?" she whispered.

"Yes. Your cousin is getting married. To a very decent and good man. In view of how I know Mr Darcy feels both about you and Miss Bennet, I have no difficulty in offering my congratulations to all her family. It is a good and happy match. And everything I should wish both for him and her."

With that he left her looking at the letters on the table and removed himself. As he reached the door, he spied Hamish quietly coming in. Baugham smiled and ruffled the boy's hair.

"Well," he said in a cheerful voice, "had enough apple loaf to get you through til dinner, eh? I hope you left some for me, for I have tedious work ahead of me — not unlike you — and I quite depend upon it to sustain me for quite a while longer."

Hamish looked at him under his fringe and smiled.

"It's very good, sir," he said, "and I think Mrs McLaughlin could possibly forgive me if ye went back and ate the rest I couldnae. But I didnae want to keep Miss Tournier waitin'."

"No, you're a good boy," Baugham said and smiled back as he stepped through the door. "Now run along and make yourself useful."

Hamish nodded and took a few running steps up to Miss Tournier.

"Here I am, miss," he said. "Let me help ye now."

Holly had picked up the letters and was looking at her name and her mother's in Elizabeth's distinct hand. Of course she knew what was in them; there could be no surprise there. Still, she was hesitant. Could she read it here and now? Was it advisable? Would she regret reading her cousin's intimate confessions or joyful exclamations in this room?

With Hamish looking at her expectantly, she made her decision and stuffed the letters into her apron pocket. She let her hand rest on them while she addressed the boy.

"Yes, Hamish. There's a lot to be done!"

AT THE END OF THE day, Holly walked slowly down the hall as she was leaving Clyne, steeling herself toward the possibility that he would appear out of obligation to walk her out, but he did not. She sighed; no explanation, no hint of...anything. Simply more apologies and remorse and back to work. Telling herself she was relieved, she made her way home undisturbed and occupied by her thoughts.

It occurred to her that she had never thanked him for the letters. Those long awaited, eagerly anticipated letters. Thus, she could not help but feel as if she had failed both Elizabeth and Mr Darcy in not mustering up a more enthusiastic reception. He must feel that she was not pleased or that she was incapable of rejoicing on her cousin's behalf. Lord Baugham was right, it was a good match and everything she wanted for her cousin, too.

She squared her shoulders and forced him out of her mind once more, patting the letters thorough her apron for the tenth time that afternoon. This had nothing to do with him and she would not let him interfere with what was a joyful family concern! She pictured Elizabeth in her mind's eye: how she must have smiled and laughed while writing, how happy she must be now that all her uncertainties and struggles were at last resolved. This was about her beloved Elizabeth, and Holly determinedly kept that thought foremost in her mind as she walked, and when she reached Rosefarm, she once more turned her thoughts away from the uncertainty and doubt that the messenger of the letters had induced in her.

"Mother!" she shouted as soon as she opened the door. "I have news!"

She knew exactly where to find her. Her mother sat with her feet up on a stool in front of the fire, reading a book in the parlour.

"News? From Elizabeth?"

"From whom else?" Holly smiled. "They were delivered to Clyne Cottage with Mr Darcy's letter to Lord Baugham." She congratulated herself for hardly hesitating at all when mentioning his name.

"Shall we guess what's inside?" She waved the letters in front of her mother dramatically.

Mrs Tournier laughed. "Two? May I chose which one?" She took her feet off the stool and Holly slipped onto it. She placed her mother's letter in her lap. "I can wait a few moments more. Open yours first and read it aloud!"

Her mother gave her a sly smile and carefully broke the seal.

"*Dear Aunt,*" she read.

"*I have a few facts to relate to you, which you and Holly may discuss amongst yourselves. Furthermore, to ensure you have topics on which to speculate that meet with your standards of both currency and depth, I have added a few points on which I would have your reactions to post haste.*

"*I am marrying Mr Darcy within the month. I love him very much and he is devoted to me. So far, there has been not a single matter for dispute among the two of us during*

271

our engagement (besides who is the more worthy of adoration, of course), but I do not expect that to last for very long. Then again, neither would I wish it to always naturally be so. One would not want to be forced to create artificial bones of contention with one's spouse based on merely a desire for lively discussion, after all.

"— *The wedding will be on the 20th.*

"— *You must both come as soon as possible and I will arrange it all.*

"— *You must stay at Longbourn.*

"— *You must wear something gay for the wedding and let your boldness for once outweigh your sense.*

"*Brevity is the soul of wit and so I embrace both of you warmly and close this in anticipation of your quick answer.*

"*Your,*

"*Eliza*"

Holly gave a smile. Her mother looked up from the letter and met her eyes.

"Oh she is a sly girl! Poking fun like that, but I suppose brides-to-be may be as sly as they want while they still have time, before marriage effectively cures them of it."

"Do you think Elizabeth will be cured of it?" Holly said surprised. "I think not. It is who she is. And after all, Mr Darcy seems to be a great admirer of her pert opinions. I should think she would take care not to change, wouldn't you?"

Mrs Tournier smiled at her daughter. "If I should hazard a guess, I think Mr Darcy will be the sly one for a while after they are married. But let us not speculate about the intimacies of a marriage that has yet to take place," she hastily added when her daughter gave her a curious look and opened her mouth to ask what she meant. She couldn't possibly explain *that* bit to her daughter.

"Do you think they will be happy?" Holly asked thoughtfully.

"No one knows," her mother answered. Holly looked a little disappointed. "Oh, I don't mean they do not stand an excellent chance of coming to an understanding and finding many unexpected things to delight in one another. But no one knows. I hope they will."

"I think they will," Holly said determinedly. "Although she will be very grand, will she not? Oh! Do you think they will invite us to Pemberley! I would love to see it!"

Mrs Tournier smiled. "Now *that* I am certain they will."

Holly sat quietly for a moment, lost in daydreams of what a grand house such as Pemberley might be like inside and picturing her cousin ruling over it all with grace and benevolence. She was interrupted by her mother's impatient fidgeting.

"And your letter, Lie-lie? Have you any plans to read it anytime soon?"

Smiling, Holly opened her letter and held it out so they could read it together. She could almost hear Elizabeth's voice ringing through the words, see her beaming face and she sighed in what she assumed was happiness and anticipation.

"So…we may go, may we not, Maman? If it is all arranged?" At Mrs Tournier's assurance that she would not miss the event for the world, Holly ventured another hopeful question. "Maybe…do you suppose that we might…buy gowns for the occasion? Gay ones, as Elizabeth says. Do you think?"

Mrs Tournier looked at her girl. Her little girl, who was not so little anymore except in some cases. She smiled.

"I think I can very well do without one, my dear. If you like, I will dye an old feather and stick it in my hair in a savage fashion and that will do for gayness on my part. But you — well, I think you might rather have at least two thirds of a new gown. I suppose that can be managed. In fact, it must be managed. Perhaps the two of us could pay Mrs Peterson a visit tomorrow and I'll see if I can bully her into redoing something for you for a pittance. Something appropriately gay."

HOLLY SAT DOWN ON HER bed and took out Elizabeth's letter from her pocket again. She had hardly had time to read it properly before. Now she was alone with the sheet of paper burning between her fingers, and she could finally give it her undivided attention.

Longbourn
Hertfordshire

My dearest, sweetest cousin,

I must, of course, as is polite and right, start by offering my excuses for being so lacking in my correspondence. Wedding preparations, as you must understand, take up a large amount of time just thinking about things to be done and remembered. Brides-to-be are notorious for thinking the needs and wishes of everyone else can very well wait while they ponder ribbons and the very demanding question of veil or not. Even dear Jane, as good and considerate as she is, is not beyond such selfishness, I have found. The colour of the wedding gown alone is a matter worth several hours of study and reflection, I have learned.

So there is to be a wedding! And you are cordially invited, as is my aunt (I will send her the particulars in a separate letter — I know how she despises receiving invitations through someone else). I shall be very happy to see you if you should be able to spare the time, for I miss you very much even though it is but a short time since we last saw one another. However, if you cannot, both bride and groom in their infinite sweetness and evenness of temper will quite understand and look forward to seeing you at some other time.

Nonetheless, there is another wedding taking place at the same time and I warn you right now that this bride will not be so sanguine about your inability to attend as her sister might. In fact, it is very probable that she will shut herself into her room and weep, only to emerge armed with fantastic accusations and presumptions towards you in her grief. It will most likely send the groom into a frowning state and he will dash off to Clanough to ascertain for himself the whys and wherefores of your refusal. That is his habit, as you know.

So please, Holly, say you will come! Say you will be there with me for I cannot think of anything that could make my day happier or more perfect. No protest is accepted. It has all been arranged.

As for the details of my happiness and how it came to such a joyful conclusion, I will not tell you anything here in the hope that you will soon be with me and I can tell you everything in person. I shall only venture to say what you already know and that is that I am very happy and both proud and humble in my affection for Mr Darcy, as — he has assured me on countless times — he is in mine. We are fortunate in that we will be very well suited, I think, for we already know the worst of one another's character and can now spend a lifetime finding out the best.

And as far as breaking our mutual vow, I promise you I will only break our pact once. After I've married my Mr Darcy, I shall happily forswear all other men for the rest of my life.

Your affectionate cousin,
Eliza

P.S. You may also congratulate me on my goodness in still having thoughts for others than myself at such a time. In my cleverness I have chosen to have Mr Darcy include this letter and the one to my aunt in his missive to Lord Baugham. That way, I shall have done my dear aunt a service by forcing that secluded peer out of his hiding place at Clyne and into her parlour, where I know she likes him to be and where he enjoys himself despite his protestations of solitude. I hope that will go some way to make you happy, too, Holly. If nothing else, leave the two by themselves and take my letter outside while you send good thoughts and make arrangements for our imminent reunion! E.B.

As she ploughed through it, contemplating every arch of the letters and the distance between the lines, her heart jumped and skipped at Elizabeth's words. It was as if she was speaking to her, sitting right here beside her. But as she reached the postscript, her vision suddenly blurred. She tried to blink the tears away, but they stubbornly welled up again and obscured the text.

"*Make me happy too . . .*" she whispered to herself, unable to actually see the lines of her cousin's letter. "Oh Elizabeth!" And with that she sunk down on her bed and buried her head beneath her blankets, where she helplessly felt her tears spill into her pillow, ending up pressing cold, wet fabric against her hot cheeks.

THE DINING TABLE OF LEDWICH House was covered with scattered pages of manuscript and was repeatedly circled by two gentlemen in the process of sorting them into something resembling an orderly progression.

"I must commend you, McKenna," the older gentleman remarked. "You have accomplished more in this past fortnight than you have in all the years I have known you. I am happy to see that you are finally becoming serious about advancing in your field." McKenna just gave him a sheepish smile so he continued, "There is no reason to feel guilty about wanting to put forth your research and findings, and if, in the process your name becomes more recognisable and a few opportunities happen to come your way, there is no harm in that either."

"I think categorising the minerals by region of origin rather than by properties would be best, Sir John." McKenna acted as if he had not heard him and began shuffling the stacks around. "Highlands. Midland Valley. Southern Uplands. And the Hebrides." As he worked, he commented, almost in afterthought. "You know, Sir John, if I divide them up regionally, what do you think about including some illustrations of the landscape — nice ones, you know. Almost like those colour plates you had done…"

Sir John's eyes shot toward the young man, they grew a bit brighter but betrayed nothing. The doctor continued with his thoughts, while still busily sorting and leafing through the piles and pages.

"And I suppose I should do something about these abysmal sketches of mine. I doubt I will impress anyone with my knowledge if it appears that I cannot distinguish granite from slate."

A knowing smile spread across Sir John's face, but he simply said, "I like your idea of the landscapes, they could add interest and colour, and I absolutely concur on the wretched quality of your sketches. Perhaps you need an illustrator."

"Precisely what I was thinking," McKenna agreed, keeping as unstudied a look on his face as he could. "Any ideas as to whom?"

"Hm…" Sir John thoughtfully paused, "There's always Bigsby. He has a fairly good eye and is well-travelled — he ought to do a passable job."

"And if I want more than passable?"

Sir John sat down, closed his eyes and leaned back as if in thought.

"Then it's Carruthers you want." He did not let on that he heard the sigh of his colleague, but after a brief pause he added, "Of course, he's extremely busy and you might have to wait quite a while for him… but then, you have already waited all this time. What would a little longer matter?"

"And if I don't want to wait any longer?" a slightly impatient McKenna rejoined.

"Why then," Sir John opened his eyes and announced in triumph, "you must ask Miss Tournier! Of course."

"Of course," McKenna said casually, but after noticing Sir John's smug expression, gave up all pretence and smiled broadly. "My thoughts exactly."

"Good, because I was beginning to worry about you, boy. Not only is Miss Tournier an excellent artist needing work, she is a fine girl with a sweet disposition. Very pretty, too, in case you have not taken the trouble to notice."

"I have." McKenna inexplicably felt his face flush.

"So I would hazard a guess that to spend time with her in such an endeavour would not be disagreeable to you?"

"Sir John," the doctor smiled, "you are anything but subtle, but I don't expect that my employing Miss Tournier would entail a great deal of time spent together. No more time than you spent when she illustrated your book. But if my commission will bring her peace and comfort, I am happy to be of service."

Sir John sat, thoughtfully rubbing his chin with his thumb as he tilted his chair back on two legs.

"Now, Philip, let's not be too hasty," he said. "This is your first major work, very important to your profession — it would not do to take any aspect of it too casually. I would advise you to oversee all the details carefully — even going so far as to take temporary leave from your position here so you might devote all of your time to it."

He gestured to the table.

"What you have here is an excellent beginning, but you need to organise, to edit, to polish your text, and you need each and every illustration to be exactly what you envision." A mischievous grin appeared on the old man's face.

"Yes, that's it. As your advisor and friend, I insist that you take some time off, take yourself away from the city to more…remote environs, a small village let's say, and devote yourself to your pursuits — whatever they may be."

McKenna could not mistake his meaning, but he had not thought about taking such a bold step himself.

"Take a leave? For how long?"

Still looking at him with that sly smile, Sir John simply said, "For as long as it takes."

276

Chapter 25

*In which the State of Things and Feelings are Reviewed Before
the Reader is Introduced to New Facts and Events*

AT this point in the story, dear reader, a curious kind of contradiction reigns. Just as in winter, nature settles into a period of recuperation and quiet before the bustling activities of springing to life once more, so man also withdraws in the prevailing season. He stops his frantic activity and stays inside. The dark days take their toll and man becomes generally dull and fond of his after meal naps. Nowhere is this truer than in the country. Unpredictable weather, bad roads and dark evenings restrict society; social intercourse slows down or goes into hibernation. So it is also with our protagonists. But their outward resignation to the mood of the season is deceptive, because within them great spring storms and restless, unseasonable stirrings of life rob their supposed repose of comfort. Furthermore, for them there is no long rest in sight. Very soon they must challenge nature's state of slumber, only to be thrown into events that change their lives. But this they do not know yet and so cannot prepare themselves. As is so often the case, they sit and regard their current state as incomprehensible and even reprehensible, yet are unwilling or unable to change it, believing themselves to be forever trapped in winter, whereas spring is even now, slowly and inexorably rolling in over the sea to sweep everything away.

So Lord Baugham wrote his letter to Mr Darcy, saying everything that was proper and expressing his genuine happiness at the news. He assured his friend he was most eager to be of service and would happily meet up with him and his affairs in Town. He informed Mrs McLaughlin of the joyful news as well, so she could have the pleasure of claiming intimate and timely knowledge of what was surely one of the most important social events of the year. He allowed Riemann to speculate on what implications the news held for his lordship's wardrobe and travel engagements. And then he failed completely to commit to fixing any plans.

He did not quite understand it himself. If ever there had been incentive to move on, surely he had enough of it now, but he told himself he must still be happy at Clyne because he felt no inclination to leave, even though the actual feelings of happiness eluded him. Still, the recurring circle of these thoughts and speculations would not leave him alone, regardless of how resolved he claimed to be.

In Edinburgh, papers were sorted, notes were organised and a brief leave of absence was arranged as Dr McKenna embarked on the preparations necessary for his long-delayed entry into the world of academic publication.

Holly still ventured out into the elements almost daily in continuance of her duties as librarian and, after that initial yet painful conversation, the uncomfortable subject that stood between her and her employer was never mentioned again. They each acted as if the unfortunate lapse had never happened, and a fragile equilibrium and working relationship began to grow between the two of them. She also wrote a letter, and if her cousin, upon receiving it, expressed puzzlement at the fact that such a long, loving letter contained only one line on herself stating that she was well, perhaps one could blame the omission of personal details on the wish to award the bride-to-be all the attention.

Mrs Tournier was also forced to cease her most industrious work and, although seasons hardly impressed her with the need for reflection, she was not above succumbing to the worst consequences of them. She caught a violent cold and retired to her sofa to bear it out.

Lying in the sitting room tapping her fingers on the windowsill, Mrs Tournier was swaddled in shawls and propped up with pillows, her left leg lying on even more pillows. She was seldom ill, which was a blessing to her household, for a more inconvenient patient was hard to find. If she suffered other people's ailments and illnesses badly, she was truly trying when she was obliged to give in to her own occasional weaknesses.

"Lie-Lie," her mother said while gazing out the window, snivelling and puffing. "I am feeling perfectly miserable and no amount of rest is going to improve my mood. What could improve it though, would be to direct my attention to other things that bother me excessively; like you, for instance. You will call me unfair, but you cannot call me wrong when I say you are back to sighing inopportunely and showing a dull face again. What on earth is going on? There was colour back in your cheeks, no doubt due to spending so much time in argument with any guests we might have, but I had hoped your cousin's news and enjoyable work could have induced a permanent improvement. You are not still harking back to Hockdown, are you?"

Holly's pencil, which had been mindlessly scribbling in her journal, stopped abruptly at these questions and she kept her head focused down on the page. She had thought she had been able to look and act the same as she always had, as if nothing out

278

of the ordinary had occurred. Her mother's questions came as an unwelcome shock.

"No, Maman, I have put Hockdown behind me. I am just trying to come up with a respectable purchase list for his lordship's library. That is all."

Mrs Tournier blew her nose and, grinning, took another sip of her tea.

"Your work ethic is admirable. However, I know that you have been diligently listing your ideas since you first began this job. Why it should cause you such struggles now, I cannot fathom. Unless it is something *else* about his lordship's library that has been giving you trouble."

Keeping her eyes resolutely away from her mother's, Holly concentrated on her 'list', hoping she sounded composed when she asked, "Why should his lordship's library give me trouble?"

Mrs Tournier narrowed her eyes. It was too good to miss and she was feeling highly irritated at such nonchalance.

"Why, one would think perhaps the dust, or the climbing on high ladders or, knowing you, even the neglect and carelessness could give one cause for anxiety."

"Not at all, Maman, things are coming along nicely."

"Well, I'm glad to hear it. So, if past injustices or his lordship's library are not to blame, what is the cause for your moods then?"

Holly put her work aside and started toward the door.

"I am sure I am not having any moods, Maman. You are angling where there is no hope of a catch. Now, why don't I get you some more tea? And isn't it time for another dose of Agrimony? Is the fire warm enough? Maybe I should go fetch some more wood…"

"Ah, killing me and my misgivings with kindness, are you, dear? Well, it only adds fuel to my flames. You know, if I am wrong, all you have to do is tell me so. There is nothing one can argue against there, but this evasion is highly suspicious and, for an old bulldog like me, highly tempting.

"Oh, and you really must develop some means of disguising your feelings if you wish me to ignore them. After all, I am your mother."

Holly became uncharacteristically snappish with her, "Since you are such an expert on my feelings, why don't you share your vast knowledge… then we both will know what they are!" and she flopped back down in her seat.

Mrs Tournier cocked her head to one side and watched her fuming daughter.

"Now that is exactly what is so infuriating in this equation, is it not? Something is obviously wrong — that is easy to read in your countenance and air — but what that something specifically is, cannot be read in the same way. One could hope you would develop a sign language of some sort to make my task easier. As it is, I am reduced to coaxing, threatening and goading to satisfy my curiosity and maternal compulsion."

Holly straightened her posture and tried to regain some degree of composure and dignity.

"Maman, you may give your curiosity and your compulsions *and* your imagination a rest. I do believe your cold has made you feverish… Are you sure there is nothing I might get for you?"

"I might very well be feverish. It would only be from boredom, after all. And to relieve it I need entertainment and stimulation, which you have not provided me with in any form except as an object for scrutiny. And that pursuit is turning even more tedious than my ailment.

"Oh, if you don't want to speak of it, you will not, I know. But I wish you *would* tell me what is bothering you so that I might help you and not be forced to tease it out of you. I can't very well lie back and be meek and quiet. That kind of behaviour would seriously alarm you, and no doubt persuade you I am mortally ill and, however wicked I am, I could not do that."

Holly hated being in this situation and had just about exhausted her attempts to re-direct her mother's questions without again resorting to dishonesty. Before he had… before that day, she had never found herself in a place where she did not feel she could confide completely in her mother, but to tell her what had happened in the garden was an impossibility.

There was no predicting how Mrs Tournier would react to the intelligence, and more to the point, as she had discovered when she tried to write to Elizabeth, there was really nothing to say. No beginning, no conclusion to the story — he had kissed her and then… nothing. How does one confess such a thing without dissolving into humiliating admissions of one's own feelings about it?

She blinked back the tears that were just beginning to gather and raised her head to face her mother.

"Maman, I am sorry but I have nothing to tell you that would provide you with entertainment or stimulation. You have my word that there is nothing bothering me and so you may cease your scrutiny."

"Well," Mrs Tournier said dryly, "if that is the case, I beg you would invite his lordship over for tea tomorrow. He has not been by in quite some time and you may tell him that I miss his company."

Holly tried to hold her gaze after her last act of defiance, but found she could not. She dropped her eyes to her hands clasped tightly on her lap, "Yes, Maman."

The Caledonian Thistle was a strangely bustling place for a blustery weekday evening, but driven out of doors by an unceasing restlessness, Baugham decided to stay. He found an empty place at the bar and accepted the mug that was immediately drawn and placed before him. He was not in a mood for socialising, so he sat back and let the voices and conversations flow over and around his own scattered thoughts.

"Hey Joe, you leavin' that bride o' yours home alone fer once? How'd you get her to let ye out o' the house?"

"Aye! She'll make him pay well enough once he gets home fer cockin' the wee finger here wi' the lads!"

Joe sat smugly, smiling into his drink, "Aye lads, say what ye will, but my lass is a damn sight prettier than any o' ye."

Across the room another man was bragging on his young son's prowess in learning to shear sheep and another man was taking a ribbing from his companions upon sharing the news that his wife was expecting their first child.

They were conversations centred around day to day domestic life, some good natured, some serious, and Baugham was just thinking how different it all was from the gossip and tittle-tattle of Town, when Mr Robinson leaned across the bar toward him.

"If ye don't mind my askin', m'laird, how are the ladies from Rosefarm faring these days?"

With a look of confusion, his lordship said, "They are well as far as I know, Robertson. Why do you ask?"

The proprietor looked slightly embarrassed. "Well now, it's just that the missus is friends wi' their Mrs Higgins and yer Mrs McLaughlin and they been talkin' and such…and after seein' that scoundrel Pembroke last week, I've been wondering…"

"Pembroke?" Baugham broke in. "He was there again?"

"Nae, he didnae stay, just come through on his way, but then when I heard what he was doing about their rent…well, the ladies have been here long enough that we almost think o' them as one o' us, ye know, but it's nae so easy to ask it o' such proud women, so if there be anything we can do t' help them, m'laird, we'd be pleased if ye could let us know. The missus and me, that is."

Baugham was stunned and, despite his natural curiosity and professed fondness for gossip in general, he was torn between a need to know more and a curious sense of protectiveness. Nevertheless, he tried to press Robertson gently until he was able to discover what one housekeeper had said to another and then passed on to the postmaster by way of his wife.

A short time later he found himself riding down the lane leading to Rosefarm Cottage. Night had come early, a cold wind was blowing and the sky was spitting snow. He pulled his horse to a stop outside the gate and then simply sat there. He could see the parlour window glowing with a warm light, and shadowy figures moving behind the lacy curtains on the window. It was an inviting sight and in his thoughts he could hear the crackling of the fire and informed opinions, he could smell the fragrance of the unconventional teapot. His mouth watered when he recalled the sharp taste of all the honey-sweetened, herb-stretched cups he had partaken of in that room. There was no use denying it or excusing it away, the truth was he wished he was in that warm parlour as well. Immediately following that thought was the realisation that he had no rights to ever be in that parlour again, no rights to concern himself with their struggles, no rights to even be in possession of knowledge about their situation.

He was not sure how long he sat there on that road, in the icy wind and spitting snow, but eventually his horse's restless movements brought him back to the present and he turned the beast around and spurred him back towards home. Tomorrow would be another day of strained politeness, of avoidance and pretending that, wherever he was in his house, his thoughts were not always centred on what was happening in his library.

"AND ... IS HE very rich, ye say?"

Mrs Higgins gave her cousin a smiling look of the knowing and turned to their friend, Mrs Campbell.

"Och aye! Ten *thoosand* a year!"

"And a great estate down south in Derbyshire!"

"And such a handsome gentleman, too. But I will say Miss Bennet is every bit as gentle and fine as he is and she deserves him very well."

"Aye," her cousin chimed in, "Miss Bennet will be just the wife for him. A very charming and fine lady she is."

"And did ye see them often together then?" Mrs Campbell said, clutching her basket, a little warily in the face of all this praise.

"Well..." Mrs Higgins said.

"Ye only needed to take one keek at them together to see how it was," her cousin said staunchly. "Wouldn't ye say so, cousin? I seen it as soon as I set eyes on them."

"Aye. Aye, I did that, too. Did I nae tell ye so, cousin?"

"Right well ye did!"

"So..." Mrs Campbell took a step closer and lowered her voice to a dramatic whisper, "it was...*love*?"

Mrs Higgins cast a glance at a farmer's wife behind the stall who was suspiciously arranging her turnips as close to them as possible. Mrs McLaughlin sent the woman an unfriendly eye and looked back at Mrs Campbell.

"Aye, *love* to be sure. And something else, an all, I daresay!"

Mrs Higgins smiled in understanding and Mrs Campbell was pleasantly scandalised.

"Ooh," she said blushing with excitement, "what a fine thing! And to think, here in Clanough!"

All three women nodded their heads in agreement.

"And what a fine thing for Miss Holly," Mrs Campbell continued, eager to add to their delicious speculations.

Mrs Higgins looked surprised. "Miss Holly? How so?"

"Well, such a good connection in the family! And his lairdship such a near friend! And as she is now employed in his library..."

Poor Mrs Campbell! Her eager partners in speculation vanished and were replaced by incredulous females instead. Mrs Higgins looked sour and turned around to give the turnips another look. "Och, well, as fer that..." Mrs McLaughlin raised her eyebrows at the audacity and looked around for Mr Scott and his promised fresh eggs. "Ay, well, I dinnae think..."

Of course, both Mrs Higgins and Mrs McLaughlin had each privately entertained exactly the same train of thought, but since neither of them had yet to mention it to the other or consolidate their opinions as experts in the matter, they certainly were not about to let Mrs Campbell rob them of making their own novel deductions together in private when they were ready to do so.

"Miss Tournier is a fine and upstanding lady," Mrs McLaughlin said. … *but surely she couldnae be setting her sights 'that' high,* she thought.

"Oh, indeed!" Mrs Higgins said, "A real lady." *And much too good for anybody as flichterie as he. Even if he is a laird an all.*

Longbourn
Hertfordshire

My Dearest Sister Arabella,

I just had to take this opportunity, when I found that Mr Bennet was writing to you about your travel arrangements, to add my own entreaties for you and my niece to come and witness the happiest day of my life as I am certain he did not stress that point nearly as much as he should have! Three daughters married, and such fine and well-to-do husbands! God has been very good to me although I do worry about poor Kitty and Mary, too, now since Lydia has gone away. I don't know that Jane and Lizzy listen to me at all when I talk to them about their sisterly responsibilities. I can only do so much myself, you know, and they should care for their sisters' futures, not to mention my own!

But can you imagine, dear sister? My dearest Lizzy and Mr Darcy! He is very rich, you know, and has a fine estate and Lizzy will be as good as a Baroness, or something! Well, I suppose you can imagine it since I am told that much progress between them was accomplished while Mr Darcy was visiting his fine friend and my dearest Lizzy was with you in Scotland. I will, of course, be forever grateful for your hospitality to her now that everything turned out so well.

You must tell me what you know about Lord Baugham for I'm sure you did your best. Dear Lizzy tells me you are quite fond of him, but I do hope you do not intend on being selfish or scheming about it. Mr Darcy tells my dearest Lizzy that his lordship is to be here for some time before the wedding itself, and I have high hopes that my Kitty may catch his eye, since I am determined to keep him far away from those scheming Lucases. It would suit Lady Lucas very well I am sure, to have Maria married to a Lord, as well as having Charlotte as the Mistress of Longbourn after your brother is dead. Some people are only out for what they can get.

Oh dear, Mr Bennet is checking his watch incessantly and has taken away my second sheet of paper so I must conclude. It is no shame, however, since we will be seeing you soon enough and there is so much to do to prepare for the weddings and the guests. I don't complain, but we are always in uproars here lately, when I so much prefer to live a calm and simple life. The gentlemen are coming to dine tonight, as they do every night. Oh...and you must find out his lordship's favourite foods and send word of them as soon as possible, I would not wish to be caught unprepared once he arrives!

Your affectionate sister Bennet.

THE DAYS PASSED, BUT HIS lordship was still unable to concentrate on the documents and ledgers before him. He ought to go down to Cumbermere and let his steward explain the meticulous entries himself, or at least he should go to London where he might effectually forget about their existence. Instead, he slid down in his chair in his study and was miles away in his thoughts from any duties connected with the books in front of him. Suddenly, as he was sharpening his quills, his feet leisurely resting on the desk, and having no intention of putting them down for a long time or using those sharpened and trimmed quills for anything resembling work, he was startled by a loud crashing noise coming from the library, accompanied by shouts. He stood up instantly, his first reaction being that the roof had surely caved in. He strode to the door and approached the library while other possibilities presented themselves — some of them more, some of them less alarming.

As he opened the door he could, to his great relief, note that at least the roof was intact and that no loss to human life or limb seemed to be the case. Miss Tournier was kneeling over what looked like books flung over the floor in a haphazard manner and with some of the pages flown away and the bindings broken.

"Miss Tournier," he asked, "are you quite alright?"

In a voice laced with frustration Holly answered, "Oh, I am fine, perfectly fine. Just incredibly ridiculous!" She lifted her face up. "This is what I get for trying to hurry through my work. And I am sorry to say that a few of your books have paid the price as well."

He bowed down and picked up some stray pages that had scattered across the room.

"Hmm. Virgil," he said while he looked through them. "And a volume that brings back unimaginable Latin translatory horrors under the auspices of Mr Grimsby. Please, Miss Tournier, think nothing of it. You have fulfilled the hidden but violent ambitions of a fifteen-year-old schoolboy."

Trying not to look as upset as she felt, she crossed the room to retrieve the pages around his feet and held her hand out for those he held. She then sat down and hurriedly stuffed them back into the broken bindings.

"I will take care of this...I am sure that the bookseller in Edinburgh can repair them..." she sighed. "Stupid...so clumsy..."

He watched her return to the desk and helplessly sort through the pages. He was silent for a while as he heard her sigh and then absentmindedly spied another page lying behind a chair and went to pick it up.

"Oh, I think not," he said as he fingered part of the Aeneid. *"At regina graui iamdu-*

dum saucia cura uulnus alit uenis et caeco carpitur igni', indeed. In fact, this particular volume is surely not worth the effort. I think you will find that the bookseller would agree with me, that the newly edited compilation by that clever fellow Finney — a Cambridge man, by the way, so it would not do to doubt his reputation — is vastly superior both in print and form to this old cheap thing. I think you would also find he would refuse to restore this one for me and would give you a very good price for the new one, which is exactly what I wish you to do. Please add a new edition to your purchasing suggestions, if you would be so kind. When you get as far as that, of course."

Holly's mind was so taken up by his first words that she did not comprehend the end of his speech for several moments. Due to her parents' unorthodox views of equality and the importance of female education, Holly had received instruction in many areas that were considered most unusual for a female — Latin being one of them.

She cursed the perversity of chance that Lord Baugham should randomly pick a page from Book IV as her mind automatically translated the lines he read:

But anxious cares already seiz'd the queen:
She fed within her veins a flame unseen

And then supplied the lines that followed:

The hero's valor, acts, and birth inspire
Her soul with love, and fan the secret fire.
His words, his looks, imprinted in her heart,
Improve the passion, and increase the smart.

"Unhappy Dido burns..." she quietly said to herself before looking up again, irrationally wondering if he picked those lines purposely and what he might have meant by it.

He was looking at her expectantly, but not with any meaning other than that he was apparently waiting for her to speak — grasping on to what little she heard of his latest words she attempted a reply.

"Finney from Cambridge...yes, certainly. I should order one then?"

"Yes, please do," he smiled, apparently relieved that she answered. "I don't know the man myself — he was before my time — but I believe no library should be without one. Whatever earlier editions might have done to destroy the appetite for poetry of the owners."

He looked around the room.

"It is coming along nicely, I see," he said. "Soon perhaps one might start referring to this as a collection again."

When she had arrived in the morning, Holly had every intention of relaying the invitation from her mother for him to come for tea, but a few dropped volumes and some lines of Latin convinced her that she was not up to it. She cursed herself for being so stupid. She was going to have to learn to come to terms with this sooner or later ... *She must get past it!*

Gathering her courage she turned to him, ready to extend the invitation, "My lord ... "

Baugham half-turned towards her and let a lazy smile creep over his eyes and lips.

"Oh, you are quite right, of course. A collection of miscellaneous whims and fancies is probably all it will ever amount to. But I will follow your recommendations, if you care to make any, as to how best to make it a *good* collection of whims and fancies."

She let out an exasperated sigh. He either was not listening to her, or had decided he already knew what she was thinking or what she would say.

Presumptuous! she thought, but she had to admit that it felt better to be angry at him than to be so tentative and unsure as she had been lately.

"As I was beginning to tell you ... I must leave here early today. Maman is suffering from a cold, but she has instructed me to invite you to tea."

The way he lit up at the simple invitation was almost pathetic. However much she tried to hold on to that brief flash of anger, it nevertheless touched her to see his obvious insecurity and delight and she found herself smiling back.

"It would be my pleasure!" his lordship said. "Thank you! I ... Tomorrow then? I just received a parcel of newspapers from London. Perhaps your mother would enjoy them?"

Holly heard herself give a little laugh. "Oh, by all means! In fact, I would be grateful if you did bring them, for, I confess, I should be very much relieved if something else was able to entertain her a little besides my own person and faults."

He grinned. "Well, persons and faults are to be found in abundance in our esteemed press! I should be happy to be of some small service."

There was a small pause where they found themselves foolishly grinning at one another, at loss of what to say next, but rather relieved that there had at least been something. Then Holly could stand the silence no more and reached for her notebook on the table.

"Finney," she said, turning around and leaning over it.

Baugham watched her leaf through the pages until she found the place she was looking for.

"By all means," he said. "Finney. And tea tomorrow?"

"By all means," Holly said still with her back turned and was grateful he could not see how she winced at her own stupidity. But had she seen him she would have known he did not think her ridiculous. His quiet smile, however, might not have made her any more comfortable and so it was a good thing she briskly gathered up her things.

"Well, I sent Hamish home ages ago," she said and looked around for her bonnet and gloves. "I should go, too. Until tomorrow then."

Lord Baugham merely smiled when she hastily let herself out of the door, but when she was safely out of earshot he once again smiled and muttered, "By all means."

Then he laughed.

Chapter 26

How Despite the Cold Season People Change Abode and Grow Busy

UNBEKNOWNST to Holly, Dr McKenna had arrived in Clanough late the previous evening, tired and cramped from the day long ride in the post chaise. His bags and cases were taken down and he acquired a room at the Caledonian Thistle Inn for an indeterminate length of time. He took a late meal and then settled into his comfortable accommodations to reflect over his next step. Not an ambitious man by nature, and with no need to make his fortune or any mark on the world, McKenna had never gone farther than vague plans to publish his research — someday. But there he was, in a small room in a small village, all the time in the world with only his manuscript and notes for company... and plans to meet his illustrator the following day.

He smiled in anticipation of that meeting, made plans to dispatch a note to Mrs Tournier first thing in the morning and to visit as soon as was convenient after that. So it was that as Holly was walking home from Clyne Cottage after relaying her mother's invitation and need of diversion from her illness to Lord Baugham, Dr McKenna was even then filling that very office in the Rosefarm parlour.

Thoughtfully tugging at her bonnet strings, she backed into the door to close it. It had been a slow walk home, perhaps even slower than she had intended. She had taken a detour and walked by the great elm by the crossing where Elizabeth had run when she had first seen Mr Darcy after church and where they had met up and talked. Now all her doubts of him, his character and intentions must be completely swept away. Holly could never imagine her cousin marrying without being completely convinced of a mutual affection and worthiness, so it must be true. Elizabeth was going to marry her Mr Darcy. *"And live happily ever after,"* Holly mouthed and sighed, smiling wistfully.

She stayed by the elm for a while. It felt good to rest a little just in between Clyne Cottage and Rosefarm Cottage and she felt closer to her cousin here, out in the fresh air. "A little too fresh perhaps," she muttered after a while and wrapped her cloak around her before heading home. She was still lost in her thoughts about Elizabeth and her future as Mrs Darcy when she pulled off her bonnet in the darkened hallway at home and groped around for the peg to hang it on. Suddenly her foot bumped into something black and large on the floor in front of her. It looked like several large, black boxes lined up on their side.

"What on earth…?"

She was just about to bend down to take a closer look when her mother appeared from the small dining room.

"Ah, there you are, Lie-lie!" she said. "Where have you been? Tea's long gone by now. Again."

"Maman," Holly ignored her mother, "what in the world are these?"

"Rock samples," her mother said, as if nothing could be more natural.

"Rock samples?"

"My dear, you are being repetitious and dull. It will not do. You must try to appear industrious and clever."

Finally Holly looked up to see her mother's face. Mrs Tournier looked very well, with not a hint of her former complaints although her cheeks were perhaps a little flushed and her eyes slightly more shiny than usual.

"Well, don't look at me like that," she said. "It's all your doing. Your friend brought them!"

"My friend?"

Her mother gave her an exasperated look. "Come in by the fire, dear. Maybe that will make your brain thaw a little and you can assume some of your usual vitality. Dr McKenna has come all the way from Edinburgh to see us!"

Dr McKenna sprang out of his seat by the table as Holly came in. He lit up at the sight of her and Holly could not but wonder if her mother had been pressing him for more commissions or extracting promises from him that he was ill-equipped to make, since she sensed such obvious relief in him at her entrance.

"Miss Tournier!" he said and came forth to meet her. "You must excuse my impulsivity! I know I should have given you notice of my coming, but I was much too eager to be on my way. I only arrived last night."

"Last night?" Holly asked, puzzled. "Oh, but it very good to see you again, of course! If, I must say, a little strange to see that my mother has offered you a seat in our dining room."

Here she cast an inquiring glance at her mother, who shuffled some documents that were lying on the table.

"Oh go on, Doctor," she said, "you can tell her and act the hero in this play."

Apparently Dr McKenna had no objections to that, but assumed a happy expression and cleared his throat.

"Well," he began, "I, of course, am here to begin work. I am finally in a position to start compiling my findings and research into printable form and as your mother's express assured me that you were available immediately — "

"Immediately? Is that so?" she turned to her mother with a raised eyebrow. "By express, Maman?"

"Yes," was the short reply, "by express."

Momentarily taken aback by the almost terse exchange between mother and daughter, Dr McKenna continued with a nervous smile, "Sir John has been most warm in his praise of your talents and, having seen your work myself, I heartily concur and he further says it is my good fortune to be able to secure you. For my illustrations," he added hastily. "Of rocks and minerals."

"*Rocks*, Holly," Mrs Tournier said with a raised eyebrow.

Holly gave her mother an impatient look before the doctor went on.

"Of course," he hastened to add, "Mrs Tournier has now informed me of your current obligations, and I will understand if you do not feel that you can take this on immediately after all.

"However," he went on with a hopeful look, "I confess that I am very selfishly counting on your talents and, as I will be in Clanough for some time, I am prepared to wait for as long as it takes until you can begin."

"Oh," Holly said, somewhat flustered, "I don't know that you need to wait very long…I mean, I *do* have my other work, but it doesn't take all of my time and…" she paused and gathered her thoughts, continuing in a stronger voice, "I welcome the opportunity, Dr McKenna, as I am thankful for the offer. Perhaps you can come by tomorrow?"

The doctor's smile was wide and immediate.

"Tomorrow would be perfect, Miss Tournier. Yes, I am very happy to come by tomorrow! Of course, I would not take you away from your current commitments, as it is I have plenty to do on my own, which is one of the reasons I have taken a room — to work in peace and tranquillity."

A short time later the doctor took leave of a pleased, yet confused, young woman and a self-satisfied older one, claiming that he did not wish to intrude any further on their evening together. He returned to the Thistle in time for dinner, quite pleased with his progress this day.

ANOTHER DAY, ANOTHER MYSTERIOUS NOISE to investigate, thought his lordship. There was light streaming out of his library and a loud thumping sound emanating from behind the door. Baugham arrested his progress down the hall and took a peek. Hamish was standing on a ladder just by the door, holding a book in one hand and fingering the growing row on the shelf.

"A,b,c,d,e,f,g,i,j,h…" he muttered. "No, a,b,c,d,e,f,g,h… There!"

Baugham smiled and admired the boy's concentration for a moment before clearing his throat.

"My laird!" Hamish said surprised. "Miss Tournier is nae here today," he added and tried to scramble down.

"Yes, I see that," Baugham said and leaned against the doorpost. "So what are you doing here, Hamish?"

The boy reached the floor and looked at his employer sideways under the long fringe of his hair.

"I…" he began. "Would ye rather I left, sir?" he said.

Baugham looked around him. The library was still dominated by stacks of books and miscellaneous heaps of what looked like rubbish to him, but apparently had not earned that official label yet since so far they had not been thrown out. One chair, the one in front of his desk, was cleared and he fit his long frame into it and looked at Hamish again.

"Of course not," he said softly. "I told you that you were welcome to stay. I am just curious as to why you should want to, when you are all alone here."

Hamish's eyes grew big. "Alone?" he said. "Well, I daresay I am, but I really dinnae mind, sir. Truly I dinnae."

"Ah…" Baugham smiled, "Captain Bob is still keeping you company, is he?"

Hamish returned his smile. "Yes. But I did promise Miss Tournier I'd put the novels up on the shelf alphabetically if I had the time."

Baugham looked up at the new order Hamish had been busy with at his interruption. "Novels, eh? And on the highest shelf? Do you suppose I have works that my librarian does not approve of? Or is the whole genre offensive to her?"

Hamish shook his head. "No, sir. They are fine books, Miss Tournier said, but they're in a terrible state. But she said she jist didnae have the heart to throw them out even if she was going to get new editions and have some of them mended."

Baugham gave a little laugh at that. "So she showed pity to the poor tattered, despised novels! Well, I suppose I should have expected it. I wonder if she shows as much charity to the other sad parts of the library."

"Well… some of them are too dirty to even burn."

His lordship laughed even more at that candid statement and confessed to Hamish that he suspected his housekeeper agreed. Hamish grinned and climbed up on the ladder again with a few more volumes. Baugham followed his progress for a while, but then his gaze wandered down to his desk. In front of him were two large boxes filled with cards edgeways and with different slips of paper sticking up. He ran his hand over them. Half a dozen quills and two different coloured inks, together with blotting paper and sand, were carefully organised at the head of the desk. Picking up the quills, he tested their sharpness with the tip of his finger. Two heaps of paper sheets lay beside his elbow. One of them seemed to be pages from old books, the other was full of scribbles and notes: "*Seneca, Oxford 1788, not 1792!*" said one. "*History of the Saxon People. Ask Mr Griggott. Also: MacCauley, Benson and Taylor,*" said another. Long lists and notes on what she had discussed with Mr Griggott, the small bookseller in Clanough, were followed by addresses to publishers in Edinburgh. There were a bunch of first pages ripped out of books with "discarded" written in bold letters on them. And then there was a hasty sketch, in the corner of a page with listed prices, of a boy sitting on the floor with his head in his hand and a book opened on his knee. "*Hamish. 29th Nov, lunch break,*" it said.

Baugham looked down at it and smiled. It was a good enough likeness, but more than the features, the artist had managed to capture the way the opened book and the story within it had caused the boy's surrender. He was interrupted when the subject of that drawing cleared his throat high above him.

"My laird," he said anxiously, "I would beg of ye not to touch anything. Miss Tournier wouldnae like it and…she is most pernicketie, sir."

Carefully Baugham put the drawing back where he had found it. Contrary to his usual habits and inclination, he straightened the sheets and made certain everything was exactly as he had found it.

"Yes, she is, isn't she?" he said and left Hamish to his chores and Captain Bob.

THERE WAS A NASTY WIND reaching into his collar and up his sleeves past his gloves as he walked through the fields towards Clanough. In this kind of weather it was no surprise Hamish had preferred to plead working engagements indoors, which included a chance at literary adventures on the High Seas, and had made the journey to attend to his dilapidated novels in his deserted library. Actually, Baugham reflected, there was a reason why he had made his way there that morning as well and it could not all be blamed on the weather.

His library was his favourite place. It was comfortable despite the obstacles and the dust, it was welcoming despite the chaos, and it was interesting even if he was there all alone — not that he ever was alone in his library these days. Although, of course, things had changed lately. She seemed preoccupied when she worked now and, as much as he really could not blame her, he was saddened by it. Perhaps it was always going to be awkward and painful, but he missed her spirit which seemed to have been replaced, through his imprudence, with withdrawal and cautiousness. It was only natural of course, and it was his fault, but once again his thoughts rambled on in the same track they always did when he got thus far. He had kissed her — insulted her — and as much as he still was unable to reconcile his reasons for doing so, he was forced to admit that, amid his regrets there was a feeling of fond reminiscence too. And one thing that made his memory so pleasant was her response. Or should that be her lack of the expected response? Or perhaps the surprise of a response at all?

He had pulled away, aghast at what he had done, realising too late that he was committing a serious offence against a lady, but her realisation of having been used so shamefully had hit her rather late it seemed. Or was she simply stunned? No, stunned was not the word for her reaction. He might be an expert at moulding his world according to what suited him for the moment, but not even he could fool himself into thinking that she had been simply stunned or shocked.

But what he had felt her to be was really of no consequence; her expressed wishes and words were his guide, and there she had been adamant. "And so," he said aloud, "I promised…"

He hit some innocent shrubbery viciously with his cane a few times and felt ridiculous, but slightly relieved all the same. What did this invitation for tea mean if not forgiveness and progress? If Mrs Tournier knew about his trespasses, it seemed she was not about to put too much importance to them. The more likely explanation was, of course, that Miss Tournier had not told her mother and simply wished to return to things as they were before.

As they were before…

He should stop hitting bushes and slap himself instead, he thought as he turned onto the lane leading up to the village. He walked briskly over the bridge. It had begun to rain. A tiny drizzle that hit him in the face as the wind turned it sideways with surprising sharpness. Damned inhuman weather. Exactly the sort of conditions when a sane man would count his blessings in front of a roaring fire and turn his back on prospects of the outdoors.

He quickened his pace, as much to leave his thoughts behind him as because of the weather. In the end, he successfully managed both as he was shown into the parlour by Mrs Higgins, where, to his great astonishment, he discovered that tea was already in progress and a guest was already being entertained. A man sat conversing with Miss Tournier in hushed tones by her drawing table, which was over-run with what looked like a manuscript and rough sketches. Miss Tournier sat with pencil in hand, sometimes chewing on it, turning the sketches around as if to understand their right angle. She looked up and the frown on her studious face disappeared for an instant, but was back again with doubled intensity before he could react, but whatever her daughter's reaction, Mrs Tournier looked pleased when his lordship descended on her straight away and in teasing accents inquired after the state and spirits of the invalid.

"Well," she said gracefully, "I suffer a vast deal, of course. There is really nothing else to be claimed. But I shan't bore you with the details for however much you confess you want to hear them, you really do not, and even less do I want to tell. You may fetch yourself some tea and then introduce a topic for our mutual amusement."

Baugham confessed he knew he had been summoned all the way from Clyne to perform this duty so he had not come unprepared. He fished out the London Gazette and its lists of appointments to the Court, saying she no doubt would find the governmental appointees of interest.

"And tea comes with scientific company this time, my lord. Dr McKenna, Sir John Ledwich's good friend and another hapless victim of his concern for us, is here to ascertain whether my daughter's skill as an illustrator encompasses the challenge of drawing rocks to his satisfaction. Rocks!"

By that time Holly had risen and was at the tea tray, pouring a cup for their newest guest. The two gentlemen exchanged greetings and Holly could not help but secretly study his lordship's face for some reaction. She did not know…she did not admit what she might have been hoping to discover from it, but as she saw nothing

292

but polite interest directed toward the doctor, she only let a small sigh escape her before handing him his cup. Lord Baugham thanked her with friendly politeness, while she met his eye as indifferently as she could — and though his face was open, she thought she could detect a slightly guarded expression in his eyes as he looked at her, a guardedness which had not been there when he spoke to her mother.

So, that is that, she thought, realising that at some level, she had been anticipating some difference when encountering him here at Rosefarm. *There is nothing. He does not care …*

Baugham prepared his tea thoughtfully as Miss Tournier returned to her seat next to the doctor, and even then it took him a moment to notice. The pitcher contained rich cream — no honey or treacle to be seen, the sugar bowl was filled to capacity with no frowning Mrs Higgins hovering about standing sentinel, and the aroma rising from his cup … pure black tea. His eye wandered back to the visitor with greater curiosity, but McKenna had already resumed his conversation with Miss Tournier and they were both once again bent over the pages on the table.

He took his cup and briskly walked to a nearby chair.

"So, Dr McKenna, is it?" he asked. "Have you come all the way to Clanough to steal my librarian from me?"

The doctor smiled easily and leaned back in his seat, "Not at all, my lord; Miss Tournier and I have already discussed it and she will work on my sketches as time allows. I still have a great deal to do on my own, and after giving the ladies the opportunity to review my writings, I find I might have a little more than I had thought."

"Good thing that," his lordship said amiably and twirled the tea cup in his hand. "I'm afraid my particular workload is rather like an Augean stable."

"Does that mean I am expected to display Herculean efforts to ever be free of dust and crumbling bindings?" Holly asked, gently smiling.

"Well, at the moment," Baugham said and gave a wry smile, "it certainly looks like it. Although I should hasten to add that I have no doubt you will perform miracles — eventually."

"It seems you will be surrounded by the natural cycle of scientific publications, then," Dr McKenna smiled. "Laborious birth and drabbling with multiple manuscripts in an attempt to add to the advancement of mankind and then witnessing that glorious final product disintegrate at the other end and being made redundant, perhaps only fit for firewood!"

A quick, spontaneous look passed between Baugham and Holly. "In the case of my collection, not even fit for that, I'm afraid," his lordship said dramatically. "But take heart, Doctor, perhaps your work will be cared for by a librarian with a fondness for hopeless cases even if they are tried by ungrateful times and owners."

"Or it will end up more famous for its illustrations than its thesis," Mrs Tournier interjected. As her daughter gave her a look she retorted, "It has been known to happen!"

Baugham laughed and Dr McKenna confessed he had nothing against that notion. "I should be so lucky; a picture says more than a thousand words. And if those were to be the wrong words..." He shrugged.

"At least the pictures will be pretty!" his lordship quipped.

"Pretty!" the ladies cried at the same time and turned their eyes to Dr McKenna.

"Oh, now I suppose all of you will turn to me and demand to know whether my scientist's sensibilities are offended by having my 'rocks' deemed 'pretty'!" he laughed.

"And I will have to amend my appalling manners by finding a way to profess illustrations of geological specimens to be perfectly impressive and interesting, even though the picture that portrays them is decidedly pretty," Lord Baugham smiled. "I think I must admit defeat and practice my apology instead."

"I should hope so," Holly said with a smile, keeping her eyes on the doctor. "While I will aspire to be accurate and true, and although some of the doctor's specimens are very lovely indeed — there are certain samples here that can in no way be rendered both accurate and *pretty*."

Her eyes shifted quickly to Lord Baugham, "I expect to find the work both fascinating and challenging."

"I hope," McKenna laughed, before his lordship could comment, "that I will be able to engender in you at least *some* interest in my field, Miss Tournier, as we work. I will give you this much instruction now: one should not presume so much based upon first appearances."

With that he rose and pulled a few stones out of his case.

"Now, do you see this unassuming bit of sandstone?"

A curious audience gathered round him and all let out gasps of surprise when he turned it over to reveal the imprint of a strange looking creature imbedded within the stone. Then he showed them what looked to be an ordinary, roundish, grey rock. With Mrs Tournier's permission and a few tools he deftly broke it open on her desk, revealing a glittering treasury of smoky violet and white crystals.

Holly could not help but reach out for it and he smilingly handed it to her. "Oh, Dr McKenna, it's beautiful."

Baugham leaned towards her, curious as well, and together they studied the rock in Holly's hand like small children, their heads almost touching as Holly tipped it so that the light from the fire reflected in the shimmering middle.

"Amethyst?" asked Baugham as he studied it.

"Yes," Dr McKenna smiled. "And quartz. I found it in the Tayside region, just outside of Monifieth. They are not plentiful, so it takes a bit of searching to find them, but they are worth the effort to seek out, are they not Miss Tournier?"

Holly looked up, transfixed by the dancing light in her hands.

"It is one of the most marvellous things I have ever seen!" she said beaming at McKenna. "Hidden away like that!"

Dr McKenna returned her warm smile and gave Mrs Tournier a look. "Quite a pretty rock, wouldn't you say?"

"Oh," Holly gasped and returned to admire the small miracle in her hand. "After seeing this I should be very happy and proud, indeed, if I could produce something that could show just how pretty — nay! — how beautiful your rocks are..."

She reluctantly held the rock out to the doctor, but he insisted that she keep it. He looked at her closely, "It is a good lesson, is it not?"

Baugham watched her nod in agreement, a smile slowly growing on her face and somehow felt that there was something being shared that did not include him. He turned to Mrs Tournier for support, but she was watching the scene before her with interest.

Chapter 27

Things Finally are Resolved in his Lordship's mind as the Evidence Mounts

BAUGHAM stirred his coffee cup and reflected he had no idea whether he had added one or two spoons of sugar and that in all probability that meant he had added at least three and would be forced to discard the drink and begin all over again when he finally got around to tasting it. He sighed heavily. Lord, this preoccupation was annoying! He was preoccupied with thoughts of Darcy and the increasing urgency of needing to arrange for his departure, but also the obvious happiness evident in his letter that not even his friend's natural reserve could hide. It was a happy event that would bring Baugham into Hertfordshire to see for himself how such a long struggle would end in perfect happiness in a little village church in a town of no consequence called Meryton. He sighed again and pushed the cup around. What was this restlessness in the face of that prospect?

The house was quiet. Well, the house was always quiet — that was the way he liked it and although Darcy's visit surely had not brought any discernable or even unwelcome change to that fact, it seemed as if the silence was what was now annoying him. Yesterday had also been quiet, but Miss Tournier had been working away in the library and they had exchanged careful comments on the prospect of the happy event between her cousin and his friend. He had detected a sadness in her and thought that perhaps she was missing her cousin or feeling wistful at the romance that had been played out before them so honestly. Maybe she was worried she would not see as much of the future Mrs Darcy now that she would be married, but then surely a trip into Derbyshire would be easier than a journey to and from Hertfordshire? Well, he had confessed his envy at their apparent happiness and she had looked at him without comment, which had made him very uncomfortable and he had left soon after.

He looked down at the drink in front of him and decided to be brave. Just as he thought, he had to put it down again hastily, but to his surprise he found that he had not added any of the sugar he thought he had and that it was still salvageable. Carefully counting the spoons he added the sugar and then got up to look out of the window. Quiet, quiet, quiet. Even nature was subdued and dull—and upon this thought his thoughts turned automatically to the one place he knew was never dull. He would pay a visit to Rosefarm. Here was an excellent time to fulfil Darcy's long delayed commission and assure that Mrs Tournier intended to take advantage of the arrangements made for her and her daughter to travel to the weddings. A perfect excuse for a visit, if there ever was one. The prospect arrested him when he put down his cup and quite unexpectedly he smiled broadly. "I am such a simpleton," he said. "I should just stop."

Once arrived at that entertaining location, he found Mrs Tournier sitting in her usual seat enjoying the blissful solitude and quiet dignity that came from spending an afternoon undisturbed by servants, scientists or young people in general. Not for long though, and she had given a wry smile when the gravel path outside her window betrayed the grating sound of determined male footsteps. She therefore displayed no surprise when his lordship slipped in through the door and greeted her with his brilliant smile. Mrs Tournier noted dryly that, unlike some of her youthful visitors, at least he had the excellent manners not to let a shadow of disappointment wash over his face when he found her alone in her parlour.

"Well, so you are the one daring to interrupt my solitary enjoyment of a quiet read, my lord? I'm afraid you have caught me feeling very smug with myself, having sent my daughter out for an extensive walk. Will you not sit down?"

His lordship happily proclaimed Mrs Tournier's company to be no sacrifice and he settled down after telling her he was pleased to see her again. He let his eye wander around the small but comfortable room and noticed a slight change in the arrangement of the furniture in the corner. There was a second chair pulled up very close to the old, wobbly table where Miss Tournier was accustomed to work, and a shipping crate sitting close by.

"Yes," his hostess told him, "it's just arrived this afternoon. Courtesy of my daughter's newest employer, I presume. Can I interest you in some tea, Lord Baugham?"

He confessed she could and gave the table and the rest of the arrangement another glance before he concentrated wholly on his hostess again.

HOLLY WAS HAPPY THAT SHE had agreed to accompany Dr McKenna on his outing that morning rather than spend another day indoors in the library. They had walked over miles of woodland, wilderness and creek bed, the doctor collecting specimens and pointing out to her how they appeared in their natural state.

He was a pleasant companion, his knowledge extensive and interesting, his enthusiasm contagious, and soon Holly was picking out intriguing specimens on her own to ask and learn about. So even though the day was cold and the wind colder, she had enjoyed herself very much. She was especially glad to have a partner in conversation with whom she could be completely relaxed — Dr McKenna was comfortable and easy to talk to, with none of the misunderstandings or awkwardness that had lately plagued her interactions.

The two of them stepped through the door upon their return to Rosefarm and burst into laughter as they each got a good look at the other's appearance. With the doctor's hat and Holly's bonnet commandeered for the transportation of the numerous mineral samples they had collected, their morning outdoors had left them looking decidedly windblown.

"Miss Tournier," the doctor said in an amused voice, "I must say that you look…exhilarated!"

She could feel her cheeks and nose tingling in the warmth of the room as she entered the parlour and unceremoniously dumped the contents of her bonnet into a pile on a table.

"Exhausted is more to the point!" She reached out for the doctor's hat. "Maman, you would not believe how far the doctor led me today in his quest for ro — " Holly turned to her mother as she spoke and stopped cold. Sitting next to Mrs Tournier, completely unexpectedly, was Lord Baugham!

She had lately been able to face him with some measure of composure because, knowing when and where she would meet with him, she could adequately prepare herself beforehand and keep her features and emotions under control. But to see him so unexpectedly like this — she felt a familiar stab of pain and confusion shoot through her before she hastily turned away. She could not be sure what, if anything, her face might have betrayed or whether anyone had noticed her bewilderment. After a moment to regain her poise, she turned back again.

"Lord Baugham, this is a surprise."

A PAUSE IN CONVERSATION HAD naturally occurred in the parlour at the sound of the door, but when Lord Baugham took in the scene in front of him, he had to force himself not to betray a reaction. The first thing that struck him was that she looked very happy. And on reflection, so did Dr McKenna. *She makes him happy,* was his spontaneous conclusion, and he, her. The implications of that conclusion rushed around in his brain, and he quickly decided the tangle of thoughts they entailed was best unravelled later. Seldom had he been less inclined to speak, but speak he must and soon. He stood up and concentrated on displaying a friendly front.

"Dr McKenna. Miss Tournier. A surprise, you think? Oh, I don't know. Since the very man who seduced me into a whirling social discourse with your family has so cruelly left me, I cannot seem to go back to my hermitical ways again. So your mother was very kind to ask me to stay for tea."

"As compensation for yet another batch of newspapers," Mrs Tournier said dryly. "Which is a mixed blessing, for how am I ever going to get down to reading them when there are travel plans to make and an endless stream of young men walking through my door?"

Dr McKenna poured himself a cup of tea and took his accustomed chair next to the drawing table with an air of comfortable familiarity, then looked from one face to another within the small parlour. He could not be sure if Baugham had noticed Miss Tournier's sudden discomposure, but *he* certainly had — as had her mother. He speculated as to its probable cause and found he was not happy with the direction his observations took him.

Suddenly Miss Tournier spotted the crate.

"Maman? What is this?" she asked, her eyes bright with curiosity. "Where did it come from?"

"Oh!" the doctor unexpectedly exclaimed from his quiet corner. "It has arrived?"

The rest of the party remained silent as McKenna rose and quickly crossed the room. He knelt down before the crate and pried the front panel open.

"Come and look."

They watched her step up and pulled the packing material away. Her hand flew up to her mouth and she gasped in surprise and disbelief. It was a bright oil lamp and a cask of oil. Another smaller parcel within contained pencils, crayons, papers...more materials than she had ever seen outside of a supply house.

Mrs Tournier followed her and picked up the objects one by one and examined them closely.

For a few moments she was speechless — her eyes were wide with wonder and confusion — but soon she was able to spit out a few syllables,

"But...why?...what is?...why?"

Dr McKenna could not help but smile at her excitement.

"I hope I did not overstep my bounds, but I thought you might like a better...a brighter light. Now you and your mother can both work in the evenings if you wish."

There was a loud snort from Mrs Tournier and a murmur of, "hm...India rubber..."

"Shall we get it set up?"

HOLLY SAT AT HER TABLE and arranged and sorted the various stacks of paper, the boxes of pencils, pastels and charcoals. She looked up and blessed the bright light suspended on its stand overhead that made her squint in its intensity — no longer would she be drawing in her own shadow.

"Let's see if it works, Doctor, shall we?"

But she could see McKenna already looking critically at one of her illustrations. She shook her head, smiled and leaned in closely to see what he had noticed.

"Yes, Doctor? What is it now?" she asked in a voice of good-natured weariness.

He leaned over to point out an area of her sketch.

"The angle of this outcropping is still not quite right."

She leaned in more.

"What? I am sure I drew precisely what you told me to draw."

"I am quite sure you did, Miss Tournier," he said with a laugh, "but it is obvious that what I told you was wrong!"

She laughed also, sat down, and in a tone that suggested the opposite, retorted, "My, my... what a surprise that would be."

They sat, heads together and hands nearly touching as the doctor pointed out just how some particular detail should look and she worked with her pencil to make it come to life.

After a moment of working together comfortably and well, Holly suddenly gave a jolt and looked at her mother and his lordship, silently watching the scene.

"Oh but..." she said.

Dr McKenna hastily got up from his seat. "But of course," he said. "That can wait. You must excuse me," he smiled to his hostess and moved over to her, "I know it is ridiculous but the phenomenon of watching one's ideas and theories emerge on paper is too fascinating for me."

Mrs Tournier said she understood completely, but as Dr McKenna chatted easily with her, Holly gave his lordship a look and, before he turned away and busied himself with the remains of his tea, she was startled to find his ice-cold gaze on her in what she could only interpret to be disdain. It almost shocked her and she wished she had not been so eager to display her easy manners with the doctor. Then she stopped herself. No, she had done nothing wrong, and if he felt she had been rude, she had plenty of reproaches she could hurl back at him. How he looked so coolly at her as if nothing had happened, how he crept into her thoughts when she didn't want him to, how he had made her uneasy when she should be the happiest she had ever been, how solitude these days was both a relief and a burden...

A short time later both the doctor and his lordship warily and carefully inched towards commonly taking their leave and wishing the ladies a pleasant evening. There was no invitation to dine, which, perhaps, had been the innermost wish of each of them, but Mrs Tournier refused to extend an invitation that would prolong the evening when the conversation had grown increasingly forced and halting, to the extent that she felt herself losing patience with guests and daughter alike. So in her selfishness and fully aware of Holly's questioning look, she allowed the gentlemen their right to profess they had stayed too long and would now leave.

THE TWO MEN WALKED DOWN the lane in silence for a short while until they reached the crossroads in front of the Thistle.

"My lord," McKenna ventured, "would you care to join me for some 'liquid reinforcement' before attempting the long journey back to Clyne?"

Baugham smiled. "Splendid idea! Tea is all very fine, but it does make one awfully thirsty. Shall we?"

The warmth of the indoor air in the Thistle's taproom surrounded the two men as they settled down. Hats and gloves were quickly divested of, jackets slung over the backs of chairs, neck cloths loosened, pints ordered — with an advisement to the server to have a sharp eye and quick action to prevent the occurrence of any empty mugs.

After taking a long draught of his drink and stretching his legs out under the table,

Dr McKenna leaned back in his chair and emitted a noise halfway between a sigh and a groan. He nodded in greeting to a fellow patron, then gave his companion a careful look.

"Do you know Mr Grant?"

Baugham turned and looked at the man. "We have been introduced, but scarcely more than that," he replied, giving the gentleman a nod of his own. "At a gathering of Lady Tristam's."

The doctor appeared to hardly be listening as he continued his thoughts on the subject. "I met him this morning. It seems he has been out of town visiting family…" he hesitated and Baugham wondered, with a small, inexplicable knot developing in his stomach, at this turn of conversation.

After a brief pause, McKenna added, "It's just that…when I first arrived here and in some conversation or other with Robertson, I let on about my business here…Robertson commented that Miss Tournier would not be in need of continually finding work if she would just get on with marrying Grant. He spoke as if they were formally engaged, but — and I admit I have not know the lady long, nor the gentleman at all — but, having met him, I just cannot see it."

In the face of his lordship's stony expression and silence, he was forced to come to the point bluntly.

"My lord…you are a close friend of the family… *is* there any agreement between Miss Tournier and Mr Grant or…perhaps expectations regarding him or any other gentleman?"

Baugham swallowed his ale and put down his tankard slowly, first avoiding the doctor's inquisitive eyes but then leaning back and meeting his gaze.

"I would suppose," he slowly said, "that is a question for Miss Tournier to answer."

He paused slightly weighing his words and forcing himself to go on with his reply. His voice was level and distant, but his eyes hardened slightly as he tried to search the doctor's purpose in the dim light.

"But to my knowledge there is no understanding with Mr Grant. With anyone," he felt compelled to add. Why this should have been so difficult he did not understand. It was, after all the truth. "Why?"

McKenna leaned forward on his elbows, toying with his mug.

"I hope you don't find me…impertinent. It is just that I thought I should ask before…Yes, that I *should* ask. Perhaps it is just that I can not believe my luck. I'm sure you with your experience of society in much more sophisticated place would have to agree. To find such a woman, hidden away in this small village and to find that no man has had the wit to see and appreciate her? Well, except apparently, this Mr Grant…"

He made a depreciative face but it was not returned. Baugham quickly looked up from his tankard, but kept his quiet.

There was a pause in the conversation as each man appeared to be lost in his own thoughts. Empty mugs were expeditiously refilled by the attentive bar maid, who walked off disappointed at the inattention of her patrons. The silence threatened to grow awkward, but soon the direction of at least one of the gentlemen's reflections was diverted when Baugham looked up again and abruptly changed the subject.

"So are you a sporting man, then?" Baugham asked. McKenna at first seemed to have difficulty comprehending his lordship's line of questioning, but then confessed he was and for a while the men were pleasantly, if formally, engaged on the neutral territory of shooting, boxing and horse riding.

Halfway through his second ale on a stomach bereft of dinner, McKenna opted for candour about his curiosity regarding the previously severed topic. His green eyes fixed upon his companion's blue ones.

"My lord, you will forgive me if I spoke plainly just before. But I must admit I still cannot quite understand the fate of my new illustrator. You know her, I suppose. It just seems to me...well...I suppose I simply cannot imagine how Miss Tournier is not already spoken for — yet she sometimes gives off the air that her heart is...I had thought that maybe there was someone..."

He took a breath and plunged ahead, "But perhaps she is surrounded by fools who look no further than her lack of fortune, which could be no matter to someone who can appreciate her real value, don't you agree? At least one can say that in Grant's favour. He can see what is right in front of him. What does fortune matter to a man of means? True, I am a second son, but I am well enough provided for and have no inclination to let such matters hinder me — not when the possibilities hold so much promise."

He looked at Baugham pointedly, "So I may take it that you — personally — do not know of any impediments in the matter? I should like to be confident of that before I follow my own inclinations or seem presumptuous. I am a man of honour, sir."

Baugham could not help but sigh and push his tankard around. There was something uncharacteristically hard around his mouth that could almost be described as sinister but he kept his voice light all the same. "'Impediments'? What a curious word, Doctor. As I said, I am not aware of any understanding between Miss Tournier and anyone. I do not think I can be plainer than that or more forthcoming without being presumptuous myself."

Baugham quickly emptied his tankard and suddenly felt hazarding the prospect of an icy ride home would be more preferable than pursuing this subject with Dr McKenna any further.

"I must beg your pardon. I fear the ale and long day has robbed me of my manners. And with that in view, I think I must return to Clyne."

He smiled and got up, gathering his personal effects. He held out his hand to Dr McKenna to shake and wished him a good night. The solitude and peace at Clyne now seemed his salvation.

THE SKY WAS DARK WITH ominous clouds when he awoke the following morning, the frozen wind blew relentlessly from the north and each minute that the snow held off only increased the anticipation of what was inevitably to come. As the hours passed, Baugham grew restless and agitated; he paced, he stared out the windows at the lane leading from the village, he sighed and paced some more. It was very cold, certainly

302

too cold for Miss Tournier to be walking all the way from the village, and despite her infernal stubbornness and insistence on refusing his assistance, he had half a mind to order his carriage anyway and compel her to accept the ride. Thrice he strode to the door with that very intention, but thrice he turned back with a sigh. Such a move on his part could very well provoke another angry confrontation, the consequences of which could either shatter the fragile equilibrium they had developed, or…he forced his mind away from the contemplation of any other possibilities. As the gloomy morning turned to dreary afternoon, his worry and irritation turned to something akin to disappointment. The weather had obviously been enough to keep Miss Tournier home.

He, on the other hand, as he told himself, knew the Scottish climate too well to put any restrictions on his own movements simply because of the weather. He pulled on his gloves and secured the collar of his riding cloak tightly about his neck. What was a little cold compared to hours of listlessness in a library — although it must be admitted that a very fine and well-organised library it was beginning to be these days. But one could not sit around admiring an unfinished work when it reminded him of the need to take leave of its architect.

Riemann gave him an anxious look — or possibly it was directed more at his boots and attire — but Baugham paid him no heed. He gave him a smile and lifted his riding crop as a goodbye as he strode out the door. Yes, the wind was of the infuriating, ice-cold kind, and the threatened snow began to fall in icy sleet that somehow forced itself through any protective clothing and made the horse giddy. Well, no matter. He would be off and there would be tea and company at the other end, which was all he needed.

The ride down to the village was tolerable once he worked his horse up to a brisk pace. The snow was growing heavier and he already felt it gathering inside his collar. His breeches were damp all the way up his thigh but his boots and his cloak kept him tolerably warm and dry after all. His face was wet as well, which he thought was a blessing, for he did not want to work up a sweat, however much he was keen to be on the inside of Rosefarm Cottage.

His progress toward that refuge halted at the edge of the village when he noticed a familiar figure — familiar though bundled thoroughly against the cold — just outside the Caledonian Thistle. So, Miss Tournier *was* out on such a day! Briefly he wondered if she was on her way to Clyne after all, but then he saw her turn and walk up the steps and into the inn.

Impulsively, he turned his horse, jumped off, threw the reins over the post in front and nearly knocked her over as he walked through the door.

"Oh!" she cried in surprise.

"Miss Tournier! I beg your pardon! I was just…I was on my way…" he stammered, then swept off his hat, "I hope you are well."

"Yes, thank you," she curtsied hurriedly, "and you?"

"I am well, quite well." He stood for a moment awkwardly before noticing the bundle in her hand. "You came for the mail, then? Ah, I wondered what could bring you out of doors on such a day."

"On such a day as this?" she asked in disbelief. "Why, it is only a little wind and snow, why should that keep me indoors?" Her eyes snapped and, for some reason, his apprehension melted away and he could only reflect how very lovely she looked, her face pink and glowing from the cold. Suddenly the room felt crowded and the fire felt very warm...

"And what brings *you* out on such a day?" she was asking, her head tilted up in that familiar defiant attitude.

"A steadfast resolution," he smiled once he recollected himself. "I have something important I wanted to discuss with you and... well, ask your opinion on. I was on my way to visit you as a consequence but first... Well, I saw you just now and I thought I might as well... catch up with you, I suppose. If you are at leisure, that is," he added.

She wrinkled her brow and he watched as her fingers went to her earlobe and absentmindedly rubbed it. He knew it meant she was contemplating his reply and as much as he enjoyed it, he felt a little pang of guilt at his selfish reasons for teasing her.

"Yes, of course," she appeared confused. "Would you care to come back to Rosefarm with me then? For tea," she added almost reluctantly. "I was just getting the mail," she shook her head and gave a disgusted look that was clearly directed at herself, "as you know, of course."

"Yes," he smiled. "I see that now. When I saw you, I wondered if you were perhaps meeting the doctor for another exploratory outing." When the question he nearly asked hung unanswered in the air, he added, "As you did not come to Clyne."

"Oh, well," she looked down, "it is nearly finished. The library, that is." She raised her eyes and found his fixed upon her intently.

"I am rather surprised," there was a slight gruffness in his voice, "that you did not come then. I expect that you will be glad to be done with... the job."

"You had something to discuss with me, my lord?" she asked as the hand unconsciously crept up again.

Baugham pulled his eyes away and offered his arm instead.

"Allow me to escort you home, if I may. Tea sounds delightful."

HE TOLD HIMSELF THAT HE was neither surprised nor offended when she did not take his arm, but rather clutched her bundle of mail close to her chest and walked ahead after a brief nod. Tossing a coin to Tommy to see to his horse, he followed her in silence. Finally the little house was before them, its walls and features exposed since all the protective vegetation had been stripped of its leaves. Miss Tournier accompanied him to the parlour, placed the letters on the spinet, then excused herself to help Mrs Higgins with the tea. The fire quite obviously had just been fed and Mrs Tournier was sitting in a deep chair, strategically placed as near the hearth as was safe, with a book in hand.

"Madam!" Baugham greeted her. "This cottage is always a haven, but I find on this day it is a positive sanctuary!"

His hostess smiled at him and quite willingly lowered her book. She eyed his wet appearance and gestured to another deep chair by the wall.

"I think you had better follow my example, my lord, and let this most extravagant fire of ours do the trick."

He thanked her and did as he was bid. As he sank down with a sigh he sent her a mischievous look.

"It just so happens, madam, I cut down a tree yesterday that would fit this particular hearth most splendidly. If you can forego another dinner of game, I thought I might show my friendship through firewood instead."

"Wood would be much appreciated; frankly, more so than grouse. I have seldom looked forward to the pheasant season more than this year..."

Baugham chuckled and settled his long legs to rest on the fender.

"Very nice and quiet here these days," he commented after a while since his hostess seemed to feel familiar enough in his company not to force any conversation. "I find myself strangely reluctant to leave Scotland, whatever the joyful reasons surrounding the departure."

"Hmph..." Mrs Tournier said enigmatically.

"Oh, and you must promise to not cause trouble for me with Mr Darcy and ultimately with Miss Bennet. He swore me to ensure your safe and expedient departure to Longbourn on Miss Bennet's behalf. You know, I would not want to be on the receiving end of displeasure with this particular bride-to-be. She has a very formidable champion in her future husband."

"Have no fear," Mrs Tournier smiled, "arrangements have been made. We are leaving on Wednesday next."

"Excellent! The roads are torture at this time of year, of course, but I will forever be in your debt if you would lie to Mr Darcy and claim I took care of that, too."

Mrs Tournier gave him a searching look. There was something desperately cheerful about him. Restlessness coupled with affection. "And you?" she said quietly.

Baugham smiled and for a moment a calmer, truer man flickered through. "Well...I must leave. Soon. But," the desperate cheer returned, "knowing that you are in good hands, now I may do so in good conscience."

"In good hands?" she turned and looked at him intently. "And whose hands might those be, my lord?"

"Ah...well, Dr McKenna. He is a gentlemanly sort, and I know your daughter is grateful for the employment."

"As well as the friendship," she said with a curious smile.

"Yes, of course. The friendship. Quite right," he said. "It is only right they should become friends. Quite."

"Hmph..." Mrs Tournier repeated. Thankfully he was saved from further contemplation by the entrance of Miss Tournier and Mrs Higgins and a fully-laden tray. The little ceremony with the arrival of the tea was then conducted in silence and reverence. Miss Tournier poured out, first for her mother, then his lordship, who got up to receive it from her hands, and then she sat back down in the deep chair focusing on her own cup.

His lordship eyed her with complaisance. This sort of quiet domesticity, although surely rarely as deceptively calm and ordinary as it appeared in this house right now, made him feel strangely quiet.

"So, Lie-lie," Mrs Tournier's voice broke the silence, "it rather amazes me that you came across anyone as foolhardy as yourself on your foolish outing today. What brings you out on such a day, my lord?"

Immediately his eyes sought out Miss Tournier's and they both burst into laughter.

"The same thing that brings your daughter out, apparently," he grinned. "A truant, restless disposition."

"A callous disregard and lack of respect for the season, more likely," Mrs Tournier mumbled.

The laughter, the fire, the tea and — yes, she must admit to herself — the company, all joined to dissolve the remnants of her discomfort and she relaxed back into her chair with a smile.

"I believe it was more like a steadfast resolution, Maman." She turned to Lord Baugham, "I rather like those words my lord, yes...I shall have to remember that phrase the next time I am accused of being foolhardy or unreasonable." Her smile broadened, "Or, I should say, 'in the unlikely event that I would *ever* be accused of being stubborn or unreasonable'? For I think I am always reasonable...though not everyone will see it."

"Well, in that *highly* unlikely event," he said, his eyes twinkling dangerously as he glanced at her over his tea cup, "I think you'd do best to remind any accuser that such doubts could make you '*stark mad or wonderfully froward*'. Either way, I think you will be allowed to keep your steadfast resolution well enough."

She twinkled back at him.

"Oh, yes...I can see clearly how such a reminder would advance my cause. There is nothing that can attest to my rationality more than the threat of becoming irrational if I am crossed. Now that I think of it though, I may have tried just that same tactic once or twice before as a little girl. You can imagine how well it worked with my mother."

Mrs Tournier huffed, but she was still quiet, for some reason being content with remaining a spectator in this sport

Holly could not help herself. She was home, warm and mostly dry, comfortable and enjoying his company. It would likely be different tomorrow, or tonight, or five minutes from now. But right now...she would be content with right now.

"However, since you are now undoubtedly convinced that I am always sensible, I would be happy to give you my opinion on whatever 'steadfast resolution' has brought you out on such a day as this."

He gave a mischievous smile. "Yes, I know you well enough to be convinced of that."

He put down his tea cup and leaned slightly forward. "It concerns Hamish. He is a good lad and I could not help but notice that Mrs Tournier's estimation of his

306

talents and character was very apt. However, as you say, the work at Clyne will soon be finished, and I will be leaving myself, and as much as I would like, I cannot keep him on for the purpose he has so far been engaged. However, I do feel he should somehow be helped to pursue his obvious talents. I was wondering whether you had any ideas?"

Holly's expression grew more serious as she mirrored Lord Baugham's posture and leaned forward toward him in thought.

"I'm sorry, but I'm afraid that for all the thinking and wondering I have done on that same subject, I am at a loss. As long as he is with his family — his father in particular — there is not much that can be done for him. What if…" Her brow wrinkled in concentration, "what if we found him some sort of position or apprenticeship here in Clanough? But I'm just so afraid…he could be so much more! No," she looked at him boldly, "he needs to go away to school, my lord. And he needs friends that will help him to do so."

Baugham wrinkled his brow mirroring her very serious expression and nodded slowly while he tapped his finger on his pursed lips.

"Quite…" he seriously said. "And yet…I'm afraid…the costs…"

She looked at him anxiously, but also narrowing her eyes. Suddenly he could control his expression no more and broke out into a wicked grin.

"Well, I would say the boy is singularly well-provided for then! If you can provide the school, I can provide the help and I dare say we can persuade Mrs Tournier to help us with the friends-bit."

Mrs Tournier looked at him under her eyebrows.

"With such benefactors as the two of you, how could I fail him?"

Holly leaned back with a satisfied expression on her face. "That's very good, Maman, because I am afraid it is going to fall to you to convince Mr Nethery to let him go.

"I know of several very good schools — I will begin writing inquiries tomorrow." She turned grateful eyes upon Lord Baugham. "Thank you, my lord. Such an opportunity will mean the world to a boy like him. Thank you indeed."

He smiled back at her and reflected how good it felt to have her look upon him with such a look. Not angry, not disappointed and not weary. At this moment he held out a hope that they could perhaps truly be friends again. He wondered if she wanted that too. Could she perhaps see it in his eyes as they lingered holding hers? How much he wanted to put past mistakes and stupid impulsive behaviours behind them?

"Well, I would like to view this as an opportunity for the world as well. He is a very talented and clever boy and he will go far and be a benefit to his country, I am certain. Unless the high seas and the footsteps of Captain Bob irrevocably claim him first, that is."

He was speaking, she could hear him…something about Hamish and the high seas. But she could not pull her eyes away from his — his expression drew her in and she returned his look, wondering what he was thinking and not realising how much time had passed until her mother not so discreetly cleared her throat.

"Lie-lie! My cup is empty."

Holly jumped up and gathered all the cups, carrying them back to the tea tray. Mrs Tournier slowly rubbed her hands together as if for warmth.

"Lord Baugham, would you be so kind as to throw some wood on the fire?

Baugham thoughtfully stoked the fire. When he was finished, he turned around and saw Mrs Tournier still watching him. He stood up and threw a glance at her daughter, still busy with piling the delicate china on top of one another and he could hear the gentle clinking of the spoons against saucers.

"Well, I must say it is a great comfort to have Hamish's future taken care of and to be able to lay his fate in your capable and caring hands. That does make my other steadfast resolution easier to execute."

He was aware of Miss Tournier interrupting her chores and turning around.

"Had enough of what Scotland can offer you in the way of blizzards, sleet and fog at this season, have you?" Mrs Tournier said with a smile that did not quite reach her eyes.

Baugham returned the smile graciously enough, but Miss Tournier's face did not change. She wore a small frown now and was obviously waiting for more explanation.

"Yes, I'm leaving," he said and then realised he had not quite meant to be so abrupt. "That is to say, I cannot put off my promise to join Mr Darcy in London any longer. I understand Mr Bingley is quite anxious for Mr Darcy, and thus me as well, to join him at Netherfield. Apparently he finds spending time with his bride-to-be is being burdened by the bride's family."

Mrs Tournier gave a short laugh. "From what I hear, Mr Bingley is a most affable man."

"Yes he is. Which makes me think Mr Darcy's sole companionship is not going to be of as much assistance as he might wish."

Baugham threw Miss Tournier a glance again. Still she said nothing.

"My man informs me that I will be ready to travel the day after tomorrow," he went on. "But, of course, once you arrive I shall be very happy to see you both again."

Mrs Tournier and his lordship exchanged a smile and when he tried to include the daughter in it, he found that she had once more turned her back and the spoons were again being gathered and the saucers piled on top of one another.

Suddenly the air was filled with the goodbyes he had said and the distance he was already busy putting between them. It was time to go. He kissed Mrs Tournier's hand, who assured him she would be very happy to rescue him from any duties that were placed upon him by his insensitive friends. Then he stood and walked over to Miss Tournier, who was now holding the tea tray and effectively blocking him from performing the same goodbye to her.

"Of course, if you have plans to visit Clyne tomorrow, this is not our final farewell."

She nodded and shifted the tray closer to herself. Since she said no more, Baugham found he had no choice but to find his hat and, with a bow, simply leave her by wishing her a good evening.

Chapter 28

*Where Some Move Away and Some Move Forward and Yet
Some Wonder about Directions in General*

A RESTLESS night and a fanciful notion of nostalgia made Lord Baugham spend the next day in the saddle. He rode across his small estate and beyond as if saying goodbye to the hills and fells and the river, all the while puzzling over his purpose at staying on for so long after so much had gone so wrong. In ordinary circumstances he would have left ages ago. Probably soon after Darcy had gone, and certainly right away upon receipt of his letter. He really did not know what made him stay. Heaven knew he had obligations elsewhere that he should not have so long delayed, but for some strange reason he felt a force that held him to Clyne, even now, stronger than the one that pulled him away.

As if testing that force he stayed out until the early dusk of a grey winter day crept over the fields and in through the woods. He then turned back and realised as he saw the lighted windows of Clyne from a distance that the pull was still there as strong as ever, even though his plans were fixed and he was most assuredly leaving in the morning. He left his horse in the stable and as he walked around the house, it was already growing darker.

Strolling by a window, he paused as he realised he was just outside the library. The room was lighted and shadows moved across the window. He approached and could clearly see Miss Tournier walking back and forth with a few books in one hand and a piece of paper in the other, apparently immersed in her work. An odd stabbing feeling caught him in his stomach — there she was, in his house, busily working, and he was outside in the dark watching her while she had no idea she was being observed. That was a poignant thought he did not wish to dwell on further, but it did drive him into the house and straight to the library after he had changed his clothes and given himself a few stern comments on his folly and the courtesy and reassurance he owed the lady downstairs.

HOLLY LOOKED AROUND HER WITH a bittersweet feeling. She and Hamish had methodically worked their way around the room for so long and now they were just ready to shelve the last book. She held it out to the boy, "I would be pleased if you would do the honour, sir."

Hamish grinned and took the book from her. He struggled within himself for a moment, knowing that the honour should really be Miss Tournier's, yet very pleased and proud that she would turn it over to him. He glanced up at her with a questioning look that competed with barely concealed pride and excitement. She smiled.

"Hamish, you have been a fine assistant. All of this is as much your accomplishment as it is mine; I could not have done it without you. Please ... it will make me very happy indeed if you were to have the privilege of shelving this last book."

Hamish thought he would do anything to make Miss Tournier happy. He looked around with the same mixed emotions as she was feeling. It had been very hard work, no doubt about that, but he had loved every minute of it — well ... almost every minute. His lessons, his time with Miss Tournier and Lord Baugham, who both taught him by word and example how to be a better person. All these books ...

Dashing away the tears that threatened to fall with the back of his hand, Hamish felt he was not ready to have it all end quite yet.

"Miss, do ye nae think his lairdship should be here for the last?"

"Oh, he is probably much too busy to come ..." Holly began, but when she saw the boy's face fall, she relented. "But it doesn't hurt to try, does it? Why don't you go and knock on his study door and invite him?"

Hamish clutched the volume against his chest, nodded and walked carefully out of the library to gain admittance to his lordship's study. He knocked on the door once with no answer and then boldly tried a little harder. There was still no answer. He looked down at the book against his chest and contemplated his options. This seemed to be a very important moment somehow and he wanted to be absolutely certain.

He made one last attempt at producing a knock that would have roused any peers sleeping behind the door, but still there was no sound. He sighed and admitted defeat. As he did so he heard soft footsteps in the hall behind him and, turning around, saw Riemann crossing the hall to mount the stairs. Now, Mr Riemann was an enigma to young Hamish. Besides being a quiet man — he did not think he had ever exchanged one word with him for all the time they had spent in the same house — he was obviously a foreigner and that was a fact that should put anyone on their guard these days. Especially one aspiring to be ready for any adventure and challenge to his bravery and the defence of the honour and security of the realm as Hamish was. But suspicious and mysterious men were always to be confronted bravely, he had learned, and so he raised his voice and asked the valet where his Master was.

"I believe his lordship has just come in," was the quiet answer and there was no opportunity for further inquiry before he slipped away again.

Hamish was slightly taken aback by this intelligence, but he also had to reflect that that man was someone to watch with his strange, barely hidden accent and footsteps quiet enough for any villain. He turned around again and, as he headed back to the library, he could see the tall frame of Lord Baugham coming down the corridor.

Hamish shyly approached him, but not without some pride. His lordship turned around and smiled at him and, feeling much encouraged, Hamish held out the book he was still clutching.

"This is the last one, m'laird."

She was already putting her things in order when he knocked on the door and caught her.

"Miss Tournier?" he said "Were you leaving? I have been out all day, but I am glad to have returned in time. I understand I have been invited to a ceremony of some importance! I must say I am honoured!"

Holly turned, surprised that he had come, "My lord! I didn't expect to see you today. I assumed you would be busy with preparations."

"Oh, I prepare to leave in quite different ways than my man does. And mostly as far away from him as possible." He smiled politely, Holly smiled politely and the ensuing silence threatened to grow awkward. Again.

Baugham cleared his throat, "I hope you and Hamish have been adequately fed and attended to?"

She gave him a small but genuine smile. "Do you think we could be otherwise with Mrs McLaughlin in charge?"

They stood, looking at each other, looking at their feet, until an impatient sigh from Hamish caught their attention. Holly's expression brightened a bit more as she remembered her purpose in inviting him to the library. She turned and gestured around the room.

"But have you not noticed, my lord? The piles are gone!"

Baugham looked around.

"And so they are!" he said and smiled. "Goodness, but if there isn't almost an echo in here now! A temporary echo, I presume."

He had his library back, just as he was leaving it behind. The shelves were obviously lacking in inventory and all the miscellaneous piles and bric-a-brac were cleared away, leaving them bare and strangely gaping, and his desk was still claimed by her correspondence, notes, papers and cards with no room for his own work but it certainly was a library — *his* library — again. She was obviously and justifiably proud of her accomplishment and he made all the appropriate comments to that effect.

She returned his smile.

"Thank you, sir. Now, Master Nethery and I are preparing to place the final book into the final shelf of the final section; we have long felt that such an occasion should be treated with the respect and dignity it deserves. We would be honoured if you would join us."

She nodded to Hamish who, with a very serious expression on his face, crossed the room holding the book out in front of him as if it were a sacred relic. He carefully and deliberately, with a bit of a dramatic flourish, slid it into its rightful place. He turned, grinning, and Holly beamed back at him, her face full of tenderness and pride.

"Thank you," Baugham said softly as he watched the two of them. Turning to Hamish he shook the boy's hand in an adult and dignified manner. "Excellent work, young man!" he said and clasped his shoulder. "I am very proud of you. I can think of no more appropriate additional award for your hard labour than a trip to the kitchen. Give my compliments to Mrs McLaughlin and she will see that you are well taken care of. Miss Tournier and I have the small matter of a bill to settle."

Hamish thought Mrs McLaughlin's pastries could very well fit into the celebratory nature of the occasion and happily took his leave. Baugham pulled out a chair at the opposite end of the writing desk and invited Miss Tournier to sit down.

"No my lord, you mistake me. There is still much to be done. I have only just begun the catalogue, my purchase list is not complete... please... there is much more to do before we settle the bill."

"Ah, but this is my last opportunity to be able to do so in person. Please indulge me; any future compensation will have to be settled through my bankers."

"I take it, then, you have no plans to return to Scotland soon?" She bit her lip in concentration. "I suppose once you get back to London, you will be quite busy with social obligations and... friends. I hope you will find the time to travel to Hertford-shire after all."

Baugham shuffled through the piles looking for a blank sheet of paper.

"Yes well," he said slowly while he searched again for a quill, "Hertfordshire is quite settled. It all depends on Mr Darcy, of course; I have placed myself at his mercy and pleasure, but I suppose I shall not be obliged to dash out into the country again immediately upon my arrival in London. At least I should hope not."

He prodded the tip of the quill with his fingertip and handed the equipment over to his librarian. "There! Go on, make your demands and don't be gentle!" but she was looking back at him with something like disapproval.

"What?" he found himself reacting impulsively. "Have I not expressed adequate enthusiasm over my friend's upcoming marriage? Very well, I hope he will be very happy and I am sure he will be, but I am not overly thrilled at the thought of spending time at another country house in another quaint country village in the anticipation of the event. And so I hope to go down later rather than sooner." He gestured to the paper on the desk, "Now, if you would be so kind..."

Holly stared at the quill in her hand. What was she supposed to do with this?

"You mean you have given no thought to what this job is worth? You wish *me* to make that determination? I am sorry, but I think that is for you to decide. I fear it is too much responsibility for a simple *country* girl like me."

Baugham gave a little snort. "My dear Miss Tournier, please do not tell me a woman like you is not aware of exactly how much an hour of her work is worth!"

Holly gasped and put down the quill.

"A woman like me? And what exactly does that mean, a woman like me?"

Baugham looked at her, puzzled. "Really, Miss Tournier. You work for a fee; what is that fee? Or does your mother keep you in the dark as to how much your efforts are worth when she settles things for you on your behalf?"

It was a reasonable question, if not put forth in the most reasonable manner, but Holly could not see it.

"Yes, yes she does. I am completely at her mercy in such matters," she replied, her voice dripping with sarcasm. "I am just as much in the dark as you must be, as it appears your bankers are the only ones who know how much you pay your employees."

Baugham made no attempt to disguise his surprise. He snatched the paper back from where it had been lying in front of her and picked up a new quill.

"Well, yes, I do have quite a number of them," he snarled. "Besides you."

He started scribbling on the paper. "What is your estimation then? Are you worth as much as a valet or a housekeeper? Perhaps you are nearer to a tailor or a butcher?"

Holly drew herself up to her full height. "You, sir, are insulting me," she said in an ice-cold voice.

"And you, ma'am, are acting irrationally."

"That may be so, but…" she broke off, "but so are you if you trust an employee to set their own wage. I might just as well say I require fifty pounds! And if I did so, you would come back with what your idea of an appropriate fee is, the idea you most assuredly already have in your head.

She flopped back in her chair in a very unladylike manner, arms crossed defensively, "You might just as well say the figure at once and spare us both the discomfort."

"I thought," he said calmly once again, "I was just asking you to do that."

"Well then," she said, equally calmly, "I will say fifty pounds!"

"Very well," he said, "that sounds fair as an annual wage for a librarian and secretary."

"Very true," she smirked, "but as I have no intention of continuing in your employ for any longer than necessary, perhaps you will be so kind as to suggest a fair wage for the duties of a *temporary* librarian."

He got up in a hasty gesture that startled her and leaned down on the desk.

"So you really want me to do that? You want me to put a price on this? You want me to *appraise* you? And what then? What if I offer too much, too little? What will you do? Will it be a triumph for you either way, Miss Tournier?"

Holly pulled away from his cold, angry eyes, and stood up from the chair sputtering, "I…but you…you expect me to do the same…I cannot…" She walked away, keeping her back to him and he could see her shoulders rise and fall with the deep breaths she took.

"I think now is not the time…" She turned around a moment later with a lift her

313

chin, "I think that I would like your secretary or banker to determine the proper amount."

"I think he had better," he answered, obviously concentrating hard on controlling himself, "because however much you ask me to, I *cannot* and I *will not*."

"Neither can I," Holly said, almost in a whisper.

Silence filled the room. Baugham searched desperately for something to say to take the edge of his last statement and Holly fought frantically to master her own feelings, not to make a fool of herself here in front of him again. Thankfully the creaking of the door soon shattered it and they each knew without looking that it was Hamish. Holly jolted into action and walked over to the boy.

"Well, Hamish? Have you eaten Mrs McLaughlin out of all her pastries already?"

"Aye, miss," the boy smiled sheepishly, "Well, not quite. She sent these, miss. And some tea for ye, miss." Hamish carefully put down the tray on the table among the piles of paper. "But I thought I might read a wee bit before I walk home. If that's alright, that is."

Baugham watched the boy come in and break the tension and he was relieved. Relieved and incredibly frustrated at the same time, funnily enough. He stayed in the room, unwilling that their last encounter should end in such a way, and once Hamish was firmly settled into his book, curled up in another corner of the room, he cleared his throat and tried again.

"You have earned some rest as well, Miss Tournier," he said quietly. "As well as some tea and pastry. The transformation is already enormous and I am grateful."

Her discomfort was evident but she answered him calmly.

"As I have said, there still is quite a bit of work left for me here, but I think I must also now concentrate on things closer to home. I still have my work with Dr McKenna...he is anxious to spend more time on it than we have been able to do so far."

He was quiet for a moment and she looked up at him. His next words were slow and thoughtful.

"Yes, I imagine he is. Dr McKenna is a good man and an excellent scientist. His good opinion of you and your work is certain to lead to opportunities for you that are to your advantage." He smiled wryly. "Science *and* flattery. A very tempting prospect, and, in the right hands, difficult to resist I imagine."

"Opportunities?" she blurted out. "Opportunities!?" What a thing for him to say! She could read his meaning clearly enough! He meant to push her off on the doctor on his way out of town and then he could leave it all behind without a second thought or regret. Very well then, she would show him that she had no regrets either. "But you are right," she said defiantly, "he is a good man. A very good man, and I look forward to becoming even better acquainted with him."

There was a moment of silence when it seemed she was daring him to respond, but he told himself he did not wish to risk another spate of harsh words, so he quickly changed the subject.

"So..." he said slowly. "This wedding in Hertfordshire...you must be looking

314

forward to seeing Miss Bennet again, and the rest of your family, in this happy time. And, after all, it is a splendid romance as well as a splendid match, don't you find? That is rare these days and worth celebrating."

"Yes, quite," Holly answered, her voice tight with frustration,

"And yet, the charms of Hertfordshire will not long keep either of us, I expect. I will be off on my neglected business soon after the wedding, and you will want to get back as well…to the doctor and his rocks."

"Yes, quite," she repeated and suddenly crossed the room and sat down by the table again. "And with that in mind, you really must excuse me."

Baugham watched her as she turned her back on him and bowed over her work. However, she sat quite still with quill in hand and paper before her without giving it any attention, instead listening intently for him to walk away.

ONCE HE CLOSED THE DOOR behind him, Holly leaned back and sighed and briefly closed her eyes. When she opened them again, she spied the sugar bowl, crammed in with the rest of the serving paraphernalia on the table between stacks of books and loose papers and cards. It was silver, with two fine handles that curled down on the shiny sides like the top of a Corinthian pillar. The fine snowy white crystals twinkled in the light. Softly, the silver spoon had shaped small hills and dales from where someone before her had carelessly scooped an appropriate amount to sweeten and break the strength of the strong tea.

So he was leaving. Tomorrow. For London. To assist Mr Darcy. In preparation for the wedding. In Hertfordshire.

She did not quite know what she was doing or, more importantly, why she was doing it, but Holly slowly lifted her finger to her mouth while still contemplating the silver bowl. Then she resolutely stuck her finger into the sugar so that the fine crystals parted and pushed upwards on the sides with a small crunching noise. Not until the tip of her finger touched the bottom did she stop. Then she slowly withdrew it again, watching the sugar crumble back into the hole she had made.

She lifted her finger to her mouth and carefully closed her lips around it. Slowly — very slowly — she swirled her tongue around her finger and nail. She felt the sharp taste curl around her tongue and seep through every corner of her mouth. It was heavenly. She could feel the sweetness all around and as the crystals turned liquid and ran down her throat, she smiled and very carefully removed her finger. Carefully pushing whatever miniscule traces might be left in the corners of her mouth between her lips, she swallowed again.

The taste still lingered and Holly could not stop smiling to herself. An indescribable and surprising sense of triumph rushed through her. She licked her lips once more, then turned to her library cards and went back to cross-referencing.

Chapter 29

Events Move to the Great Metropolis while Life Goes on in the Village

As the carriage drew up before Sunderborn House in Berkeley Square four days later and very late at night, his lordship felt more exhausted from this journey than he had ever felt in his whole life. The journey down from Clyne at this time of year was draining in itself, but, in addition, his mind was in disarray. He had not adhered to his usual whims of departure and as a consequence, instead of feeling a relief and anticipation to be on his way, he had suffered exceedingly from the long miles of travel. He had furthermore been cursed with the most unimaginable winter weather in living memory and the fog that had rolled in over London was so thick that his coachman had lost his way twice between Tyburn turnpike and Berkeley Square. Indeed, his lordship wryly reflected, the peculiar air certainly reflected his growing impatience to see the end of this trip, the end of these wandering thoughts and his repeated failure to bring them into any order.

He was greeted by his butler, who with great ceremony and obvious concern, ushered him quickly into the house, lamenting about how this sort of weather brought out the worst kind of criminals and mischief in the streets, and how he and the whole household had been most anxious and Cook had wanted to send Will, the footman, out since yesterday to try to meet his lordship and assure his safety. It bore testament to Lord Baugham's distraction of mind that he let these obvious expressions of affection and concern pass him by without countering them with either impatience or incredulity, but rather thanked his butler and bid him convey the news of his safe return to the rest of the staff.

"Should you like your bath now, sir?" Townsend asked as he folded away the heavy winter travelling coat and stowed away hats, gloves and personal effects.

A great wave of fatigue washed over him. His staff stood eager and ready to see to his every need... yet, what he most needed, they could not provide. Peace, both within himself and within the realm and world. A very simple request and yet a fancy not to be dwelt upon further. A bath would have to suffice.

"Yes, I should!" was his lordship's adamant answer as he freed himself from his last pieces of outer clothing. "Yes, I can see you notice how I reek even from that distance. Dirty business travelling. A bath — that would be marvellous.

He then gave instructions for a roaring fire to instantly be lit in the principle rooms of the house, most particularly his library. He was met by his footman at the door as he proceeded up the staircase.

"Good to have you home again, my lord!" he shouted as he watched his master ascend. "You were very much missed!"

"I highly doubt it," his Master muttered between his teeth, but continued his way. All the same, the simple sentiment touched him and made him feel grateful. *If servants are all the family one is to have,* he thought resignedly, *it is nice that they show a measure of affection toward one.*

After his tea and attending to the most pressing business at hand that was his bath and the removal of strange smells and the dirt and grime of the road, his lord-ship took a stroll through his house with the intent of finishing in his library, where he could linger comfortably until dinner. Sunderborn was a small but comfortable house, perfectly fulfilling both the requirements of easy bachelorhood and Earldom. Where size had been bartered for the sake of convenience and expense, elegance and refinement had not been spared. It reflected his personality well, Lord Baugham thought, that outward luxury and taste would never stand in the way of functional-ity and expediency.

The sitting rooms and drawing rooms had benefited in style from the absence of family heirlooms, the most precious and ostentatious pieces having been sold off long ago by his late father to feed his gambling habits, the un-sellable ones being stowed away at Cumbermere Castle against the unlikely day such artefacts would tickle anyone's fashion fancy once more. Contrary to what might have been expected of a gentleman, Lord Baugham favoured light colours and fabrics and easy seating arrange-ments, with no guns, trophies or battle scenes adorning any part of the establishment.

Baugham walked slowly into the library and felt himself ease into his house. Here there was none of the affection he felt for Clyne — for outside, and on occasion even inside these walls, society pressed upon him an adopted role and persona he used for pleasure, entertainment and diversion, but which was not his own — but as he sank into his familiar chair and measured this comfort against the previous days on the road and in the inns, he realised he was happy to have arrived and would even call this his home of sorts. From where he sat, he could look out of his window onto the square — or could if the shutters were not closed. The nearest one he could nudge with the tip of his boot, but the other he was obliged to move out of the chair to open. He parted the curtains and looked out, surprised by the stillness and the tranquillity of the foggy scene. It felt soothing and it calmed him down to the degree that he even entertained thoughts about how much beauty there was in the world and in the things before him. He turned around and, from having stood in the coolness reflecting from the windows, he now recognised a new smell: the smell of his home. Familiar, dusty, warm — he searched his mind for appropriate attributes.

As usual, he slowly went through the room to match his memory of it with reality. The bookshelves in this library bore no resemblance to the ones he had left up north. Even before he had invited chaos into his life and library, the shelves at Clyne had been a shambles. His library in London was quite different. Lord Baugham was no collector; he had no patience for the cultivating of relationships to publishers or vendors, or building stratagems for purchase. He tended to buy what he fancied and it was to his credit that he generally fancied very fine pieces, and those pieces he displayed and enjoyed on his London shelves.

As his eyes fell upon 'Tam O'Shanter' lying on its back on one of the tables, never put away among its prouder brethren, yellow from age and covers missing, he gave a wry smile. He picked it up. In a very long and looping hand on the title page his mother's name stared back at him. For a long time he let his eyes rest on the letters and old thoughts and feelings slowly welled up within him.

She had loved that poem. "Come here, David, let me read Tammie for you," she would say, asking him for his favourite passage. "Anything you like, Mama," was always the answer and it was true. He loved all of it because she loved all of it. She was a good reader but then, as she told him, she had to be. All the Welsh were poets and singers and though perhaps, she laughingly would admit, strictly speaking there was not so much Welsh in her as she might want there to be, she did love a good rhyme. "And this old Gaelic fool is as good as any of them," she had said. He agreed even now. Even on impartial evidence, disregarding his mother's fondness and his own bias as a result, "Tammie" was a marvellous poem.

Although he had another, better copy somewhere, this was the one he had left out, and he picked up the old battered volume and sat down on the sofa to look through it. But his thoughts wandered. He realised that the wit and recklessness of Burns had been more than a love of rhyme for his mother: it had been a way to adapt to her circumstance and fate. She had taken refuge in books and rhyme to try to bring some meaning and order to a failed marriage and a disappointed life. That had been her gift and lesson to him. But, as much as she had given him and as much as he still loved her for it, when the room grew darker and the words on the page grew more obscure, he could not keep his mind from questioning whether that strategy was not so supreme after all. Perhaps there was something to be said for not merely accepting facts as they were, but challenging them and conquering them instead of ignoring and abandoning them.

Truth was a frightening thing and never as compatible with one's ambitions as one might wish. Truth was a capricious master, devoid of feeling and fickle in its consequences. Truth did not always set you free — the walls of your prison could be crafted from bitter truth, as his mother had discovered. But then, he had never seen her attempt to break those walls, to stare truth in the eye, to make her peace with it. Perhaps she had not had the strength to try; perhaps a woman in her circumstances had very little choice and too much to lose. But what exactly did *he* have to lose? Why was his own mind rebelling against him, never allowing him to see a truth that did not seem impossible, complicated, or foolish? How was he to discover what he really needed and what he wanted, and was there necessarily always an honest difference between the two?

'Tam O'Shanter' had been lying on his knee for a long time already when he realised he was sitting in the dark and the room had grown cold. He shrugged and got up, carefully putting the book back where he found it and giving the *Ex Libris* one more affectionate caress before he left.

Now, wha this tale o truth shall read,
Ilk man, and mother's son, take heed:
Whene'er to drink you are inclin'd,
Or cutty sarks rin in your mind,
Think! ye may buy the joys o'er dear:
Remember Tam o Shanter's mare.

LIFE IN CLANOUGH FELL INTO a quiet routine after Lord Baugham left for London. Every day Holly would walk to Clyne Cottage after breakfast, share a cup of tea with Mrs McLaughlin before spending the rest of the morning in the quiet library, cataloguing the existing inventory, making additions as new purchases arrived and giving Hamish his lessons. Afternoons were spent at home, more often than not working with Dr McKenna until late evening.

On one such evening very much like all the others, she pulled out a sheet of paper and held her pencil at the ready. Dr McKenna pulled a second chair up close.

"Why don't we try the slate quarries in Ballachulish?"

As Holly began to sketch to his words, Mrs Tournier interrupted her own work to watch the couple. That the doctor was interested in her daughter was obvious, but what her daughter felt she could not know. A wave of frustration washed over her as she reflected on Holly's recent behaviours. There had never before been such reticence in their relationship; Holly had not kept secrets from her for many years, but ever since that day when she and his lordship quarrelled in the garden, she had been silent and mysterious. Why that particular quarrel should cause such a change when so many previous misunderstandings had occurred and been forgotten, she could not understand, nor would Holly explain. Her daughter was troubled, she could see that, but it appeared no inducement would be sufficient to convince her to share those troubles with her mother.

Her hand unconsciously reached up and she fingered the locket around her neck: *Yes, yes … I know she's a grown woman now,* she said to her long absent husband, *but*

I don't have to like it. And I don't have to stop worrying because of it. The sound of soft laughter pulled her attention back to the present and she saw the two young people smile at each other over the page that Holly was now diligently erasing. Dr McKenna's smile was beaming and Holly's was soft, but it was a smile nonetheless. Mrs Tournier quietly closed her books, stacked her papers and rose and, after watching them for a moment longer, she slowly withdrew, quietly closing the door behind her and going up to her own room.

In the parlour the efforts continued on, the workers oblivious of their companion's departure.

"The hill rises roughly at a thirty degree angle...no, not quite that steep...yes! That's better. And the deposits are ninety feet up the slope...about two-thirds of the way...yes, good..."

Holly smiled.

"If you would be so good as to hand me that volume on the window sill, Doctor? And the sample box? I don't want my imagination to run away with me too much."

"If you'll forgive me for saying so, Miss Tournier, it is doing no such thing. I think you must be able to read my mind. That is exactly what I wanted to portray. Now, if you could make the drift on the left side of the hill sharper, you could then insert a more detailed description of the boulder in accordance with this sample here..."

"That is a beautiful stone. It's so dark. I hope I can catch its lustre."

"Oh yes, and you have to imagine the whole cliff wall shining in the sunlight! Spectacular, absolutely spectacular!"

Holly smiled again.

"The way you speak of it certainly makes slate acquire new and exciting dimensions, Dr McKenna. I never thought stone could be quite so inspirational."

He smiled at her as she put her pencil to the page again and asked, "Tell me how the boulder is situated."

And so the evening passed as every other evening passed. A quiet dinner, sometimes with the doctor for company, sometimes just the two ladies. Afterward, they would read or talk, and then, to conserve candlelight, early to bed. It was the life of peace that Holly had always dreamt of when away from home, but though she appreciated it when it settled around her like a warm secure blanket, in the moments she was honest with herself, she knew she could not quite feel content with it.

"So here you are! Enjoying yourself, are you?"

Mr Darcy looked up from his correspondence and saw his friend leaning in the door opening.

"Baugham," he said. "You took your time."

His lordship shrugged and studied his fingernails. "Roads. Weather. The usual excuses."

Darcy shook his head.

"But I am certain you were able to manage splendidly enough on your own with lawyers and bankers and such," Baugham went on.

Darcy grinned and leaned back in his seat. "I'm certain I was."

Both men smiled a little and Baugham moved to take the chair opposite his friend.

"You must stop doing this soon, you know," Darcy said trying to look stern, but not succeeding entirely.

Baugham sighed. "The shackles of marriage rob more people than just the spouses of their freedom to come and go as they please. Ghastly business. Don't know why you put yourself through it."

"Believe me, I made cautious calculations and weighed the matter most carefully and have concluded that the gain will clearly outdo any losses, if you will pardon me for admitting so in your presence."

"Well, you would have. I would be interested to see those calculations put down on paper, I must admit. The logical argumentative process must be somewhat lacking for my taste, I am sure."

"Not at all. You are just not in the possession of the right factual premise."

"Well, without true facts one cannot reach a factual truth."

Both men smiled, thinking of youthful debates that were more about truth than understanding.

"You are staying for dinner?" Darcy said casually.

"Of course. I think I can very well listen to any professed truths about love, marriage and even the future Mrs Darcy if your Cook performs as usual."

"I'll make certain he does," Mr Darcy said and laughed when his friend rolled his eyes at him.

HOWEVER, MR DARCY WAS NOT a man whose tongue was loosened with the violence of his affections and so talk on love, marriage and the future Mrs Darcy was swiftly done with. Neither was he in the habit of influencing the conversation of his friend when there was plenty to be had of it, and so Lord Baugham was able to talk sports, horses, politics, current affairs (in the wide sense), speculations on the war and the even the general state of policing in the Capital as opposed to the provinces and Scotland in particular, without interference from him. It was not until seated with brandy, fire and nightfall that Mr Darcy fixed his friend with a scrutinising eye and became inquisitive.

"And how are our friends at Rosefarm?"

Just as he thought he would, Baugham gave him a look of studied surprise and indifference. "What about them?"

"I was wondering why you have not mentioned them."

"There was no need. You did."

"But only just now."

"True. Still, I think Lord Sidmouth's difficulties and the annual exploits of the Quorn are more fruitful topics for discussion."

"Be careful, Baugham, snide comments from you make me suspicious."

"Suspicious of what?"

"That all is not well with you and the ladies of Rosefarm."

Baugham suddenly sprang out of his seat and walked over to the fireplace to lean against its mantelpiece, glass still in hand.

"Rest easy on that score. All is as it should be."

There was a pause while Darcy tried to read meaning into Baugham's silence and his lordship tried to kill the topic by his.

"I am given to understand," Darcy said finally, "by the means of which Miss Bennet's letter was delivered to her cousin, that Miss Tournier is at present employed by you to reinstate your library."

Baugham threw him a quick look.

"Yes."

"A laudable effort."

"Well, it was in shambles. You never stopped telling me so."

"And how is it progressing?"

Baugham shrugged. "Well enough, I suppose." He gave Darcy a tired look. "You're not going to start that lecture on 'my behaviour' again, are you? It is not necessary, I assure you."

Something in Baugham's tone of voice made Darcy frown.

"I see no need to be defensive, Baugham. I admit the circumstance of Miss Tournier as an employee in your home is highly unusual — and some might well question the wisdom of such an arrangement — but, tell me… are you completely clear in the delineation between your so-called Scotland self and the man you present to the rest of the world? In your own mind. Now that you have come back, has the London rake returned in full measure? No doubt your Scotland friends would be surprised to see him."

Baugham watched his friend with a distinctly hostile eye.

"Calling me a rake, Darcy, will not get you anywhere. Questioning my actions concerning the employment of Miss Tournier to reinstate my library without full knowledge of all the facts and motivations is imprudent, and doubting my morals and sense of honour is insulting. And I am very capable of performing *self*-flagellation should the need arise."

"Oh. I have no doubt about that. It is rather your consistency I worry about."

"Consistency?"

"Yes. You are a good man, Baugham, I know you are. I know it because you act upon it often enough and I have seen it first hand. But I doubt whether you know it yourself. Really."

Baugham looked at his friend. His first impulse was to dismiss his comment as nonsense. His second to laugh at him. But somehow he was capable of neither.

"I am the same man as I was when I left Scotland," he muttered. "I have not changed. Everything is the same."

"And will it change do you think?"

Baugham looked at Darcy. There was really nothing arrogant about him, he thought. No censure in his voice or disapproval in his attitude. It was rather curiosity and concern. It was one of those rare moments in their friendship where only the men — not the names or titles or fortunes — sat in the room talking. Last time this had happened was when Darcy's father had died. Such a very long time ago now, but Baugham remembered the way they had talked then in this very room. "My world will never be the same," Darcy had said and whereas the death of his own father had actually come as a relief and as a release into freedom for him, he knew that Darcy felt exactly the opposite. "You will always be the same to me," his lordship had said and had meant it sincerely. That was still true.

"I may be the same man as when I left Scotland," he therefore said quietly, "but I am not the same man I was upon leaving London. What kind of man I am now, I am not certain of, but I hope…I want him to be the man you say you recognise in me. The one, I hope, who was always there in spite of everything."

Darcy gave a smile. "That makes me happy to hear. I like that man."

"Thank you. I can only hope others may as well."

HOLLY LAY IN HER ROOM under a thick layer of blankets, with only the light of the moon to illuminate the darkness. They had spent the day in preparation and the evening in packing, so both Rosefarm women were ready to leave for Hertfordshire first thing in the morning. Once her eyes adjusted to the low light, she absentmindedly stared up at the drawings on her ceiling, too keyed up to sleep. Two things made her smile — just before they made her frown. She was excited at the thought of seeing Elizabeth again, but, at the same time, she knew that this would be a good-bye as well. Elizabeth was about to become Mrs Darcy and things would never be — *could* never be — the same between them again. And, as silly and vain as she knew it to be, she was excited about the re-worked gown that was placed with great care at the top of her trunk. She had modelled it for her mother before packing it away and both ladies were pleased with the result. No one would ever be able to tell that the dress was several years old. It was silly, useless, she knew, but when she saw her reflection in the window glass as she twirled around in it, she could not help but wonder what Lord Baugham might think of it.

A deep sigh filled the small, dark room. Lord Baugham. He would be at the wedding, of course, and however much she tried to convince herself otherwise, she knew she *wanted* him to be there. She wanted to see him. No matter that he would probably scarcely notice her now that he had returned to his exciting life in London. *It will be good, really,* she told herself, *in such fine company as will be there, he will have no reason to notice me, and I need to see that. And then, once this wedding is over, there is no reason for us to ever cross paths again. I will go home, forget him once and for all and move on with my life.*

Move on…*just how am I to move on?*, she wondered.

She knew that Dr McKenna had some interest in her and that a very little encouragement would secure his attentions — she grimaced as she recalled how Lord Baugham had pressed her in that very direction just before he left. She was already well aware of the doctor's sentiments and she was being very careful not to give a wrong impression while she tried to sort out her confused feelings, but it was so very galling to have the man she loved, even if he was ignorant of that fact, attempt to push her into an alliance with someone else.

That was when she had realised, truly realised, that all her hopes were impossible and that she was better to look ahead and stop wasting her time on unattainable dreams. Thunderbolts out of the blue did not happen to former schoolmistresses in Scottish villages.

Part of her said that there was no need to hurry any decision, but the other part reminded her that even in this remote little corner of the world time did not stand still. The future for herself and her mother was by no means secure; their income being derived from commissions they managed to procure with no promise of more in the future. Mr Pembroke would never grow any kinder or more generous and they would constantly be seeking to keep the wolf from the door. She had told Elizabeth that she was giving up her dreams and lofty goals and would dedicate her life to taking care of her mother — and there was only one way for her to do so with security.

She could not marry Mr Grant — as respectable as he was, every feeling within her revolted at the idea. Dr McKenna was a good man. Nice, handsome, comfortable and easy to talk to, gentle like the rain...and he was here and interested now. Not off in London doing who knows what before...*Stop it, Holly!* she reprimanded herself and returned her thoughts back to the subject of the doctor. It would be wrong of her to mislead him or keep him dangling in the hopes that...well, in a vain hope for the thunderbolt. She knew she must either give up hope or give in to it — though she really could not bear the thought of either one.

I will give myself until after the wedding, she determined, *once we return home, I will give Dr McKenna all the encouragement he needs and I will move on with my life. Once and for all.*

LORD BAUGHAM HEARD THE DOOR close behind him as he entered his house. In the hall, he was relieved of his outer clothes and he lingered a while, aimlessly shuffling through what certainly would seem a respectable number of cards and invitations on the table. There was one thing to be said for hanging about that tired old maze of chambers and antechambers they call Whitehall, conducting business and greeting colleagues: he had missed three separate acquaintances who had tried to call that morning. Beside the cards, there were the usual invitations and billets. He turned one over and could not disguise his surprisingly strong reaction to the inscription on the back. Lady Merriwether apparently was entertaining again and he had been restored to her guest list. He looked at the directions without reading them. Memories and random words, accusations, and looks assaulted him suddenly:

You trifle and charm and flirt and play your way through the lives of people you hardly know and think you can go back to your London circles and everything will be as it has always been here...

And those words had been followed by more harsh words, and then he had stared, and taken a step and reached out to pull her to him and... he shook his head violently. Why? Where had that come from?

You think you can go back to your London circles and everything will be as it has always been here. Well, it will not!

As it always has been there... But, she was right. No matter how much he had wished and hoped that his leaving Scotland behind would solve this unsettled feeling within him, no matter how he desired to be able think of them as quiet and unchanging and going on peacefully with their lives, he knew that was conceit on his part. He had acted unpardonably and caused her pain; he could not turn back the clock and he had no inkling of how to make up for it, and as a consequence, he had done exactly what she accused him of doing.

Do you imagine that we disappear into our little holes as soon as we are not needed for your entertainment anymore? Well, we do not! We are left with exactly what you leave us with in terms of irresponsible behaviour and hopes and interpretations...

They would not disappear, even from his thoughts. Life for them would move on, only without him; time would pass, the rent would come due, roses would bud and bloom, and her work with Dr McKenna — a good man, a good friend, but more to the point, a man who knew the treasure he had found there in the remote village of Clanough — would continue.

He wondered if she would marry him, and concluded that she very likely would. It would be a good match, he acknowledged. She and her mother would be well cared for, and the doctor would treat Miss Tournier with kindness and respect as his wife. His wife. Baugham realised he was crunching Lady Merriwether's invitation in a tight grip. Away, he must throw this silliness away, and stop allowing senseless regrets and recriminations to preoccupy his mind. Quickly he took all the remaining letters, cards and notes and bolted for his study, where in one violent gesture he flung the morning's correspondence into the fire. Despite the early hour, he poured himself a generous helping of brandy and watched the papers turn into curling sheets of ash and smoke.

You make it your business to charm and endear yourself to every female you happen upon... I am sorry if it disappoints you that I do not wish to be among that number...

No, of course it doesn't, he thought, *but…*

The fire crackled as a log collapsed on top of another one and sent a myriad of tiny sparks upwards. Then it was quiet.

Baugham took a deep drink. What if he didn't stop at that 'but'? What if he, for once, could let down that infernal guard he always held so tightly over his thoughts and permit them to wander in the direction they would? And so, after another fortifying swallow, he let them.

The first thing that wandering brought to mind made him smile. Her flashing eyes and quick tongue and all the ways she had reprimanded and infuriated him. Why should that make him smile? She had shown him grace and very pretty behaviour, too, but oh, that pride of hers! Oh, that stubbornness that had the exact opposite affect on him than she no doubt intended! But when she smiled and when she sat in concentration at her work and when she looked at her mother, there was a calmness to her, a sense of purpose and beauty that was irresistible.

Irresistible…he sighed and suddenly he knew. He had, from the very beginning, been resisting her and what she made him think, and feel, and want. And when it came to Miss Holly Tournier, in every encounter — disastrous or unexpectedly pleasing — he wanted more than he could have. He wanted to go further than he told himself he could or should go. He wanted more of *her*. The truth, the most curious truth of all, now stared him boldly in the face; he wondered how he had never come to see it before. Standing in his London study, staring into the fire and thinking over his many failures, his heart burst and revealed itself to him — too late.

"So what am I to do?" he sighed aloud. "I must love her. I can do nothing else. I *must*." Hearing the words hang in the air made them real, and as if to punish himself he repeated them. "I do love her, and I have wronged and degraded her, and then practically handed her over to another man — a man who is *not* a damn fool! But, it is nothing more than I deserve. And after all, what indication is there that I would not have added injury to insult if I had done anything else than finally left her alone…just as she wanted." He slid down in his chair in front of the hearth, clutching the bottle in his hand and thanking whichever providential power that had not forsaken him, that it was nearly full.

MCKENNA STOOD LOOKING OUT THE window of his room at the bustling scene below. He resisted the urge to go downstairs as he had already said goodbye to the ladies the night before. There was no reason; he was in no such standing with them to warrant another leave taking at the moment of departure.

He clenched his fists open and closed, watching the scattered leaves blowing down the lane in the cold wind and Miss Tournier bracing herself against it as their effects were stowed and secured. He could not tear his eyes from her — the girl that had bewitched him so quickly and so innocently from the first moment of their acquaintance. A chuckle escaped him as he remembered that party at Rosefarm — Sir John's pyrotechnics in the kitchen, the jig she and her cousin had danced so unaffectedly and

326

joyously, the lovesick suitor she kept trying to avoid. *What was it about her?* Was it the way she was so...well, sensual was the only word he could use to describe her. The way she would always turn her face toward the warmth of the sun or the movement of the wind. How she would stop everything right away when she got hungry, and then, when he would work her too long, how she would stretch like a cat and declare she must stop and get some rest. How — with her French father, English mother and Scottish upbringing — she had this unusual way of pronouncing certain words that was quite endearing. This girl...

This girl that probably had feelings for another man.

He was not a stupid man, and he had seen enough to know that there was something between his lordship and Miss Tournier — but not enough to know what that something was. And she was, in effect, going to him right now. In fairness to all concerned, whatever feelings were there must be resolved before he could take any sort of action, but he fervently hoped that Lord Baugham would continue his indecisive ways. He had too much at stake to expect it, and he did not think that any man could be so blind indefinitely, so he tried to prepare himself for whatever might come. However, if his lordship should still chose to do nothing, once Miss Tournier returned to Scotland he would know what to do.

His eyes rested on her as she beckoned to her mother who had been waiting inside out of the cold. She was smiling, but her eyes were distant and a little sad.

She is unhappy, he thought as he watched the door to the carriage close and the vehicle begin to move away. But there was nothing he could do for her right now — maybe later, but not now. He prayed that he would get that chance.

Chapter 30

There is a Party Gathered for a Wedding in a Small Village in Hertfordshire

THE coach creaked and rocked as it travelled on the last leg of the journey from Clanough to Hertfordshire, but in a pleasant change of circumstance, Mrs and Miss Tournier were now the sole passengers. Though it was mid-afternoon, the light coming in from the windows grew increasingly dim and Holly looked across to see her mother squinting at her book. She smiled faintly and reached out her hand to rest on the pages.

"It is beginning to rain outside, Maman. You should give your eyes a rest."

Mrs Tournier closed the book and turned her attention to her daughter, who was once again, as she had been for the majority of the three days previous, staring out the window at the passing scenery.

"It's a bit hard to believe that we are going back to Hertfordshire again," she said thoughtfully. "So much has changed since that day I dropt you at your Aunt and Uncle Bennet's for the summer. I was afraid you would never forgive me for leaving you...and then when I came to get you at the end of the summer, I was afraid you would never forgive me for taking you away."

Holly smiled, but her mother talked on.

"And now, Elizabeth, that little slip of a girl, is going to be married, and Jane too," she mused, almost to herself. "So many years have passed, so much of good and of bad has happened, and now you girls are all grown and will be leaving your child-hood homes behind."

"I do not want to leave Rosefarm, Maman, not after I am back at last."

"That may be so, but you will. It must, it ought to happen sooner or later, and I rather get the feeling that it will be sooner. And I will be painfully blunt and tell you

328

I will not have you using me or my feelings as an excuse not to."

She directed a glance at her daughter who sighed but said nothing, settling back into the shadows of her seat so her face was not discernable.

"Besides, I find myself looking forward to being a grandmother, especially if my grandchildren are close by. Say...in Edinburgh?"

"Maman!"

"I am merely stating a fact."

"There is no such thing as a 'fact' about it, Maman!"

But Holly's indignation had to surrender in the face of her mother's arched eyebrow and her own need to finally share the thoughts that had been plaguing her by running through her mind and leaving her no peace since they had left home.

"Oh well, perhaps," Holly sighed. "Perhaps there is an...opportunity for it. And perhaps that is just what I ought to do."

"What you *ought* to do? Yes, and one ought to get a bad tooth pulled when it is necessary too, but I would expect a little more enthusiasm from you when discussing your choice of husband. Holly," she leaned forward earnestly, "it is obvious to anyone who cares to see — and I do care to see — that Dr McKenna only wants a little encouragement from you to declare himself and offer marriage. That is a fact, but — and I am surprised at you for making me feel the necessity to add — do not by any means contemplate giving that encouragement unless you are absolutely certain it is what you want. Both for you and for him."

"I don't know why would I not want to marry a handsome, kind, and respectable man and have a home and family of my own," Holly said almost irritated at the way her mother's ignorance of *all* her thoughts made her treat such a matter as so simple. "I would be a fool to turn my back on the opportunity. It would be a privilege to be the wife of such a man and I would certainly be very lucky!"

"That is true, Lie-lie, however, I am not blind and I am not a simpleton and I rather take offence at being treated as such. Besides regard and respect for the doctor, I also see unhappiness in you and I would do anything in my power to steer you away from that."

Holly leaned her head back in frustration, but managed to send her mother a desperate look.

"You are a grown woman," her mother continued, "and you can make your own decisions, and I am more than happy to respect those decisions provided they are made sensibly — and if you think I am advocating sense over sensibility you are even more of a fool than I thought. Still, I want for you to be happy and sometimes in order to be so you must stop looking for things in persons that — "

"I am not looking for things in anyone," Holly interrupted, "Not any longer..." She broke off abruptly and then went on in a more subdued voice, "But you are right and that is what I'm trying to do. I really am, Maman. It is time to open my eyes to what is around me, time to accept reality. I think, perhaps, I can be content in a life of quiet comfort with a man I esteem and respect and that is what I want. Hoping

329

for more is just — well — it's just a foolish waste of time and will make me miserable. As you say — impossible."

She dropped her eyes to her lap, but looked up a moment later.

"A good man can be like the gentle rain, can he not, Maman, rather than a thunderbolt?" Her question was almost a plea. "One can be happy with kindness and caring and intelligence; it can be no sacrifice to become a wife to such a man and give him a happy life. And what is so appealing about lightning and thunder, after all? The rain can be enough; no flash, no noise, no surprises…just comfort…there is nothing wrong with the rain…"

Mrs Tournier shook her head, a feeling of sorrow swept over her in hearing the resignation and dullness in her daughter's words. With every word she uttered her suspicions about the state of her daughter's heart were confirmed and it made her sad beyond words and at a loss over how to counsel her. Hoping for more might well be fruitless, but settling for less could have unhappy consequences for more than just her. In her heart she feared the joyous family occasion of a wedding would turn out a heavy and disappointing business indeed.

"No, Lie-lie, there is nothing wrong with the rain, if that is the life you choose and if it suits well with your nature. I hope I have taught you that being honest with yourself is the best way to achieve happiness. It may look like rain now but the weather changes. For everyone."

Closing her eyes and leaning back into the seat, Holly had to choke back a sob.

"Oh, Maman, what does it matter? What does honesty help? Or preferences, when one's choices are made for them?"

The carriage was quiet, except for the creaking of the springs and the periodic squeak of the turning wheels, for a long time. Mrs Tournier waited for Holly to go on; Holly wished she could take back every word she had just uttered.

"Dear," her mother said, "all I am saying is that safety and comfort are important considerations when the alternatives are uncertainty and a broken heart, there is no doubt, and not to be lightly dismissed. Life very rarely turns out to be what you think it will, seen through the hazy perspective coloured by strong emotion. You and I know that, don't we? But don't ever think I am advocating shutting out your heart and disregarding your happiness as well as your security, before you make any decision. That is what is meant by 'knowing thyself'. This what the road to hell looks likes when you set out with your good intentions and even though your goal is to make everyone happy you may very well end up failing miserably on everyone's account."

It had been a long day and a tiring journey, the gloomy weather combined with the waning season brought an early and profound darkness and suddenly Holly was very tired.

"But Maman, what if I decide to hold out for what I really want and it never comes? What if I see hope and I have no other proof than my heart and my faith? What if I am wrong and I lose everything?"

IT HAD BEEN A VERY long time since he had cause to deal with the unpleasant after effects of a night of excessive drink, but even in his unhappy condition, Baugham counted it as a blessing to be preoccupied with the state of his head and stomach rather than with the newly discovered, and infinitely more wretched, state of his heart. The journey from London to Netherfield was passed wallowing in intense and self-inflicted misery; the subsequent journey some time later from Netherfield to Longbourn was passed swallowing a sudden, irrational panic.

A quick glance around the small parlour told him what he already knew — they had not yet arrived. Of course they had not yet arrived; he shook his head at his own stupidity even as he let out the breath he had been holding. There was no possibility they would come until tomorrow at least. He had time. By the time he was faced with her again, he would be in control of himself.

That quest would have to wait, because the small parlour was in danger of growing even smaller with Mrs Bennet's advancing verbal onslaught once the gentlemen's entrance was noticed. Predictably, and not from a sense of spatial charity either, Darcy instantly moved to Miss Elizabeth's side as soon as the introductions had been performed, and although he spoke little, it was evident that he was not going to let anything as mundane as an old friend distract him. Bingley lasted a little longer and for several minutes chatted amiably with his lordship and future mother-in-law, but after Miss Bennet had sent about half a dozen warm looks his way, his concentration faltered and he started to make plans for claiming a seat closer to her, instantly losing all ability to carry a conversation.

Unfortunately, conversation in the Longbourn parlour was anything but wanting as Mrs Bennet then turned her attention from her sons-in-law to her guest.

"My dear Lord Baugham," she gushed, "how good of you to come to celebrate with us. Weddings are such festive occasions, do you not agree? And we have certainly not had a shortage of them in our family."

"Yes, I imagine you are quite — " he began, but before he could continue, his head was shot through with a sharp, stabbing pain by the piercing voice of his hostess.

"Mary! Kitty! Come here!" Mrs Bennet then turned to him with a most genteel smile, "My lord, may I introduce my other, *remaining*, daughters?"

If his lordship's poor head was pained by the shrill call, or if his smile tightened slightly as the summoned daughters came forth, he was able to keep it from the notice of his hostess and soon he was flanked by the younger Miss Bennets. Miss Mary was handsome enough, if she would just smile, he thought. She was obviously studious, as she had been immersed in a book before her mother called and she came forward with the volume still clutched in her arms, but Baugham could not help but consider that her cousin, Miss Tournier, could well counsel her that a young woman could be educated and thoughtful while still maintaining an air of liveliness and spark.

However, with the next introduction, it was obvious that Mrs Bennet had singled this daughter out for his particular attention. He suppressed a groan as he smiled woodenly and agreed that she was, indeed, nearly the prettiest of all her daughters and how fortunate it was that Mr Darcy and Mr Bingley had not met her first of all the sisters. Privately, his thoughts took a different turn; Miss Catherine Bennet was a pretty thing, but she was hardly more than a girl! She scarcely had any business being "out" of the schoolroom at all, much less to be pushed forward as an object of interest to a gentleman such as himself. His indigestion growing worse by the moment, he turned to Darcy in search of rescue from the attentions of the zealous mother and smiling daughter, but his friend was apparently engrossed in some aspect of Miss Elizabeth's countenance. No help would be forthcoming from that quarter.

Miss Kitty smiled and simpered in all the appropriate places and, prompted by her mother, stayed close to his side. Baugham politely inquired after her studies, which, he found to his surprise, were nonexistent, but he valiantly kept up a stream of small talk. Of course, the obvious topic of conversation was the upcoming dual wedding, though she declared she was heartily sick of the entire affair and would be happy when the whole thing was over with. The only consolation for having to endure such trials was her new gown, but what a lovely gown it was, pink, just the right colour for her as everyone says, and trimmed in the prettiest...

"Miss Catherine," he smiled in as brotherly as fashion as an only child could muster and patted her arm, "I trust you will forgive the interruption if I release you to find company more interesting than my own. I simply must go greet your sister properly. You run along now and enjoy yourself."

Kitty sent him a look that he did not take time to decipher, he just mumbled as she stomped off, "There's a good girl..." before turning to capture the attentions of Darcy's beloved away from him.

"Miss Bennet!"

"My lord!" She clasped his hand warmly as he finished kissing hers. Her eyes sparkled with what he supposed was happiness and love or certainly confidence in being loved and giving happiness, because Darcy still had not deviated from her side and was still looking rather more at her than at anything else going on around them. "I hope you come with good news!" she said.

"Oh yes!" Baugham smiled. "I have it on very good authority — your aunt's in fact — that the Rosefarm party will be joining you here very soon. I think tomorrow, in fact."

"Oh splendid!" Miss Elizabeth said and smiled at him. "I cannot tell you how happy that makes me. I so wanted my cousin and my aunt to be here for the wedding and now they will be!"

"You absolutely do not need to tell me that, it is perfectly obvious from your countenance. Furthermore, you must believe me to be in earnest when I confess to you I could not have withstood disappointing both you and Darcy and — I must admit — myself in failing to see to it that your wish was fulfilled."

"Wish?" said Darcy, and belying the dryness of his tone by sending his betrothed an openly adoring gaze. "Demand was more like it..."

332

THE INTERIOR OF THE CARRIAGE was completely dark and no words had been exchanged for at least an hour, though neither passenger had succumbed to boredom and monotony by falling asleep. Each woman was acutely aware that the other was across from her, awake and alert, and waiting, and when the silence was finally breached, it was almost comical that, after so many weeks of reticence, both parties spoke almost at once. Quiet words floated across the darkness and met in the middle.

"Holly, I wish you would speak to me — "

"Maman, I have not been honest with you — "

Mrs Tournier heard the bleak despair in her daughter's voice and she moved to her side and took her hand.

"My darling girl," she said, ignoring for the moment the words and concentrating on the feelings. "What do you mean? Don't you know you can tell me anything?"

Of course, in the face of such motherly compassion Holly's resolve broke down and for a few moments could only weep in her mother's arms. After so many weeks of holding back, of pretending that everything was as it should be, the release was welcome indeed.

"I lied to you. That night when you asked me if I was upset, if something was wrong…I said no…but there is. There *is* something wrong and I *am* very upset."

Mrs Tournier sighed and turned her daughter's face towards her.

"Ah, well, my dear, but what could be so wrong, Lie-lie? What has happened that you felt it necessary to lie about it to me?"

"I did not tell you because I was unsure of your reaction. Indeed, I am still not sure what I wish your reaction to be."

Holly trained her eyes on the blackness across from her and began.

"A few weeks ago, the day after the Martinmas Fair when his lordship came for tea…do you remember he left quite abruptly? Well, it was not for the reason I gave you…He left because I was upset and confused…you had sent him out to find me, and we quarrelled, and then…quite suddenly…" she turned her eyes to meet her mother's, "Maman, Lord Baugham kissed me."

She dropped her eyes again and waited for the result of her admission.

It was seldom Mrs Tournier confessed to such a thing, but at this moment she had no choice but to admit that she was at a loss for words.

"Well!" she finally said in honest astonishment and still had take another moment to bring order to her thoughts. Despite everything, despite her pride in her observation and intelligence she had not thought she would be faced with a confession such as this!

"My dear," she went on in what she hoped was a calm voice that would inspire rational explanation and that would settle her beliefs and perceptions of the state of things as well, "why do you suppose he did that? What else happened?"

"He would not say why…" Holly murmured, her head still down, "only that he was sorry…mortified…it was a terrible mistake…it would never happen again…Nothing else happened — he begged my forgiveness, I gave it. He left, I returned to you."

Mrs Tournier narrowed her eyes and struggled to understand.

"Child," she said in an earnest voice, "tell me the truth, did he force himself on you and did you reject him?"

Holly's voice grew very quiet as she struggled to control her breathing.

"No, he did not. That is, he did not ask my permission, but...I did not even have time to reject him before he was apologizing. It was not at all like that...I am not fearful around Lord Baugham, just confused."

"Dear," her mother went on just as quietly, "you do not have to answer this, but I must ask for I do think I am beginning to understand and I don't mind telling you it is most upsetting. Do you regret the act or the circumstance?"

Holly leaned on her mother's shoulder, silent tears falling freely. "Maman, would you understand if I answered both yes, and no?"

Mrs Tournier sighed and kissed her daughter's hair while she gently wiped away her tears.

"Yes, I would," she said. "It makes my heart ache for you, but I certainly would. And he?"

Holly shook her head and could barely utter the words through her tears. "I don't know," she whispered. "But I think... I felt... I saw..." But that was all she could say.

They sat quietly for a while. Mrs Tournier had a fair inkling of what was going through her daughter's heart even if her mind was muddled, but added to this a revelation of a most serious kind had left her own mind and convictions in turmoil. Suddenly behaviours she had tolerated and merely thought foolish took on a new meaning and she found herself trying to understand aspects of her friend she had never thought were any of her concern. She had seen enough with her own eyes to fit in some pieces of the puzzle and to readily acknowledge his lordship's own troubles. Funnily enough, this understanding of his personality and appreciation for his character only brought on a fresh wave of sadness and frustration. What had he done? What did he think he was doing? How on earth did he think he could get away with it? Did he not realise there were two- Nay! Three. Nay! *Four* hearts involved in this blind and foolish game of his?

Conflicting feeling raged within her maternal heart. The burden of a meeting in Hertfordshire with her daughter's feelings what they now obviously were, battled with the burning longing to physically slap that infuriating man into sense or even responsibility! Her palm itched with the desire as she could not curse him out loud. And then, out of the very core of her understanding and affection, not to mention her own sad experiences, crept a melancholy sort of tune that took over her heart strings and made her reflect that in truth, not even a mother's crusade against anyone out to wrong her child could ignore that more needed to be protected and championed than Holly's heart. Life had left wounds and scars on more than one young person dear to her, and in truth, she had no inkling if true healing was even possible for either — much less for both together. So in silence she contemplated her choices while she absentmindedly caressed the hand she still held in hers.

Finally Holly lifted her head, sniffed loudly and took the already soggy handkerchief out of her mother's hand to blow her nose and compose herself.

"So," Mrs Tournier said and clasped her hands in her lap, "you are going to make up your mind about … this?"

Holly dried her eyes and squared her shoulders,

"Yes, I think I have to. It is time to put that foolishness behind me. I know what I need to do.

"And are you going to give yourself to Dr McKenna, a gentle, quiet and respectable man, in an attempt to forget Lord Baugham?"

"No Maman," Holly quietly answered. "Not to forget. To accept."

Mrs Tournier's jaw clenched and a strong, stiff feeling crept up her spine as she watched and listened to her child grasping for action that would quell her confused feelings in a desperate gamble that she could heal her heart by burying her hopes.

Holly repeated herself a moment later without realising her mother had formed her own resolutions in the meantime. "To accept, Maman. Some things just cannot be."

THE FOLLOWING DAY, MRS ARABELLA TOURNIER looked around the entrance hall of her childhood home. She had not seen it, except briefly, for twenty odd years and she found that her mental picture of it matched reality perfectly. Nothing had changed. Well no, something had changed. She could not quite put her finger on it so she took in the walls and the floor and the furnishings as she slowly shed her garments.

Her brother stood watching her and her sister nervously fiddled with a piece of cloth between her fingers that Mrs Tournier assumed was a handkerchief. It was obvious that Mrs Bennet had not quite yet decided whether she was too nervous of her sister to speak or too nervous to keep silent.

Behind her, Mrs Tournier's nieces were lined up: Jane, Elizabeth — casting merry looks at her and her cousin beside her mother, obviously impatient to have this ceremony over and done with — Mary and Catherine.

"Sister," Mr Bennet finally said and kissed her cheek. His wife fluttered nervously when she realised some kind of greeting was expected.

"Brother," Mrs Tournier said calmly and looked expectantly at her sister.

"Oh," said Mrs Bennet, "I most sincerely hope your journey was comfortable. Mr Darcy arranged it all, you know, and he is the most particular man, I find."

"Quite," Mrs Tournier said and let her eyes wander to her niece Elizabeth. She received a gentle kiss on the cheek by her oldest niece and a full fledged hug from Elizabeth while her younger nieces obviously felt a curtsey was as close to their Aunt Arabella as they ever wished or dared to be.

As Holly received an even warmer welcome and even a few shrieks and a bit of girlish chatter, Mrs Tournier let her eyes scan the room once more.

"New wallpaper," Mrs Bennet instantly volunteered.

"Really?" Mrs Tournier answered.

"How was your journey," her brother asked as Mrs Hill departed with the last of the traveller's effects.

"Excruciating," his sister answered dryly.

"Well then," Mr Bennet said and showed his sister the way to his library and then closed the door firmly behind them.

LORD BAUGHAM TRANSFERRED HIS GAZE from the open fireplace back to his opened book. As he did so, he spotted Miss Caroline Bingley wagging her slippered foot up and down and glancing at him. Lord Baugham sighed. During the time they had already spent together in the same house he had come to know Miss Bingley fairly well and from all he had been forced to learn about her, that gesture meant she was planning some course of action to break the silence of the evening that most assuredly would include him. To be perfectly honest, his lordship thought to himself, it was impossible to tell whether he feared or welcomed such an interruption as an alternative to blankly staring at the pages in his book.

The other gentlemen were there as well, but they were not of very much help with Miss Bingley. Mr Bingley did give his sister smiles at her attempts at conversation, but when asked for an opinion, he started in his chair as if woken from a deep reverie and stutteringly admitted he was somewhat at a loss over the details of what was being discussed. Darcy did not even keep up pretence of attending to his surroundings. He steadfastly sat with his book on his knee and his gaze never wavered from its pages. However, as Baugham was quite certain Francis Bacon never wrote anything humorous on purpose, and Darcy never previously had found him unintentionally ridiculous, the slight tugging at the corners of his mouth that he displayed every once in a while and the twinkle in his eye very much gave him away.

The reason for Bingley's and Darcy's enforced stay at their own house was not out of a feeling of too much familiarity with the Bennet family being imminent, but rather that more visitors were expected at Longbourn — all the way from Scotland. He had expected Bingley and Darcy to be half finished with breakfast when he came down that morning and busily discussing how large a portion of the day could be spent either at Longbourn or in the vicinity of Longbourn, and in the company of certain young ladies in residence. But no. Out of consideration for the weary travellers and family reunions, the Netherfield party had sacrificed a day of courting.

Baugham sighed again.

To be perfectly frank, the expectation of the Tournier women joining the wedding party and the impending prospect of talking with and seeing them once again, clearly overshadowed any expectations of enjoyment he held for witnessing the ceremony between his friends and their respective brides. That would be quickly enough accomplished and no great rituals or lavish arrangements were expected, and after that was over, he would certainly waste no more time in Hertfordshire. Seldom had his long overdue business up at his estate seemed like a better alternative to staying were he was. But before that…yes, before that…

Oh, he could not help it. It *would* be good to see her; he pondered the upcoming meeting with equal parts anticipation and dread and he was anxious to get on with it rather than continue to wait around in uncertainty. He was not so much concerned with her reaction and feelings as he was with his own. A selfish thing to confess, to be sure, but even so, all his energies must of course be spent to assure that he did not betray himself or act irrationally. However skilled he was at hiding his true feelings and true self from the world, a practice he had been perfecting since he was a boy, this was truly uncharted ground.

Yet, if the prospect of seeing her, here among her family, under the guise of a wedding, was confusing to his resolve and temper, seeing both of them would remind him of better days, of a calmer existence, of a truer self — someone he liked better than what he was in other company. Of course, he must start by apologising and putting right the rather strained way they had parted. But as he did so — and he had no doubts he would be forgiven — perhaps they could talk and be as they had been. And then… Still avoiding Miss Bingley's eye, Baugham smiled at his page. Would anything have changed in removing south, he wondered? Would it be easier and would he be spared this restlessness? Whatever the case, it would be very good to see her again. *And* her mother, too.

Right then a languid voice interrupted his thoughts.

"I have always thought," Miss Bingley said right above his shoulder, "that the charm of the country lies in the contrast it offers to Town. Just as you can find something soothing in old buildings despite their discomfort, draughtiness, dullness and impractibility."

Baugham looked up and noticed Mr Bingley ducking his head to avoid his or his sister's gaze.

"You're not fond of the country, Miss Bingley?"

She gave a little laugh. "Oh, Lord Baugham. 'Fond' I certainly am. As long as there is always the reliability of the season that will allow me to quit it in time."

In one long, graceful movement she descended on the other end of the sofa and placed her arm to decoratively rest along the back of it.

"Am I to understand you share my attitude? I have heard you are very fond of your country estate — as long as it does not interfere with your London pleasures."

Baugham frowned. Was this woman hinting at his past troubles and his flight to Clyne? But no, how could she know. She was not an intimate of his, regardless of her insinuations and he had never come across her as part of polite society in Town. As for Clyne and his reasons for taking up residence there… Well, presumably there had been gossip, but that had died down long ago and no one cared about that anymore.

"Scotland," Miss Bingley prompted with a small smile. "What on earth did you find so enticing in *Scotland*?"

"The same you found in Town, I suppose," Baugham smiled back. "Novelty."

Miss Bingley looked down on her string of pearls and managed to look both amused and offended.

"But," Baugham amended, "even if that was what lured me there, novelty was never what kept me coming back."

"Are you a romantic, my lord? An avid admirer of scenery? A finder of truth in nature?"

That Miss Bingley could have come so close to reading his heart and yet been so mistaken at the same time amused him.

"Truth," he mused. "Yes, I think that is exactly it, Miss Bingley. I did find the truth and as we both know, that is one thing neither one of us will ever find in London."

"Sit ye down, Rose, and rest yer feet."

Mrs McLaughlin abandoned the dust covers she was spreading out over the furniture and sunk down into the soft chair upon her cousin's arrival. Mrs Higgins threw her a quick look and followed her example, putting her feet up on the fender in front of the small and economical fire as well. She lifted the small glass Mrs McLaughlin had given her and sniffed.

"Elderberry?"

"Aye. I made fifteen bottles of it and now there's no one here to drink it."

"Well, the ladies will be back after the wedding…"

"Ye're right, Rose, I'll pack a few bottles in yer basket afore ye leave. This is dusty work."

The women sampled Mrs McLaughin's homemade potion and licked their lips in silent appreciation.

"Och," Mrs McLaughlin finally said, "an empty house again…"

"But he stayed longer this time than usual, dinnae he?"

"Aye, that he did. I was thinking he'd never be gone."

She had meant it to be a dry comment indicating she treasured her reclaimed peace and quiet, but Mrs Higgins knew it was the confession of a hope that his lordship would have stayed even longer.

"And when will he come again?" she asked.

Mrs McLaughlin shrugged. "No one knows. Mebbe when the salmon fishing starts."

The women sighed in unison.

"I'll tell ye something, Rosie," Mrs McLaughlin said, "and I dinnae mind if ye think I'm daft but I did think… Well, I thought the reason he stayed so long was mebbe… I mean, he always liked his stay here, I know he did. It is a shelter for him, he says, a sanctuary that he treasures and even when he does leave he is already looking forward to coming again, even if he doesnae know when that'll be. But this time, with him staying so long an all, I thought that mebbe there was some new… attraction that kept his interest. Ye'll think I'm daft, I'm sure."

"No-oo Heather," her cousin said, "I'll match yer confession and own up I… well, I know that it is presumptuous of me, but one does hear things, and see things, and sense things, even if they do go on in a respectable parlour under the eyes of a chaperone like Mrs Tournier…"

"Well, Mrs Campbell was wrong then," Mrs McLaughlin said. "Although…"

"Yes," sighed her cousin and looked into the fire.

For a while they each contemplated the if's and delicious consequences of what the realisation of their fancies would have brought, but since there was nothing to be done about that and plenty to be done about his lordship's drawing room, they soon abandoned their empty glasses and set about rolling the carpets aside and covering the ornate candle holders on the walls to shut all the rooms of Clyne Cottage except the library.

Chapter 31

The Days that Led up to the Big Event

THE parlour was filled with women, all sitting in a circle and busily sewing. In the middle of the night, Mrs Bennet had been struck with the sudden realisation that she had not ordered nearly enough handkerchiefs for Mrs Bingley and Mrs Darcy to begin their married lives with, so every available seamstress was recruited to remedy the oversight. Arabella Tournier plied her needle alongside the rest and watched as her daughter valiantly tried to keep pace with her more skilled cousins. She saw, too, how Holly's smiles looked slightly strained, and how, as thrilled as she obviously was with her cousins' good fortune, there was a dullness about her that she did not like — as well as a question that hung, unasked, in the air. She decided to take the initiative in the one area she could.

"So, Sister," she turned to her brother's wife, "Has his lordship arrived in Hertfordshire yet?"

At one and the same time, her sister's exclamations and her daughter's cries filled the room.

"My dear sister, how kind of you to ask...!"

"Ouch! Oh, it's nothing, just a prick. I'm so clumsy..."

Holly was tended to by her solicitous cousins who wrapped her finger and declared that she would be excused from any further needlework if she would instead consent to read to them while they worked, but not before Elizabeth looked up to meet her aunt's eye. The young woman's questioning gaze was met by the older woman's wiser one and Elizabeth returned to her work with the belief that perhaps her cousin was suffering from another sting as well. Mrs Bennet's effusions were not so readily dealt with.

"Oh yes, indeed he has and he graced us with his presence the moment he arrived. Who would have thought I would be entertaining an Earl in this very parlour…"

She abandoned her smug face for a moment and leaned forward in confidence.

"He is an odd man, as far as I can tell, a nervous, restless sort and I could not interest him in my poor Kitty, though she did try her best. Snubbed her is what he did."

"It is no matter, Mama," Kitty replied, "he talks too much anyway."

Elizabeth, who had sent her cousin a searching look, but been assured by a quick shake of Holly's head that she was fine and it was nothing to remark upon, noticed her aunt still watching her daughter with narrowed eyes.

"I think you must take great care, Kitty," she said in an attempt to steer the attention away from Holly and let her surprising clumsiness be forgotten. "I distinctly remember sitting in this very parlour and comforting Mama with the promise of never dancing with Mr Darcy when he had been so unforgivably rude to me at the Assembly Rooms last Michaelmas. And now it seems I am expected to dance with him at every event we ever find ourselves at together again," she finished with a dramatic sigh.

Kitty looked at her sister and scrunched her face in disbelief, but Mrs Bennet put down her work and looked at Elizabeth.

"Yes, yes… That is very true, I suppose…" she said, a mercenary hope kindling in her eye. "I remember it distinctly. Kitty, you know there may still be…"

"*The Lady of the Lake?*" Holly said quickly and picked up a book from the side table.

"Oh yes, please!" her cousin said, instantly regretting that she planted such a thought in her mother's fertile imagination.

"Perhaps if he could be persuaded to come and dine and even a little dancing afterwards," Mrs Bennet persisted and turned to Kitty. "And you must wear your blue gown — "

"*Harp of the North!*" Holly suddenly exclaimed, a little more loudly than necessary. Elizabeth's eyebrows shot up and Mrs Bennet gave a start in her chair and lost her train of thought. Mrs Tournier's lips tightened and she turned her attention to the lace in front of her while Holly lay the book on her lap and continued in a more subdued tone. "*That mouldering long hast hung, On the witch-elm that shades Saint Fillan's spring, And down the fitful breeze thy numbers flung…*"

As Holly drew her breath at the end of the tenth stanza, Mrs Bennet had already grown tired of verse and seized the opportunity to return to her favourite subject.

"As to your kind inquiry, Sister, perhaps I should add that the gentlemen have been here every day. Except yesterday, unfortunately, because… well, I'm glad you are settled in now and I dare say they will come running again as soon as they've… well, done whatever it is gentlemen —*fine* gentlemen — do in the mornings before going visiting."

Mrs Tournier gave her daughter a look. "How about some more of those '*wondrous scenes*', Lie-lie?

Holly quickly picked up again, but she had not been reading for long before Mrs Hill announced the arrival of the gentlemen from Netherfield. All pedestrian sewing was hastily put away and replaced with delicate embroidery, a move performed with the deftness and skill that could only come from much practice. The gentlemen entered, the ladies rose in greeting, introductions were made, bows and curtseys were exchanged and Holly paled a little at the sight of Lord Baugham among them.

Thankfully...? yes she decided, thankfully, she was spared the necessity of speaking to him right away, because once he had politely extricated himself from his gushing hostess, he strode directly to Mrs Tournier and greeted her enthusiastically.

She watched their exchange out of the corner of her eye. To her dismay, her mother was short in her tone and her facial expression showed none of the regard she knew she held for him. *Oh no,* Holly thought, *she is going to tell him. She is going to let him know she knows... Oh, I should not have said anything.* Her thoughts were muddled and she turned away from the scene in an effort not to see, not to hear.

She could have cried with relief when Mr Darcy approached and smilingly sat in a nearby chair. They talked amiably and as Elizabeth came up to his side, his whole being lit up and the smile, which had seemed almost apologetic and sheepish earlier, turned into a definite satisfied grin.

Had Holly not turned away from her mother and Lord Baugham's exchanged greetings, she would, perhaps, have been comforted to know that not even her mother's staunch resolution to give his lordship a piece of her mind could override what she knew was expected of her in her sister's salon.

Thus she restricted her words to an absolute minimum and very soon gave him to understand she was very eager to greet Mr Darcy and become acquainted with Mr Bingley rather than enter into any extended conversation.

The affianced couples having gradually separated themselves slightly from the group, Mrs Tournier purposefully moved over to Mr Darcy and Elizabeth's side. Mrs Bennet was flitting around the parlour and trying to position Kitty to her best advantage and Holly again found herself somewhat at loose ends. She had no fine sewing to turn her attention to, as Mary had quickly done, and her reading could be no longer wanted, so she retreated to the fireplace and stood quietly, ostensibly admiring the screens. However, it was not long until she felt a presence behind her, and knowing exactly who it was, she turned to him.

"My lord."

"Miss Tournier."

Baugham found his puzzlement over Mrs Tournier's reticence was forgotten as soon as her daughter spoke to him. He pasted a smile on his face and set about his task. He would act as if everything was as it had always been between them — and that called for playful insult and flattery.

"What are you doing here, skulking alone by the fireplace?"

His voice was warm and soft. Despite herself she felt her stomach flutter and she involuntarily blushed and looked away.

"Sir," she said, squaring her shoulders and gazing out over the room, "I absolutely never skulk."

"Of course you don't. Perhaps you are just prudently waiting for me here so I can tell you how much I have missed your company."

"Is London really so dull, my lord?"

"Frightfully. No one has scolded or abused me for an entire week. Just look at Darcy! I held high hopes for him to perform when I finally arrived at his doorstep, but all he can think about is his bride and for some reason his docility is quite frightening."

Holly smiled, but still did not meet his eye. "I think you don't miss my bad temper as much as you miss your library at Clyne. I am very happy to report it is coming along very well. So you have absolutely no excuse to pick a quarrel with me, however much you feel you need one."

"I'm glad to hear it. But what on earth shall we do with one another if there is no dispute to be had?"

"How about a stab at some civil conversation? I'm sure we can manage it if we try."

"Hm. And what if we grow unspeakably bored very soon? Will you abandon me to the tedious admiration of other people's blatant happiness straight away again?"

"No," Holly smiled, "I suppose I will just return to my skulking and leave you to fend for yourself, as you always do so well. But, have you truly grown tired of bearing witness to so much bliss?"

"Bliss is, in itself of course, all good and well, but it does not make for very exciting conversation. So you see, I have missed you."

"Sir, that is the second time you profess such personal sentiments to me. Are you fishing for me to express reciprocal feelings?"

Baugham's smile faltered and he began to grow desperate as she met each of his attempts at humour with mere polite conversation. He struggled to keep the bitterness out of his voice when he replied. "Oh no. You may lie to me as much as you like."

Her eyes darted to his immediately. "Lie?" A wave of relief washed over him as he saw a familiar spark of defiance in her expression. "You mean you wish for me to tell you that for the past fortnight, life in Clanough has been just as dreary as life in Town has apparently been? I should flatter you that, without your presence, nothing whatsoever of interest could ever happen?"

"That would be a very good start, Miss Tournier. But would that be a lie?"

Once she finally met his eyes, it was hard to look away. He was very beautiful, she found herself thinking. Just as he was, bordering on impertinence, his blue eyes twinkling and his smile widening. It was a dangerous and foolish time and place to do so, but she so wanted to give in to the temptation to let go of the tight control she had held over herself for so long. Each word he spoke cut sharply, but she had to admit that she preferred the pain over the deadness of feeling she had been left with lately. She dropped her defences and strode bravely into the line of fire.

"I think I must leave that up to you to determine. Am I being truthful, or merely taking advantage of the liberties you have just offered me? What say you, my lord? Will you call me a liar?"

If it was possible, his smile grew even bigger, his eyes even more blue as he stepped closer. Leaning in, he said almost in a whisper: "Liar."

He was so close; it was hard to breathe, hard to think. One of them should move back, she thought, if he would not, then she ought to. They should maintain a proper space between them, but at the same time she had to fight the almost irresistible urge to close what little space was left between them and…what? Swallowing the silly lump that rose in her throat, she drew herself up with dignity and smiled shakily, teasing back as best she could.

"Sir! Is it really gentlemanly to rise to every bait that is laid before you, even when it is most imprudent?"

He was now impossibly close to her, his voice was soft, almost intimate. "Oh, Miss Tournier, I think we both know that as far as you are concerned, self-control is not an option."

As soon as he said it, he regretted it. He watched her staring in confusion for a moment; she moved forward, then blushed scarlet and turned quickly away, only managing to utter a confused, "Oh…" before suddenly bolting away. As he stood, kicking himself for going so far, for judging her and their meeting so falsely, for stupidly pushing what should have been a friendly greeting between acquaintances into flirtation and embarrassment, he could feel the eyes of Mrs Tournier boring into his back from across the room.

His sense of failure was complete, there was no denying it. He decided there and then to abandon all pretence of equilibrious relations with the Tournier family and tread very, very carefully instead.

Taking refuge the only way he could and inflicting suitable punishment on himself in the process, Lord Baugham hastily engaged Mrs Bennet in conversation. He was engaged in a long discussion on the trials of providing a house full of girls with an appropriate education, with the youngest Miss Bennet called upon by her mother to provide an example for his lordship of how well she had succeeded in preparing her daughters for *any* social sphere.

Thankfully, a first meeting cannot, in all politeness, be dragged out for the best part of the day, however much the hostess does not mind and the other guests would have it so, and so the gentlemen were forced to leave. Tomorrow they could come early and make a day of it.

Baugham, being faced with the prospect of freedom again, was all smiles and said everything that was right and proper in taking his leave. He looked across the room and tried to catch Miss Tournier's eye, but she appeared to be deep in conversation with her cousin, Miss Mary, and would not look up. The goodbyes between the engaged couples dragged out and he stood alone waiting for Mr Bingley to have the glove on his right hand buttoned carefully by his fiancée.

"My lord. A quiet word if you please."

Mrs Tournier's low voice made him give her a surprised look as he found her suddenly standing beside him.

"Certainly, madam! How may I be of assistance?"

"You can stop indulging yourself at the expense of others inferior and dependent upon you, and you can exercise a little good sense and honour for a change."

Her voice was still low, but it held an ice-cold tone that Baugham had never heard her use before. No sarcasm, no mocking — just pent up anger and barely controlled contempt.

"I'm sorry, madam," he said and looked at her, puzzled, "I really have no idea what — "

"Oh, I think you have a perfectly good idea. And should you be even more adept at self-delusion than I give you credit for, I suggest you find yourself a deep and comfortable chair at Netherfield tonight, where you can give that sharp mind of yours some well-deserved exercise and dwell on what you owe to yourself and to others."

Of course he knew to what she was alluding. What confused him was her turn of phrase. 'Self-delusion'? 'What he owed *himself*'?

He tried to catch her eye, but she was still looking out over the room, tea cup in hand and refused to give him the attention.

"My daughter, strange as it seems to some, and most probably due to the effects of a rootless existence as a child ending in disappointment, has a morbid appreciation for the truth in all its wretched form. It is what she wants and, through it, she can perhaps attain what she deserves."

"Yes," he said simply and sheepishly, "I should. I…I apologise…But…"

That was when, with a quick flick of her head, she looked at him. "I cannot quite decide whether you are a thoughtless coward or a lazy fool, but I *have* quite decided that neither my daughter nor I need put up with either any longer. Do I make myself clear?"

Even if she had not, Baugham felt he needed to escape the scorching heat of her disapproval. "Indeed, madam, crystal clear," he mumbled. As she replaced her cup on her saucer and prepared to walk away from him, he managed to send her a pleading look.

"Am I…am I too late?"

After letting him linger in his obvious shame and misery, Mrs Tournier let her fingers briefly brush over his sleeve in a corrective, but protective gesture. "You don't deserve to know that through me," she said and then he was left by the door to wait for Darcy and Bingley.

HOLLY LOOKED OUT INTO THE hall, where her mother and Lord Baugham were talking. She could tell, both by his lordship's sheepish demeanour as he put on his hat and gloves alone by the door, and her mother's severe face when she returned, that the one thing she dreaded had indeed taken place. She abandoned her place by the door and hastily made her way to her mother back in the parlour.

"What did you say to him, Maman?" she whispered sharply.

Mrs Tournier gave her daughter a calm look and emptied an extra spoon of sugar into her tea as a reward for a job long overdue and now well done.

"I told him to stop being such a presumptuous, blundering fool."

"Oh no!" Holly whined. "Oh please, Maman. Really. I told you it is all well. Over and done with."

Mrs Tournier gave her daughter a contemptuous look. "It is not well and it is not all over. He needed a slap to his head, and if you are incapable or unwilling to give it, it was necessary for me to do so. Let's hope he finally uses his sense and takes note of the foolery he's been indulging in, which is causing more misery than he is even aware of."

"I still wish you had not set him down here and now," Holly said quietly, unable to deny her mother's words. "It is of no great consequence. After all, after the wedding we will hardly see him again. Surely."

Her mother snorted, gave Holly a scornful look, and stalked off to enjoy her tea out of the presence of fools.

Mrs Bennet was an extremely happy woman. Had she been any happier she would have purred in her chair. Sir William Lucas might hold a knighthood and his daughter might regularly be on the receiving end of singular condescension in the drawing rooms of an Earl's daughter and a great lady, but for the second day in a row, Mrs Bennet had an Earl and a fine lord in her own parlour. *Her* own parlour! If she progressed in this thought and contemplated the fact that he was unmarried to boot, there would have been a real danger she might have swooned on the spot from excitement! Instead, she smiled benevolently at Lord Baugham again. As if his presence was not fortune enough, he was standing beside his friend, Mr Darcy — practically a lord himself! — who was betrothed to her dearest Lizzy! Mrs Bennet sighed once more in her happiness and felt her heart nearly burst at the seams.

On the sofa sat good, dear Lizzy, her other good, sweet daughter, Jane and her odd niece, Holly. The girls kept up the conversation, reminiscing about Elizabeth's recent Scotland trip, walking in the north and walking in the south and what was to be missed and what appreciated in the different corners of the Kingdom.

Suddenly Elizabeth clasped her cousin's hand and jumped up.

"Oh Holly!" she said. "The tree house! Do you remember the tree house?"

Her cousin laughed. "How can I forget? Is it still there?"

"Let's go and see!" Elizabeth pulled her out of her seat. "Let's go now!"

Mrs Bennet felt her contentment with the magnificent scene in front of her eyes threatened by her second eldest's appalling lack of judgment.

"Lizzy!" she said. "Really! With such fine visitors! You cannot be serious? You'll catch your death of cold! And only two days before your wedding? Do you want to be married with a red nose?"

Elizabeth still held on to her cousin's hand, but sent Lord Baugham a poignant look. It took a moment for his lordship to realise he was being appealed to.

"Oh!" he said and gave Mrs Bennet his most brilliant smile. "Really ma'am, far be it for me as a guest to come between Miss Elizabeth and her fondness for the outdoors in any manner of weather. In fact, I must say it sounds like a delightful scheme and I wholeheartedly embrace it."

"Holly?" Elizabeth said pleadingly. Her cousin laughed.

"Oh!" said Mrs Bennet grasping for straws. "Well! Ah! Mr Bingley...?"

"I should love to!" Mr Bingley said hastily and grabbed Jane's arm to pull her up from the sofa, too.

"A small stroll before dinner, Mama," Jane said and smiled at her mother.

"The way you keep your table, Mrs Bennet, I am sure we will need a vast deal of exercise in order to do it justice," her betrothed went on.

"Oh!" Mrs Bennet said, suddenly well pleased. "Of course! By all means!"

Kitty Bennet had left her sewing at the table and quickly got up when everyone else did.

"Mama…" she said. "Maria…"

"Yes, yes," her mother said impatiently.

The party gathered in the hall to don their outer clothing while Mrs Bennet could not let go of the thought that she was sending her daughters out to catch a dreadful cold and ruin the best day of her life in advance with worry. She fussed around them and whereas Jane let her tuck an extra scarf around her and send for a muff from Mrs Hill, Elizabeth ignored her and very quickly threw on her clothes.

"A tree house, you say? You, my dear, are entirely too sly for your own good," Mr Darcy told his bride-to-be as he ushered her out of the door.

"You, sir, do not know the half of it," Elizabeth smiled sweetly and cast a glance at her cousin as his lordship caught up with them.

Mr Bennet watched the brood of youngsters shuffle out of the parlour and listened to the noise grow fainter as they moved towards and out the door. His sister seemed to be oblivious to the commotion and only lifted her head when quiet once more returned to the room. Mrs Bennet could not hide her displeasure at being left with three people balancing reading material on their knees for companionship and she opened her mouth to complain.

"Did I tell you I acquired Mr Hume's first edition lately?" Mr Bennet intercepted her, addressing his sister while still looking down at his newspaper.

"I don't believe you did, no," Mrs Tournier said and turned the leaf of the letter she had been reading.

Wordlessly the two siblings rose and removed themselves to Mr Bennet's library. Mrs Bennet watched them as they moved past her chair.

"But dinner!" she exclaimed. "You mustn't forget! It's venison stew! And fish, too!" Her protestations died out and she threw a glance at the only remaining person beside herself in the room.

Mary Bennet straightened her back and returned her mother's look. "I think we must be thankful for what little reflective solitude is allotted us at such a time," she said. "The gravity and solemnity of the upcoming events, I fear, is in grave danger of being overshadowed and cheapened by all this merriment and superficial socialising, which can only result in…"

Mrs Bennet shuffled in her chair and sighed after silencing her daughter with an exasperated look.

"They will be back for dinner," she muttered a little sourly until she realised the thought, indeed, did give her some comfort in her now so empty parlour. "They will *all* be back for dinner."

IT WAS A LIVELY AND talkative group that made its way down the lanes — losing the youngest Miss Bennet on the way to her friend at Lucas Lodge — through the hedgerows, beyond the village, passing by the willows shadowing the little stream with their empty branches behind the green and through Farmer Wilson's pastures until they came to the woods and the remnants of the tree house.

Holly was still mortified that her confession had caused her mother to so thoroughly take Lord Baugham to task over his behaviour, and even though she had to admit to some measure of satisfaction in the knowledge that he was experiencing *some* suffering on that account, she could not help but feel sorry for him, especially on seeing how very carefully, even solicitously, he was now acting in her company.

Lord Baugham, meanwhile, found himself exceedingly thankful that the group had not paired off as he had feared it might. More often than not, Miss Tournier was helped over rough patches or steered around muddy spots by Mr Darcy or Mr Bingley, while he was called upon to render the same service to one or the other of the Miss Bennets. A good thing that, he reflected, since she tended to flinch as if burned whenever it fell to him to perform the duty and he could not in all honesty say he was completely reconciled to his exchange yesterday with Mrs Tournier. At the same time, his dissatisfaction with her refusal to answer his question caused a growing feeling of urgency to build within him. He could not spend so much time in her company and remain in doubt. Something had to happen. He had to do something.

At last they stood before the dilapidated structure and Lord Baugham's thoughts gave way again.

"It looks so small, Eliza. I remember it being so much bigger."

"Oh, it was Holly. Don't you remember? It was as big as the whole world!"

Holly smiled as she reached out to tug on the boards, still nailed crossways onto the trunk. "I remember. We could see all the way to America from up there, couldn't we? And Paris and India." After testing all the boards, she turned a sly look upon her cousin.

"No, no Holly! Don't you dare challenge me! I am practically a married woman, much too dignified and respectable for such antics."

"Well, one of us will have to do it, for old time's sake. And you have an able assistant, who I am certain would not object to raising you up a few feet if you are feeling faint of heart."

"Faint of heart! Very good, Holly! You do know just how to tempt me, but I am determined neither to undermine my dignity in the eyes of my betrothed, since it is as very fragile as it is, nor am I to be gauged so easily!"

But Elizabeth's smile could not be suppressed, nor the twinkle in her eye when she fixed her gaze on Holly and issued her own challenge.

"Go!"

A big grin spread across Holly's face, "I will!"

Before the squeals of disbelief could even properly issue forth from Elizabeth and Jane, or the exclamations to not be foolish and to take care could be uttered by the gentlemen, Holly had scrambled up the ladder and was standing on the platform. Elizabeth rushed up behind her and peered up through the branches, laughing.

Holly smiled as she shielded her eyes from the sun and exclaimed at the exotic sights that were still visible from the heights, but in reality, she felt a little sad inside — for really it was only treetops and nearby farms, and she wished she had not climbed up after all.

"Miss Tournier, please! You must come down now before you hurt yourself," a stern male voice commanded. She looked down and saw five pairs of eyes, in varying degrees of delight, concern and consternation looking back up at her, so she consented and allowed herself to be helped down by three pairs of hands. Feeling a bit ridiculous, she nevertheless said brightly, "Well. Now that that foolishness is over, shall we head back?"

The walk back saw the groupings revert to the more traditional pairings, with each couple moving along at its own pace, and Lord Baugham found himself accompanying Miss Tournier back to Longbourn. He could not forget the sight of her, eyes bright, scrambling up that ladder. He could have kicked Darcy in the shins for interfering in what so obviously was a treat for her although, of course, it was quite silly to be climbing up like that on the spur of the moment. Nevertheless, she had looked exhilarated and at no point had he seen any danger in the escapade.

"You must have some very fond memories of your childhood, Miss Tournier. You are very lucky in that."

She turned to him, with a slight frown. "A few, yes. Most of them shared with my cousin. And most of them better left to the past, it would seem."

"Not at all," Baugham said softly. "It was quite charming."

She said nothing, but an unwillingness to let an uncomfortable and possibly unbreakable silence descend upon them made him try again.

"You must be happy to be able to spend time with your cousin again, before the wedding. With both of them. And I suppose be able to talk. About things."

"It is nice. However, with the wedding rapidly approaching, I am understandably more often called upon by the brides to listen rather than talk." Holly looked back for those brides, and to her dismay, neither couple were anywhere to be seen. Had they taken a wrong turn?

"Yes," he said, "I suppose that is true. But I daresay your cousins will have the opportunity to return the favour. At...uh...some point," he added awkwardly. "Sooner or later, I mean."

"I daresay they will, at some point," she replied without emotion, still arching her neck to find any trace of them and not really paying attention to his words. "Sooner or later."

Baugham cleared his throat in an effort to transfer her attentions but to no avail.

"Right. Yes."

"I cannot see them anywhere. Do you see where they might have gone?"

Baugham looked around the winding wooded path through to the fields. He shrugged.

"I think they are probably taking all the enjoyment out of a solitary walk as they can and rather feeling cold weather is to their advantage. Do you wish to wait for them?"

Holly looked back still trying to spy either of the two couples, but it seemed Lord Baugham was right. Elizabeth and Mr Darcy and Jane and Mr Bingley were more than happy lingering in the shelter of the woods. She hesitated.

"Nothing at all to fear, Miss Tournier. If we are too long missed, I have no doubt that your cousin will come out on an anxious search for you." He smiled. "Much like the search you went on, that night when we found her and Mr Darcy walking together. Remember? Though…" He grimaced, realising his mistake too late, "of course, the outcome…will not…I mean…" He gave up. "Miss Elizabeth appears quite happy. As does Darcy, of course."

She was too busy scanning the horizon for any sign of her cousins, and no doubt wishing herself anywhere but where she was, to reply. When it was obvious they were not to be found, she smiled briefly and set off toward Longbourn. Baugham followed, stupidly thinking that if he kept talking, at some point he would say something that would pull him out of the hole he was digging for himself. Unfortunately, his next comment was not that something.

"If a man as resolute as Darcy can succumb to its siren song, it makes one quite wonder about just how far-reaching the powers of romance might be," he said.

Holly's eyes shot to his face.

"The powers of romance?" she said, more sharply than he expected. "It's a pretty idea, my lord, but one more fit for fairy tales…and other people!"

Perversely enough, Baugham felt his heart swell at her confessed lack of interest in romance, but he was interrupted from pursuing the subject by Miss Tournier looking down at her feet and sighing, "Oh, dear…"

Lord Baugham looked to where her eyes were directed and noticed they had walked right into a sea of mud stretching all around the area of a turnstile by the fence by the edge of the wood. He lifted his feet tentatively and smiled wryly at the noise every child delighted in and every valet dreaded.

"Perhaps more people know about that tree house after all," he smiled.

Miss Tournier did not look as amused as he did, for her boots were wholly immersed in mud and filth and there was no saving her skirts from being soiled either. She shifted on her feet, clearly looking for an escape.

"Perhaps we can flee this by retracting our steps a little," he said and moved sideways slightly.

To his great surprise, Miss Tournier simply looked at him with a frown and did not move.

"Your plan is a good one except for the fact that I seem to be stuck."

She moved her skirts aside, determining that she had sunk up to her ankles in thick, sticky mud. She pulled up with her right foot but only succeeded in raising it an inch or two against the strong suction before nearly losing her balance. Lord Baugham reached out to steady her then withdrew his hands again as quickly as possible.

She huffed in frustration and with hands on hips, looked around for something, anything, that might give her an idea for getting out of this predicament, but no remedy presented itself.

Baugham played with the idea of either placing his hands around her waist and lifting her up, or of extending the end of his walking stick for her to grab and then to pull her out, but both seemed inappropriate. He therefore finally reached out his gloved hand to her and said, "Here. Let's see if I can pull us out of this."

With no other alternative presenting itself, she reached out and took his hand. He tugged at her arm while she tried to lift her foot.

After a long time, being pulled so hard that she felt like her arm would come out of its socket, her foot suddenly broke free. Unfortunately this only caused her other foot to slip in the mud and she lost her balance again, nearly tumbling headlong into his lordship. She could not help but nervously laugh at his obvious confusion and discomfort as he tried to set her aright without actually touching her. Once she was steady again, she reached out both her hands, "Maybe we should try it this way."

He looked down at her as he heard her laugh. It was incredible how the sound lifted a weight off his mind and how the sun seemed to break out from behind all those heavy, grey and forbidding clouds that had hung over and between them.

She should laugh more, he found himself thinking. *If only she would laugh more. If she had laughed more, maybe…*

Slowly he reached out his two hands to meet hers and he could feel his face break out into a relieved smile.

"Yes," he said, "that is a very good and practical idea. Just the thing, in fact."

She put her hands into his and allowed him to slowly pull her, one step at a time, across the muddy crossroads. Most of her attention was focused downward, keeping her feet from slipping, and the rest of it was concerned with keeping her skirts untrodden and muddying them up worse than they already were.

Eventually they reached the grassy roadside and she looked up to thank him for his assistance. He still had hold of her hands and when she met his gaze she felt a familiar jolt. He was looking at her with tenderness in his eyes — the same way he had looked at her right after he kissed her. For a moment, he looked as if he was going to speak. She held his eyes, waiting…

But he dropped her hands and turned his head; she dropped her eyes and commented on the state of her boots. They moved on in silence.

They walked for some time, staring straight ahead. Baugham's feelings were a mixture of relief at the moment of cooperation and familiarity between them and fear that the strange discomfort they were now feeling would affect it. He had wanted to say it; he had nearly done so. Why had he not said it when the moment presented itself? He risked a glance in her direction, though he could only see the top of her bonnet, and shook his head. Before he laid himself open to … well, he could not even consider it without first ascertaining her circumstances. In that moment of hesitation, between impulse and prudence, he had once again lost an opportunity. At the same time, he also did not want to allow the resulting silence to damage the little bit of progress they had made. Still looking ahead, he quietly began again, this time actually uttering a few tentative words.

"You must allow me to apologise, but I wonder — "

"No," Holly interrupted. "Please. No."

"Miss Tournier, I fear I have upset you again and please allow me…" The look on her face as she turned to him made him stop, but only for a short time. He had to say something, at this moment he didn't care why, but he had to try so he rushed the words out. "…to tell you, you are absolutely right about Mr Darcy and about romance being for other people… too… people like your parents. For you, in fact."

"For me? Who are you to…" she broke off and looked away momentarily, but as she took a breath and fixed her eyes on him again, he felt a surge of admiration for her courage, despite the words she said next. "I never said I didn't… I never did not want to… thank you for the reminder — yet again, my lord, but only a fool holds out for childish notions."

"Childish?" He felt compelled to press the point, "Or brave? If you choose the right battle, isn't it foolish to surrender without a fight?"

"Choose battles? Just exactly what is the one you have chosen, my lord? And why do you plague me with it? There is no point in fighting a battle that is already lost. Perhaps I am guilty of cowardice there, but I don't know that I have the strength to do otherwise. I may be a fool, but I am not such a fool as that."

"Is it foolish to dare to trust your own heart?" he pushed.

Holly felt a lump growing in her throat and her breath becoming shaky, but she knew she must answer somehow. Something was happening, something was being addressed and this might be the only time she would be able to speak to it. She looked up at him and met his eyes solemnly and squarely.

"What about those who do *not* even know their own hearts? What about those who might love such a one as this? What is to become of them?

"How long should they wait before they admit that the thunderbolt has passed them over and there is nothing to fight for? Are they not better off to look elsewhere and learn to be content with the gentleness of the rain?"

She held his gaze and did not look away.

Baugham swallowed. "Are you? Are you happy with the rain then?"

"Happy?" Holly's cheeks were flaming red and her breath came short. "Rain?! My lord, at the moment the whole meteorological world is in suspension! Seemingly the weather gods cannot quite decide what to subject this poor mortal underling with! All I know is that inevitably the heavens *will* open up on me and right now I have no protection against anything whatsoever!"

352

He looked back at her steadily, thinking to himself how good it felt to have her complete concentration even though it seemed to be effectively hindering him from releasing the words he wanted to say. "I can say nothing against the gentle rain," he smiled sadly, "it can be a blessing where the earth is scorched and dry, and thunderbolts are admittedly frightening when one has lived in the desert all one's life. They can easily be misconstrued. No, I could never take offence at the gentle rain. But perhaps, there ought to be more than looking for a way to make the desert easier. Perhaps it is a matter of having the courage to find a better place to live. Or perhaps there just has never been anyone who — "

Just then the sound of distant shouts could be heard and they saw Mr Bingley and Mr Darcy walking toward them, waving. Holly turned to his lordship.

"My credit now stands on such slippery ground, that one of two ways you must conceit me — either a coward or a flatterer," she blurted out in a rush. Then she tilted her chin defiantly at his increasing frown. "Are you acquainted with Julius Caesar?"

"Acquainted with whom?"

"Julius Caesar. Act three."

"I have read all five acts, Miss Tournier. But what does that — "

"Antony's speech," she said abruptly. "It surely puts the matter much more succinctly than what has been attempted by either of us just now by debates on battles or the weather. Which are you, my lord? Coward? Or flatterer?"

Baugham drew back instinctively. He had gone too far, while at the same time being nowhere near his goal, but she was, as always, infuriating in her ability to pinpoint his faults. Why was she always so quick to judge, so quick to accuse and presume at his motives?

"Well, I expect that you would have no trouble charging me with both, Miss Tournier. *'What should such fellows as I do, crawling between heaven and earth?'* It seems I am doomed in that respect, regardless of my sincere efforts." He turned away from her and waved to the approaching gentlemen.

"Ho, Darcy! Bingley! Here."

Holly froze momentarily at the studied casualness to his tone that appeared so readily — he kept his gaze forward and any hint of tenderness that might have shown itself before was carefully masked. But it was no matter; she drew in a deep breath and followed him to the waiting men.

BAUGHAM WAS BEGINNING TO BREATHE more easily, thankful for the gentlemen's belated interference. The four new arrivals had healthy blushes on their faces and it was evident that their dawdling had a pleasurable reason. The frosty roof tiles of Longbourn were clearly visible behind the trees and Baugham longed for a change of scenery, a chance to regroup, to disappear behind normal social discourse. In his relief at being rescued from the uncomfortable direction in which the conversation with Miss Tournier had gone, and in an attempt to draw her cousins around her, he spoke brightly to the ladies as they caught up with them.

"Miss Bennet, Miss Elizabeth, you may rest easy. I have brought your country cousin safely back from her romp in the mud."

A cold voice sounded behind him.

"My romp in the mud? Their *country* cousin?" Baugham closed his eyes and sighed. Here it was, he could feel it building. Their halting conversation had left them no choice, it seemed. It was about to happen ... again, and this time they would be performing for an audience. But no matter, it was inevitable, unstoppable. He turned around, appearing a little cold himself. Yet Miss Tournier had already stalked off in a furious pace, leaving him behind with four pairs of puzzled eyes upon him.

"I beg your pardon ..." Baugham muttered and took a few long strides to keep up with her. He hoped the rest of the party would have the sense to revert to their slow pace, but he realised Miss Bennet, and therefore also Darcy, were closely following.

He caught up with her in the courtyard of the house.

"Miss Tournier, please forgive me. I was wrong and I didn't mean to — "

"No," she interrupted, "of course you didn't. You never *mean* anything do you? You go through life speaking and acting and never meaning *anything*, you pompous, arrogant, thoughtless, over-privileged London *clown!*"

He realised Miss Bennet and Darcy were close behind him, but at that moment, he did not care.

"If I was not so busy defending myself to you at every single turn, perhaps you could let your preconceptions go for once and *understand* my meaning instead of turning everything I say or do against me! Eloquence in the face of hostility is not very easy to accomplish!"

Holly gasped. Elizabeth had entered the yard and looked dumbfounded at her cousin and Lord Baugham. Mr Darcy opened his mouth to interfere, but Elizabeth put up her hand to hold him back.

Holly turned around and walked up to the door, which inconveniently enough had been opened to let the returning party in as soon as possible. She stopped at the threshold and spun back around to answer his accusation.

"How can one understand anything about your meaning when you are always acting without reason, speaking without thought, and then running away without explanation? If I compel you to defend yourself against that, my lord, I cannot apologise for it."

"That I have difficulty with my mode of expression must be a singular personal opinion of yours, since you seem to be the sole sufferer thereof!"

"If that is the case," Holly spat out, marching back onto the walk toward him. "I would suggest that you continue to restrict yourself to the society of those that have neither discretion nor understanding. It is only when you are in decent company, apparently, that your shortcomings are exposed."

"Baugham, should we — " Mr Darcy stepped out from behind Elizabeth, but she grabbed his hand impulsively, which was enough for him to forget to go on and shift his focus back to her.

"I beg your pardon, I'm sure." Baugham, ignoring his friend, was nearly shouting,

354

"I never knew decent company that felt their only course for redress against feelings of maltreatment was to behave like a common fishwife!"

"When one is treated in a common way, I suppose that reaction is only natural."

Her face was flushed and her eyes were shooting daggers at him. Her breath came quick and her brows were drawn together in a truly menacing look. Wisps of hair had come lose from under her bonnet and she tugged her earlobe in an effort to control herself.

This is all wrong, he thought, *if I could just smooth out that brow, take her hand and reassure her I mean no harm. I never meant any harm, if I could just make her see that. If I could just tell her, ask her, explain to her, kiss her...*

He moved toward her, but stopped himself abruptly.

"I see that my vulgar behaviour has shocked you into silence. I am happy for it," Holly said. "I shall make note to try to inspire the same reaction in you as often as possible henceforth, for I do confess I prefer it!" She brushed past him on her way to the door, "Even if I *am* a mere country girl, as you take every opportunity of reminding me."

Nearly speechless with confusion and anger, Baugham could only retort to her back, "You are not...! I do *not*...It is you who are always...!"

He strode to catch up to her, oblivious to all the eyes upon him, but she had stalked in through the door and even though she was met by Mrs Bennet, eager for her guests return, her mother, who had quit the library as soon as she saw her daughter stomping over the green, and Mrs Hill, who just stood staring with her arms held out in readiness to accept any garments anyone cared to dispose of with her, Holly did not care.

"I will be in my room, changing for dinner," she told no one in particular. "*Getting rid of the mud*!" she added a little more loudly.

Lord Baugham had stopped just outside, leaning against the outer wall, eyes closed and struggling to control his breathing, but Elizabeth came flying through the door, followed closely by Darcy.

"Holly!" she called, but her cousin was already at the top of the stairs. Elizabeth raised her eyebrows almost to her hairline and sent her fiancé a telling look and an excited smile.

"What?" Mr Darcy said, completely puzzled.

Elizabeth frowned and looked for her aunt. Their eyes met, but Mrs Tournier did not look as excited as Elizabeth expected. In fact, she appeared distinctly furious. After a moment of silent communication and questioning, Mrs Tournier turned on her heel and returned to the library. Mrs Bennet found her speech as her oldest daughter and Mr Bingley came through the door offering profuse apologies for having tarried so long, and a quieter, more subdued Lord Baugham joined them, smoothly admitting he was looking forward to dinner with the immense appetite they had all worked up in the frosty weather, but resolutely refusing to look anywhere but into the roaring fire.

Chapter 32

*We witness Several Persons being Dissatisfied with the State of Affairs
and Learn of their Various Ways of Coming to Terms with It*

Mrs Bennet shuffled her meat around on her plate and looked anxiously down her table. Something had gone wrong and she could feel one of her spells coming on. It was a disaster, but she had no idea what had happened. Of course, that strange scene when her niece had burst in and been most violent in her speech against one of her fine guests had been quite out of the ordinary and now her dinner — her dinner was ruined!

She glanced at Lord Baugham sitting beside her. Was he offended at the early hours of the dinner? Oh, she should have kept late Town hours, but Mr Bennet *would* insist on adhering to backward country customs. Was that why his lordship's thin smile seemed to turn into a grimace only a few seconds after she addressed him and tried to engage him in conversation? It couldn't be the fish — surely not! It was a fine piece of fish and yet he had hardly touched it. Mr Bingley and Mr Darcy had eaten well enough and Mr Bingley had even complimented her on it. No, it couldn't be the fish.

It could very well be her peculiar sister, sitting opposite him, and in that case she could hardly blame him and could only curse her own stupidity for seating her in his lordship's vicinity. They kept exchanging glances. Or rather, Mrs Tournier kept sending him glances and he kept avoiding them by offering very strange comments on really quite ordinary things: the silver, the light, the weather, and the wine. But not the fish.

As a consequence, the conversation she was desperately trying to hold up at her end of the table slipped downwards and rested firmly between her daughter Elizabeth and Mr Bingley, with occasional interjections from Mr Darcy and support from Jane.

They seemed happy enough, although Elizabeth in turn kept throwing comments and questions at her niece, Holly, who was next to Mr Bennet and her younger cousins at the far end of the table. She seldom answered more elaborately than in monosyllables. By the time the stew arrived Mr Bennet, had for some reason, decided to enter the fray. This particular circumstance, Mrs Bennet decided, was a most grave and suspicious thing indeed.

"Climbed up to the tree house did you, eh, Holly? And none of these gallant, protective gentlemen tried to stop you, my dear?"

The gallant gentleman at the farthest end of the table staunchly looked down at his plate and, chewing the same piece of meat that he had been chewing for the past five minutes, tried to ignore the conversation and what it did to his feelings. But Mr Bingley confessed Miss Holly had looked so competent that he would not have dared interfere. Mr Darcy muttered that she did come down soon enough, so there had been no real worry.

"I think, sir, you will want to profess more surprise at the fact that I did not join her," Elizabeth said. "A decision I regret already."

"I cannot agree with you there," Mr Darcy smiled.

"Oh, I suppose you think only trees at Pemberley are good and safe enough for me to climb henceforth," Elizabeth laughed. "And I do suppose you are right. I am quite certain in your devotion to your property you have already made them so."

"Pemberley does have some excellent trees..." Mr Bingley offered.

"I simply meant that I personally could not have assured the safety of two treebound young women and, since your cousin first claimed my attention and protection by her speed and determination, I was already committed to her safety and would not have been pleased to weigh my responsibilities between my betrothed and her beloved cousin."

"Oh Darcy!" Bingley said, laughingly. "As if neither of us remaining gentlemen could have assisted you."

Miss Tournier seemed to make a loud snorting noise, but instantly lifted her handkerchief to hide a cough.

"That is very gallant of you, Mr Bingley," Elizabeth smiled. "I am having a grand time now picturing the two of us wantonly falling from trees, only to be caught by chivalrous gentlemen! When you come to Pemberley, Holly, we must make a habit of it."

Mr Bennet laughed with his daughter, but was acutely aware of his niece sitting beside him being more than quiet, and although he was not exactly well acquainted with her, the way Elizabeth was sending her cousin anxious glances and trying to draw her in made him curious. The few glances Holly did direct anywhere else than at her plate, lap and the walls were directed to the other end of the table, and so Mr Bennet turned his attentions to a study of his sister. He was well enough acquainted with her to be able to tell *her* dull face and quiet habits masked a raging temper. Having missed the earlier spectacle, he wondered what had set her off. The immediate and obvious answer, when considering the demeanour of his niece, was a mother-daughter quarrel, but Arabella was no quarreller. She was a debater. Not only that, she rarely succumbed to anger in the process, so the way her mouth was pressed into a thin line and her conversation was severely curtailed was indeed unusual and not indicative of any family dispute. The distressed undertones of his wife's conversation turned his attention across the table to another guest who was being uncharacteristically taciturn: Lord Baugham. Hm…

"Now, Holly, my dear," he said, turning back to his niece, "I suppose you must be very pleased with Elizabeth's feat of capturing a man who will transport her nearly one hundred and fifty miles closer to you."

Holly pushed her potatoes around in the gravy. "I could say so, but then my pleasure would be at your expense, Uncle. I know how much you will miss her."

"Well, well. I confess, life has ill prepared me for loss of any kind, most certainly in areas I care so much about, but I don't mind admitting your gain and my defeat to you. As long as you properly appreciate it."

Holly smiled faintly. "Of course."

Mr Bennet watched her for a moment. "You know my dear," he said, "I think you and I should form a plan. I think one or the other of us — or, come to think of it, both of us — should rush up to Pemberley as soon as an invitation can be contrived and then we must establish ourselves in a pair of its smaller, but still fine, rooms, refuse to budge and thus shut ourselves out from the world around us. No one would ever find us. Would that not make a grand plan? If we need intelligent society that will not show us up in its superiority, but rather lend silent distinction to our frivolity, we shall send for Mr Darcy, and when we need lively company that will make us seem wise and contemplative in our silence, we will send for Mrs Darcy."

Despite herself, Holly smiled.

"That is a grand plan, Uncle. Except I do not know that I want to shut myself out of the world."

"Don't you?" her uncle said shrewdly. "You certainly give a fair impression of it this evening. And you mustn't blush or protest, my child, for I find myself liking you very much for it."

Mrs Tournier saw her brother engaging his niece in conversation and even noticed him being able to draw a smile over Holly's sour face. She found herself thankful to her brother for the effort. Words she wanted to utter to the guest opposite her burned in her throat and had not Mr Darcy on her side been solicitous enough to offer the occasional comment or question for deliberation, she was rather sure she would have succumbed to the temptation.

When dinner was over and the ladies excused themselves, she found some relief in speaking to her oldest niece while Holly was coaxed into a game of some sort with Elizabeth — who was still behaving as if Holly needed her for a crutch to lean on through the evening — and with Mary and Kitty. Slowly, she noticed colour returning to Holly's cheeks in the heat of the game and she even gave a small triumphant laugh when laying down a winning hand.

"You let me win that, Elizabeth," she said. "Shame on you!"

"I did not! But if you are so certain about it I will claim the same from you, with interest, in the next round."

As expected, her brother had not been able to keep two young lovers away from the parlour for long, even with the aid of his best wine. Mr Bennet and Lord Baugham sauntered idly behind the more energetic gentlemen, deep in conversation and obviously in no great hurry themselves to return to the ladies. For some reason, this circumstance incensed Mrs Tournier beyond reason and she was once again out of sorts.

"Music!" cried Mrs Bennet. "Shall we not have some music?" But as much as she tried to steer Kitty towards the pianoforte, the rest of the room paid her no heed and since Kitty was not prepared to claim any attention by performing, Mrs Bennet was forced to give up. She was comforted by the fact that Jane and Mr Bingley took pity upon her and she could happily entertain herself for the next hour by describing Jane's wedding clothes and assuring Mr Bingley he would not be disappointed in his wife's choices. In this she had a very sympathetic and faithful audience and so she was happy.

Mary Bennet liked to sit by her aunt. She did not like to talk to her; regardless of her local reputation as an intelligent and informed woman, Mary hardly ever understood a word of what her Aunt Arabella said to her. But she sat beside her and tried to emulate her frown, which Mary thought quite intimidating and therefore probably a useful thing to learn. She also approved wholeheartedly of her aunt's penchant for sending Lord Baugham sharp looks, and was pleased to see her aunt shared her opinion on flighty young men who brought no worthy arguments to any discussion and rather seemed to thrive on frivolity. She could perfectly well see how her aunt tensed when his lordship moved closer to her cousin, Holly, again, although this time he stayed at a respectable distance and seemed only to utter a few words to her, to which she replied with equal economy.

Mrs Tournier could just make out three words that were repeated between the two. "I am sorry." She scoffed. Indeed. It was a sorry affair, indeed, and there was nothing she could do about it. On very few occasions since her husband's passing had Mrs Tournier felt helpless, and never on her own behalf. It was not in her nature to admit to such a possibility, but, just as she had for her husband when he lost his hope and will to live and ideals to believe in, she now felt powerless on behalf of their daughter.

Holly was strong, yes, but in order to stay strong one must sometimes give in to weakness, and surrender to desperate feelings, and the truth. Time would heal wounds caused by that surrender and she was certain Holly would continue being strong exactly because she so bravely lived in those feelings and acknowledged them, but to witness it was sad and hard. Nevertheless, the hopeless feeling persisted, because there was another who refused to do the same. As *his* friend, she hoped fervently he would give due consideration to her words and would act accordingly. As *her* mother she wished him nothing but ill. It was not an easy place to be herself, she reflected, and come nightfall she hoped she could find some peace in a make believe conversation with her husband once again.

Baugham sat in his chair in front of the fire in his bedroom, having absentmindedly undressed and prepared for sleep that he knew would not come easy tonight. What another singular day it had been! For some time now he felt he had been placed in the middle of a stage play: things were happening to him instead of him directing what he wished to touch his life. Today was a prime example. Such a day would have been unthinkable a short time ago.

And would to God that could still be the case! he thought violently and stretched his arms above his head before he slumped back again. Here he sat, in a strange bedroom, embarrassed like a schoolboy for misbehaving, confused by irrelevant quotes from imperial plays and long drawn out analogies about the weather, and frustrated because he had failed so spectacularly in his mission. She really was a most exasperating woman!

But that was an empty show of defiance which he did not believe in himself anymore. As he reached for a familiar, battered volume, in the quiet, the words of Miss Tournier once again came back to him:

My credit now stands on such slippery ground, that one of two ways you must conceit me — either a coward or a flatterer.

He had to own it, that was a sharp and daring question for her to pose. And more to the point, it was a question that he knew he had to answer, if only to himself: *Which are you, my lord? Coward? Or flatterer?*

A coward, he thought.

He sighed and stretched his legs towards the fire and reached for his glass, lifting Tam O'Shanter up from his knee. Turning a few pages he followed the lines with his eyes:

While we sit bousing at the nappy,
An' getting fou and unco happy,
We think na on the lang Scots miles,
The mosses, waters, slaps and stiles.
That lie between us and our hame…

But a mention of Scots mosses, waters, slaps and tiles was all he needed before his mind predictably began to wander in exactly the direction not endorsed by Mr Burns.

Her world was in suspension, she had said, and she had no protection against whatever may befall her. Something jabbed at his heart when he thought about that. She would not admit to him to have an attachment, but she would berate him for posing the question. Was he a complete fool to see that as a sign of hope? Was he deluded to think that her anger and indignation was all the proof he needed? If she had set out on another path — a path away from him — she would not have abused him so terribly, would she? She would not have dared him to reveal himself…

But pleasures are like poppies spread;
You seize the flower, its bloom is shed.
Or like the snow falls in the river,
A moment white—then melts forever.

All his adult life he had sought pleasure, believing that 'moment white' was enough. To seek after more was to risk exposing something within him that he had spent his entire life protecting. The very thoughts now spinning through his mind frightened him but... it was time to let go and believe in something new, something more. He would finally believe in his mother's words when she told him she wanted him to be happy, and that happiness was not attained through protection against the heart, but only through exposure and risk.

Now, however, he did see the solution clearly. He had all the indication of her feelings and situation he had the right to expect. The rest was up to him and he must show as much daring as she. It was only fair, after all, and he knew he owed it to her. He needed to atone for his trespasses and mistakes against her by being as honest as he could be. In no other way could he truly make up for what he had done to her (and himself, he added sadly) in the garden at Rosefarm that cold and windy day. He felt exhilarated; she deserved to know the truth, now that he recognised it, about why he kissed her. She deserved to know he had wanted to kiss her, not to insult her, and if the truth be told — and it must — he still wanted to, and then to offer himself to her to abuse and berate and jab and finally kiss some more. That was all he wanted of her — everything. Somehow, he would find a time and a place to tell her how he felt and explain himself.

Suddenly her feelings hardly mattered; she might despise him, and rightfully so, but he would declare himself all the same. He hoped she would not be uncomfortable, but he also hoped he could be clear and leave no doubt as to his feelings. Considering those feelings were still somewhat newly formed and acknowledged, he foresaw some difficulties. The way he had used her, he owed her the chance to throw it back in his face, and he could in no way be certain that she would not do exactly that. But, giving her that chance, putting himself at her mercy; that was the only way he could ever truly be forgiven. She had certainly abused him, and rightfully so, but she had also been brave, braver than he could hope to be. She had challenged him to be honest with her, he recognised that now, and he had been a coward not to accept it. He had to put his faith in her, knowing her as well as he did. She had every right to punish him, but she possessed a generous heart and he knew that if there was no hope for him, she would not have been so bold.

Despite the revolution that was now spreading from his heart to his mind and the resolutions he was so bravely forming in spite of his hesitations, Baugham had to smile to himself. He could trust Miss Tournier. He knew her well enough. Yes, he truly did know her better than he thought he did, and besides tender feelings, like fragile buds only just daring to raise their heads from the dark soil of his neglected heart, there was trust and admiration. Despite whatever he had been guilty of, there had always been that, and she deserved to know that too, and so much more besides.

He would choose his moment and, until then, let hope live within him for once and not quell it under veiled inquiries, reason and pretexts. If there could be the remotest chance of her ever letting him kiss her again, some risk taking would certainly be worth it. If she could not return his feelings — and he could very well understand how that could be for a variety of reasons — if she did reject him, he could and must live with that, because she would know the truth and the truth was what he owed to her above all. But maybe...just maybe...she might feel the same.

OF COURSE, HOLLY WAS NOT sleeping, but it was late and she had no wish to speak to anyone and so she lay absolutely still in her bed, determined to ignore the scratching on her door. It was Elizabeth, of course, and so the scratching would not stop simply because there was no answer. Holly sighed. Just as she prepared to call out a greeting, Elizabeth popped her head around the door.

"Holly," she whispered, "don't tell me you're asleep."

"Very well, I won't," Holly answered dryly.

"Good," her cousin said and crept in to sneak up on her bed.

"You shouldn't be here, Elizabeth," Holly said gently, "you have a busy day tomorrow."

Elizabeth scoffed. "Nonsense! What I really should not do is let my dearest friend go to bed alone and obviously miserable."

"That is very kind of you, but you should also not think of me at this time. If I am miserable it's only because I have failed you and my family by behaving very badly and for that I ask your forgiveness."

"No apologies please Holly! But an explanation would be nice."

Holly tried to smile but she could not quite manage it. Instead she sat up against her pillows.

"I'm sorry, Eliza, I don't think I can do that tonight. I really am quite tired."

Elizabeth crept closer and took her cousin's hand. "Holly, I know it's terribly selfish of me, but I do want my wedding day to be perfect. And if you are not happy, it cannot be perfect."

"Well, as sorry as it makes me to have to say it, I'm afraid your wedding day cannot be perfect then, Elizabeth," Holly said and fought to hold back her tears.

"But why?" Elizabeth asked and put her hand to her cousin's cheek to soothe her. "Why, Holly? What is the matter?"

Holly stared at her idle hands in her lap. She did want to tell everything but should she? Could she?

"Don't you want to tell me?" Elizabeth asked quietly.

"Yes," Holly said abruptly. "Oh yes! But it is difficult. So very hard...to say it."

"Well," Elizabeth said and crept closer, "try..."

Holly swallowed hard a few times. "Yes. I'll try. It's...I feel like such a fool. It's just...he..."

362

She broke off, uncertain of how to say the words to her friend, to *his* friend's future wife.

"He?" Elizabeth prompted. "Holly? Which he?"

"What do you mean by that, Eliza?"

"I have eyes, Holly, and I do not think that doctor you were telling me about is the one causing you so much present unhappiness."

No," she shook her head. "It's nothing. I need to…see…that it's nothing. It doesn't matter."

Elizabeth sat up in alarm. "Of course it matters, Holly! How can you even contemplate marrying another man when you — "

"When I what, Elizabeth?" Holly sat up and snapped back. "When I could instead live the rest of my years in genteel poverty and spinsterhood? That is a fine thing for you to suggest to me two days before your own most advantageous wedding!"

Refusing to be goaded into a distracting argument, Elizabeth said calmly, "You are right. I am indeed getting married in two days, and I will become the mistress of a great estate. And that, Holly, presents you with another choice, a better choice. I will hear no protests and no proud rebuttals. I love you, you are my dearest cousin and you deserve to be happy and secure for the rest of your life. I will be in a position to care for you, Holly, to include you in my new home as a sister if you are ever, ever, ever in need of it."

"And why should I live as a dependent in your home if I can have a home of my own? Why should I consent to having you care for me when I can instead care for my mother?"

"Holly," Elizabeth spoke plainly, "I am very well aware that a marriage founded on mutual esteem and respect rather than love can be successful. I do however believe that you cannot hope to find peace or contentment in a marriage if you are in love with another man. Not you! And just think — "

A strong rap on the door pre-empted Holly's reaction and both girls jumped.

"Lie-lie?" Arabella Tournier's strong voice rang out. "I need to speak to you."

Holly swiftly dried her eyes with the back of her hand and Elizabeth shuffled to the edge of the bed.

"Shall I let her in?"

"No, I will," Holly jumped up and ran to open the door, intensely thankful for the intrusion.

"Oh, I see," Mrs Tournier said, when she saw her niece, but Elizabeth shook her head faintly and could not reassure her. Mrs Tournier's face fell again and with a sigh she strode into the room. Elizabeth wished them both a good night and started out the door.

"Sleep well, Eliza," Holly said and tried to sound cheerful. "Busy day tomorrow."

"Yes," her cousin said. "Will you be there with me? I need you."

"Of course." This time Holly's smile was genuine.

"Good. Thank you."

Mrs Tournier waited until Elizabeth left the room before she sat down on the edge of her daughter's bed.

"Quite popular tonight, aren't you, dear?" she said and looked at her.

"Oh, I think not," Holly said and looked down into her lap again, refusing to meet her mother's eye. "Quite the opposite, really. I spent most of the evening apologising."

"And did anyone apologise to you?"

Holly nodded. Then she sighed and looked at her mother with sadness, but also with hard determination in her eyes. "I do not wish to discuss it," she said firmly but quietly.

Mrs Tournier ran her hand over her daughter's cheek and then her hair. Holly had hastily plaited it into one thick, careless braid and half of the front had already come undone as if she had tossed and turned all night instead of just for the past hour.

"Did you do your one hundred?"

Mrs Tournier was referring to the one hundred brush strokes she had taught her daughter to subject her hair to every evening before bed. It had been a pleasant ritual in Holly's childhood, but now as an adult she was less than diligent about it.

"No Maman," she therefore smiled, "there was no point to it. I will have to wash my hair tomorrow anyway."

"All the more reason, Lie-lie!" her mother said. "Come here; let me do it for you."

Holly still smiled as her mother picked up her brush from the small armoire in the corner and she shuffled closer to her. Mrs Tournier gently untied her hair and gathered it over her back to set to work. The first brush strokes were hampered by tangles and Holly's head was snapped backwards several times. But the long strokes soon did their work and the rhythmic sounds were very soothing and soon Holly felt herself relax under her mother's care.

"Maman, you mustn't think..."

"Hush, Lie-lie," her mother interrupted her, "no talking during the counting. Twelve, thirteen, fourteen, fifteen..."

So Holly stayed silent and her mother slowly went through the ritual and soon her scalp was tender from the bristles of the brush and her hair was shiny and flighty from the treatment.

"One hundred," Mrs Tournier said and put down the brush. "There."

"Thank you, Maman."

"It is certainly a while since I have done that. My hand will be aching in the morning."

Holly felt her hair and wound a few tresses between her fingers. "I won't bother to braid it again before bed, I think," she smiled.

"Good idea," her mother said. "Was there something you wanted to say to me?"

"No. Not really. But perhaps I could just... For a little while you could simply..."

"Of course, my precious child," Mrs Tournier said and closed her daughter in her arms.

"My lord!"

Baugham shifted his gaze with a start to rest on his valet instead of the wall. Riemann looked at him strangely. It was true, he often looked at him quite exasperated and even sad when his lordship showed blatant disregard for the finer points of his work, but this time he looked positively... angry.

"My dear fellow, what's the matter?" Baugham said, puzzled.

"My lord," Riemann said and visibly tried to gather himself before he spoke. "I would beg you to get out of your clothes and pay attention. I have coats to brush, shoes to polish, neckties to attend to for tomorrow and since it appears you are not going visiting, I would beg to attend to that coat as well in the process. It is your best. I need to get on with it. Tomorrow is a big day and it warrants the proper preparations."

Baugham was stunned, but he obeyed his valet and struggled out of his coat. That was the longest speech he had ever heard him utter. It appeared this was to be one of those days when he seemed separated from the rest of the world by some sort of strange language barrier. Suddenly people spoke the most appalling nonsense at him and he seemed, completely unawares, to have switched his own speech to some incomprehensible foreign language his fellow Englishmen had trouble understanding.

It had begun at breakfast. After a night of heavy sleep, he had cheerfully gone down to catch Darcy and Bingley and to take part of their plans to visit Longbourn that day. But once he got there, his friends were eating a leisurely breakfast in silence while Miss Bingley and Mrs Hurst were chattering away on what a lovely day it was turning out to be, completely ignoring the fact that a heavy, icy mist was hanging over the landscape and reducing the view from the windows to a few feet.

"Still here?" Baugham had cheerfully greeted the two men. "So at what time are we going to Longbourn today?"

Bingley looked up and stared at him open-mouthed and Darcy looked him up and down apparently remarking to himself on his fine coat and elegant dress with a grim look. Miss Bingley, however, seemed to find his friendly enthusiasm for visiting amusing.

"Oh, my lord!" she smiled slyly. "Really! Not even you can expect the Bennets to entertain any visitors *today*. I'm afraid you will really have to do with us."

Baugham felt sheepish. "Ah," he said and concentrated on choosing a piece of bread exactly the right size. "If you say so, Miss Bingley."

"I'm afraid my sister and I have you gentlemen to ourselves the whole day," she smiled and pushed her own chair back from the table, turning towards him and making an inviting gesture to the empty chair beside her.

"Ah," Baugham said again when he was forced to accept it. "How delightful."

He contemplated for a moment the possibility of going over to Longbourn himself in the guise of a morning ride, but then thought the better of it. Despite having exchanged embarrassed apologies yesterday with Miss Tournier, he had no doubt he had left her in a state of mind that would ensure she would have no qualms stabbing him with a sewing needle or strangling him with a lace ribbon if he should happen to demand her attention alone.

So perhaps it was for the best, he conceded, despite the fact that his musings and decisions from last night were demanding urgent action now to finally be settled. It would be good to let things calm down a little before he could see her tomorrow.

But his thoughts on the prudence of biding his time were severely tested by mid-afternoon. He had thought Darcy pretty sly when claiming he had some papers he wanted his lordship to attend to in the study and had actually looked forward to a nap — well, thinking disguised as a nap behind a newspaper, really — when it turned out the damn fellow really had papers he wanted him to look at! How in God's name it was his business how Darcy, after he was married, settled his affairs on his wife and his sister and various theoretical off-spring was beyond him, but apparently some sort of witnessing was needed and he spent a good while glancing longingly at the chair and the paper draped across it while struggling through legal paragraphs, and signatures, seals, and attachments.

When he finally could sink into the chair and spread out his newspaper with its soothing rustling sound, Bingley set off. It was quite obvious that Charles Bingley was growing nervous about marrying his angel after all. The problem was rather that instead of confessing to his qualms and calling them by their proper name so that either Darcy or he could put him at ease, he insisted on making large transliterations of his dilemma in strange metaphors about making turns in country dances and playing more fiddles than one at the same time.

Darcy soon gave up and retired behind his paper, but Baugham could not quite bring himself to stop trying to decipher the curious workings of Mr Bingley's mind and so he was stuck for a good while.

Luncheon, on the other hand, was a slightly less tedious affair, and he found refuge in keeping Darcy's sister company and chatting with her about London. It was rather hard work though, and not so much from Miss Darcy's natural fatigue after a long journey or her youth, which made it necessary for him to adapt the conversation rather out of his own customary sphere of interest, but because Miss Bingley kept interrupting and claiming their attention through exaggerated compliments directed at Miss Darcy's accomplishments and acquaintances and Lord Baugham's wit and conversation.

Lord Baugham did escape for a ride into the fog and icy cold weather. His spirits improved temporarily and had he been more familiar with the geography of this part of Hertfordshire, he might well have braced Miss Tournier's certain disapproval, defied social conventions and gone down to Longbourn after all. But he returned to his prison and was awarded with more of Bingley's conversation on the difficulty of balancing one's necessary show of ardour for one's beloved against the possibility of frightening the angelic creature away if one does not perfectly go about it.

After a dinner where the entire household was completely obsessed with the coming wedding — the service, the clothes, the weather, the breakfast, the cake, the behaviour of others and the stature of oneself, Baugham was very grateful when Miss Bingley withdrew with her sister to go through Miss Darcy's trunks undisturbed and choose for her a gown in a fashion complimentary to themselves for the next day's ceremony. Hurst was sleeping in what seemed to be his assigned chair, although Baugham was beginning to have his doubts on just how deep that slumber was in the face of Bingley's ongoing speculations.

"I hope she will not display nerves tomorrow," Bingley went on. "I mean, a blushing bride is very charming and of course one can't expect her not to be nervous and apprehensive, but I do hope she gets a good night's sleep tonight, for I know she confesses to being so much more calm and confident when she is not tired and I know I would not want to — "

"Bingley." Baugham stood up and looked down on his host. Behind his newspaper Darcy made a menacing rustling sound, but he paid it no mind. "You love Miss Bennet. She loves you. She will marry you tomorrow morning. You will make her your wife in every sense of the word by tomorrow night. And after that I have no doubt you will both remain just as charming, easy, courteous, forgiving, indulging, adoring, and obliging as you ever were. Now, in anticipation of the coming month when you will have nothing to do but dwell on the perfections of your bride and enjoy her charms, please find something else to speak about until then, man!"

Bingley stared, dumbfounded, but having exhausted his mental resources by being patient, civil and social to those around him while in the throes of his own turmoil and anticipation for the coming day, Baugham withdrew with his last strength and stalked off to his bedroom to plead his surrender.

It was true; he looked forward to the next day as much as anyone downstairs, but for completely different reasons than those anxious to witness or participate in the ancient ritual that would usher in a new order and life.

Riemann was still giving him a jaundiced eye when he helped him undress and Baugham pleaded exhaustion and lack of patience from the nonsense he had been subjected to all day. Riemann offered no comments — he never did — but moved around his master in silence that was all the more loud for being so quiet.

"Oh, stop it, man," Baugham mumbled and stretched his back. "You are not the injured party here, despite my lack of interest in what constitutes a properly brushed coat."

The unspoken disbelief in his valet's eyes at that comment caused Baugham to retreat.

"Oh, maybe you are right," he said. "I should look my best tomorrow. If only to grant her the fullest satisfaction when she casts me from the highest cliff."

Riemann's frown softened. "Early start tomorrow, my lord," he offered. "Shall you want your book and a glass of wine all the same as usual?"

"No," Baugham said firmly. "I am going straight to bed. And then tomorrow will come all the more quickly. Thank God."

Chapter 33

The Lovers Finally Get Each Other

THE hallways were still dark when Holly, barefoot and in her nightgown, moved quickly and deliberately through the door, slipped into Elizabeth's room and quickly crawled into her bed.

"Holly?" a sleepy voice beside her questioned.

"Shh…" she answered. "Go back to sleep."

But it was too late; Elizabeth turned toward her and took her hand.

"I'm glad you are here. Today is going to be so hectic and I was afraid I wouldn't have time to seek you out. Talk to me Holly, tell me it will all be well…I am thrilled and frightened and happy and sad all at once. And I am worried about you…"

"Hush!" Holly whispered. "None of that! This is your day, Eliza, yours and Jane's, and it will be perfect because you deserve nothing less. You aren't to think of anything unpleasant, least of all me and my silliness. I just wanted a minute, before everyone wakes up and it all begins…to say a proper goodbye…" she swallowed hard, "and to tell you how much I love you and will miss you. And how happy I am for you."

She could feel Elizabeth reach out and pull her into a hug.

"How many times have we lain just like this, Holly? Whispering together in the dark, making plans and sharing dreams? Not nearly enough, I know, but I cherish every single memory. You know that no matter what I am called or where I live, I will always love you, don't you? Nothing will change."

"Don't be silly, Elizabeth," Holly smiled, "everything will change, just as it should — most especially your partner for whispering together in the dark." She could not see, but she knew Elizabeth would smile at that. "I just wanted this one last moment."

They talked together quietly while the house began to stir. A few times Elizabeth tried to turn the conversation in her direction, but Holly deflected it and, as is only right and proper, the talk mostly focused on ceremonies, breakfasts, travelling clothes, touring plans and a fervent insistence on regular letters and frequent and long visits once she was established.

All too soon a summoning knock sounded on the door, and Holly scooted out of her cousin's bed after giving her a kiss on the forehead. Already as she walked back to her own room she could see that the pandemonium had begun — trays were coming up, dresses, flowers and ribbons floated from one end of the hall to the other, the smell of curling hair wafted through the air mixing with the aromas of the cooking preparations downstairs, amidst it all were the happy shrieks and giggles of the Bennet girls and the excited exclamations of her aunt.

HE COULD TELL BY THE way Darcy hitched up his right eyebrow that he was surprised to see him waiting at the bottom of the stairs.

"I'm early," Darcy said.

"Well," Baugham said and straightened his waistcoat for the umpteenth time, "I'm earlier."

Despite having been fussed over by his man like never before that morning, after a hasty cup of coffee and a little makeshift breakfast in his room, Lord Baugham had still descended the stairs first of all the gentlemen. The ladies were not expected to journey to the church until later and so Lord Baugham had waited in fidgeting silence at the bottom of the stairs for Darcy and Bingley to join him.

Even if he had called his valet's ministrations a "damned fuss," Lord Baugham knew Riemann's work had been impeccable. If nothing else, he could take comfort in the knowledge that whatever trials he would experience today, he would do so cutting a very distinguished and elegant figure. Darcy looked him over and a silent smile of approval played on his lips. Baugham countered with a hitched eyebrow of his own and drew out his watch to relieve his impatience.

Just then they heard quick steps on the landing above them as Mr Bingley made his way to join them.

"Darcy!" he cried only half way down. "My lord! Here you are! Splendid! All set?"

Yesterday's nervousness seemed to have been exorcised and the man was all smiling affability and good humour. His lordship suddenly remembered his own mission that morning and waved at the footman to call for clothes and carriage.

"Well then, let's get this misery over and done with, shall we?" he muttered and pushed the grooms towards the door.

"THERE, MAMAN," HOLLY SAID AS she fastened the last button. "You are beautiful."

In the hallway they could hear the sounds of opening and closing doors and footsteps rapidly running up and down the staircase, but Mrs Tournier's room was much more subdued. As if by unspoken agreement, very little was said as they helped

369

each other with the finishing touches of their own toilettes. Examining herself in the full-length mirror with a critical eye, Arabella Tournier pronounced a clipped, "I'll do, I suppose," before turning her attention to her daughter. As she busied herself with Holly's buttons and arranging the skirt of her newly re-made gown just so, she could not help but feel relief — for her daughter's sake — that the festivities would soon be at an end and they would, in a short time, be back and safe at Rosefarm, just the two of them. An irritated breath escaped her just then and though Holly looked at her curiously, she did not bother to explain.

There would be no such thing as 'safe at Rosefarm' any longer, not with that devil Pembroke in control. And just the two of them... well, she knew that if she tried, she might be able to dissuade Holly from her plans to encourage the doctor's attentions. What she did not know was whether she ought to try.

The sounds outside the door were dying down and they could hear the carriages coming up the gravel drive below them. *Now is not the day to dwell on these matters,* Mrs Tournier silently declared to herself and, as she shared a look with her daughter, she knew Holly had just determined something similar.

"You look very nice yourself, my dear," she said, "and since you know I have an aptitude for understatement you may take that as an admission that, in my eyes at least, you are in danger of upstaging the brides."

Holly gave her mother a look, but she thought silently to herself she had made the best of things and that she could at least take comfort in the fact that she had nothing to be ashamed of in her appearance in front of the more fashionable part of the family.

She held out her hand to her mother, and sooner than she could have expected, they were watching the Bennet carriage carry the brides and their parents down the lane to the church and then they too were on their way in Mr Darcy's carriage. The big day had arrived.

To his great annoyance, weddings in the country did not seem the quiet family affair one would expect. It was uncertain how many of the spectators would actually have the audacity to claim a seat inside the church for the ceremony, but a great many of them appeared to be perfectly happy standing around the churchyard to catch a glimpse of the bridal party.

"It was only to be expected," Darcy said calmly as Bingley accepted a few words of congratulations from some forward villagers and Baugham frowned.

It was a fine day. Cold and crisp, but it did seem as if the sun was going to honour the proceedings now that she had been persuaded to rise above the rooftops to spread her pale and cold light. Baugham wondered which force would have won out with the inhabitants of Meryton had they been forced to contend with both the spectacle of local girls marrying wealthy, handsome young men and the icy fog that had kept most of them firmly indoors yesterday. The attraction of the Bennet wedding was not to be tested today, however. The brides were blessed with weather that, as was the general consensus of the onlookers, was only rivalled by their own beauty.

Baugham positioned himself by the door after Darcy extracted Bingley from another matronly well-wisher and watched the grooms disappear inside the small church. Soon enough, he was able to greet the rest of the Netherfield party. Just as Miss Bingley let her hand leave his sleeve after begging him not to tarry outside in this cold weather, Baugham spotted two carriages draw up.

And then there she was. After his heart had settled in his chest again, his focus was suddenly clear — so much clearer than it had ever been sitting in a chair or pacing around Netherfield. The party made their way up the slope, Mrs Bennet in a flurry behind her husband escorting his daughters and Mrs Tournier leading the younger cousins, leaving her daughter to the rear carrying her older cousins' effects.

The sight of the brides sweeping past him made him smile. He executed an elaborate bow and congratulated Mr and Mrs Bennet. Mrs Bennet was about to offer him a comment before she noticed Jane's train was askew and needed immediate attention. Mrs Tournier greeted him silently and led the even more silent girls inside. But just as Miss Tournier was about to enter, he stepped forward and lightly laid his hand on her elbow.

"Miss Tournier."

She hesitated, but did not pull away directly even though she stayed looking down at his hand.

"I must speak to you," he said almost brusquely, aware he had only a few seconds.

She gave him a look that was hard to interpret.

"Please?" he added, his voice softer.

Holly stared at him. This handsome, impeccably dressed man with piercing blue eyes boring into her and holding onto her arm just as she was about to step into church and witness her cousins' wedding, was begging her for a meeting in a soft voice. She felt confused.

"Now?" she asked hesitantly. "We really must be getting inside."

"After church," he went on. "Can we — "

"No," she said. His heart sank. "The wedding breakfast," she added. "After that, I suppose. But — "

Before she could finish, he broke out into a smile and stepped back.

"Thank you. The willows? Where we walked last?"

How could she say anything when being smiled at like that? When blue eyes full of sparkle and cool fire looked into her own and willed her to consent? She nodded hastily and, with her heart beating in her throat, hurried away from him. She must get away from him.

How she found the pew where her mother was sitting, Holly did not know, but she was grateful that there was no time for questions, for the ceremony was just about to begin. A small rustling sounded behind her and she knew that he had come in and was taking a place on the other side of the room; she could feel him there. For a moment, the fog of her thoughts cleared and her whole attention was taken up by the two couples taking their place at the front of the church. Elizabeth and Jane were beautiful. Jane radiated a peaceful joy, quiet and deep while Elizabeth sparkled with delight, bright and dazzling, and the sight of them took her breath away.

But, as they turned to face the reverend and the ceremony began, Holly could not keep her thoughts on the proceedings. A picture flashed in her mind, she felt again the touch on her elbow:

I must speak to you...

It's just because he will be leaving, Holly, she told herself. *It's one more apology before he goes...just like all the others before it. That's all.*

His face fell when she had said, "No," and his voice as he said, "Please?" So soft. Vulnerable even.

You both behaved badly, and he just... His smile when she agreed... *Stop!*

She forced her mind away from those thoughts just at the moment when both couples turned and were introduced to the congregation. She smiled and hoped that the tears that sprang to her eyes would be taken as a sign of joy and pride.

THE DINING ROOM AND PARLOUR of Longbourn were filled with the sounds of clinking silver, low and not so low conversations, laughter, tears and good wishes and hovered between very full and crowded. Holly found herself wandering around the rooms in the midst of the talking and eating, making new acquaintances and renewing old ones and very determinedly *not* paying attention to the whereabouts of Lord Baugham. If he was standing alone near the fireplace, she paid no mind. Likewise when he filled his plate and took a seat at the dining table near to Mr Phillips. Nor did she note the duration of his short conversation with Mr Bingley. He was very difficult to ignore, however, because she seemed to always be able to sense where he was in the rooms, but as his request for a word with her was certainly nothing more than his need to deliver another apology she did not care to hear, she was firm in her resolve to succeed. The morning passed slowly, excruciatingly slowly, as Holly watched the newly-wed couples greet their guests and accept well-wishes and suddenly Holly realised that she no longer could feel his lordship's presence in order to disregard it.

She turned and scanned the rooms, but she could see nothing. He was not there! She knew he was not there and she had a sinking feeling that he had grown tired of waiting and changed his mind. Before she had a chance to admit her disappointment to herself, the sound of a voice behind her made her jump.

"Lose something, Holly?"

"Oh!" Holly shrieked before recognising the voice. "Oh, Elizabeth, it's you. Or, should I say Mrs Darcy?"

Her cousin's smile was brilliant, "Oh, by all means, say Mrs Darcy — I don't believe I will ever grow tired of the sound of it.

"But, Holly, you are standing here looking positively distressed. Is something wrong?"

"Oh, it's nothing..." Holly said, taking a breath and forcing herself to relax. "It's just that Lord Baugham mentioned that he wanted to speak to me and...well, I suppose he has thought better of it. Wise decision, I should think, we wouldn't want to ruin your morning with another quarrel." She laughed weakly at her joke.

Elizabeth's eyebrows drew together. "He asked to speak with you? Here?"

Although she tried to keep her attention on her cousin, Holly really could not help but continue to scan the clusters of chatting guests.

"Well…no…" she admitted casually, or so she thought. "He asked if I would meet him…"

Elizabeth's eyebrows shot up. "Meet him? Where?"

Holly's eyes darted to Elizabeth's face. "The willow grove."

Elizabeth was suddenly very much in danger of losing her composure.

"The willow grove! Holly! Why are you not there?"

"This is your wedding breakfast, Eliza. I would never forgive myself if I were not here to see you off."

"I would!" Mrs Darcy quickly retorted, before taking her cousin by the shoulders and propelling her through the crowd and down the hallway, "Go!"

"Elizabeth, I'm sure it is nothing important. It can wait." Her protests fell on deaf ears. She tried again, "But what about Jane…"

"I will make your excuses to Jane. She will understand."

Holly found herself at the door, where her cousin threw her cloak over her shoulders and quickly tied her bonnet under her chin. Elizabeth fixed her with an intent look and kissed her cheek.

"Holly. Trust this. Go!" The last was punctuated by a stamp of her foot.

After a moment's pause, with the smallest gleam of hope lighting her eyes, Holly decided.

"I will!"

And with that she was out the door.

HE LOOKED AT THE WATER slowly flowing past the barren banks and naked trees. A few leaves were still clinging on the branches, but they looked very forlorn and would soon have to give up to another heavy storm or even the first real snow.

As he watched, one leaf gave up its struggle against the inevitability of time and, though no breeze or movement had disturbed the stillness of the air, it released its hold on the safety of the branch and softly fluttered down to the surface of the water. He followed it until it floated out of sight. In truth, he felt a kinship to it, like he had been carried to this point by an innocent, bubbly mountain stream and before he knew how, he was now quickly being drawn through the rough and wild river current towards the waterfall. There was nothing else to do, the banks were too far away and held no real rescue; he had to take that plunge over the edge. He only hoped the water would carry him and give him some strength and purpose before he was either thrown on the rocks underneath or into unknown and dangerous waters.

Absentmindedly he snapped off another twig from the willow. He fiddled with his watch and wondered if the breakfast was anywhere near its end. He should have stayed, but it had been impossible, and now he found that even if waiting in a calmer location might not be as perilous to the sensibilities of the guests in the bridal party, it certainly did nothing for his own sense of peace. After having taken a few turns to pass the time, he had no desire to continue giving in to this restlessness, but concentrated on the faint sound of the rippling water and prodded the tufts of wilted grass with his cane.

Thus she saw him standing on the side of the path. As he noticed her approach, he lifted his head; a flush of excitement, then nervousness, rose within him and gripped his stomach and his face broke out in a curious mix of a smile and a frown.

She stopped a good ten feet away from him and he greeted her softly.

"Thank you for meeting me here, Miss Tournier. You can have no doubt..." He stopped himself and smiled sheepishly at her. "That is, I *hope* you can have no doubt of my need to speak to you alone."

While rushing to the river bank, Holly had been trying to keep her thoughts and questions, hopes and fears under control — but what did he wish to say to her? What if he was not there? Why did he pick the willow grove? What on earth would she do if he insisted on continuing that infuriating line of argument and questioning from the last time they had spoken? She did not know the answers to any of these questions, but she refused to give in to wishful thinking.

At least that is what she kept telling herself.

She took a moment to steady herself and her breathing — ruthlessly suppressing the spark of hope that his words gave rise to in her heart — before she could answer him.

"My lord, when it comes to you and your purposes, I must confess I am often in doubt."

He studied the ground in front of him as he smiled.

"Yes, I am certain that is a very fair estimate of my faults and trespasses against you."

He took a step closer and met her eyes. He was hoping to find encouragement and some clue of how to begin there, but she returned his look with a puzzled and wary expression.

He sighed and decided that in order not to enforce her rightful objections to his conduct towards her, he now quickly needed to change tactics and try straightforwardness at the expense of diplomacy.

"My need to speak to you alone is actually a consequence of trying to rectify the many instances in which I have erred against you, but also against myself. The most blatant example of that being that day in your mother's garden. I hope you will forgive me and show patience with me for bringing that up again, but it is of crucial importance that I start by putting that... incident in its rightful perspective."

A look of pain flashed across her face and he was momentarily taken aback.

"I'm sorry," he mumbled, "the memory of it causes you discomfort, I know. I am not willingly trying to be selfish in my defence here. I... I need to say something."

"Oh..." She said faintly and looked out over the riverbank. "If you have brought me all the way out here to offer another apology, my lord, it was not necessary."

"No, that is not why I…I have offered too many empty apologies of late, but I have come to realise that the only way for me to put right what I have wronged is to give you something of greater value. And the most precious and rare thing I have to give to anyone — to you — is the truth. I must be truthful. To you and also to myself. And you must do with it as you will.

"I pride myself on being a rational and reasonable man, Miss Tournier. But that day I was far from it. Had I been rational and reasonable, I should have realised my true offence. For you see, in truth, I very much *wanted* to kiss you that day. I think I had wanted to do so for a very long time, and I was a fool when I did not realise it was not so much a spontaneous outburst rather than the quite rational expression of a more long-standing need…"

She coloured and her eyes darted here and there, looking everywhere but at him, her breath coming rapidly. It was obvious that she was embarrassed and bewildered, but he pressed forward, afraid to stop once he had begun. It must out. All of it needed to be said to leave no doubt either in her mind or his. Not anymore.

"Pardon me, I do ramble on," he said more quietly. "I think I must offend you. I know I did so then. In so many ways. I was so dishonest and such a coward, I can very well understand if you should never forgive me. All I can say is that I am honest — painfully so — now."

He tried to meet her eyes, but she continued to look flustered and turn away.

"My heart, you see, is a new-found companion to me," he went on, smiling a little, apologetic smile. "It has been a stranger to me until now. Until you. And now it has taken me over and speaks with my voice. It says to me that you are essential to my happiness. That my life, in truth, already circles around you and it needs you to feel complete. All else is pretence and rationalisation. And the urge to kiss you was just a desperate expression of that hitherto suppressed need."

She lifted her eyes in one hasty movement and looked at him. Encouraged by the fact that she looked more bewildered than disgusted, he decided to push on.

"So, my heart says, ever since that day, I have in truth wanted to do it again. But that is a trifle difficult since I did promise not to. Do it again. But now, I thought, in view of what I now know…hope…if I might ask…very politely…Do you think…? Would I…could I kiss you again, Miss Tournier?"

HOLLY COULD NOT BELIEVE WHAT she was hearing. She looked into his eyes, they were brilliantly blue and open and sincere — no masks. It seemed an eternity without sound, just the world spinning around her and his words echoing in her ears. That and the faint realisation that he was laying his feelings — his honest feelings — before her. Was her mind playing tricks on her? He wanted to kiss her? She grasped for words but none came out. Only a small whimpering, desperate sob.

His eyes had not let go of her. They were still watching her, steadily, with hope and fear and desperation in them that belied all the casual eloquence of the simple question he had just put to her. Hardly trusting her voice, she gave a hasty smile that

375

dissolved into an incredulous look.

"You want to kiss me?"

"I do. More than anything. May I, you think?"

"Why?" was the unexpected answer. "Why now?"

"Because..." he smiled nervously, looking down and fidgeting with his hands again. "Forgive me. I'm a fool." He took a breath and smiled again. "Miss Tournier. I am so sorry but I ... I love you. That is why I kissed you then, and that is why I want to kiss you now."

After swallowing hard she gave a quick bob with her head and his face broke out into a relieved smile.

"Really? You mean...?"

"I..." She shook her head, "I don't know, but right now ... yes. Oh yes!" And then she looked up into those blue eyes, wondering if her heart had been put into an empty barrel and was rolling down a steep and bumpy hill, while she waited with a fluttering stomach and a tiny bit of terror as he leaned in toward her.

Just before he was close enough for her to feel his breath on her face, he drew back a little, reaching out his hand. She took it slowly, as if uncertain whether her actions would shatter the moment, but when he closed his fingers around hers all she could hear was the sound of her heart beating. He held on to her tightly and opened his other hand, palm up. In it lay a twig of willow, twisted and braided, soft and supple from the work and moulded into a ring.

"No. I should ask you something else first. Something even more important," he smiled hesitantly. "Will you marry me ... Miss — Holly ... please?"

Despite his almost overwhelming nervousness, he almost had to laugh when he saw her reaction; her eyes grew wider and her mouth dropped open as she looked from the willow ring in his hand up to his face and down again several times.

"Are ... are you in earnest?"

"Never more so in my life, my sweet."

Her eyes softened and she smiled the most beautiful smile he could imagine. She lifted her hand and clasped it in his; the little willow ring between their palms. When she looked at him again, there was a decided gleam in her eye and with a lift of her eyebrow, she gave him her answer.

"I will have to think about it. But you may kiss me in the meantime."

That was all the encouragement he needed and he drew her closer as a wave of relief and happiness washed over him. There were no sharp rocks at the bottom of this waterfall after all. In her eyes he had found a calm, deep pool of still water that he would happily drown in.

"Oh no," he said, feeling her closeness. She looked up at him expectantly, her lips already parted. "I will not make the same mistake twice. I have been so unforgivably foolish and I fear I must know now. So, madam," he muttered as he caught a wisp of hair come loose and slowly tucked it behind her ear, "I will gamble everything, I will stake my heart. This is a package deal this time I'm afraid: will you be mine *and* let me kiss you...now and for the rest of your life?"

She was trembling. His closeness, the touch of his hand as he played with her hair, the sound of his voice as he whispered so softly and intimately, the look — the almost overwhelming look in his eyes. She wanted to resist, to say, "Wait! There is so much to consider" — this was so sudden...

But she could not tear her eyes away from his, and she could not resist what she saw in them. All she could manage was an almost imperceptible nod and a barely whispered, "Yes."

"Oh, good," he simply said, and then everything else was secondary.

It was just as he remembered. She smelled sweet and warm and tasted of honey and dew. Her hand never left his and he clasped it tightly to make certain she would understand he would not let go before his time — this time — and more than anything, he felt like the missing piece of a puzzle had finally been found and fitted perfectly into a very awkward and hitherto curious void within him. There was so much promise in her answer, there was so much happiness to be discovered and she would marry him. She would be his and he would be hers: to torture, to tease, to test every inch of the way and to kiss, to love, and to openly adore and enjoy and to never, ever let go.

He released her lips and rested his forehead against hers.

"Thank you," he said. "You have made me a very happy and a very relieved man. I thought it was too late. I thought I was too flawed. I thought I had driven you away the very moment I dared listen to my heart alone."

Holly felt as if she was dreaming. She was in his arms, and this time instead of feeling shock and surprise, she felt at home, safe and warm, like she was finally in the one place she had always belonged. The cold hurt and loneliness that she had carried within her heart since her father's death began to loosen and thaw with his kiss.

When it was over, he was still there, speaking words she could scarcely believe, showing himself and his heart to her, unguarded and vulnerable.

"You are welcome — you are so very welcome. I should be ashamed to admit it, but what you did that day, that was not what offended me. In truth, it helped me to know my heart as well, but afterwards..."

He still held onto her one hand tightly, but her other hand had somehow slid under his coat and rested on the small of his back. He felt so warm and strong and she knew she should take her hand away, but the thoughts of what had happened before made her want to hold him all the more tightly.

"But afterwards...you pulled away...you will not pull away from me again?"

He smiled and let his arms encircle her tightly.

"No, I will not. Ever. Look!"

He released her and took her left hand in his, slipping the willow ring over her finger. It was too big and it chafed against her other fingers, but he lifted her hand to his lips and kissed it.

"It's neither grand, nor valuable but it would bend, like me, around your finger for as long as you will have it. This willow will not weep, it will turn and follow and draw you back if you ever regret having sat down by its feet. That I promise you, sweetest, dearest, busiest bee of my heart."

She smiled as she fingered the ring.

"It may not be grand, but it means the world to me."

Everything was still around them. It seemed even the water that had been bubbling and chattering before had slowed its pace and rested. There was no wind; there were no birds, just a steady heartbeat where she rested her head against his chest that was in perfect harmony with her own still sounding in her ears. She slipped her arms around his waist, wondering if she could ever again feel as happy as she did at this moment.

Chapter 34

The Romance at Longbourn Continues

THEY were slowly — very slowly — making their way up the village road back to Longbourn. She was leaning on his arm, a weight he cherished, and he was doing his utmost to keep her as close to him as possible. Sometimes her head would briefly lean against his shoulder and he would stop their walk to have a better look at that sweet face so infuriatingly hidden beneath the bonnet.

Very little had, in truth, been said. He felt it was a relief for once to let his actions and expressions speak for him and to do so without control or qualms. He was delighted with the way his every true word or look caused her to reward him with the same. She laughed a great deal and sighed happily a great deal more. He used every excuse to draw her towards him and delay their return and she did not put up much resistance.

"Do you think she will forgive me?" Baugham asked when she laughingly accused him of once again employing underhanded tactics to prevent her from returning to her mother. "I have kept you out here to myself for a scandalously long time, and when I do bring you back, it is only to tell her that I will be taking you away from her for good. I believe I might truly be frightened to face her. She has had no qualms in letting me know she is already most displeased with my behaviour of late." He kept his grip on her and despite the fact that they were in full view of the road, he slipped his arms around her.

"Ah, my love," he sighed, pushing her bonnet back. "To think my triumph could be this great after my faults have been so grave. It is, I declare, positively immoral."

She smiled and lifted herself on her tiptoes and kissed his lips lightly, keeping her hands on his shoulders possessively.

"I admit your behaviour has been quite vexing, and not only to Maman, but she has been equally cross with me recently, so she may not at all mind your taking me off her hands. However, this brings up a very important matter that should be discussed. Have you thought this over carefully? Are you absolutely sure this is what you want? I most likely will not make a very good wife, you know."

He raised his eyebrows and caught hold of her waist with both of his hands.

"Discuss? Matters? Dearest, are you trying to scare me off? Here I am making violent love to you — at long last, one might add and against all my silly notions of self-preservation — and you want to discuss 'matters'?"

He lowered his head closer to hers and brushed his lips over her cheek and temples on his way to finding her lips once again. He let his hands bring her even closer, his blue eyes intensifying as she was once more drawn to rest against him.

"No, it seems you will not make a very good wife at all, will you?" he murmured.

"I think I just told you that. Just remember that I have done my duty and warned you."

He gave a throaty little laugh that for some reason sent a thrill down her spine.

"I rather think you will make a perfect wife...for me. But yes, I've thought this over carefully. I've thought of nothing else for days, and this is exactly what I want.

He rested his chin on her hair and softly asked, "Now, are there any other serious matters of import you would like to discuss, madam, before I kiss you again?"

"Actually, there is one other thing."

"And what might that be?" he asked, tilting her chin up with his finger and teasing her mouth with his.

"Tell me why," she managed to ask.

"Why I want to kiss you?" he teased, his breath warm on her cheek. "I thought I answered that already. I love you."

"Oh..." was all she could say and despite having quite happily slipped into familiarity with him so quickly, she blushed.

He simply smiled and tenderly draped the shawl that had fallen down over her shoulder again, taking much time in assuring it was lying snugly against her neckline. Then he kissed her and gently nudged her on, still holding on to her waist.

They wandered out onto the main road leading to and through the village. Baugham was slightly disappointed to note that most of the good citizens of Meryton and its surroundings who passed them as they made their way back seemed in a hurry to be somewhere else out of the chill air and not inclined to take notice of his singular cause for happiness or his beautiful future bride. They picked up their pace, her hand entwined through the crook of his arm, and there rested a contented and peaceful silence between them.

When they spied the roof of Longbourn peeking over the hedges at the end of the lane, Baugham stopped and took her hand.

"Dearest...Holly?" he said softly. "May I come in and speak to your mother yet today?"

She smiled at him, neatened the folds of his cravat and straightened the lapels of

380

his coat.

"You had better. If you think I will consent to you going back to Netherfield and leaving me to wonder whether all of this has been a dream, or to fend for myself in this singularly light-headed state you've reduced me to, without going inside and making this official with my mother, you are sadly mistaken."

She fingered the circle of willow still adorning her left hand, "Though, what she will have to say about your choices in jewellery... I cannot tell."

He smiled and, determined to steal one more kiss in the shelter of the shrubberies, he encircled her and drew her close.

"Well, whatever she does, I have high hopes she will congratulate herself on a very well directed lesson in propriety after all."

Holly was just going to ask him what he meant when he executed his ambition and engaged her in a long, thorough and breathless kiss that effectively emptied her mind of anything except his presence.

MRS TOURNIER PURSED HER LIPS and let both of her hands rest, obscuring the text of her open book lying in her lap. How long was that daughter of hers going to walk the country lanes in her sorry state? She had seen her slip out after talking to Elizabeth earlier, but when she questioned her niece she would say nothing about Holly's disappearance.

The bridal couples had departed, and the older generation of the Bennet family was quietly sitting in the parlour digesting the day's events. Mrs Tournier glanced at her brother in the chair beside her reading his paper. That he had stayed with them, rather than retire to his study, was a testament to the contemplative silence in which they were immersed, each sunk into his or her own thoughts, each unwilling to share them. Even Mrs Bennet was silent, blissfully basking in the great fortune of having daughters sensible enough to attract such wealthy and fine husbands, when the door opened and her niece stumbled in, bright-eyed, cheeks flushed, breathless and followed by an only slightly less animated Lord Baugham.

A stunned silence followed where the older Bennets stared, and the young people exchanged sheepish glances and tried to catch their breaths and composure.

Finally, Mr Bennet folded his newspaper over his knees and gave his sister a look.

"Perhaps you should like to make use of my study, Arabella?"

Mrs Tournier found herself quickly and replied in a calm voice.

"It certainly appears that I should," she said and abandoned her book.

She stood and walked down the hall and the young lovers trailed after her, aware that their movements were being followed by the other occupants of the parlour — one slightly bemused and one keenly curious. Once they entered the room and the door was shut behind them, there was a strange silence as Holly shuffled with her skirts and his lordship shifted his gloves from one hand to the other and finally deposited them into his hat. Mrs Tournier noticed something peculiar in their postures. They stood a little too close together and there was a little too much eagerness in their avoidance of meeting any eyes.

"Well!" said Mrs Tournier, turning around to face them. "Either you have caused another monumental scene with one of your incomprehensible quarrels or I had better ask his lordship not to take a seat until he has spoken!"

The brightness of Holly's eyes belied the attempt at calmness in her voice.

"Maman, I believe you should offer Lord Baugham a seat. He...he wishes to speak with you."

The object of their debate could not resist sending her a look he knew spoke plainly of all the feelings he had so recently attained her permission to express.

"I dare say Mrs Tournier is perfectly right," he smiled. "What I wish to say to her does have a better, more appropriate, ring to it done formally."

Mrs Tournier, in turn, sent him a look which almost made her daughter tremble, and then settled herself regally in a chair by the fire. But his lordship sent his love a reassuring smile and addressed himself to her mother.

"No doubt the singularly silly grin on my face speaks volumes to a shrewd and impatient observer such as yourself, ma'am. I have a perfectly good reason for it, however, which must speak in my defence. I have asked your daughter if she would honour me with her hand in marriage and, to my great relief and happiness, she has accepted me."

"Indeed?" said Mrs Tournier, contemplating which of her several honest sentiments she should express first.

"Oh, madam, please don't tell me you are rendered speechless! Rather let me suggest to you that wonder at how I ever made it to this point, or even self-congratulation on your part, would be far more appropriate."

Mrs Tournier pursed her lips but could not suppress the twinkle in her eye.

"I only wonder at what my daughter did to finally bring you to your senses, my lord."

Baugham looked at his betrothed, still steadfastly standing by his side.

"She laughed," he simply said. "She frowned. She smiled. She crept into my heart and kindled a fire. She had the courage and conviction to look me in the eye long enough for me to see promises of things I never thought I would see. And," he added with a wry smile, "she bothered me until I thought I should go distracted."

"Yes," Mrs Tournier said tartly, "she has a tendency to do that."

One look at her daughter's face after his little speech told the woman all she needed to know. The girl was far gone. The both of them were far gone. She leaned forward in her chair and held out her hand to Holly while addressing his lordship.

"I would say that you are even on at least one score, Lord Baugham, for you have caused sufficient bother and distraction in this family to consider yourself fully repaid for whatever troubles you may have experienced. I have questions and concerns, make no mistake about that, but since it is obvious that neither of you has room for any thoughts beyond your present bliss, I will defer any conversation on matters of business for another day.

"Well, I suppose if you must have her, I *can* have no objections. I warn you though, Tournier ladies come in pairs."

382

His lordship laughed. "Of course! And let us not forget, madam, which of you enticed me first to give up my secluded existence. I shall never forget that first afternoon's tea, when I was so pleasantly disabused of all my prejudiced notions regarding my Scotland neighbours."

Mrs Tournier gave a quick smile and shook her head before turning her attention to Holly.

"I know you are happy, Lie-lie, and I am happy for you. You do not need my consent, but as long as your young man there satisfies me of his love for you and his intention to take care of you, you will have my blessing. It is good to see you smile again. You look just like your Papa when you smile so…"

Holly, who had been watching their exchange with her heart in her stomach and a lump in her throat, was completely overwhelmed with emotion when her mother spoke those words and she was only able to choke out, "Oh, Maman…" before the tears came. She dropped to her knees and embraced her mother, still sitting in her chair, laughing as she cried because she knew how silly she was being. After a time, she composed herself enough to loosen her hold and accept the handkerchief offered by a slightly uncomfortable, yet still smiling, Lord Baugham.

"As much as tears distress me, my dear, and in particular, I have found, your tears," he said while she wiped her eyes, "it must be a remarkable testament to my blissful state that I cannot stop grinning even now."

He then noticed Mrs Tournier glancing down at her daughter's hand she was still holding on to with a look of surprise.

"What in the world is this?"

His lordship pulled up a stool to sit beside the chair and answered sheepishly, as he took Holly's hand from her mother's and fingered the willow ring.

"This, ma'am, is evidence of the sorry state your daughter has brought me to. I would accuse her of toying with me by her delay in meeting me, if I were not convinced there is not a touch of guile in her. The longer I waited for her this morning, the stronger the realisation became that I did not care to be without her — ever — and all the time I worried she would not come. By the time she finally arrived, I knew I must propose without delay. If she said yes, I would not wait another day to put a ring on her finger and so provide the world with visible evidence of my good fortune. Call it a selfish impulse if you must…" he squeezed her hand and smiled tenderly into Holly's face, "but it is an impulse I am very glad I gave in to."

To his surprise, Mrs Tournier only smiled distantly as her hand rose up to the locket around her neck. A few moments' reflection brought a change however, and with slightly narrowed eyes she turned again to Lord Baugham.

"Well then, with such a happy ending to such a bizarre affair, I trust that you will keep all other…impulses you may have under good regulation henceforth?"

Holly blushed scarlet at this and was about to sputter a protest, but his lordship merely smiled.

"You have my word as a gentleman. I will treat your daughter with all the respect, honour and dignity that such a lady as she is, deserves and if she scolds me for my numerous trespasses — old and new — I will only love her more."

The smells of cooking dinner wafted their way through the house and into the study, reminding Holly that she had been unable to eat very much at the wedding breakfast. More than ready for a proper meal, she scrambled up from the floor.

"You will stay to dinner, my…my lord? I shall just inform my aunt…" before giving two separate hands a squeeze and exiting the room.

Holly delivered her message quickly and did not stay around for the inevitable torrent of questions from her aunt, instead she slipped down the darkened hallway into the empty morning room. It was dim and cold, but she needed a moment alone to think and reflect. The events of the day had been so sudden, so wonderful and so surprising that she could scarcely believe them to be real — only the little bit of twisted willow and the very real recollection of the feeling of his arms around her was proof that it all had actually happened. She thought wistfully of Elizabeth, wishing that she was still there so she could share her joy with her dear cousin — but with a smile and a blush, she realised that Elizabeth most certainly would *not* wish to be back at Longbourn this night.

So instead, with the sounds of her Aunt Bennet's frantic preparations for a distinguished and unexpected dinner guest in the background, she closed her eyes, remembering his words, his looks, his embrace…and she allowed herself a child-like bounce or two and a tiny squeal of joy before collecting herself once again and slipping out, returning to the warmth of the occupied rooms. She paused outside the door to the study, smiling as she realised that she needn't have closed her eyes to see him, he was waiting for her just inside. He turned at the sound of the opening door and looked at her with such affection that she wondered if it were possible for a person to expire from sheer happiness — if it were so, she thought, there was a very real danger she would never live to see the morrow.

THE DINNER WAS A QUIET affair. The events of the day had effectively quelled any need for joyous outbursts and loud congratulations. It seemed, to everyone, there had been an abundance of them already and all were content with sitting back and admiring the one happy couple left for them to study. In keeping with the day's events, it certainly seemed nothing but logical and right that young love should not completely abandoned Longbourn all in one sweep. Mrs Bennet could not help sending wistful looks down to Miss Catherine, but then the inclination to be content with the more distant family connection to a peer overtook her and that night, when she sent for the after dinner fruit and sweets, she was actually a very happy and fulfilled woman.

Holly hardly looked at her lover all through dinner, but she could feel him sending her frequent looks and smiles between his easy chatter to her mother and Uncle. She smiled almost continually herself and felt a warm glow of contentment inside. The day had been a long one and an evening spent in polite conversation in a parlour was to neither Holly's nor Lord Baugham's tastes. Holly felt she needed to catch her

384

breath and Lord Baugham felt like he needed to catch his equilibrium in quiet. It had been a revolutionary day and the feeling of happy exhaustion was enough to send his lordship back to Netherfield earlier than expected.

"Oh!" Holly said just before they reached the door to take a long drawn-out farewell away from the prying eyes and formal rituals of the parlour. "I completely forgot. I meant to ask you, I tried to find you at breakfast, but you had disappeared. Why?"

He smiled. "I couldn't stand it anymore. Two more minutes and I would have bitten Mr Bingley's infuriatingly smug and happy head off. People kept expecting me to concentrate on the wedded couples and all I could do was to gawk at you. It was embarrassing."

"I never noticed you gawking at me."

"Well, I was. I still am."

A satisfied smile appeared on her face, "Hm."

After such a day and evening, Holly was not able to accompany him outside and say the goodbye she would wish to. She had to content herself with his offering of a tender kiss on her cheek and a squeeze of her hand on the threshold... and a kiss to the forehead... and softly running his finger along her cheek and under her chin... and a tug on a loose curl... and a kiss to her hand... then to each finger... until the rattling of a newspaper and the sharp sound of a closing book in the parlour, not to mention the giggles from down the hallway, made them recall the presence of numerous chaperones in the house.

"Right. Well, then," he said, as he at last stepped out into the night, donning his hat, "Good night... Holly."

There was a draught from the open door, but Holly could not bring herself to close it completely.

"Will I see you tomorrow?" she said.

"Yes."

"And will you be early?"

He smiled. "Yes."

"It seems such a long time away. I wish it were morning already."

"Yes." He leaned in over her and kissed her soundly. "You sleep well. You will need all your strength and patience when I call again. Tomorrow. Early."

She smiled. "Yes."

He started moving towards the carriage and she was suddenly struck by a practical question.

"Oh... dearest?" she said, hesitating a little while taking a few steps out into the courtyard. "What do I call you now?"

He turned around just before getting into his vehicle and a smile broke out over his features. "Whatever you like. As always," he said and waved goodbye.

Holly wrapped her shawl around her and watched the carriage leave with a strange warm feeling rushing all through her. "Dearest," she whispered. "As always..."

That night Mrs Tournier once again subjected her daughter to her one hundred in silence before bedtime. Sometimes, when the whole world changes, old routines become all the more precious and important. There's no need to mourn them as such, but obeying them one more time takes on a significance that can only be seen and known when they will soon disappear from our daily lives forever.

LORD BAUGHAM SAUNTERED INTO THE lower drawing rooms at Netherfield whistling a ditty that was distinctly romantic in nature and happy in its tune, dealing — he seemed to recall — with the delights of a shepherd boy being able to steal a kiss from the dairy maid and in French, no less. It was an empty house with the staff having been allowed to take advantage of their Master's big day and early departure for his honeymoon to some other part of the country. But Miss Bingley sat in front of the fire, deeply immersed, it seemed, in a solitary game of *Patience*.

Baugham sank down in the sofa and gave her a happy wink of his eye. Miss Bingley looked slightly taken aback, but continued her careful placing of the cards before addressing him.

"So," she said slowly, "here we are."

"Oh yes!" he said, but he could not stop thinking of the last bit of verse he could remember. "*Si tu le veut, ah, tant mieux!*" And he hummed a little of the remaining chorus.

"You look very sly, my lord," Miss Bingley said. "I wouldn't suppose it has anything to do with your successful evasion of the last hour of the wedding breakfast?"

"Oh, Miss Bingley. Nothing escapes you!" Baugham said cheerfully. "Are you telling me you did not enjoy it?"

Miss Bingley abandoned her cards and looked thoughtfully at him. "I must confess," she said carefully, "I am not overly fond of country weddings, never having had much experience of them. It is altogether a far too...public affair for my taste. It is, after all, a contract, an arrangement, a domestic issue, not a public ritual at all. And it so very vulgar to be gawked at by people one does not know and has no connection to. Though, at such events it is vulgar to be gawked at even by people one *does* have a connection to, I suppose."

"I certainly agree with you there," Baugham said. "There is something to be said for private ceremonies."

"Ye-es." Miss Bingley smiled. "Special licences really are a God send."

"An expensive God send," Baugham said, but was now looking at her with interest.

"Of course," Miss Bingley agreed. A little smile played around her lips as she turned back to her pursuit. "Oh, but it really was a lovely wedding all the same. As far as country weddings go, I suppose. And dear Jane was such a lovely sight to behold. I think...yes, I am quite certain we shall be the best of friends and the happiest of sisters!"

"And what about you, Miss Bingley?" Baugham asked. "It seems Netherfield has a new and benevolent Mistress. How will you take to that?"

"Oh..." Miss Bingley shuffled together her cards and gave a little laugh. "I love my family very much. We Bingleys are all very close and extremely fond of one another.

That will surely not change regardless of this latest…addition to our family circle. Although, hopefully, within moderation as to certain extended family members."

She gave his lordship an exaggerated sigh and arched her eyebrows in a disgusted gesture. Baugham could very well see she wanted him to ask her meaning, but he found he had no wish to and so he ignored her. Instead he smiled to himself. He was beyond hope. He had no interest in gossip! Truly this had been a most extraordinary day!

"Well," his companion continued as no response was forthcoming, "the Bennets are what they are. All I am concerned about is dear Charles' happiness. And I do think dear Jane will make him very happy."

"She seems to have a general talent for that," Baugham smiled, "so your sentiments must be ever so slightly tainted by self-interest as well, I should think."

Miss Bingley did not wish to answer that so she took up her cards again.

"Oh but I shall be very happy to quit the country, now that the deed is done," she said. "It is such a strain on one's nerves to be away at this time of year. I fancy I shall see you in Town soon as well, my lord?"

Baugham could not help but let a smile break out on his features. "I think you shan't have the privilege, my dear Miss Bingley," he said. "You see, it seems I shall have to overcome my own dislike for country weddings and start busily arranging one of my own."

As he got up, he gave her another wink and his most brilliant smile and decided to make an early night of it in order to honour his promise to his country bride and be back at Longbourn again early the next morning.

Chapter 35

The Groom makes his Preparations to take Himself and his Bride north, which Receives a Mixed Reaction

"COME and sit yourself down, my love, and let me confess my foolishness to you. Then we can see what you will call me today," Baugham said and patted the window seat beside him in the small hall outside Mr Bennet's study.

Holly smiled and obliged him. "Although after what you just did to me I am inclined to be in a very charitable mood with you."

"And if I repeated my performance in front of your relations in the parlour, what would you do then? I confess I had a hard time waiting until I had you for myself, so I should like to know for future reference."

"I should most probably be forced to slap you, my lord, and then request you do it again twice in private."

Baugham laughed. "Very well. I might have to become a repeat offender because I was about to tell you I am about to desert you."

"You would not dare," she said lightly, but with an incredulous pout.

Baugham reached out and gently ran his finger over the creases of her frown, pleased that he now had the liberty to indulge in his earlier wishes of smoothing it away. "No, I would not, if I had not already made the arrangements to go north to Cumbermere right after the wedding. Today, in fact."

"Oh!" Holly said and could not help looking rather despondent.

"My dearest little bee," Baugham said softly and caressed her cheek. "If you only knew how much I adore your inability to disguise your feelings."

Holly smiled faintly. "I... It's just, I had hoped — "

"So had I," he sighed. "I don't know what incredible stupidity made me go against my fondest hopes and wishes and fix an engagement on the other side of the Kingdom just when I was about to see you again.

"But go I must, although I can well postpone it for a day or two and blame the weather, the roads, letters, social engagements, cleaning up after the bridal party...everything but the real reason."

They exchanged a lingering look and Baugham caught her hand and kissed it. "In fact, I do think Mr Tilman, my steward, would be shocked were I to promptly present myself at the expected hour. Mustn't do that."

"Well, if you must go, you must go," Holly said, a little placated by his obvious look of adoration and deciding she could well afford to be generous.

"Well, my dear, I think that I am not alone in that. You, after all, must go, too."

Holly shrugged a little. Her mother had mentioned no plans and it seemed to her she was quite happy to sit in her brother's study for a while yet.

"Do you know what is my highest wish?" her betrothed muttered while still holding her hand to his lips.

She was shaken out of her reverie and gave him an indulgent smile.

"Oh, I see I have effectively destroyed my reputation for anything else than flirtation and courting," he laughed. "Very well, I must redeem myself. I am going to adopt the role of Lord and Master sooner than you had ever imagined and will arrange for you and your mother to accompany me as far as Nottingham. Can you live with that?" he asked more softly.

Her smile told him she was quite happy to practice wifely subservience in this instance to match his newfound interest for husbandry.

He looked at her shrewdly. "And if I tell you I will be finished with my business within a fortnight only to rush across the border to your side and return to Clyne?"

Her face brightened. "Oh!"

"So, in view of all that information, what would you call me today?"

She gave a little laugh and swung the foot she was resting on her other leg. "Oh, I cannot tell you! I tossed and turned for hours in bed last night thinking of how to call you!"

He did not say anything, but the way the light shifted his eyes to a darker shade and he held her gaze for just a trifle too long, made Holly blush without knowing exactly why and avert her eyes to her hands in her lap instead.

"Well," said Baugham slowly, "don't fret, love. The only thing that matters is that you will be able to call me husband soon enough."

She nodded, at a loss over why her heart beat a little faster and her breath came a little quicker still.

"So, in that vein, tell me, are you one of those women who feel it would be a sin to pass up the chance of a society wedding?"

"Oh, not at all!" she said quickly. "That is...unless you..."

"God forbid! I could not imagine anything more tortuous than escorting the love of my life up and down the vestry to sign the register at St George's Church in

Hanover Square. I think we should get married in Scotland."

Holly smiled. "Because it is the quickest way."

"Not at all." He returned the smile and caught her hand to hold it between his. "Because it is your home and I love it."

"Well, that is a good thing. Weddings in Scotland have some dubious connotations where young, unmarried Englishmen are concerned."

Baugham laughed again. "I'm not that young! And thankfully, my dear, neither are you!"

IT IS NOT EASY FOR young lovers to make love in a house while still adhering to the demands of polite society, especially in a house already suffering from the deprivation of two beloved daughters and their well-tolerated suitors. The couple draws attention when they would prefer neglect, and are teasingly accused of behaving either foolishly or adoringly — depending on the perspective and expectations — when instead of providing entertainment for the listless household, they would much rather secret themselves in a private corners, away from amused glances and knowing observations, and proceed with their mutual adoration in peace.

Still, they bravely try and discuss the wedding that took place recently without slipping into too much speculation on their own, compliment the hostess on her taste and fare without wistfully confessing they would much prefer to be home, and engage the mother in talk about general things without somehow making every thing relevant to the bride. Plans for leaving are quickly suggested and when no one except the Mistress of the house can find any arguement against the scheme, practical arrangements and concerns are quickly dispensed with normal social intercourse must once again be attempted.

At some point, however, the elders grow weary and the youngsters grow itchy. Then there is nothing else to do but to cast an admiring glance out the window and profess a great desire to take some enjoyment in the fresh air despite rain, hail or icy winds and then quickly accompany one's beloved outside where there, curiously enough, is plenty of opportunity for combining propriety with pleasure.

"Do you realise," Holly said, leaning on his arm as they walked around the house in perfect contentment and ignorance of the ice cold wind on their faces, "that this is the very garden where Lady Catherine tried unsuccessfully to warn Elizabeth away from Mr Darcy? She told me she called it a 'prettyish kind of wilderness'." Holly looked around, "And it is very pretty in the summer…"

"That may be," his lordship murmured as he leaned forward, past the brim of her bonnet to kiss her cold cheek with his warm lips, "but I think I like your garden at Rosefarm better — a perfect mixture of regimentation and exuberance that I absolutely insist you bring to my home and my life as well."

After brushing his lips over hers, he continued leading her around the barren grounds. "So, that is where the women in your family are afflicted with their obstinate streak? In the garden? I should have guessed. I suppose in learning to challenge the iciest winds and fiercest drizzle there, you would thus have no problem standing up to a mere Lady Catherine. But poor woman, I'll warrant she had not reckoned on facing such a stubborn adversary."

"I do not have an obstinate streak!"

"Of course you do," he laughed, "and quite a charming one."

He felt her stiffen ever so slightly.

"As much as my bad qualities are under your protection, sir, and though I have a great many faults that I will own up to, I will not have you adding to that list unnecessarily. I *do* have strong opinions, but I am *not* obstinate."

Leaning in very close he whispered in her ear, making her shiver, "Then, prove it."

"How?"

A sly smile spread across his face, "Accompany me to that bench over in that corner, sit down beside me and let me kiss you."

Holly rolled her eyes. "That bench over there? Away from the windows and out of sight? After all the significant frowns and 'watch yourself' looks I had to endure from Maman before she would let me out the door just now? And really, how is that supposed to prove your case at all? You surely can't expect me to — "

"Of course I didn't!" he cried triumphantly. "As I already said, you're obstinate!"

As he expected, her brows nearly met in the middle and she turned flashing eyes to him, muttering, "I'll show you obstinate." She turned and pulled him directly to the bench, grumbling all the while, plunked herself down in the middle of the seat and turned a saucy smile upon him, "There...who's obstinate now?"

He sat down next to her, close, so very close, and removed his gloves and hat and reached across to place them on the seat on the other side of her.

"I am impressed, madam. But, if I recall, the bench was only the first part of the challenge." He leaned in and ran his finger softly underneath her chin, "Now we must ascertain whether you are too stubborn to let me kiss you — on this bench in the corner, away from the windows, and out of sight."

He leaned in and touched his forehead to hers and smiled. He felt her quick intake of breath, he watched her eyes grow deep and dark and felt her hand slide around to his back, and then, *she* was kissing *him*, and in such a way that he very quickly lost all awareness of where he was — all he knew was her...his Holly...the tickle of her breath on his skin, the taste of her mouth, the soft insistence of her fingers on the back of his neck as she drew him closer, the curve of her waist and the roundness of her —

With difficulty he pulled back, but she looked at him with a broad smile.

"Who is being stubborn now?" she teased, not realising the extent of control he had had to master. "I think, now that I have given in, I could stay out here and let you kiss me all morning."

Baugham cleared his throat, drew in a deep, shuddering breath and turned to face forward.

"Well, love," he smiled wanly, "*could* and *should* are not exactly the same thing, now are they? Talk to me instead." He leaned forward, his elbows on his knees, "Tell me

391

what you plan to do while I am away, once you return to Rosefarm."

"Talk to you?" Holly asked, puzzled. "After all your scheming to get me over here and out of sight, you want me to *talk* to you?"

"Yes, actually," he smiled softly and relaxed a little. "After all, when we are married I intend to be highly unfashionable and spend a great deal of time together. It would be nice if we could learn to hold a civil conversation just the two of us. I don't think a little practice would do us any harm, do you?"

MRS TOURNIER STOOD IN FRONT of the window of her brother's study — the study that had been their father's before him and that had barely changed since the day she had left her childhood home so many years ago. Their father had smoked a pipe and there was still the faint smell of tobacco lingering in the fabric and walls even though her brother was not a smoker himself. The study was a curious place. It was either the place for exchanging harsh words or even dealing out punishment for misdemeanours or a place for silent companionship through reading. Yesterday, and on two occasions not so long ago before that, it had been the place for releasing a dearest child into the care and guardianship of a man professing violent, but honourable, affection for her.

Violent and honourable... Mrs Tournier watched her daughter walk past the window with her betrothed. She sighed and turned away from the prospect only to find that her brother was watching her.

"I know how you feel," he said. "And I have gone through it twice."

"Then you have had some practice, with still more opportunities to become even better at it. I am not so sure I did so very well at all and now I have no one left to redeem myself over."

"I can only improve, because I will not care as much," her brother said.

They exchanged feeble smiles and Mrs Tournier sat herself down.

"What a harsh thing to confess, Brother," she said lightly.

"The truth nonetheless. And who says that old age should only leave wisdom and resignation? I am quite selfishly angry and miserable at the same time, and I do not intend to deny it. It is a comfort of sorts."

"I'm sure it will be. Once I get that far."

Mr Bennet folded away his newspaper. "Are you worried about her, Arabella? Do you think she has done something foolish?"

"No. Rash, certainly, but not altogether unexpected or even avoidable. I have faith in the reason and affection of them both. I dare say they will be well suited, but I am convinced they will have to both work hard and learn humility if they are to get what they want out of this marriage. And I think each of them wants so very much from it."

"Marriage doesn't always oblige you that way."

"Some degree of disappointment in one's spouse is inevitable."

There was a long silence between the siblings.

"There is one thing that I keep turning around and around in my head," Mrs Tournier finally said. "Do we chose who we love because of the people who did not

392

love us? Those we wanted love and affection from, but who were unable to give it? And, if that is the case, how much can we expect rationality to save us? Is not false judgement based on misconceived rationality far worse than a mistake made by the heart?"

"That's three things, my dear," Mr Bennet smiled.

"Give me one omnipotent answer to all of them then."

But Mr Bennet shook his head. "No Arabella," he said, "I cannot give you that. I am the last person on earth who could. But I do think — yes, I will admit as much — that had you not gone away to London all those years ago, I might not have had to say goodbye to exactly the daughters I now have."

Mrs Tournier turned around and stared at him. "What do you mean?"

"I mean I missed you. I missed your wit and your courage and your relentless older sister dismissals of my arguments."

Mrs Tournier reached out her hand and her brother took it. "I miss Father," she said. "Every day. When Jean-Baptiste died all I could think of, for months, was that he was no better than Father."

"And yet," her brother smiled, "here we are. The source for another generation's faltering steps to finding themselves through others. What do our flaws and mistakes matter, Arabella, as long as we can say we truly loved them and they know it?"

"Not much. Perhaps not so much after all."

Longbourn
Hertfordshire

My dearest Elizabeth,

Yes, I am back to calling you Elizabeth just as you must always call me Holly regardless of what either of us may change into. I sit here at Longbourn still, at your own desk in your own room — well, your old room — a room so filled with you that I truly think any minute you will come bursting through the door and tell me to come and look at something downstairs immediately. And if you should come bursting through the door, Mrs Darcy, I should still not be afraid of you but tell you, just as I always do, that ordering me about will get you nowhere and that I have a very important letter to write that I will not put off on any account.

Maman and I will start our journey North tomorrow and before I start packing and saying my goodbyes, I must send you this note, hoping that your honeymoon at Pemberley is everything you dreamed it would be and that you might actually have time to read it.

You may ask yourself why I insist on claiming your attention only to profess my boldness and the pleasure of using your quills and paper. Well, I can promise you a little more than that. Oh, Eliza, I can scarcely say the words — how can I write them down for you! Best to just bravely charge ahead, I think, and extravagantly devote much space to one single simple line.

Lord Baugham asked me to marry him and I said yes and I am so happy I could burst!

There, are you shocked? Are you amazed? Would you care for me to elaborate? I shall tell you then that it is quite true, although the letters stare back at me too and I cannot but marvel at how strange they appear. But it is true. I love him very much — well, perhaps you suspected that already — but he loves me too, Elizabeth. I am certain of it. And the truth is, as strange and unbelievable as it seems, my acceptance has made him as happy as his offer has made me. It certainly is a strange thing to have someone admit to such attachment that he will not even let me go back home alone, but plots and insists on Maman and me travelling in his carriage all the way to Nottinghamshire under his protection before he takes to his estate in Cheshire to settle his business and we catch the post further North. Would you believe how happy I am to succumb to his highhanded ways? He has promised that once finished he will return to Scotland and we will be married right away!

My dearest Eliza, thank you so much for sending me out into the cold December morning to meet my fate! And thank you for keeping the hope alive for me that I might be loved to such a degree that my knees go weak, my heart flutters and bubbly laughter mingling with tears of happiness arises at the most inopportune moments! And thank Mr Darcy for the arrangements to bring me and Maman all the way here from Rosefarm! I so long to talk to you and have you laugh at my childish happiness at such a turn of events. And maybe we shall do so very soon. I sincerely wish it.

But for now you must content yourself with being happy with your Mr Darcy, the beauty of Pemberley and the knowledge that your cousin wishes you every happiness to match her own. I will go to Clanough, wait for my prince, read the letters he promised to send me every day and occupy myself with work until he can come back and claim me. Not that it is necessary. I live and breathe in my love for him and have done so for such a long time it seems already that nothing can be left wanting.

Your faithful cousin always,
Holly

Chapter 36

The Strain of Confinement Wears on the Nerves of one
Traveller and on the Restraint of Another

WHEN Lord Baugham handed the hired mount over to the ostler at the Nottingham inn, he stretched his sore limbs and revelled in the sensation of discomfort due to exercise rather than circumstance. He was a poor traveller under the best of circumstances; his restless disposition did not take well to being confined within even a very fine carriage for hours and days on end, and by the middle of the second day of travel with his future bride and mother-in-law, he could take no more. It was not that the company was unpleasant, or even that he could not overcome his usual distaste for confinement. In this particular instance, his dilemma was quite the opposite in that the company was entirely too pleasant, too distracting, too tempting, and with Mrs Tournier keeping her attention in her book for the greater part of the day, and succumbing to the drowsiness of the road in the evenings, he had entirely too much time to ponder just how pleasant, distracting and tempting the woman was who sat across from him.

He sighed and could not help but regret how badly a restless temperament tolerated a long journey in such circumstances. No wonder it had all ended so queerly, finding him now waiting for them, half grateful and half frustrated, watching horses being led about and counting the moments until his carriage would appear while at the same time dreading that very appearance because of the words left hanging in the air upon their separation.

He sincerely hoped Mrs Tournier had been wrong earlier when she announced in a clear voice, as he sat watching and Miss Tournier sat being watched, that a few days' travel across the country in a carriage taught one more about one's fellow travellers than twenty years of polite marriage could do.

"Not that this marriage looks like it is going to be burdened with that particular characterisation," he muttered to himself while kicking an overturned bucket, innocently laying by the yard pump.

So, if one cannot make love to one's betrothed on a confined, bumpy carriage ride, one must occupy oneself in other ways. As in conversation with one's future mother-in-law about one's betrothed.

"I hope you don't object to a speedy marriage," his lordship asked Mrs Tournier.

"I would think in this instance it was a sign of prudence," was the answer.

There was a quick look from Holly, but Baugham avoided lingering on this self-evident conclusion of their marriage plans by a wink and a smile. She settled back, but he could tell her attention was piqued, so he decided to continue this successful line of speculation.

"Excellent! I was thinking St Thomas' Day, the twenty-first of December, would be suitable. Soon enough for discretion, yet far enough away to make the proper arrangements. I will have no makeshift, blacksmith Scottish wedding either," he said, still smiling. To his surprise, his bride frowned, so he explained further. "I have given this some thought and I have every intention of marrying you in a ceremony that is valid in England as well as Scotland."

"Of course, you have! I never doubted that," Holly said testily, "but Scottish marriages are perfectly valid marriages and seem to do very well for many Scottish people."

"Exactly! *Scottish* people. Which we certainly are not. When it comes to the English, we can never be too careful with Scottish marriages, I'm afraid."

Mrs Tournier abandoned her daughter in her gallant defence of Caledonian customs and owned that she agreed with his lordship. Holly looked down at her hands and pressed her lips together.

"And since we have no intention of getting married in London — "

"In Hanover Square, that is," she interrupted him. "I thought we only agreed on not wanting a society wedding."

Baugham looked surprised. "You want to get married in Town now?"

"No, I don't. That is to say I would not object to getting married in Town if that was easier for our purposes, since you just spoke so damningly about Scottish weddings, but — "

"Well then!"

He directed this last comment to the mother, who nodded and let her eyes sweep over the two young people with some interest. Holly's only reaction was a sigh and the act of parting the curtains on the small window and looking out through the mud-stained glass at barren fields.

"I will see to the right arrangements," Baugham went on in a slightly more conciliatory tone, not realising that it was too late to for appeasement. "I will not drag my bride down the aisle for any ceremony that will cast doubt on the validity of our marriage, nor will I consent to any repeat performances for the English authorities.

I want to marry her properly, in front of God and in the faith of my fathers in which I was raised and which my sovereign has sworn to uphold and defend. I believe there is an English church over at Melrose and I will have the Episcopalian minister there marry us in the same communion and with the Archbishop's approval. If you can stand travelling the extra miles to have it done, that is. But I think I had better warn you. I have a strong suspicion that if you want to challenge this plan and St Andrew's as your wedding church, you will likely have to fight both me and your mother."

Mrs Tournier nodded. "Now as for the settlements..."

Baugham waved away the question. "Of course. All will be properly seen to. I'll have my man in Edinburgh, Mr Crabtree, come down to Rosefarm, shall I?"

"Excellent idea," Mrs Tournier agreed.

"What about personal arrangements for my daughter?"

Baugham sat back in a satisfied manner. "Riemann tells me he intends to write to my London staff at once and direct Mrs Townsend to immediately begin inquiries into finding a suitable abigail."

Holly shuffled uncomfortably in her seat and took to twirling her willow ring nervously between her fingers.

"And I swear the willow ring will be gone before it is worn through," Lord Baugham said with an indulgent smile.

"I like the willow ring!" was the quick answer.

Both his lordship and Mrs Tournier met this bit of fancy with a small laugh. After that, Baugham now realised, he had committed the grave error of launching into further detail about the wedding breakfast at Clyne, mistakenly taking his bride's silence as a sign of interest and approval. Granted, he was thoroughly deceived as to the prudence of discussing all these important matters right then and there by Mrs Tournier's relentless quizzing as to his future plans: his return from Cheshire, whether he had made any travel plans for the honeymoon period, and where he intended they would settle afterward, were each examined in detail and he prided himself with the fact that he had ready answers to give for each of her inquiries. So much so, that when the conversation turned to the sticky point of whether the prospective bride should honour her current employment obligations, and if so, how, they were so immersed in the subject they did not notice that bride's features growing positively forbidding.

After at least an hour of deliberation and still unable to come to an immediate solution that could be satisfactory to all parties, he and Mrs Tournier agreed to put the subject aside for the time being; she picked up her book again and he turned his attention back to his lovely, but now silently staring, beloved. As he sat watching her gaze thoughtfully at the passing scenery through the window glass, contemplating just how much he was looking forward to wedded bliss, and so quickly back to the same distressing dilemma as before, he felt a pair of sharp eyes peering over the book at him. He coughed, fidgeted, smiled sheepishly and turned his own attention out the window, and at the next roadside establishment they passed, rapped on the roof of the carriage with his walking stick.

His fiancée had not been very understanding of his sudden desire to hire a horse and ride ahead to secure lodgings on this last night before they were forced to part ways, and she made no secret of the fact. In fact, it seemed to him through their heated exchange of words while the horses were changed and he was procuring his own mount, that she was dissatisfied with his every gesture and word. The quarrel that took place out in the lawn before the tavern had not only attracted the amused attention of several other travellers, it also reinforced his desperate resolution that a separation was indeed for the best.

After securing three more than adequate rooms, and partaking of a warm meal and a hot bath, he felt much better, and when his carriage arrived, he greeted the occupants with equanimity.

His future bride met his greeting with a narrowed-eyed look of frustration.

"Well, I see you obviously have benefitted from our separation, my lord," she said tartly. "You have me at a disadvantage, I'm afraid."

Her mother gave her one exasperated look before she swept up the stairs to the building and away from the rush of horses, vehicles and traffic around them

"You need a bath," she told her daughter, "though I might just take the opportunity of washing out your mouth myself!"

Baugham had the good sense to hide his amusement behind a wide-eyed incredulous look and said nothing.

"I'm sorry," he said and then concentrated at drawing his betrothed away from the menacing movements of the horses and ostlers rushing around them. "I am a miserable traveller, but I should not have expected your sufferings to be considerably eased by just removing myself. I wish I could have made you fly."

"Fly!"

Holly's frustrations at having been forced to sit with all her objections and pent up frustrations for the better part of the afternoon came out in a disgusted cry. It now was impossible for his lordship to ignore it.

"You're still upset with me." Once again he was awarded with a disgusted noise. "I'm sorry," he said again. He took her arm and gently steered her up to the front of the Inn. "Now about that bath..."

Her eyes flew open. "Don't tell me you've arranged that, too!"

"I've arranged it all. It is what we agreed, after all," his lordship defended himself, not a little perplexed. "What? You don't like to bathe?"

"It is what *you* agreed," she retorted with a sigh. "I have scarcely been able to draw breath lately without something being agreed about me."

His stare intensified and had she known him a little better there would have been enough warning signs in the way he looked at her to realise she had tread on sensitive matters.

"You resent my actions on your behalf?"

"Not really," she muttered, fully aware she was pouting like a schoolgirl, but desperate to regain some control. It seemed she had given up every semblance of that in her life lately. Since agreeing so happily to marry him, so much was already being decided for her, she felt she was not her own mistress anymore — not of her feelings, her thoughts, her obligations... What would happen to her if she no longer could rule herself? Would she disappear behind a strange noble title and Holly would be no more? Would she be sent around to strange estates among strange people in strange carriages with or without her husband? Would she float away at the mercy of her husband, society, unknown persons and expectations, and be lost to herself for ever? Who would she be then? And would she become forever completely helpless?

"But," she said hesitatingly, "there is so much! You have no idea! My whole life... and all in a short time... You and Maman in that carriage... it will all be gone and I don't know... Oh, I suppose I am frightened!"

They stayed away from the door where people were walking in and out. Standing in the shade of a nook in the ancient building, Holly felt his arm settle lightly around her waist.

"Not of me, I hope." There was a softness to his tone, and even a playfulness, that refuted any possibility of her being so, but this time it was evident from the way he looked at her that he was thinking of other things, too.

She stepped slightly away and fixed her gaze steadily on him.

"Of you most of all," she admitted. A look of concern flashed across his face but she continued, "I am afraid of how very much you mean to me... the power you have even now over my heart and happiness and the power you will soon have over everything else. And when you plan out my future above my head as if I am not even there... it frightens me how willing I am to place everything I am in your hands and how little and how futilely I object."

His first reaction was to protest, to question her trust in him and be hurt in the standard convention of lovers, but before the words reached his lips he realised that she was putting a name to the same fears that he, too, knew and struggled with. That she would look him in the eye and share those fears with him so plainly, spoke of more trust and love than he felt he had any right to expect. He reached out and lightly took her hand, brushing the twisted willow ring lightly with his thumb.

"You're right. You will not regret it," he promised, "I cannot swear that I will always be right or perfect, but if your heart and happiness are in my hands, they are also inescapably joined with my own, which are in yours. I think, I *know*, we will be very, very careful with each other, and therefore ourselves."

He brought her hand to his lips and he saw her expression soften.

Both of them concentrated on that little piece of twisted wood, already so fragile and abused in love and affection.

"The willow ring stays?" he said.

"The willow ring stays," she said firmly.

"Can I give you another one, too?"

"Another willow ring?"

He shrugged. "Or whatever material seems appropriate and is available."

She suppressed a smile. "Oh, very well. As long as you stop speaking so harshly about Scottish weddings and embarrassing me with monetary details. I felt like you were going to put a price on my head next!"

"I'm sorry. Those matters are important, though."

"But not in closed carriages."

"No," he conceded. "Now," he said with a tender smile, "shall we venture back inside and see if we can't make the most of this last evening together?"

LORD BAUGHAM WAS AS OBSESSED with horseflesh as the next typical gentleman, but his interest often took curious detours out to strange stables where he could chat with professional handlers, and quietly observe as they carried out the familiar, soothing rituals of caring for the dependable beasts. While waiting for his fellow travellers to take the baths he had so imperiously arranged for them, he walked up and down the stables at the back, paused to witness the dance of coordinated chaos as horses were changed and led away and then sat himself outside the inn to watch the busy road out of Nottingham gradually quiet down in the growing dusk of the early winter evening. Soon, there was nothing left to see. Even the dogs had gone home and the few people venturing out at all were bearing lights against the dark, even though it was barely dinnertime.

That thought awakened expectations in both his lordship's stomach and mind, so he got up and sauntered back to the inn. With the last of the posts departed and most of the cold and weary travellers having retired to their well-earned rest for the night, the stately Clarion Inn was very quiet. There was sure to be more life in the taproom, but his lordship realised he was not in a taproom frame of mind since he was waiting for his bride-to-be and her mother to join him for dinner, so he hung about the stairs, at first politely answering inquiries and looks from staff and fellow inhabitants but soon growing restless and unable to ignore the growling noises from his stomach.

Then he heard a door close and footsteps in the gallery above his head; it surprised and pleased him to realise that, even in such a place, he immediately recognised to whom they belonged. He turned on his heel and took the first three stairs in one go on his way up the narrow stairwell to meet the one who was long overdue to spend her time with him.

The moment he set foot on the landing, he saw her disappear into her room. He walked down the hall and just as he reached the doorway, the door was flung open and he was face to face with a flurry of light coloured skirts and a whiff of a feminine smell he knew very well. Nearly losing his balance, he caught her in her rush, taking several steps forward to steady himself until he was pushed against the wall just inside her room with a bump. Not deterred in the least, he noticed to his delight he had caught hold of her around her waist and that she was leaning against his chest with only her shawl in a bundle between them.

"Oh!" she said faintly

"Well, oh, indeed!" he said and smilingly raised her up again, leaving the support of the wall behind him, but not loosening his grip one bit. "In a hurry somewhere, madam? I am, perhaps, in your way?"

A slow smile spread across her face. He was the last person she had expected to run into upstairs, but though she was very surprised, it was a most pleasant surprise.

"What are you doing up here? You should not be in here. I was coming down to meet you."

"Too late," he smiled slyly. "Too slow. I had to find you most urgently."

With one hand still holding her shawl, she leaned into him and looked up into his face with an amused expression.

"Well, now you have found me. What do you intend to do with me?"

"Hm, well let me see... I could tease you with the fact that I have taken it upon myself to order your entire dinner for you and insist you come down to the dining room and eat it this instant. Or I could jealously ask you if you have made plans to escape my tyranny since you are clasping your outer garments so passionately to your person... Or I could begin the difficult work on trying to balance my faults with my virtues and keep you right where you are... "

"Ye-es, you do have a great many faults for which to atone. Perhaps a recitation of your virtues would be beneficial to your cause."

He tightened his hold on her just a little and was pleased to notice her breath quickening slightly and a faint blush creeping over her cheeks.

"On the other hand, actions speak louder than words. And, of course, if one would persuade, one must appeal to interest rather than intellect... "

Giving him a look that could only be described as saucy, Holly tilted her chin up in playful defiance.

"I will have you know that I highly prize my intellect and I fail to see how a right and proper listing of your good qualities would fail to convince me." Her smile turned sly, "And I'm sure I do not know what you mean when you accuse me of having interests."

An overwhelming feeling welled up in him; he could not tell if it was love, appreciation or gratitude, or perhaps all three, but he delighted in the fact that she was there with him, alone and playful, yet without a hint of playing games.

"At this moment I find the thought of pursuing anything remotely intellectual, tedious in the extreme." He leaned in closer. "As for your interests... perhaps you would allow me a small demonstration. I believe it will prove my point."

And indeed his point was well made. There were a number of things she was suddenly very interested in — his arms, his hands, his mouth, his scent, his warmth, his ability to make her feel so completely out of control and beyond her own knowledge.

She lost her grip on the shawl as she wrapped her arms around his neck and it fell to the floor between them in a flutter. Neither of them paid it any attention. He walked her back against the wall and along with the hard panelling against her shoulders, she could feel him pressed against her on the other side, just as hard and unyielding — and yet she found she wanted to draw him even closer still. When his lips released hers and moved over her temple and down her cheek and over her ear, she moaned slightly and then gasped in surprise.

"Holly," he murmured in her ear, his breath tickling her, his elbows moving to both sides of her head, leaning against the wall behind her. "Oh Holly…"

"Yes," she said without really understanding what she meant by saying it, but it was an answer to something and it came instinctively from deep within her. "I…yes…"

He lifted his head and met her eyes. She was shocked by what she saw in them. His eyes, a dark violet with unimaginable storms raging behind them, bored into her and she almost lost her ability to breathe. In fact, she was distinctly short of breath and her body trembled with something…something deep within her spreading throughout her stomach, down to her legs, arms and finally head, making her eyes lose their focus and her cheeks flame with heat.

When he kissed her again, she did not even flinch when she opened up to him, so ready to have him come even closer, even further, even harder…

But then suddenly he broke off and she grabbed the lapels of his coat in desperation as he pulled back, certain she let out a cry as well. His breathing was rapid and harsh. His hands were on the wall behind her again and he held himself away from her.

"Oh Lord," he said in a strangled voice. "This won't do. It won't do. I think I must go…"

"No, don't go. Please." Struggling for control herself, Holly tried to speak evenly. "I am sorry. I should have…I should have not…"

"You have nothing to be sorry for, Holly," Baugham took a step backwards and ran an agitated hand through his hair, "No *shoulds,* no *should nots.* My mistake, my fault…When you are this close, I lose all sense of myself. I lose all sense of anything but you…I should just leave now…"

"No, you can't. Please don't leave like this. We'll have dinner. We can walk down, talk, wait for Maman…"

He looked at her smilingly, a little calmer.

"No, my dear. We cannot, *you* cannot, go in right now. Look at yourself."

While she blushed, tugged, straightened and adjusted in front of the mirror, he looked up and down the hallway and tugged at his coat and waistcoat nervously.

"It really is quite a good thing I will go tomorrow," he said quietly. "To Cheshire. It is no use, I cannot…We have some time yet to get through until we are married — everything must be done properly, arrangements, settlements, matters of great importance that I will not allow to be rushed or poorly done just because I cannot control…it has hardly been four days and look what I am doing. Look at what a desperate fool and graceless cad I am. It is your mother's garden all over again…"

She finished her adjustments and he held out his arm to her.

"I'm sorry, too," she whispered, taking it cautiously and allowing him to lead her slowly down the stairs. "About now and…about earlier, when you left. I don't want to lose my temper with you but when you…something just happens…"

If she could have seen his face fixed on the stair ahead of them she might have felt slightly offended again, because Baugham indulged in a wide, impish grin.

402

"I know, my love, something does."

"I suppose it is because you break through every wall I have built around me that I feel the need to defend myself, to lash out at you. In a good way, I mean."

Baugham's smile turned tender and he looked at his bride-to-be. "A very good way, love," he said, addressing her in a soft voice. "You'll see. All will be perfectly well. We will just have to wait a little while longer and I am certain that when we ... get to know each other even better, everything will be just as it ought."

"I do love you," she muttered, "and I don't understand why I should ... "

Baugham shushed her and in a quick gesture, just before rounding the last corner of the corridor, turned her chin upwards, kissing her soundly and holding on tightly to her elbows, both to keep her near and far enough. For now.

"But soon," he said while looking down at the increasing floor space between them. "On St Thomas' Day ... my wife." A smile spread across his face. "In everything and every way." Only then did he dare look at her and she saw he was almost physically hurt with the effort he had just displayed.

"I cannot wait," she whispered. "I ... I want so very much to ... " she dropped her eyes, "In every way ... "

"I thought that was my confession to make," he smiled impishly. "I very nearly did not just now ... wait, that is. You are ... you are all that I could wish for."

She reached out her hand and he took it, once again putting it through his arm but keeping the distance between them. Holly looked at him awkwardly and he returned it with a sheepish smile. She was bewildered, disoriented and a bit short of breath.

"I think dinner," he said gesturing towards the door to the dining room. "Don't you?"

THEY WALKED THROUGH THE DOOR and found Mrs Tournier already seated at a table close to the fireplace. Her expression changed from irritation at being kept waiting to expectation when she noticed their entrance to curiosity upon their coming closer. She said nothing as Lord Baugham pulled out the chair for her daughter, but when they were both seated she noted dryly, "You were quite right in forgetting your shawl after all, my dear. I think even you will have to agree that his lordship did splendidly in his highhanded arrangements this evening, providing us with seats close to the warming fire."

She nearly startled when, within seconds, first one then the other jumped up and cried:

"Oh, my shawl. I must have dropped it! I'll go and ... "

"No! Please, allow me ... "

"Goodness!" Mrs Tournier commented, not a little alarmed, before turning to his lordship and saying crisply, "Did you plan that, too?"

Apparently, Mrs Tournier reflected, she had hit a raw nerve because Lord Baugham rose with a murmur and hastily walked out. She cast her daughter a glance, but Holly was arranging her skirts and saying something inane about heat and fires. When his lordship returned, he was carrying the missing garment as if it was a rag of undeterminable origin and instead of returning it to its owner, he gave it to her with another murmur.

"Maman thought I might be cold," Holly said in a queer voice. "She didn't know...we didn't know about the fire."

"Oh, I didn't light the fire!" his lordship protested and then pointedly looked about for the staff.

"No, of course you didn't," his betrothed said. "No, you couldn't have known about the fire. Being so hot, I mean."

"But it is good," Lord Baugham said while still eyeing the room. "Hot fires are good. Just as they should be on cold...cold winter...nights. And all the way into spring of course."

"Of course," his bride agreed enthusiastically. Mrs Tournier narrowed her eyes.

"You must be hungry," she said slowly. "You are no doubt affected by the excessive heat after your extended wanderings around cold hallways."

She noted that at exactly the moment she chose to deliver this observation, Lord Baugham's imperious look finally attracted a servant and Holly chose to take the shawl out of her mother's hands and busily fold it into exemplary neatness.

Mrs Tournier sighed. So there was a "garden" in this place, too, but instead of abruptly finding business with his horse like the last time, his lordship had come into dinner with them. She decided to make the best of the evening and its incomprehensible conversation and thank the heavens that a separation was forthcoming.

The conversation part was perversely entertaining. Everything she said was met with excessive interest while the comments of the other party were met with hasty acceptance and monosyllabic replies — and no eye contact. The obvious trespass on polite intercourse and decorum from earlier in the day was compensated by such formal drawing room manners that Mrs Tournier was certain she was going to lose all patience.

But, it had to be owned, this obvious state of affairs did cause her some relief as well. It had been a curious and very quick courtship and it was to some degree reassuring to see her daughter so free from doubt, not to mention his lordship so single-minded. Nevertheless, Mrs Tournier decided as she watched her daughter accidentally brush over his lordship's fingers as they both reached for the salt shaker, the situation probably warranted a candid discussion with her daughter on the ways of the world. She may be touching in her defence of Scottish marital customs, but she had a very short memory if she was likewise putting her faith in the social customs of small Scottish villages. Yes, there were plenty of reasons for a small chat and enthusiastic endorsement of a wedding before Christmas.

WHEN THE POST CHAISE AT last pulled into the Caledonian Thistle yard on the last leg of the journey home, all she could think about was the hope that Mrs Higgins had kept supper warm and lighted the fire in her bedroom. If she never set her foot in a carriage again, it would not be too soon!

It had been a difficult goodbye and that last kiss he had stole while her mother had

404

her back turned and was arranging her skirts over the seat was too rushed and too desperate to make up for the morning's frantic scheming to have a last moment alone.

"I'll think of you with love," she had whispered, "even when I curse you for being so far away."

His smile was unmistakable and he had quickly twined his fingers through hers before parting on the top of the stairs. So she had to do with just the memory of those pressing fingers, that smile and the hasty lips on hers as she sat and watched the landscape change and the northern climate claim ground.

The next morning when she woke up in her old bed in her small room, it took several minutes for her to reconcile the events of the previous days with her present surroundings, but soon she was lying back on her pillows and remembering. Soon after that she jumped up and hastily pulled on her dressing gown. She skipped down the stairs on her way to the kitchen to share her good news with Mrs Higgins, but as she passed the parlour door she suddenly stopped. It was empty, but the sight of her worktable, scattered with papers and pencils, rock samples and specimens, halted her in her tracks. She had said in her letter to Elizabeth that nothing could be wanting to make her happiness complete, but she now knew that everything was not, in fact, perfect.

A feeling akin to regret and guilt welled up in her stomach. She did not, by any means, regret the events in Hertfordshire or her engagement to Lord Baugham, but she did hate the thought that Dr McKenna would be made unhappy and she felt guilty over the fact that he had done so much and been so kind to her. She did not believe any of his actions had been taken in order to create an obligation, but the truth was she did feel thankful to him, and obliged, for his kindness and generosity and she could not think of how she was going to tell him of her engagement. He had always treated her in a manner signifying only friendship and esteem, but the expectation that she would have been able to successfully encourage him beyond friendship, added to the knowledge that she had planned on offering such encouragement, made her feel awkward and uncomfortable.

She ran her fingers over one of her sketches and picked up a rock sample, hefting it in her hand, then allowed it to fall back on the table with a clatter. She left the room, closing the door behind her and went to the kitchen, but not quite as excitedly as she had begun.

MRS HIGGINS STRUGGLED UP THE last slope towards Clyne Cottage with the distinct metallic taste in her mouth from near exhaustion. She still held on to her skirts in one hand to ease her step and clutched her basket in the crook of her arm while panting heavily from her more than brisk pace. A woman her age should not be scampering across the fields with her skirts hitched up like some young slip of a girl, but she was in a hurry. She never stopped to socialise as she usually did on the way to visit her cousin, but pressed on ahead without more than a mutter of an apology to her neighbours and their greetings. Mrs Higgins was in a hurry, because she was in sole possession of earth shattering information and if she did not reach Mrs McLaughlin as soon as possible, someone else might claim knowledge and familiarity with the extraordinary intelligence that had just reached her from her young lady's own lips and that would not do. It was most especially urgent since a letter was expected and it was a sure thing Mrs Robertson would not hesitate to spread the word once it arrived.

Not far now. She had been rehearsing her announcement ever since Mrs Tournier had dismissed her from the parlour and Mrs Higgins had spontaneously walked up to Miss Tournier and given her a hug and her heartfelt congratulations including a few tears and pinching of young cheeks. Very soon after that had she abandoned her post in the kitchen and set off. And now she was almost there. Just a few more steps around the house...through the kitchen garden...up to the door and...Better take just a few seconds and catch the breath...although, of course, that was equally possible inside...

Mrs Higgins burst into the kitchen at Clyne Cottage just as Mrs McLaughlin was serving her husband his tea. Both of them looked up in amazement and ceased their activities as soon as Mrs Higgins came in unannounced and set her basket down on the table with a resounding bang.

"Rose?" Mrs McLaughlin said frowning. "What on earth? Is everything alright?"

Mrs Higgins tried to catch her breath and steady herself at the table. Mr McLaughlin, having neglected his neeps for the moment it took him to realise it was not an escaped beast nor a whirlwind that had broken down the door to the kitchen, calmly went back to his meal.

"Come here, cousin," Mrs McLaughlin said. "Sit yerself down. Ye're in a right state!"

"I...am...well," Mrs Higgins said and tried to swallow the bile that crept up her throat.

"For certain yer nae such thing!" Mrs McLaughlin said sternly. "Yer red as a lobster in the face and yer eyes are about to pop out of their sockets. Ye'll give yerself an apoplexy! Sit down!"

Mrs Higgins did as she was told for she could do nothing more and she needed her strength to impart her knowledge, not to argue with her imposing cousin.

"Now, don't tell me ye've been running all the way from Clanough, Rose, ye know right well it's nae good fer ye. Yer nae as young as ye used to be and with the cold in yer lungs and the way ye exhaust yerself in this cold weather, ye'd be a fool to..."

"Laird Baugham!" Mrs Higgins managed to spit out. Her cousin stopped her tirade instantly.

"What about his lairdship?"

Mrs Higgins thought she might have started out at the wrong end anyway for all her careful planning.

"That is..." she attempted, but had to clutch her chest again and swallow a few times. "Miss Tournier really..."

Now her cousin was looking at her with a distinct frown and sat down beside her.

"What in God's name are ye blabberin' about? Do ye have news of his lairdship through Miss Tournier?"

406

Mrs Higgins nodded. "They're getting married."

It sounded so flat the way the words almost wheezed out of her between her attempts to steady her breaths, but the effect they had on Mrs McLaughlin was mesmerising nonetheless. Her mouth dropped open, her eyes bulged and she sat absolutely frozen in front of her, just staring back without making a single sound. Mrs Higgins sat back in silence herself and let her heart slowly slip down her throat and back into her chest again.

This singular constellation was enough for Mr McLaughlin to glance up from his meal at his wife and her kin.

"Humpf," he concluded after a while. "Weel, nae ferlie. That was a teed baw.[1]" And he wiped his mouth and left the table.

Pemberley House
Derbyshire

My dear, sweet, excellent Holly,

I am stealing time from all my various obligations like congratulatory visits, answering felicitations (who <u>are</u> half of these people who write me to tell me they are so happy for me?!), learning to navigate in and outside of my already beloved Pemberley and, most especially, my dear Mr Darcy, to send you my love and heartfelt congratulations. How happy, happy you have made me with your wonderful news! Mr Darcy sits by me as I write this, admiring my hand and style, as he should at every opportunity from now on, and although he is quite jealous of my attention, he expresses full confidence in my ability to adequately portray his delight and happiness for you as well. We are both so pleased about the news! He, it must be confessed, is also astonished, but I told him it was only his blindness for my own charms that stupidly led him to ignore his lordship's obvious feelings for you. I think he almost believes me.

Oh Holly, I wish I could find the words to tell you about married life! It is wonderful! But it is more than that, it is bewildering, confusing, so strong and at times almost feverish in its expression but it really is the most wonderful thing. And, as you too will no doubt have the joy of discovering, the stronger sex can be so weak while the weaker sex so strong that the promise of complete harmony of one mind and one flesh in a perfect state of bliss really is attainable. I do not know if one is supposed to discuss it or even how, but you will see what love can do. And when we next see one another we will drink our tea in silence and elegance, look at each other and just <u>know</u>.

I am so happy for you! Of course, I am happy for myself for being such an excellent cousin in my perseverance in subjecting you and his lordship to one another's company

---

1 Well, no wonder. Cut and dry from the start.

and for being so clever as to boldly impose on two people and thus make four persons happy in one go. And I am so very happy I could extract that promise from you not to swear to things no one has the right to forsake in the name of principles. You will be very happy, I know it, and when you send that piece of wedding cake to me I shall cry a little for the childhood friends who are now so very grown-up and established beyond their wildest dreams. They will be happy tears, Holly, because of all the people in the world, I can think of no one who deserves to be happy more than you!

All my love and sincerest congratulations once more.

Your cousin
Elizabeth

McKenna thought he had braced himself. He had spent the time of Miss Tournier's absence preparing himself for any possible outcome of her time in England in the company of Lord Baugham again. Once he heard that she had returned, he made himself wait several days, but this morning when he was breakfasting at the inn, Robertson stopped by his table and asked if he would drop something by Rosefarm if he was planning to go that day, and he readily agreed.

He thought he had braced himself, but when he realised he was being commissioned to deliver a letter to Miss Tournier he felt a sinking in his chest, and when he saw a return address of Cumbermere Castle, Cheshire, he knew that he had not really been prepared at all. He tried to give it back to the landlord, but Robertson was already rushing back to the bar to address a billing dispute with another patron.

So he set out for Rosefarm Cottage unenthusiastically, but he came upon her in the lane on the way. She appeared distracted and did not see him coming her way until she was nearly upon him.

"Oh! Doctor!" she exclaimed, before quickly dropping her eyes, "It's ... it's good to see you."

So there he was, standing face to face with Miss Tournier on the road and not knowing how to approach the subject of the letter that weighed so heavily in his chest pocket. She was obviously uncomfortable and casting about for something to say, but as much as he might understand, and even sympathise with her discomfort, he was also at a loss.

"We just returned," Miss Tournier finally broke the silence, "I mean, it's been several days, of course, but, well ... I am on my way to the post office."

Her words pulled him out of his stupor. Here was the opening if ever one was to present itself. He reached into his coat pocket.

"Then it is lucky we met, Miss Tournier, for now I can save you the trip. Mr Robertson has asked me to deliver this to you."

He watched as her eyes brightened, "A letter?" She started to reach out for it, but then she let her hand drop slowly.

"Yes. He thought you might want this particular one right away." He held it out to her and she took it from his hand thoughtfully and ran her finger over the seal.

"You have seen who it is from, of course."

"I have."

"I think I should..."

"No need, Miss Tournier. No need at all."

They stood motionless again for some time, both staring at the letter she held in her gloved hands. McKenna at last cleared his throat.

"Well, I think I had best be getting back. Please accept my congratulations and give your mother my best."

"Thank you," Holly raised her eyes to him, "I will, thank you. But will you not come to tea, or perhaps...we could do some work?"

"No," he shook his head slowly, and smiled, "Tomorrow, I think. I am sure you will need to recover from your journey. Perhaps...yes, tomorrow."

"Of course."

Stiff bows and curtseys followed and then the lady and the gentleman slowly turned and walked back in the directions they had come. McKenna returned to his room to work for the rest of the day in silence and solitude. Holly returned to Rosefarm, climbed the stairs slowly and closed herself in her bedroom.

Too ambivalent about the scene that had just passed, she could not bring herself to break the seal at first. She crawled up onto her bed and sat cross-legged, holding the letter in her lap and trying to reclaim her earlier excitement at the thought of receiving this very letter. She closed her eyes and pictured him, his smile, his eyes, that way he had of looking at her. She looked at the silly willow ring still on her hand and smiled as she twirled it around her finger. She examined the seal and the written direction and imagined him sitting at his desk writing to her. And eventually, her unease lessened and her anticipation grew; she broke the seal and began reading her very first love letter.

CLANOUGH WAS A SMALL VILLAGE, and like every other small village, town, or community throughout the world and throughout the ages, its inhabitants were closely connected and intimately concerned with the goings-on of all its other inhabitants. Births and deaths, one man's habits of drunkenness or sloth, one woman's long-suffering endurance or propensity to nag, family quarrels, financial blessings or struggles, causes of rejoicing or causes for despair — all were viewed as the rightful knowledge and property of the entire populace. And, like most small, intimately acquainted communities, the sudden elevation of one of their own to unexpected fortune and prosperity was not always greeted with rejoicing. In too many homes the cry, upon hearing the news sweeping through the neighbourhoods like wildfire, was, "Why her and not me...or you...or our Meg...?" This was something Holly should have been aware of, having spent so many years in the small community of schoolgirls that was Hockdown, but she was not thinking of such things this day.

This day, all she could think of was her need to get out of the house.

It was the low murmur of voices that pervaded the rooms — the voices of her mother and Mr Crabtree as they negotiated over her worth and her future — that drove Holly out into the cold wind to run Mrs Higgins' errand to the butcher for the day's meat.

Slowing down her steps as she neared the post office, she wondered if she should take herself inside to inquire after letters. There had been one yesterday — a very lovely letter that had put colour in her cheeks and a lump in her throat and that had convinced her that her betrothed was the sweetest, most charitable, loving and poetic man on earth. A reply had already been dispatched with Mrs Higgins that morning, but as he had said he would write to her every day...

Still she was hesitant. It had surely been nothing, Mrs Robertson was known for her good natured lack of tact, but lately it seemed that there were always others there too. And especially Mrs Campbell, who was really an awful gossip.

Holly shook her head and kicked a stone in her path sending it scrambling along towards the road. She wanted a letter from him more than she feared local gossip and stupidity. Had it not always been so? She had always been subject for talk and speculation and ill-advised references to "the Jacobin's lass" and the "radical girl." It had calmed down in later years because she was no longer a daily feature of village life and people had grown used to the war. Besides, these days there were plenty of animosity towards the powers that be in the home countries and a war weariness that could not be bothered with who was and was not of an enemy race and so talk had moved on. Those foolish people, they were like that stone in her path she had just kicked. You nudged them a little in their deep set beliefs and away they rattled for a while until they came to a standstill and lay waiting in the path of someone else to put some fuss into their dreary lives.

Holly winced to herself. That Mrs Robertson. She really had no use for any more stupidity. She was restless and had difficulty concentrating on the Doctor's work as it was and his sad looks and obvious new reticence followed her whenever she let her thoughts wander beyond what was before her. The only thing that soothed her were *his* letters — his darling letters that she slept with and carried around in her pocket, fingering them at every opportunity and tried to read, listening and trying to imagine how he would say the words on that paper, how he would say he missed her, how he loved her.

"Oooh!" Mrs Robertson had said so cheerfully and winked first at Holly and then at Mrs Campbell. "I kno why ye're here, dearie, don't I?"

Maybe her smile could have been friendlier and a little warmer, but Holly really could not stand Mrs Robertson at the best of times and so she had thought it would be better to stay calm and unaffected.

"Do you have any letters for me, please?"

Mrs Robertson gave a cooing noise and rubbed her hands together. "Aye, I do indeed. I have been waiting all morn to give it to ye, I certainly have!" She shuffled through her post and Holly wished she would hurry up or even address Mrs Campbell

410

because she definitely did not want to get into a conversation with her.

"Aye, here it is!" Mrs Robertson held up a folded sheet of paper for both Holly's and Mrs Campbell's inspection. "Such a neat hand," she went on. "Very rare in a man. Very. And I do have some experience in that field," she added seriously. "Quality."

Holly had thanked her and made for the door. "And generous, too," Mrs Robertson cooed more in the direction of Mrs Campbell again since Holly was about to walk out the door with the object of her interest. "Why, fancy him sending all that money to the mister to cover the postage! It was a canny work that caught him, my dear. Aye, but she's always been the clever one!"

Now that she had the letter, she was in no hurry to complete her task and return to the house. She would instead savour the anticipation, holding off on breaking the seal until the last possible moment. Therefore she took her time wandering the high street, looking in shop windows, admiring the latest offerings on display and ignoring the proprietors' new-found interest in her as they stood at the glass and beckoned for her to enter. She nearly succumbed to the temptation at the milliner's, debating whether that lovely new bonnet in the window was too extravagant a purchase to add to her trousseau, and as she hesitated in the doorway, she overheard a conversation between Miss Primrose Tristam and her sister Prudence as they walked past without seeing her.

"But Primmie, you mustn't say things like that. You have no reason to think..."

"Don't be a simpleton, Pru," Miss Tristam scoffed. "How else do you think she could pull off such a coup?"

"But you really cannot suggest... Primmie, we have never known her to act in such a way."

"Prudie, if you can explain why a man like him would offer marriage to a girl like her if he didn't have to, I would like to hear it."

Prudence blinked stupidly, "Don't you suppose he loves her?"

"You really are a fool," a deep disgusted sigh escaped from Miss Tristam. "Mark my words. She got up to something in England, I am sure of it. She waited until he was among his own people and society and she got him into some kind of compromising position. It's not like she hasn't done it before, you know."

"Primmie, no!" her sister gasped in disbelief. "Tell me!"

"Mr Pembroke says that she tried the very same thing with him!" she said with a knowing smile. "Of course, that was years ago and he wasn't fool enough to fall for it, like Lord Baugham did, but believe me, I'm sure his lordship had no choice in the matter..."

Their voices faded as they moved down the street, but Holly had heard enough. Was this what people were saying of her? Her face turned scarlet and she felt alternately hot with shame and cold with fury. She stood, no longer seeing the beautiful display in the window, until she could steady her breathing and resist the urge to follow Primrose and scratch her eyes out.

After she was able to regain her composure, telling herself that whatever Primrose Tristam might think of her had no importance on what she knew to be the truth, she left the milliner's and headed straight to the butcher shop to fetch Mrs Higgins' chicken so she could go home and read her letter. The desire for delayed gratification gave way to the need for immediate assurance. Passing the Thistle on the way back, she arrived just in time to see Dr McKenna quickly stepping out the door. She drew in a breath and prepared to deliver a greeting when the door opened again and Mr Grant, obviously intoxicated, lurched out in pursuit of the doctor and crying out in a loud voice, "Walking away won't change a thing! No matter how you look at it, or try to excuse it, you know good and well she toyed with us both, McKenna!" he shouted to his back.

Dr McKenna's face was grim and set when he turned around to face Mr Grant.

"Grant, I've told you once already that I will not hear any more slanders you have to say against Miss Tournier. I am sorry you were disappointed and I can sympathise with and understand your feelings, but what you say is untrue and too much to be borne! I would strongly advise you to keep your tongue. Now and ever."

Mr Grant answered, speaking in such a loud and rash tone that Holly, frozen to the spot in horror, felt she wanted to die from the mortification.

"She kept me on the rope for years, until you and that lord showed up — and then after stringing you along, she tosses you aside in a moment, just like she did me, when she could get her greedy claws into something better. How can you defend her?"

Before she could see how it happened, Dr McKenna had taken hold of Mr Grant's coat and Mr Grant was being propelled over to the outer wall of the inn.

"Grant," he spoke in a voice of deadly calm to the man pinned against the wall, "Miss Tournier has never implied nor offered anything more than friendship to me — and I am sure she was equally honest and forthright with you. I understand your regrets, but hopes are not expectations, and polite friendship is not encouragement. And if I should hear that any such talk has passed your lips again, I will bring it to his lordship's attention — and if he is not here to defend Miss Tournier's honour, I will take that privilege upon myself. I hope I have made myself clear."

McKenna released him then and Holly watched in shock as Mr Grant stumbled away, mumbling to himself, but she was not able to take herself away before the doctor turned and saw her.

"Miss Tournier!" he called to keep her from walking away, as she was poised to do. She waited while he quickly stepped over to meet her. "I am sorry that you were here to witness that, but please...do not take any of it to heart. He could not have...he did not mean it, I know."

"Then how could he speak so?" Holly asked quietly, refusing to meet the doctor's gaze, "What would make him, make anyone, say such things?"

McKenna let out a breath and ran his hand over his forehead, "People can say and think many things that they don't necessarily believe when they are upset and disappointed. I know —"

"You know?" Holly interrupted. "How do you know? What makes you so certain that Mr Grant did not mean what he said?"

A small smile played across Dr McKenna's lips, "I know, Miss Tournier, because I know you. As Mr Grant knows you. And both he and I, and anyone else who knows you, will never believe that you are capable of acting improperly, or selfishly. It's just talk, Miss Tournier, and talk will blow over."

"Dr McKenna, you are too kind, truly." Holly felt uncomfortable receiving such praise from him of all people, but she did not know how to express herself without alluding to the subject that had as yet, and always would, remain untouched between them. "But I thank you for speaking in my defence."

"Not at all," it was his turn to mumble. "I do it gladly and sincerely."

There was an awkward pause, where many things could have been spoken and none were, but then, after he had ascertained that she was quite alright, and she had politely but firmly declined his offer to see her home, Holly said goodbye. She mechanically made her last purchases, wondering if every friendly smile or curious stare masked ugly and unkind thoughts like the ones she had been subjected to already. When she walked back to Rosefarm, her mind was whirling with thoughts, questions and doubts.

Chapter 37

*In which we Learn that the Pen is the most Effective Weapon
when Moving Opposing Armies Closer to One Another*

HOLLY came home to the same voices of her mother and his lordship's solicitor droning on about settlements, pin money, jointures and trusts. She delivered her purchases and told Mrs Higgins she was fatigued and would be going up to her room for a nap. The housekeeper smiled and pinched her cheek and told her to take good care of herself.

Up in her room, Holly slipped off her shoes, loosened her laces and crawled under her blankets, her mind still swirling with what she had heard that day, feeding the lingering doubts that ever hovered around the outskirts of her thoughts.

Why *would* a man like him offer marriage to a girl like her?

She shook her head to clear it of doubt and drew out his letter.

Cumbermere Castle
Cheshire

My Dearest, most Ravishing Bride,

The most fatal thing about you, my dear, is that you always seem to make me act against my own better judgement. Don't think I blame you for that trait, because in actual fact I praise you for it. It has, on the whole and particularly of late, made me a very happy man. However, this letter of yours that I have just read under the eyes of my valet — a man who knows me and my bad habits and traits better than I do myself — will and must awaken that very instinct in me, make me act impulsively

414

and raise alarm in anyone who knows me. When you write that you miss me and wish for my return, it is all I can do not to order my horse at once and be on my way to Scotland without a second thought. What does it matter that not everyone shares my opinion of just how right that would be? Good sense be damned, my love calls me and I am powerless to resist...

It was a sweet sentiment and she could not help but smile, but still her doubts would not rest. Did she truly, as he claimed, make him act against his better judgement? She could not deny that had most certainly been the case in the early days of their acquaintance. But even recently... her mind wandered, as it frequently did, to that moment at the inn in Nottingham. He had nearly lost control then; he said he nearly lost all sense of himself and he had berated himself for it. The question suddenly troubling her was: was he acting against his better judgement now? Was this engagement and proposed marriage merely an impulsive decision that sounded feasible when he was so far away from home, and desirable when he was surrounded by the happiness and celebration of a friend's wedding? Would he come to regret his rash proposal and wish he had used his judgement more wisely? Would he come to believe, as everyone else in the world appeared to, that she had set out to secure him for her own financial and social gain? Would he end up despising her for it?

Rosefarm Cottage
Clanough
Selkirk

It is dark, but I sit here burning a candle so that I can read your last letter once again and try, somehow, to find some peace amid all my doubts and fears. But what strikes me at this moment are not your professions of love or the examples of your wit or gift of language. Instead I read your first paragraph over and over and wonder that you can so blithely exclaim over the loss of your good sense in matters involving me – and I wonder what it will mean, for you and for me, when that good sense returns, as it must. Too, I wonder if your mention of it indicates that you are beginning to see that things cannot be what you want simply because you want them, and I wonder if you are now asking yourself some of the same questions that are plaguing me.

I need to say something, but first I must tell you that my feelings for you are un-changed, nor will they ever change. I love you. I have loved you since that first kiss and before — every time you came to my rescue, every time you made me angry, every time we quarrelled and every time we enjoyed each other's company — my love was growing, though I did not know. When you kissed me, I knew. I still know. But that is beside the point... maybe it isn't even enough.

I wonder if marriage between two people such as you and me can ever be. Maybe we are too different, maybe I am not what you think I am, or maybe I am exactly what you think I am, but not at all what you need.

So now I am beginning to think that you should stay in Cumbermere for a longer time. While there, you will have time to think, to decide, perhaps to seek counsel before you are bound to me forever to your regret. If it was a momentary impulse that made you offer marriage to me, a matter of being swept up in some whim or fancy, then I will release you from your promise without reproach or condition. The thought of us marrying, as wonderful as it might seem, was probably too fantastic to be real anyway.

This I offer to you. What I ask in return is a timely answer to what your decision will be.

H.

MR RIEMANN WAS LYING ON his bed, his midday meal satisfactorily shared with the rest of the staff below stairs and with one biscuit transported for his personal enjoyment in his hand. He lay back, happily taking advantage of the peace surrounding his Master's impending meal and that same gentleman's habit of either taking a small nap in his library or — as was more usual these days — closeting himself into his study with his steward or some other member of his staff for a long afternoon of actual work.

After thoughtfully savouring the biscuit to the last crumb, very carefully lest he should end up with evidence of his indulgence either on the bed or on his person, he crossed his legs and then his arms behind his head and felt himself drift off into well-deserved relaxation while doing a mental inventory of what was still needed to supplement his Master's wardrobe for the upcoming nuptials. His thoughts had just slipped over into that unregulated state between rational thought and untamed dreaming when he heard rapid footsteps approaching his chamber through his lordship's dressing room.

Before he had time to fully get off the bed, the door flew open and Lord Baugham pushed his head through.

"Riemann," he said in a queer voice, "we are leaving."

Neither the order itself nor the manner of it came as a surprise to the valet.

"Very well, sir," he said calmly and discreetly buttoned his waistcoat. "And where to, my lord?"

Strangely enough, his lordship paused for a moment. "Clyne," he then said forcefully and left the valet's room.

When Riemann caught up with him a few minutes later in his lordship's own bedroom, Lord Baugham was rummaging through a pile of books on the table.

"Put these into my trunk," he said. "And I have some more downstairs that belong at Clyne. And then I need the papers. Let's leave in an hour."

416

"My lord," he said, "I think you mean *you* will leave in an hour."

He was answered with a waving hand and receding steps towards the door. "Certainly!"

Mr Riemann watched his Master walk out the door leaving him to his chores and he started preparing his lordship's riding satchel, mentally calculating weather conditions, the distance and necessary stops at inns along the way while trying to recall what — if anything — he had left at Clyne in the way of adequate clothing. He was despondently thinking he would have to reconcile himself to the fact that before he could reach Clyne with the rest of his lordship's effects, his Master would already be roaming around his Scottish hideaway, making his social visits and doing his courting in his less than his best clothes. That was when he discovered a letter that had been left under the pile of books and he carefully removed it. It was a lady's hand — long, neat and dutifully crossed. Without reading any further, Riemann noticed it had been scrunched by a strong hand and he instinctively smoothed out the page, re-folded it in the same neat fashion and, smiling a little to himself, decided to deposit it in his Master's already cramped luggage.

HOLLY'S HANDS WERE COLD. SHE held them in front of her mouth and blew on them to keep them warm. Her nose was cold, too. She touched it with her sleeve and rubbed it gently to warm it up, but as soon as her hand left her face she could feel the tip of it go numb again. She could, of course, have moved away from the cold window and stopped staring out of it at the even colder view outside, where a few people passed their house swiftly to be out of the freezing weather as soon as possible, but she found she could not. If she did, if she abandoned her vigil, she would have had to find something else to do and she was paralyzed and unable to concentrate on anything other than her rambling thoughts.

Hot tears stung her eyes and she leaned her forehead against the window glass. Her mother had no idea she was so miserably idle. She thought she was in her room attending either to her sewing, or her letter writing, or even her lists for Lord Baugham's library. She had no idea her daughter stood staring out of the window, listlessly wondering in how many ways good intentions led one straight to a personal hell.

No letter today! Still! Mrs Robertson had told her with a barely concealed smirk. Those words, and the smug sentiment behind them, rang over and over again in her head. So perhaps he was doing what she had asked of him. Perhaps he was taking some time to deliberate. She was surprised at how his obedience and consideration felt so...hurtful. Like she had been pushed into a prison cell of her own making and the very door she had asked to be shut had slammed her in the face. Would she never hear from him again? Should she really have sent that letter at all? Perhaps it could have waited, but then...No. She shook her head and shifted her feet, pressing her other sleeve against her cold face. That would not have been right. It would not have been right towards him and if she had not told him the truth and given him a choice he would surely have ended up despising her if...

Eyes drawn to a commotion in the distance, in a moment Holly realised that the rider tearing down the lane with no regard of life or limb, either for his beast or the surrounding people, was destined for her own door, she felt a swift stab of terror run through her. He had come! But why? The possible answers to that question only served to terrify her. Unable to move an inch, as if in a dream, she watched that familiar, tall figure hurl himself off his horse and just throw the reins over the gatepost without one look behind him. She heard his steps — steps of determination. Bad or good determination? Doom or salvation? She swallowed when she realised she must go down and meet him. Instinctively she knew mere propriety and a flight of stairs would not keep him from barging into her chamber if she did not cut him short. So she flung herself out of the room and to the stairs, only to find him already waiting for her at the foot of them, hatless, gloveless, red-faced and breathing heavily, looking up at her with a raging ice-storm in his blue eyes.

Neither of them said a word and Holly felt her heart beating in her throat and her hands were now hot and clammy. Just as she was about to offer some stammering statement on his surprising presence, her mother emerged from her parlour. For a moment, time stood still until Mrs Tournier swept past her daughter up the stairs.

"I will search for my Thesaurus in my room," she said. "Thoroughly."

It broke his spell on her and she moved awkwardly, still holding on to the banister. When she could look at him again, his eyes had shifted to a duller colour and a look of desperation had overtaken them.

"Holly..." he said.

Her first overwhelming urge was to run down to him and throw herself in his arms, but she was only two steps down when she remembered her doubts. She stopped herself and gripped the banister tightly.

"You didn't write."

"I am here," he said in a voice strangely hoarse.

"I know," she murmured, her voice sounding distant and oddly calm. "You must be cold."

He turned his hand in a dismissive gesture, but let it fall half way. Then the silence enveloped them again and Baugham fought the urge to take the very few steps that were needed to close the gap between them. Instead he recalled his purpose and asked the question that had been plaguing him for nearly three days now.

"What happened?"

All those hours in the saddle, all those thoughts spinning around in his head making him lose track of time and distance, all those dark evenings at inns waiting to be off again, the fears, the doubts, the anger, the frustration all came out in that one question. He had no idea what type of reception he was expecting upon his arrival, he had thought only of getting there, but this cold and distant welcome was not it. But this was what he had needed to know — something had happened.

Holly looked at him squarely, but failed to answer. How could she answer without damning herself?

418

"That was a nice letter you sent," he then went on crisply, offended at her aloofness. More than offended, he was terrified, and it caused him to retreat from her, from the feelings that threatened to make him lose control and throw himself at her feet. And that — the fear, the vulnerability — made him angry. "I cannot tell you how much I appreciate having my word and my character and my future happiness thrown into doubt so ably and succinctly. You have quite the gift."

"It is your future happiness that concerns me the most. And mine." She gripped the railing so hard that her hand began to ache.

"And so you have decided...when?...suddenly?...after much deliberation?... that I don't know my own mind? That I cannot be happy with you, or you with me?"

It was supposed to come out in a dry and matter-of-fact way, but he felt the desperation well up from within him. Was it all in vain? Had he been wrong?

Struggling hard to keep her voice steady, she said, "I begin to wonder if that might be so, at least in your case. And if you are not happy, I could not be so."

His voice rose in pitch, "I see I must thank you for taking it upon yourself to determine how I am to be happy, in opposition of everything I have sworn to you of my feelings. You are indeed too wise, too kind for me..."

But suddenly he had no more strength for anger or sarcasm. His whole body ached, his bones, his head, his eyes and, feeling his legs go weak from exhaustion, he had to steady himself at the banister and look down at his feet — dirty and throbbing within their boots — willing them not to fail him.

"Can we sit...somewhere? Please?"

She was down the rest of the steps in the matter of a moment, and his arms were around her and she could feel him leaning on her for support as he rested his head against hers and whispered in her ear over and over.

"What happened, Holly? Why? Why would you say...? Why would you *think*...?"

She felt him wavering again so she led him to the parlour sofa.

"Wait here, I'll be right back."

His head shot up, his eyes suddenly clear again.

"Wait? No, Holly, waiting is what I have been doing for three torturous days. Now I am here; you must explain this to me."

"I will, just allow me to fetch you some wine." She even managed a smile at this strange turn of events, as she mirrored the service he performed for her at the Tristam's *soiree-musicale*. She did not wait for his protests, but slipped out and returned again quickly with a generous glass. Handing it to him, she sat down stiffly on the edge the chair opposite him. She looked down at the dark, red liquid in the glass he held.

"People talk;" she said almost soundlessly, "sometimes what they say is true."

He drank greedily, but stopped once he heard her words.

"Who is talking? Have they told you something? Something about me?"

"No, nothing about you," she said, pre-occupied and needing to continue while she still had the nerve. "Not about you...about me."

"I don't understand." It was true. He was at a complete loss. What did that have to do with her altered feelings for him? "What did they say?"

She concentrated on her hands clasped on her lap and told him everything that she had overheard from Mr Grant and Dr McKenna, from Mrs Robertson, Miss Tristam and her sister.

"And," she continued, "the way they look at me as I walk down the street, the things they say... it makes it seem like you would never have loved me if I had not set my heart on capturing you, by design, or deceit, or by entrapment. And then I remember the inn, and your letter came and I began to wonder if it was true after all and maybe I am not what *you* think I am... maybe I am what *they* think I am, because... Perhaps we should... wait."

He leaned back with a sigh and closed his eyes for just a moment. The words came flooding out of her and hit his tired brain and exhausted body like a punch in the stomach. Gossip. Small minded people in places where everyone thinks they know everyone else and their business. Everywhere they were all the same. Whether in Clanough or in London. All the same. Lord he was tired.

"They have no idea what you are," he said and opened his eyes. "But I do. They have no idea why I love you. They have no idea how you made me love you. But I do."

He reached out his hand to her and she slowly slipped hers onto his big, warm palm. "They know nothing about you and me," he whispered. "The way we fought so hard, so uselessly and how much it hurts to hear you say that the sweet surrender, after all that fruitless fighting, was a mistake or a whim. It wasn't. It *isn't*. Don't ever tell me it is. Don't tell me *anyone* knows that better than you or I."

He could see her swallow and fight the tears, but they rolled silently down her cheeks anyway. "I need you, Holly," he said and carefully touched one of the tears with his thumb. "Don't shut me out just when I have found you. If you need me to convince you of my love I will do it a thousand times over, but please don't reject me like this. I don't want to be outside of your love anymore."

She took her other hand and enclosed his, pulling it on to her lap, but would not meet his eyes.

"And," she said in a voice barely above a whisper, "what if it is true?"

His stomach sank and his heart lurched.

"What if what is true?"

"What they have been saying about me. What if Primmie is right? What if I really did try to force you into a compromising position where you had no choice? I hadn't thought of it before, but I never told Maman about that kiss while you were here. You know when I told her? It was when we were on our way to Hertfordshire — just like Primmie said — I waited until you were among your own people and society. What if I really did that to you, to try to trap you?"

"Trap me?" Baugham sat up straight again and removed his hands. "This is madness! *Trap* me? As if I have not spent a lifetime avoiding traps and attachments that I could not break out of at a moment's notice! If I did not want to be *trapped*, I would not be here. I would not have ridden like a madman for days, half terrified I was going to be cast aside on a whim and half furious that you could doubt my honest feelings just when I am so absolutely convinced of them myself for the very first time! What do you think I am? What does Miss Tristam think I am? A sheep? A cuckold? An idiot?"

"No! But I…"

He sprang out of his seat. "Miss Tristam thinks you went hunting for me among 'my own people'? Snaring me against my own intentions? Forcing me into a compromising position? I have never heard such nonsense in my life! What about me? What about my behaviour? Does Miss *Tristam* think it is commonplace courtship for a man to abuse his intended at every turn? Accuse her of trespassing and ignorance? Use harsh words against her and her judgement in front of her friends and family and on public roads?! Or does Miss *Tristam* think that is all part of your very special and successful brand of entrapment, planned and induced by you against my will?!"

He pressed his fingertips against his temples and rubbed them slowly while he felt his purpose and grip on the situation slowly fade away with his renewed anger.

"No…this is not about Miss Tristam. I will not have her in this conversation. This is about us."

"But, it is *not* just about us. It is about perceptions, and what maybe others can see in us that we do not see ourselves. And I cannot honestly say that if I had known of a way to secure your love, I would not have attempted it. What does that then make me?"

"Holly, I refuse to hold other people's perceptions of my conduct as the mirror in which I view myself. I will answer for my actions with my word and reputation as a gentleman and on the Day of Judgement. Other than that I will not have gossips besting my own conscience on what is right and wrong. And neither should you. Why do you even listen to that rubbish — your conscience and your feelings are clear! Enough of Miss Tristam and gossip and slighted lovers and jealousy! I did not come here for them. I came here for you!"

"My feelings are very clear!" Holly cried in agitation. "I *know* what I feel for you. But my conscience is not. If you came here for me, you have the right to know what I am. There is more, something else I need to tell you. Mr Grant…he was right about one thing. When I came back to Clanough from Elizabeth's wedding, I had every intention of…taking another path. But then I found something better — you — just as he said." She buried her face in her hands, "You came along just in time and I was so happy I never gave a thought to anyone else but myself. Now, what does *that* make me?"

Baugham stared at her.

"But please do not think…Nothing was ever spoken, or assumed, or implied. It is just that you would not see, and then you left and I thought you were happy to get away from me…and I was so very upset and wondered if I should just be practical and…"

She tried unsuccessfully to blink back her tears while still avoiding his eyes.

"But it was not what I wanted. Everything I have ever wished and hoped and prayed for came true for me in that willow grove. I just never believed it could, and I was sad and afraid. But all along I wanted you…and so I did exactly what Mr Grant accused me of doing."

He felt panic rise in his throat. Did she think she did not *deserve* him? Was she going to throw him aside because she had wanted him, but had been prepared to settle for someone else? What about the promise they had made and the promise of happiness he had so clearly seen growing between them? Was she going to doubt that for the sake of a principle? Suddenly he felt exhausted. He had no fight left in him. He had thought he would not have to fight anymore — fight himself, fight her, fight the world.

He slowly sank down beside her feet and gently took her hand, holding it to his cheek after kissing it.

"Holly," he said quietly, fearfully, "you are frightening me. What are you going to do?"

It was automatic, instinctive; she pulled his head down into her lap and stroked his hair, even as she spoke the words that would release him from his promise to her. "I just — " her breath caught in her throat and she had to begin again, speaking as steadily as she could, "I just needed you to know the truth. What I will do is up to you."

There was a deep sigh somewhere in the folds of her dress and a barely audible murmur.

"The truth..."

She looked down at his head in her lap, and it was so comfortable for him to be there like that, so natural for her to run her fingers through his hair. He looked tired; his eyes were closed but she could see the pain in his face.

"The truth then," she took a deep breath and from somewhere deep within found the courage to bare herself to him, "The truth is — I love you. I want very much to be your wife." He raised his head and looked at her as she continued, "But I only want to be your wife if you love me as well. If you still want me. If you are sure of me, of who and what I am. If you do not, if you regret or question your offer, I want you to release me, as I will release you."

"Do you really think I do? Do you think that is why I rode over here like this? Why I now lie here and never want to get up? Why, despite everything you said and I said just now, I'm somehow smiling because you told me the truth — that you love me?"

He turned his face and without even attempting to restrain himself drew a deep breath, feeling her warmth, her smell and the soft fabric of her dress against his cheek.

"You are such a foolish little bee," he muttered, "and I will never let you go. From now on, whatever comes, it must be the two of us. It can be no other way without tragedy for our poor, doubtful souls. And in view of that, please let me rest here like this just a little while before I must get up. Smack my foolish, impertinent head if you will, but let me stay."

The cold fist of fear and confusion, of guilt and pain slowly released its grip on her heart. She bent down and instead of giving his head a smack, she gave it a kiss and whispered, "Stay."

She could feel the warmth of his breath touch her skin through her skirts as he spoke, eyes closed again, "And what else?"

"I will marry you. I love you."

422

"Love. My final plea before I surrender. I cannot wait any longer. Marry me soon. Very soon. No talk of waiting."

She brushed a stubborn wisp of his hair away from his temple and looked on as she felt his jaw clench once more.

"I will," she whispered.

She felt his body relax; he murmured, "Thank God" just before he dozed off still resting on her lap, his arms still clutching her knees.

The room gradually grew dim in the late winter afternoon, but Holly was unwilling disturb his rest, so she sat perfectly still, playing with his hair until he stirred and opened his eyes. Reluctantly he pulled away from her and sat back on his heels with an embarrassed smile.

"Forgive me. I don't know why I... I'm sorry, Holly."

"Don't be. You were tired."

He rubbed his hands over his face and tugged at his waistcoat, his face suddenly brightening.

"And now I'm restored. I hope," he said, moving to the sofa opposite her once more, "that you have put all these silly doubts and worries behind you, because I have something for you."

She pulled just a little away, sat straighter and, like all women, could not disguise the alighted interest in her eyes.

"For me? Now? You brought me something even after my letter?"

"Call it a foolish, or even a desperate, optimism, but yes, I carried them with me in hopes — "

"Them?"

"Yes," he said teasingly. "There are two things. One is old, one is new."

He grinned as her eyes flashed and her expression changed into a slight pout.

"Oh heavens, are you going to punish me by making me do riddles?"

He kissed her and reached into his waistcoat pocket. "Here is the first." Withdrawing his hand, he opened it up to reveal a thin gold ring. She gasped and stared at it.

"Remember you promised I could give you another?" he said. "This one is a little more durable, which in view of what we have just gone through I should say is most appropriate, and I hope it proves to you my love isn't a fancy or a feeling. *'Nor will it change, though all be changed beside'.*"

"Quoting poetry to aid your wooing, my lord?" she asked with a smile. "And such a fanciful poet like Mr Coleridge."

"Oh, I have done much better than that," he said with a self-satisfied air as he handed her the ring. "Take a look."

She held it up to look at the engraving — a delicate filigree design on the outside and, on the inside, these words: *'To adore thee is my duty — Goddess o' this soul o' mine!'*.

"Oh," she sighed in delight. "Burns."

"Who else?"

"Oh, my... love, it is perfect! I could not want for a better... " she stammered at a loss for words, so she reached out her left hand. The battered willow ring was still there, dangling precariously and looking as if it might fall off any moment.

"You do it, love," she said. "It's only proper."

His eyes warmed and he took the golden ring and slipped it on above the willow one. She gave a little laugh and drew herself up to the crook of his arm again and lifted up her hand to admire it. He took it and caressed her hand with his fingers.

"Yes, it is perfect, isn't it? But there is still something else."

Her eyes lit up and she looked at him eagerly.

"As if this wasn't enough," she said and smiled.

"Well," he said as he dug further in his waist pocket, "when it comes to trinkets I do not think there can be such a thing to a woman's mind as enough. And in your case I wholeheartedly agree."

He finally withdrew his hand and handed her a faded, battered box. In it lay a small reddish-gold locket on a delicate golden chain.

"Try it," he said.

There was no question that the locket was ancient. Directing her questioning eyes at him, she took it with her trembling fingers and held it up for inspection.

"It's beautiful," she whispered. "Whose is it?"

"It's yours, of course. But before that it was my mother's," he said simply. "I think she was given it on the marriage of her sister when she was a bridesmaid. It is not worth much in monetary value, but since it is the only piece of her jewellery left that my father did not…well, that is left, it is very valuable. I sent for it from London, where it's been stashed away with the bankers. First time it has seen daylight in years."

Holly turned it over and narrowed her eyes at the faint engraving on the inside.

"Lady Amelia Isabel Gwenllyan Richwood?" she read. "That was your mother?"

"Yes," he smiled, "before she married my father."

She looked at him, detecting a hint of withdrawal in his eyes and she hastily decided not to ask what she so wanted to ask this time. He took the locket from her and, leaning in close, reached around to fasten the clasp at the back of her neck. The soft brush of his fingers against her skin sent gooseflesh down her entire body. He kissed her lightly as he drew back, meeting her soft gaze with his own.

"It's beautiful. You are beautiful."

She was indeed beautiful; her face was beaming as she held her hand out again to admire the thin band. She then raised her hand to the locket and fingered it, reading the inscription once again before turning to him with a look of concern.

"You should go," she tentatively touched his cheek. "I still cannot believe you are actually here, but you look so tired." she smiled. "I have abused you so terribly in making you come because of that letter and yet I am so glad you did. But I will be selfish no more. You must rest."

He briefly leaned into her palm before taking her hand and kissing each finger tip and then gave a grimace as he got to his feet.

"I suppose I must. But I will be by tomorrow again and that will be even more heart-wrenching because I understand you have been receiving regular visits from a certain Mr Crabtree?"

Holly smiled. "Maman has."

Baugham cast a glimpse up the stairs as he put his gloves on. "Is it very hard to find your mother's Thesaurus?" he asked.

"Almost impossible sometimes."

"Ah."

He met her gaze and hesitated. "May I?" he said and caught her hand again, pulling her closer. "Before I go?"

She nodded her consent and the kiss they shared served as the sweetest balm to their wounded hearts. When he at last let her go, she took his head possessively in her hands and looked at him closely.

His hair was flat to his head from too many hours under his hat, the grime of the road showed on his face and clothing, he smelled like horse and sweat — and he had never been more beautiful to her. He was like wine to a mouth grown weary of water — and he was looking at her with warmth and love and desire and total surety. And she knew that everything was right and good.

Holly watched him disappear down the lane from the front step of the house until she could hardly keep from shivering from the cold. Then she re-entered the house and quietly latched the door behind her.

ON THE LAST OF HIS leg home, his lordship recited nursery rhymes to himself not to fall out of his saddle. His trusted mount could probably have taken him straight home even in an unconscious state, but since Weimar was known to sometimes put his own interest before his Master's, Baugham did not trust him not to forsake his normal box in the stable at Clyne and instead take refuge in some farmer's barn nearer by. But when he was close enough to Clyne Cottage for Weimar not to be tempted any longer, he struggled out of his seat, patted his horse on the rump and sent him to the stables on his own for the last few yards.

Thus he arrived on foot and he automatically steered his steps towards Mrs McLaughlin's kingdom. The Queen was, indeed, at home, nursing a small nick that she had sustained while cutting turnips in the perfect sized chunks for mutton bone stew while her mind was occupied elsewhere. She had just finished cursing and was reaching for a cloth to wind around her finger when the door opened.

"Bless me!" was all she could utter when the very person she had been thinking about walked into her kitchen. "Laird, bless me lownly!"

"Don't worry, Mrs McLaughlin," the Master of Clyne said, drawing out a chair and sitting down immediately. "I shan't drag mud all over the house. I think I'll just camp out here and rest a bit before I go upstairs, if I may."

But Mrs McLaughlin paid his words no heed as she put the kettle on in one stroke and then watched his lordship leaning his head in his hands at her kitchen table, sighing deeply.

"Is ought wrong, sir?"

"No," he said not looking up but rubbing his neck with his hands, "thank God, no."

Mrs McLaughlin turned into her larder. Wordlessly bread and cheese and meat appeared in front of his lordship, who just eyed the offerings while he played with the knife. Finally the housekeeper reached up on to her highest shelf and brought down a bottle and a glass.

"Here," she said and poured him a measure. "From my cousin up in Aiberdeen. It cures any trouble so ye don't have to fear I'll bring out the tonics next and gar 'em on ye in yer feeble state."

Lord Baugham accepted her offering with a smile. "Ah yes," he said having finished it in one go. "Quite."

Mrs McLaughlin took a step closer and looked down at the young man in his sweaty and dirty clothes, pale face and sagging posture. She slowly eased him out of his coat as he sat and let his fingers play over the now empty glass and then lay it over her arm while picking up his hat and gloves.

"Ye eat now," she said. "Ye cannae wash or go to yer bed hungrysome. I'll prepare it for ye meantime."

Baugham nodded. In the doorway Mrs McLaughlin halted and looked around once more.

"Did ye see her?"

Still he did not answer her in words, but his countenance told her all she needed to know.

"Things will be unalike here from now on. That's good. She is a good woman, that I know. And she brought ye back here, my laird, and for that I will always love her."

With that Mrs McLaughlin climbed the stairs with a light heart, curiously stinging eyes and constricted throat to prepare his lordship's bath, lay out his nightclothes, put extra blankets in his bed and fluff his pillows to perfection, so he could rest under her care for until it was no longer her sole duty.

IT IS OFTEN SAID THAT all things must come to an end and this is often said with regret at the passing of what was thought or even hoped to be a permanent state of affairs. Our present state is often more comfortable and preferable than changes we have willingly or unwittingly invited into our lives. Even if that change is welcomed and sought after, few of us can leave our old habits and arrangements behind without some slight regret. Who of us has not been guilty of sentimentality and lack of faith in what the future might bring when one season has come to pass and the next is yet waiting to be ushered in? We dwell on the passing and, because man is a creature who likes his history, we parcel our experiences into small narratives, hoping to give meaning and value to the eras of our lives that will soon be delegated to memory.

It is safe to assume, however, that the close friends we have met in our little Scottish village had few or no regrets in the changes that this new season would bring. Yet, they could not help but realise that the upcoming St. Thomas' Eve would also bring many comfortable and beloved aspects of their present lives to a close. The end of a daughter and mother in a small cottage together, the end of independence, and even an end to mothers' exclusive caring concern, whether the object be one's own daughter, or a charge loved as dearly as a son. However, each of them knew and welcomed this change as far more than just an end. They very clearly saw the beginning as well, and that is the thought we wish to leave our reader with as well. Every end is a beginning and it is never more true than when the story is a love story.

It would be foolish and unfair to extend our original analogy of two equal armies marching toward confrontation any further. After all, the purpose of this campaign was never the complete victory of one party over the other, but rather a mutual surrender on favourable terms for each. Still, it is the nature of our combatants that arms and strategies will not be easily abandoned, even though they aim for peace. There are many targets to lay siege to and conquer yet, many campaigns and marches to struggle through. It is a happy story, for it is a story about life and love and in every end along the way there is a promising new beginning. In the future, love will change and grow. Love will spread and multiply. Love will be tested and ignored. Love will be in peril and it will be fought for. Lord Baugham and his bride showed much courage in Mrs Tournier's parlour, for they recognised that their fates lay with the other despite dangers and uncertainties. It is perhaps good to bear in mind that courage is usually rewarded and that Love, if it is trusted, can be stronger than any adversary. But that, as has been said above, is another story.

> *But as all several souls contain*
> *Mixture of things they know not what,*
> *Love these mix'd souls doth mix again,*
> *And makes both one, each this, and that.*
> — John Donne

428

Lightning Source UK Ltd.
Milton Keynes UK
173811UK00001B/71/P